The Ghastly Gothic Tomes

Vol. 7

The Ghastly Gothic Tomes

Vol. 7

Published by NRM Books.

ISBN: 978-1-965179-10-9

CREDITS
Cover Art by: Nathan Reese Maher

COPYRIGHT

The Ghastly Gothic Tomes are protected under the copyright laws of the United States of America. Any reproductions or unauthorized use of the contents herein including, but not limited to, artwork and text is prohibited without written permission from the author. Novels, poems, plays and short stories published herein are part of the public domain.

Copyright 1st Edition October 14th, 2024, all rights reserved.

Table of Contents

"The Mummy!"
by Jane Webb (Mrs. Loudon)
Published 1827, p. 2-434

"Rappaccini's Daughter"
by Nathaniel Hawthorne
Published 1844, p. 465-461

"The Custom House & The Scarlet Letter"
by Nathaniel Hawthorne
Published 1850, p. 462-662

The Mummy!

By Jane Webb (Mrs. Loudon)

INTRODUCTION.

I have long wished to write a novel, but I could not determine what it was to be about. I could not bear any thing common-place, and I did not know what to do for a hero. Heroes are generally so much alike, so monotonous, so dreadfully insipid—so completely brothers of one race, with the family likeness so amazingly strong—"This will not do for me," thought I as I sauntered listlessly down a shady lane, one fine evening in June; "I must have something new, something quite out of the beaten path:—but what?"—ay, that was the question. In vain did I rack my brains—in vain did I search the storehouse of my memory: I could think of nothing that had not been thought of before.

"It is very strange!" said I, as I walked faster, as though I hoped the rapidity of my motion would shake off the sluggishness of my imagination. It was all in vain! I struck my forehead and called wit to my assistance, but the malignant deity was deaf to my entreaty. "Surely," thought I, "the deep mine of invention cannot be worked out; there must be some new ideas left, if I could but find them." To find them, however, was the difficulty.

Thus lost in meditation, I walked onwards till I reached the brow of a hill, and a superb prospect burst upon me. A fertile valley richly wooded, studded with sumptuous villas and romantic cottages, and watered by a noble river, that wound slowly its lazy course along, spread beneath my feet; and lofty hills swelling to the skies, their summit lost in clouds, bounded the horizon. The sun was setting in all its splendour, and its lingering rays gave those glowing tints and deep masses of shadow to the landscape that sometimes produce so magical an effect. It was quite a Claude Lorraine scene; and more fully to enjoy it, I entered a hay-field, and seated myself upon a grassy bank. The day had been sultry; and the evening breeze, as it murmured through the foliage, felt cool and refreshing. "It is a lovely world," thought I, "notwithstanding all that cynics can say against it. Our own passions bring misery upon our heads,

The Mummy!

and then we rail at the world, though we only are in fault. Why should I seek to wander in the regions of fiction? Why not enjoy tranquilly the blessings Heaven has bestowed upon me?"

I felt too indolent to answer my own question; a delicious stillness crept over my senses, and the heaving chaos of my ideas was lulled to repose. A majestic oak stretched its gnarled arms in sullen dignity above my head; myriads of busy insects buzzed around me; and woodbines and wild roses, hanging from every hedge, mingled their perfume with that of the new-mown hay. I reclined languidly on my grassy couch, listening to the indistinct hum of the distant village, and feeling that delightful sense of exemption from care, that a faint murmur of bustle afar off gives to the weary spirit, when suddenly the bells struck up a joyous peal — the cheerful notes now swelling loudly upon the ear, then sinking gently away with the retiring breeze, and then again returning with added sweetness. I listened with delight to their melody, till their softness seemed to increase; the sounds became gradually fainter and fainter; the landscape faded from my sight; a soft languor crept over me: in short, I slept.

It would be of no use to go to sleep without dreaming; and, accordingly, I had scarcely closed my eyes when, methought, a spirit stood before me. His head was crowned with flowers; his azure wings fluttered in the breeze, and a light drapery, like the fleecy vapour that hangs upon the summit of a mountain, floated round him. In his hand he held a scroll, and his voice sounded soft and sweet as the liquid melody of the nightingale.

"Take this," said he, smiling benignantly; "it is the Chronicle of a future age. Weave it into a story. It will so far gratify your wishes, as to give you a hero totally different from any hero that ever appeared before. You hesitate," continued he, again smiling, and regarding me earnestly: "I read your thoughts, and see you fear to sketch the scenes of which you are to write, because you imagine they must be different from those with which you are acquainted. This is a natural distrust: the scenes will indeed be different from those you now behold; the whole face of society will be changed: new governments will have arisen; strange discoveries will be made, and stranger modes of life adopted. The restless curiosity and research of man will then have enabled him to lift the veil from much which is (to him at least) at present a mystery; and his powers (both as regards mechanical agency and intellectual knowledge) will be greatly enlarged. But even then, in his plenitude of acquirement, he will be made conscious of the infirmity of his nature, and will be guilty of many absurdities which, in his less enlightened state, he would feel ashamed to commit.

"To no one but yourself has this vision been revealed: do not fear to behold it. Though strange, it may be fully understood, for much will still remain to connect that future age with the present. The impulses and feelings of human creatures must, for the most part, be alike in all ages: habits vary, but nature endures; and the same passions were delineated, the same weaknesses ridiculed, by Aristophanes, Plautus, and Terence, as in after-times were described by Shakspeare and Moliere; and as they will be in the times of which you are to write, — by authors yet unknown.

"But you still hesitate; you object that the novelty of the allusions perplexes you. This is quite a new kind of delicacy; as authors seldom trouble themselves to become acquainted with a subject before they begin to write upon it. However, since you are so very scrupulous, I will endeavour, if possible, to assist you. Look around."

I did so; and saw, as in a magic glass, the scenes and characters, which I shall now endeavour to pass before the eyes of the reader.

CHAPTER I.

In the year 2126, England enjoyed peace and tranquillity under the absolute dominion of a female sovereign. Numerous changes had taken place for some centuries in the political state of the country, and several forms of government had been successively adopted and destroyed, till, as is generally the case after violent revolutions, they all settled down into an absolute monarchy. In the meantime, the religion of the country had been mutable as its government; and in the end, by adopting Catholicism, it seemed to have arrived at nearly the same result: despotism in the state, indeed, naturally produces despotism in religion; the implicit faith and passive obedience required in the one case, being the best of all possible preparatives for the absolute submission of both mind and body necessary in the other.

In former times, England had been blessed with a mixed government and a tolerant religion, under which the people had enjoyed as much freedom as they perhaps ever can do, consistently with their prosperity and happiness. It is not in the nature of the human mind, however, to be contented: we must always either hope or fear; and things at a distance appear so much more beautiful than they do when we approach them, that we always fancy what we have not, infinitely superior to any thing we have; and neglect enjoyments within our reach, to pursue others, which, like ignes fatui, elude our grasp at the very moment when we hope we have attained them.

Thus it was with the people of England:—Not satisfied with being rich and prosperous, they longed for something more. Abundance of wealth caused wild schemes and gigantic speculations; and though many failed, yet, as some succeeded, the enormity of the sums gained by the projectors, incited others to pursue the same career. New countries were discovered and civilized; the whole earth was brought to the highest pitch of cultivation; every corner of it was explored; mountains were levelled, mines were excavated, and the globe racked to its centre. Nay, the air and sea did not escape, and all nature was compelled to submit to the overwhelming supremacy of Man.

Still, however, the English people were not contented:— enabled to gratify every wish till satiety succeeded indulgence, they were still unhappy; perhaps, precisely because they had no longer any difficulties to encounter. In the meantime, education had become universal, and the technical terms of abstruse sciences familiar to the lowest mechanics; whilst questions of religion, politics, and metaphysics, agitated by them daily, supplied that stimulus, for which their minds, enervated by over cultivation, constantly craved. The consequences may be readily conceived. It was impossible for those to study deeply who had to labour for their daily bread; and not having time to make themselves masters of any given subject, they only learned enough of all to render them disputatious and discontented. Their heads were filled with words to which they affixed no definite ideas, and the little sense Heaven had blessed them with, was lost beneath a mass of undigested and misapplied knowledge.

Conceit inevitably leads to rebellion. The natural consequence of the mob thinking themselves as wise as their rulers, was, that they took the first convenient opportunity that offered, to jostle these aforesaid rulers from their seats. An aristocracy was established, and afterwards a democracy; but both shared the same fate; for the leaders of each in turn, found the instruments they had made use of to rise, soon became unmanageable. The people had tasted the sweets of power, they had learned their own strength, they were enlightened; and, fancying they understood the art of ruling as well as their quondam directors, they saw no reason why, after shaking off the control of one master, they should afterwards submit to the domination of many. "We are free," said they; "we acknowledge no laws but those of nature, and of those we are as competent to judge as our would-be masters. In what are they superior to ourselves? Nature has been as bountiful to us as to them, and we have had the same advantages of education. Why then should we toil to give them ease? We are each capable of governing ourselves. Why then should we pay them to rule us? Why should we be debarred from mental enjoyments and condemned to manual labour? Are not our tastes as refined as theirs, and our minds as highly cultivated? We will assert our independence, and throw off the yoke. If any man wish for luxuries, let him labour to procure them for himself. We will be slaves no longer; we will all be masters."

Thus they reasoned, and thus they acted, till government after government having been overturned, complete anarchy prevailed, and the people began to discover, though, alas! too late, that there was little pleasure in being masters when there were no subjects, and that it was impossible to enjoy intellectual pleasures, whilst each man was compelled to labour for his daily bread. This, however, was inevitable, for as perfect equality had been declared, of course no one would condescend to work for his neighbour, and every thing was badly done: as, however skilful any man may be in any particular art or profession, it is quite impossible he can excel in all.

The Mummy!

In the meantime, the people who had, though they scarcely knew why, attached to the idea of equality that of exemption from toil, found to their infinite surprise, that their burthens had increased tenfold, whilst their comforts had unaccountably diminished in the same proportion. The blessings of civilization were indeed fast slipping away from them. Every man became afraid lest the hard-earned means of existence should be torn from his grasp; for, as all laws had been abolished, the strong tyrannized over the weak, and the most enlightened nation in the world was in imminent danger of degenerating into a horde of rapacious barbarians.

This state of things could not continue; and the people, finding from experience that perfect equality was not quite the most enviable mode of government, began to suspect that a division of labour and a distinction of ranks were absolutely necessary to civilization; and sought out their ancient nobility, to endeavour to restore something like order to society. These illustrious personages were soon found: those who had not emigrated, had retired to their seats in the country, where, surrounded by their dependants, and the few friends who had remained faithful to them, they enjoyed the otium cum dignitate, and consoled themselves for the loss of their former greatness, by railing most manfully at those who had deprived them of it.

Amongst this number, was the lineal descendant of the late royal family, and to him the people now resolved humbly and unconditionally to offer the crown; imagining, with the usual vehemence and inconsistency of popular commotions, that an arbitrary government must be best for them, as being the very reverse of that, the evils of which they had just so forcibly experienced.

The prince, however, to whom a deputation from the people made this offer, happened not to be ambitious. Like another Cincinnatus, he placed all his happiness in the cultivation of a small farm, and had sufficient prudence to reject a grandeur which he felt must be purchased by the sacrifice of his peace. The deputies were in despair at his refusal; and they reurged their suit with every argument the distress of their situation could inspire. They painted in glowing colours the horrors of the anarchy that prevailed, the misery of the kingdom and despair of the people; and at last wound up their arguments by a solemn appeal to Heaven, that if he persisted in his refusal, the future wretchedness of the people might fall upon his head. The prince, however, continued inexorable; and the deputies were preparing to withdraw, when the prince's daughter, who had been present during the whole interview, rushed forward and prevented their retreat:—"Stay! I will be your queen," cried she energetically; "I will save my country, or perish in the attempt!"

The princess was a beautiful woman, about six-and-twenty; and, at this moment, her fine eyes sparkling with enthusiasm, her cheeks glowing, and her whole face and figure breathing dignity from the exalted purpose of her soul, she appeared to the deputies almost as a supernatural being; and regarding her offer as a direct inspiration from Heaven, they bore her in triumph to the assembled multitude who awaited their return: whilst the people, ever caught by novelty, and desirous of any change to free them from the misery they were enduring, hailed her appearance with delight, and unanimously proclaimed her Queen.

The new sovereign soon found the task she had undertaken a difficult one; but happening luckily to possess common sense and prudence, united with a firm and active disposition, she contrived in time to restore order, and to confirm her own power, whilst she contributed to the happiness of her people. The face of the kingdom rapidly changed—security produced improvement—and the self-banished nobles of the former dynasty crowding round the new Queen, she chose from amongst them the wisest and most experienced for her counsellors, and by their help compounded an excellent code of laws. This book was open to the whole kingdom; and cases being decided by principle instead of precedent, litigation was almost unknown: for as the laws were fully and clearly explained, so as to be understood by every body, few dared to act in open violation of them, punishment being certain to follow detection; and all the agonizing delights of a law-suit were entirely destroyed, as every body knew, the moment the facts were stated, how it would inevitably terminate. This renewal of the golden age continued several years without interruption, the people being too much delighted with the personal comforts they enjoyed, to complain of the errors inseparable from all human institutions; whilst the remembrance of what they had suffered during the reign of anarchy, made them tremble at a change, and patiently submit to trifling inconveniences to avoid the risk of positive evils.

This generation however passed away, and with it died, not only the recollection of the past misfortunes of the kingdom, but also the spirit of content they had engendered. A new race arose, who, with the ignorance and presumption of inexperience, found fault with every thing they did not understand, and accused the Queen and her ministers of dotage, merely because they did not accomplish impossibilities. The government, however, was too firmly established to be easily shaken. The judicious economy of the Queen had filled her treasury with riches; her prudent regulations had extended the commerce of her subjects to an almost incredible extent; and her firm and decided disposition made her universally respected both at home and abroad. The malcontents were therefore awed into submission, and obliged, in spite of themselves, to rest satisfied with growling at the government they were not strong enough to overturn. At this time, however, the Queen died, and the state of affairs experienced an important change.

It has been before mentioned, that the religion of the country had altered with its government. Atheism, rational liberty, and fanaticism, had followed each other in regular succession; and the people found, by fatal experience, that persecution and bigotry assimilated as naturally with infidelity as superstition. A fixed government, however, seemed to require an established religion; and the multitude, ever in extremes, rushed from excess of liberty to intolerance. The Catholic faith was restored, new saints were canonized, and confessors appointed in the families of every person of distinction. These priests, however, were far from having the power they had possessed in former times. The eyes of men had been too long opened to be easily closed again. Education still continued amongst the lower classes; and though, at the time this history commences, it was going out of fashion with persons of rank, its influence was felt even by those most prejudiced against it. During the reign of the late Queen, the minds of the public not having any state affairs to occupy them, had been directed to the improvement of the arts and sciences; and so many new inventions had been struck out, so many wonderful discoveries made, and so many ingenious contrivances put into execution, that poor nature seemed degraded from her throne, and usurping man to have stepped up to supply her place.

Before the Queen died, she chose her niece Claudia to succeed her; and as she enacted that none of her successors should marry, she ordered that all future queens should be chosen, by the people, from such female members of her family as might be between twenty and twenty-five years of age, at the time of the throne's becoming vacant. Every male throughout the kingdom who had attained the age of twenty-one, was to have a voice in this election; but as it was presumed it might be inconvenient to convoke these numerous electors into one place, it was agreed that every ten thousand should choose a deputy to proceed to London to represent them, and that a majority of these deputies should elect the Queen. This scheme, however, though feasible in theory, seemed likely to present some difficulties when it was to be put in practice; but of these, the old Queen never troubled herself to think. She had provided against any immediate disturbance by choosing her own successor, and she left posterity to take care of itself.

Queen Claudia was one of those fainéant sovereigns of whom it is extremely difficult to write the history, for the simple but unanswerable reason, that they never perform any action worthy of being recorded. However, though she did not do much good, she seldom did any harm: she thus contrived to escape either violent censure or applause; and, in short, to get through life very decently, without making much bustle about it. She continued the same counsellors that had been employed by her predecessor, appointing the sons, when the fathers died, to save trouble. She left the laws as she found them for the same reason; and, in short, she let the affairs of government go on so quietly, and so exactly in the same routine as before, that for two or three years after her accession, the people were scarcely aware that any change had taken place.

The commencement of the year 2126 was, however, marked by symptoms of turbulence. The malcontents, secretly encouraged by Roderick, King of Ireland, and suffered to gain strength under the easy sway of Claudia, rose to arms in different parts of the kingdom; and marching to London, attempted to seize the person of the Queen. For the moment, the regular forces of the kingdom seemed paralysed, and the insurgents would have succeeded in their daring attempt, but for the presence of mind and valour of Edmund Montagu, a young officer of ancient family, a captain in the Queen's body-guard, who had the good fortune to rescue his sovereign.

This circumstance was decisive; the rebels, disappointed in their hopes, and imperfectly organized, gave way everywhere before the regular troops, who had now recovered from their stupor; whilst the Queen, whose gratitude for the timely succour afforded by Edmund Montagu was unbounded, made him commander of her forces in Germany, and the youthful hero quitted England to take possession of his post.

CHAPTER II.

High and distinguished as was the favour shown to Edmund Montagu, it was by no means greater than he deserved. His face and figure were such as the imagination delights to picture as a hero of antiquity; and his character accorded well with the majestic graces of his person. Haughty and commanding in his temper — ambition was his God, and love of glory his strongest passion; yet his very pride had a nobleness in it, and his soldiers loved though they feared him.

Very different was the character of his younger brother Edric, whose romantic disposition and contemplative turn of mind often excited the ridicule of his friends. As usual, however, in similar cases, the persecutions he endured upon the subject, only wedded him more firmly to his own peculiar opinions; which, indeed, he seemed determined to sustain with the constancy of a martyr; whilst he put on such a countenance of resolution and magnanimity whenever they were assailed by jests or raillery, as might have been imagined suitable to an expiring Indian at the stake. Unfortunately, however, his friends did not always properly estimate this dignified silence; and their repeated bursts of laughter grated so harshly in the ears of the youthful Diogenes, that he became gradually disgusted with mankind. He secluded himself from society; despised the opinion of the world, because he found it was against him; and supposed himself capable of resisting every species of temptation, simply because, as yet, he had met with nothing adequate to tempt him. Older and more experienced persons have made the same mistake.

The education of these two young men had been entrusted to tutors of characters as essentially different as those of their pupils. — Father Morris, who had had the care of the elder, was an intelligent Catholic priest, the confessor of the family. Whilst Doctor Entwerfen, who took charge of the younger, was a worthy inoffensive man, whose passion for trying experiments was his leading foible; but whose good-nature caused him to be beloved, even by those to whom his follies made him appear ridiculous.

Sir Ambrose Montagu, the father of Edmund and Edric, was a widower, and these two sons constituted his whole family. The worthy Baronet was no bad representative of what an old English country gentleman always has been, and of what it still continued, even in that age of refinement. He was as warm in his feelings as hasty in his temper, and as violent in his prejudices, as any of his predecessors. In fact, the same causes must always lead to the same results; and there is something in a country life that never fails to produce certain peculiar effects upon the mind.

Sir Ambrose, however, was far superior to the generality of his class, and amongst innumerable other good qualities, he was an indulgent master and an affectionate father. His foible, however, — for alas! where shall we find character without one, — was a desire to show occasionally how implicitly he could be obeyed. In general, he was easy to a fault; and it was only when roused by opposition, that the natural obstinacy of his disposition displayed itself. Edmund was his favourite son; the early military glory of the youthful hero was flattering to his parental pride, and his eyes would glisten with delight at the bare mention of his darling's name.

It was one fine evening in the summer of the year 2126, when Sir Ambrose Montagu, such as we have described him, was sitting in his library, anxiously expecting intelligence from the army. To divert his impatience, he had ordered the attendance of his steward Mr. Davis, and endeavoured to amuse himself by hearing a report of the affairs of his farm; whilst Abelard, an old butler, who had been in the Baronet's service more than forty years, stood behind his master's chair holding a small tray, on which was placed an elegant apparatus for smoking, and a magnificent service of malleable glass, made to fold up to a pocket size, when not in use, containing the baronet's evening refreshment.

Sir Ambrose was above seventy; and his long white hair hung in waving curls upon his shoulders, as he now sat in his comfortable elastic arm-chair, leaning one elbow upon the table before him. His features had been very handsome, and his complexion still retained that look of health and cleanness, which, in a green old age, is the sure indication of a well-spent life. His countenance, though intelligent, was unmarked by the traces of any stormy passions; the cares and troubles of life seemed to have passed gently over him, and content had smoothed the wrinkles age might have made upon his brow; whilst the tall thin figure of Mr. Davis, as he stood reverentially bending forward, his hat in his hand, and his whole demeanour expressing a singular mixture of preciseness and habitual respect, contrasted strongly with the dignified appearance of his master.

The windows of the library opened to the ground, and looked out upon a fine terrace, shaded by a verandah, supported by trellis-work, round which, twined roses mingled

The Mummy!

with vines. Below, stretched a smiling valley, beautifully wooded, and watered by a majestic river winding slowly along; now lost amidst the spreading foliage of the trees that hung over its banks, and then shining forth again in the sun like a lake of liquid silver. Beyond, rose hills majestically towering to the skies, their clear outline now distinctly marked by the setting sun, as it slowly sunk behind them, shedding its glowing tints of purple and gold upon their heathy sides; whilst some of its brilliant rays even penetrated through the leafy shade of the verandah, and danced like summer lightning upon the surface of a mirror of polished steel which hung directly in face of Sir Ambrose.

"What a lovely evening!" exclaimed the worthy baronet, gazing with a delighted eye upon the rich landscape before him; "often as I have looked upon this scene, methinks every time I see it I discover some new beauty. How finely that golden tint which the sun throws upon the tops of those trees is relieved by the deep masses of shadow below!"

"It is a fine evening," said Davis, bowing low, "and if your honour pleases, I think we had better get the patent steam-mowing apparatus in motion to-morrow. If the sun should be as hot to-morrow as it has been to-day, I am sure the hay will make without using the burning glass at all."

"Do as you like, Davis," returned his master, taking his pipe, "you know I leave these matters entirely to you."

"And does not your honour think I had better give the barley a little rain? It will be all burnt up, if this weather continues; and if your honour approves, it may be done immediately, for I saw a nice black heavy-looking cloud sailing by just now, and I can get the electrical machine out in five minutes to draw it down, if your honour thinks fit."

"I have already told you I leave these things entirely to you, Davis," returned the baronet, puffing out volumes of smoke from his hookah. "Inundate the fields if you will; you have my full permission to do whatever you please with them, so that you don't trouble me any more about the matter."

"But I would not wish to act without your honour's full conviction," resumed the persevering steward. "Your honour must be aware of the aridity of the soil, and of the impossibility that exists of a proper development of the incipient heads, unless they be supplied with an adequate quantity of moisture."

"You are very unreasonable, Davis," aid Sir Ambrose; "most of your fraternity would be satisfied by being permitted to have their own way; but you — —"

"Excuse my interrupting your honour," cried Davis, bowing profoundly; "but I cannot bear it to be thought that I was capable of persuading your honour to take any steps, your honour might not thoroughly approve. Now as to the germinization and ripening — —"

"My good fellow!" exclaimed Sir Ambrose, smiling at the energy with which Davis spoke — his thin figure waving backwards and forwards in the sunshine, and his earnest wish to convince his master, almost depriving his voice of its usual solemn and sententious tone. "As I said before, I give you full and free liberty to burn, dry, or drown my fields, as you may think fit; empowering you to take any steps you judge proper, either to germinate or ripen corn upon any part of my estate whatever, only premising, that in future you never trouble me upon the subject; and so good night."

This being spoken in a tone of voice Davis did not dare to disobey, he slowly retired, apparently as much annoyed at having his own way, as some people are at being contradicted; when suddenly a brilliant flash of light gleamed on the baronet's polished mirror. "Ah! what was that?" exclaimed Sir Ambrose, starting up, and dashing his pipe upon the ground.

He gazed eagerly upon the mirror for a few seconds in breathless anxiety, bending forwards in a listening attitude, and not daring to stir, as though he feared the slightest movement might destroy the pleasing illusion. The flash was repeated again and again in rapid succession, whilst a peal of silver bells began to ring their rounds in liquid melody. "Thank God! thank God!" exclaimed the aged baronet, sinking upon his knees, and clasping his hands together, whilst the big tears rolled rapidly down his face, "My Edmund has conquered! my Edmund is safe!"

The faithful servants of Sir Ambrose followed the example of their master, and for some minutes the whole party appeared lost in silent thanksgiving; the silver bells still continuing their harmonious sweetness, though in softer and softer strains, till at last they gradually died away upon the ear. Sir Ambrose started from his knees as the melody ceased, and desiring Abelard to summon Edric and Father Morris, he rushed upon the terrace, followed by Davis, to examine a telegraph placed upon a mount at little distance, so as to be seen from one end of it: the light and music just mentioned, being a signal always given, when some important information was about to be transmitted.

The sun had now sunk behind the hills, and the shades of evening were rapidly closing in as the baronet, with streaming eyes, watched, the various movements of the machine. "One, two, and six!" said he; "yes, that signifies he has won the battle, and is safe. My heart told me so, when I saw the signal flash. My darling Edmund!—two, four, and eight—he has subdued the Germans, and taken the whole of the fine province of France. Six, six, and four—alas! my failing eyes are too weak to see distinctly. Davis, look I implore you! The signal is changing before we have discovered its meaning! For mercy's sake, look before it be too late! Alas! alas! I had forgotten your eyes are as feeble as mine own. Oh, Davis! where is Edric? Why is not he here to assist his poor old father at such a moment as this?"

In the meantime, Edric was, as usual, engaged in those abstract speculations with Dr. Entwerfen, which now formed the only pleasure of his existence, and which he pursued with an eagerness that made all the ordinary affairs of life appear tasteless and insipid. His imagination had become heated by long dwelling upon the same theme; and a strange, wild, indefinable craving to hold converse with a disembodied spirit haunted him incessantly. He had long buried this feverish anxiety in his own breast, and tried in vain to subdue it; but it seemed to hang upon his steps, to present itself before him wherever he went, and, in short, to pursue him with the malignancy of a demon.

"What is the matter with you, Edric?" said Dr. Entwerfen to his pupil, the day we have already mentioned. "You are so changed, I scarcely know you, and your eyes have a wild expression, absolutely terrific."

"I am, indeed, half mad," returned Edric, with a melancholy smile; "and yet, perhaps, you will laugh when I tell you the reason of my uneasiness. I am tormented by an earnest desire to communicate with one who has been an inhabitant of the tomb. I would fain know the secrets of the grave, and ascertain whether the spirit be chained after death to its earthly covering of clay, condemned till the day of final resurrection to hover over the rotting mass of corruption that once contained it; or whether the last agonies of death free it from its mortal ties, and leave it floating, free as air, in the bright regions of ethereal space?"

"You know my opinion," said the doctor.

"I do," replied the pupil; "but forgive me if I add—I do not feel satisfied with it: in fact mine is not a character to be satisfied with building my faith upon that of any other man. I would see, and judge for myself."

"I do not blame you," resumed the doctor; "a reasonable being should believe nothing he cannot prove;—however, to remove your doubts, I am convinced we have only occasion to step into the adjoining church-yard, and try my galvanic battery of fifty surgeon power, (which you must allow is surely enough to re-animate the dead,) upon a body, and then——"

"Hold! hold!" cried Edric, shuddering. "My blood freezes in my veins, at the thought of a church-yard:—your words recall a horrible dream that I had last night, which, even now, dwells upon my mind, and resists all the efforts I can make to shake it off."

"Tell it to me, then," resumed the doctor; "for when the imagination is possessed by horrible fantasies, it is often relieved by speaking of them to another person."

"I thought," said Edric, "that I was wandering in a thick gloomy wood, through which I had the utmost difficulty to make my way. The black trees, frowning in awful majesty above my head, twined together in masses, so as almost to obstruct my path. Suddenly, a fearful light flashed upon me, and I saw at my feet a horrid charnel house, where the dying mingled terrifically with the dead. The miserable living wretches turned and writhed with pain, striving in vain to escape from the mass of putrescence heaped upon them. I saw their eye-balls roll in agony—I watched the distortion of their features, and, making a violent effort to relieve one who had almost crawled to my feet, I shrank back with horror as I found the arm I grasped give way to my touch, and a disgusting mass of corruption crumble beneath my fingers!—Shuddering I awoke—a cold sweat hanging upon my brows, and every nerve thrilling with convulsive agony."

"Mere visionary terrors," said the doctor. "You have suffered your imagination to dwell upon one subject, till it is become morbid.—However, though I do not see any reason why your dream should make you decline my offer, I will not urge it if it give you pain."

"Is it not strange," continued Edric, apparently pursuing the current of his own thoughts, "that the mind should crave so earnestly what the body shudders at; and yet, how can a mass

The Mummy!

of mere matter, which we see sink into corruption the moment the spirit is withdrawn from it, shudder? How can it even feel? I can scarcely analyse my own sensations; but it appears to me that two separate and distinct spirits animate the mass of clay that composes the human frame. The one, the merely vital spark which gives it life and motion, and which we share in common with brutes, and even vegetables; and the other, the divine ethereal spirit, which we may properly term the soul, and which is a direct emanation from God himself, only bestowed upon man."

"You know my sentiments upon the subject," replied the doctor, "therefore I need not repeat them."

"I know," resumed Edric, "you think the organs of thought, reflection, imagination, reason, and, in short, all that mysterious faculty which we call the mind, material; and that as long as the body remains uncorrupted they may be restored, provided circulation can be renewed: for that you think the only principle necessary to set the animal machine in motion."

"Can any thing be more clear?" said the doctor. "We all know that circulation and the action of the lungs are inseparably connected, and that if the latter be arrested, death must ensue. How frequently are apparently dead bodies recovered by friction, which produces circulation; and inflation of the lungs with air, which restores their action. If your idea be correct, that the soul leaves the body the instant what we call death takes place, how do you account for these instances of resuscitation? Think you that the soul can be recalled to the body after it has once quitted it? Or that it hovers over it in air, attached to it by invisible ligatures, ready to be drawn back to its former situation, when the body shall resume its vital functions? You cannot surely suppose it remains in a dormant state, and is reawakened with the body; for this would be inconsistent with the very idea of an incorporeal spirit."

"Certainly," resumed Edric, "the spirit must be capable of existing perfectly distinct from the body; though how, I own candidly my imperfect reason cannot enable me to comprehend."

"I wish you would overcome your childish reluctance to trying an experiment upon a corpse, as that must set your doubts at rest. For if we could succeed in re-animating a dead body that has been long entombed, so that it might enjoy its reasoning faculties, or, as you call it, its soul in full perfection, my opinion would be completely established."

"But where shall we find a perfect body, which has been dead a sufficient time to prevent the possibility of its being only in a trance? — For even if I could conquer the repugnance I feel at the thought of touching such a mass of cold mortality, as that presented in my dream last night, according to your own theory, the organs must be perfect, or the experiment will not be complete."

"What think you of trying to operate upon a mummy? You know a chamber has been lately discovered in the great pyramid, which is supposed to be the real tomb of Cheops; and where, it is said, the mummies of that great king and the principal personages of his household have been found in a state of wonderful preservation."

"But mummies are so swathed up."

"Not those of kings and princes. You know all travellers, both ancient and modern, who have seen them, agree, that they are wrapped merely in folds of red and white linen, every finger and even every toe distinct; thus, if we could succeed in resuscitating Cheops, we need not even touch the body; as the clothing it is wrapped in will not at all encumber its movements."

"The idea is feasible, and, as you rightly say, if it can be put into execution, it will set the matter at rest for ever. I should also like to visit the pyramids, those celebrated monuments of antiquity, whose origin is lost in the obscurity of the darker ages, and which seem to have been spared by the devastating hand of time, purposely to perplex the learned."

"You say right," cried the doctor with enthusiasm. "And who can tell but that we may be the favoured happy mortals, destined to raise the mystic veil that has so long covered them? we may be destined to explore these wonderful monuments — to revive their mummies, and force them to reveal the secrets of their prison-house. Cheops is said to have built the great pyramid, and it is Cheops whom we shall endeavour to re-animate! what then can be more palpable, than that it should be he who is destined at length to reveal the mystery."

"Every word you utter, doctor, increases my ardent desire to put our scheme into immediate execution: but how can we accomplish it? How obtain my father's consent? You know it has long been his intention to marry me to the niece of his friend the Duke of Cornwall, and you know how obstinate both he and the duke are."

"Then if you remain in England, it is your intention to marry Rosabella?"

"I would perish first."

"If that be the case, I confess I do not see the force of your objection."

"True; for as long as I refuse to marry her, their anger will be the same, whether I travel or remain in England. In fact, I shall be happier at a distance than here, where I shall be annoyed by having the subject constantly recurred to. Yet it pains me to speak upon it to my father. He has so long cherished the idea of my marriage, and dwelt upon it so fondly—"

"Then you had better stay,—relinquish all thoughts of scientific discoveries, and settle contentedly on an estate in the country; employing your time in regulating your farm, settling the disputes of your neighbours, and bringing up your children, if you should happen to have any."

"How can you torment me so?—If you could imagine the struggle in my bosom, between inclination and duty, you would pity me."

"Do you think your presence necessary to your father's happiness?"

"No—if Edmund be with him, he will never think of me."

"And do you not think—nay, are you not certain, that an union with Rosabella would make you miserable?"

"It is impossible to doubt it. Her violent temper, and the mystery which hangs over the fate of her father, which she cannot bear to have even alluded to, forbid the thought of happiness as connected with her."

"It is strange, so little should be known of her father. I never heard the particulars of his story."

"No human being knows the whole, I believe, but the duke and my father. However, I remember to have heard it rumoured when I was a child, that he had committed some fearful crime, and that he was either executed, or had destroyed himself."

"Then it is not surprising that it should pain Rosabella to hear him spoken of. But to return to our subject: your answers have removed the only doubts that can arise; and after what you have confessed yourself, I cannot imagine what further hesitation you can feel—"

At this moment they were both startled; and the words were arrested on the doctor's lips by a gentle tap at the door. It was old Abelard the butler. Half ashamed of the unphilosophic terror he had evinced, the doctor felt glad to be able to hide his emotion under the appearance of anger, and demanded peevishly, what was the matter. "Have I not told you a hundred times," continued he, "that I do not like to be interrupted at my studies! and that nothing is more disagreeable than to have one's attention distracted, when it has been fixed upon an affair of importance!"

"I do not attempt to controvert the axiom you have just propounded," returned Abelard, speaking in a slow precise manner, as though he weighed every syllable before he drawled it forth: "for undeniable facts do not admit of contradiction. However, as the message with which I stand charged at the present moment relates to master Edric, instead of yourself, I humbly opine, no blame can attach itself to me, on account of the unpremeditated interruption of which you allege me culpable."

"And what have you to say to me?" demanded Edric.

"That the worthy gentleman, your respectable progenitor, requests you instantly to put in exercise your locomotive powers to join him on the terrace, to the end, that there your superior visual faculties may afford soulagement to the mental anxiety under which he at present labours, by aiding him to develop the intelligence conveyed to him by the telegraphic machine."

"What!" exclaimed Edric, eagerly, and then, without waiting a reply, he darted forward, and in a few seconds was by the side of his father.

Abelard gazed after him with amazement: "There is something very astonishing," said he, addressing Dr. Entwerfen, "in the effervescence of the animal spirits during youth. I labour under a complete acatalepsy upon the subject; I should think it must arise from the excessive elasticity of the nerves. Ideas strike—" but here, happening unfortunately to look up, he too was struck to find Dr. Entwerfen had vanished with his pupil, and unwilling to waste his eloquence upon the empty air, he also departed; slowly and solemnly, however, according to his custom, to join the party assembled on the terrace.

CHAPTER III.

When Edric and Dr. Entwerfen reached Sir Ambrose, they found Father Morris at his side, explaining with his usual promptness and clearness the meaning of the different signs of the telegraph.

"My dear Edric," exclaimed Sir Ambrose, throwing himself into the arms of his son, "my dear, dear Edric! your brother has gained the battle! The Germans are completely overthrown. He has taken their king, and several of their princes prisoners; and the fine province of France is ceded to us entirely!"

"I am rejoiced to hear it," cried Edric, returning his father's embrace with emotion, "and he, I hope, is safe?"

"I hope so too," replied Sir Ambrose; "though he says nothing of himself: but you know Edmund: 'Our troops won this,' 'our army gained that!' — 'the soldiers fought bravely!' — he never speaks of himself. To hear him relate a battle, nobody would imagine he had ever had any thing to do with it."

"It is too dark to see any more," said Father Morris, who had been for some time watching the telegraph, and now turned from it in despair; "the machine is still in motion, but it is too dark for me to decipher what it means."

The attention of all present was directed to the sky as he spoke. It was indeed become of pitchy blackness, a general gloom seemed to hang over the face of nature; the birds flew twittering for shelter, a low wind moaned through the trees, and, in short, every thing seemed to portend a storm.

"Had we not better return to the house?" said Dr. Entwerfen, looking round with something like fear at these alarming indications, for his heated imagination had not yet quite recovered the effect of the awful speculations he had so lately been indulging in. "What is that black spot there? I declare it moves! Good heavens, what can it be?"

"Really, doctor!" returned Abelard, "you provoke the action of my risible faculties. That opaque body which you perceive at a little distance, and which seems to have occasioned such a fearful excitement of your nervous system, is only a living specimen of the corvus genus, who has probably descended upon earth to search for his vermicular repast."

"I beg your pardon, Mr. Abelard," rejoined Mr. Davis, speaking with his usual precision, "but, according to my humble apprehension, you labour under a slight mistake as to that particular. The feathered biped that has so forcibly attracted your attention, appears to me, not one of the corvi, but rather one of the graculi; a variety of extremely rare occurrence in this vicinity, and which are sometimes called incendriæ aves, from their unfortunate propensity to put habitations in combustion, by picking up small pieces of phlogisticated carbon, and carrying them in their beaks to the combination of straw and other materials, sometimes piled upon the apex of a house, to defend it from the inroads of pluviosity."

"It is of no use," sighed Sir Ambrose, still straining his eyes to endeavour to decipher the movements of the telegraph, the outlines of which only now appeared, stamped as if in jet, and strongly relieved by the dark grey sky beyond.

"It is of no use," reiterated Father Morris, and the whole party were preparing to retire, when suddenly a vivid light flashed upon them from the hill, and instantly a long line of torches seemed to stream along the horizon. "He is coming home, but will write more to-morrow," exclaimed the whole party simultaneously; for all knew well by experience, the meaning of that signal. "He is coming home, thank God!" repeated Sir Ambrose, his pallid lips quivering, and every limb trembling with agitation.

"Look to my father," cried Edric, "he will faint."

"Oh no, no!" repeated Sir Ambrose: "thank God! thank God!"

"Lean upon me, at least," said Edric, affectionately.

Sir Ambrose complied; and, supported by his son, still gazed anxiously on the torches, their red glare shedding an unnatural light around them, and making the surrounding darkness only appear still more intense. Thunder now growled in the distance, and rain began to fall in large drops; yet still Sir Ambrose gazed upon the torches, and could not be persuaded to leave the terrace. These wild, fearful looking lights, gleaming through the tempest, seemed a connecting link between him and his darling son; and it was not till they were obscured by the thick heavy rain, and even the outline of the telegraph vanished in the gathering clouds around, that he could be induced to seek for shelter.

The Mummy!

Sir Ambrose slept little that night: the sleep of age is easily broken, and perhaps the joyful agitation of his spirits had produced a slight access of fever. He rose with the dawn; and, long before the rest of his family had descended, summoned Abelard, that he might dispatch him to inform his most intimate friend the Duke of Cornwall of the news.

"Go," said he, as soon as the drowsy butler made his appearance. "I am sure the duke feels nearly as great an interest in the success of Edmund as myself, and will not be displeased if he be disturbed a little earlier than usual upon such an occasion."

"I obey," replied Abelard. "I will shake off my somnolent propensities, and speed with the velocity of the electric fluid to the castle of the noble chieftain."

"Take heed you do not forget your message by the way," repeated Sir Ambrose, smiling.

"Not all the waters of Lethe could wash such somnifugous tidings from my memory," replied the butler. "Your honour's words are imprinted upon the mnemonic organ of my brain; and my sensorium must be divided from my cerebellum ere they can be effaced."

The Duke of Cornwall had been the intimate friend of Sir Ambrose almost from infancy. They had been companions at school and at college; besides which, peculiar circumstances which had happened in their youth, had linked them together in indissoluble ties. What these circumstances were, however, no one exactly knew, except the parties concerned, and they always avoided alluding to them. All that was generally understood upon the subject, being, that Sir Ambrose had, in some manner, been instrumental in saving the duke's life; but how, when, or where, was never clearly explained.

The Duke of Cornwall was of the Royal family of England, and closely allied to the throne. His father had been brother to that prince who had so stedfastly refused the crown when it was offered to him by the ambassadors from the people; and as that prince had left no male descendants, the duke might be considered as legitimately entitled to reign. The thought of disturbing by his claims the female dynasty now established, had, however, never entered into the mind of the duke; who, with half the sense of his friend Sir Ambrose, possessed, at least, ten times the obstinacy; and having taken it into his head that he would marry his daughter Elvira to Edmund Montagu, and his niece Rosabella to Edric, he turned all his thoughts, plans, and wishes to the accomplishment of this object, and suffered no other idea to interfere with it.

Those, however, who were acquainted with the characters of the young people, thought the duke had quite reversed the natural order of things by this arrangement; and that the strong mind and haughty spirit of Rosabella would have suited better with the ambitious Edmund; whilst the soft yielding disposition and feminine graces of Elvira seemed to harmonize exactly with the taste of the philosophic Edric. No persuasions, however, could induce the duke to deviate in the slightest degree from his design. Like many of the higher classes of society in those days of universal education, he affected an excessive plainness and simplicity in his language; so much so, indeed, as sometimes almost to degenerate into rudeness, in order that it might be clearly distinguished from the elaborate and scientific expressions of the vulgar; and when urged upon the subject of these intended marriages, he would roughly say, "Don't talk to me; there is nothing like a little contradiction in the married life. If two people were to agree to live together, who were always of the same opinion, they would die of ennui in six months. No, no, I'm right, and so they'll find it in the end."

He would then shake his head, and put on such a look of positive determination, that his friends would generally retire in silence, feeling it perfectly in vain to attempt to alter his resolution. As to consulting the inclinations of the young people themselves, the idea never entered his imagination. "Children don't know what is good for them," he would reply sharply, if any one presumed to suggest such a thought, "and it is the duty of parents and guardians to decide in such matters."

Sir Ambrose, wishing the connection for his sons, and respecting even the whims of his friend, had as yet never interfered, and the young people had also appeared silently to acquiesce. Rebellious spirits, however, were hidden under this apparent calm; and the duke was soon to learn from experience, that human beings were rather more difficult to manage than a drove of turkeys, or a flock of sheep; a fact, of which before he did not seem to have the slightest suspicion.

The duke had already risen, and was in his garden, when the messenger of Sir Ambrose arrived panting for breath, and quite exhausted by the velocity which, as he expressed it, he had employed in endeavouring to execute with the utmost expedition, the implied wishes of his master. The duke was surprised to see him.—"What brings you out so early, Abelard?"

demanded he.

"Oh, your grace," replied the butler, gasping for utterance, "the haste I have made has impeded my respiration; and the blood, finding the pulmonary artery free, rushes with such force along the arterial canal to the aorta, that—that—I am in imminent danger of being suffocated."

"Pshaw!" said the duke.

"Besides," continued Abelard, "a saline secretion distils from every pore of my skin, in a serous transudation, from the excessive exertions I have made use of."

"And what has occasioned these violent exertions?"

"The earnest desire experienced by Sir Ambrose to transmit with all the expedition possible, to your grace, the intelligence he has just received of the acquisition of a victory by Master Edmund, in the hostile territory of Germany."

"Victory!" shouted the duke, "Victory—Rosabella! Elvira! where are you, girls? Here's tidings to rouse you from your slumbers.—And how is he, Abelard? Is the brave boy safe himself? God bless him! victory will be nothing to us, if we are to lose him."

"It occasions me excessive chagrin," replied Abelard, "that I am totally unable to resolve that interrogatory to your grace's complete satisfaction. Taciturnity, however, upon some subjects, is, I believe, generally considered synonymous with prosperity; and, as Master Edmund, to the best of my credence, conveyed no information relative to his sanity in the communication made by him to his paternal ancestor, I humbly opine that there are no reasonable grounds for supposing it has suffered any material deterioration in consequence of the late sanguinary encounter in which he has been engaged."

The duke had not patience to wait the conclusion of this speech; but hobbled away as fast as his infirmities would permit, vociferating for Elvira and Rosabella, in a voice that might have silenced Stentor; and Abelard, finding himself alone, was fain to follow his example, marvelling as he went along, however, at the excessive impatience of the fiery spirits of the age, which would not permit people to remain stationary, even to hear, what he called, a compendious replication to the very questions which they themselves had propounded.

Whatever faults might fall to the share of the Duke of Cornwall, that of a cold heart was certainly not amongst the number, and the delight he felt on hearing of Edmund's triumph could not have been greater if the youthful hero had been his own son. His eyes, indeed, absolutely sparkled with transport, when he communicated the intelligence to his niece and daughter; and his tidings were not bestowed upon insensible ears, for the breasts of both his youthful auditors throbbed with pleasure at the news, though the causes of their emotions were different. Elvira had been the idol of Edmund's homage from her childhood; and she fancied she returned his passion with equal fervour; but she deceived herself, and love was as yet a stranger to her heart. Endowed with great beauty and superior talents; accustomed from her earliest infancy to be worshipped by all around her; surrounded by flatterers, till even flattery itself had lost its charm, Elvira was as yet insensible to love; why she was so, we leave to philosophers to explain; we merely state facts and leave others to draw conclusions.

Rosabella's character was essentially different from that of her cousin. Passion was the essence of her existence; and her dark eyes flashed a fire that bespoke the intensity of her feelings. She loved Edmund, but though she loved him with all that overwhelming violence, that only a soul like hers could feel, yet she would not have scrupled to sacrifice even him to her revenge, if she had thought he treated her with negligence or contempt. She scorned the opinion of the world, and regarded mankind in general but as slaves, whom she should honour by trampling beneath her feet. Ambition, however, was her leading passion, and even her love for Edmund struggled in vain for mastery against it. This feeling was now highly gratified by the tidings of Edmund's victory. She triumphed in his glory; and a deeper glow burnt upon her cheek, from the proud consciousness she felt that she had not placed her affections upon an unworthy object.

"We have no time to lose, girls," said the duke. "I would not miss being with Sir Ambrose when he receives his letter, for kingdoms. Here, Hyppolite! Augustus! get a balloon ready, and let us be off directly. How tedious these fellows are! They might have removed a church steeple in the time they have wasted about that balloon."

"If your grace would have a moment's patience," said Hyppolite, holding the cords of the balloon. But his Grace had no patience; it was an ingredient Nature had quite forgotten to put into his composition; and, without waiting for the

The Mummy!

ascending ladder to be put down, he sprang into the car in such haste the moment the balloon was brought to the door, that he was in imminent danger of oversetting it. "So! so!" said he, "very well! that will do,—and now girls, that you are safely embarked, we will be off. Hyppolite! you will steer us:—and, Abelard, go you into the buttery, and let my fellows give you something to eat; you will want something after your fatigues. There! there, that will do; don't let us hinder a moment— —;" and the rest of his speech was lost in air, as the balloon floated majestically away.

"It has often appeared very astonishing to me," said Abelard, after watching the balloon till it was out of sight, "to observe how partial great people are generally to an aërial mode of travelling; for my part, I think the pedestrian manner infinitely more agreeable."

"De gustibus non est disputandum," replied Augustus, the duke's footman, to whom this observation was addressed:—"But I think I observe symptoms of lassitude about you, Mr. Abelard. Will you not adjourn to the apartment of Mrs. Russel, our housekeeper, to repair by some alimentary refreshment, the excessive exhaustion you have sustained in the course of your morning's exertions?"

"Willingly, Mr. Augustus.—I own candidly, I feel the want of a little wholesome nutrition. I shall, besides, be extremely happy to avail myself of the opportunity fortune so benignantly presents, of paying my respects to Mrs. Russel, whom I have not seen these three days."

The worthy housekeeper was equally rejoiced with Abelard at this instance of fortune's benignity; a sort of sentimental flirtation having been going on between them for the last thirty years. She accordingly stroked down her snow-white apron, re-adjusted her mob cap, and smoothed her grey hairs, which were divided upon her forehead, with the most scrupulous exactness, before she advanced to welcome her visitors. "What will you take, my dear Mr. Abelard?" said she, as soon as he was within hearing; "what can you fancy? I have a delicious corner of a cold venison pasty in my pantry."

"Words are altogether too feeble to express the transports of my gratitude at receiving so gracious an accolade, beauteous Eloisa," replied the romantic butler; for thus, in allusion to his own name, was he wont to call her. "But though you had only the rigours of the Paraclete to invite me to, instead of the comforts of your well-stored pantry, still would words be wanting to express the feeling of my bosom on thus again beholding you."

"Spare my blushes!" said Mrs. Russel, casting her eyes upon the ground, and playing with a corner of her apron. "I feel a roseate suffusion glow upon my cheeks, as your flattering accents strike upon the tympanum of my auricular organs."

"Oh, Mrs. Russel!" sighed Abelard, gazing upon her tenderly;—then, after a short pause, he continued: "As to the aliments with which your provident kindness would soulage my appetite—though venison be a wholesome viand, and was reckoned by the ancients efficacious in preventing fevers, and though the very mention of the savoury pasty makes the eryptæ, usually employed in secreting the mucus of my tongue, erect themselves, thereby occasioning an overflow of the saliva, yet will I deny myself the indulgence, and content myself simply with a boiled egg, as being more likely to agree with the present enfeebled state of the digestive organs of my stomach."

"You shall have it instantly," cried Mrs. Russel.

"And will you have the kindness to superintend the culinary arrangement of it yourself?" rejoined Abelard. "I do not like the albumen too much coagulated; and I prefer it without any butyraceous oil, simply flavoured by the addition of a small quantity of common muriate of soda."

The egg was soon prepared and devoured. "Thank you, thank you! dear Mrs. Russel," said Abelard; "this refection was most acceptable. I had felt for some time the gastric juice corroding the coats of my stomach; and still, though I have now given it some solid substance to act upon, I think it would not be amiss to dilute its virulence by the addition of a little fluid. Have you any thing cool and refreshing?"

"I have some bottled beer," replied Mrs. Russel; "but I am afraid the carbonic acid gas has not been sufficiently disengaged during the process of the vinous fermentation to render it wholesome; and there is scarcely any alcohol in the whole composition——"

"That is exactly what I want," said Abelard; "for my physicians have expressly forbidden stimulants. Provided the gluten that forms the germ was properly separated in the preparation of the malt, and the seed sufficiently germinated to convert the fecula into sugar, I shall be perfectly satisfied."

The Mummy!

"I can guarantee the accuracy of its preparation both with regard to the malt and the beer," repeated Mrs. Russel; and the frothing fluid soon sparkled in a goblet, to the infinite satisfaction of the thirsty butler, who, after a hearty draught, vowed nectar itself was never half so delicious; and that all the gods on Olympus would envy him, if they could but taste his fare, and see the blooming Hebe that was his cup-bearer.

CHAPTER IV.

When the balloon of the duke approached the habitation of Sir Ambrose, its occupiers perceived the worthy baronet walking with hasty strides towards the mount of the telegraph, which commanded an extensive view of the surrounding country, followed by Edric and Dr. Entwerfen, who appeared vainly endeavouring to persuade him to relax a speed so little suited to his advanced years.

"Talk not to me of going slowly, when I expect news of my darling Edmund!" exclaimed Sir Ambrose, continuing his rapid pace—his heart beating with paternal pride, and his countenance beaming with exultation.

"I am also anxious to hear of my brother," said Edric, "but after the information we have already received by the telegraphic dispatch, it appears to me that we have little more to learn of importance."

"Edric, you are not a father, and you can have no idea of a father's anxiety," replied Sir Ambrose, hurrying on to the mount, as though he hoped the rapidity of his motion would afford some relief to the impatience of his mind; whilst the party of the duke, seeing the point to which he was hastening, opened the valves of their balloon, and made preparations to descend upon the same spot.

The duke and Sir Ambrose were always glad to meet, but as the present occasion was one of more than ordinary interest, so they now greeted each other with more than ordinary pleasure. The duke had always been warmly attached to Edmund, and his voice actually trembled with agitation as he exclaimed:—

"Well, my old friend, you see your brave boy is determined to keep us alive still. Our blood would stagnate in our veins, if he did not give us a fillip now and then to rouse us. But what does the young rogue say of himself? I hope he's not wounded?"

"He never mentions himself," replied Sir Ambrose, tears glistening in his eyes, as he pressed the hand of his friend warmly in his own; "Edmund loves his country too devotedly to think of either peril or reward in her service."

"But he shall have a reward!" cried the duke, laughing; "ay and a fitting one too! Eh, Elvira, what say you?"

The Mummy!

Elvira blushed, smiled, and looked down, as young ladies generally do upon such occasions; whilst Sir Ambrose, who had now reached the summit of the mount, was too eagerly looking round in every direction to hear his friend's remark.

In those days, the ancient method of conveying the post having been found much too slow for so enlightened a people, an ingenious scheme had been devised, by which the letters were put into balls and discharged by steam-cannon, from place to place; every town and district having a piece of toile metallique, or woven wire, suspended in the air, so as to form a kind of net to arrest the progress of the ball, and being provided with a cannon to send it off again, when the letters belonging to that neighbourhood should have been extracted: whilst, to prevent accidents, the mail-post letter-balls were always preceded by one of a similar description, made of thin wood, with a hole in its side, which, collecting the wind as it passed along, made a kind of whizzing noise, to admonish people to keep out of the way.

The mount on which Sir Ambrose now stood, commanded an extensive view, and the scene it presented was beautiful in the extreme. On one side, innumerable grass fields, richly wooded, and only divided from each other by invisible iron fences, appeared like one vast park; whilst, on the other, the waving corn, its full heads beginning to darken in the sun, gave a rich glowing tint to the landscape. But Sir Ambrose thought not of the prospect, he did not even see the murmuring brooks and shady groves, the smiling vales and swelling hills, that constituted its beauty; no, his attention was wholly occupied by a small black spot he had just discovered on the edge of the horizon. In breathless anxiety, his eyes almost starting from their sockets, he bent eagerly forwards, gazing on this small and at first almost imperceptible speck. It gradually grew larger and larger — it rapidly approached! and in a few seconds a slight noise buzzed through the air, as the long-expected balls whizzed past him.

Sir Ambrose's agitation was excessive; with trembling limbs and livid lips, he hurried to the nearest station, which luckily was close at hand, and round which several of his household were assembled, in their impatience to hear the news. Sir Ambrose could not speak, but the person whose province it was to sort the letters guessed his errand, and opening the bag held forth the ardently expected treasure. Gasping for breath, Sir Ambrose eagerly attempted to take it, but his hands were unequal to the task, the violence of his emotion overpowered him, and after a short, but fruitless struggle, he fell senseless on the ground.

The confusion produced by this unexpected incident, was indescribable. The old duke walked up and down, wringing his hands, and exclaiming, "What shall we do? What will become of us?" whilst the rest of the party endeavoured to give assistance to Sir Ambrose.

"Parental affection," said Davis, who had an unfortunate propensity for making long speeches precisely at the moment when nobody was likely to attend to him, "Parental affection has been universally allowed by all writers, both ancient and modern, to be one of the strongest passions of the soul, and the most exalted instances might be produced of the surprising energy of this universal sentiment."

"For Heaven's sake help me to raise my father," cried Edric: "Give him air, or he will die!"

"Patience," continued Davis, "is necessary in all things, and is perhaps one of the most useful and estimable qualities of life. It enables us to bear, without shrinking, the bitterest evils that can assail us. Without patience, philosophy would never have made those wonderful discoveries that subjugate nature to our yoke."

"Fetch me some water," exclaimed Edric, "or he will expire before your eyes."

"It appears to me," said a labourer, who had been mending a steam digging-machine in a neighbouring field, and who now stood leaning upon his work, and looking on gravely at all that passed, without attempting to offer the least assistance;—"It appears to me that it would be highly improper to administer the aqueous fluid in its natural state of frigidity, under the existing circumstances. The present suspension of animation under which Sir Ambrose labours, is evidently occasioned by want of circulation. Now, as it is the property of hot liquors, rather than cold ones, to supply the stimulant necessary for the reproduction of circulation, I opine that hot water would answer the purpose better than cold."

In the mean time Father Morris had brought some water from a neighbouring fountain, and throwing it on the patient's face, Sir Ambrose opened his eyes: for some moments he stared wildly around him, but, as soon as he began to recollect what had passed, he implored Father Morris to give him his ardently desired letter.

The Mummy!

"You are not yet equal to reading it," said Father Morris compassionately; "I fear the exertion will be too much for you."

"Oh give it me! give it me," exclaimed the poor old man; "if a spark of mercy remain in your soul, do not keep me in this agony!"

It was impossible to resist the tone of real anguish that accompanied these words, as Father Morris put the letter into his hands. — Sir Ambrose took it eagerly; though he trembled so, that he could scarcely break the seal. At last, he tore it open and gazed at its contents, but he could not read a word; he dashed away his tears, and rubbed his eyes impatiently — all was in vain — the writing was still illegible — "Read! read!" cried he, in a voice trembling with agitation, "For Heaven's sake, read! — will no one have pity on me?"

Father Morris took the letter, and read it aloud, whilst Sir Ambrose sate — his eyes raised to Heaven, his hands clasped together, and the tears rolling down his aged cheeks, listening to his words, and drinking in every syllable. After giving a circumstantial account of the battle, and assuring his father that he had not been wounded, Edmund proceeded thus. "The Queen has written me a letter of approbation in her own hand, and has been graciously pleased to signify her intention of honouring me with a triumphal entry into London; she has likewise conferred upon me letters of nobility. The goodness of my sovereign makes a deep impression upon my breast; but for the rest, I assure you that neither the applauses of the multitude, nor the privilege of writing Lord before my name, can afford a moment's satisfaction to a heart that pants only for the pleasure of seeing again those most dear to it; nor shall I enjoy my triumph unless those I love be present to give it zest."

"I congratulate you, my dear patron!" exclaimed Father Morris, as soon as he had finished; "I congratulate you from my inmost soul!"

"Go to his triumph!" exclaimed the duke, rubbing his hands in ecstasy; "Yes, yes, that we will; won't we, my old friend? God bless him! I'm glad he is not hurt, though. And so, you see, in spite of all his glory, he can't be happy without us. How prettily he says that! — 'Not all the approbation of my sovereign, the praises of the people' — nor — nor — what is it? I don't remember the exact words, but I know the sense was, that he couldn't be happy without us, and, God bless him! I'm sure I'm as happy as he can be, at the thought of seeing him."

Sir Ambrose could not reply, but the tears ran down his aged cheeks like rain, as his heart breathed a silent offering of thanksgiving to the Almighty Being who had thus bestowed victory upon his son; and his lips murmured some inarticulate sounds of transport; whilst Elvira and Rosabella mingled their tears with his, for joy often becomes painful and seeks for a relief like grief.

The party now slowly returned to the mansion of Sir Ambrose, so completely occupied in discussing Edmund's letter, as to be totally unaware that Edric had not accompanied them; yet such was the case. The youthful philosopher's heart had swelled almost to bursting, as he had listened to the reading of his brother's letter, and he now rushed into a thick wood, shelving down to a romantic stream, which formed part of the pleasure-grounds of Sir Ambrose.

Almost without knowing where he was going, Edric plunged amongst the trees, and threw himself upon a grassy bank under their shade, upon the border of the rivulet. The gentle murmuring of the water, gave a delightful sense of refreshing coolness, particularly agreeable from the burning heat of the day; and Edric lay, his eyes fixed upon the sparkling waves as they danced in the sunbeams, with both his hands pressed firmly upon his throbbing temples, endeavouring in vain to analyze the new and strange emotions that struggled for mastery in his bosom. By degrees he became more calm; and though his heart still beat with feelings he could not quite explain, he felt soothed by the softly gliding streamlet; and the stormy passions of his breast seemed lulled to tranquillity as one hand fell carelessly down by his side, and the other merely supported the head it no longer constrained.

It was not envy that occasioned Edric's emotions; but shame and indignation burnt in his bosom when he recollected that he was wasting his days in comparative obscurity, whilst his brother, only a few years older than himself, was ennobling the name bequeathed to him by his ancestors.

"And cannot I also become famous?" thought he, his heart swelling with emulation. "Though I abhor the profession of a soldier, are not other ways open to me of attaining eminence? Why should I not exert myself? I will remain in indolence no longer. I, too, will prove myself worthy of my forefathers, and show the world that the exalted blood of the Montagus has not degenerated in my veins!" His eyes sparkled with the thought, and he half raised himself, as though eager to put it into immediate execution. A moment's reflection, however, restored him to himself, and he could not help smiling at his own folly. "And yet I call myself a philosopher," thought he: "Alas! alas! how little do we know ourselves; and after all, the pursuit of knowledge is the only employment worthy of a man of sense: the transitory applause of the multitude, it is beneath him to accept. Nature is the goddess I adore; and if it should be granted to me to explore her secrets, I shall be the happiest of mankind. But why should I pass my life in anxious cravings never destined to be realized? The events of to-day have only proved yet more clearly the little value my society is of to my father. Were I absent, I should soon be forgotten. Why then should I not travel and satisfy these restless wishes that gnaw at my heart and poison every pleasure? I was not born to rest contented with the dull routine of domestic life, and I detest hypocrisy: I will seek my father; and, explaining my real sentiments, break off this hated marriage and set off for Egypt immediately."

Satisfied with this resolution, Edric rose and walked hastily towards his father's mansion, with all that inward vigour which the consciousness of having made up one's mind is certain to bestow; and which, perhaps, is one of the most agreeable sensations that can be experienced by the human mind, as that of suspense or indecision is undoubtedly one of the most unpleasant.

Edric found his father and the duke busily engaged in consulting upon their intended journey, which was an event in both their lives; for as, since the universal adoption of balloons, journeys were performed without either trouble or expense, the rich had lost all inducement to undertake them, and it was rare for a man of rank to quit his family mansion unless he had some post at court.

"I have a palace in London," said the duke, "which I hope you will make your home; though it has been so long unused that I doubt whether it will be fit for your reception."

"Do not distress yourself about making arrangements for my family," replied Sir Ambrose; "for you know I have a brother living in London, and though we have not seen each other for years, I think upon such an occasion as this I ought to forget all animosity, and visit him, if he will receive me."

"True," rejoined the duke; "I never thought of that: but you are quite right. Though he did make a foolish marriage, the ties of blood are too strong to be easily shaken off, and this is an excellent opportunity for a reconciliation."

"Another thing also weighs with me," continued Sir Ambrose: "you know that though I was so much hurt at his marriage, I was in some measure the cause of it."

"You the cause of it!" exclaimed the duke, in excessive surprise.

"You know," resumed Sir Ambrose, "my brother was always a bookworm; and the last time I visited him, I found him so uncomfortable, and his domestic affairs so dreadfully neglected, that I advised him to get an active managing woman to act as housekeeper. He did so, and in twelve months made her—Mrs. Montagu."

"I always thought your brother was too learned to know any thing useful, and too clever to be able to take care of himself; but I own I never suspected him of being such a fool as to marry."

"Perhaps I was a greater one than himself in resenting his conduct, for I believe they get on very well. Mrs. Montagu does not want sense."

"I do not doubt her abilities, or that she was extremely well fitted for her original station; but very different qualities are required in the wife of Mr. Montagu from those which were suited to his housekeeper."

"I know it; and also that there is perhaps nothing more difficult than for a person in her situation to preserve the medium between affectation and vulgarity. However, I am told that though Mrs. Montagu cannot quite divest herself of the pedantry she acquired at a charity-school in her youth; and though she still talks as learnedly as if she had never ventured beyond the precincts of the kitchen; yet, that she makes my brother a good wife, and they say her daughter Clara is a charming girl."

"I can imagine nothing good springing from such a source."

"Prejudice! my dear duke, sheer prejudice!"

"Well, well, I will say no more about it; for, as you justly say, if Mrs. Montagu makes your brother a good wife, and he is happy with her, I don't see any right any body else has to trouble himself about the matter: and so, as I don't like quarrels in families, I think you are quite right in wishing to see your brother. However, if they do not make you comfortable, I hope you'll remember you have another friend, and so we'll now wish you good day: come, girls!"

And the old duke trotted off, followed by his fair companions. Edric's heart throbbed violently when he found himself alone with his father; the moment was arrived he had been so ardently wishing for, and yet he was silent. He had scarcely had patience to wait the end of his father's conference with the duke; and whilst it had lasted, he had been arranging and re-arranging a thousand times in his mind, the phrases he meant to make use of; yet now they seemed to have all vanished from his memory, and he stood gazing through the open window, his mind feeling a perfect chaos, and without being able to recollect one single word of what he had determined to say. Sir Ambrose, in the mean time, felt perfectly happy, and in the buoyancy of his spirits tapped his son upon the shoulder.

"What all amort! Sir Knight of the Woeful Countenance," said he; "Come, come! I will have no gloomy looks to-day. But, heyday! what is the matter with you, Edric? You don't smile—are you unhappy? You look as if you had something upon your mind."

"I have something upon my mind, my dear father," said Edric, solemnly; "and something that I wish to communicate to you." He stopped when he had said this, but Sir Ambrose did not reply, and, for some minutes, neither spoke. At length, Edric broke the pause, which had been one of perfect agony to him, and, speaking very fast, he exclaimed, "Yet I don't know why I should hesitate. It is that I do not love Rosabella—that I never can marry her—that I should be entirely miserable even to think of it—and, that this is my fixed and unalterable determination."

"Heyday!" cried Sir Ambrose; "what is all this? Not marry Rosabella!"

"Never; no tortures should induce me! I am convinced she would make me wretched," continued Edric, hurrying through what he meant to say. "Our tempers don't assimilate. We should both be miserable. I should be very sorry to cause either you or the duke a moment's uneasiness—very sorry—I would die first! But to marry Rosabella would be worse than dying a thousand deaths—we should be the most wretched of human beings, and you would be unhappy at seeing me so."

"Mercy on me!" cried Sir Ambrose, heaving a deep sigh, and feeling almost out of breath at the volubility of his son. "I thought you dumb just now, but I see that you can use your tongue fast enough when the subject pleases you. Not marry Rosabella! Is the boy mad? Is she not young, beautiful, and highly accomplished? What would you have, I wonder? You certainly must be out of your senses to refuse such a woman; and one too, so superior to yourself, in rank and fortune."

"In fortune I allow her to be superior; but I think the mystery attached to the name of her father, more than compensates for any difference of rank."

"Don't talk about what you can't understand. Duke Edgar is dead, and his faults should be buried with him; besides, it is hard the girl should suffer for the sins of her father."

"What were those sins, my dear Sir? I have often heard them darkly hinted at, as something almost too dreadful to mention; but I never heard the particulars."

"Edric," said Sir Ambrose, solemnly, "if you have the least regard for my feelings, or entertain any duty for me as a son, never again advert to that subject. Circumstances there are relating to it, of a deep, awful, and mysterious nature, with which I am well acquainted, but which I have taken a solemn oath never to reveal. Never speak of them again; the bare remembrance makes me shudder — oh! would to Heaven I could forget them!"

"I am very sorry, Sir, that my question was such as to give you pain: but rest assured that my curiosity shall never again annoy you."

"I am not angry with you, Edric. You could not know the feelings your question would create in my bosom, and it was natural you should wish to know something of the father of your intended wife. However, think no more of him. Consider the present duke as your future father-in-law; and if possible forget that such a person as Duke Edgar ever existed."

"You forget, Sir," said Edric, firmly but respectfully, "that I have before declared my determination never to marry Rosabella."

"Nonsense!" rejoined his father, "you don't know what you are talking about. The world would call me as mad as yourself if I were to let you act so foolishly: besides, what would the duke say?"

"To speak candidly, Sir, that is what principally annoys me; for I trust that your good sense and affectionate disposition will soon enable you to see the affair in its proper light."

"That is to say, you think I am an old fool, and that you can coax me to any thing you please. But you shall find your error. You shall learn I will not be coaxed; I will be obeyed. You shall marry Rosabella, or you shall leave my house."

"My dear father!" said Edric, attempting to take Sir Ambrose's hand.

"Away, Sir!" cried his father, shaking him off, "obedience far outweighs words. If I am your dear father, you will act in compliance with my wishes; and if you do not, it is a mockery to call me 'dear.'"

"I cannot marry Rosabella."

"Was ever such obstinacy! — such folly! The world will think you distracted."

"I care not for the world!" cried Edric, impatiently.

"Youth like!" returned his father. "It is very strange no one will be contented to take experience at second-hand. They must buy it for themselves, and sometimes pay very dear for it before they profit by its lessons. You talk like a child, Edric: when you get a little older, you will find practice and theory very different things. You say you despise the world: but you are wrong, the world must not be despised; nay more, it ought not to be even slighted. As long as you live in it, you must conform to its opinions: it is ridiculous to think otherwise. I don't like to hear people say they don't care for the world; the world must be cared for; and when people pretend to scorn it, it is generally because they are aware they have done something to make it scorn them."

"But, my dear father! you would not wish me to sacrifice my conscience to its dictates."

"And pray, Sir, what has your conscience to do with the matter in question?"

"Should I not sacrifice it by marrying a woman I feel I could never love? In my opinion, nothing can be more sacred than the marriage vow; and with what feelings could I enter into this solemn engagement in the presence of Almighty God, calling upon him to witness it, when I knew my heart was at variance with my words? My soul would recoil with horror at such blasphemy."

"You talk about your conscience, Edric,—but should you not rather say your inclinations? The person of Rosabella does not please your fancy, I suppose; and to gratify a capricious whim, you would destroy the happiness of your father, and ruin your own prospects for ever."

"It is not of the person of Rosabella that I complain, my dear father;—I allow her to be beautiful as a Venus, and that her talents even exceed her personal charms: but when I see her large black eyes flashing fury, and her rosy lips curved into an expression of indignant scorn, I forget her beauty, and think only of the fearful passions of her soul."

"Your objections are futile, Edric; at any rate, they are of no avail. You must marry her—I am sorry it is against your inclination, but I will not have my authority disputed:—besides, the disappointment to the duke would be dreadful. It was but this morning that he proposed, that as soon as you and Edmund should marry, I should give up my estate to you, and he his to your brother, whilst we two old folks should retire to the cottage on the hill; and pass the remainder of our lives in contemplating with rapture the happiness of our children."

"I own the duke is so obstinate—"

"So, you have discovered that, have you? Well, you are right there; for when he has taken a fancy into his head, no arguments can turn him from his point. But there is a difference between obstinacy and firmness. Now, though I am not obstinate like the duke, you shall find I can be firm, Edric. However, as I have always been an indulgent father, I do not wish to decide hastily now, and I give you a week to make up your mind: at the expiration of which time you shall marry Rosabella or quit my house for ever. No reply, young man, I will not hear a word. Begone; leave me now, and in a week's time let me know your decision."

It was in vain to attempt a reply; and Edric left his father's presence oppressed by that strange, mysterious presentiment of evil, which, like a fearful cloud, dark, gloomy, and impenetrable, sometimes hangs upon our thoughts, foreboding horrors; though so dimly and indistinctly, that, like all the gigantic phantoms we sometimes fancy through the mist of twilight, their terrors seem increased tenfold by the very uncertainty that half shrouds them from our sight. Mingled with these feelings, however, was one of wild, unearthly joy. Driven from his father's house, he would be free to travel—his doubts might be satisfied—he might, at last, penetrate into the secrets of the grave; and partake, without restraint, of the so ardently desired fruit of the tree of knowledge. Nothing would then be hidden from him. Nature would be forced to yield up her treasures to his view—her mysteries would be revealed, and he would become great, omniscient, and god-like. His mind filled with a chaos of thoughts like these, which he strove in vain to arrange, and which seemed to swell his brain almost to bursting, Edric involuntarily strolled again into the wood he had so lately quitted, and again throwing himself upon the banks of the murmuring stream, he was soon lost in a reverie.

CHAPTER V.

In the mean time, different emotions were agitating violently the bosoms of the two lovely heiresses of the duke. When they reached the castle, each of them retired to her separate apartment to ruminate upon what had passed. Confidence did not exist between them, for confidence requires congeniality of mind, and those of the fair cousins were essentially different. Each princess, however, had a favourite attendant, or rather a companion, in whose bosom she was in the habit of pouring her thoughts; and, on their arrival at the castle, they parted immediately, equally eager to find their respective confidants, and inform them of all that had happened. Marianne had been the attendant of Rosabella from her childhood; and haughty as the Princess naturally was, she was, like many other haughty people, completely the slave of her servant. Marianne was perfectly aware of her power, and she occasionally used it tyrannically: on the present occasion, however, she was really alarmed at the glowing cheeks, sparkling eyes, and agitated frame of Rosabella, and asked, with an appearance of deep interest, if she were ill.

"In mind, though not in body," replied Rosabella, throwing herself upon a sofa, and hiding her face in both her hands. "Oh, Marianne! what a wretch I am!"

"What is the matter?" asked the suivante.

"He loves her! he adores her!" cried Rosabella, starting from her couch and traversing the room rapidly. "Curses on her beauty! O that a look of mine could wither it! or that she could feel the burning fire that rages here!" Then stopping suddenly, she gazed upon her attendant with the wildness of a maniac, and, pressing her hand firmly against her side, threw herself again upon her couch, exclaiming, "Oh, Marianne! why am I not beloved like Elvira?"

"And are you certain that she is beloved?"

"Certain!" reiterated Rosabella, wringing her hands; "Alas! alas! would I were not so certain; but can I doubt the evidence of my senses? This day—this very day! I saw Father Morris put a letter into her hands, which was enclosed in that addressed to Sir Ambrose. I saw a blush of conscious pleasure glow upon her cheeks as she perused it, and I could have stabbed her to the heart,—yes, and exulted in her dying agonies—triumphed in her groans. Oh, Marianne! is it not extraordinary that one so great, so noble, and so exalted as Edmund, can love such a poor, weak, feeble being as Elvira? But she loves him not; at least not as he should be loved. She is incapable of it."

"I wonder Father Morris gave her the letter."

"He could not help it, Marianne. It fell from its enclosure when Sir Ambrose tore it open; but she saw it fall. I even saw her eye rest upon the address; Father Morris merely picked it from the ground, and placed it in her hands."

"I thought he would not have given it to her voluntarily."

"No; I think not. I believe the father is my friend, though I own sometimes it appears strange to me, Marianne, that he should seem to prefer my interest to that of every one else, when so many ties bind him to Sir Ambrose's family, and so few to me: nay, though I am often peevish and unreasonable with him, he never is offended, and appears to remain still as warmly attached to me as before:—I cannot account for it."

"He has ties that bind him to you that you know not of," said Marianne, in a low, under voice; "he was your father's friend."

"Was he?" cried Rosabella, eagerly; "then perhaps he may enable me to clear off the shade that has so long hung upon my father's name. By heaven! neither the gratification of my love nor of my revenge would give me half the pleasure."

"You had better not ask him," said Marianne, in the same low, mysterious tone; "you can learn nothing upon that subject which it would give you pleasure to hear." Then changing her voice, she added, "But what said Edric to the news of his brother's glory?"

"I know not—I care not! Ice itself cannot be colder than Edric. When we met, and he offered his hand to greet me, his touch seemed to freeze my very veins. Cold, prudent, calculating, and cautious, he has all the vices of age without its excuses:—I hate him!"

"You do not then, I suppose, long for the moment when you are to become his bride?" asked the companion, with a sarcastic smile.

"Long for it, Marianne?" cried Rosabella, starting from her couch, and clasping her hands together with energy—"long for it! No; if all other resources fail, death shall free me before the hated moment arrives." And as she spoke, Rosabella walked up and down the room, in a state of violent agitation.

"But your uncle?" resumed Marianne.

"My uncle!" repeated Rosabella, stopping short, "yes, yes; my uncle is positive—and I—a poor dependant, and in his power. But even that shall not control my will. Poor and dependant as I am—I am free; and sooner would I labour for my bread, sooner would I perish in the streets, or endure unheard of torments, than live in a palace surrounded by crowds of adoring slaves, if the price were that I must call Edric husband."

Marianne, satisfied with the ease with which she found she could play upon the feelings of her mistress, now touched a chord that thrilled to softer emotions.

"I can never believe," said she, "that a mind so noble as that of Edmund, can long remain in the thraldom of Elvira. When he comes to know her better, and to feel the feebleness of her soul, he must despise her."

"Ah! do you think so?" cried Rosabella eagerly. "But you deceive yourself, Marianne; Edmund is so blinded that he fancies her very faults perfections."

"But that blindness cannot last for ever, and when it wears off, disgust must ensue."

"Oh, Marianne, if it were so!" exclaimed Rosabella; and, sitting down, she rested her elbows on her knees, and pressed her hands against her beating forehead, concealing her face and remaining apparently lost in meditation. Marianne did not disturb her. She was aware that she had given her active imagination a theme to work upon, and she left her to enjoy it; tranquilly resuming her usual avocations without seeming to notice her abstraction.

Whilst this scene was passing in the apartment of Rosabella, Elvira was informing her confidant, Emma, who had been her governess and remained her companion, of the pleasure she had experienced from hearing of the success of Edmund, and from the tenderness of his letter. "How I wish I could love him as he deserves," said she, "but, alas, I fear it is not in my nature. I can scarcely even comprehend what he thinks I ought to feel, and the violence of his manner terrifies me beyond expression. Is it not extraordinary, Emma, that this passion, which seems so universally extended throughout all nature, should be alone a stranger to my breast—that I alone, should be debarred from feeling its influence? Edmund complains of my coldness; and I feel that he has reason to do so. I feel that his love is different from mine: I esteem and respect him; I have even a sincere friendship for him, and no one values his worth more than I; I should also be very sorry if any misfortune were to befall him; but this is all, and I do not think I am capable of feeling more for any one."

"Indeed you deceive yourself," replied Emma; "I am sure a heart so kind and affectionate as yours is capable of love. Do not marry Lord Edmund; I am certain you do not love him as you will love one day: and if a day should arrive, when you feel a real passion, what will be your horror at the recollection of the sacred ties which bind you to one who is indifferent to you. I shudder at the thought."

"And so should I, Emma; but that it is impossible such an event can happen. If I were married to Edmund, I never could love another, even if my nature were susceptible of the passion: a fact I much doubt."

Emma shook her head incredulously. "Oh!" sighed she; "how little do you know of love!"

"I know more of it than you imagine. In my opinion, people would never fall in love, if they had abundance of other thoughts to occupy their minds. They would marry, of course: but that, as every body knows, is quite a different thing."

"Then you disbelieve in love entirely?"

"Not entirely; but I think what is generally called love is the offspring of idleness. When people have nothing to do, particularly if they happen to have warm imaginations, they amuse themselves by picturing an idol of perfection. This they endow with all kinds of virtue probable and improbable; and they are enchanted with the fantasy, because it is their own creation. They soon find a face or figure that pleases them, and to this they attach the charms they had before given their imaginary idol—no matter whether they accord or not. When people are what is called in love, they are like persons in green spectacles, they see every thing of a colour that does not really belong to it. Marriage, however, lifts up the magic veil, and displays the real faults and imperfections of each individual. The self-deluded mortals then find out their mistake, though too late; and start back aghast at the appalling spectre that presents itself, crying out bitterly against deception; whilst, in fact, they have been only deceiving themselves."

"You reason admirably; but it is only from the head, not the heart. If you had ever felt, you would perceive the fallacy of your arguments."

"I think not; for I am convinced the experience of ninety-nine persons out of a hundred would confirm what I say, if they could but be persuaded to avow their real sentiments. This, however, they are always, in such cases, very reluctant to do, as no one likes to own himself deceived."

"And do you think all love is like that you have been speaking of?"

"Heaven forbid!—No—no, Emma, do not imagine I am such a heretic as to deny the existence of true love. I only think it is very difficult to be met with. That it does exist, I firmly believe; but few, very few are the bosoms that are capable of feeling it."

"Now I agree with you perfectly. I thought you could not mean all you before asserted."

"Excuse me, Emma, I did mean what I said. But I did not then speak of real love; I spoke only of the passion, or rather fancy, that usurps its name. Real, pure, undefiled love is that absorbing affection that prefers another's happiness to its own; that devotion that would sink unknown to the grave, to procure another's happiness; that seeks not its own gratification, but would sacrifice all the world can give, to promote the welfare of another; that can taste of no pleasure and partake of no delight, unless it be participated by the beloved object, and even then, joys in his satisfaction more than in its own. This is what I call love. I can imagine such a passion, though I shall never feel it. However, that it may be felt I am firmly convinced: though even you must acknowledge, it is rare to find it."

"Alas! my dear mistress!" said Emma, sighing heavily. "Every word you utter, convinces me you deceive yourself. For God's sake, do not marry Lord Edmund. You could have no idea of the romantic feelings you describe, if your heart were not open to receive them. Lord Edmund does not——"

"Hush! hush, Emma!" exclaimed Elvira, playfully interrupting her. "It is of no use. Say what we will, like most people that argue, we are sure to remain of the same opinion when we have done. I don't believe anybody ever yet was convinced by words; we must wait for facts, and, en attendant, suppose we consult upon what dress will be most becoming for us to wear at the approaching ceremony."

Emma gladly consented; and the princess and her companion were soon involved in a maze of ribbons, crapes, gauzes, silks and satins, from which it would be quite in vain for me to attempt to extricate them.

When Edric next saw his father, after the partial explanation that had taken place between them, he was excessively surprised to find him behave exactly as usual. The youthful philosopher was rather disconcerted at this conduct, which completely deranged all his speculations. In the course of his meditations in the grove, he had magnanimously made up his mind to endure every species of persecution rather than submit in the slightest degree to alter his opinions; and such is the strange and whimsical inconsistency of the human mind, that he was actually disappointed when he found there appeared little prospect of his heroic resolutions being called into practice.

It may seem strange to those who are feelingly convinced of the substantial comforts of an hospitable mansion and well supplied table, that any one should be found quixotic enough to lament that he had lost the chance of being deprived of them; but Edric's was the age of romance. His life had hitherto passed in one dull monotonous round, and the prospect of bustle and adventure has, in such cases, most irresistible charms. He also knew nothing of the world; and was almost as ignorant of the real evils of life, as the French princess, who, hearing that some persons had died of hunger, wondered at their folly, and said that for her part, rather than be famished, she would eat bread and cheese. Thus, as we said before, Edric was rather chagrined than delighted, when his father greeted him the morning after their conference as affectionately as before, and very amicably proposed that as soon as breakfast was ended, they should take a walk together to the castle of the duke.

Unwilling to vex his father needlessly by refusing, and yet fearful of compromising his firmness, by appearing to accede to what might be treachery on the part of his opponents, our young philosopher gave a rather ungracious assent to this proposition, and remained apparently absorbed in meditation during the whole walk. They found the duke extremely busy. Like many other people who have few real affairs to occupy them, he was quite delighted with any thing that seemed to promise a little bustle, and was firmly resolved to make the most of it. He was then giving orders for an illumination, and a public dinner to his tenants; bell-ringing, speech-making, and a variety of other things, we have really neither time nor patience to enumerate. Busy as he was, however, he was glad to see our friends, and greeted them most cordially.

"You are come in the very nick of time," said he: "I was just upon the point of sending for you. Do you know, Sir Ambrose, it has struck me that this triumph of Edmund's will be an admirable opportunity for his marriage; ay, and for yours too, Edric. What say you, Sir Ambrose?"

"Oh! of course I can have no objection."

"And of course," resumed the Duke, "I do not suppose the young men can have any. What do you say, Edric?"

But Edric did not speak: for, to own the truth, he did not exactly know what to say.

"Edric is so delighted, that it has deprived him of the power of utterance," observed the baronet, rather maliciously, perceiving the duke grow impatient.

"I trust your grace will excuse me," said Edric, at length recovering himself; "but— —but— —"

"But what?" said the duke, impatiently.

"I thought," resumed Edric, with considerable hesitation, "that your grace did not intend that the princesses should marry—till—till they had passed the age that would render— that is to say, that does render them eligible candidates for the throne.—"

Edric did not express himself very clearly; as he was not altogether certain of what he was saying. The duke, however, heard enough to put him into a passion.

"So I did," exclaimed he, "I know that perfectly; but I have altered my mind, I tell you: Claudia isn't above thirty, and she's likely to live these fifty years,—so it is of no use waiting for her death. Besides, I should like to see my children married before I die. I am getting old; and anxiety in these respects increases with declining years."

"Then my anxiety ought to be greater than yours, duke, for I am the eldest," said Sir Ambrose.

"By a couple of years, at least," returned the duke, laughing, "for I suppose that is about the difference in our ages. But you don't answer me, Edric. Do you think you have eloquence enough to persuade your mistress to relinquish the prospect of a throne in your behalf?"

"I would not wish her to make any sacrifice upon my account," replied Edric.

"Confound such coldness! why, when I was a young man, my heart would have beat like a pendulum in perpetual motion at such a proposition. Go to her, man! and try your fortune.—

'She is a woman, therefore to be wooed;

She is a woman, therefore to be won;'

or rather what, perhaps, will be better, I will send for her here, and tell her my will. Egad! I have a mind to surprise Edmund, and let you grace his triumph as bride and bridegroom."

"Rosabella would never consent to such a proposition," exclaimed Edric, willing to postpone the dreaded explanation as long as possible.

"I think not," resumed the duke, "if you woo her with that face. However, you need not distress yourself, as you will have nothing to say till you get to the altar. I'll take all the rest upon myself, and I've a notion I shall prove the better suitor. I know women well, and how to manage them. I'll defy any woman in the world to have a will of her own whilst she is in my custody. I know how to quiet them and bring them round. You shall see how I will manage Rosabella. She won't have a word to say for herself. Here Augustus, tell the Princess Rosabella I wish to speak with her."

"Hold!" cried Edric, "I cannot allow you to send for the princess till I have first explained my real sentiments— —"

"Nonsense!" said the duke. "However, I see there is no occasion to send for her; for yonder she comes. I will meet her and explain my sentiments, and then it will be quite time enough to talk about yours."

So saying, he broke from Edric, who attempted to detain him; and advanced to meet Rosabella.

"Good God!" exclaimed Edric, "what will become of me? this obstinate old man will tell her, I wish our union: and for worlds, I would not mortify the proud spirit of Rosabella, by publicly declining her hand. What shall I do? I must request a private interview, and throwing myself upon her mercy, persuade her to reject me."

"Then you still persist in your determination," said Sir Ambrose. "I had hoped my kindness in appearing to forget what passed yesterday, had disposed you to comply with my wishes. However, since you seem inclined to adhere to your resolution, you cannot be surprised that I should follow your example, and I can only repeat, that if you do not marry Rosabella, you know the alternative."

"I do," said Edric, firmly; "and I am prepared to meet it."

In the mean time, the duke had met Rosabella, and had evidently begun to declare his wishes to her, for the colour had fled from her cheeks, and her eyes were cast upon the ground, whilst her strongly compressed lips, as she walked silently by his side, showed that it was with infinite difficulty that she controlled her feelings sufficiently to hear him with patience.

"In short," said the duke, as they drew near Sir Ambrose and his son, "I have fixed upon the day after to-morrow for your wedding, and, though I own the time is somewhat short to make preparations, you must be satisfied to have your wedding clothes after your marriage instead of before, which I should think need not make much difference. So now all you'll have to do, will be to tell your cousin; and the day after to-morrow your name will be Montagu."

"And do you know of whom you are disposing so unceremoniously?" asked Rosabella, raising her brilliant eyes from the ground, and fixing them upon him with a look of proud scorn. The duke shrunk involuntarily from the withering glance, which seemed to fall upon him with the fabled power of that of the basilisk.

"Of whom I am disposing?" stammered he, unconsciously repeating her words, "Of whom I am disposing? Why, of my niece, to be sure," he continued, arranging with difficulty his scattered ideas. "You are my niece, are you not?"

"Yes," returned Rosabella, "unfortunately I am your niece; and I blush for an uncle who does not scruple to abuse so barbarously the last legacy bequeathed to him by an unfortunate brother. Yes, my lord duke, I am your niece—your protégée—your dependant. I am not ashamed to own that I owe my daily bread to your bounty; but notwithstanding all this, I am not aware that I am your slave, nor do I think the pecuniary obligations I am under to you, sufficient to give you the right of disposing of me as an article of furniture, or a beast of burthen."

The Mummy!

"You mistake the matter entirely, Rosabella," said the duke; "I do not wish to hurt your feelings."

"Do you think, then, that I am formed of stone or iron, that I am to be told to marry when and where you list, without having my inclinations consulted or my affections gained? Look at the bridegroom for whom you destine me. Certainly I must be insensibility itself to resist such overwhelming ardour."

"You are right, Rosabella," replied the duke; "he is enough to provoke a stone. I admire your spirit; a woman should not unsought be won, and he, I own, looks as if he expected you to go down upon your knees, and beg him to accept of your hand."

"You are mistaken," returned Edric, now taunted into the necessity of avowing himself, in spite of his former resolutions; "it is not merely coldness that dictates my conduct. I should have explained myself before, had you permitted it, though I would willingly have spared the princess this public declaration. However, as I am now forced to avow my real sentiments, I openly and solemnly protest, that no torments shall ever force me to become the husband of Rosabella. I am sorry — —"

"Spare your pity, Sir," said the princess, haughtily, and interrupting him — "I, at least, have no occasion for it; for know, that I too would sooner experience a thousand deaths than become your wife. Nothing but the respect I owe my uncle has prevented my declaring my sentiments sooner."

"And only my affection for my father kept me silent."

"What a considerate pair! and how highly we ought to feel obliged to them!" said the duke, ironically. "And pray, if your respect and affection permit you to answer the question, what may it be your high will and pleasure to intend doing now?"

"Whatever you please," replied both Edric and Rosabella, almost at the same instant.

"Dear me! how amazingly condescending! So, as long as you are permitted to have your own way, we may have the honour of suggesting plans for your approbation whenever we please. How astonishingly kind! I am afraid we shall never be able to show ourselves properly grateful, Sir Ambrose."

"This irony, my lord," said Edric, firmly, "is unworthy both of yourself and us. I will allow that you and my father have both reason to be displeased with our conduct, as it has disappointed hopes which you have long cherished; but permit me to say, that if you had expressed your displeasure in serious, manly, and open terms as he did, it would have been much more befitting your high rank and the importance of the subject, than the taunting irony you have thought proper to make use of."

"Schooled too! by St. Wellington!" exclaimed the duke. "Upon my word, these are fine times, when a man of my age and rank is to be lectured by a beardless stripling!"

"I did not mean to offend your grace," said Edric; "and I am sorry the violence of my feelings compelled me to use language unbefitting my youth, and disrespectful to an old and valued friend of my father."

"Say no more, young man," replied the duke, "apologies only double an offence. If such are your sentiments, I would rather you declared than concealed them, as I think even insolence preferable to hypocrisy. However, after what has passed, I can never meet you amicably again, and I shall even avoid entering the house of my friend, Sir Ambrose, whilst you remain in it." This was spoken with dignity, and a majestic firmness of tone. The duke's voice, however, trembled a little as he continued—"I shall be sorry to lose the society of my old friend, and I should be equally sorry to induce him to desert you, but I cannot willingly expose myself to insult; and I must accordingly decline all farther intercourse with your family."

"Decline all farther intercourse with our family!" exclaimed Sir Ambrose. "This from you, duke! And Edmund! my darling Edmund! is he to suffer for the faults of his brother?"

"How do you know that the loss of my daughter would make him suffer?" asked the duke, sneeringly. "Perhaps when the moment came for me to give her to him, he too would make a bow, and humbly asking my pardon, beg leave to decline the honour. Oh! curse such politeness!"

"My dear duke, I would answer for Edmund with my life. He adores Elvira, and loves you as a father. You, too, have always professed to love him—"

"And so I do. Didn't I rejoice like an old fool at his triumph? Didn't I determine to give my daughter, and bestow my estate upon him? And were not these proofs of love?"

"They were, they were! my dear friend! and, as he has never done any thing to offend you, why should not your favourable intentions continue? Why should you punish him on account of this ungrateful idiot, whom I renounce for ever."

"Oh, my father! my dear father!" exclaimed Edric; "do not say for ever!"

"Yes, for ever! I repeat," resumed Sir Ambrose. "Begone and let me never see you more. I told you yesterday my determination, and as you have chosen to incur the penalty, you must take the consequence. Come, my friend," continued he, taking the arm of the duke, "let us leave him to his own reflections. Thank God! we are none of us answerable for the faults of our children; and it would indeed be sad, if you and I were to break a friendship that has lasted half a century, on account of the childish folly of an inconsiderate boy!"

"It would, indeed," returned the duke; "and it would have broken my heart to have quarreled with my darling Edmund. Yet, it is hard, at my time of life, to be disappointed in one's fondest hopes."

And as he walked away with Sir Ambrose, the tears actually streamed down his cheeks. Both Edric and Rosabella were affected, but, wisely considering that they could say nothing likely to allay the storm, they remained silent till the old men had gradually disappeared.

CHAPTER VI.

When Sir Ambrose and the duke thus withdrew, Edric and Rosabella were left alone together, and remained for some moments in perfect silence, for both felt keenly the awkwardness of their situation. After standing for some time looking as foolish as their enemies could reasonably desire, Edric bowed, and would have made good his retreat, but Rosabella stopped him.

"Let us be friends, Edric," said she, smiling and holding out her hand, "though we are no longer lovers."

Edric took the offered hand, and involuntarily pressed it to his lips. "Upon my word, you improve!" continued Rosabella gaily; "I declare I never saw such an instance of gallantry from you before, during the whole course of our courtship!"

Edric smiled as he replied, "If you knew the burthen that has been taken from my mind by the explanation of this morning—"

"Hush! hush!" cried Rosabella laughing, "Now you have spoiled all again. I was afraid your gallantry was too great to be lasting."

"I acknowledge," replied Edric, joining in her mirth, "that it is not very polite in me to rejoice in being freed from your chains: but I am no flatterer, and—and—"

"A truce with apologies," exclaimed Rosabella; "as my uncle very justly observed just now, they only make the matter worse. The case is simply this: you and I were not suited for each other; we found it out, and we are both glad to be released from ties that we discovered were incompatible with our happiness. 'Can any thing be more clear?' as Dr. Entwerfen says. You, I presume, are going to travel, and to gratify your natural love of variety and wish to acquire information; whilst I, poor unfortunate damsel that I am, must remain at home and wear the willow, till I am fortunate enough to meet with a swain who has the penetration to discover my charms."

"And most ardently do I hope that it may soon be the case!" said Edric, astonished at her affability, and feeling more kindly disposed towards her than he had ever done before. "You are right in supposing I wish to travel; but, alas! I have not now the power. My father is too much offended to afford me the means; and without money—"

"Travelling is far from agreeable," interrupted Rosabella, smiling: "is not that what you would say? Why not apply to Father Morris, then; he can, and I am sure, will help you. For myself, I am powerless, except as far as giving advice."

"Your advice, however, is excellent," replied Edric, regarding her with still increasing amazement; "and I assure you I will follow it to the letter. I never thought of applying to the reverend father, though I now feel it is the best thing I can do."

"Why then do you look at me so incredulously?" continued Rosabella; "I can have no motive for deceiving you; and yet you look as suspicious as though you thought I had. I own my behaviour towards you is changed; but remember the different circumstances in which I am now placed. Formerly I feared even to speak to you, lest my words should be deemed an encouragement of the pretensions I supposed you to entertain to my hand. Now that we are both free, that reason no longer exists; and besides, I feel grateful to you for declaring your sentiments so openly, and thus saving me from my uncle's displeasure. 'Can any thing be more simple?' as your friend Dr. Entwerfen would say."

Notwithstanding Rosabella's apparent openness, however, and the plausible reasons she gave for her conduct, Edric could not divest himself of the idea that she wished to get him out of the kingdom as speedily as possible, for some other motives than those she thought proper to avow. There likewise appeared some mystery in her speaking so confidently of the assistance of Father Morris; for as the duke's family had a regular confessor, Father Murphy, it seemed strange that Rosabella should have an intercourse with any other priest, beyond that required by the common forms of society; and so slight an intimacy could scarcely warrant the positive assertion she had made use of. Edric, however, was too anxious to avail himself of any opportunity that offered of proceeding to Egypt, to trouble himself with long investigation of the subject; and when he quitted Rosabella, he proceeded in search of Father Morris as a matter of course, and almost without any volition of his own.

The suite of rooms appropriated to Father Morris in the mansion of Sir Ambrose was in a wing partly detached from the main dwelling; and thither Edric bent his steps. As he approached, however, to his great surprise he heard a sound of blows followed by deep groans. Knowing that it was the hour of dinner for the domestics, and that none of the other inmates of the mansion were at home but the friar and himself, he could not at first account for this strange and fearful noise; but finding, as he advanced, the sounds proceeded from the inner chamber of the priest, where no one but himself ever ventured, he soon became satisfied that Father Morris was performing a penance of self-flagellation; and as it was deemed impious to interrupt a penitence, he seated himself quietly in the outer chamber, waiting the priest's leisure; wondering, however, to himself, what crime so holy a man could possibly have committed, that could require so severe an expiation.

When Father Morris made his appearance, it was with his usual downcast eyes and composed look. He expressed his astonishment at seeing Edric, but made no allusion to the penance he had just been performing, and listened with a cold unmoved aspect to Edric's communication.

"Then I am to understand," said he, when it was finished, "that you are like the prince we were reading of the other day, in a book we found in your tutor's library. You cannot be happy because you have never been miserable; and you are going to plunge into all the cares and troubles of the world, merely to learn how to enjoy retirement."

"Not exactly so, father;" rejoined Edric; "I have two other motives,—the anger of my father, and the earnest tormenting wish I before confessed to you, of diving into the secrets of the grave."

"And how is that to be accomplished by your leaving England?"

"I wish to try to resuscitate a mummy."

"The scheme is wild, vague, and impracticable."

"Not if Dr. Entwerfen's hypothesis be true. For, supposing the souls of the ancient Egyptians to be chained to their bodies, and to be remaining in them in a torpid state,—it is very possible that by employing so powerful an agent as galvanism, re-animation may be produced. I have already seen some wonderful instances of the vivifying power of the machine; and as the Egyptians took care to preserve the bodies of their dead quite entire, probably from the idea I have just alluded to,—I think the mummies are the best subjects we can possibly fix upon for our experiments."

"The ancient Egyptians did not imagine the souls of their dead remained in the bodies, but that they would return to them after the expiration of a certain number of years; so that your hypothesis, as far as it rests upon their opinions, falls to the ground."

"Do not call it my hypothesis," returned Edric, "it is that of Dr. Entwerfen; my own opinion is decidedly different—for I cannot imagine any idea of death that does not imply a separation between the body and soul. The subject, however, is curious; to me highly interesting; and I own, candidly, there are many mysteries connected with it, which it would give me the highest satisfaction to have explained."

"And these mysteries, which have vainly excited the speculation of the learned since the commencement of the world, you think your journey to Egypt will enable you to unravel," said Father Morris, with a sardonic sneer. Edric felt irritated at his manner, and replied warmly:—

"I am not presumptuous, father; but as even you must allow, man is often but a blind instrument in the hands of fate, it is possible that the racking desire I feel to explore these mysteries may be an impulse from a superior power, and a proof that I am destined to be the mortal agent of their revelation to man. Egypt is a country rich in monuments of antiquity; and all historians unite in declaring her ancient inhabitants to have possessed knowledge and science far beyond even the boasted improvements of modern times. For instance, could we attempt to erect stupendous buildings like the pyramids, where enormous masses are arranged with geometrical accuracy, and the labours of man have emulated the everlasting durability of nature? Are we even capable of conceiving works so majestic as those they put in execution? No; assuredly not. In every point they surpassed us."

"Even in their religion?" asked Father Morris sarcastically.

"No," returned Edric; "every scheme of religion falls infinitely below the divine perfection of Christianity; but as Christianity was not in the times we are speaking of, revealed, it cannot be denied that the Egyptians made some approach to wisdom even in their devotions. They worshipped Nature, though they disguised her under the symbols of her attributes, and gratified the vulgar taste by giving them tangible objects to represent ideas too sublime for their unenlightened comprehension. That they entertained the divine idea of a resurrection, and of rewards and punishments in a future life, is evident, not only from their favourite fable of the Phœnix, and the use they made of the now hackneyed image of the Butterfly;

but by the care they bestowed upon the preservation of the body; their mournings for the loss of Osiris, and rejoicings when he was found; and the kind of trial to which they subjected the human corpse after death, when, if serious crimes were alleged, and proved against it, it was denied the rites of sepulture, and left to rot, unlamented. Then, can any modern institutions excel the wisdom of the laws enacted by the Pharaohs? or can any modern magnificence equal that displayed in the cities of Memphis and Thebes? And since this will hardly be disputed, what country can be more fitting than that once so highly favoured, to be the scene of the most important discovery ever made by Man? Deride me if you will; I feel a superior power inspires my wishes. I feel irresistibly impelled forward. I feel called upon to act by a force far superior to my own, and I will obey its dictates. You smile, and secretly ridicule my projects; but remember that excessive incredulity sometimes savours as strongly of folly as credulity itself, and that both are alike injurious to the progress of science."

"I do not doubt it," said Father Morris, with provoking coldness; "though it must certainly be allowed not to be the prevailing foible of the present day. However, without staying to discuss that point at present, I humbly suggest, that, as I happen unfortunately to be rather pressed for time, it may be as well to condescend to bestow a few minutes' attention upon the best human means of enabling you to fulfil the high destinies that await you in Egypt—as, notwithstanding the imperious nature of the impulse that invites you there, I presume you are aware that the vulgar agency of money will be necessary, as well as the scientific one of galvanism."

The feelings of Edric were too highly wrought to bear this irony; and, snatching up his hat, he rushed out of the room, casting a look of indignation at the priest, who vainly endeavoured to stop him. Maddened by the conflicting emotions that struggled in his bosom, and disgusted alike with himself, Father Morris, and all the world, Edric hurried on, totally unaware which way he was going, till his career was stopped by his coming suddenly and violently in contact with another person, who was running equally heedlessly with himself, but in an opposite direction. Both recoiled some paces from the shock, and Edric found, to his surprise, it was Abelard whom he had greeted so unceremoniously. Curiosity to know what could have occasioned the abstraction of the worthy butler, (he being generally remarkable for his peculiar attention to matters of ceremony,) diverted the thoughts of Edric from himself, and he, for the moment, forgot his own woes, whilst he inquired into those of Abelard.

"Alas! alas!" said the old man, shaking his grey head, whilst the tears streamed in torrents down his wrinkled cheeks, "that I should ever have lived to see this day! Oh, Master Edric! how could you irritate your respectable progenitor? Alas! alas! I feel my lachrymal gland suffused almost to overflowing, whenever the recollection of what has passed shoots across my piamater."

"For Heaven's sake! tell me what is the matter!"

"Oh dear! oh dear!" sobbed the unhappy butler, "that such longevity should have been granted me only that I might see so promising a young gentleman turned out of doors."

"Tell me the worst; though, indeed, I now fear I comprehend your meaning but too well."

"Sir Ambrose commands that you depart immediately, and never enter again into the mansion of your paternal ancestors."

"What will become of me!" exclaimed Edric, clasping his hands together, and raising his eyes to Heaven; then, after a short pause, he added more composedly, "Well, come what will, I am resigned. Fate urges me onward with irresistible violence, and I feel it would be in vain to attempt to combat against her dictates. I, at least, am prepared to execute her will."

"But where will you go?" sobbed Abelard. "You will want money and friends. Alas! alas! that I should ever see the son of my old master stand in need of pecuniary assistance!"

"He but repeats the words of Father Morris," said Edric; "and yet how differently his doubts affect me. The irony of the priest drove me to despair, but the grief of this old man soothes my wounded spirit. He surely loves me."

These words were uttered in so faint a key, that the name of Father Morris only caught the ear of Abelard, and he replied:

"I don't like Father Morris, and I never did; though it is now twenty years since he first entered the family, and though I have never seen any thing in him to censure particularly, throughout the entire of that long period, yet my aversion remains undiminished. I suppose it must be a natural antipathy, and that the pores of my body don't assimilate in shape with the atoms that emanate from his."

"He drove me almost to madness," said Edric.

"I am not surprised at that," returned Abelard; "for I know he can take a fiend-like pleasure in tormenting. He can employ the most provoking, tantalizing expressions, and yet preserve the same soft, smooth voice, and keep his palebræ half closed, and his visual organs fixed upon the ground. Indeed, I never saw the iris of his eyes dilated in my life; and then he has such a manner of raising his supercilia, curving his nose, and drawing down his depressor anguli oris when he listens to any one or replies to them, as to give the expression of a perpetual sneer to his saturnine countenance."

Edric's own recent personal experience bore testimony only too forcibly to the justice of those remarks; and as the wounded man shrinks from the slightest touch, so did Edric find the words of Abelard jar upon his nerves; as turning away from him to hide his emotions, he encountered the earnest gaze of Father Morris himself.

"Why do you appear astonished?" said the priest, smiling. "You are an infant, Edric; you quarrel with your best friends, and then appear surprised that you do not find them as capricious as yourself. You fancy you are very angry with me, for instance, and yet I am not conscious of having done any thing to offend you. Was it a crime to attempt to moderate an enthusiasm that I feared might mislead you? was it a fault to warn you against the dangers of a world of which as yet you know so little? No, no; I am confident your own reason and excellent good sense will acquit me, if you will but suffer them to act. Your imagination is too vivid, Edric; it sweeps away all before it, like a torrent. If you would view things calmly, you would perceive your folly. The world will teach you wisdom. Go then, travel; experience personal privations and evils of every description, that you may learn to enjoy the pleasures that even now lie within your grasp, but which you spurn from you with contempt. So true it is that we never learn the real value of any blessing till we have experienced the misery that attends its privation."

"If this be the case," replied Edric, soothed in spite of himself, by the insinuating manner of the monk, "why should my feelings be an exception to the general rule? And since all our pleasures acquire a new zest by the force of contrast, and mine have long since lost all relish, is it not even wisdom to try the effect of change?"

"And yet it seems a folly," said Father Morris, in his smooth, plausible, hypocritical voice, with his eyes again fixed upon the ground, "to incur a certain evil in the hope of attaining an uncertain good."

Edric started, and fixed his eyes upon him, with an expression the monk well understood; and, not wishing again to provoke him past endurance, he continued in a different tone: "But it is useless for age to preach lessons of prudence to youth, and as your father says, every one must purchase his own experience; so we will now, if you please, change the subject to that of making preparations for your journey. You are still determined to visit Egypt, I suppose?"

"It is my most ardent wish."

"Return then to your own apartment, and by to-morrow all shall be ready for your departure."

"He must not enter the house!" said Abelard; "alas! alas! that I should live to say it! Sir Ambrose has forbidden him even to cross the threshold."

"Can you not remain concealed in the apartment of Dr. Entwerfen?" asked Father Morris, after a short pause; "no one enters there but himself; and one of the windows looks upon this terrace, so that you may reach it unobserved; Abelard, I am confident, will not betray you; and I will accompany you, as I wish to consult with the doctor respecting your intended voyage."

Edric hastily assented, and bidding Abelard an affectionate adieu, he and Father Morris easily climbed through the window that led to the adytum of Dr. Entwerfen, whilst Abelard, clasping his hands together, exclaimed as he retired, "God bless him! Well, he shall not want for pecuniary assistance at any rate, if Mr. Davis and I can help it; that is one comfort."

When Edric and Father Morris entered the study of Dr. Entwerfen, they found him engaged in what, certainly considering his age and station, seemed a very extraordinary amusement. He was apparently dancing a hornpipe, drawing his heels together, and alternately rising and sinking like a clown in a pantomime, twisting his face, in the mean time, into the most hideous grimaces.

"What is the matter?" cried Edric and Father Morris, both at the same instant, gazing at him with surprise.

"I—I—I am galvanized," cried the doctor, in a piteous tone; nodding his head with a sudden jerk, that seemed to threaten every instant to throw it out of its socket; and then, suddenly starting, he kicked out one leg horizontally, and twirled round upon the other with an air of an opera dancer.

"How did it happen?" cried Edric, excessively shocked at the unnatural contrast exhibited between the doctor's serious countenance, and involuntary antics.

"I can't—exactly—tell," replied the doctor, bolting forth his words with difficulty, and still swimming, grinning, and capering, to the inexpressible horror of his companions, till by degrees his grimaces subsided, and he was enabled at last to stand tolerably steady. He now informed his friends, that trying some experiments with his galvanic battery, he had unfortunately operated upon himself; and in his turn listened to their account of what had passed between Edric and Sir Ambrose. Instead of expressing sorrow, however, when he found his pupil had quarrelled with his father, the doctor's eyes sparkled with joy—"Then you must inevitably travel," exclaimed he. "We shall visit the pyramids, we shall animate the mummies, and we shall attain immortality."

There was something in this violent expression of the doctor's transports that did not quite harmonize with Edric's feelings, especially as he fancied he perceived a satirical smile lurking round the lips of Father Morris.

"When shall you be ready to set off?" asked he abruptly.

"To-morrow, if you will," replied the doctor. "I have foreseen this result some time, and I have been preparing every thing accordingly. I never knew a young Englishman in my life, Father Morris, who was not fond of travelling. The inhabitants of other countries travel for what they can get, or what they hope to learn; but an Englishman travels because he does not know what to do with himself. He spares neither time, trouble, nor money; he goes every where, sees every thing; after which, he returns—just as wise as when he set out. Not that I blame curiosity—no—I admire it above all things!—it is that which has led to all the great discoveries that have been made since the creation of the world, and it is that which now impels us to explore the pyramids."

Edric looked excessively annoyed at the conclusion of this speech, and, to change the subject, hastily asked the doctor, if he thought his galvanic battery powerful enough for the experiment they meant to try with it.

"Powerful!" exclaimed the doctor; "why I feel it even now tingling to my fingers' ends. I should think, Sir, the effect it has had upon me is a sufficient proof of the force of the machine."

"Undoubtedly!" replied Father Morris; "nay, if we are to judge by that, I only tremble lest you should animate the pyramids as well as the mummies, and you must allow it would be an awkward sight to see them come tumbling and slipping along the plain."

"Sir!" said the doctor, staring at him.

"Do you intend visiting any other country than Egypt?" asked Father Morris, fearful he had gone too far, and wishing, for reasons he did not openly avow, not to offend his companions.

"I should like to see India," said the doctor; "some black-letter pamphlets in my possession, allude to its being once governed by an old woman; and as the regular historians make no mention of the fact, I should like to see what traditions I could gather respecting it on the spot. The religion of the ancient Hindoos, before they were converted to Christianity, has been said to have resembled that of the ancient Egyptians; by comparing the monuments of both, one might be made to illustrate the other. I should also like, before we quit Africa, to see the celebrated court of Timbuctoo. I have long been in correspondence with a learned pundit there, who has communicated to me some of the most sublime discoveries."

"The whole of the interior of Africa must be interesting," observed Father Morris, "particularly the rising states on the banks of the Niger. It is generally instructive as well as amusing to watch the birth and struggles of infant republics; and to remark first how fast the people encroach, and then the governors. Whilst the rulers are weak, they are always liberal; but their exalted sentiments in general decrease in exact proportion as they become powerful."

"In short," resumed the doctor, "I would willingly traverse the whole world; I know but one country that I should dislike to visit."

"And which is that?" asked Edric.

"America," replied the doctor. "I have no wish to have my throat cut, or my breath stopped by a bowstring. I have a perfect horror of despotic governments."

"Then how do you endure the one we live under?" asked Father Morris.

"The case is quite different," returned the doctor. "With us, the spur of despotism is scarcely felt; and the people, being permitted occasionally to think and act for themselves, are not debased and brutalized as the slaves of absolute power are in general. Despotism, with us, is like a rod which the schoolmaster keeps hung up in sight of his boys, but which he has very seldom any occasion to make use of. From such despotism as that of the Americans, however, Heaven defend us!"

"Amen!" said Edric; "for, as we are happy now, we should be idiots to desire a change."

"What an unphilosophical sentiment!" exclaimed the doctor: "I am really quite shocked that you, Edric, should utter such a speech. What an abominable doctrine! Remember, that if you once allow innovation to be dangerous, you instantly put a stop to all improvement—you absolutely shut and bolt your doors against it. Oh! it is horrible, that such a doctrine should be ever broached in a civilized country. You could not surely be aware of what you were saying?"

"To-morrow," said Father Morris, addressing Edric, and without noticing the indignation of the learned doctor, "you must proceed to town, where you can remain at the house of a friend of mine, till you are ready for your voyage to Egypt. I would not, however, advise you to stay long before you go there; for, as your father intends visiting London in a day or two, you might meet, and the consequences, be unpleasant. I have already dispatched a carrier-pigeon to advise my friend, Lord Gustavus De Montfort, of your arrival; he, I am sure, will give you a hearty welcome, and not only afford you the shelter of his house, but afford you all the assistance in his power, to enable you to make preparations for your journey; for which purpose, also, I will take care to supply you with money. No thanks," continued he, stopping Edric, who was about to speak, "I detest them. If you really feel obliged to me, you will prove it by remaining silent. I must leave you now, as my longer absence might create suspicion. Adieu! God bless you! A balloon will wait for you to-morrow morning, at the corner of the wood. The doctor will, of course, accompany you. I think you may safely rest here concealed till then. Once more, adieu!"

"Now Father Morris is gone," said Doctor Entwerfen to his pupil, "I have a treat for you. I will show you a curious collection of ballads, all of which are at least three hundred years old, which a friend of mine picked up in London for me the other day, and sent me down this morning by the stage-balloon. They are all of the genuine rag paper, a certain proof of their antiquity; for, you know, the asbestos paper we now use has not been invented more than two hundred years. But you shall see them: follow me."

So saying, the doctor trotted off to his library, that paradise of half-forgotten volumes, most of which had been accidentally saved from their well-merited destination of covering over butter, and wrapping up cheese, to be drawn from the dust and obscurity in which they had lain for centuries, to ornament the shelves of Doctor Entwerfen; and whose authors, if they could have taken a peep upon earth, and beheld them, would have been quite astonished to find themselves immortal. Entering this emporium of neglected learning, the doctor hastily advanced to a table, on which lay his newly acquired treasures, and holding them up, exclaimed, "Look, Edric, how beautifully dirty the paper is; no art could counterfeit this dingy hue. This sooty tinge is the genuine tint of antiquity. You know, Edric, in ancient times, the caloric employed in culinary purposes, and indeed for all the common usages of life, was produced by the combustion of wood, and of a black bituminous substance, or amphilites, drawn from the bowels of the earth, called coal, of which you may yet see specimens in the cabinets of the curious. As these substances decomposed, or rather expanded, by the force of heat, the attraction of cohesion was dissolved, and the component parts flew off in the shape of smoke or soot. This smoke, rising into the air, was dispersed by it, and the minute particles, or atoms, of which it was composed, falling and resting upon every thing that chanced to be in their way, produced that incomparable dusky hue, which the moderns have so often tried, though in vain, to imitate. I beg your pardon, Edric, for using such vulgar language to express what I wished to say, but really, treating upon such a subject, I did not know how to explain myself elegantly."

"Oh! I understood you very well, Sir. After all, the only true use of language is to convey the ideas of one person to the understanding of another; and, provided that end be attained, I really do not see that it is of any consequence what words we make use of."

"True, Edric dear! you make very just observations sometimes. Well, but the ballads; I was going to show you my treasures, — my jewels! as the Roman lady said of her children. Look what beautiful specimens these are! A little torn here and there, and with a few of the lines illegible—but genuine antiques. I'll warrant every one of them above three hundred years old. Look, it is real linen paper; you may tell it by the texture; and then the spelling, see what a number of letters they put into their words that were of no use. Look at the titles of them. Here is the 'Tragical end of poor Miss Bailey'—and here 'Cherry Ripe'—and 'I've been roaming.' Here is 'The loves of Captain Wattle and Miss Roe'—and here are 'Jessy the flower of Dumblane,' and 'Dunois the brave.' But this is my Phœnix—here is what will be the envy of collectors! here is my invaluable treasure. This, I believe, is absolutely unique, and that I am so blest as to possess the only copy extant. The date is wanting, but the manners it describes are so unpolished, that I should almost think it might be traced back to the times of the aboriginal Britons.—Thus it begins:—

'At Wednesbury there was a cocking,

A match between Newton and Scroggins;

The nailers and colliers left work,

And to Spittle's they all went jogging.

Tol de rol lol.'

I used to be very much puzzled at this burthen, which is one of frequent recurrence in ancient songs. At first, I thought it a relic of some language now irrevocably lost. Then it struck me, it might be an invocation to the deities of the aborigines. In short, I was quite perplexed, and knew not what to think, when a learned friend of mine hit upon an idea the other day, which seems completely to solve the difficulty. He suggests that it was an ancient manner of running up and down the scale; and that 'Tol de rol lol' had the same signification as 'Do re mi fa;'—which solution is at once so simple and ingenious, that I am sure you, as well as myself, must be struck by it. I here omit a few stanzas, in which the author enumerates his heroes exactly in the Homeric manner. The names are so barbarous, that I am afraid of loosening my teeth in pronouncing them:—

'There was plenty of beef at the dinner,

Of a bull that was baited to death;

Bunny Hyde got a lump in his throat,

Which had like to have stopt his breath.'

What a beautiful simplicity there is in that last line,

The Mummy!

'Which had like to have stopt his breath.'

Oh, we moderns have nothing equal to it! —

'The company fell in confusion,

To see this poor Bunny Hyde choke,

So they hurried him down to the kitchen,

And held his head over the smoke.'

"This develops a curious practice of antiquity. You know, Edric, I explained to you just now the manner in which combustion was formerly effected, and the causes of the production of what was called smoke. I own, however, it seems a strange way of reviving a half-suffocated man, to hold his head over smoke, which, being loaded, as I said before, with innumerable atoms of all sorts and sizes, would, one might think be more likely to impede respiration than restore it. The fact, however, is undoubted; and it not only affords a curious illustration of the manner of the ancients, but is of itself a strong proof of the authenticity of the ballad; for such an idea never could have entered the head of a modern. To return to poor Hyde —

'One gave him a kick o' th' stomach,

And another a thump o' th' brow,

His wife cried throw him i' th' stable,

And he will be better just now.'

This unfeeling conduct of his wife does not say much in commendation of the ladies of those times. Here follows an hiatus of several stanzas: I find, however, by a word or two here and there, that they celebrated the exploits of two gallic heroes: —

'The best i' th' country bred;

The one was a brassy-wing black,

And the other a dusky-wing'd red.'

These unfortunate victims of the cruelty of man seem both to have perished. There is a stanza, however, before this catastrophe, which seems to relate to the combat.

> 'The conflict was hard upon each,
>
> Till glossy-wing'd blacky was choked,
>
> The colliers were nationally vex'd,
>
> And the nailers were all provoked.'

This passage seems very obscure: 'Nationally' is evidently a sign of comparison, but I cannot say I ever saw it employed before. It is, however, another proof of the amazing antiquity of the ballad. After this, it appears that the people broke in upon the ring, and both cocks were crushed to atoms. I don't know whether you are acquainted with the manner in which these gallic combats were conducted, Edric. A kind of amphitheatre was formed, upon which the birds were pitted one against the other, whence the name cock-pit. The combatants were armed with large iron spurs, and the victor generally left his rival dead upon the field. The ballad proceeds:—

> 'The cock-pit was near to the church,
>
> As an ornament to the town;
>
> One side was an old coal-pit,
>
> And the other was well gorsed round.'

Gorse was a kind of heath or furze.

> 'Peter Hadley peep'd through the gorse,
>
> In order to see the cocks fight;
>
> Spittle jobb'd his eye out with a fork,
>
> And said, "Blast you, it sarves you right."'

This is very spirited and expressive, though the false quantities render it difficult to read.

> 'Some folks may think this is strange,
>
> Who Wednesbury never knew,
>
> But those who have ever been there,
>
> Won't have the least doubt but it's true.

For they are all savage by nature,

And guilty of deeds that are shocking,

Jack Baker he whack'd his own feyther,

And so ended the Wednesbury cocking.'"

"It is very fine certainly," said Edric, who was half asleep.

"Upon my word," returned the doctor, "I don't think you have heard a single word I have been saying."

"Oh! yes, I have," replied Edric, "every syllable. It was about a man killing his own father, and putting his eyes out with a fork."

"Eh?" cried the doctor, somewhat annoyed at this unequivocal proof that though his words might have struck upon the auricular organs of his pupil, they had not reached his brains. The exclamation of the doctor restored Edric to his senses, and he began to apologize.

"I am really very sorry," said he, "but you must excuse my inattention. Sometimes, you know, the mind is not in tune for literary discussions, even when proceeding from the most eloquent lips. This is my case at the present moment. My mind is so occupied by the important change that has just taken place in my affairs, that, I own, even your learning and eloquence were thrown away upon me."

"If that be the state of your mind," replied the doctor, with chagrin, "it is of no use to show you any more of my literary treasures; else I have some of matchless excellence. Here is a letter addressed to Sheridan, a witty writer of comedies, in the eighteenth century, which has never been opened,—and here is a tailor's bill of the immortal Byron, which may possibly never have been looked at. But here is the most inestimable of my relics. Look, at least, at this. This piece of paper, covered carelessly with irregular strokes and lines, was once in the possession of that enchanting, that inimitable novelist of the nineteenth century, generally distinguished in the works of contemporary writers by the mysterious title of 'The Great Unknown!' See, here is half the word 'Waverley,' written upon it, and doubtless all these other irregular marks and scratches proceeded directly from his pen. I confess, Edric, I never contemplate this relic of genius without a feeling of reverence, and almost of awe. 'Perhaps,' say I to myself, when I look at it, 'when these letters were formed, the first idea had but just arisen in the mind of the author of those immortal works, which were afterwards destined to improve and delight mankind. Perhaps, at that very moment gigantic thoughts were rushing through his brain, and a variety of new ideas opening their treasures to his imagination.' Oh, there is something in the mere random stroke of the pen of a celebrated character, inexpressibly affecting to the mind;—it carries one back to the very time when he lived—it seems to make one acquainted with him, and to let us into the secrets of his inmost thoughts. But I see you are not attending to me, Edric!"

"I am very sorry—another time I should be happy—but now—I cannot. However, when we return, perhaps—"

"It may be then too late," said the doctor, with solemnity; and locking up his cabinet, he led the way back to his common sitting-room, in high dudgeon.

CHAPTER VII.

The morning after the events just recorded, as Mr. Montagu, the brother of Sir Ambrose, was sitting at the breakfast-table with his wife and daughter, they were all startled by the unexpected arrival of a letter from Sir Ambrose. "Bless me!" cried Mr. Montagu, moved for once to forget his usual habits of indifference—"I do believe it is a letter from my brother."

"Your brother!" screamed Mrs. Montagu, starting up to examine it, and in her agitation overturning a patent steam coffee-machine, by which coffee was roasted, ground, made, and poured out with an ad libitum of boiling milk and sugar, all in the short space of five minutes. "Oh!" continued she—"I am scalded to death!"

"I hope not, my dear," said Mr. Montagu, calmly taking up his letter, and carefully examining it on all sides without opening it. "Yes," continued he, "it is indeed from my brother, and I hope it contains no ill news, for I do not perceive any signs of mourning about it." And so saying, he very tranquilly laid his letter again upon the table, and recommenced sipping his coffee.

"La! papa, hadn't you better open your letter and read it?" asked Clara, who was busily employed in assisting her mother.

"Ah!" resumed Mr. Montagu. "True! I never thought of that—I think I had." Then again taking the letter in his hand, he broke the seal and gave it to Clara to read.

"And do you think my daughter is to leave me when I am in this miserable condition, Mr. Montagu, to read letters from your brother, Mr. Montagu—a man who has always treated me with such disrespect, Mr. Montagu,—and I half scalded to death!"

"I am sure I'm very sorry, my dear," began Mr. Montagu.

"Oh, spare your sorrow," exclaimed his wife—"for I'm sure you don't care one single straw about me. You're a cruel man—"

"Hadn't I better read the letter?" asked Clara, trembling at the thought of the domestic sparring she saw about to ensue.

"Yes, yes! read, my dear," said her father, glad of any pretext to avert the coming storm: for though he seldom disturbed himself about any thing, provided his study was not swept oftener than once a month, and he was not obliged to submit to the insupportable fatigue of arranging his ideas in the tense form, necessary for conversation; he had yet a most inconceivable horror of his wife's fluency of tongue, thus affording a striking proof of the ingratitude of mortals, who often ungraciously find fault with the very things for which they have most occasion to be thankful; as it must be allowed that nothing could really be more convenient for a man of a taciturn disposition, than to have a wife who could manage to talk at once for him and herself too.

Notwithstanding the encouragement of her father, Clara, however, still paused, looking with a timid eye towards her mother, for that lady's permission to begin. Curiosity struggled powerfully with anger in the breast of Mrs. Montagu for some minutes; but at last the former prevailed, and with a nod she permitted Clara to read. She immediately began as follows:—

"My dear brother."

"Humph," observed Mrs. Montagu, "his last letter began—Sir. He's getting wonderfully civil, I think."

"Pshaw!" exclaimed her husband.

Clara continued,—"I am happy to inform you, that my dear Edmund has gained a glorious victory."

"And what is that to us, I should like to know?" said Mrs. Montagu: "for my part, I have too much pride to trouble myself about people, who don't trouble themselves about me."

Clara went on.—"We are all coming up to London, to be present at a grand triumph the Queen is going to give him; and thinking it a pity there should be a misunderstanding——"

"Ah! what's that, child?" exclaimed Mr. Montagu, laying down a problem which he had been studying ever since she began.—"Read that again, Clara."

"And thinking it a pity there should be a misunderstanding any longer existing between you and me, we being both fast approaching to the grave, I intend, with your and Mrs. Montagu's permission——"

"Mrs. Montagu's permission!" cried the delighted Mrs. Montagu; "are you quite sure he says that, Clara?" and she pressed over her daughter's shoulder to ascertain the joyful fact. "Well, well, I do declare he really does says so. Look, my dear, there it is, — 'Mrs. Montagu's permission.' He never called me Mrs. Montagu before. God bless him! a nice old gentleman! I am sure I shall be very glad to see him and his brave son, too. Only think, my dear! what an honour it is to have a hero in one's family! Read on, Clara; I feel quite interested to know all the particulars of my nephew's victory. You know, he is my nephew, Mr. Montagu, as well as yours, as I am your wife, and he is your own brother's son; so, read on, Clara, and let us know all about him."

Clara obeyed the moment her mother gave her an opportunity. "I intend, with your and Mrs. Montagu's permission, to take the opportunity of visiting you. I remain, with kind remembrances to Mrs. Montagu and my niece, to whom I long to be introduced, your affectionate brother,

"Ambrose Montagu."

"Very well," said Mr. Montagu, "I shall be very glad to see him; I always loved my brother, and I was quite sorry when we were not friends."

"Here is a postscript," resumed Clara, and she read:

"I quite forgot to inform you, that the Queen has conferred a title upon my son, and that I shall have to present him to you as Lord Edmund."

"I am very glad to hear it," exclaimed the gratified uncle.

"And so am I," reiterated his wife. "My nephew, Lord Edmund Montagu. I wonder when they will be here: I must set about making preparations for them immediately. Strike the kitchen automaton, Clara, to summon all the domestic assistants together, that I may give my orders. Dear me! what a bustle I am in."

In one corner of the room stood a kind of organ, by playing certain notes upon which, intimation was given in the lower regions of what was wanted in the parlour; the organ having long tubes communicating with the kitchen, through which the sound was conveyed. Clara accordingly sat down, and by striking a few chords, soon assembled all the domestics of her father.

"I expect company," said Mrs. Montagu, with an air of excessive consequence. "My brother-in-law, Sir Ambrose Montagu, and my nephew, Lord Edmund Montagu, are coming to stay with us during a triumph, with which her most gracious Majesty the Queen intends to honour Lord Edmund, my nephew. When did my brother-in-law, Sir Ambrose, say that he and my nephew, Lord Edmund, intended coming, Mr. Montagu? Clara, look at Sir Ambrose's letter. 'I intend,' says he, addressing Mr. Montagu, 'with your and Mrs. Montagu's permission, to be with you on such a day,' but I forget what day he mentions."

"He does not say which day," replied Clara, consulting the letter.

"Well, at any rate, it will be very soon," resumed Mrs. Montagu; "and we must prepare accordingly. You know, the connexions of my brother-in-law, Sir Ambrose, are very high, and I do not doubt but his intimate friend, the Duke of Cornwall, will call to see him—nay, perhaps, he may dine at my table with the two princesses, his daughter and niece. Indeed there's no knowing, but, perhaps, even her most gracious Majesty the Queen may condescend to enter my humble doors. Do you hear, all of you?—you must all be attentive. You Angelina, as cook, will have the most upon your hands—remember, nothing can be too plain for great people. Fricassees and ragouts are only devoured by the canaille."

"I am instructed of that, Ma'am," replied Angelina, a great, fat, bonny-looking cook,—"but I flatter myself I know how to concoct dishes——"

"That is the very thing I want to avoid," interrupted her mistress. "It is the fashion now for great people to have only one dish, and that as plainly cooked as possible. I have been told by a friend of mine, who got a peep at the great dinner the Queen gave the other day to the foreign ambassadors, that there was nothing in the world upon the table, but a huge round of boiled beef, and a great dish of smoking potatoes, with their jackets on."

"Well, Ma'am," returned Angelina, "I will rally both my physical and mental energies to afford you all the satisfaction in my power; notwithstanding which, I am free to confess, that, in my opinion, the gastronomic science is now cruelly neglected, and that I do not think the digestive powers of the stomach can be properly excited from their dormant state by such unstimulating food as that you mention. Besides, the muscular force of the stomach must be strained to decompose such solid viands, and I should think the diaphragm seriously injured—"

"You, Alphonso," continued Mrs. Montagu, addressing the footman, and cruelly interrupting the learned harangue of the cook, "must have a new suit of livery. In the mean time, arrange properly the best drawing-room, and clean the pictures. There is a fine large painting of one of the old English artists, over the door, the colours of which are quite faded; I am afraid you have used something improper to clean it."

"Indeed, Madam," returned Alphonso, "I think the fault is in the picture itself. It did not dry well originally; I don't think the oil that was used in its composition had the carbon and hydrogen mingled in proper proportions. You know, Madam, that oil in general has an amazing affinity for oxygen, and absorbs it rapidly; now, though the oil of this picture has been exposed for years to the action of the common atmospheric air, yet it has never thickened properly into a concrete state."

"Eustace! you, as butler, must take care not to bring any variety of wines to the table: nothing is drunk now but port and sherry; and even they are going out of fashion. Have plenty of strong ale, however, and porter, for they are now reckoned the most elegant liquors for the ladies."

"I shall do my utmost endeavour to obey your injunctions, Madam," said Eustace, bowing respectfully, "but I cannot imagine that any species of corn, even if it have undergone the vinous fermentation, can produce a liquid so agreeable to the palate, as well as conducive to the sanity of the body, as the juice of the grape."

"And you, Evelina and Cecilia," continued Mrs. Montagu, addressing her housemaids, "must superintend the arrangement of the dormitories: let the air out of the beds and re-inflate them—examine the elastic spring mattresses—mend the gossamer curtains—sweep the velvet carpets, and take care the tubes for withdrawing the decomposed air, and admitting fresh, are in proper order;—also, clean out the baths attached to each chamber, and take care there is an abundant supply of water."

"I am told that ablution in the common aqueous fluid is becoming more fashionable than any medicated baths," said Evelina, "and that some people of rank actually use a composition of alkali and oil to remove the pulverous particles that may have lodged upon their epidermis in the course of the day."

"I fear from the commands you have issued, Madam," rejoined Cecilia, "that you were oblivious of the alteration that has been effected in the superior dormitory. The air there is no longer changed by means of tubes—but there is a fan-feather ventilator fixed in the ceiling, which by its gentle undulations occasions a free circulation of the aëriform fluid; I do not think, however, that it is quite adequate to supply the place of the tubes; as upon entering the room the other morning, I perceived a strong sensation of azote, and I am confident that the proportion of nitrogen more than trebled that of oxygen in the air contained in the whole apartment."

"I am sorry for that," said Mrs. Montagu, "as it is the best sleeping-room: however, as it is too late to change it, we must do the best we can; and so go all of you and attend to my directions, for I should be very sorry to have my brother-in-law Sir Ambrose, and my nephew Lord Edmund, put to any inconvenience, during their sojourn in my dwelling; to say nothing of the great and noble guests who may perchance also honour the mansion with their presence."

Whilst this bustle was taking place in the house of Mr. Montagu, Edric and his tutor were on their way to London. It was with infinite difficulty, however, the doctor could be persuaded to set off without alarming the family; for, again and again, he would return to survey the treasures he was leaving behind, and the moment Edric thought he had him safe, he would recollect some indispensable requisite for their journey, and hurry back again to find it. At last they were fairly started, and a favourable wind blew them rapidly towards London. Edric had never seen this vast metropolis, and his astonishment and delight, when its magnificent palaces, its superb streets, its public buildings, its theatres, and its churches, broke upon him, was quite beyond description. His transports and exclamations, indeed, at length became so violent, as quite to annoy the learned doctor.

"If you feel such rapture at the sight of London," said he, peevishly, "I suppose you will be reluctant to quit it; and I dare say you already repent having proposed to travel."

"Oh! what is that?" cried Edric, without attending to him, as, lost in amazement, he saw a house in the suburbs gently slide out of its place, and glide majestically along the road, a lady at one of the windows kissing her hand to some one in another house as she passed. "Do my eyes deceive me, or does that house move?"

"Certainly it does," replied the doctor. "Did you never see a moving house before? You must have heard of them at any rate, for nothing can be more common. It certainly is convenient, when one wants to go into the country for a few weeks, to be able to take one's house with one: it saves a great deal of trouble in packing, and permits one to have all one's little conveniences about one. You see there are grooves in the bottom of the houses that just fit on the iron railways; and as they are propelled by steam, they slide on without much trouble. It does not answer, however, with any but small houses, for large ones can't well be made compact enough. However, you must postpone your admiration of that, as well as of the other wonders of London, for here we are at Lord Gustavus's door. What a noble mansion! is it not? This street, Edric, is called the Strand, and is the most fashionable in London; because it adjoins the Queen's favourite palace at Somerset House."

"Is that the palace?" said Edric. "It seems a noble pile of building."

"The gardens are fine," replied the doctor; "but as they are thrown open to the public, and nothing is paid for admission, it is reckoned vulgar to walk in them. You English do not like any thing you do not pay for; but more of this hereafter. We must now prepare to pay our respects to our noble host."

Lord Gustavus de Montfort received them very kindly, but Edric found something in his voice and manners excessively forbidding. He had a pompous disagreeable manner of speaking, with a nasal accent so strong, that it was absolutely torture to Edric, whose sense of hearing was uncommonly fine, to listen to him. He had also a conceited dictatorial way of delivering his opinion, which Edric thought extremely unpleasant. He generally commenced his speeches with "Thinking as I think, and as I am positive every one who hears me must think, or at least ought to think;" and this exordium formed an epitome of his character; as he was firmly persuaded that every one who differed in the slightest degree from his opinion, was decidedly wrong, whilst the possibility of his ever being mistaken himself never entered his imagination. His father had been one of the counsellors of the late Queen, and his eldest brother having declined to take the father's place upon his death, Lord Gustavus had been appointed to it. Thus he was really a person of some consequence in the state; and though his being so was quite a matter of chance, arising from the circumstances above-mentioned and the indolence of the Queen, he affected to regard it as a matter of personal favour to himself, and endeavoured to persuade his hearers that the affairs of government could not possibly go on without him. Knowing his foible of wishing to be thought of importance in the realm, and feeling the want of a leader of rank, some of the discontented spirits of the kingdom had endeavoured to gain him over to their party; and though Lord Gustavus was strictly loyal, and even particularly fond of talking of her gracious Majesty the Queen, and boasting of the confidence she placed in him, yet his vanity could not altogether resist the able attacks made upon it by the rebels. He wavered, he began to talk of reform, and to mingle boasts of his popularity amongst the people, with those he had before indulged in, of enjoying the favour of his sovereign. Thus he hung upon the balance, ready to incline to either side, according to the circumstances that time or chance might produce.

"I am extremely happy," said he, as he advanced to meet his guests, "that my worthy and respected friend Father Morris has procured me the honour of such illustrious visitors. The holy father has informed me of the sublime purpose that animates your bosoms and leads you to traverse realms of air, to explore the hitherto undiscovered secrets of the grave. His partiality for me has also led him to imagine that my humble means may perchance prove conducive to so great an end, and he has requested me to give you all the assistance in my power to promote the gigantic objects you have in view. Thus you may rest assured, no efforts shall be wanting on my part to fulfil his wishes, and as, though insignificant in myself, I am so happy as to be honoured by the protection and favour of her Majesty the Queen, my most gracious sovereign; and also as my feeble attempts to promote the public good have been rewarded by the gratitude of the people; it may perchance be in my power to serve you; and in the mean time I hope you will do me the honour to partake of such hospitality as my humble mansion can afford." So saying, Lord Gustavus led the way through a sumptuous suite of rooms, to one where an elegant cold collation was laid out, of which he invited his guests to partake. Nothing could be more splendid than the furniture and embellishments of this apartment. The rooms were hung with crimson silk, trimmed with gold; valuable paintings decorated the walls; statues of inestimable price filled each corner, and magnificent mirrors increased tenfold the magic of the scene. Lord Gustavus secretly enjoyed the astonishment and admiration painted upon the countenances of his guests; and whilst he openly affected to talk of his "poor house," and his "humble attempts to entertain them," &c. his heart covertly exalted in the grandeur around him, and his eyes sparkled with pleasure at the effect he saw it produced upon the strangers. Nothing makes one so much disposed to be in a good humour with the world, as being in a good humour with oneself; and nothing is so certain to produce that delightful sensation, as to see what we possess excite the admiration of others. Thus, as the flattery conveyed by looks far outweighs that expressed by words, and as the looks of Edric and the doctor unequivocally declared their sentiments, Lord Gustavus was quite enchanted with his visitors, and spared no pains to render them equally happy as himself. He ordered a large apartment to be prepared for the doctor, that he might make his arrangements for the intended Egyptian expedition quite at his ease; he commanded his servants to obey his directions implicitly, and he directed tradesmen to supply every thing that might be wanted at his own expense.

Having thus given the doctor carte blanche, he next turned his attention to Edric, and, finding it was his first visit to London, volunteered to show him all the wonders of that immense metropolis, which then, spreading enormously in every direction, seemed like the fabled monster of the Indians, to stretch its enormous arms on every side and swallow up all the hapless villages which were so unfortunate as to fall within its reach.

In the mean time, Sir Ambrose had begun to repent, though secretly, of the unwarrantable severity with which he had treated his son. It is a trite though undeniable observation, that we never know the real value of any possession till we have lost it; and thus Sir Ambrose, though he had thought nothing of the respectful and dutiful attentions of his son, whilst he was in the habit of constantly receiving them, now felt their want, and regretted bitterly the ill-timed harshness that had deprived him of them for ever. Still, however, he was too obstinate to own he had been wrong; and though he knew that by recalling his son he should restore his lost happiness, he, like many other persons in similar situations, most magnanimously determined to persist in being miserable.

The Duke of Cornwall was quite astonished, and even indignant, at what he termed the inconsistency of his friend. "How can you be so weak as still to regret the loss of that peevish boy?" said he, as, on the second morning after Edric's departure, he entered the library of Sir Ambrose, attended by his confessor, Father Murphy. "Depend upon it, it is bad policy; for patience robs care of its bitterest sting, as this holy father says. You often preach that doctrine to me, don't you, Father Murphy?" Father Murphy was an Irishman, and gifted with a rich brogue, which, aided by his comely figure, round rosy face, and little laughing black eyes, gave a peculiar raciness to every thing he said. He had not long filled the office he then held, and though he had been recommended to it, on the death of the duke's late confessor, by Father Morris, yet no two human beings could be more different than he and that reverend personage. Father Murphy, indeed, was a general favourite, and the whole household of the duke concurred in thinking him quite a nonpareil of a priest; for, as he was not very fond of doing penance himself, so he was not very rigid in imposing it upon others, and consequently he and his penitents were always upon the best terms imaginable. In short, he seemed especially designed by Nature to be good friends with all the world; and on his side he certainly did the utmost not to thwart the beneficent old lady's kind intentions.

He now smiled good-humouredly at the duke's question, and replied, "Och! and is it me ye're quoting from, yere Grace? And where's the use of that, pray? when ye know I'm just here and ready to quote for myself."

"If all your observations are as good as that the duke has just repeated," said Sir Ambrose, "I don't know any body that might be quoted from with more advantage."

"Sure! and is it of myself ye're saying that?" asked Father Murphy, "for if ye are, ye never made a better spach in all your life; only there's a little mistake if ye think the observation ye're talking of came out of my own head, for it didn't do any such thing."

"Do not be alarmed," said Father Morris, who now approached, and who spoke with his usual satirical sneer: "No one who knows you will ever suspect you of any thing so atrocious."

"Good-nature and integrity are sometimes more than equivalent to brilliant talents," said Sir Ambrose bitterly.

"True," rejoined Father Morris, in one of his softest, most insinuating tones; "but they become inestimable when united, as in the example before us:" bowing to Father Murphy as he spoke. Sir Ambrose turned, and looked earnestly at the tall thin figure of the monk as he stood before him, his arms crossed upon his breast, and his head, as usual, bent towards the ground, but he did not speak. A short pause ensued, which was broken by the duke's suddenly exclaiming, "Did you not say Dr. Entwerfen has gone off with Edric?"

"Certainly, I did."

The Mummy!

"Then, depend upon it, the whole was a planned thing. They have taken some wild scheme into their heads, and they are gone to execute it."

"Impossible!" exclaimed Sir Ambrose.

"I see no impossibility in the business," resumed the duke. "I think the case is clear. They did not know how to get off decently; and so Edric pretended to quarrel with you and me, to give the thing a face."

"I cannot fancy Edric guilty of such meanness," cried Sir Ambrose passionately.

"I don't think the matter admits of a single doubt. But what do you think on the subject, Father Morris?"

"Men devoted to austere professions like myself," replied the priest, without raising his eyes from the ground, "know but little of what is passing in the world. Thus, though my body be no longer shrouded in the gloom of a cloister, my mind remains still too much abstracted from the busy scenes around me, for me to be a competent judge of the effect of human passions."

"Och, then, ye are very right to say nothin' about them," cried Father Murphy; "for though I'm in a passion every day of my life, I nevher know what to say when I begin to talk of it. And so I jist think it's the wisest way to holdth my tongue."

Neither Sir Ambrose nor the duke made any reply; and after settling that they should commence their journey on the following morning, they separated.

CHAPTER VIII.

The journey of the duke and Sir Ambrose to London had nothing in it to distinguish it from hundreds of other journeys, and they did not meet with a single adventure worthy of being recorded.

It happened by one of those singular coincidences in real life, which would be called improbable in a novel, that Mr. Montagu's mansion adjoined that of the duke, Mrs. Montagu having, like most of the parvenu genus, a most violent penchant for the neighbourhood of the great; perhaps, in the hope that gentility might be infectious, and that she might catch a little by being near it. Both houses were in the Strand, which was, as we have before stated, in those days the most fashionable part of London, and both had beautiful gardens shelving down to the Thames.

Mrs. Montagu received her brother-in-law with all that awkward overstrained civility, with which persons raised above their original grade in society, generally endeavour to show their respect to those whom they consider as their superiors; whilst Mr. Montagu welcomed him with warm affection, and presented his daughter Clara to her uncle with all the fondness of a parent.

Clara Montagu well deserved his partiality, for she was a charming girl; and her light fairy form and animated features seemed to realize all that poets feign of Hebe. Sir Ambrose was delighted with her, and half his dislike of the mother banished, as he contemplated the budding charms of the daughter. It was well he had such an antidote, for poor Mrs. Montagu, in her over-anxiety to render herself agreeable, contrived to be most excessively annoying to him. Perhaps, indeed, there are few things more troublesome than this vulgar attempt at politeness, and the good temper of the baronet was almost exhausted ere he retired for the night.

Abelard, who had accompanied his master to town, and who often officiated as groom of the chamber, assisted him to undress, and, as usual with servants in those days, took the liberty of giving his opinion freely of their hostess. Sir Ambrose felt no interest in his remarks, but he did not check them, as he hoped, after he had exhausted this theme, he might turn the conversation upon Edric. The baronet was indeed excessively anxious to hear some news of his son, though he was by far too proud to make any inquiries respecting him.

The Mummy!

"So you really think Mrs. Montagu disagreeable, Abelard," said Sir Ambrose.

"She is a perfect nuisance, your honour, to all civilized society. Why, I have observed her all day, and I verily believe she has never left your honour for ten minutes, nor ever ceased for more than half an hour at a time, pressing your honour to eat."

"True," said Sir Ambrose, laughing, "one would think she took me for a slave, and wanted to feed me up fat before she sent me to market to be sold."

"Then she is so curious and inquisitive," resumed Abelard. "When she saw me bow to Master Edric just now, she was quite in a fever to know who he was; but I would not satisfy her."

"Master Edric!" exclaimed the baronet. "What, then! have you seen my son?"

"Yes, your honour, and it startled me so that it made me raise the adnatæ of my visual organs like one of the anas genus when the clouds are charged with electric fluid; and my heart leaped from its transverse position on my diaphragm, and seemed to stick like a great bone right across my œsophagus."

"How did he look?" asked Sir Ambrose. "Not that I feel the slightest anxiety respecting him. No—no, his own conduct has quite precluded that."

"He was in a balloon, and when he saw me, he wrote something on a piece of paper with a pencil, and threw it down, desiring me to give it to your honour."

"Where is it?" cried Sir Ambrose, endeavouring to conceal his anxiety.

Abelard searched his pockets, and opened a large pocket-book, which he carefully examined, but in vain. "I am afraid I have lost it, your honour. No; here—here it is. Yes,—no. These are some verses of my own, in the acromonogrammatic style, only every line begins with the same word with which the last ended, instead of the same letter. Shall I read them to your honour?"

Sir Ambrose groaned in the spirit, and the unmerciful Abelard, taking that for a token of assent, deliberately unfolded the paper, and read as follows:—

"ON LOVE.

"Of all the powers in Heaven above,
Above all others, triumphs Love:
Love rules the soul—the heart invades,
Invades the cities and the shades.
Shades form no shelter from its power,
Power trembles in his courtly bower.
Bower of beauty—art thou free?
Free thou art not—nor canst thou be!
Be every other class released,
Released from love, thy woe's increased;
Increased by all the weight of care,
Care flowing from complete despair."

"Humph!" said Sir Ambrose.

"I hope your honour is pleased with this little effusion of my Muse?"

"Oh yes, it is very fine, Abelard."

"And your honour thinks it well turned, and well expressed."

"Excellently! only I own I don't understand why despair comes in the last line."

"Despair—despair: oh! to rhyme with care, your honour."

"That reason is unanswerable," returned Sir Ambrose, smiling.—"And so you are quite sure you have lost Edric's note!—Not that it is of the least consequence, as nothing he could say, can possibly alter my opinion of his conduct; but, if you had had it—I thought I might as well have read it, to avoid the imputation of obstinacy."

The Mummy!

"It is irrevocably gone, your honour."

"Well then, good night; and, if you should see Edric again, you may as well tell him the fate of his note;—for, shamefully as he has behaved, I would not give him reason to accuse me of obstinacy."

This was the second time the baronet had made the same observation; and ill-natured people might have said;—but what do the remarks of ill-natured people signify to us? We hope all our readers will be good-natured ones, and as they will assuredly put the best possible construction upon Sir Ambrose's conduct, we will not be so malicious as to suggest an evil one.

Edric was exceedingly agitated by his encounter with Abelard; and, feeling convinced his father was in town, he determined to delay his journey no longer, as his dread of meeting him was excessive. He therefore resolved to seek his tutor, and, if he found him still inclined to procrastinate, to set off without him. On reaching the doctor's chamber, however, he found half his anger converted into laughter at the ludicrous situation of the poor philosopher, who, surrounded as he was on every side by a crowd of tradesmen clamorous for orders, looked something like Mercury encircled by a tribe of discontented ghosts upon the banks of the Styx.

"Yes, yes, Mr. Jones," said he; "I see you understand me. The coats are to be those woven in machines, where the wool is stripped off the sheep's back by one end, and the coat comes out completely made, in the newest fashion, at the other."

"Very well, Sir," said Mr. Jones, wagging his ears in token of assent; for in those days of universal education, even the muscles of the head were trained to perform functions which in former days it was only supposed possible they might attain: "You are quite right, Sir,—no person of fashion ever wears any thing else now."

"Oh, Edric!" cried the doctor, "I shall be ready to attend to you directly;—and so, Mrs. Celestina, you must make the soup, if you please, water-proof; and you, Mr. Crispin, must have the boots ready to dissolve, at a moment's notice. Oh, dear! oh, dear, what a perplexity I am in, my head is going just like a steam-boat, at the rate of sixty miles an hour!"

"Upon my word, doctor," said Edric, looking round in dismay, "if we are to take half the things assembled here, I do not know where we shall find a balloon large enough and strong enough even to raise us from the ground."

"I will show you one," replied the doctor, mysteriously; and solemnly drawing forth from his bosom a key, which appeared to have been suspended by a ribbon from his neck, he slowly opened, with great difficulty, a secret drawer in his escritoire, and produced from its inmost recesses a small bottle of Indian rubber. The gravity of the doctor's manner, and the length of time that he had employed in this operation, had excited Edric's curiosity, and he burst into a violent and uncontrollable fit of laughter when he saw the result.

"What is the matter, Edric?" asked the doctor, with the utmost solemnity; "what can be the occasion of this unceremonious and ill-timed levity?"

"Parturient mountains, my dear doctor," replied Edric, still laughing,—"you know the rest."

"Ridicule, Edric," said the doctor gravely, "is by no means the test of truth. Fools often,—nay, generally, laugh at what they cannot understand, and when I shall have explained the motives of my conduct, I trust you will feel ashamed of your present weak and unseasonable mirth.

"Caoutchouc, Edric, is a substance capable of astonishing dilation and contraction; whilst the peculiar elasticity and tenacity of its fibres give it a strength and solidity, very rare in bodies when in a state of extreme tension. There are several very extraordinary phenomena relating to elastic bodies, which I am happy to have an apposite opportunity of explaining to you." (Edric yawned.) "You know, elastic substances have the power of wonderfully resisting a force which would annihilate solids, apparently infinitely stronger than themselves, as a feather-bed will repulse a cannon-ball that would penetrate with ease through a thick table. Now the reason for this is clear: the elastic body has the power of summoning all its forces to its assistance, for the effect of a blow may be traced even to its remotest extremity; whereas the solid substance can only oppose its enemy by the mere resistance of the identical part struck."

"Certainly," said Edric, striving to suppress a yawn; "nothing can be more clear."

"Nothing," resumed the doctor. "I was sure you would admire the force of my reasoning; indeed, I see the excess of your admiration in the involuntary yawns in which you have been indulging. On some occasions, Edric, man shakes off the artificial restraints of society, and breaks forth into the full freedom of honest and unsophisticated nature: — thus it was with you, Edric. In ancient times, the extension of the jaws was held synonymous with the extension of the understanding, and the opening of the mouth and eyes was considered as the greatest possible sign of pleasure that could be given. In the works of an ancient author, whose poetry was doubtless once esteemed very fine, since it is now quite unintelligible, we find the following passage: —

'And Hodge stood lost in wide-mouth'd speculation.'

Again,

'His eyes and mouth the hero open'd wide.'

— And divers others, which — — "

"We will leave till a more convenient opportunity, if you please," said Edric, interrupting him. "At present, do favour me for five minutes with your attention. We cannot take all these things."

"Why not?" asked the doctor, gazing at his pupil with surprise; "for my part, I do not think we can dispense with a single article."

"These cloaks," said Edric, "and those hampers, for instance, cannot be of the slightest use."

"I beg your pardon," returned the doctor. "The cloaks are of asbestos, and will be necessary to protect us from ignition, if we should encounter any electric matter in the clouds; and the hampers are filled with elastic plugs for our ears and noses, and tubes and barrels of common air, for us to breathe when we get beyond the atmosphere of the earth."

"But what occasion shall we have to go beyond it?"

"How can we do otherwise? Surely you don't mean to travel the whole distance in the balloon? I thought, of course, you would adopt the present fashionable mode of travelling, and after mounting the seventeen miles or thereabouts, which is necessary to get clear of the mundane attraction, to wait there till the turning of the globe should bring Egypt directly under our feet."

"But it is not in the same latitude."

"True; I did not think of that! Well, then," sighing deeply, "I suppose we must do without the hamper?"

"Certainly; and without those boxes and bottles too, I hope."

"Oh no! we can't do without those. Those bottles contain my magic elixir, that cures all diseases merely by the smell:—a new idea that. You know it has been long discovered, that the whole materia medica might be carried in a ring, and that all the instruments of surgery might be compressed into a walking-stick. But the idea of sniffing health in a pinch of snuff is, I flatter myself, exclusively my own."

"Very likely; but we cannot be encumbered with your panaçea in our aërial tour."

"Then that box contains my portable galvanic battery; that, my apparatus for making and collecting the inflammable air; and that, my machine for producing and concentrating the quicksilver vapour, which is to serve as the propelling power to urge us onwards, in the place of steam; and these bladders are filled with laughing gas, for the sole purpose of keeping up our spirits."

"The three first will be useful," said Edric; "but I will positively have no more."

"Adieu! adieu! then, my precious treasures!" exclaimed the doctor, looking sorrowfully around: "Dear offspring of my cares! children of my mind! and must I leave you to some rude hand, which, heedless of your inestimable worth, may scatter your beauties to the winds? Alas! alas!"

"Breakfast is ready, and my lord is waiting!" interrupted the shrill voice of one of Lord Gustavus's servants.

"Then we must go!" said the doctor; and the rest of his pathetic lamentation remained for ever buried in his own bosom.

Lord Gustavus was already seated when they entered the room, with two gentlemen, whom he introduced to our travellers as Lord Noodle and Lord Doodle. These noble lords were both counsellors of state as well as their illustrious host, and had attained that high honour in exactly the same way, viz. they had both succeeded their respective fathers. It is not easy to

The Mummy!

be very diffuse in their description, as they were members of that honourable and numerous fraternity, who never take the trouble of judging for themselves, but contentedly swim with the stream, whichever way it may flow, and have nothing about them to distinguish them in the slightest degree from the crowd. Lord Gustavus was at present their leading star, and they might very appropriately be termed his satellites. Thus, when any new idea was started, they cautiously refrained from giving an opinion till they found what he thought of it:—they would then look wise, shake their heads, and say, "Exactly so!" "Certainly!" "Nobody can doubt it!" or some of those other convenient ripieno phrases, which fill up so agreeably the pauses in the conversation, without requiring any troublesome exertion of the mental powers of either the hearer or the speaker. These gentlemen had now visited Lord Gustavus, for the purpose of accompanying him and Edric to the Queen's levee, and as soon as they had taken breakfast, the whole party, with the exception of Dr. Entwerfen, proceeded to court.

When arrived there, however, they found the Queen had not yet risen. "Her Majesty is late this morning," observed Lord Maysworth, a gentleman loaded with orders and decorations, addressing Lord Gustavus:—"I am not surprised," said his lordship, "for her most gracious Majesty told me the other day, that she has slept badly for some time."

"Which, of course, caused you great grief?" asked Dr. Hardman, a little, satirical-looking gentleman in a bob-wig.

"Thinking as I think," said Lord Gustavus gravely, "and as I am sure every one here must think, or at least ought to think, her Majesty's want of sleep is a circumstance of very serious importance."

"Oh! very!" exclaimed Lord Noodle, shaking his head. "Most assuredly!" cried Lord Doodle, shaking his.

"Why?" demanded the doctor; "of what possible consequence can it be to her subjects, whether her Majesty sleeps soundly or has the night-mare?"

"Of the greatest consequence," replied Lord Gustavus solemnly.

"Nothing can be greater!" echoed his satellites.

"Well!" observed Lord Maysworth, "for my part, I am such a traitor as to think we might exist, even if the Queen did not sleep at all."

"Or if she slept for ever," rejoined the doctor significantly.

"Oh, fie!" cried Lord Gustavus; "what would become of us, if the great sun of the political hemisphere were to set!"

"We must watch the rising of another, I suppose," said Lord Maysworth.

"Yes," continued Dr. Hardman: "and then the energies of the people would be roused. They want awakening from their present slumber—they have slept too long under the paralyzing effects of tyranny. The government wants reform; corruption has eaten into its root, and it must be eradicated ere England can be free, or its people happy. Would to Heaven I might live to aid in the glorious struggle; that I might see the people assert their rights, and the fiend, Despotism, sink beneath their blows."

"I have ever admired," said Lord Maysworth, "the high integrity and fine principles of the worthy doctor, which have not only obtained for him the applause of England, but the admiration of Europe. The courage, wisdom, and purity of his mind cannot be too highly extolled; and all who know him concur in calling him the firm and devoted friend of mankind. I also have been an humble supporter of plans of economy and retrenchment; and it was I who had the honour of suggesting to the council the other day, that an humble petition should be presented to her Majesty, requesting her respectfully to order a diminution of the lights in her saloon, proving incontestably, that there were, at least, six more than were absolutely necessary."

"Thinking as I think, and as I am sure every one here must think," began Lord Gustavus,—but ere he had time to finish his exordium, the folding doors at the back of the audience chamber were thrown open, and the Queen appeared, sitting upon a gorgeous throne, and surrounded by the officers of her household all splendidly attired.

The usual ceremonies then took place:—Claudia smiled graciously on Edric, as he kissed her hand, and inquired when he intended to depart. Edric informed her on the morrow; when, condescending to express regret, and desiring to see him on his return, she wished him an agreeable voyage, and dismissed him.

The Mummy!

During their ride home, Lord Gustavus could talk of nothing but the graciousness of the Queen, upon which he was still expatiating, when the balloon stopped; and Edric, who, though he felt grateful for her kindness, was annoyed by hearing so much said of it, hastened to leave him as soon as he possibly could with propriety. On his road to his own apartment, however, he heard a strange and fearful noise, like the voice of some one screaming in an agony of rage and pain, which seemed to proceed from the chamber appropriated to his learned tutor; and he was going there to ascertain the cause, when the agitated form of the unfortunate philosopher burst upon him.

Sad, indeed, was the condition in which this splendid ornament of the twenty-second century now presented himself before the eyes of his astonished pupil. His face glowed like fire; his hat was off, and water streamed from every part of his body till he looked like the effigy of a water deity in a fountain.

"Here is management!" cried he, as soon as his rage permitted him to speak; "here is treatment for one devoted to the service of mankind! But I will be revenged, and centuries yet to come, shall tremble at my wrath."

In this manner he continued, and being too much occupied in these awful denunciations, to be able to give any information as to what calamity had brought him into this unseemly plight, it will be necessary to go back a little to explain it for him.

When Dr. Entwerfen left the breakfast-room of Lord Gustavus, which he did not do till a considerable time after the rest of the party had quitted it, he was so absorbed in meditation that he did not know exactly which way he was going; and, happening unfortunately to turn to the right when he should have gone to the left, to his infinite surprise he found himself in the kitchen, instead of his own study.

Absent as the doctor was, however, his attention was soon roused by the scene before him. Being, like many of his learned brotherhood, somewhat of a gourmand, his indignation was violently excited by finding the cook comfortably asleep on a sofa on one side of the room, whilst the meat intended for dinner, a meal it was then the fashion to take about noon, was as comfortably resting itself from its toils on the other. The chemical substitute for fire, which ought to have cooked it, having gone out, and the cook's nap precluding all reasonable expectation of its re-illumination, the doctor's wrath was kindled, though the fire was not, and in a violent rage he seized the gentle Celestina's shoulder, and shook her till she woke.

"Where am I?" exclaimed she, opening her eyes.

"Any where but where you ought to be," cried the doctor, in a fury. "Look, hussy! look at that fine joint of meat, lying quite cold and sodden in its own steam."

"Dear me!" returned Celestina, yawning, "I am really quite unfortunate to-day! An unlucky accident has already occurred to a leg of mutton which was to have formed part of today's aliments; and now this piece of beef is also destroyed. I am afraid there will be nothing for dinner but some mucilaginous saccharine vegetables, and they, most probably, will be boiled to a viscous consistency."

"And what excuse can you offer for all this?" exclaimed the doctor, his voice trembling with passion.

"It was unavoidable;" replied Celestina, coolly; "whilst I was copying a cast from the Apollo Belvedere this morning, having unguardedly applied too much caloric to the vessel containing the leg of mutton, the aqueous fluid in which it was immersed, evaporated, and the viand became completely calcined. Whilst the other affair—"

"Hush, hush!" interrupted the doctor; "I cannot bear to hear you mention it. Oh, surely Job himself never suffered such a trial of his patience! In fact, his troubles were scarcely worth mentioning, for he was never cursed with learned servants!"

Saying this the doctor retired, lamenting his hard fate in not having been born in those halcyon days when cooks drew nothing but their poultry; whilst the gentle Celestina's breast panted with indignation at his complaint. An opportunity soon offered for revenge; and seeing the doctor's steam valet ready to be carried to its master's chamber, she treacherously applied a double portion of caloric: in consequence of which, the machine burst whilst in the act of brushing the doctor's coat collar, and by discharging the whole of the scalding water contained in its cauldron upon him, reduced him to the melancholy state we have already mentioned.

The fear of the ridicule attached to this incident, in a great measure reconciled the doctor to Edric's project of a speedy departure, and the following morning they bade adieu to Lord Gustavus, and, stepping into their balloon, sailed for Egypt.

CHAPTER IX.

No event of any importance occurred to our travellers in the course of their aërial voyage. They were too well provided with all kinds of necessaries to have any occasion to rest by the way, and in an incredibly short space of time they were hovering over Egypt. Different, however, oh! how different from the Egypt of the nineteenth century, was the fertile country which now lay like a map beneath their feet. Improvement had turned her gigantic steps towards its once desert plains; Commerce had waved her magic wand; and towns and cities, manufactories and canals, spread in all directions. No more did the Nile overflow its banks: a thousand channels were cut to receive its waters. No longer did the moving sands of the Desert rise in mighty waves, threatening to overwhelm the way-worn traveller: macadamized turnpike roads supplied their place, over which post-chaises, with anti-attritioned wheels, bowled at the rate of fifteen miles an hour. Steamboats glided down the canals, and furnaces raised their smoky heads amidst groves of palm-trees; whilst iron railways intersected orange groves, and plantations of dates and pomegranates might be seen bordering excavations intended for coal pits. Colonies of English and Americans peopled the country, and produced a population that swarmed like bees over the land, and surpassed in numbers even the wondrous throngs of the ancient Mizraim race; whilst industry and science changed desolation into plenty, and had converted barren plains into fertile kingdoms.

Amidst all these revolutions, however, the Pyramids still raised their gigantic forms, towering to the sky; unchanged, unchangeable, grand, simple, and immoveable, fit symbols of that majestic nature they were intended to represent, and seeming to look down with contempt upon the ephemeral structures with which they were surrounded; as though they would have said, had utterance been permitted to them—"Avaunt, ye nothings of the day. Respect our dignity and sink into your original obscurity; for know, that we alone are monarchs of the plains." Indestructible, however, as they had proved themselves, even their granite sides had not been able entirely to resist the corroding influence of the smoke with which they were now surrounded, and a slight crumbling announced the first outward symptom of decay. Still, however, though blackened and disfigured, they shone stupendous monuments of former greatness; and Edric and his tutor gazed upon them with an awe that for some moments deprived them of utterance.

The doctor, however, who was too fond of reasoning ever long to remain willingly silent, after surveying them a few minutes, broke forth as follows:—"What noble piles! What majesty and grandeur they display in their formation, and yet what dignified simplicity! Can the imagination of man conceive any thing more sublime than the thought that they have stood thus frowning in awful magnificence, perhaps since the very creation of the world, without equals, without even competitors,—mocking the feeble efforts of man to divine their origin, and seeing generation after generation pass away, whilst they still remain immutable, and involved in the same deep and unfathomable mystery as at first."

"It is very strange," observed Edric, "that, in this age of speculation and discovery, nothing certain should be known concerning them."

"It is," returned the doctor; "but the thick mysterious veil that has rested upon them for so many ages, seems not intended to be removed by mortal hands. They remind one of the sublime inscription upon the temple of the goddess Isis, at Sais:—'I am whatever was, whatever is, and whatever shall be; but no mortal has, as yet, presumed to raise the veil that covers me.'"

"Your quotation is apt, doctor," resumed Edric, "for both relate to Nature. Indeed, Nature appears to be the deity which the ancient Egyptians worshipped, under all the various forms in which she presents herself; and their strange and animal deities were but reverenced as her symbols. It was Nature whom they worshipped as Isis; it was Nature that was typified in the Pyramids; and the good taste of the Egyptians made them prefer the simple, the majestic, and the sublime, in those works which they destined to last for ages. Formerly, from the immensity of their population, and high state of their civilization, labour was so divided, and consequently so lightened, that multitudes were enabled to exist exempt from toil. These persons, devoting themselves to study, became initiati; and either enrolled themselves amongst the priesthood, or passed their lives in making themselves masters of the most abstract sciences. The consequences were natural: they followed up the ramifications of creation to their original source; they penetrated into the most profound secrets of Nature, and traced all her wonders in her works: aware, however, of the taste of the vulgar for any thing above their comprehension, and of the natural craving of the human mind for mystery, they wrapped the discoveries they had made in a deep and impenetrable veil, and concealed awful and sublime significations under the meanest and most disgusting images."

"You are right," said the doctor, "in your observations upon the religion of the ancient Egyptians; but it does not appear to me that the Pyramids were erected by them."

"What! I suppose you draw your conclusions from the want of hieroglyphics in their principal chambers; and, from what Herodotus says of their having been erected by a shepherd, you think they were the work of the Pallic race."

"No; though I allow much may be said in favour of that hypothesis, particularly as Herodotus says the kings under whom they were erected, ordered all the Egyptian temples to be closed, which we know the shepherd or Pallic sovereign did; but I cannot imagine that an ignorant, Goth-like race of shepherds, men accustomed to live in tents or in the open air, and possessing no talents but for war, were capable of constructing such immense piles. No, no, the Pyramids required gigantic conceptions, highly cultivated minds, and unwearied perseverance; all qualities quite incompatible with a warlike wandering race. No, I do not think the Palli were capable of imagining such structures, much less of constructing them. I think they were the work of evil spirits."

"Evil spirits!" exclaimed Edric.

"Yes," returned the doctor. "We are told that the evil spirits, after their expulsion from Paradise, were under the command of the Sultan, or Soliman Giam ben Giam, as he is called by Arabic writers, but who is supposed to have been the same as Cheops; and that he employed them in this vast work."

"I do not know by what analysis etymologists can draw the name of Cheops from that of Giam ben Giam: but, supposing the fact to be correct, that they designated the same person, I think it only proves more strongly my hypothesis; for the Palli came from Mount Caucasus, where the evil spirits were said to have been enchained, and if Cheops was a Pallic king, it is possible the Egyptians might poetically call their conquerors evil spirits."

"That is a good idea, Edric; though I do not think it by any means certain that Cheops was a Pallic king. However, we shall soon be able to see his tomb, and judge for ourselves; for we have now approached near enough to the Pyramids to descend. Foh! what a smoke and what a noise! It is enough to rouse the mummies from their slumbers before their appointed time, and without the aid of galvanism. Have you opened the valves, Edric? Oh yes! I perceive we are getting lower; we will not lose a moment before we visit the Pyramid. But what a crowd of brutes are assembled to witness our arrival! they stare as though they had never seen a balloon before. Egypt is certainly a fine country, but the inhabitants are a century behind us in civilization."

An immense crowd had gathered together to witness the descent of our travellers, and they did indeed stand staring, lost in stupid astonishment at the strange sight that presented itself; for though the Egyptian people had occasionally seen balloons, they had never before beheld one made of Indian rubber. The odd figure of the doctor, too, amused them exceedingly, as he sat wrapt up in the most dignified manner in an asbestos cloak, his bob-wig pushed a little on one side from the heat of the weather and the warmth of his argument; his round, red, oily face attempting to look solemn, and his little, fat, punchy figure trying to assume an air of majesty. The Egyptians were amazingly struck with this apparition, and being, like most colonists, somewhat conceited and not very ceremonious in their manners, they looked at him a few minutes in silence, and then burst into immoderate fits of laughter.

The doctor was exceedingly indignant at this rude reception, and rising, shook his fist at them in anger; a manœuvre, however, that only redoubled the mirth of the unpolished Egyptians, whose peals of laughter now became so tremendous, that they actually shook the skies, and occasioned a most unpleasant vibration in the balloon. Edric, who was almost as much annoyed as the doctor, had yet sufficient self-command to continue calmly making preparations for his descent; and without taking the least notice of the crowd below, he screwed the top upon the propelling vapour-bottle; he let the inflammable air escape from the balloon, which rapidly collapsed as they approached the earth, and throwing out their patent spring grappling-irons, they caught one of the lower stones of the Great Pyramid, and in a few moments the car in which our travellers were sitting, was safely moored at a convenient distance from the earth for them to alight. Edric now unloosed the descending ladder, and reverentially assisted the doctor, who was encumbered with his long cloak, to reach terra firma in safety, — amidst the bustle and exclamations of the crowd, who thronged round them expressing their wonder and astonishment audibly, in broad English.

"Where the deuce did this spring from?" cried one; "the car would load a waggon!"

"And what is gone with the balloon?" said another; "it is clean vanished!"

"Well, I never saw such a thing in all my life before!" exclaimed a third; "I think they must be come from the moon."

"Hush! hush," cried an old gentleman bustling amongst them, who seemed as one having authority. "What's the matter? what's the matter?"

"We are strangers, Sir," said Edric, advancing and addressing him: "we come here to see the wonders of your country, and we wish to explore the Pyramids — but the reception we have met with — —"

"Say no more — say no more!" interrupted the worthy justice, for such he was. "Get about your business, you rapscallions, or I'll read the riot act! Here, Gregory, call out the posse comitatus, and set a guard of constables to keep watch over these gentlemen's balloon, whilst they go to explore the Pyramids. Eh! but where is the balloon? I don't see it. I hope neither of the gentlemen has put it in his pocket!" laughing at his own wit.

"No, Sir," returned Edric, smiling, "though it is a feat which might easily be accomplished, for that is our balloon," pointing to the caoutchouc bottle, now shrunk to its original dimensions.

"Very strange, that!" said the Justice; "Very curious, very curious indeed! Well, gentlemen, if you wish to proceed immediately, you'll want a guide of course. These cottages at the foot of the Pyramids are all inhabited by guides, who get their living by showing the sights. They are sad rogues, most of them, but I can recommend you to one who is a very honest man. Here, Samuel," continued he, knocking against a small door, "Samuel! I say!"

Samuel made his appearance, in the guise of a tall, raw-boned, stupid-looking fellow, with a pair of immensely broad stooping shoulders, which looked as though he could have relieved Atlas occasionally of his burthen, without much trouble to himself. Coming forth from his hut in an awkward shambling pace, he scratched his head, and demanded what his honour pleased to want.

"You must show these gentlemen the Pyramids," said the Justice.

"Ay, that I will with pleasure!" returned Samuel; "I've got my living by showing them these fifty years, man and boy; and I know every crink and cranny of them, though I'm old now and somewhat lame. So walk this way, gentlemen."

"We are very much obliged to you, Sir," said the doctor, bowing to the Justice; who was in fact one of those good-natured, busy, bustling men, who are always better pleased to transact any other person's business than their own; and are never so happy as when a new arrival gives them an opportunity of showing off their consequence. Indeed, there is a pleasure in showing wonders to a stranger, that only those who have little else to occupy their minds can properly estimate: a man of this kind feels his self-love gratified by the superiority his local knowledge gives him over a stranger; and, as it is, perhaps, the only chance he ever can have of showing superiority, they must be unreasonable who blame him for making the most of it. Justice Freemantle was accordingly exceedingly delighted with travellers who seemed disposed to submit implicitly to his dictation; and he returned a most gracious reply to the doctor's thanks.

"Don't mention it! don't mention it, my dear Sir!" said he; "I am never so happy as when I can make myself useful. Is there any thing else I can do for you? You may command me, I assure you; and you may depend upon it, no injury shall be done to your luggage, whilst you are away."

"What a very civil, obliging, good-natured old gentleman," said the doctor, as they walked towards the entrance of the Pyramids; "I declare he almost reconciles me to the country, though, I own, I thought at first the people were the greatest brutes I had ever met with."

"Which Pyramid does your honour wish to see?" asked the guide.

"That which contains the tomb of Cheops, man!" cried the doctor solemnly; who, encumbered with his long cloak, and loaded with his walking-stick and galvanic battery, had some difficulty in getting on.

"Won't your honour let me carry that pole and that bag?" said the man; "you'd get on a surprising deal better, if you would."

"Avaunt, wretch!" exclaimed the doctor, "nor offer to touch with thy profane fingers the immortal instruments of science."

The Mummy!

The man stared, but fell back, and the whole party walked on in perfect silence.

In the mean time, Edric had walked on before his companions, completely lost in meditation. A crowd of conflicting thoughts rushed through his mind; and now, when he found himself at the very goal of his wishes, the daring nature of the purpose he had so long entertained, seemed to strike him for the first time, and he trembled at the consequences that might attend the completion of his desires. With his arms folded on his breast, he stood gazing on the Pyramids, whilst his ideas wandered uncontrolled through the boundless regions of space: "And what am I," thought he, "weak, feeble worm that I am! who dare seek to penetrate into the awful secrets of my Creator? Why should I wish to restore animation to a body now resting in the quiet of the tomb? What right have I to renew the struggles, the pains, the cares, and the anxieties of mortal life? How can I tell the fearful effects that may be produced by the gratification of my unearthly longing? May I not revive a creature whose wickedness may involve mankind in misery? And what if my experiment should fail, and if the moment when I expect my rash wishes to be accomplished, the hand of Almighty vengeance should strike me to the earth, and heap molten fire on my brain to punish my presumption!"

The sound of human voices, as the doctor and the guide approached, grated harshly on the nerves of Edric, already overstrained by the awful nature of the thoughts in which he had been indulging, and he turned away involuntarily, to escape the interruption he dreaded, quite forgetting for the moment from whom the sounds most probably proceeded.

"Lord have mercy on us!" said the guide; "I declare that gentleman looks as if he were beside himself! and see there! if he hasn't walked right by the entrance to the Pyramid without seeing it! Sir! Sir!" halloed he.

Excessively annoyed, but recalled to his recollection by these shouts, Edric returned.

"These Pyramids are wonderful piles," said the doctor, as he stumbled forward to meet him. "I really had no adequate conception of the enormity of their size. They did not even look half so large at a distance as they do now."

"Immense masses seldom do," replied Edric; compelling himself with difficulty to speak.

"True," returned the doctor; "the simplicity and uniformity of their figures deceive the eyes, and it is only when we approach them that we feel their stupendous magnitude and our own insignificance!"

"They give an amazing idea of the grandeur of the ancient kings of Egypt," said Edric, without exactly knowing what he was saying. "Their palaces must have been superb, if they had such mausoleums."

"How absurdly you reason, Edric!" replied the doctor peevishly; for, being annoyed with his burthens and his cloak, he was not in a humour to bear contradiction. "I thought we had settled that question before. In the first place, I think it very doubtful whether the Egyptians had any thing to do with the building of these monuments; and if they had, I think they were meant for temples, not mausoleums; and in the next place, even if they were intended for tombs, their greatness affords no argument for the splendour of the surrounding palaces; as the Egyptians were celebrated for the superiority of their burying-places, and for the immense sums they expended upon them. Indeed, you know, ancient writers say they went so far as to call the houses of the living only inns, whilst they considered tombs as everlasting habitations;—a circumstance, by the way, that strongly corroborates my hypothesis, at least as far as their opinions go; as it seems to imply that both soul and body were designed to remain there."

They had now entered the Pyramid, and were proceeding with infinite difficulty along a low, dark, narrow passage: "Observe, Edric," said the doctor, "how the difficulty and obscurity of these winding passages confirm my opinion: you know, the religion of the ancient Egyptians, like that of the ancient Hindoos, was one of penances and personal privations; and, granting that to be the case, what can be more simple, than that the passages the initiati had to traverse before they reached the adytum, should be painful and difficult of access. Besides this, as you know, the bones of a bull, no doubt those of the god Apis, were found in a sarcophagus in the second Pyramid, it seems probable that it was sacred to his worship: and its vicinity to the Nile, which was indispensable to the temples of Apis, as, when it was time for him to die, he was drowned in its waters, confirms the fact. Indeed, I am only surprised that any human being, possessing a grain of common sense, can entertain a single doubt upon the subject."

"How do you account for the tomb we are about to visit being placed in the Pyramid, if you think they were only designed for a temple?" asked Edric.

"The question is futile," said the doctor. "A strange fancy prevailed in former times that burying the dead in consecrated places, particularly in temples intended for divine worship, would scare away the evil spirits, and the practice actually prevailed in England even as lately as the nineteenth or twentieth century. Indeed, it was not till after the country had been almost depopulated by the dreadfully infectious disease that prevailed about two hundred years ago, that a law was passed to prevent the interment of the dead in London, and that those previously buried in and near the churches there, were exhumed and placed in cemeteries beyond the walls."

Edric did not reply, for in fact his ideas were so absorbed by the solemn object before him, that it was painful for him to speak, and the doctor's ill-timed reasoning created such an irritation of his nerves, that he found it required the utmost exertion of his self-command to endure it patiently. The passage they were traversing, now became higher and wider, shelving off occasionally into chambers or recesses on each side, till they approached a kind of vestibule, in the centre of which, yawned a deep, dark, gloomy-looking cavity, like a well.

"We must descend that shaft," said the guide, "and that will lead us to the tomb of King Cheops; but as the road is dark, and rather dangerous, we had better, each of us, take a torch."

As he spoke, he drew some torches from a niche where they were deposited, and began to illuminate them from his own. The red glare of the torches flashed fearfully on the massive wails of the Pyramid, throwing part of their enormous masses into deep shadow, as they rose in solemn and sublime dignity around, and seemed frowning upon the presumptuous mortals that had dared to invade their recesses, whilst the deep pit beneath their feet seemed to yawn wide to engulf them in its abyss. Edric's heart beat thick: it throbbed till he even fancied its pulsations audible; and a strange, mysterious thrilling of anxiety, mingled with a wild, undefinable delight, ran through his frame. A few short hours, and his wishes would be gratified, or set at rest for ever. The doctor and the guide had already begun to descend, and their figures seemed changed and unearthly as the gleams of the torches fell upon them. Edric gazed for a moment, and then followed with feelings worked up almost to frenzy by the over-excitement of his nerves; whilst the hollow sound that re-echoed from the walls, as they struck against them in their descent, thrilled through his whole frame.

No one spoke; and after proceeding for some time along the narrow path, or rather ledge, formed on the sides of the cavity, which gradually shelved downwards, the guide suddenly stopped, and touching a secret spring, a solid block of granite slowly detached itself from the wall, and, rising majestically like the portcullis of an ancient fortress, showed the entrance to a dark and dreary cave. The guide advanced, followed by our travellers, into a gloomy vaulted apartment, where long vistas of ponderous arches stretched on every side, till their termination was lost in darkness, and gave a feeling of immensity and obscurity to the scene.

"I will wait here," said the guide; "and here, if you please, you had better leave your torches. That avenue will lead you to the tomb."

The travellers obeyed; and the guide, placing himself in a recess in the wall, extinguished all the torches except one, which he shrouded so as to leave the travellers in total darkness. Nothing could be now more terrific than their situation: immured in the recesses of the tomb, involved in darkness, and their bosoms throbbing with hopes that they scarcely dared avow even to themselves, with faltering steps they proceeded slowly along the path the guide had pointed out, shuddering even at the hollow echo of their own footsteps, which alone broke the solemn silence that reigned throughout these fearful regions of terror and the tomb.

Suddenly, a vivid light flashed upon them, and, as they advanced, they found it proceeded from torches placed in the hands of two colossal figures, who, placed in a sitting posture, seemed guarding an enormous portal, surmounted by the image of a fox, the constant guardian of an Egyptian tomb. The immense dimensions and air of grandeur and repose about these colossi had something in it very imposing; and our travellers felt a sensation of awe creep over them as they gazed upon their calm unmoved features, so strikingly emblematic of that immutable nature which they were doubtless placed there to typify.

It was with feelings of indescribable solemnity, that the doctor and Edric passed through this majestic portal, and found themselves in an apartment gloomily illumined by the light shed faintly from an inner chamber, through ponderous brazen gates beautifully wrought. The light thus feebly emitted, showed that the room in which they stood, was dedicated to Typhon, the evil spirit, as his fierce and savage types covered the walls; and images of his symbols, the crocodile and the dragon, placed beneath the shadow of the brazen gates, and dimly seen by the imperfect light, seemed starting into life, and grimly to forbid the farther advance of the intruders. Our travellers shuddered, and opening with trembling hand the ponderous gates, they entered the tomb of Cheops.

In the centre of the chamber, stood a superb, highly ornamented sarcophagus of alabaster, beautifully wrought; over this hung a lamp of wondrous workmanship, supplied by a potent mixture, so as to burn for ages unconsumed; thus awfully lighting up with perpetual flame the solemn mansions of the dead, and typifying life eternal even in the silent tomb. Around the room, on marble benches, were arranged mummies simply dried, apparently those of slaves; and close to the sarcophagus was placed one contained in a case, which the doctor approached to examine. This was supposed to be that of Sores, the confidant and prime-minister of Cheops. The chest that enclosed the body was splendidly ornamented with embossed gilt leather, whilst the parts not otherwise covered were stained with red and green curiously blended, and of a vivid brightness.

The mighty Phtah, the Jupiter of the Egyptians, spread its widely extended wings over the head, grasping in his monstrous claws a ring, the emblem of eternity; whilst below, the vulture form of Rhea proclaimed the deceased a votary of that powerful deity; and on the sides were innumerable hieroglyphics. The doctor removed the lid, and shuddered as the crimson tinge of the everlasting lamp fell upon the hideous and distorted features thus suddenly exhibited to view. This sepulchral light, indeed, added unspeakable horror to the scene, and its peculiar glare threw such a wild and demoniac expression on the dark lines and ghastly lineaments of the mummies, that even the doctor felt his spirits depressed, and a supernatural dread creep over his mind as he gazed upon them.

In the mean time, Edric had stood gazing upon the sarcophagus of Cheops, the sides of which were beautifully sculptured with groups of figures, which, from the peculiar light thrown upon them, seemed to possess all the force and reality of life. On one side was represented an armed and youthful warrior bearing off in his arms a beautiful female, on whom he gazed with the most passionate fondness. He was pursued by a crowd of people and soldiers, who seemed rending the air with vehement exclamations against his violence, and endeavouring in vain to arrest his progress; whilst in the background appeared an old man, who was tearing his hair and wringing his hands in ineffectual rage against the ravisher.

The other side, presented the same old man wrestling with the youthful warrior, who had just overpowered and stabbed him; the helpless victim raising his withered hands and failing eyes to Heaven as he fell, as though to implore vengeance upon his murderer, whilst the crimson current was fast ebbing from his bosom. The dying look and agony of the old man were forcibly depicted, whilst upon the features of the youthful warrior glowed the fury of a demon.

The sarcophagus was supported by the lion, emblem of royalty, the symbol of the solar god Horus; and above it sat the majestic hawk of Osiris, gazing upwards, and unmindful of the subtle crocodile of Typhon, that, crouching under its feet, was just about to seize its breast in its enormous jaws. Neither of the travellers had as yet spoken, for it seemed like sacrilege to disturb the awful stillness that prevailed even by a whisper. Indeed, the solemn aspect of the chamber thrilled through every nerve, and they moved slowly, gliding along with noiseless steps as though they feared prematurely to break the slumbers of the mighty dead it contained. They gazed, however, with deep but undefinable interest upon the sculptured mysteries of the tomb of Cheops, vainly endeavouring to decipher their meaning; whilst, as they found their efforts useless, a secret voice seemed to whisper in their bosoms—"And shall finite creatures like these, who cannot even explain the signification of objects presented before their eyes, presume to dive into the mysteries of their Creator's will? Learn wisdom by this omen, nor seek again to explore secrets above your comprehension! Retire whilst it is yet time; soon it will be too late!"

Edric started at his own thoughts, as the fearful warning, "soon it will be too late," rang in his ears; and a fearful presentiment of evil weighed heavily upon his soul. He turned to look upon the doctor, but he had already seized the lid of the sarcophagus, and, with a daring hand, removed it from its place, displaying in the fearful light the royal form that lay beneath. For a moment, both Edric and the doctor paused, not daring to survey it; and when they did, they both uttered an involuntary cry of astonishment, as the stern, but handsome, features of the mummy met their eyes, for both instantly recognized the sculptured warrior in his traits. Yes, it was indeed the same, but the fierce expression of fiery and ungoverned passions depicted upon the countenance of the marble figure, had settled down to a calm, vindictive, and concentrated hatred upon that of its mummy prototype in the tomb.

The Mummy!

Awful, indeed, was the gloom that sat upon that brow, and bitter the sardonic smile that curled those haughty lips. All was perfect as though life still animated the form before them, and it had only reclined there to seek a short repose. The dark eyebrows, the thick raven hair which hung upon the forehead, and the snow-white teeth seen through the half open lips, forbade the idea of death; whilst the fiend-like expression of the features made Edric shudder, as he recollected the purpose that brought him to the tomb, and he trembled at the thought of awakening such a fearful being from the torpor of the grave to all the renewed energies of life.

"Let us go," whispered the doctor to his pupil, in a low, deep, and unearthly tone, fearfully different from his usually cheerful voice. Edric started at the sound, for it seemed the last sad warning of his better genius, before he abandoned her for ever. The die, however, was cast, and it was too late to recede. Indeed, Edric felt worked up to frenzy by the overwrought feelings of the moment. He seized the machine, and resolutely advanced towards the sarcophagus, whilst the doctor gazed upon him with a horror that deprived him of either speech or motion.

Innumerable folds of red and white linen, disposed alternately, swathed the gigantic but well-proportioned limbs of the royal mummy; and upon his breast lay a piece of metal, shining like silver, and stamped with the figure of a winged globe. Edric attempted to remove this, but recoiled with horror, when he found it bend beneath his fingers with an unnatural softness; whilst, as the flickering light of the lamp fell upon the face of the mummy, he fancied its stern features relaxed into a ghastly laugh of scornful mockery. Worked up to desperation, he applied the wires of the battery and put the apparatus in motion, whilst a demoniac laugh of derision appeared to ring in his ears, and the surrounding mummies seemed starting from their places and dancing in unearthly merriment. Thunder now roared in tremendous peals through the Pyramids, shaking their enormous masses to the foundation, and vivid flashes of light darted round in quick succession. Edric stood aghast amidst this fearful convulsion of nature. A horrid creeping seemed to run through every vein, every nerve feeling as though drawn from its extremity, and wrapped in icy chillness round his heart. Still, he stood immoveable, and gazing intently on the mummy, whose eyes had opened with the shock, and were now fixed on those of Edric, shining with supernatural lustre. In vain Edric attempted to rouse himself;—in vain to turn away from that withering glance. The mummy's eyes still pursued him with their ghastly brightness; they seemed to possess the fabled fascination of those of the rattle-snake, and though he shrunk from their gaze, they still glared horribly upon him. Edric's senses swam, yet he could not move from the spot; he remained fixed, chained, and immoveable, his eyes still riveted upon the mummy, and every thought absorbed in horror. Another fearful peal of thunder now rolled in lengthened vibrations above his head, and the mummy rose slowly, his eyes still fixed upon those of Edric, from his marble tomb. The thunder pealed louder and louder. Yells and groans seemed mingled with its roar;—the sepulchral lamp flared with redoubled fierceness, flashing its rays around in quick succession, and with vivid brightness; whilst by its horrid and uncertain glare, Edric saw the mummy stretch out its withered hand as though to seize him. He saw it rise gradually—he heard the dry, bony fingers rattle as it drew them forth—he felt its tremendous gripe—human nature could bear no more—his senses were rapidly deserting him; he felt, however, the fixed stedfast eyes of Cheops still glowing upon his failing orbs, as the lamp gave a sudden flash, and then all was darkness! The brazen gates now shut with a fearful clang, and Edric, uttering a shriek of horror, fell senseless upon the ground; whilst his shrill cry of anguish rang wildly through the marble vaults, till its re-echoes seemed like the yell of demons joining in fearful mockery.

How long he lay in this state he knew not; but when he reopened his eyes, for the moment, he fancied all that had passed a dream. As his senses returned, however, he recollected where he was, and shuddered to find himself yet in that place of horrors. All now was dark, except a faint gleam that shone feebly through the half-open gates; these ponderous portals slowly unclosed, and the form of a man, wrapped in a large cloak, and bearing a torch, entered, peering around as it advanced, as though half afraid to proceed. Edric's feelings were too highly wrought to bear any fresh horrors, and he shrieked in agony as the figure approached. The sound of his voice subdued the terrors of the intruder, and the doctor, for it was he, shouted with joy, as he rushed forward to embrace him.

"Edric! Edric! thank God he is alive!" exclaimed he. "Edric! my beloved Edric! for God's sake, let us leave this den of horrors! come, come!"

Reassured by his tutor's voice, Edric arose, and taking one hasty, shuddering glance around as the light gleamed on the sarcophagus, he hurried out of the tomb. Neither he nor the doctor spoke as they passed through the vestibule, where the colossal figures still sat in awful majesty; indeed, as their torches were extinguished, their gigantic forms looked still more terrific than before, from the wavering and indistinct light thrown upon them. Edric shuddered as he looked, and hurried on with hasty strides to the place where they had left the guide, whom they found kneeling in a corner, hiding his face in his hands, and roaring out, "O Lord, defend us! Heaven have mercy upon us! Lord have mercy upon us! Heaven have mercy upon us!"

"He has been in that state for more than an hour," said the doctor mournfully; "for, after I came to myself again, I tried to rouse him, but all to no purpose."

"Then you also fainted?" said Edric, with difficulty compelling himself to speak.

"Why," resumed the doctor with some hesitation, "I don't know that you can exactly call it fainting; but the fact was, that when I saw you touch the plate upon the mummy's breast, and start back, looking so horribly frightened, I—I thought I had better call for assistance; so as I ran for that purpose, somehow or other, I fell down, and lay insensible I don't know how long. When I came to myself, however, I tried to rouse the guide, and when I found I could not, I came to seek you; but now that we are both recovered, I really don't know what is to become of us; for this fellow will never be able to show us the way out, and I'm sure I don't know the road."

"Let us try to find it, at any rate," said Edric faintly.

"Oh, for God's sake, take me too!" screamed the guide. "If you have any mercy, don't leave me in this fearful place."

"Take the light then, and lead the way," said Edric. The guide obeyed, shaking every limb, and every now and then casting a terrified look behind, whilst the quivering flame of the torch betrayed the unsteadiness of the trembling hands that bore it. In this manner they proceeded, starting at every sound, and frightened even at their own shadows, without daring to stop till they reached the plain.

"Thank God!" cried the doctor, the moment they stepped out of the Pyramid; looking round him, gasping for breath, and inhaling the fresh air with rapture.

"Thank God!" reiterated Edric and the guide, as they walked rapidly towards the place where they had left their balloon. When arrived there, however, they looked for it in vain; and fancying themselves under the influence of a delusion, they rubbed their eyes, and again looked, but without success.

"Dear me, it is very strange!" said the doctor; "this is certainly the place, and yet, where can it be?"

"Where, indeed!" repeated Edric; "horrors and unaccountable incidents environ us at every step; I am not naturally timid, yet—"

"Ah!" screamed the doctor, as he tumbled over a man lying with his face upon the ground; "Oh!" groaned he, as Edric and the guide with difficulty raised him; "would to Heaven I were safe at home again in my own comfortable little study, indulging on pleasing anticipations of that which I find is any thing in the world but pleasing in reality."

CHAPTER X.

We left Dr. Entwerfen in the last chapter uttering a very moral, if not a very new, exclamation on the vanity of human expectations; which had scarcely escaped from his lips, ere cruel Fate, resolving not to be accused in vain, supplied him with yet more abundant cause for lamentation. We have before mentioned, that the doctor had stumbled as he quitted the Pyramids, and that his friends raised him from the ground; but what was his consternation and dismay, when, on looking round to thank them, he found he was surrounded by armed men, who commanded him in the royal name to surrender! Sadly did the doctor turn his woeful eyes upon Edric, but, alas! he was in the same predicament as himself; and, in spite of their entreaties, they were marched off to prison, without being at all informed of what crime they had committed.

Sadly passed the night, and gloomy dawned the day upon the unfortunate travellers, whose minds were harassed and bewildered by the extraordinary success of their awful experiment, and whose misery was infinitely increased by the suspense they had to suffer, both on account of their ignorance of the crime of which they were accused, and its probable punishment if they should be found guilty. Soon after daybreak, however, a summons for them arrived, and they were conducted as criminals before the same magistrate who, the day before, had treated them with such officious kindness.

Very different, however, was the solemn judge who, clothed in all the insignia of magisterial dignity, now sate upon the bench, from the easy, good-tempered gentleman of the Pyramids; and the unlucky travellers saw, in an instant, that they were not likely to experience any favour from their previous acquaintance with him. The court was thronged with people, and the prisoners saw that they were regarded with curiosity, mingled with horror and supernatural fear. It is not agreeable to feel oneself an object of disgust to any one; and though Edric magnanimously and frequently repeated to himself that it was quite indifferent to him what such ignorant wretches as Egyptians thought of him; yet, if he would have avowed the truth, he would have been quite as well contented to have found himself the object of their admiration instead of their hatred; and he would have been very glad to have been safely at home again; whilst the doctor openly and loudly lamented the much regretted comforts of his own dear delightful study at Sir Ambrose's. Little time, however, was allowed for reflection; for as soon as the prisoners were placed at the bar their examination commenced.

"So, gentlemen!" said the learned judge, "you stand convicted—no, I mean accused, of a most horrible, heinous, and sacrilegious offence—an offence that makes our hair start with horror from our heads, and every separate lock rise up in vengeance against you." The justice paused, that the prisoners might admire his eloquence; but, alas! such was the absorbing nature of self-love, that they were only thinking of what was going to be done with them, and to what this terrible exordium was likely to lead. After a short pause, Edric, supposing they were expected to speak, addressed the judge, and begged to know of what crime they were accused.

"We are strangers," said he, "and gentlemen. We were attracted to your country by an account of the wonders it contained; we declared our purposes openly; we have affected no concealment; and we have done nothing we need blush to avow—"

A confused murmur ran through the court as he spoke, expressive of the utmost disgust and abhorrence; Edric felt indignant, and he looked round proudly as he added:—

"Yes, I repeat we have done nothing we need blush to avow, and nothing derogatory to our characters as Englishmen and gentlemen."

"Sorcerers! wizards! demons in disguise!" cried the crowd. "Down with them! burn them! guillotine them! destroy them!"

"Is this fair? is this generous?" asked Edric. "If we have done wrong, let our crime be proved, and we are ready to submit to any punishment you may think proper to inflict; but do not condemn us unheard. In England, every man is deemed innocent until he be proved guilty. You boast of having imported and improved upon all the useful regulations of the mother country, and cannot surely have omitted her most glorious law. Let us then have a fair trial, and God forbid that the course of justice should be impeded."

"You talk well, Sir," said the judge; "but it's of no use here. My chair, Sir, is made of witch-elm, and the whole court is lined with consecrated wood; so you may take your familiars to another market, for here they will avail you nothing."

"Good God!" exclaimed Edric, wringing his hands, "what ignorance! what gross superstition! And yet, in this man's power are our lives!"

The Mummy!

"Oh! oh!" said the judge, who saw his despair, though he did not exactly know the cause; "I have brought you to, have I? Yes, yes; I tell you, no incantations will be of any avail here; and so, clerk, call the witnesses—"

The first person examined was the man who had been left in charge of the balloon, and he deposed as follows:—"Why, Sir," said he, scratching his head, as though he supposed wisdom dwelt in his fingers, and that their touch might give a little to his brain, "your honour told me to call out the posse comitatus, and set a guard of constables over the gentlemen's whirligig; but I thought as how, seeing it was but a queer-looking thing, and not likely to tempt anybody to steal it, I might as well save the gentlemen from throwing their money away upon a parcel of idle fellows, and keep watch over it myself."

"And so get the reward instead of them," observed the judge.

"Why, your honour," said the fellow, grinning, "I thought they might give something that might do me some good, but that it would be nothing amongst so many."

"Very true!" remarked the judge; "Go on Gregory."

"Well," continued Gregory, "as I was sitting there, thinking of nothing at all, and somehow, I believe, I had fallen into a bit of a doze, I heard a queer sort of a buzzing, and I opened my eyes, and there I saw the gentlemen's whirligig buzzing and puffing like a steam-engine on fire, and i' th' midst o' the smoke I'll take my oath I saw the mummy of King Cheops as plain as I see his worship there sitting in his throne."

"Oh!" groaned the horror-struck crowd; "Oh!" groaned the judge and jury.

"Yes," continued the man; "I'll take my oath, if it was the last word I had to speak, that I saw him there vomiting fire, and his big eyes flaring like a fiery furnace."

"Oh!" groaned the judge, crowd, and jury, a degree louder than before.

"And then," resumed Gregory, "something went whiz, and off it all fled together like a flash of lightning—"

"Oh!" shrieked the whole court, in a convulsion of horror. Some of the fair sex in particular, screamed and covered their faces, as though they feared the next exploit of the redoubtable magicians would be to blow up the court, and send them all flying after the resuscitated mummy.

"With your permission, Sir," said Edric, as soon as the tumult had somewhat abated, "this proves nothing against either my friend or myself. We are, in fact, injured by it, and we have a claim against you instead of your being able to substantiate a charge against us. We left our balloon, containing valuable articles, and money to a considerable amount, in your charge, or, at least, in the custody of a man whom you recommended. When we quitted the Pyramid, we, of course, inquired for our balloon—it had vanished; and instead of making us amends for our loss, you throw us into prison and tell us a wild, extravagant story of the disappearance of our property, which no man in his senses can possibly believe."

Another confused murmur, though very different in its character from the former, ran through the court on the conclusion of this speech; and the judge, if such an expression be not profane when speaking of a representative of justice, looked most excessively foolish.

"Had not your worship better call the other witnesses?" whispered the clerk, pitying the dilemma of his principal.

"True, true!" said the Lycurgus of Anglo-Egypt; "your observation is premature, young man; when the case has been proved against you, it will be time enough for you to think of your defence."

Edric bowed assent, and the examination continued. The guide was the next witness.

"Well, Samuel," said the judge; "what do you know about this matter?"

"Why, Sir," replied Samuel, "ye see, my dame and I were sitting by the fire, and we'd got a black pudding, as we was a going to have for our dinners. And so says dame, 'I likes it cut in slices and fried,' and so says I——"

"Hold, fellow!" cried the judge, with great dignity. "Don't abuse the patience of the Court. We have nothing to do with your dame or the black pudding; it is quite irrelevant to the matter now before us. Go on."

But Samuel could not go on; and, like his predecessor in the witness-box, he only stood still and scratched his head.

The Mummy!

"Why don't you speak, fellow?" asked the clerk.

"Because I doesn't know what to say," replied Samuel.

"You must tell all you know about this affair," pursued the clerk.

"But I doesn't know where to begin!" rejoined the perplexed witness; "his worship says it is not reverent."

"Begin with the Pyramid," said the judge; "and, if you can, give a clear account of all that happened after you left the old passage by the moveable block in the wall that was last discovered."

"Why I can't say there was any thing very particular happened, as I know of, Sir," said Samuel, "after that, till we got to the shaft, and then we went down, Sir, you know, as we always does, till we came to the tomb of King Cheops; and then I turned the gentlemen in by themselves, as we always does, for the 'fect, as Parson Snorum calls it. And then I sits me down i' the vault, to wait for 'em, and I'd just rolled myself up, and was dozed asleep, when I hears such a noise as if the Pyramids were all coming tumbling about my ears. So up I jumped and rubbed my eyes, for I did not know very well where I was; and then I saw something that seemed to strike the torches out of the hands of the two great sitting figures, and put them out; and then I saw a great tall figure come gliding by me; and when he came up to the light, I saw his great flaming eyes; and then I fell upon my knees, and he laid hold of my shoulder and griped it. Look, your honour!" laying bare his shoulder as he spoke, and showing the deeply indented marks of the bony fingers of the Mummy. Again a groan of horror and indignation ran through the Court; and when another witness proved that the sarcophagus of Cheops had been examined, and was found empty, the judge seemed to think it was a clear case, and called triumphantly upon Edric for his defence.

"I do not see that what has been proved," said Edric, shuddering in spite of himself, "can affect either my tutor or myself. These people say that a mummy has revived, and, quitting the Pyramid in which he had been so long immured, has flown away with our balloon: but, supposing the tale to be true, what proof have you that we were at all implicated in the business? We were in the Pyramid, it is true; but so was also this man, whom you have brought forward as a witness against us. Supposing it was the intervention of some human aid that roused the Mummy from its tomb — a fact, by the way, by no means proved, why may not he be the agent instead of us? What is there to fix the charge against us? Have we gained any thing by the adventure? Have we not, on the contrary, been serious losers by it? Where is our balloon, and the valuable articles it contained? If we are wizards, it must be confessed that we are very foolish ones; for we have lost our property, and thrown ourselves into prison, without reaping the smallest possible advantage! And if we have the power you seem to attribute to us, why do we stay here to be questioned, when we might so easily fly away in a flame of fire, or turn you all to statues, and walk quietly off without your being able to follow us?"

Every one shuddered, and many turned pale at this speech, seeming to fear that Edric was about to put his suggestions into execution; whilst the judge seemed posed, and in vast perplexity as to what he had better determine; — and the people were dreadfully afraid, lest they might, after all, lose the edifying spectacle of of an auto-da-fé, for which they had been so impatiently longing.

Edric marked the hesitation of the judge, and endeavoured to improve it to his own advantage. — "For my part," continued he, "I am a British subject, and as such, under the protection of my own Court; my Sovereign has a consul here, and to him I make my appeal. I am neither ignoble, nor unknown in my own country, — my name is Montagu, and I am brother to the celebrated general of that family, — whose victories, no doubt, have reached even this remote province!"

"My dear Mr. Montagu!" said the judge, "I really beg your pardon: why did you not acquaint me sooner with your dignity? I dare say there is no truth at all in the charge: — only assure me upon your honour that you did not touch the mummy, and that you know nothing of what is become of it at present, and I will instantly order you to be set at liberty."

"I certainly do not know what is become of it," replied Edric. "But—"

"No!" interrupted Dr. Entwerfen, coming forward with the air of a determined martyr, "I will not suffer such equivocation. —I would rather perish at the stake, than disavow, for a moment, my opinions, or betray the sacred interests of science with which I feel I am entrusted. No, Sir! my pupil cannot make the public declaration you require. I know he would not—and he cannot if he would;—on the contrary, I avow the fact. We came here for the express purpose of endeavouring to

The Mummy!

resuscitate the mummy of Cheops, and I glory in the proud thought that we have succeeded." (A groan of horror.) "Yes, Sir, I do not hesitate to avow openly, that the grand object of my life, for several successive years, has been to detect in what consisted the strange, inexplicable secret of life. We live, Sir, we die: we are born, and we are buried: we know that time, sickness, or violence, may kill us; but who can say in what the mysterious principle of life consists? Various theories have been broached, with which, no doubt, a gentleman of your intelligence and extensive information is well acquainted; — and life has been successively stated to depend upon the heart, the brain, the circulation of the blood, and the respiration of the lungs. All, however, are fallacious; the heart has been wounded, and the brain has been removed, and yet the patient has lived, whilst the operations of respiration and circulation have been kept up for hours, in a body from which the vital spirit had departed. Weighing all these and divers other arguments in my mind, it has struck me, and indeed I may say, that after mature deliberation, I have confidently arrived at the conclusion, that both the faculties which we call life and soul depend entirely upon the nervous system. Do not all philosophers agree that we receive ideas merely through the medium of the senses? And can our senses be operated upon otherwise than through the influence of the nerves? Ergo, the nerves alone convey ideas and sensations to the mind — or rather, the nerves alone are the mind. Not a single instance, I believe, is known in which life remained after the sensorium had been destroyed, or even seriously injured. What then can be more simple than to suppose life resides there? Pursuing this idea, I have long been convinced that where the nervous system remained uninjured, and the appearance of death was only occasioned by a suspension of the operation of the animal functions, that life might be restored, if, by the intervention of any powerful agency, the nervous system could be excited to re-action; and as this, of course, could not be effected where any kind of decomposition had taken place, it appeared to me that a mummy was the only body upon which the experiment could be tried with the least prospect of success. From various circumstances, however, it has never till now been in my power to realize my wishes on this head; but for a few weeks past, my pupil has entertained similar longings to myself; and yesterday saw our hopes accomplished. Yes; I flatter myself there cannot now remain a shadow of doubt to the world, that, in ordinary cases, before decomposition has taken place, that resuscitation is not only possible, but probable, and that dead bodies may be easily restored to life."

The horror and consternation produced by this extraordinary speech, amongst the Anglo-Egyptians who heard it, far exceeded any human powers of description. Their terror at what they considered as the doctor's daring impiety, being considerably augmented by their not understanding above one-tenth part of what he said,—and when he had finished, there was a dead pause which no one dared to interrupt, till a sudden gust of wind happening to blow open the door of the justice's retiring-room, the terrified crowd fell back aghast one upon another, pale and trembling, as though they absolutely expected his Infernal Majesty to appear before them in propriâ personâ.

When tranquillity was in some degree restored, the judge ordered the prisoners to be reconducted to prison.

"After the dangerous and impious speech we have just heard," said he, "it would be madness to trust such suspected persons at large; and yet, I would willingly take time to consider the case, and to ascertain whether this young man be indeed the person he represents himself; as, I own, I should be sorry to inflict the full penalty of the law upon the brother of her Britannic Majesty's Commander-in-chief."

Remonstrance was useless, and the prisoners were again conducted to their dungeon where they were heavily chained, and left to ruminate upon the calamities that had befallen them. Far from agreeable were these meditations; for Edric was too angry with the doctor's ill-timed candour to be inclined to speak; and the doctor was too much ashamed of the effect already produced by his eloquence, to wish to make any farther display of it. At length, as his eyes became accustomed to the faint glimmering light admitted into the dungeon, he perceived the wall to which he was chained was covered with hieroglyphics, and endeavoured to divert his chagrin by examining them.

"I congratulate you, Sir," said Edric, when he perceived this, feeling rather indignant at his tutor's coolness—"I congratulate you most sincerely upon your philosophy, and most earnestly do I wish that I could imitate it."

"Ah, Edric!" returned the doctor, "all men are not equally gifted."

"With either the art of making blunders, or forgetting them," said Edric pointedly.

The Mummy!

"These hieroglyphics are very curious," observed the doctor, who had his own reasons for not wishing to pursue the subject; "see how beautifully the ancient Egyptians worked in granite. The fine polish they contrived to give this hard substance would be perfectly astonishing, if we did not recollect that they always edged their tools with emerald dust."

"Humph!" said Edric, in a tone which seemed to imply "and what does it matter to me if they did?" The doctor, however, was unabashed, and continued: "You see, as usual, the figure of the bull is frequently repeated here. This wall is evidently built of stones gathered from some ancient ruin. By the way, Edric, I don't think I ever explained to you why the ancient Egyptians chose a bull as one of their deities, or, rather, as their principal one. You know, that anciently the year began in Taurus, though, by the precession of the equinox, it has now advanced past Aries. Well, as the ancient Egyptians found that the sun began its career in Taurus, what could be more natural than that they should identify a bull with the vivifying principle? The same theory may account for that legend of the Chaldeans, which supposes the world to have been produced by a bull's striking chaos with his horn—which horn, by the way, was probably the origin of the fable of Amalthea, or the Horn of Plenty."

Edric made no reply, and the doctor dreading a pause, which might give his pupil an opportunity of upbraiding him, went on:—

"Though the Egyptians had a number of divinities, they clearly worshipped only two, viz. the principles of good and evil. Osiris, Isis, Cneph, Phath, Horus, and all their host of inferior deities, were clearly types of the first, and light and life were their essence; whilst Typhon, Campsa, and the malignant deities, exemplified the second, and their attributes were invariably darkness and death."

"For Heaven's sake!" cried Edric, "say no more upon the subject, for it is not in the power of language to describe the horror I have at the mere thought of any thing Egyptian. Let us escape from this fearful country, and I most sincerely hope nothing may ever happen to recall even its recollection to my imagination."

"Such and so changeable are the desires of human life!" said the doctor. "But a few short weeks since, Egypt was the goal of your wishes, and the prospect of re-animating a corpse—"

"Oh! do not mention it!" cried Edric, shuddering. "Oh God!

how justly am I punished, by the very fulfilment of my unhallowed hopes! — even now the fearful eyes of that hideous Mummy seem to glare upon me; and even now I feel the gripe of its horrid bony fingers on my arm!"

"Oh yes, no doubt," exclaimed the doctor, "he pinched hard. He was a king, and kings should have strong arms, you know."

"For God's sake! do not jest upon such a subject," returned Edric; "a subject so wild and fearful, that I can still scarcely believe but that all which has passed was a dream."

"If it be," said the doctor, "it is one from which I freely avow I should be very happy to awake, for I must confess this prison is not at all to my taste."

"And yet, is it not your fault — ?" began Edric.

"Recrimination, Edric, is always folly," interrupted the doctor, who did not now feel very proud of the part he had acted before the magistrate, nor very anxious to have it alluded to; — "and instead of losing time in regretting past errors, it is the part of a wise man to endeavour to find means of remedying them, and avoiding them in future."

"Agreed!" returned Edric; "and as I presume you are now convinced your learned dissertation on the probable seat of human life was, to say the least, ill-timed, we will drop the subject. But, even if we get out of prison, what is to become of us? Our money and valuables were all in the balloon; and here we are, in a foreign country, entirely destitute."

"Not entirely, Edric — not entirely!" cried the doctor, a glow of satisfaction spreading itself again over his face; "no, no; I have guarded against that; ah, what a thing it is to have foresight! Well! some persons are certainly singularly gifted in that line, and it is a happy thing for you that you have somebody to think for you. See here!" displaying the things as he spoke; "here is a bed, bolster, and pillows, ready for inflation; a portable bedstead, linen, soap, pens, ink, paper, candles, fire, knives, forks, spoons, and money; all snugly packed up in my walking-stick!"

"Your supporter," returned Edric, smiling, "as you used to call it; and as it now seems likely to prove, in more senses than one."

"Yes, yes!" cried the doctor, "let us only get out of prison, and

The Mummy!

all the rest will be easy."

"But that only, doctor."

"Of that we must take time to consider."

"Well, it is some comfort that we are likely to be allowed time enough, as my hint respecting the British consul did not seem thrown away upon the judge. Oh, doctor, if you had not spoken!"

"Why, surely you would not have given him the declaration he required?"

"There was no occasion. He neither wished nor expected more than I had already said. After what I had mentioned of my family, he only wished a decent pretext for setting us at liberty."

"At any rate," said the doctor, by way of changing the subject, "you see my doctrine is proved completely by the resuscitation of the mummy, for it must have been perfectly restored to life and consciousness, or it could not have flown away with the balloon."

"For my part," returned Edric, "I can scarcely believe what has occurred to be real: there must be some deception. And yet, by whom can a deception have been practised, and for what purpose? In short, I am quite bewildered."

The doctor being much in the same condition, could only sympathize with his pupil; and in this state we must leave them, whilst we inquire respecting the mysterious object of their speculations.

The mummy thus strangely recalled to life, was indeed Cheops! and horrible were the sensations that throbbed through every nerve as returning consciousness brought with it all the pangs of his former existence, and renewed circulation thrilled through every vein. His first impulse was to quit the tomb in which he had been so long immured, and seek again the regions of light and day. Instinct seemed to guide him to this; for, as yet, a mist hung over his faculties, and ideas thronged in painful confusion through his mind, which he was incapable of either arranging or analyzing.

When however he reached the plain, light and air seemed to revive him and restore his scattered senses; and gazing wildly around he exclaimed, "Where am I? what place is this?

Methinks all seems wondrous, new, and strange! Where is my father? And where! oh, where, is my Arsinoë? Alas, alas!" continued he wildly; "I had forgotten—I hoped it was a dream, a fearful dream, for methinks I have been long asleep. Was it, indeed, reality? Are all, all gone? And was that hideous scene true?—those horrors that still haunt my memory like a ghastly vision? Speak! speak!" continued he, his voice rising in thrilling energy as he spoke—"speak! let me hear the sound of another's voice, before my brain is lost in madness. Have I entered Hades, or am I still on earth?—yes, yes, it is still the earth, for there the mighty Pyramid, I caused to be erected, towers behind me. Yet where is Memphis? where my forts and palaces? What a dark, smoky mass of buildings now surrounds me!—Can this be the once proud Queen of Cities? Oh, no! I see no palaces, no temples—Memphis is fallen. The mighty barrier that protected her splendour from the waste of waters, must have been swept away by the encroaching inroads of the swelling Nile. But is this the Nile?" continued he, looking wildly upon the river; "sure I must be deceived. It is the fatal river of the dead. No papyrine boats glide smoothly on its surface; but strange, infernal vessels, vomiting forth volumes of fire and smoke. Holy Osiris, defend me! where am I? where have I been? A misty veil seems thrown upon the face of nature. Awake, awake!" cried he, with a scream of agony; "set me free; I did not mean to slay him!" Then throwing himself violently upon the ground, he lay for some moments, apparently insensible. Then slowly rising, he looked at himself, and a deep, unnatural shuddering convulsed his whole frame. His sensations of identity became confused, and he recoiled with horror from himself: "These are the trappings of a mummy!" murmured he in a hollow whisper. "Am I then dead?" The next instant, however, he broke into a wild laugh of derision:—"Poor, feeble wretch!" cried he; "what do I fear?— Need I tremble, in whose bosom dwells everlasting fire? No— no! let me rather rejoice. I cannot be more wretched; why then should I dread a change? I should rather welcome it with transport, and bravely dare my fate."

At this moment the car of the balloon caught his eye: "Ah! what is that?" cried he; "I am summoned! 'Tis the boat of Hecate, ready to ferry me across the Mærian Lake, to learn my final doom. I come! I come! I fear no judgment! My hell is here!" and, striking his bosom, leaped into the car, and stamped violently against its sides.

At this instant Gregory awoke; his terror was not surprising. The dried, distorted features of the Mummy looked yet more hideous than before, when animated by human passions; and his deep hollow voice, speaking in a language he did not understand, fell heavily upon his ear, like the groans of fiends. Gregory tried to scream, but he could not utter a sound. He attempted to fly, but his feet seemed nailed to the spot on which he stood, and he remained with his eyes fixed upon the Mummy, gasping for breath, while a cold sweat distilled from every pore. In the mean time, Cheops had stumbled over the box containing the apparatus for making inflammable air, and striking it violently, had unintentionally set the machinery in motion. The pipes, tubes, and bellows, instantly began to work; and the Indian-rubber bottle became gradually inflated, till it swelled to an enormous magnitude, and fluttered in the air like an imprisoned bird, beating itself against the massive walls to which it was still attached.

"Still it goes not," cried Cheops, again stamping impatiently. The quicksilver vapour bottle had fallen beneath his feet, and it broke as he trod upon it. The vapour burst from it with inconceivable violence, and tearing the balloon from its fastenings, sent it off through the air, like an arrow darting from a bow.

CHAPTER XI.

In the mean time, Sir Ambrose Montagu had been presented to the Queen, and the evening after his arrival in town he attended her drawing-room. The splendour of the English Court at this period defies description. The walls of the room in which the Queen received her guest, were literally one blaze of precious stones, and these being disposed in the form of bouquets, wreaths, and trophies, were so contrived as to quiver with every movement. These magnificent walls were relieved by a colonnade of pillars of solid gold, around which, were twined wreaths of jewels fixed also upon elastic gold wires, so as to tremble every instant. The throne of the Queen was formed of gold filigree beautifully wrought, richly chased and superbly ornamented, whilst behind it was an immense plate of looking-glass, stretching the whole length and height of the apartment, and giving the whole the effect of a fairy palace. The carpet spread upon the floor of this sumptuous saloon was so exact an imitation of green moss, with exquisitely beautiful groups of flowers thrown carelessly upon it, that a heedless spectator might have been completely deceived by the delicacy of their shape and richness of their colouring, and have stooped to pick them up, supposing them to be real. The suit of rooms appropriated to dancing was equally splendid, and fitted up in the same manner, save that the floors were painted to imitate the effect of the carpet, and rows of trees were placed on each side, hung with lamps. This imitative grove was so exquisitely managed, that the spectator could scarcely believe it artificial; and the music for dancing proceeded from its leaves, or from automaton birds placed carelessly amongst its branches.

The dresses of the Queen and her attendants were worthy of the apartment they occupied. Brocaded silks, cloth of gold, embroidered velvets, gold and silver tissues, and gossamer nets made of the spider's web, were mingled with precious stones and superb plumes of feathers in a profusion quite beyond description. The most beautiful of the female habiliments, however, were robes made of woven asbestos, which glittered in the brilliant light like molten silver. The ladies were all arrayed in loose trowsers, over which hung drapery in graceful folds; and most of them carried on their heads, streams of lighted gas forced by capillary tubes into plumes, fleurs-de-lis, or in short any form the wearer pleased; which jets de feu had an uncommonly chaste and elegant effect. The gentlemen were all clothed in the Spanish style, with slashed sleeves, short cloaks, and large hats, ornamented with immense plumes of ostrich feathers, it being considered in those days extremely vulgar to appear with the head uncovered. It would, perhaps, have been difficult to imagine more perfect models of male and female beauty than those which now adorned the Court of Queen Claudia, for the beau ideal of the painter's fancy seemed realized, nay surpassed by the noble living figures there collected. The women were particularly lovely, and as they stood gathered round their Queen, or lightly threaded the mazes of the graceful dance, dressed as above described, their brows bound with circlets of precious stones, and their glossy hair hanging in rich luxuriant ringlets upon their ivory shoulders, they looked like a group of Houris, or the nymphs of Circe, ready with sparkling eyes and witching voices to lure men to destruction.

Claudia was very handsome, and though her countenance wanted expression, her noble figure and majestic bearing well qualified her to play her part as Queen amongst this bevy of beauties, with becoming dignity. There is something in the habit of command, when it has been long enjoyed, that gives an imposing majesty to the manner, which the parvenu great strive in vain to imitate; and Claudia had this in perfection. The consciousness of beauty, power, and high birth swelled in her bosom; and even when she wished to be affable, she was only condescending.

She now, however, received Sir Ambrose most graciously; she gave him her snowy hand to kiss, and addressed a few words of compliment to him, which sank deep into his heart. It is one of the privileges of greatness easily to excite emotion; one word of commendation from those above us, far outweighs all the laboured flattery of our inferiors. Thus the words of Claudia, and the warm praise she bestowed on Edmund, gave the purest transport to his father's heart; and affected him so violently, that he would have fallen at her feet, had he not been supported by a young man who stood near him.

"You seem faint, Sir," said the youth; "will you permit me to lead you to a seat."

"Thank you, thank you," cried Sir Ambrose, gratefully accepting the proffered aid, and leaning on his youthful supporter as they left the presence. The stranger carefully placed Sir Ambrose upon a sofa, under the harmonious trees we have already mentioned; and as he stood before him, asking if he should procure him some refreshments, Sir Ambrose had full leisure to survey his face and figure: both were handsome in the extreme. The youth seemed scarcely to have passed the age of boyhood, and his well-proportioned form displayed all the lightness and activity of youth; but wit and good-humour laughed in his bright blue eyes, whilst animated features and an enchanting smile completed an ensemble which few bosoms were frozen enough to resist. Sir Ambrose was irresistibly pleased, and longed to know to whom he was indebted for so much kindness. But he felt too delicate to ask the question in direct terms, and there was nothing in the youth's exterior to mark decidedly to what rank in life he might belong.

He was handsomely dressed, and his air and manner appeared slightly foreign; though this might be fancy, arising from Sir Ambrose's ignorance of the manners and habits of the Court. There also seemed something droll about him, and the air with which he submitted to Sir Ambrose's scrutiny was excessively comic.

"Is there any thing I can do for you?" asked he at length, when he thought the baronet's curiosity had had time to satisfy itself.

"Nothing," replied Sir Ambrose; "but—"

"But—you would like to know who I am?" said the stranger.

"I own," returned Sir Ambrose, blushing, "I would fain know to whom I am so much obliged."

"My name is Henry Seymour," replied the youth. "I was born in Spain, of English parents. I am an orphan and in want; and have been introduced to the Queen, in hopes of getting a place at Court, by one of her Majesty's physicians, Dr. Coleman."

"I am quite ashamed," said Sir Ambrose, "that my indiscreet curiosity—that is, that you should have thought—I mean, that I should have asked for—"

"In short," interrupted the youth, "you think, perhaps, that I meant to call you rude by giving such a long account of myself: but I always do so in similar cases; it saves trouble."

Sir Ambrose smiled. "You are a singular youth," said he; "I should like to know you better."

"And I," returned the stranger, "should be proud to obtain the friendship of Sir Ambrose Montagu, and shall always reckon the day that introduced me to his notice, as one of the happiest of my life."

A glow of pleasure spread over the animated features of the youth as he spoke, and Sir Ambrose fancied his accent sounded slightly Irish: convinced, however, that he must be mistaken, he did not remark it, but only exclaimed, "You know me, then?"

Before the stranger had time to utter a reply, the Duke of Cornwall, and the Princesses Rosabella and Elvira approached, and prevented him from speaking.

"How do you find yourself, my dear friend?" said the duke; "they told us you were ill."

"I have been slightly so," returned Sir Ambrose; "and I believe I should have fainted, and paid my respects to my Sovereign quite orientally, if this gentleman had not saved me."

"I am sure we are very much obliged to you, Sir," said the duke, turning to the youth.

"Indeed, we feel most grateful," said Elvira.

The stranger made a suitable reply, and after a short conversation, in which Dr. Coleman joined, that worthy gentleman having been also drawn to the spot by the report of Sir Ambrose's illness, he requested the favour of Elvira's hand for the dance.

"That is a very nice young man," said the duke, when he was gone to join the dancers: "I admire him much."

"He deserves every thing you can say in his favour," returned Dr. Coleman: "I have known him long, and I love him as a son."

When Elvira retired to her chamber that night, she sighed so often, and so deeply, that Emma, who assisted at her toilet, could not avoid remarking her uneasiness. "Are you ill, my dear mistress?" asked she, in a tone of feeling; "what else can have produced this sudden change?"

"I am quite well," said Elvira, again sighing.

"Why then do you sigh and look so thoughtful?"

"I was thinking of Lord Edmund."

"Indeed! I did not think he had the power to make you sigh. He has reason to feel flattered."

"Oh, Emma! I wish he were like Henry Seymour!"

"And who is Henry Seymour?" asked Emma, smiling, and beginning to suspect that she had been rather hasty in fancying Lord Edmund had occasion to flatter himself on account of the Princess's tristesse.

"One of the most fascinating of human beings," returned Elvira; "so gay, and yet so tender. He is not, perhaps, so regularly handsome as Edmund, but he has such expressive features, and his soul gives such animation to his countenance."

"Poor Edmund!" thought Emma: but as she was too discreet to say so, Elvira was not aware of the interpretation that might be put on what she was saying; and she went on, raving of the pleasures of the ball, till she was fairly in bed.

The following day was appointed for the triumphal entry of Lord Edmund, and the greatest part of the night preceding it, was passed by Sir Ambrose in the greatest agitation. He could not sleep; he rose several times from his bed, in excessive anxiety, to listen for the repetition of noises which he fancied he heard: once he opened his window—all was still. His room looked into the garden of Mr. Montagu, which, as we have already mentioned, shelved down to the Thames, and the calm moonlight slept peacefully upon the tall, thick trees, and verdant lawn that spread before him. The evening breeze felt cool and refreshing; but Sir Ambrose sighed, and a strange fear of something he could not wholly define hung over him.

He again retired to bed, and at length sank into a feverish and uneasy doze. At daybreak, however, a thundering of cannon announced the arrival of the important day. Sir Ambrose started from his pillow at the first discharge, and the solemn sound thrilled through every nerve as it pealed along the sky. Scarcely had its echoes died upon the ear, when another, and another peal succeeded; and the heart of Sir Ambrose throbbed in his bosom almost to suffocation, as he sate, resting his head upon his hands, and striving, though ineffectually, to stop his ears from the solemn sound, which seemed to absorb his every faculty, and strike almost with the force of a blow upon his nerves.

Whilst he was still in this position, Father Morris entered the room.—"Come, come, Sir Ambrose!" cried he, "are you not ready? The Queen has sent for us, and the procession is just ready to set off."—Sir Ambrose started: he attempted to dress himself, but his trembling hands refused to perform their office, and Father Morris and Abelard were obliged to attire him, and lead him down to join his friend, the duke, who was waiting for him impatiently.

It has often been said that the anticipation of pleasure is always greater than the reality: this, however, was not the case in the present instance, as the brilliancy of Lord Edmund's triumph was far greater than even the imaginations of the spectators had before dared to conceive. The duke and Sir Ambrose, attended by Father Morris, found the individuals who were to compose the procession of the Queen assembled in the extensive gardens belonging to the superb palace of Somerset House. These fine gardens, spreading their verdant groves along the banks of the river, adorned by all the charms of nature and art, and enriched by some of the finest specimens of sculpture in the world, were now crowded with all the beauty and rank of England, who, waiting for the arrival of their Sovereign, formed an ensemble no other nation in the world could hope to imitate.

In the centre walk, appeared the superb Arabian charger of the Queen, led by his grooms, and magnificently caparisoned. His bridle was studded with precious stones, and his hoofs cased in gold; whilst his blue satin saddle and housings were richly embroidered and fringed with the same metal. The noble animal, whose flowing mane and tail swept the ground, paced proudly along, tossing his head on high, and spurning the ground on which he trod, as though conscious he should perform a conspicuous part in the grand pageant about to take place. All now was ready, but yet Queen Claudia did not appear.

"It is very strange, but lately it is always so," said Lord Maysworth to Lord Gustavus de Montfort, who had been for some time engaged in earnest conversation with Father Morris. Lord Gustavus started at the sound of his friend's voice in some apparent confusion, whilst Father Morris replied in his usual soft, insinuating tones, "Perhaps her Majesty may be indisposed, and have slept rather longer than usual."

"Most likely," returned Lord Maysworth; "yet it is strange the same thing should happen so often. — If you remember," continued he, again addressing Lord Gustavus, "I made the same observation the morning of her last levee. Indeed I have frequently made it lately, and I have observed that she looks pale and languid."

"Here she comes, at any rate! and for my part, I think I never saw her look better," said Dr. Hardman, who had now joined them, and who, notwithstanding his violent politics, was one of the physicians of the Court. The indolence of Claudia, which, indeed, seemed daily increasing, having induced her to overlook what another Sovereign would have resented.

Claudia did indeed look well, and her dress suited well with her style of beauty. Her trowsers and vest were of pale blue satin; whilst over her shoulders was thrown a long flowing drapery of asbestos silk, which hanging in graceful folds, swept the ground as she walked along, shining in the sun like a robe of woven silver. On her head, she wore a splendid tiara of diamonds; and in her hand, she bore the regal sceptre, surmounted by a dove, and richly ornamented with precious stones. Thus gorgeously attired, surrounded by the ladies of her household, she issued from her palace; and whilst her kneeling subjects bent in humble homage around her, she mounted her noble charger. Cannon were now fired in rapid succession; the bells of every church rang in merry peals, and martial music mingled in the clamour. The palace gates were thrown open, and the procession poured from them along the streets, where crowds of human beings bustled to and fro, eager to catch a glimpse of the sumptuous spectacle.

First advanced a long double line of monks, arrayed in sacerdotal pomp, and bearing immensely thick lighted tapers in their hands; chanting thanksgiving for the victory. They were followed by chorister-boys, flinging incense from silver vases, that hung suspended by chains in their hands, and chanting also; their shrill trebles mingling with the deep bass voices of the priests in rich and mellow harmony. The Queen next appeared, her prancing charger led by grooms, whilst beautiful girls, elegantly attired, walked, on each side of their Sovereign, scattering flowers in her path from fancy baskets made of wrought gold. Behind the Queen, rode the ladies of her household and the principal nobles of her Court, the superb plumes of ostrich feathers in the large Spanish hats of the latter, with their immense mustachios, and open shirt collars, giving them the air of some of Vandyck's best pictures. As they rode slowly along, their noble Arabians paced proudly, and champed the bit, impatient of restraint.

The ladies of the Court, superbly dressed in open litters, next appeared, borne upon the shoulders of men splendidly clad in rich liveries. Amongst these, were Elvira and Rosabella.

These were followed by monks and boys as before, but singing a somewhat different strain. It was now a chant of glory and triumph that swelled upon the ear, for these preceded the duke and Sir Ambrose; who, the one as uncle to the Queen, and the other as father of the expected hero, occupied the post of honour. The two venerable old men sate hand in hand in a sumptuous car drawn by two Arabian horses, and were followed by a large body of the Queen's guards.

The costliness and variety of the dresses worn this day, were quite beyond description. Many of the ladies had turbans of woven glass; whilst others carried on their hats very pretty fountains made of glass dust, which, being thrown up in little jets by a small perpetual motion wheel, sparkled in the sun like real water, and had a very singular effect.

In this manner the procession advanced towards Blackheath Square, said to be the largest and finest in the world, where the meeting between the Queen and her general was appointed to take place. Amongst the numerous balloons that floated in the air, enjoying this magnificent spectacle, was one containing Father Murphy, who had been prevented, by a sprained ankle, from joining in the procession, and the family of Mr. Montagu—and nothing could be more enthusiastic than their delight, as they looked down upon the splendid scene below them. Few things, indeed, could be imagined finer than the sight of this gorgeous cortège, winding slowly along a magnificent street, supposed to be five miles long, leading from Blackfriars' Bridge, through Greenwich, to Blackheath.

Sumptuous rows of houses, or rather palaces, lined the sides of this superb street; the terraces and balconies before which, were crowded with persons of all ages, beautifully attired, waving flags of different colours, richly embroidered and fringed with gold, whilst festoons of the choicest flowers hung from house to house. We have already said the air was thronged with balloons, and the crowd increased every moment. These aërial machines, loaded with spectators till they were in danger of breaking down, glittered in the sun, and presented every possible variety of shape and colour. In fact, every balloon in London or the vicinity had been put in requisition, and enormous sums paid, in some cases, merely for the privilege of hanging to the cords that attached the cars, whilst the innumerable multitudes that thus loaded the air, amused themselves by scattering flowers upon the heads of those who rode beneath.

Besides balloons, however, a variety of other modes of conveyance fluttered in the sky. Some dandies bestrode aërial horses, inflated with inflammable gas; whilst others floated upon wings, or glided gently along, reclining gracefully upon aërial sledges, the last being contrived so as to cover a sufficient column of air for their support. As the procession approached the river, the scene became still more animated; innumerable barges of every kind and description shot swiftly along, or glided smoothly over the sparkling water. Some floated with the tide in large boat-like shoes; whilst others, reclining on couch-shaped cars, formed of mother of pearl, were drawn forward by inflated figures representing the deities or monsters of the deep.

When the Queen reached a spot near Greenwich, where, through a spacious opening, the river, in all its glorious majesty, burst upon her, she paused, and commanded her trumpeters to advance and sound a flourish. They obeyed, and after a short pause were answered by those of Lord Edmund; the sound, mellowed by the distances, pealing along the water in dulcet harmony. Delighted with this response, which announced the arrival of Lord Edmund and his troops at the appointed place, the procession of the Queen was again set in motion, and in a short time arrived at Blackheath.

The noble square in which the meeting was to take place, was already thronged with soldiers; whilst every house that surrounded it was covered with spectators. No trees or fantastical ornaments spoiled the simple grandeur of this immense space; the houses that surrounded it, built in exact uniformity, each having a peristyle supported by Corinthian pillars, and a highly decorated façade, looked like so many Athenian temples. As the cortège of the Queen entered the square, the soldiers formed an opening to receive it, and reverentially knelt on each side, with reversed arms, and bending banners as she passed. In the centre was Lord Edmund, surrounded by his staff, all in polished armour; for since an invention had been discovered of rendering steel perfectly flexible, it had been generally used in war. Lord Edmund's helmet, however, was thrown off, and his fine countenance was displayed to the greatest advantage, as he and his officers threw themselves from their war steeds to kneel before the Queen. Claudia, also, descended from her charger, and as she stood in her glittering robes, surrounded on all sides by her kneeling subjects, she looked, indeed, their Sovereign. With becoming dignity, she addressed a few words of thanks and commendation to Lord Edmund, as he knelt before her, his thick, dark, brown hair falling in clustering curls over his noble forehead. His graceful figure was shown to the utmost advantage, by his closely fitting armour, over which, however, upon the present occasion was thrown a short cloak of fine scarlet cloth, richly embroidered with gold, and fastened in front by a cord and superb tassels, made entirely of the same metal. He looked a living personification of the God of War.

The Queen raised him from the ground in the most gracious manner; and then turning to the still kneeling soldiers, she made a short speech to them, of the same nature as that which she had addressed to Lord Edmund: after which, again mounting her palfrey, she made Lord Edmund ride by her side, and prepared to return to town. Edmund's quick eye had discovered, and exchanged looks of affection with his father and friends, though the etiquette of his present situation did not permit him to do more; and he now rode proudly by the side of the Queen, gracefully bowing to the assembled crowd as he passed along, his heart beating with pleasure at the thought that his triumph was witnessed by those most dear to him; whilst his noble Arabian tossed his head and champed his bit as he pranced forward, as though he also knew the part he was performing in the splendid ceremony.

Acclamations rent the sky as the procession advanced, and showers of roses were rained down upon the Queen and her general from the balloons above; from which, also, flags waved in graceful folds, and flapped in the wind, as the balloons floated along the sky. Every one seemed delighted with the grandeur of this splendid pageant; but no one experienced more pleasure than the occupiers of the balloon of Mr. Montagu. Even that oblivious gentleman himself was moved to exclaim, that he never was more enchanted in his life; whilst the raptures of his spouse were so excessive, that, like the spectators of the stag-hunt on the lake of Killarney, she was in imminent danger of throwing herself overboard in her ecstasy: and Clara clasped her hands together, in all the transports of childish delight, her sparkling eyes and animated looks bearing ample witness to her gratification.

"What shouting! what a noise!" exclaimed Mr. Montagu; "I declare it puts me in mind of the acclamations in the time of Nero, when the Romans shouted in concert, and birds fell from the skies with the noise!"

"La! papa, is that true?" asked Clara.

"Och, and that's a strange kind of a question," said Father Murphy, "and one I wouldn't like a child of mine to be putting."

"And why not?" asked Mr. Montagu, somewhat indignantly.

"Because a child ought always to belave what his father says, before he hears him open his mouth."

"How well the Queen looks!" observed Mrs. Montagu, to whom the reverend father's remark was far from agreeable. "It was said a short time since, that she had lost her appetite and could get no rest; but I think she doesn't seem to have much the matter with her now."

"My nurse says she's being poisoned," cried Clara, "and that it would be no great matter if she was, for then the people would have to choose a Queen for themselves, and they might make what terms they pleased with her."

"And is this the kind of servant you suffer to attend on my daughter, Mrs. Montagu?" demanded the indignant father, roused from his usual lethargy by the importance of the occasion; "Clara shall go to a boarding-school to-morrow, and her nurse shall be dismissed. My child shall not be taught to utter treason."

"Dear me! Mr. Montagu," replied the wife, "what a serious matter you make of a little harmless gossip!"

"Gossip do you call it?" repeated her husband; "it is such gossip as might cost me my head, and you your fortune, if it were to reach unfriendly ears."

An awkward pause followed this speech, which no one seemed inclined to break, till Clara exclaimed, "Dear me! what a pretty horse my cousin Edmund rides!"

"I think that's a prettier that comes after him," said Father Murphy.

"What, that one with his head hanging down and his mane sweeping the ground?" asked Mrs. Montagu.

"Yes. — And it's a very handsome young man also, that walks by the side of him," replied Father Murphy.

"His hands are chained as if he were a prisoner; and he looks like a foreigner," observed Mr. Montagu, who had relapsed into one of his fits of abstraction: "I wonder what can bring him there!"

The Mummy!

"La! Mr. Montagu, how you talk!" exclaimed his wife, "you know my nephew Lord Edmund, has just gained a battle, and what can be more natural than that he should have taken prisoners?"

"True," rejoined Mr. Montagu with the utmost naïveté, "I never thought of that!"

"Och, and it's a barbarous custom that of putting chains about the hands of the prisoners," said Father Murphy, "as if it was not bad enough to be a prisoner without looking, like one."

"Poor fellow!" cried Clara, "I should like to go and let him loose. He looks very melancholy!"

"How great my nephew Lord Edmund looks!" continued Mrs. Montagu: "I declare it he were a real king he couldn't have a grander appearance. And then to see the poor old gentleman his father, my brother-in-law, Sir Ambrose, sitting there hand-in-hand with the Duke of Cornwall himself — I declare it does my heart good to look at them!"

Whilst Mrs. Montagu was thus exulting in the reflected grandeur that shone upon her, from being sister-in-law to the person who sat hand-in-hand with the duke, the joy and delight of that exalted personage had been almost as great as her own.

His impatience during the whole procession from London had been excessive; and the moment he saw Edmund, he rubbed his hands in ecstasy, and jumping up in his seat almost overturned Sir Ambrose, who was also bending forward eagerly gazing upon his son. "There! there he is!" cried the duke. "Look how handsome he is! Oh the young rogue! there'll be many a heart lost to-day, I warrant me! Look at him, how the colour comes into his cheeks as the Queen speaks to him! Look! Now he helps her on her horse — and now see, he's looking round for us! There I caught his eye — see, Sir Ambrose! don't you see him? — Surely you ar'n't crying, my old friend? Why you'll make me as great a fool as yourself — God bless him! I am sure I don't know any thing we have to cry at; but we are two old simpletons."

Father Morris, who had joined the procession of monks, was almost as much affected as his patron. Indeed his affection for Edmund seemed the only human passion remaining in his ascetic breast. Cold even to frigidity in his exterior, Father Morris seemed to regard the scenes passing around him but as the moving figures of a magic lantern, which glittered for a moment in glowing colours, and then vanished into darkness, leaving no trace behind:—whilst he, unmoved as the wall over which the gaudy but shadowy pageant had passed, saw them alternately vanish and re-appear without the slightest emotion being excited in his mind. Under this statue-like appearance, however, Father Morris concealed passions as terrific as those which might be supposed to throb in the breast of a demon: though never did his self-command seem relaxed for a moment, but when the interests of Edmund were in question. On the present occasion, however, joy swelled in his bosom almost to suffocation, as he raised his eyes to Heaven, and, wringing his hands together, exclaimed, "Oh! it is too—too much!"

There is something indescribably affecting in seeing strong emotion expressed by those who are generally calm and unimpassioned; and Sir Ambrose, by whom this burst of feeling from his confessor was quite unexpected, gazed at him with the utmost surprise, and, strange to tell, though the monk had now lived nearly twenty years under his roof, it was the first time he had seen his head completely uncovered. Father Morris's cowl had now, however, fallen off entirely, and displayed the head of a man between forty and fifty, whose fine features bore the traces of what he had endured. His noble expressive brow seemed wrinkled more by care than age, and his sable locks had evidently become "grizzled here and there," prematurely. Sir Ambrose gazed upon him intently, for the peculiar expression of his features seemed to recall some half-forgotten circumstance to his mind, dimly obscured, however, by the mist of time. The earnestness with which he consequently regarded the monk, seemed at length to recall the latter to himself. He started, and, whilst a deep crimson flushed his usually sallow countenance, he hastily resumed his cowl, and appeared again to the eyes of the spectators, the same cold, unimpassioned, abstracted being as before.

The ovation had now nearly reached Blackfriars' bridge, at the entrance to which, a triumphal arch had been erected. The moment the Queen and her heroic general passed under it, a small figure of Fame was contrived to descend from its entablature, and, hovering over the hero, to drop a laurel crown upon his head. Shouts of applause followed this well-executed device; and the passengers in the balloons, wondering at the noise, all pressed forward at the same moment to ascertain the cause of such continued acclamations. The throng of balloons became thus every instant more dense. Some young city apprentices having hired each a pair of wings for the day, and not exactly knowing how to manage them, a dreadful tumult ensued; and the balloons became entangled with the winged heroes and each other in inextricable confusion.

The noise now became tremendous; the conductors of the balloons swearing at each other the most refined oaths, and the ladies screaming in concert. Several balloons were rent in the scuffle and fell with tremendous force upon the earth; whilst some cars were torn from their supporting ropes, and others roughly overset. Luckily, however, the whole of England was at this time so completely excavated, that falling upon the surface of the earth was like tumbling upon the parchment of an immense drum, and consequently only a deep hollow sound was returned as cargo after cargo of the demolished balloons struck upon it; some of them, indeed, rebounded several yards with the violence of the shock.

Amongst those who fell from the greatest height, and of course rebounded most violently, were the unfortunate individuals who composed the party of Mr. Montagu, an unlucky apprentice having poked his right wing through the silk of their balloon, in endeavouring to avoid the charge of an aërial horseman, who found his Æolian steed too difficult to manage in the confusion. The car containing our friends was in consequence precipitated to earth so rapidly, as for the moment to deprive them of breath.

"Och, and I'm killed entirely!" cried Father Murphy.

"Oh, my bonnet! my beautiful bonnet!" sobbed Mrs. Montagu; whilst Clara, dreadfully frightened, began to cry; and Mr. Montagu, whose ideas were generally a long time travelling to his brain, particularly upon occasions of sudden alarm, stood completely silent, stupidly gazing about him, as though he had not the least notion what could possibly have happened. Indeed, it was not till a full hour afterwards, that he found himself sufficiently recovered to exclaim, "Dear me! I do think we were very near being killed!"

In the mean time, the confusion in the air still continued; piercing screams that demons were in the air, mingled horribly with the crashing of balloons, the cries of the sufferers, and the successive falling of heavy weights. The situation of the crowd below, however, was infinitely worse than that of those above. The momentum of the falling bodies being fearfully increased by the distance they had to descend, those below had no chance of escape, and were inevitably crushed to death by their weight, whilst the agonizing shrieks of the unfortunate wretches who saw their danger coming from a distance, yet were so jammed together in the crowd that they could not fly, rang shrilly upon the ear, and pierced through every heart.

At this moment a dreadful scream ran through the crowd, and the horse of Queen Claudia, his bridle broken, his housings torn, his nostrils distended, and his sides streaming with gore, rushed past—"Oh God! the Queen! the Queen!" burst from every voice, and one general rush took place towards the spot from whence the cry had proceeded.

Beneath the triumphal arch, and partially sheltered by its shade, lay the bleeding body of Claudia, supported by Edmund. By her side, knelt Rosabella, who, assisted by Father Morris, was applying restoratives; whilst Henry Seymour was endeavouring to restore Elvira, who had fainted in the arms of her father, and Sir Ambrose, his face streaming with blood, stood at a little distance amongst a group of courtiers, several of whom had also experienced severe injuries. The tumult in the air still continued; groans and shrieks and exclamations, that the atmosphere was supernaturally haunted, were heard in many places; and some persons declared the accident to be the work of demons. A current of wind had blown those balloons that had become unmanageable across the city, while the others, terrified almost to madness, appeared still contending with some fearful monster in the sky.

The courtiers, however, heeded not this disturbance; for all their attention was occupied by the apparently expiring Queen, whose long-drawn sighs, and convulsed bosom, seemed to threaten her instant dissolution.

"She's gone!" cried Lord Gustavus de Montfort, as her bosom heaved with a deep, heavy sigh, and then all was still.

"Yes, she's dead!" repeated Lord Noodle.

"She is certainly dead!" reiterated Lord Doodle.

And then these sapient counsellors of the apparently departed Queen shook their wise heads in sympathy.

"Hush! she breathes!" cried Lord Edmund.

For some moments, the courtiers stood in breathless anxiety watching the body, and fearing to move lest they should break the awful silence that prevailed, though their hearts throbbed till the pulsations were almost audible.

The Mummy!

Fearful was the pause that now ensued! All were suffering from the torments of hope or fear; for all knew that the interests of the whole community hung upon her breath. Most of the courtiers also either hoped to gain places, or feared to lose them, whilst all trembled at the uncertainty that seemed to rest upon their future destiny, and the prospect of the anarchy which the purposed mode of electing their future Sovereign might create. The interest which the fate of the Queen excited was thus intense, and the courtiers hung over her body with streaming eyes and motionless limbs to watch the result.

At this instant, a fearful and tremendous yell ran through the air; and the car containing the Mummy, which had been for some time entangled with the other balloons, fell to the ground with tremendous force, close to the expiring Queen. The gigantic figure of Cheops started from it as it fell — his ghastly eyes glaring with unnatural lustre upon the terrified courtiers, who ran screaming in agony in all directions, forgetting every thing but the horrid vision before them.

END OF VOL. I.

CHAPTER XII.

The tumult had now nearly subsided. The late busy crowd had flown, uttering shrieks of horror and dismay; and of all the countless mass of human beings that had so lately thronged around, none now remained but Edmund and Father Morris, who supported Claudia; and the Duke and Henry Seymour, who still remained near the insensible form of Elvira; the eyes of all being chained, as though by magic, upon the horrid vision before them; whilst they, pale and immovable as the sculptured marble of the tomb, waited in fearful expectation of what was next to happen, and scarcely dared to move or breathe; the solemn silence that prevailed being only broken by the convulsive gasps of the expiring Queen:—an awful change from the busy hum of thousands which had so lately filled the air!

"Where am I?" exclaimed Cheops, gazing wildly around—his deep sepulchral voice thrilling through every nerve:—"Where is Arsinoë? Where is she? They seize her! They tear her from me! Curses on the wretches!—May Typhon's everlasting vengeance pursue them with its fury, and may their hearts wither, gnawed by the never-dying snake!"

The Mummy gnashed his teeth as he spoke, and the gloom that gathered on his dark brow grew black as night. All shuddered as that horrid glance of eternal hatred seemed to freeze their blood. They turned away involuntarily; and when they looked again, the spectre had disappeared. The shattered remains of the balloon lay before them; for happening to cross London just at the moment of the greatest confusion, it had become entangled in the crowd, and, notwithstanding the strong material of which it was composed, had been rent asunder in the scuffle, and had fallen with its fearful occupier to the ground.

"Good God!" cried Father Morris, after a short pause; "what a horrid vision! what can it mean?"

"It seemed an Egyptian Mummy," said Edmund, shuddering; "and it spoke that language. But what can have resuscitated it? What human power can have recalled to life, a being so long immured in the silent tomb!"

"Perhaps the vehicle he came in may contain something to explain the mystery," said Henry Seymour.

At this moment several persons ran past screaming with terror, and exclaiming that they had seen a demon. When the confusion excited by these trembling fugitives had a little subsided, a few of the courtiers began also to make their appearance, and return to their posts near the Queen. But all were pale, and they started at every sound, seeming ready, at the least alarm, to take flight again as expeditiously as before.

Claudia still lay insensible; her heaving chest and deep convulsive sobs for breath, alone betraying signs of life. But her fate no longer excited the deep, overwhelming interest it had done before. Whispers of wonder and superstitious horror mingled with the hopes and fears inspired by her danger; and her removal to the palace was almost regarded with indifference, so completely were the minds of men occupied by the strange spectacle they had so lately witnessed.

Every one, indeed, neither thought nor spoke of any thing but the Mummy; and a thousand rumours, each more extravagant than the last, spread from mouth to mouth respecting it. Men stood in groups whispering to each other, and scarcely daring to stir without a companion: nay, even then, creeping from place to place, looking cautiously around, and starting at every noise, as though they feared the awful visitor was returned: whilst the sages of the country gravely shook their heads, and declared that what had taken place was evidently a visitation from Heaven, in punishment of the sins of mankind. An indefinable presentiment of evil hung over the spirits of all. Gloom, indeed, spread through every class of society: all dreaded they knew not what—and all shrunk with horror from the thought of supernatural agency. There is an invincible feeling implanted by Nature in the mind of man, which makes him shudder with disgust at any thing that invades her laws.

The body of the Queen being removed, attended by her physicians and the ladies of her household, the rest of the assembled courtiers gathered round the balloon; and exclamations of terror and surprise broke from their lips when they discovered it to be the same in which Edric and Dr. Entwerfen had so short a time before taken their departure for Egypt. The whole truth now seemed to flash upon them.

"I thought how it would be," said Lord Maysworth; "you know I told you, Lord Gustavus, that in my opinion it was an expedition that could never possibly do any good—but you were of a different belief."

"My Lord," returned Lord Gustavus, solemnly, "thinking as I think, and as I am convinced every one who hears me must think, or at least ought to think, it is my deliberate opinion, that the expedition of my youthful friend and his learned tutor was both admirably planned and well concocted, and that if it have failed in its ulterior object, it has been solely owing to some of those unforeseen events which sometimes do occur even in the best regulated arrangements, and which it was utterly impossible for any human ability entirely to ward off and avert."

"Edric's balloon! Impossible!" cried Sir Ambrose, rushing forward to ascertain the fact, and forgetting all his anger against his son in his anxiety for his fate. "Yes! yes!" continued he, looking at some of the things, as they were drawn forth and exhibited by different persons in the crowd; "those were Edric's books — that was his desk. Oh! my son! my son! what is become of him?"

Many sympathized with the unfortunate father, and more eagerly questioned each other as to the probable meaning of what they saw. No one, however, could give any explanation; and all was confusion and dismay. The bosom of Edmund, after the first moment of excitation had passed, was racked with anguish too bitter to allow him to feel curious even to know his brother's fate. But a few hours before, love and fortune seemed to unite in showering their choicest blessings upon his head, and now he was the most wretched of mankind; for if Claudia died, Rosabella or Elvira must be queen; and if Elvira should be chosen, all hopes of becoming her husband must be lost.

"Oh, God!" cried he, striking his forehead in agony, "why was I reserved for this? Why did I not perish fighting the battles of my country? And why was I saved only to be mocked with the hope of happiness, which, just as it seemed within my grasp, flies from me for ever? Wretch that I am! would that I had been never born, or at least had died in my nurse's arms, and thus escaped the tormenting pangs that now drive me to distraction!"

Whilst Edmund thus raved, the eye of Rosabella followed his every movement, and seemed with a fiend-like pleasure to exult in his agonies. "I am avenged," thought she; "he now feels what I have so often suffered. But this is not all; he must be probed to the quick ere he can know the bitter vengeance of a woman scorned."

Whilst these violent emotions were convulsing the bosoms of all around, the old duke knelt by the side of Elvira, gazing upon her with the most intense anxiety. Her gentle and feminine nature had been overpowered at seeing the blood of

The Mummy!

Claudia, and she still lay insensible, looking more exquisitely lovely than fancy can conceive. The beauty of Elvira was of the most soft and feminine description; long silken eyelashes shaded her dark hazel eyes, and gave them an expression more voluptuous than brilliant, whilst nothing could exceed the delicacy of her complexion, or the beauty of her full rosy lips. The figure of Elvira might not have served as the model of a courageous heroine, but it would have suited admirably for an Houri; and lovely as she always was, she had perhaps never looked more so than at this moment, as the returning blood softly retinted her cheeks, and her eyes gradually unclosed. Lord Edmund gazed upon her, till, maddened by the thought that he must lose her for ever, he could no longer endure his own sensations, and, darting amongst the crowd, he endeavoured to fly from the world and from himself.

The duke, on the contrary, saw the recovery of his daughter with unalloyed transport, for though he loved Edmund, and wished to have him for a son-in-law, he was by no means insensible to the prospect of seeing his daughter a Queen, and his breast throbbed with violent emotions, which had long been a stranger to it.

In the mean time the Mummy had stalked solemnly through the city, urged more by instinct than design; the mist that still clung over him, making him seem like one wandering in a dream. Yet still he advanced; his path, like that of a destroying angel, spreading consternation as he went, and all he met flying horror-stricken from his sight: many, however, when the monster had passed, crept softly back to gaze after him, and amongst this number was Mrs. Montagu, in whose breast curiosity, that vice of low minds, reigned predominant.

The whole family had reached home in perfect safety, the lady herself hurrying her return, the moment the accident of the Queen was made known: lest, as she said, in the confusion that might ensue, her servants might be induced to leave her house, and some evil disposed personages might strip it of its contents. Urged by this prudent motive, Mrs. Montagu had hastened home, and finding all safe, was just about to retire to re-arrange her disordered dress, when one of the servants rushed into the room with the account of a fearful spirit having been seen in the Strand, whose mysterious appearance, coupled with the singular accident that had happened to the Queen, seemed to portend some dreadful calamity that was about to fall upon the country.

"What is it like?" asked Mrs. Montagu; "have you seen it, Evelina?"

"Oh yes, ma'am!" cried the panting girl; "its eyes flare like fire, and it stares so wildly round it! and as it went along it saw a dead cat lying in the street; and it knelt down and took the creature up, and kissed it, and lamented over it in such a strange way, and in such a strange language! I never heard any thing like it in my life."

"Oh, dear! I should like to see it!" cried Mrs. Montagu, flying to the door, and holding it half open to secure a retreat in case of necessity. Just as she reached the street, however, fate, as though willing to gratify her curiosity, occasioned the Mummy to turn back; and with that kind of half pleasure and half pain, with which the good people of England sometimes delight to gaze upon any thing horrible, Mrs. Montagu continued to look as it rapidly approached her dwelling, till, as it reached the door, to her infinite horror it stalked towards it. Awe-struck and trembling, Mrs. Montagu retreated. The Mummy followed her. He stretched his hand out to her. She shrunk back aghast from his touch. "Lead on!" cried he with a voice of thunder. Mrs. Montagu could bear no more, and she fled screaming to the parlour, where her husband was already lost in some of his beloved calculations.

Absent as Mr. Montagu generally was, however, he was roused by this unexpected intrusion, and the blood ran chilly through his veins, as he saw the tall majestic figure of Cheops stride across the apartment. His athletic stature, his dark swarthy complexion, and his strongly marked features, aided by the fearful lustre of his piercing eyes, gave to his figure, swathed as it yet was in the vestments of the grave, a supernatural grandeur that thrilled through every nerve of Mr. Montagu's frame, and he shrunk back with horror as his fearful guest stalked past him.

Cheops saw his terror, and smiled in proud disdain as he threw himself upon a couch, placed near a window looking upon the garden, which, as we have before stated, shelved down to the river. There he lay, his eyes fixed upon the majestic Thames, whilst Mr. and Mrs. Montagu gazed with trembling limbs and pallid lips at their strange guest, without daring either to approach or disturb him.

"Thus have I watched the Nile," said Cheops, his awful voice sounding as from the tomb, "whilst the gently rising waters have gradually swelled into the flood which was to pour joy and plenty over the land: — and thus, too, have I lain, gazing upon its streams, when, the purpose of all-bounteous Nature having been fulfilled, it has sunk back, slowly retiring to its natural bed. But, oh! how different were the feelings that then throbbed in my breast, to the corroding fire that now consumes me! — Oh! Osiris! what horrid thoughts flash through my brain! — they come like overwhelming floods pouring from heaven to the great deep, sweeping all before them in one mighty ruin. — Oh! Arsinoë! by the fell rites of Typhon, there's madness in the thought!"

Then springing from the couch, his eyes glared with yet fiercer brilliancy as he flashed them round, whilst Mr. and Mrs. Montagu, terrified beyond the power of expression, flew towards the door, eyeing the motions of their dangerous guest with feelings of unspeakable horror. The storm of passions in the breast of Cheops, however, though tremendous, seemed soon allayed; for ere many moments had elapsed, he sank again upon the couch in a kind of lethargy, which, if it were not slumber, seemed at least to imply a temporary cessation from pain.

"Thank God!" whispered Mr. Montagu, as he motioned to his wife to creep out of the apartment. She tremblingly obeyed; and the moment she thought herself in safety, she threw herself upon her knees, and thanked God with more fervour than she had ever done before in her whole life; whilst the servants, who were all assembled in the ante-room, crowded round her, trembling and with pallid cheeks and white lips, clustering together like bees swarming round their queen.

"Oh, madam! madam!" exclaimed Angelina, in a whisper, "what will become of us? A serous moisture transudes from every pore in my body with the chilliness of death, and my very hair erects itself with horror upon my head."

"And my heart throbs with such violence," said Cecilia, "that the whole arterial system seems deranged."

"It is evidently an Egyptian Mummy," observed Mr. Montagu, and, as he seldom spoke, every word he uttered was listened to as an oracle. "Its language and its dress bespeak its origin, but by what strange event it has been resuscitated — "

At this moment a sharp knock at the door made the terrified servants all spring closer together, clinging to each other in an agony of nervous horror, and not one daring to approach the door. The knocking and ringing, however, at length became so violent, as to rouse even Mr. Montagu to give the clamorous intruders entrance. It was Father Morris and Sir Ambrose.

"Oh, my dear brother!" cried the latter, panting for breath; "have you heard the news? The strangest vision has appeared, and the Queen is certainly dying. Every one says it is a demon."

"What, the Mummy?" asked Mr. Montagu.

"Have you heard of it then?" said Sir Ambrose eagerly.

"It is now in this house," cried Mrs. Montagu.

"In this house!" repeated her brother-in-law; whilst Father Morris, who had looked pale and exhausted when he entered the hall, became still paler, and looked scarcely able to support himself.

"To arms!" cried Cheops from the inner room; "the Palli are upon us! Cowards that we are, the enemy are at our gates!"

Screaming, and scarcely knowing where they went, the terrified servants tumbled over each other in the hastiness of their retreat, huddling themselves together in a heap, yet keeping their eyes fixed upon the door from which they expected the spectre to appear, as though charmed by the fascination of a rattle-snake.

A loud crash now produced a fresh scream; then all was still. After a long pause, which seemed of endless duration, Father Morris, evidently with a dreadful effort, roused himself and advanced—

"Death itself is not so horrid as this suspense," said he, as he resolutely threw open the door of the room, which had contained the Mummy, and entered it. It was empty—but the broken frame-work of the window seemed to point out in what manner the awful visitor had made his exit.

It was with infinite difficulty that Mrs. Montagu could be persuaded to return to the room; and when she did, the remainder of the day was passed by her, and every inhabitant of her mansion, in fear and trembling. When they spoke, it was in whispers, and when they moved, they crept along with stealthy noiseless steps, as though they feared the echo of their own footsteps: the eyes of all fixed timidly upon the broken window, through which the fearful stranger had disappeared.

The Mummy!

Slowly and heavily the hours rolled on, till the time appointed for dinner arrived: the servants, as they served the meal, looking timidly around, instead of regarding the dishes they carried in their hands, and the family scarcely daring to eat, and only speaking in whispers, whilst they started every moment, fancying the wild eyes of Cheops again glared upon them, and his deep hollow voice again rang in their ears; and their own tones sounded strangely hoarse and unnatural. Nothing, however, had terrified Mrs. Montagu so much as the laugh of Cheops; strange, wild, and unearthly, it still seemed to ring in her ears, like the yell of a demon; whilst, if any thing that happened, chanced to recall the appalling sound, her limbs shook in every joint; her teeth chattered in her head; terror blanched her lips and cheeks to a ghastly paleness, and she seemed every instant upon the point of rising from her seat and flying shrieking from the room.

In the mean time, the sensations these extraordinary events had created amongst the people were indescribable. Strange rumours and contradictory reports were circulated, and the most incredible stories invented of all that had passed. The minds of men became bewildered; they knew not what to credit nor what to think; a gloomy presentiment hung over them; they seemed to feel some fearful change was at hand, but scarcely knew what to hope or what to fear. Business was at a stand: people indeed gathered together in the shops, but it was only to whisper secretly to each other, strange mysterious stories of the late marvellous events, which they dared not breathe in public. The extremes of ignorance and civilization tend alike to produce credulity, and the wildest and most improbable stories were as greedily swallowed by the most enlightened people in the world, as they could have been even by a horde of uncultivated barbarians.

The family of Mr. Montagu retired early to rest at the close of the eventful day we have been speaking of, hoping to lose in sleep the remembrance of the harassing events they had so lately witnessed. Lord Edmund had returned soon after the disappearance of the Mummy; but he had locked himself in his chamber, and had refused to see any one, his mind being too much agitated for him to endure the common forms of society. All was soon quiet throughout the mansion.

It was midnight when a tall figure wrapped in a large cloak, appeared slowly gliding with catlike steps through the garden of Mr. Montagu. It cautiously avoided the light, and crept along the shadiest walks and thickest allies, carefully shrouding itself from observation, and endeavouring, by availing itself of the shelter of the trees, the better to conceal its movements. It has been already stated that the garden of Mr. Montagu was only separated from that of the duke by a terrace very little used; the door, indeed, leading to it from Mr. Montagu's premises, had been so long closed up, as to be nearly forgotten, and yet it was towards this unfrequented spot that the mysterious figure directed its course. The long neglected door slowly opened, and the stream of light it admitted, was obscured for a moment by a passing shade; and then all seemed dark, silent, and mysterious as before.

"It certainly went that way," said a voice, the preciseness of which marked it as belonging to Abelard; "and it was a real, tangible, material form, as I saw its shadow intercept the light when the door was opened and it passed through."

"It is quite impossible," cried Evelina, one of Mrs. Montagu's housemaids, who having been induced by the inconstant butler to take a ramble with him by moonlight, had also witnessed this strange apparition; "you must be mistaken Mr. Abelard, for that door has not been opened this age. It is even nailed up, as you may see yourself if you examine it."

"It is very strange," said Abelard, after he had tried the door and found it immovable; "I certainly saw it open."

"It must have been an optical delusion, Mr. Abelard," said Evelina; "the retina of the eye is sometimes strangely affected, and represents objects quite different to what they really are."

"I must consult Father Morris about it to-morrow," resumed the butler; "for it was certainly the Mummy spectre."

"La! do you think so, Mr. Abelard?" said Evelina, turning pale; "why then didn't you speak to it."

"I will if it comes again," returned Abelard.

"Oh! there it is!" cried Evelina; and the worthy pair flew back to the house, screaming in concert, and without once daring to look behind them. Scarcely, however, had the last echo of their footsteps died away upon the ear, when the figure emerged from the recess in which it had lain concealed, and again crept slowly towards the door leading into the garden of the duke.

"Hist! Marianne!" cried he, pausing for a reply; but all was still. "Marianne!" repeated he still louder—"Fools! dolts! idiots!" continued he, stamping violently, as he still found his call of no avail; "they have kept me so long with their cursed folly, that she is gone. Eternal misery haunt them for their officious babbling. By Heaven! if they had had the sense to climb the wall, I had been lost:—but hark, she comes!"

The door now slowly opened, and a female figure holding a light appeared.

"How is she?" cried the stranger.

"Better," returned the female.

"Then it is past the power of man to kill her," resumed the first; and rushing wildly past her he buried himself in the deepest recesses of the grove.

CHAPTER XIII.

Father Morris, when Abelard and Evelina confessed to him the following morning the strange spectre they had witnessed, treated the whole as the mere vision of their heated imaginations, and refusing to listen to any of their surmises respecting it, prepared to attend the Queen, who, finding herself sufficiently recovered to be able to attend to the duties of religion, had, from the general reputation of his superior sanctity, sent for him to confess her. Her Majesty, indeed, seemed rapidly improving, and the hopes of Edmund reviving with her health, he passed every hour he could abstract from the duties of his station, at the feet of his adored Elvira, his love for whom, seemed increased by the imminence of the danger he had just escaped, of losing her for ever.

In this manner several days had passed, and the strange visit of the Mummy, and the accident of the Queen, had already taken their place on the shelf with the other événements passés of the day; when one morning Sir Ambrose was startled by an earnest message from the Duke of Cornwall, entreating him to come to him without delay. Sir Ambrose immediately obeyed the summons, and found the duke walking up and down his study in a state of the greatest agitation, which Father Morris was vainly endeavouring to tranquillize.

"Oh, my beloved friend!" exclaimed the duke, springing forward and grasping the baronet's hand the moment he saw him approach: "my dear Sir Ambrose, Claudia is no more!"

"Dead!" cried Sir Ambrose, involuntarily looking at Father Morris, whose aspect, however, still preserved only its usual cold and statue-like appearance. "Are you sure that she is dead?—I thought she was better."

"So we all did," said the duke: "but alas! we deceived ourselves, for Father Morris has just seen her expire. Oh! where is Edmund—why is he not with you?—what will become of him? It will destroy him to lose Elvira: and I, too, that have felt so proud in the expectation of his becoming my son-in-law, oh, it will break my heart!"

"Oh!" cried Father Murphy, who was also present; "and if that's the case, why don't you let Rosabella take the crown at once, and make no more fuss about it."

"And yet," continued the duke, "I cannot bear that Elvira should be deprived of her right, she would so become a crown;

and with her inflexible sense of justice, and desire for improvement, she would do so much good that I should not feel justified in depriving the country of such a sovereign."

"Thus," said Father Morris, smiling, "do we deceive ourselves; you are ambitious whilst you think that you are only just. Believe me, if you consult Elvira's real happiness, you will not impose upon her the troublesome duties of a crown: she will make a better wife than a queen; for her gentle nature is less fitted to command than to obey. Rosabella has more firmness."

"I do not agree with you, Father," said Sir Ambrose; "in my opinion Elvira is infinitely better fitted to be a queen than Rosabella, for her passions are more under the control of reason."

"That is to say," resumed the monk, sneeringly, "they have not yet been called into play."

"What do you mean, Father?" began the duke.

"Nothing that could give you offence, my Lord," returned the priest. "Disgusted myself with the world, I naturally thought the princess most likely to find happiness where I seek it myself—viz. in a life of quiet and retirement."

"Enough," said the duke: "but where is Edmund? Let us seek him; no doubt he is with Elvira—poor things! we must spoil their billing and cooing."

Edmund was with Elvira, and was passionately urging his suit, whilst she, engaged with her embroidery frame, listened with a half abstracted mind, and Emma duteously waited behind her chair.

"You do not love me," said he, "or you could not answer with such provoking coldness."

"Indeed I do, Edmund, but you are so unreasonable. I have already told you I have no idea of that passionate overwhelming love you appear to feel, it absolutely terrifies me, and I am sure it is not natural to my character.—This silk is too dark, Emma—and so, Edmund, if you feel you cannot be happy with such love as it is in my power to bestow, we had better determine at once to separate."

"Good God!" exclaimed Edmund, striking his forehead violently with his clenched hand; "how coldly you talk of our separation!"

"What can I do? I try every thing in my power to please you. Emma, give me my scissors. But since you will not hear reason—"

"Reason!" cried Edmund fiercely, seizing her arm, and then letting it go again; "If you talk of reason you will drive me distracted!"

"You quite terrify me with your violence, Edmund," said Elvira, rising, and preparing to quit the room.

"Oh stay! stay, my adored Elvira!" exclaimed Lord Edmund, throwing himself upon his knees and catching her hand; "for Heaven's sake, stay! pardon my impetuosity—frown upon me, treat me with coldness, disdain, or contempt, but do not, do not leave me."

"I do not know what you wish; I have repeatedly told you I am ready to become your wife whenever our parents think fit; and that I will do every thing in my power to make you happy. Do you call that coldness?"

"I do—I do indeed: freezing, insulting coldness. Oh, Elvira! I would rather see you spurn me—hear you declare you hated me, or know that you doomed me to destruction, than hear you speak of our marriage in that calm, unvaried tone."

"How unreasonable you are!" said Elvira, smiling. "Hear him, Emma; is he not a singular being? And if I find it so difficult to please him now, what must I expect when I become his wife?"

"Tormenting girl!" exclaimed Edmund, "you know your power but too well."

"What ridiculous creatures these lords of the creation are!" said Elvira, playfully holding out her hand to Edmund, though she still affected to address Emma; "I really don't think any of them know what they would have; and I believe the only way to manage them is to make one's-self perfectly disagreeable."

"That you can never do," cried Edmund, rapturously kissing her hand.

At this moment a slight tap at the door announced the arrival of the duke and his friends.

The Mummy!

"So, so!" said the duke, "we have found you, have we? but you must take your leave of such tender scenes for the future."

"What do you mean?" asked Edmund.

"The Queen is dead," said Sir Ambrose. The glowing countenance of Edmund turned of a ghastly paleness; and his livid lips quivered, as he leaned against the window for support.

"Assist him!" cried the duke. "He will faint! Don't distress yourself, Edmund; the death of Claudia shall make no alteration in your prospects."

"I am better," said Edmund faintly, attempting to smile, and waving off all assistance; "'Twas but for a moment: the suddenness of the shock overcame me: I thought the Queen was better."

"She was supposed so," returned the duke; "but it seems she had some internal malady her physicians were not aware of. An inward bruise, I believe. But don't make yourself unhappy about it, Edmund; I cannot bear to see you wretched. Let Rosabella take the crown, and think no more about it."

"Your Grace wrongs me," said Edmund, his fine countenance glowing with the exalted feelings of his soul. "However I may suffer from the violence of my feelings, I can never permit them to interfere with my sense of duty. Elvira has a right to ascend the throne, and if my exertions can ensure her success, she shall be Queen."

"Thou art a brave lad!" cried the duke. "And will you really try to secure the election of Elvira, when you know, by so doing, you will deprive yourself of her for ever?"

"I shall do my duty," said Lord Edmund, pressing his lips firmly together, as though to suppress his feelings. Father Morris looked at him from under his over-shadowing cowl with a kind of sardonic smile, which seemed to say "You speak well, but let us see how you will act."

"My noble Edmund!" murmured Sir Ambrose, tears rolling down his cheeks.

Elvira's eyes thanked her lover for his disinterestedness; and the glow of anticipated triumph which flushed her cheeks, betrayed, that neither her love for Edmund, nor the grief for the loss of her cousin, could suppress her joy at the flattering prospect opened before her. "Elvira!" said Lord Edmund, gazing upon her earnestly, as though he would penetrate the inmost recesses of her bosom. "What are your wishes? Do not hesitate to declare them, for alas! much hangs upon your words."

Elvira blushed, and cast her eyes upon the ground; however, Lord Edmund comprehended but too well the meaning of her silence, and he sighed deeply. "It is enough," said he, in a mournful tone; "then the die is cast." He paused a few moments, whilst his friends, though they all looked at him with the deepest commiseration, respected his emotion too much to venture to interrupt it: then rousing himself, he hastily brushed a tear from his eye, and exclaimed, "How weak is human nature! I know my duty, and I will perform it; but yet—Oh Elvira!"

"Compose yourself, my beloved Edmund," said his father; "to-morrow you will be more calm."

"Oh, talk not of to-morrow!" replied Edmund; "to-day is the season for action. Keep the death of Claudia concealed a few hours, if possible. I will in the mean time assemble my friends: I know the army is devoted to me. A council of state will be chosen to direct the kingdom during the interregnum. I must be one of its members: some weeks must elapse before the election can take place, I think?"

"Three months is the time fixed," said the duke: "but you know the votes of all the people are to be collected, and that, with such a population as ours, will be no trifle: to be sure, it is the deputies that are to do the business, but then it will take some time to elect them."

"When the founder of the present dynasty ordained her successor should be chosen by the votes of the whole people," said Sir Ambrose; "she wisely recollected the difficulty that must arise from collecting their votes impartially, and directed they should elect deputies; but when she ordered that every ten thousand men throughout the kingdom should choose a deputy of their own rank and station to come to London to represent them, she did not calculate upon the immensity of our present population, nor think of the evils the presence of such a disorderly body of men must bring upon the capital."

"Yet any attempt to reduce their number, would inevitably overturn the government," observed Father Morris; "for as it is the only act of freedom the people have long been permitted to enjoy, they will be proportionably tenacious of it."

"And the majority of these deputies are to decide the election," said Edmund, musing; "then our business must be to secure that majority. Think you that any good can be done by endeavouring to procure the return of those who are disposed to be favourable to us?"

"Very little," returned Father Morris, to whom this observation was addressed; "for the lower classes, from their conceit and pedantry, are extremely difficult to manage. Their deputies, however, notwithstanding the ordinance of the Queen, will probably be more polished, and less learned, as the lower classes will be ill able to spare the time necessary to become deputies, whilst the country gentlemen will be delighted to obtain something to do."

"We must be prompt," said the duke, "at all events. I don't like delay."

"True!" replied Edmund, starting from a reverie into which he had fallen; "I must get myself nominated a member of the council, and we must arrange our other plans afterwards."

The party now separated, and Elvira, left alone with her companion, indulged in dreams of future grandeur. "I am sorry for the death of Claudia," said she, "but I never loved her; she was so cold and uninteresting—such a mere matter-of-fact being—she had no soul, Emma, and how can one love a being so totally passionless and insipid? I wonder," continued she, after a short pause, "what Henry Seymour will think of this?"

Emma smiled. "Poor Lord Edmund!" said she.

"I know what you would say," returned Elvira; "I am sorry for him, and I admire his conduct extremely. There is really something very noble about him."

Emma again smiled, for she saw, in spite of this admiration, that in a week poor Lord Edmund would be forgotten.

In the mean time, poor Rosabella's mind was a prey to the most violent passions. A billet from Father Morris had informed her of the death of her cousin, and of the designs brooding against her interests. "I will be revenged," said she; "I will show them mine is not a soul to dwell upon impotent grief. I will assemble my friends; my father's party was strong in the state; it cannot be quite extinct. Let me see, to whom shall I apply?"

"The Lords Noodle and Doodle (both of ancient families) were both devoted to your father, and were under great obligations to him when they were young," observed Marianne.

"But they are such fools!" said Rosabella.

"They are well connected," returned her confidant; "and power does not always attend upon talent."

"True, and, as they are so weak, I may guide them as I will."

"Do not rely upon that: folly is generally obstinate; and though there may be hopes of convincing a man of sense, fools will always have their own way."

"How then are they to be dealt with?"

"By letting them fancy they direct, when, in fact, they are directed. Apply to Lords Noodle and Doodle, as though for advice, more than assistance. Consult them how you ought to act, and suggest the advantages that will arise from your possessing the throne so artfully, that they may fancy what you say the dictates of their own minds, and then, if they advise any course, they in some measure pledge themselves to support you, if you pursue it."

"I do not doubt obtaining their sanction, and that of Lord Gustavus de Montfort; but I wish I could also obtain the countenance of Dr. Hardman, for he has many friends, and some talents," said Rosabella; "and I own I do not feel satisfied to trust myself entirely in the hands of any of the others."

"Talk of liberty and public spirit," replied Marianne; "promise a redress of grievances, and a radical reform of all evils, and you may secure Dr. Hardman. Yet he is not a fool; nay, he is even shrewd, penetrating, and persevering; but as lunatics are generally mad only upon one subject, so even men of sense have generally some prevailing folly, and his is, that of being thought of importance in the state. Indeed, in my opinion, there are very few human beings that we may not make subservient to our views, if we have but penetration enough to discover their weak sides, and art enough to avail ourselves of the discovery."

"The world is very much obliged to you for the high opinion you have of it," returned Rosabella; "however, I like your advice, and will pursue it. But do you think Father Morris will approve?"

"Oh, I will answer for him," interrupted Marianne.

"I will then write to each of the three lords," continued Rosabella; "and appoint a time and place for an interview with each. I must attend to the doctor afterwards."

"Beware," said Marianne; "you have a difficult game to play. The old proverb says, it is well to have two strings to one's bow; but four, I fear, will be too much for you to manage."

"Fear me not," cried her mistress; "impetuous as I generally am, I can be cautious when I see occasion."

In pursuance of her resolution, Rosabella wrote to the noblemen, whose assistance she wished to secure; and receiving favourable answers, the hour of twelve that night was fixed upon for a secret meeting between Lord Gustavus and herself upon the subject. The utmost secrecy was requisite, as Rosabella knew the fiery temper of her uncle, and felt confident, that if he discovered her plans before they were ripe for execution, his vengeance would have no bounds. She wished, therefore, to ascertain her strength privately; and, as she was aware a fruitless struggle would only involve her in ruin, she resolved not to betray her intentions till there appeared at least a fair prospect of success.

For this reason, when the duke informed her of the death of the Queen, she affected only the surprise she might naturally be supposed to feel at the suddenness of the event; and appeared absorbed in grief for the loss of her cousin, without seeming even to think of the consequences likely to ensue to herself; in short, she acted her part so well, that the duke was completely deceived; and when he returned to Sir Ambrose, after his conference with her, he exclaimed, "We had no occasion to alarm ourselves, or give ourselves so much trouble: I don't believe Rosabella even thinks about the throne; and I am sure she doesn't care a straw whether she has it or not. I am even confident, from what I have seen to-night, that I have only to express my wishes in favour of Elvira, to have her resign all pretensions immediately."

Sir Ambrose smiled and shook his head incredulously, and the duke was provoked; for, like all weak, obstinate men, he was extremely tenacious of the infallibility of his judgment.

"Why do you shake your head?" said he; "Do you disbelieve my assertion?"

"I do not disbelieve your assertion; I only doubt your penetration!"

"And why do you doubt that?"

"Because I know Rosabella."

"Then you think her indifference affected?"

"I think it too great to be real. Moderation is not by any means a characteristic of Rosabella. She is ever in extremes; and when she appears otherwise, depend upon it she is only acting a part, and she has some end in view that she hopes to gain by it."

"Well, let her be as sly as she will, she cannot deceive me! I'll watch her! I'll defy her to think, walk, look, or speak, without my knowing of it; and if I find she nourishes even the thought of rivalling Elvira, she shall quit my house immediately. I will encourage no vipers."

Sir Ambrose smiled inwardly at the mistaken confidence of his friend in his own judgment. Thinking it useless, however, to irritate him by farther opposition, he endeavoured to turn the conversation upon another subject. "It is strange," said he, "how frequently I have been thinking of that Mummy. If there be no deception in the business, it is a perfect miracle!"

"And what deception can there be?" returned the duke, peevishly: "you think yourself so very wise, and that you know so much better than other people, only because you are always suspecting something wrong. Now, for my part, I think, as poor Dr. Entwerfen used to say, 'Incredulity is often as much the offspring of folly as credulity'!"

"I wonder what has become of the doctor and Edric? for, ill as Edric behaved, he is still my son; and I own I should like to know where he is."

"Oh! I don't think you have the least occasion in the world to trouble yourself about him. Depend upon it, he and his mad friend, Doctor Entwerfen are rambling about Egypt, and are happier now than ever they were before in their lives."

"If you are right," said Sir Ambrose, "and they are now in Egypt; as they have lost their balloon, they may be even in want of necessaries."

"And it is very right they should be so," replied the duke; "what business had they to go away?"

The hours of this eventful day rolled on heavily with Rosabella; the important consequences of the struggle she was about to engage in forcibly impressed her mind. Ruin must inevitably ensue if she failed, and even if she succeeded, her path seemed strewed with thorns. The anxiety natural to the intrigues she was about to be involved in, also hung about her. Though haughty and vindictive, Rosabella was not naturally deceitful. Indeed the very violence and impetuosity of her passions rendered it difficult for her to appear otherwise than she really was. The secret intercourse, however, which, through the intervention of Marianne, she had long maintained with Father Morris, had somewhat practised her in concealment, but it was still repugnant to her nature. She was now anxiously expecting a visit from the reverend father, and as he was generally remarkably punctual to his appointments, his non-appearance filled her with a sensation of dread; and a presentiment of evil crept over her, that she tried in vain to overcome.

"It is long past the hour the father mentioned," said Marianne, after a long pause, during which she had been listening with the utmost attention to every sound. "I cannot imagine the cause of his absence. Surely our plans have not been discovered." And as she spoke, her blanched cheeks and livid lips betrayal the deep interest she took in his fate.

"How gloomily that heavy bell clangs in my ear!" said Rosabella; "it seems to ring the death-knell of my hopes. A gloomy foreboding hangs upon my mind, and undefinable horrors rise in dim perspective before me."

"Hark!" cried Marianne, her sense of hearing sharpened by anxiety; "he comes! yes, yes, he comes," added she, after a short pause; and in a few seconds Rosabella heard the Father's well-known step. "You are very late," said she, as he entered the room.

"Good God! what is the matter?" asked Marianne, as the haggard, agitated features of the priest met her eye. "You look like one who has held communion with infernal spirits."

"You say right, Marianne," replied the Father, in a deep hollow tone; "I have, indeed, conversed with spirits — for never could those fearful eyes that so long have glared upon me, belong to mortal."

"What do you mean?" asked Rosabella.

"I have again seen the Mummy! that fearful spectre from the tomb. I have even conversed with him, and he lives and breathes; nay even reasons, thinks, and speaks like a human being; but the cerecloths of the grave are still wrapped round him, his fearful eyes glare with unearthly lustre, and his deep sepulchral voice thrills through every nerve."

"What, that horrid creature whom we saw descend from above at the very moment of Claudia's accident? Heaven grant no horrible consequences may ensue from so awful an invasion of the general laws of nature!" said Rosabella.

"Are you certain it is no deception?" asked Marianne.

"Deception!" returned the priest, "even I trembled, Marianne, when I gazed upon the countenance of that tremendous being, and read there the traces of fierce and ungoverned passions, wild and destructive in their course as the raging whirlwind. Even I, dreaded the influence he might exert upon our destinies, and shuddered at the thought of such a creature's being released from the fetters of the tomb, and sent back as a destroying spirit upon earth. The eternal gloom that hangs upon his brow, seems to bespeak a fallen angel, for such is the deadly hate that must have animated the rebellious spirits when expelled from heaven. His look is terrific; and my blood froze in my veins at his horrid laugh, which seemed to ring in my ears like the mockery of fiends when they have involved a human being inextricably in their toils."

"It may be a fiend," murmured Marianne, in a low whisper. At this moment, the clock struck twelve.

Rosabella started at the sound. "Lord Gustavus will expect me," cried she.

"Go, then," replied the priest, "with Marianne. I will follow presently."

With trembling limbs, beating heart, and all the trepidation which the consciousness of guilt cannot fail to give even to the firmest mind, Rosabella and Marianne proceeded to the terrace, where they found Lord Gustavus waiting to receive them.

"You may think it strange, my Lord," said the agitated princess, as she advanced, leaving her confidant at the gate which led from the garden, "that I should desire this meeting."

The Mummy!

"By no means—by no means," said Lord Gustavus, condescendingly. "Indeed, I have already had some conversation with an emissary of yours, that has let me into your views; and I find from him your ideas upon several important subjects are so clear, so just, so sensible, and so accordant with my own, that I feel disposed to become your partizan, even before you utter a syllable."

"And who is this emissary?" asked Rosabella, unable to account for a reception so unexpectedly gracious, and alarmed at what she feared a premature exposure of her plans.

"Father Morris," replied Lord Gustavus, alarmed in his turn, lest he should have unguardedly committed himself: "he told me, he was an accredited agent of yours, and even induced me to—to—"

"Your Lordship need not hesitate," returned Rosabella; "I was not aware, that Father Morris had seen you, or I should not have expressed surprise."

"I have been induced then," said Lord Gustavus, "to bring with me two friends of mine, Lord Maysworth and Dr. Hardman. They are fully convinced of the justness of your ideas respecting retrenchment and reform; and they think your plans of curtailing the expenditure, by throwing all the power of the state into the hands of a few trustworthy individuals, upon whom you may thoroughly rely, (such as them or myself, for instance,) most excellent."

Poor Rosabella was here completely puzzled, as she had not the slightest idea of what plan Lord Gustavus could possibly allude to; nor indeed was it probable she should, it being entirely the offspring of the creative brain of Father Morris, invented by him solely for the purpose of the winning of the noble lords, to whom he had confided it, over to her party. Rosabella was naturally quick, and, possessing abundantly that very unexplainable, but well-known faculty, designated "tact," she instantly divined the motive that had induced Father Morris to attribute this scheme to her, and determined to avoid, if possible, betraying her ignorance.

Lord Maysworth and Dr. Hardman, who had remained at a little distance, and whom the agitation of Rosabella had prevented her before seeing, now advanced; and after having been presented to the princess, the former assured her of his devotion to her cause.

"I admire your ideas exceedingly," said he; "and particularly your intention of removing Lord Edmund from the command of the army, and placing an older and more experienced person in his stead."

"Lord Edmund!" cried Rosabella, thrown off her guard by the sudden mention of that name.

"Father Morris told me so," resumed Lord Maysworth, in surprise.

"And he told you truly," interrupted Rosabella. "Father Morris is worthy of all the confidence I can repose in him; and, in fact, he knows my inmost thoughts; but I was not aware that he had seen you."

A conversation now ensued, in the course of which Lord Maysworth detailed, with admirable minuteness, a variety of subjects calling for reform. Rosabella did not understand half he said, for his calculations bewildered her; and her mind, accustomed to soar with the eagle flight of genius, and take in oceans with a glance, could scarcely condescend to listen to the petty articles of economy in expenditure, to which it seemed principally his object to draw her attention. She assented, however, to all he said; and having let him speak as long as he liked, without showing symptoms of weariness, and having luckily said 'yes' and 'no' in the right places, he departed quite enchanted, and completely gained over to her party, declaring her to be, without exception, one of the most sensible young women he had ever conversed with in his life. To this, Lord Gustavus and Dr. Hardman assented, as she had appeared also to acquiesce in all they had said; and the noble lords and learned doctor departed perfectly satisfied.

Scarcely were they gone, when Father Morris appeared. "My dear father!" exclaimed Rosabella, enraptured at the result of the interview, "congratulate me! Lord Maysworth, Dr. Hardman, and Lord Gustavus, are our own."

"I rejoice sincerely, my child," returned the priest; "for Heaven knows I feel as great an interest in your welfare as in my own. But what did they say? Let us hear if your hopes are well founded."

"At first their expressions were rather of a negative nature — for they told me rather that a party existed against my rival, than for myself. They say the duke has many enemies, from his obstinate and conceited disposition; they said also that my father had had many friends."

"And do they exist no longer then, that you lay such emphasis on the word had?'" asked Father Morris bitterly.

"They exist, but it seems my father has been so unfortunate as to lose their friendship," returned Rosabella; "Lord Gustavus even alluded to some crime, which he said he had committed."

"Crime! Did he dare to call it crime?"

"He did indeed, and it is not possible to describe the torture that rent my bosom as he spoke. I always knew my father had been unfortunate, but I never before even suspected him of having been guilty."

"Nor was he guilty, girl! none but fools or idiots dare breathe such an accusation against his name."

"Ten thousand blessings on you for relieving my mind from the agony of believing him unworthy of my love. I am perfectly satisfied with your assurance; and yet, methinks, I would fain know his history."

"Rosabella, you never knew your father; you were but three years old when circumstances occurred that urged him to commit a deed of desperation. Seek not to inquire farther; and endeavour, since misfortune has thrown a shade over your father's name, to redeem it by the lustre of your own."

"As an obscure individual, whatever might be my will, power would be wanting."

"But it shall not be wanting. You shall be Queen. I swear it, though all the powers of heaven and earth should unite to oppose my designs, and though even blood should be necessary to seal the compact—"

He was going on when a fiendish laugh rang in his ears; and, looking up, he beheld the gigantic form of Cheops standing over him. The bright moonbeams showed, with horrible distinctness, the strange attire, savage features, and unearthly gaze of the Mummy, as his horrid laugh echoed from the wall behind them and pealed across the water. Rosabella had not before seen him, except when she knelt before the dying Queen; and, shrieking with horror, she fled for refuge to her uncle's garden, whilst Cheops thus tauntingly addressed the priest.

"You were conspiring mischief. Though the language your lips employed was unknown to me, that of your looks was clear. Men do not cast their eyes upon the earth, and murmur forth their accents as though they trembled at the sound of their own voices, when their purposes are such as will bear avowal. Make me your confidant, and by the aid of my serpent deity, my guardian Cneph, I may assist you: but force me to become your enemy, and Typhon himself never pursued Isis and the infant Horus with more unrelenting vengeance than I will follow you and destroy your plans."

Dreading alike to trust, or enrage this mysterious being, and cursing the evil chance that had led him to that spot, Father Morris, who, like all the English in those days, was an universal linguist, found himself obliged partially to obey this injunction, and inform the Mummy of his design. Cheops burst into one of his terrific laughs of derision. "And so," he said, "you would make yonder feeble girl who fled screaming at my approach, a Queen. A fit monarch for a warlike people. Can a woman's arm resist an invasion of the Palli, or a woman's hands direct the reins of Mizraim's government? Alas! alas! where am I wandering? I forgot the change wrought in my destiny, and that your people seem powerless as the sovereign you would give them. Be satisfied, I will not betray thee. Indeed, so do I hate thy countrymen, that I shall rejoice to see thee triumph in deceiving them. Beware, however, how thou attemptest to deceive me, lest my vengeance, quick, sure, and unforeseen as the secret agency of the Epoptæ, should fall upon and crush thee at the very moment of the fruition of thy wishes."

Fearing, whilst he hated the mysterious being thus strangely thrust into his most inmost secrets, Father Morris promised obedience, and the Mummy retreated within the walls of Mrs. Montagu's garden; ere he left the priest, however, he held out his hand to him. "Give me your hand," said he, "and let us seal our compact." Father Morris shuddered as he obeyed; for the words of the Mummy recalled those he had just employed, when this fearful apparition broke in upon him, and brought with them a train of thoughts he would now willingly have shaken off. He did not dare, however, to refuse, and reluctantly held out his hand: the Mummy seized it with an iron grasp, and an icy chill seemed to creep from his hand to Father Morris's heart, as he burst into one of his demon-like laughs and left him.

Father Morris, unable to shake off the horror that oppressed him, for he felt as though he had entered into a compact with a fiend, stood gazing at the supernatural appearance of Cheops as he stalked across the terrace. His gaunt figure (rendered more

The Mummy!

awful by the grave-clothes that bound it) was magnified in the moonbeams, which seemed to increase, rather than to mitigate the unearthly ugliness of the apparition they shone upon. The priest was fixed in a fearful trance: in imagination, he still felt the cold and iron grasp of the Mummy, whose eyes seemed as though they were still looking into his very soul, and whose solemn accents were even now scaring his faculties. At length, however, Father Morris recovered something of his self-possession, and fled from the spot (he scarcely knew in what direction) under the fear, at every turning, of again encountering the dreaded Mummy!

CHAPTER XIV.

When the reverend father took refuge in his chamber after this fearful and memorable interview, he felt that strange mysterious sensation of something dreadful hanging over him, though he scarcely knew what, which so often weighs upon the mind when any great and unexpected change has taken place in our destiny. He threw himself upon a sofa, and endeavoured in vain to analyze his feelings. He was not superstitious; but there was something about the Mummy that inspired him with awe in spite of himself, and he felt that he was no longer his own master, for a supernatural power seemed to mingle with his designs, and control his actions: he endeavoured in vain to recur to the plans he had that morning arranged for gaining over partizans to the side of Rosabella; he could not govern his ideas; he could no longer direct them as he wished; one sole thought occupied his mind, one sole image floated before his senses. He held his head with his hands, he pressed them firmly against his ears, and closed his eyes, as though by shutting out external objects his mind could recover its tone. It was all in vain! the gaunt figure of the Mummy still seemed to stalk before his eyes, and his fiendish laugh still to ring in his ears. Father Morris rose from his couch and threw open his window; the cool evening breeze revived him, and restored his faculties. He now began to reason with himself.

"It is very strange," said he; "but, unaccountable though it may seem, the destinies of this fearful being are evidently interwoven with mine. His appearance here at this eventful moment, and his forcing himself upon my confidence, which a secret power superior to my own prevented the possibility of my refusing him, cannot surely be accidental. No, no—he is permitted to revisit this earth for some positive and definite purpose; perchance to counteract my plans, perchance to aid them. There is no vanity in the thought; for upon my destiny, at this moment, hangs that of a mighty empire, and I feel that I am but a blind instrument in the hands of Fate, condemned to work, mole-like, in the dark, uncertain whether I be not drawing destruction upon my head at the very moment when I fancy I am attaining the pinnacle of happiness and glory. However, I will not be wanting to myself; this strange agent may be sent to aid me, and it shall not be my fault if I do not avail myself of his assistance. In his present garb he creates disgust and terror; but clothed as a human being, his superhuman eloquence, and the strange fearful interest excited by his looks and manner, might render him a powerful assistant. It shall be my present business, then, to endeavour to make him serviceable to my views; and to do this I must persuade him to adopt the dress and manners of the country."

Pleased with the resolution he had taken, and quite forgetting the lateness of the hour, Father Morris descended hastily to the usual sitting room of Mrs. Montagu; but what was his horror, on entering it, to find, instead of the usual cheerful party he expected, only the dreaded Mummy! Cheops again lay stretched upon the couch he had before occupied, his eyes fixed upon the brilliant constellation of Orion, and his lips murmuring an address to the deity he fancied it to represent.

"Yes, blessed Horus!" cried Cheops, as Father Morris entered the room; "thou wilt hear my prayer, for thou hast also been a stranger in a foreign land; forced even in thy mother's arms to fly, pursued by all the fury of fell Typhon's rage; thou knowest how to pity the unhappy! And thou too, bright Isis!" continued he, addressing the moon, "thou also hast known sorrow; when thy streaming tears occasioned the first overflowing of the Nile, and grief for the loss of Osiris rent thy bosom with despair—then becamest thou well fitted to be patroness of the wretched. O Arsinoë! could I but recall the fatal moment when I saw thee last!"

"Despair is sinful," said Father Morris, who now stood beside him; "repentance may obtain forgiveness even of the most heinous crimes."

Cheops started upon his feet at the sound of the father's voice, and burst into one of his fearful laughs: "And who art thou," cried he, "who presumest to preach repentance to me? Oh! I know thee now, thou art the priest whose confidant I am become. But though I will aid thee, think not I will be thy slave—no, rather art thou mine, for thou art in my power!"

Father Morris felt his blood curdle in his veins at this address, and, though he strove to speak, his tongue clove to the roof of his mouth, and he could not articulate a word. Cheops saw his embarrassment, and continued in a milder tone, "Fear nothing; we may be useful to each other. I would fain quit these garments of the tomb, and since I seem destined to remain some time amongst your fellow-men, I will endeavour to assume their manners. You seem to have influence amongst them; try, then, to pacify their fears, and teach them to regard me as a fellow-being."

At this moment the solemn clang of a deep-toned bell fell heavily upon their ears. Cheops started at the sound, and, springing from the couch on which he had reclined, bent forward eagerly to listen as it slowly pealed through the deep silence of the night. It was the great bell of the ancient cathedral of St. Paul, which tolled to announce that on the following day the body of the deceased Queen would lie in state.

"What is it?" cried Cheops; "whence comes that fearful knell, awful as the sound which is doomed to sink into the souls of the initiate of the Isian mysteries? Again it tolls; speak! whence comes it? what does it foretell? Is it the signal of another change of existence, strange, awful, and mysterious, as that I have already experienced? Let it come, I am prepared. The gods cannot inflict tortures more horrid than those I already suffer. Cannot! have I said? dread Osiris, forgive the impious thought! Methinks e'en now I see thy dark blue countenance frowning in awful majesty at my unguarded rashness. Forgive me, mighty Spirit! No longer will I repine at thy decrees, but teach my proud rebellious heart submission. Alas! alas! had I before done so. But it is now too late, and happiness is lost to me for ever."

Sighing, he hid his face in his hands as he spoke; and all again was silent, save the deep-toned bell, which still fell heavily at intervals upon the ear. Slowly the hours rolled on, yet still Father Morris sate gazing on the Mummy, till the first bright tints of morning broke through the dark grey sky, and a half-subdued bustle in the streets, as of people hurrying to and fro, announced that preparations were making to hang them with black.

The confused murmur—the busy voices hushed to whispers, and the still-continued tolling of the muffled bell, harmonized with the fearful form of the Mummy-visitant, which, now seen dimly by the uncertain shades of the breaking twilight, seemed to acquire fresh horrors from the obscure and wavering gleams thrown upon it. It was at this moment, when objects were gradually becoming more distinct every instant, that Lord Edmund rushed into the room—"Father Morris," cried he, "you must aid me, or all is lost!"

And as he spoke, he started back aghast; for the terrific form of the Mummy struck upon his sight. He had seen him, it was true, on his first descent; but the events that had since occurred, involving as they did the dearest interests of his soul, had almost driven the circumstance from his memory. Now, however, aided by the illusive light, the spectre appeared before him in all its frightful reality, and even the firm mind of Edmund shrunk back aghast from the appalling sight.

"Why do you shrink?" said Cheops, his deep hollow voice thrilling through the souls of his auditors; "why does my form appear to create such terror? Is it because a tomb has been my dwelling? Oh, degenerate race! know that the sons of Mizraim, bold, wise, and learned as they were, held that communion with the dead was needful to the living. They loved to gaze upon the empty casket, deprived of all that gave it value, for it taught the meanness of the body; and who could dwell upon the withering worthless clay, and not acknowledge to his soul how poor were its highest pleasures, when compared to the sublime aspirations of the spirit? Why then tremble? Virtue need fear no spectres, and vice might shudder at itself. If thine own conscience do not upbraid thee, what hast thou to fear?"

"Nothing!" said Lord Edmund firmly; "spectre or demon, whatever you may be, I fear you not! 'Twas but the infirmity of human nature; it is past, and I am again myself, and strong in the consciousness of the integrity of my own mind. It is not in the power of Hell itself to fright me from my purpose!"

"The integrity of thine own mind!" cried Cheops, with one of his horrid laughs; "Poor weak offspring of clay! ay, confide in thy boasted strength; rely upon thy vaunted firmness; but when the hour of trial and temptation shall arrive, tremble!"

Lord Edmund shuddered in spite of himself, and his blood ran colder in his veins! "Who art thou?" cried he, indignantly: "strange, terrible being that thou art?—and why art thou permitted to revisit earth to taunt me into madness?"

"I was once as thou art," returned Cheops. "Young, ardent, and impetuous, I thought the world was made for happiness, and that men were born to be my slaves. Glory was my idol, and Fame the only meed I coveted. Deeply did I drink of her intoxicating cup; my renown spread to the remotest corners of the earth, and my power became as boundless as my ambition! To immortalize my name, I caused the erection of an enormous pyramid! and my grandeur seemed beyond the reach of destiny to destroy. But I trusted in my own strength, and I fell! Tremble then, weak man! nor dare to boast how thou wilt act until the moment of temptation shall arrive!"

The deep thrilling voice of the Mummy fell upon Lord Edmund's ear as a warning from the tomb. He too was relying on his own strength, and should he too fall? Forbid it Heaven! "No!" thought he, "in some cases I might fear; but now, when the welfare of her I love is at stake, I cannot fail!"

The Mummy smiled as he read the thoughts that passed over Lord Edmund's expressive countenance. "Thus I too thought," muttered he; "and as I was, so will he be deceived! Human nature is still the same even in this remote corner of the globe. Fool that I was, then, to attempt to reverse her decrees! Forgive me, mighty Isis!" The rest was lost in inarticulate murmurs as the Mummy's head sank upon his breast.

"Oh, God!" cried Edmund to Father Morris; "whence comes this fearful spectre? what does it import?"

"I know not," said Father Morris, in a hoarse unnatural whisper, his eyes still strained upon the Mummy. Edmund started, for the unusual abstraction of Father Morris added fresh horror to the scene: his senses seemed bewildered; he scarcely knew where he was, or what was passing around him; he rubbed his eyes, and tried to wake from what appeared a frightful dream; but in vain; the vision was still there in all its horrible distinctness, and Edmund felt a terrific creeping steal along his nerves as the hollow sepulchral voice of the Mummy again fell upon his ears.

"Alas! where am I?" continued he; "can that river be a ramification of my beloved Nile? or am I indeed torn from all I prize and love, to be cast upon this secluded spot, where all seems strange and insignificant? O deity of the foaming waters! holy Sirius, hear me! Calm my troubled spirit, and grant some gracious manifestation of thy divinity to chase my growing doubts. But I deceive myself; this is not the Nile! No papyrine boats glide o'er its polished surface. No acanthus groves nor forests of lofty palm border its banks. No, no! the immortal palm, fit emblem of the soul, grows only in those favoured realms, where, spurning at oppression, it resists the feeble efforts of man to bend it to the earth, and springs upward with only added vigour from the feeble attempts made to subdue it!"

The Mummy ceased, and a solemn silence prevailed; whilst passions fierce as the whirlwind's fury flitted across his face, chilling the beholder's heart with horror at the fearful being whose bosom could conceive them.

Father Morris was not naturally timid; he even possessed uncommon strength both of nerves and mind; yet an unwonted shuddering ran through his frame as he gazed upon Cheops, and traced the workings of that demoniac mind as they were successively imprinted on his features. Involuntarily he turned away in disgust. "For God's sake, let us go!" cried he, gasping for breath; for a strange feeling that he could not define, seemed to impede his respiration.

"Yes, yes—let us go!" stammered forth Edmund; still, however, keeping his eyes fixed upon the awful object of his fear, as he slowly moved towards the door.

"Stay!" cried Cheops in a voice of thunder. Involuntarily they obeyed. "How feeble is this race of men!" resumed the Mummy; "how different from the sons of ancient Mizraim, from the Macrobian Ethiopians, or even our Pallic foes; degenerate in form as well as spirit, their souls no longer seem emanations from the divinity, though perhaps the immortal spark becomes degraded and abased from its long continuance in clay, and is sunk for ever from its pristine greatness! Stay, then!" continued he; "why should you fly me? I mean you no harm, and I swear by the sacred tomb of Osiris in Philæ, that I will not hurt you. Drive me not then from amongst you, and I may aid your projects: at least, it is your duty to receive me as the destined instrument of Fate, since Osiris decrees that my soul shall quit its transmigrations in the form of animals to re-animate this worthless body. Take me then into your counsels, confide in my power and I swear by the holy dust of Isis that you shall not repent."

"Avaunt, demon!" cried Lord Edmund, and, bursting from the room, he rushed out of the house.

What farther passed between the priest and his awful visitor, was known only to themselves; for when the family descended to breakfast, the Mummy was gone, and Father Morris appeared absorbed in his usual studies, without taking the slightest notice of the terrific occurrences of the night.

The death of the Queen being now generally known, her remains, laid in state, were exposed to the lamentations of her subjects, and the family of Mrs. Montagu were amongst the earliest visitors to the mournful spectacle.

In an immense hall, hung with black, was placed a kind of bier, covered with black cloth, supporting the body of the deceased Queen, over which was thrown a velvet pall, so disposed, however, as to display the beautiful features of the deceased, which, though now fixed in death, still retained their native expression of majestic dignity.

Immense tapers of an enormous thickness lighted the sombre walls, hung with black cloth; whilst chorister boys walked up and down chanting hymns in honour of the deceased, and flinging incense in the air from silver vessels suspended by silver chains, which they carried in their hands; thus shedding fragrance around, and chasing the fearful odour of mortality even from the very chamber of death. Priests wrapped in funeral garments also slowly paraded the room, muttering prayers, and joining occasionally their full, deep-toned voices with the shriller chant of the boys.

The space where the public were admitted, was railed off from the lower end of the hall; but near the body knelt a beautiful female arrayed in black velvet, and her fair face and arms shaded by a veil of black crape.—

"O Osiris!" cried a figure wrapped in a long dark cloak, grasping the arm of Father Morris, "who is that lovely creature? There, bending over the last awful relics of mortality, methinks she looks beauteous as the phœnix rising from the funeral pile, and triumphing in glory over the impotent malice of the grave."

"Hush! hush! for Heaven's sake!" whispered the deep, full voice of Father Morris; "it is Elvira, the rival of Rosabella, whom you have sworn to support."

"Typhon himself could not injure her," said Cheops, for it was he; and he stood with his eyes fixed upon her, apparently lost in meditation.

"For mercy's sake, let us go on!" whispered the priest, "you will excite attention — we shall be discovered. Besides," continued he in a lower tone, "did you find a crown so delightful that you think you would injure her by depriving her of one?"

"No! by the holy limbs of Osiris!" said Cheops; and, obeying the influence of the friar's arm, he moved onwards.

"Why was not Rosabella with Elvira in the hall?" asked Sir Ambrose. "I thought it was commanded by the law that all the princesses of the Blood Royal should exhibit themselves publicly as mourners by the corpse of the deceased Queen."

"Rosabella is ill," replied the duke. "Grief for the loss of her cousin has produced an access of fever, and she is unable to quit her bed."

"Indeed!" returned Sir Ambrose, incredulously; "it is very strange! I own I did not give Rosabella credit for so much sensibility."

Notwithstanding the incredulity of Sir Ambrose, however, Rosabella was really dangerously ill; though her illness did not proceed exactly from the cause she chose to assign for it. The terror she had felt at the sudden appearance of the Mummy, whom she thought a supernatural being, at the very moment she believed the death of her cousin was darkly hinted at by the monk, operating upon an over-excited imagination, had produced fever; and for some days Rosabella was in considerable danger.

The secret exertions of Father Morris, however, in her behalf, prevented Rosabella's cause from being injured by her illness; and, by the time she was able to leave her bed, Lord Gustavus de Montfort, Lord Maysworth, and Dr. Hardman, with the Lords Noodle and Doodle, had declared themselves her adherents, bringing with them all the numerous host who, finding it too much trouble to judge for themselves, are always ready to follow in the train of a great man. The day when this important declaration was made, was that on which all the nobility of the realm assembled in that splendid monument of antiquity, Westminster Hall, to choose the council of state to govern the kingdom during the interregnum. This venerable pile, which had seen so many generations successively rise and pass away, now cleared of the encumbrances with which the bad taste of the middle ages had loaded it, shone in all its original magnificence, and opened wide its ponderous portals to receive the whole nobility of England upon this important occasion.

It was a glorious, and almost an awful sight, to see so many great and illustrious characters, some of whose names were celebrated even to the remotest corners of the globe, collected together in that magnificent hall. Few however, thought of the grandeur of the spectacle; the deep interest excited by the occasion that assembled them absorbing all minor feelings. The business of the day was soon entered upon; and twelve noble individuals chosen to direct the affairs of state, till another Queen should be elected.

The Duke of Cornwall, Lord Edmund Montagu, Lord Gustavus de Montfort, Lord Maysworth, and the Lords Noodle and Doodle, were amongst the number chosen; and as soon as the election was completed, the council retired together to an apartment appropriated to their use, to consult upon the measures to be taken to secure the due election of their future Queen. Then it was, that the anxious father of Elvira was paralyzed, to hear the noble lords above-mentioned declare themselves partizans of her rival; and to see others who had till then remained neuter, seem inclined to range themselves upon the same side. In vain did Edmund exert his powerful eloquence; the weight and influence of the adverse lords far outweighed all his arguments in the breasts of the auditors; and the poor old duke returned home depressed and almost broken-hearted, from the conviction he received, that the feeling of the majority of the council was decidedly against his child.

The moment the duke reached his own palace, he repaired to the apartment of Rosabella, and found her apparently in a state of convalescence, reclining upon a sofa, supported by her confidant Marianne, with Father Morris sitting at her feet. The holy father was evidently confused at the unexpected arrival of the duke; and he rose hastily in great disorder, to endeavour to account for his appearance there. The duke, however, was too much enraged to listen to him, or, indeed, to notice the suspicious circumstance of his secretly visiting the princess; his passion was solely directed against Rosabella, and not even her present feeble and emaciated appearance was sufficient to disarm his anger.

"Wretch!" he exclaimed; "vile, ungrateful wretch that thou art! Thou hast destroyed me. Thou wilt bring the grey hairs of thy benefactor with sorrow to the grave! And so treacherously too! Oh, Rosabella! how could you plot against me whilst you were enjoying the shelter of my roof. Against me, did I say? Alas! would it were only against me! But no! with fiend-like barbarity, you have conspired to destroy my child!"

The duke had here unwittingly struck a chord that thrilled through the inmost souls of his auditors; he did not heed their confusion, however, but went on.

"Oh, Rosabella! if I could have guessed, when thou wert brought to me a little smiling infant, and I took thee under my protection to foster thee as my own child, that thou wouldst prove a serpent to sting my heart to the core! But I was told it would be so—Sir Ambrose warned me to beware. 'Your brother,' said he, 'has proved a villain; the violence of his passions has led him to commit unheard-of crimes; and may not the same furies glow in the bosom of this smiling infant? Do not desert her, but do not educate the offspring of guilt in the bosom of your own family.'"

"And did Sir Ambrose say this?" exclaimed Father Morris, grinding his teeth together, and scarcely able to articulate from the strength of the emotion that convulsed his frame. The duke, however, did not hear his question, and passionately continued—"He advised well, but I was deaf to his counsel; Fate hurried me on to my own destruction, and I nourished with the tenderest care a wretch whom I have this day discovered plotting with traitors to deprive my child of her birth-right!"

"What do you mean, my Lord?" said Rosabella; "I do not understand you."

"Yes, yes!" replied the duke, "ask what I mean; you may well assume that face of smiling innocence—too—too often it has served your purpose! Fool, idiot, that I have been, to have been so easily deceived! But your arts will now be vain. Lord Gustavus de Montfort would not have openly declared himself your friend, as he did to-day, if the most insidious arts had not been practised to win him."

"And has he done so?" asked Rosabella, her eyes sparkling with joy.

"Has he done so?" repeated the duke bitterly; "no doubt you know it but too well. Also that the prosing Lord Maysworth, the enlightened Lord Noodle, and the intelligent Lord Doodle, have enlisted their empty heads and long purses upon your side."

"Have they?" cried Rosabella, transport brightening every feature.

"Oh, Rosabella!" exclaimed the duke, passion giving way to agony, and torrents of tears streaming down his aged face; "that look of affected astonishment is intolerable! You must have known all this! I am a poor, weak, old man! there needed not such plotting to deceive me. It breaks my heart to find you guilty of hypocrisy."

Rosabella was affected by her uncle's tears: all his former kindness rushed upon her mind, and Nature resuming her powerful influence, she forgot all her ambitious projects, her hopes, her fears, and her intrigues; she thought only of the feeble, miserable, old man before her; and, attempting to throw her arms round his neck, she sought to mingle her tears with his, and, clinging to his feet, implored his forgiveness. The duke, however, could not read her heart, and, blinded by his passion, saw in this action only an aggravated insult: violently he spurned her from him, commanding her to leave his house immediately, and, by so doing, extinguished for ever every gentler feeling in his niece's breast.

Rosabella's haughty spirit did not wait a second repulse. Her tears were instantly dried, and, with eyes flashing fire and cheeks glowing with indignation, she rushed out of the room, without deigning to reply.

The duke's rage, if possible, exceeded her own; and these near relations, united as they were by the tenderest ties, parted in mutual hatred, sincerely hoping, on both sides, that they might never meet again.

Father Morris and Marianne followed Rosabella; and they found, as they expected, that the violent over-excitement of the moment had given way to hysterics. These tremendous convulsive agonies soon exhausted her enfeebled frame, and she lay upon a sofa in a state of torpid languor nearly approaching to insensibility, whilst her friends consulted upon what course they should pursue. During this pause of uncertainty and painful deliberation—for as Rosabella was entirely dependent upon her uncle, the case seemed hopeless—a letter arrived from Lord Gustavus de Montfort, offering the loan of his palace and his purse to the princess. That prudent and calculating nobleman was fully aware of the situation in which Rosabella would be thrown by his declaration in her favour, and of the advantage that would accrue to himself in after-times, if she should obtain the crown, from his having at such a moment conferred an important service upon his future sovereign.

Father Morris did not hesitate to open this letter and read it. Rosabella was not in a state to be consulted. Indeed, the case was one that did not admit of hesitation; and a conveyance having been procured, the princess was removed to the house of Lord Gustavus, before she had recovered the full use of her faculties.

CHAPTER XV.

The morning appointed for the election of the council of state was passed by Elvira in the most intense anxiety. For herself, she had no wish to be a Queen—nay, perhaps she trembled at the thought; but when she saw how earnestly it was desired by her father, and thought of the bitterness of his disappointment should she be rejected, her eyes filled with tears, and she felt ready to make any sacrifice to promote his happiness.

Thus, trembling with agitation, yet fearing alike every change, the fair Elvira sate, leaning her head upon her hand, whilst Sir Ambrose, whose rank did not entitle him to a vote, Dr. Coleman, and Henry Seymour, endeavoured to console her.

"My dear young lady," said the good doctor, "indeed, indeed, I think you distress yourself quite unnecessarily. With such supporters as your father and Lord Edmund, I do not think you can fail of success."

"You quite mistake me, doctor, I assure you," returned the princess; "I think not of the crown, yet it is not possible to express what I have suffered during the last few hours. Ere my father went to the council this morning, his agitation was so excessive that I feared it would destroy him, and my impatience for his return is become almost agony."

"Let me entreat your Highness to be composed," said Henry Seymour. "You torment yourself with vain terrors. I cannot suffer myself to imagine for a moment that the duke can be otherwise than successful."

"My dear child," observed Sir Ambrose, "exert your own good sense; nothing can be more foolish than to let imaginary horrors usurp any influence over your senses; you thus suffer doubly, and often the pains of anticipation exceed those of reality. But, see, here comes Father Murphy, and my little lively niece, Clara. Well, father, what news? Will the princess be Queen?"

"Och, and there can be no manner of doubt of it!" returned Father Murphy.

Elvira turned pale. "God in his mercy grant you may be mistaken!" said she.

"Oh, dear!" cried Clara, involuntarily.

"Why do you exclaim, fair lady?" asked the doctor, smiling.

"I am so surprised—so astonished!" said the blushing girl.

"At what?" resumed the doctor inquisitively.

"That—that," said Clara timidly, "that the princess should not like to be a Queen."

"Alas! alas!" said Elvira, smiling languidly, "you are too young, Clara, to know the awful responsibility such a situation would impose. The Queen of England must devote herself to her people; once elected, she is cut off for ever from all the happiness of domestic life. She must form no ties—she must indulge in no attachments—she can never feel the happiness of devoting herself entirely to promote the welfare of one adored object. She can never know the transports of a mother!" and, sighing deeply, Elvira cast her eyes upon the ground, whilst those of Henry Seymour were fixed earnestly upon her.

"Yet all this," said Sir Ambrose, "is rather imaginary than real. The subjects of a good Queen ought to be her children; and the glory of contributing to the happiness of thousands, and ruling nations by a nod, may well compensate for the humbler comforts of a domestic fireside."

"I do not agree with you," rejoined Dr. Coleman; "I think the situation of a Queen is one both of trouble and responsibility. We all know how difficult it is to give satisfaction even in the most ordinary occurrences of life; and how much more must that difficulty be increased in such an exalted station. Besides, it seems cruel to condemn a young and beautiful woman to the miseries of celibacy. Woman naturally seems to want support; she is to man, what the clinging ivy is to the majestic oak,—its loveliest ornament; but take away the standard tree, and she falls forlorn and unsupported to the dust. Do you not think so, Mr. Seymour?"

The youth started at this appeal, for his thoughts had indeed wandered far from the scene before him. "Yes," said he, after a short pause.

Sir Ambrose laughed heartily. "Upon my word," said he, "I congratulate you, Dr. Coleman, upon your happiness in having such attentive auditors. The princess looks as if she had not heard a single word that you have said; whilst Mr. Seymour, when you appeal to him for his opinion, only starts, and says 'Yes.'"

The Mummy!

"You are quite right, Sir Ambrose," returned Dr. Coleman, smiling good-humouredly; "and I begin to discover that reasons are quite useless when the feelings are interested."

"Och!" said Father Murphy; "and my opinion is that we have all rason to be interested; for I should not be surprised at all at all, if the King of Ireland was to take advantage of our troubles, to make a descent upon us. There is no time so fitting for throwing every thing into confusion, as when nobody knows what he is doing."

"There may be much justice in your remark, holy father," said Henry Seymour, smiling; "but, for my own part, I own I do not apprehend the King of Ireland has any such bloody-minded intentions."

"Report speaks highly of his son," observed Elvira.

"Not more highly than he deserves," cried Doctor Coleman enthusiastically. "The youthful Roderick is brave, noble, and generous; possessing every quality to fit him for a hero; and is quite incapable of any thing bordering upon meanness."

"Is he handsome?" asked Clara, with infinite naïveté, looking up earnestly at the doctor as she spoke.

"As the Achilles of the ancients," replied the doctor.

"Dear me, how I should like to see him!" said the little beauty, with the utmost simplicity:—"Should not you, Mr. Seymour?"

"I cannot say I have any curiosity," returned Henry Seymour, having infinite difficulty to help laughing.

"Dear me, how very odd!" said Clara, looking at him earnestly; "I do believe the doctor was only quizzing us, and that he's very ugly and disagreeable. Is he, Mr. Seymour?"

The air and manner with which she put this question, quite destroyed the small remains of gravity Henry Seymour had till now with so much difficulty preserved; and, bursting into a violent fit of laughter, he rushed out of the room. Every body looked astonished, and Dr. Coleman embarrassed. After a short pause, however, he seemed to recover himself. "It is very strange the duke does not come," said he, pulling out his watch. "The council must be chosen before this; and they seldom stay to deliberate long at a first sitting."

"I am miserable," cried Elvira. "If he should be ill!"

"Shall I seek him?" asked Dr. Coleman; and, reading her assent in her countenance, he quitted the room.

"The doctor is very obliging," said Sir Ambrose; "but he never did like Rosabella. He hated her father, and when Duke Edgar—but, I forget! his history is a secret which must rest for ever in my own breast."

"Do tell me, uncle!" cried Clara coaxingly; "I should so like to hear it, and every body says you know all about him."

"And what can his history have to do with such a little chit as you?"

"I don't know," said Clara with the utmost innocence; "but I am sure I should like to hear it."

"Why?" again asked Sir Ambrose.

"Because every body says it is a secret," replied Clara, clinging round him, and fondly stroking his face;—"so do tell me, my dear uncle, pray do?"

"You are a little coaxing witch," said Sir Ambrose, patting her long silky hair; "I would tell you any thing in reason, but the history of the father of Rosabella—"

"Rosabella!" cried the duke, bursting into the apartment with the fury of a maniac—"Rosabella! who speaks of Rosabella? She is a wretch, a vile, insidious wretch! She has destroyed me—she has conspired to destroy my child!"

And as he spake, the agonized old man sank into a chair, fainting with exhaustion, whilst a sanguine stream gushed from his mouth and nostrils, a blood-vessel having been ruptured by the violence of his emotions. Elvira shrieked in anguish, and, dreadfully terrified, threw herself upon her knees beside him, imploring him to speak to her, whilst Sir Ambrose, even more alarmed than herself, ran screaming for assistance. Dr. Coleman and Henry Seymour were at hand. The duke, and his daughter, who had fainted, were conveyed to their separate apartments, attended by Clara, Sir Ambrose, and the doctor, whilst Henry Seymour and Father Murphy were left together.

"O Beauty!" thought Henry Seymour, as he watched the lovely form of Elvira, looking like some fair flower drooping on its stem, carried past him, "how omnipotent is thy power! Even the savage monarch of the forest, tamed by thee, has crouched beside a maiden's feet! How heavenly does she look! pure as the immortal spirit, when, ere his breast was sullied by the grosser passions, man first conversed with God!"

"And sure if it's the princess ye're thinking of," said Father Murphy, tired of being so long silent, "ye've rason to look so sadly after her, for it's all over, and she'll never be Queen."

Henry Seymour started: the voice of the holy father sounded harsh and discordant in his ears; it had dispelled all his fairy dreams; and with a movement of impatience he threw open some folding doors, and walked into the garden. Father Murphy followed him.

"And where is it that ye're going?" asked he.

"I would be alone," said Henry in a commanding tone.

"And so ye shall be," returned Father Murphy, "when I'm after laving ye; and that I will do in a whiffey. But—"

"Begone!" cried a peculiarly low, hollow voice which sounded close to the friar's ear, He started, and as he looked up, the withering glance of Cheops fell full upon him; he screamed wildly and fled, uttering shrieks of terror.

Cheops looked after him with a scornful smile, and then fixing his superhuman eyes on Henry Seymour, he waited for him to speak. Few were the human beings who could have met that scowl unmoved. Those wild eyes, shaded as they were by the thick dark brows above them, always seemed to sink direct to the beholder's soul: Henry Seymour, however, shrank not from their gaze. A long pause ensued.

"You wish for help," said Cheops, "and it is in my power to assist you. I know you well, you are not what you seem; but fear not, and all your hopes shall be fulfilled."

"Alas! how can they?" said the youth, "when I know them not myself."

"Hear me!" returned Cheops; "you love Elvira, you would fain become her husband, and would yet not deprive her of the crown. Even now, you were revolving in your mind a scheme to reconcile these two apparently incompatible objects; but, besides innumerable minor obstacles, one great one destroys your plans—you have a father."

"In the name of Heaven!" cried Henry Seymour wildly, "who and what art thou?"

But, ere he had finished speaking, the Mummy was gone. "Fiend! demon!" cried the youth, "what means this unreal mockery? But thou shalt not escape me thus."

In the mean time, the duke had somewhat recovered, and, by permission of Dr. Coleman, Lord Edmund and Sir Ambrose were admitted to his chamber. The reverend Fathers Morris and Murphy were there already.

"I believe it is quite against the rules," said the doctor, "to allow visitors to a patient in the duke's state;—but he is so irritable, I fear keeping him in suspense might occasion a relapse."

"I am sorry to see you thus, my dearest friend," said Edmund, pressing the duke's hand warmly; "you have always been a second father to me, and, God knows! I love you as myself."

The Duke fervently returned his pressure, but he could not speak. "My dear, dear friend!" said Sir Ambrose, the tears trembling in his eyes.

"Come! come!" said Dr. Colman, good-humouredly, "I must not let you agitate my patient. Lord Edmund is only come, my Lord Duke, to take leave. He is going into the country to try to exert his influence amongst the electors."

The duke shook his head.

"I must not have you despair," said Sir Ambrose; "we shall beat them yet: not but that we must fight hard, for Rosabella is as crafty as a fox, and you see what a party she has made:—besides, she's as selfish as her father."

"No," said the duke feebly, and speaking with great difficulty; "Edgar was not selfish."

"The influence of natural affection is astonishing!" said Sir Ambrose; "since it makes you speak thus of one who has so grossly injured you."

"Edgar's faults," replied the duke, scarcely able to articulate, "were rather those of circumstance than of feeling. I am convinced of it, and forgive him. Nay, if he were alive, and I could see him, I would clasp him to my heart."

"Och!" said Father Murphy, "and that's said just like yourself; for there's nothing so like a Christian spirit as forgiving our enemies; — and so may Heaven prosper and bless all that love ye, and send all that hate ye to the Devil."

"But how does that accord with the Christian spirit you were talking of?" asked Dr. Coleman, smiling.

"Och!" replied Father Murphy, "and it's clane another thing. For none but the Devil's own brats could hate the duke, and he's a right to his own, surely."

Dr. Coleman, though not quite convinced by the sophistry of the holy father, did not attempt to controvert it; and the party, fearing to fatigue the duke, soon after separated.

A few hours after this conversation, Father Morris was walking in one of the shadiest parts of the garden of Mr. Montagu, where the thick trees spread over his head, and by their umbrageous foliage, almost shut out the light of the sun. In the very centre of this gloomy grove, a funereal urn had been erected by one of the former possessors of the mansion, over which hung a weeping willow. The monument had once been gaudily adorned with bright colours and gilding, to mark the armorial bearings and dignity of the dust that mouldered below. Now, however, damp and neglect had hastened the work of Time in that secluded spot. The once white marble was stained with a dirty green, and moss had grown round the crumbling monument of former greatness: the plaster effigies of the arms had cracked, and peeled off in places; whilst wild-flowers had taken root in the fissures, and reared their blooming heads, and twined their fantastic wreaths around the mouldering stone, hanging in wild luxuriant festoons over this emblem of decay, as though to mock the feeble efforts of man to perpetuate his name, and assert triumphantly the supremacy of Nature.

Father Morris was struck by the effect produced by this apparently simple circumstance, and he stood with his arms folded on his breast, attentively gazing upon the urn: "And for this," thought he, "yes, even for such perishable baubles as these, does man risk his immortal soul. For this, for honours that decay even whilst we gaze upon them; for fame, which the slightest breath may blow away, light as the thistle's down; for wealth and power, which, past a certain point, pall on the senses; and for ambition, we sacrifice all the mind holds dear to it. And what is ambition? What real happiness can fame, wealth, or power bestow? I will repent; it is not yet too late: — for worlds I would not harm that poor old man. Yes, he has still a heart. I am not wholly lost. Oh! how his look, his voice thrilled to my inmost soul, and awakened feelings I thought for ever dead. Oh, Julia! Julia! surely thy blest spirit would rejoice if angels can still feel for mortals, at my repentance. Oh, if one fatal act could but be recalled, and one fiend be satisfied, I might still be saved!"

And overpowered by his emotions, even his firm heart was softened; he leant his head against the mouldering urn, and, hiding his face in his cowl, he wept. Blest were those bitter tears, and sweet were the sensations that stole over the mind of the monk as they flowed; for they were the first fruits of human feeling that had long touched that savage breast. Soothed by their healing balm, and half forgetting the cares that hung about him, Father Morris still reclined against the tomb; whilst mild and pleasing images floated before his fancy, and the fairy form of Happiness rose again upon his sight, and, though dim and indistinct by distance, seemed once more to beckon him forward through the mist of time. Lost in these meditations, the most delightful he had long indulged in, the father remained unheedful of the lapse of time, till he was startled by a tap upon his shoulder, and, turning, he beheld the giant form of Cheops.

"Fiend, demon, devil!" cried he, passionately; "avaunt! and tempt me not!"

The Mummy burst into one of his frightful laughs of derision. "What!" said he, "have you forgot your friend? your confidant? your confederate? And is it thus you treat him? Have you forgot our compact and your oath? which, if it were necessary, was to be sealed with blood?" (The friar shuddered, whilst Cheops continued:) "Pshaw! pshaw! talk not of temptation! The passions in that breast defy its power; for demons scarce could credit them. Fear not temptation then, most pure and most immaculate priest! for know, I can read thy heart: and I — yes, even I — shudder at the wickedness it conceals!"

"My feelings are changed — I repent!"

"Impossible! your repentance is but as a passing shade before a glowing fire, which, even if not removed, would be soon devoured by the flames!"

The Mummy!

"I tell you, my purpose is changed:—I will no longer plot against the duke; and Elvira, if she will, may be Queen."

"'And do you think a crown so enviable then,'" said the Mummy, repeating the friar's own words, once addressed to him, "'that you think you would injure her by depriving her of its cares?'"

"Devil!" cried the father, unable to resist the feelings these words had conjured up.

"And these are mortals," said Cheops; "they sin, and they repent! Thus adding hypocrisy to guilt, and doubling their crimes by the knowledge they have of their enormity!"

"Demon!" returned Father Morris; "the words of that old man wrung my heart; and I would sacrifice all the world can give, to throw myself upon his breast, and obtain his forgiveness."

"I believe you think so now," said Cheops maliciously; "but when Rosabella shall be Queen, and wealth and dignities shall be dispensed by Father Morris; when nobles shall bend humbly before him, and, hanging upon his smile, beg favours from his hand, then—"

"Curses on thee, fiend!" cried Father Morris, rushing from the grove, and pressing his cowl round his head with both his hands, as though he feared the horrid laugh of Cheops should echo in his ears, and sting him into madness.

"Weak, feeble worm!" exclaimed Cheops, with a scornful laugh, looking after the friar as he darted from his sight; "and yet this man boasts of his intellect; ay, and rules his fellow-men almost to his will! Degenerate wretches! O powerful Osiris! if from thy dread abode thou deignest to look down upon thy votary, pity him now! condemned to waste his days amongst this hated race! And thou, fell Typhon! dread avenging deity! say, will thy awful wrath accept of victims such as these? Alas! I fear vengeance like thine will not be thus appeased! and that thy never-dying fire, will still gnaw my vitals. Oh! these mortals think they suffer: but what are their torments when compared to mine?"

As he spoke, he gnashed his teeth in fury, whilst again the expression of passions, too tremendous to be conceived by mortals, darkened on his brow.

CHAPTER XVI.

"I am really glad we have left the house of my uncle," said Rosabella to Marianne, the morning after her removal to the palace of Lord Gustavus; "for though there is something revolting to my feelings in being dependant upon a stranger, yet as it may soon be in my power to repay any obligations I may receive from him, it is better than the treachery I was obliged to practise towards the duke. There is something so mean in treachery!"

"We are always apt to feel most disgusted with those vices most repugnant to our nature," said Marian smiling, "whilst we are merciful to those we practise. However, I can't say I think there is much difference."

"What!" cried Rosabella indignantly; "do you class those vices that spring from a noble though mistaken spirit, with those that are the natural offspring of base, grovelling minds?"

"No," returned Marianne, "for I think the latter preferable, as the mind that produces them is incapable of making nobler efforts; whilst the others, by degrading their possessors, show forcibly the monstrous depravity of the human heart."

"I do not understand you," said Rosabella.

"Nor is it necessary you should:" rejoined her confidant.

Rosabella was not quite satisfied with this summary manner of dismissing the argument, and was proceeding to question her confidant's maxim, when a tap at the door announced a page from Lord Gustavus, who came to know if the princess would honour his master with an audience.

"Certainly," said Rosabella; and in a few minutes Lord Gustavus entered her boudoir.

"I hope your Serene Highness has rested well," said the noble lord with his usual pomposity; "I feel better this morning."

"I am perfectly well, I thank your lordship!" returned Rosabella; "and the relief I have experienced, by having the weight that has so long hung upon my mind relieved by my removal to your hospitable mansion, has proved an excellent soporific."

"That being the case," said Lord Gustavus, "perhaps your

The Mummy!

Highness will have no objection to indulge the noble lords who already have declared themselves on your behalf, as also some others of their friends who are anxious to enlist under your banners, with an interview: for thinking as I think, and as I am convinced every reasonable person in the kingdom must think, no time ought to be lost in a matter of so much and of such infinite importance."

Rosabella, thinking par merveille exactly the same as the noble lord, instantly gave him her hand to lead her to his library, where the illustrious personages he had spoken of were waiting to receive her. It has been already said that Rosabella was beautiful, and now that her recent illness, and the agitation natural to the novelty of her present situation had softened the usual pride and haughtiness of her demeanour, she looked perfectly lovely. It has often been allowed, that a beautiful woman never looks so well, as when in affliction; there being something in the appearance of a timid helpless female, looking up to man for protection and support, that rouses every generous and manly bosom in her behalf; whilst that wretch must indeed be lost to every sense of feeling and humanity, who could be deaf to the prayer of beauty in distress. Thus the appearance of Rosabella caused a general sensation in her behalf, whilst her usual pride and haughtiness, which were well known, only made her present diffidence and agitation, her downcast eyes and trembling voice, appear still more interesting from the strong effect of contrast they produced.

The persons collected in the library of Lord Gustavus were all affected by her manners; and though perhaps it would have been difficult to find a group of individuals more various in their usual habits and modes of thinking, yet upon this one point they were agreed. The personages who composed this worthy assemblage, were Lord Maysworth, the Lords Noodle and Doodle, Dr. Hardman, and the young Prince Ferdinand of Germany, who had been taken prisoner by Lord Edmund, and was now upon his parole of honour, till the conditions for his ransom could be arranged. He was at present the guest of Lord Maysworth, who having in his youth received great obligations from the German Emperor, was now glad of an opportunity to show his gratitude to his son; and who had now brought him to Lord Gustavus, to introduce him to the Princess Rosabella.

Prince Ferdinand was ardent and romantic, and he was just at that happy age when all appears bright and blooming, before reality has destroyed the flattering dreams of hope; when we are ready to believe all we wish, and imagine human nature without a blot. Alas! why are the delightful moments of life so transient; and why can we never partake of pleasure without having our relish for it destroyed!

Confiding, however, and unsuspicious as Prince Ferdinand was, he was certainly excessively astonished to hear Lord Maysworth, the advocate of freedom and equality, eloquently plead in Rosabella's behalf that her father was the elder brother of the present duke, and that consequently her claim was strengthened by all the magic powers of primogeniture, and he was still more surprised by his assertion that the present duke had rendered himself unpopular by advising the late Queen to rebuild the late palace at Richmond, by which several hundreds of workmen were kept in employ during the whole of the preceding winter, and saved from perishing.

"Good heavens!" cried Prince Ferdinand, "Can you blame that? Was it not better than suffering them to perish with cold in the streets?"

"No danger of that, your Highness—no danger of that," returned Lord Maysworth—"nobody can perish of cold in our streets, because, you know, we have always pipes of hot air in them to make them quite warm. And as to the palace, it is really quite melancholy to think how many thousands of the public money were expended upon it. Oh! I assure you, it is quite impossible to find a man more deservedly unpopular than the Duke of Cornwall."

"Oh, quite impossible!" said the Lords Noodle and Doodle, shaking their heads.

"Thinking as I think, however, and as I am confident every one here must think," said Lord Gustavus, "it will be imprudent to depend entirely upon the duke's unpopularity: Lord Edmund is beloved by the army; and, as he is decidedly upon the side of Elvira, we cannot be too cautious."

"Oh, no, certainly!—we cannot be too cautious," echoed the two repeaters.

"It is a glorious circumstance, however," said Dr. Hardman, "that the choice of the Queen rests entirely with the people; their voice alone will decide the glorious struggle, and their free unbiassed opinions alone give the Monarchy its future Queen."

"Yes," said Lord Maysworth, "it is true, it rests with them alone to decide the question; and for this reason do you not think it will be as well, my lords, for each of us to repair to his country seat, and endeavour, by his influence in the neighbourhood, to procure the election of such deputies as may be disposed to vote favourably to our wishes."

"The plan is excellent!" cried Dr. Hardman.

"Excellent!" exclaimed Lord Gustavus.

"Excellent!" echoed his attendant satellites.

"Then it only remains for us to put it in execution," said Lord Maysworth.

"If the princess will excuse my absence—" began Lord Gustavus.

"Oh, my Lord!" interrupted Rosabella hastily, for she dreaded his long speeches beyond the power of description, "think not of me: I must be, indeed, unreasonable, if I could complain of your absence, when it is for my service you will be employed."

"The princess speaks like an oracle," said Dr. Hardman; "and I think we cannot do better than put her wishes in execution."

"Farewell then, my friends," said Rosabella, her voice trembling with emotion as they parted, "and may success attend you; for the present, my poverty, in all but gratitude, prevents my wishes; but the time may come, when you shall find the powerful Queen will not forget the favours conferred upon the dependant princess."

"Oh!" cried the noble lords and Dr. Hardman, "do not mention reward; patriotism and the disinterested love of our country alone dictate our actions—we think of nothing else!"

"'Twould be treason, and worse than blasphemy," said Prince Ferdinand, "to mingle the thought of self-interest with such purposes. Who indeed can see the Princess Rosabella, and suffer the paltry thought of self to interfere with his devotion to her interests?"

Rosabella smiled graciously upon the youthful speaker, though she did not speak.

"If, however," said Lord Maysworth, "the interests of the state should require a general more experienced than Lord Edmund, I have served, and I would willingly forego the transports of domestic peace to devote myself to the welfare of my country.'"

"Or, if the state should need a minister," observed Lord Gustavus, "thinking as I think, and as I am sure every one else must think, she has a right to command the services even of one so devoted to retirement as myself."

"For my part," said Dr. Hardman, "I wish neither place nor pension; but if my humble services in a medical capacity—"

"Fear not," returned Rosabella, "but that all your wishes shall be gratified; for, if I should be Queen, I shall only regard myself as an agent to dispose my power to the hands of those most worthy of it."

As she said this she withdrew, having the rare happiness to leave all her auditors perfectly satisfied with her conduct. In fact, such was their delight, that each stood for some moments after her departure lost in contemplation, indulging in day-dreams of the delightful anticipations her words and manner had excited, till, like Farmer Ashfield and his dame in "Speed the Plough," they were in imminent danger of running foul of each other in their abstraction: the entrance of a servant, however, roused them from their reveries; and, feeling somewhat alarmed of having so far forgotten the dignified sentiments they had been professing, they retired to their respective homes to take measures to put the scheme that had been suggested into execution.

"How I hate that Lord Gustavus," exclaimed Rosabella when she reached her boudoir. "Even if he makes a sensible observation, he adds so many explanations to it, that the spirit evaporates."

"Yes," returned Marianne, "he has yet to learn, that to tack explanations to wit, is like adding water to wine; you diminish its strength and spoil its flavour; but even he is preferable to Lord Maysworth."

"Oh! I don't think so," cried Rosabella, "for a ridiculous fool is always better than a prosing one. I can laugh at Lord Maysworth, but Lord Gustavus sends me to sleep."

"When an important enterprize is undertaken," said Marianne, "it will not do to be very scrupulous about the tools one employs to accomplish it. It is the part of a man of talent to discover the weaknesses of the human beings around him, and make them each subservient to his purpose."

"At any rate, that is not difficult in my case," rejoined Rosabella; "for my good friends are so eager to show themselves off, that, I must do them the justice to say, they neither give me the trouble to find out their weaknesses, nor the way to win them. Prince Ferdinand is the only one who possesses a single spark of noble feeling."

"And he, I think you say, seemed struck with your appearance?"

"He appeared to be so."

"We must improve that prepossession. The alliance of Germany may be invaluable to us. You must encourage the hopes of the prince, and do all you can to fan his infant passion into a flame."

"But I love Edmund."

"Pshaw! how can you be so childish? I do not wish you to love Prince Ferdinand. If you can contrive to make him love you, it will be all that is necessary."

"But do you consider the cruelty of trifling with his feelings?"

Marianne laughed. "I did not imagine you so romantic," said she tauntingly. "Do not alarm yourself; the rage for dying of love is gone by: therefore, notwithstanding the power of your charms, you must excuse me, if I presume to doubt their murderous properties."

Rosabella was too much mortified by the manner in which her confidant treated her scruples, to wish to continue the conversation; though the reasoning of Marianne produced its full effect upon her mind, and even, in spite of herself, influenced her conduct.

In the mean time, the family of Mr. Montagu experienced considerable uneasiness on account of Clara, whose health gradually declined.

"I cannot imagine what is the matter with my daughter?" said Mrs. Montagu one day to Dr. Coleman; "I wish you would talk to her a little.—Here, Clara, my dear, do just step this way. —You will be quite shocked, doctor, at the change in her appearance. Poor girl! I don't think she has ever properly overcome the fright she experienced at the first sight of the Mummy, for she has never seemed herself since. Indeed

'It seems to me she hoards some secret care,

That breaks her rest and drives her to despair.'"

"What do you quote that from, my dear?" asked Mr. Montagu, more interested in his wife's quotation than the illness of his daughter.

"Oh! it is one of a lot I bought the other day at the patent steam-book manufactory, in Hatton-Garden. I had been buying some other things, and so I persuaded the man to throw me in a bargain of quotations very cheap. They were all quite new, and ready cut, dried, and made up into pills for use. But I never saw such a man in my life;—you think nothing at all about your daughter. I really wish you would question her a little, for she will tell me nothing."

"Very well, my dear, I will," said Mr. Montagu; but the next instant he was absorbed in his studies again, and had even quite forgotten that such a being as Clara existed.

"Really," said Mrs. Montagu to the doctor, "I do not think any poor woman in the world ever was so plagued as I am. You see what a husband I have. He never troubles his head about any thing; and if I were to take it into my head to walk off, I don't think he would even miss me; and then, my daughter—but here she comes.—Clara, I sent for you to speak to Dr. Coleman."

Dr. Coleman was excessively struck by the alteration in Clara's appearance. The beautiful, lively, blooming girl was changed to a pale shadow-like being, whose existence seemed to hang upon a thread, and whose fragile form the first ungentle breeze would annihilate.

"What is the matter with you, my dear child?" asked the doctor.

"Nothing," said Clara, sighing.

"And I don't know any thing that can be worse," said Father Murphy, who happened to be present; "for that's the speech a young lady always makes when she's in love, and I don't know any disease that's harder to cure."

"In love!" cried Mr. Montagu, roused from his lethargy by that ill-omened word, which generally grates so harshly upon the ears of parents and guardians. "In love!" repeated he, looking earnestly at his daughter; "who can she possibly be in love with?"

"Ay, that's the question," said his wife: "for I'm sure I never trust her from under my own eye; and I'll defy her to fall in love without my knowing it. No, no, she cannot be in love."

"Och! and that's no rason at all," cried Father Murphy, "for I never knew of watching doing any good at all in such matters."

"Well, Clara," said Dr. Coleman, "you hear Father Murphy's opinion; do you plead guilty to the charge?"

Clara's blushes became deeper, and her agitation so excessive, as Dr. Coleman fixed his eyes upon her, that, finding she could not bear his looks, she burst into tears, and hurried out of the room. Poor Clara! the fangs of the most cruel of passions had indeed pierced thy heart, though thou wast unconscious of it thyself!

It may be remembered, that, on the day of Edmund's triumph, Clara had been forcibly struck by the fine figure and noble appearance of a youth, who had walked as prisoner in the procession. It was Prince Ferdinand; who, having formed a strong intimacy with Lord Edmund, had been an almost constant visitor at the house of Mrs. Montagu ever since. Clara was just at the age when the human mind first begins to feel the want of something to love. In her own family, her affections had been thrown back upon herself; and, being driven to the regions of fancy to find an object to occupy her heart, she would often wander for hours together in the garden, picturing to herself adventures, which she would paint in all the vivid colours of imagination; till, lost in creations of her own, she would almost forget the tame, cold realities of life.

Of course, all these imaginary adventures could not exist without a hero; but Clara could never fix upon any definite form to bestow upon him, till she had seen Prince Ferdinand. Then, all her dreams seemed realized; and the secret God of her idolatry appeared to stand before her, in propriâ personâ. Clara was now perfectly happy; and as, from the prince's frequent visits to her cousin, she now often passed whole days in his society, though he perhaps scarcely saw her, or at most regarded her but as a pretty child, yet she was satisfied: she saw him, and she heard him speak; what more was wanting to complete her dream of bliss?

Lord Edmund's departure for the country, however, broke this magic charm. Prince Ferdinand came no more to Mrs. Montagu's; and Clara heard of him only as the devoted admirer of Rosabella. Jealousy till that moment had been scarcely known to her, even by name; but it now shot its fiercest pangs into her heart. She had never been accustomed to conceal her feelings, and they now destroyed her. The climax, however, was still to come. One day, as she was mournfully pacing the terrace in her father's garden, she was startled by the appearance of Prince Ferdinand himself: her agitation was excessive; her lips trembled, and she panted for breath; but he passed on without noticing her—yes, it was he, the cherished idol of her thoughts, the hero of her dreams;—and he had passed without seeing, or at least without seeming to behold her. Was it possible he could have seen her and passed so coldly?—was it possible she could be so totally indifferent to one who was all the world to her? Oh! there was madness in the thought! she could not bear her own reflections. What would become of her, she knew not—she cared not; and, in an agony of despair, she plunged into the thickest grove of the garden.

Though it was summer, the day was cold and chilly; a drizzling mist fell fast, and a thick fog from the river wrapped the grove in gloom. Heedless however of the weather, Clara hastened on to the spot where stood the marble urn; but as she approached it, she started back, for close beside it stood the hideous figure of Cheops, dimly seen through the gathering gloom.

"Fear not!" said he in a softened, though still hollow voice; "tell me your woes, and, if I can, I will assist you."

"Alas! it is in vain," cried Clara in an agony of despair too profound even to admit of her feeling the fear generally experienced by all who saw the Mummy; "no one can relieve me,—I have no hope!"

Cheops smiled. "Poor child!" said he, "it is always thus when Eros first creeps into the soul, covering his arrows with roses, so that they are not seen till their barbed points rankle in the heart! I cannot tell how much I pity thee! So young and lovely too, it is hard that even thou shouldst not be exempt from the common lot of mortals! Yet do not despair."

"I do despair!" cried Clara, darting away from him; "I am truly wretched!"

The Mummy!

From this moment Clara saw the Mummy almost daily, and her mind acquired new force and energy from his society, though her health visibly declined. It was not, indeed, possible for human beings to hold daily intercourse with Cheops without feeling their souls withered. The glowing tints of youth and health faded rapidly from the cheeks of Clara; she became pale and spiritless, whilst she appeared to have lost all interest in the common affairs of life. Her fits of abstraction, however, her dejection, and her solitary wanderings, at length became so evident as to excite the attention of her mother, and the scene we have just described was the result.

Nothing could be more painful to poor Clara than the questioning she had undergone. She rushed from the presence of her parents to her favourite garden, to think over what had passed, and implore the assistance of the mysterious being with whom she had associated herself. He was not there, however; and though she repeatedly called upon his name, he came not. The weather was now delicious; the autumnal tints, that had just begun to change the lovely verdure of summer into a glowing brown, gave richness to the landscape. Since the abolition of coal and wood fires, the air of London had become pure and bright, though it still remained soft from its vicinity to the river, and it was thus highly favourable to vegetation: whilst, as no house was permitted to approach within a certain distance of the Thames, the sumptuous gardens that bordered its banks were beautiful in the extreme. That of Mr. Montagu, which has been so often alluded to, was in particular laid out in the greatest taste; and its grateful shade and delicious fragrance calmed poor Clara's troubled spirits, and soothed them to repose. Nothing, indeed, could have a more lulling effect upon the harassed senses than the scene before her. The air was perfectly still; not a leaf was agitated, not a flower stirred; all nature seemed to repose, but Clara alone felt restless. The questions of Dr. Coleman, and surmises of Father Murphy, had created a variety of new feelings in her mind; and she wandered up and down, oppressed by a sensation of melancholy which she had never felt before. She could not define her own sensations; she could not analyze her thoughts; and, as she sauntered to and fro without any determinate object, she listlessly pulled the leaves from a rose that she carried in her hands.

The scattering of the rose-leaves, however, recalled her to herself, and she smiled as she saw the mischief she had done. "Alas! poor rose!" sighed she, apostrophizing the flower; "I know not why I have destroyed thee!" Then walking hastily away, she plunged into the thickest part of the grove. "Why am

I thus agitated?" said she to herself. "Why do I feel thus miserable and discontented? Can it be love? Love!" she repeated, whilst deep blushes glowed upon her cheeks, and she started at the echo of her own voice. She threw herself upon a turfy bank under a shady tree, and, resting her head upon her hand, watched through the leaves the light fleecy clouds that drifted along the sky, till, oppressed by the painful nature of her own sensations, she sighed heavily, and tears swam in her eyes.

At this moment, footsteps rapidly approached; and Clara, springing upon her feet, hastily drew her hand across her eyes, and hid herself amongst the trees.

Dr. Hardman and Father Morris, who approached, seemed absorbed in conversation; and Clara, who dreaded Father Morris excessively, kept herself concealed, to avoid meeting him. We have already mentioned, that she was simple and innocent to a degree; but hers was the simplicity of ignorance, not folly. Her natural abilities were excellent, and her mind uncommonly strong. She therefore neither screamed nor fainted, though, from her present position, she became auditor to a scene of the deepest villainy. Notwithstanding the influence which Rosabella's party had at present in state, Father Morris was not satisfied. He wished to make her election certain, and this could be only done by removing Elvira. Dr. Hardman was her physician—the rest may be easily imagined.

Clara trembled, and her flesh seemed to creep upon her bones, as she listened to this horrid conference. But her terror was even increased when they changed the subject, and spoke no longer of an intended murder, but of one which had been already committed. Clara shook in every limb, and her lips and cheeks became blanched with fear; yet she uttered no cry, nor betrayed her presence by the slightest motion. At length they went, and Clara stood like one awakened from a fearful dream, almost doubting the reality of what she had heard.

An hour elapsed, yet Clara still stood motionless. What should she do? Would her unassisted testimony be believed in matters of such awful import against the weight and influence of two persons of so much consequence in the state? No, she felt it would not. Yet, if she remained silent, she would be accessory to the murder of Elvira. What could she do? what course ought she to pursue?—she knew not. A chaos of thoughts seemed whirling through her brain, and threatened almost to drive her to madness. The longer she thought, the more she became confused; and she began to fear her senses were actually leaving her, when a solemn voice sounded in her ear. Well did she know those deep and awful tones—they were those of Cheops; and, confiding the awful secret to him, she promised to comply implicitly with his injunctions.

It was the day following this adventure, that, as Father Murphy and Abelard were conversing tranquilly together, lamenting over the degeneracy of the age, their conference was interrupted by the sudden appearance of the duke.

"Where is Sir Ambrose?" cried he in a state of violent agitation—"where is Sir Ambrose? I must see Sir Ambrose immediately."

"Calm yourself, for Heaven's sake!" said Father Morris, who had followed him unobserved. "This violent agitation will destroy you: remember your recent illness, your age, your weakness—"

"Where is Sir Ambrose?" cried the duke.

"This vehemence is unbefitting of your station," continued Father Morris: "moderate it, I entreat you—it can do no good."

"Will no one call Sir Ambrose?" reiterated the duke: and as the baronet, who had been summoned by Abelard, appeared, he threw himself into his arms, sobbing like a child.

"Oh, my dear, dear friend!" exclaimed he, "they are determined to ruin Elvira. Lord Gustavus and his adherents are gone to their country-seats to try to influence the election of the deputies; and my child can have no chance against such treachery."

"If that be all," said Henry Seymour, who had accompanied the baronet, "why not follow their example? your influence must, at least, be equal to theirs."

"He is right," rejoined Sir Ambrose. "I know not why we did not do so sooner; but, even now, it is not too late."

"And what end can possibly be produced by such a measure?" asked Father Morris, scowling darkly at the youth: "the freedom of the election should be inviolable."

"But!" hastily interrupted the duke, "if they attempt to control it, we may surely—"

"I was not before aware," said Father Morris, in his cold,

ironical manner, "that the circumstance of others doing evil was any reason for our committing sin."

"Nonsense!" cried the duke; "there can be no sin in securing the election of my daughter; and so, Sir Ambrose, we will set off to-night, if you please."

"With all my heart!" said Sir Ambrose: and the two old men and Henry Seymour hurried away, leaving the monk alone. He did not, however, long remain so, for in a few seconds Cheops was at his side.

"So, Sir," said Father Morris, scowling upon Cheops with a look of deadly hatred, "you have proved yourself my friend, in suffering this babbling boy to counteract my views. Did you not boast he was your slave?"

The Mummy met his glance without shrinking; and, bursting into one of his fearful laughs, exclaimed tauntingly, "And so he is: but I thought you had determined not to oppose the duke any longer. It seems, then, I did not understand your reasoning in the garden."

"Fiend! cursed mocking fiend!" cried the friar, gnashing his teeth.

"Nay!" returned Cheops, "why blame me? Was I wrong in believing what you said? Was it, then, only a part you were acting to deceive me?"

"Demon! thou canst read my heart; but it is thy wish to drive me to distraction."

"No, no, my good Father Morris, my worthy friend, I honour you too much! If I can read your heart, I must be charmed to see such devotion to your friends, such candour, openness, and integrity."

"Taunting devil! be my sins what they may, thy presence is a penance that might redeem them. By Heaven! hell itself were easier to endure than those bitter scoffs."

"And darest thou talk of Heaven?" said the Mummy in an awful voice, that thrilled through the father's soul; whilst his eyes glared with such supernatural lustre that the priest could not bear their beams, and sank upon one knee before him, bending his head to the ground. "'Tis as it should be!" continued Cheops, with one of his fiendish laughs. "Yes, he is mine—he bends before my will! Now will I tell thee what thy feeble reason was too powerless to discover: I am still thy friend. The duke and Sir Ambrose will only injure their cause by the ill-judged measures they will take to promote it. They had the advantage of justice, honour, and open dealing upon their side; was it nothing to deprive them of these fair sounding words? Will they in future be able to complain of corruption, when they have attempted to corrupt? Had it not been so, even if success had crowned your efforts, would not the minds of men have inclined to the side of injured integrity? for so they might have termed the party of the duke. Might they not also have said the election was secured by bribery and deceit; and upon the first discontent that arose against Rosabella's government, would they not have recurred fondly to the recollection of the honest, open dealing, plain speaking duke! Men naturally love and respect virtue, though they may be seduced for a time by the allurements of vice. Thus, though they might not have had strength of mind to resist the arts of your party, their best feelings would have still remained upon the side of Elvira. This can now no longer be the case. The duke and Sir Ambrose voluntarily throw away their strongest hold—they rush blindfold to destruction. They degrade themselves to your level; whilst, as they are unused to deceit, they will not succeed in their endeavours, and disgrace will be their only reward. Now, do you blame me?"

"Blame you!" exclaimed Father Morris; "you are my friend, my best, my only friend, my preserver."

"With regard to Edmund," said Cheops, "we must excite his jealousy. If he were detached from Elvira, her cause would perish."

"It would, it would!" cried Father Morris.

"Try then thy efforts," said Cheops; "and if thou canst excite suspicions, fan them gently to a flame, yet without seeming to do so. Do not attack Elvira openly, or assert broadly that she loves another; but hint it darkly, so that your victim cannot misunderstand, and that the damning certainty may flash upon his mind with greater force than mere words can give. Well knowest thou what I mean, and well hath Nature modelled thee for such a part. That downcast look, that insinuating voice, and half ironical manner; the infernal deity himself could not well have wished a more fitting agent to execute his designs on earth than thou. Work then upon Edmund, and success cannot fail to follow your attempts."

"Thou Machiavel!" cried Father Morris; "my friend, my dearest friend, my benefactor: oh! how I could fall down and worship thee!"

A sardonic smile curled the haughty lips of Cheops. "Learn then to obey in silence," said he, "nor dare again to blame designs far beyond your comprehension!"

CHAPTER XVII.

The day following was appointed for the departure of the two families of the duke and Sir Ambrose for the country; and the whole preceding evening was passed by the two old men in arranging their plans, and forming new schemes to ensure success. Elvira took no part in this conversation, though certainly the person most interested: she was thoughtful and distraite; she was too restless to remain in one place. She walked to the window; she returned, and she again sat down. She attempted to work, to read, to draw — all was in vain; all seemed tasteless and insipid. Again she went to the window, and, opening its folding doors, stepped out upon the balcony. It was a delightful night, and the air felt soft and warm. Vines, laden with their luscious fruit, twined from pillar to pillar of the balcony, forming a kind of verdant network, whilst the moon shone bright upon the lovely scene beyond. Below, a smooth green lawn stretched forth like a velvet carpet, bounded on each side by Chinese rose-trees, the delicate tints of which looked still more transparently beautiful in the lovely light. Behind these, rose trees of a loftier height and deeper shade, whilst at the extremity of the lawn wound the river. The clear moon-beams trembled on the gently rippling stream, and gave a transparent brightness to the graceful foliage of a weeping willow, which hung over the water, and quivered in every passing breeze.

Elvira gazed upon the fair scene before her, and sighed heavily as she gazed. A gentle sigh softly echoed hers, and she started to find that Henry Seymour was standing before her.

"How beautiful is Nature," said he, "when undefiled by the follies and sins of man. Here one might forget the world, and all its busy turmoil of deceit. When one gazes thus upon the sublime and lovely face of Nature, how poor do all the arts, the ambition, and the pitiful contrivances of man appear. The soul seems elevated to its proper sphere, and to long to throw off the frail covering of clay, which yet chains it down to the grovelling passions of earth, and to soar triumphant to its native skies."

His fine eyes were turned to heaven as he spoke; and Elvira gazed upon them and his noble countenance beaming; with enthusiasm, till she quite forgot to reply.

"Do you not agree with me, Elvira!" said he, in a tone of the softest melody, fixing his eyes upon hers with a look that sank deep into her heart. Again she sighed deeply, but she could not speak. "Oh, Elvira," continued he, taking her hand; "will you forget me? will not the remembrance of this night form a tie between us, when we shall be far, far apart?"

"Apart!" cried Elvira, almost with a shriek of surprise.

The youth sighed; and, gazing earnestly upon her blushing face, whispered tenderly, as he pressed her hand to his heart, "O that I could flatter myself sorrow mingled with that sigh."

"Why, what is this?" said the old duke, bustling to the window; "the doctor tells me you are going to leave us. Surety you might contrive to stay till after the election."

"I am very sorry, Sir," said the youth; "but the circumstance that calls me away—"

"Ay, ay, the doctor told me; a near relation dangerously ill, that can't die in peace till he's seen you. Well, well, my boy, such things must be; and if he's doomed to die, I only wish him an easy death, and you a good legacy."

"I cannot tell you how sorry I am to part with you," said Sir Ambrose, who now advanced, "nor how sincerely I wish you good fortune."

"Thank you, thank you, Sir," said the youth: "alas! I now feel how poor words are to express my gratitude for all your kindness. But—"

"I am sorry to hasten you, Mr. Seymour," said Dr. Coleman, who now approached; "but time wears apace."

"True, true," said Henry, "I had forgotten. Once more farewell. God bless you all!" and he hurried away, as though fearful of his own resolution if he ventured to stay another second. For the rest of the evening, Elvira was silent and abstracted; the suddenness of the blow seemed to have stunned her, and she felt like one wandering in a dream. Was he really gone? Should she never see him more? were questions she scarcely dared even to ask herself. "He was nothing to me, a mere common acquaintance," she repeated incessantly; and yet she felt a wearisome void, a sickening disgust and impatience at every thing around her, which she had never experienced before. "What can be the matter with me," said she peevishly; "I shall never see him again; and it is the excess of weakness to feel an interest in the fate of one, who is evidently so indifferent about me; and yet he seemed affected when he said we were about to part. Was he really so? But of what consequence to me is it whether he were so or not. I shall never see him more." And Elvira sighed involuntarily at the thought. "I am devoted to other prospects. I—in short, I will think of him no more." And, in pursuance of this magnanimous resolution, she thought of nothing else all night.

The following day, Elvira and her friends went into the country; but, as Cheops had predicted, the duke and Sir Ambrose proved quite unequal to the task they had undertaken, and they only lost their popularity by the attempt. Men were disgusted to see personages hitherto considered so respectable descend to meanness, and the shallowness of the artifices by which it was intended to impose upon them excited their contempt. In the mean time, Lord Edmund was not more successful in London than his friends in the country: he had marched a chosen body of troops within a convenient distance of the metropolis; in consequence of which ill-judged measure, the members of the council, to show that they were not influenced by the fear of military authority, and to vindicate their independence, invariably opposed every measure that he suggested.

As the law, however, forbade any decisive promises till the actual day of election, there was still hope, though the friends of Elvira struggled on, rather from a wish not too hastily to abandon her cause, than from any rational, well-founded prospect of success.

In the midst of these anxieties, Elvira's health indeed seemed rapidly declining. A weight that nothing could alleviate, hung upon her spirits; she made no effort to secure voters; but pale, silent, and melancholy, she glided about—the ghost of her former self. Still, however, she was lovely; the increased delicacy of her complexion, and shadowy lightness of her form, harmonized well with the general style of her beauty; whilst her fine eyes, shaded by their long silken lashes, only shone more brilliantly from the glowing hectic of the cheek below.

The time fixed for the important ceremony now rapidly approached; the election of the deputies was concluded, and the families of the duke and Sir Ambrose prepared to return to town. The night, however, before they departed, the duke gave a grand fête champêtre to the neighbouring gentry; and as a considerable number of the deputies were expected, he particularly enjoined Elvira to exert herself to the utmost to win their suffrages. Never perhaps had Elvira looked more beautiful than she did that night, as, pale, trembling and timid, she received her numerous guests; and never, perhaps, was effect more magical than that which her appearance produced. Her very diffidence and modesty attracted; and the reserve, with which she shunned, rather than sought the attention of the crowd, completed the enchantment.

"It is her fear of seeming to wish to interest us," whispered one deputy to another, "that makes her treat us so coldly."

"Yes," replied the other; "and I like her the better for it. If she were to attempt to make herself agreeable, I should hate her; the duke and Sir Ambrose have sickened us of that!"

The fête was given in the gardens of the duke, which were beautiful and extensive, and now brilliantly illuminated by lamps suspended from the trees. There was something, however, not quite congenial to Elvira's taste in thus marrying the gorgeous splendour of art to the simplicity of nature, and she sighed heavily as she watched the flaring lamps scorching the calm pale verdure of the trees.

"Now this is as it should be," said the old duke, as he led his daughter to the pavilion appointed for her to receive her guests; "Elvira now looks like herself. Does she not, Dr. Coleman?"

The doctor shook his head: "I fear," began he—

"Oh! we will have no fears to-night!" cried the duke gaily; "remember, Elvira! every thing now depends upon you. Play the part of the smiling, condescending hostess; win the hearts of the deputies, and you will make that of your old father leap for joy. We shall have a gay party, sha'n't we, doctor?" continued he, eyeing the groups as they advanced. "I wish your friend, Henry Seymour, were here amongst us."

Elvira started, and deep blushes suffused her cheeks at the mention of this name. The doctor eyed her attentively, though he replied as though he had not noticed her agitation. "It was urgent business, you know, that obliged him to leave England."

"He was a charming youth," said the duke; "so gay and yet so fearless. I think, however, I observed that his spirits seemed much depressed the last time I saw him."

"You know he said it was the death—I mean the illness of a relation, that compelled him to go."

"Young men don't generally feel so much for the illness, or even death of old ones," returned the duke: "now, if I were to judge, doctor, I should think it far more likely it was some love affair. But we can't stay talking about it now. I must go, and attend to my guests: and do you mind, Elvira, and make yourself agreeable."

Poor Elvira, however, was, perhaps, never less fitted to obey her father's injunctions than at this moment; for the conversation she had just heard, had quite deranged her nerves. Her father's supposition inflicted a deep pang on her heart; and though she went through the duties of her station mechanically, her mind wandered to Henry Seymour.

It was a lovely night, and the general effect of the scene, as groups of elegantly-dressed people flitted to and fro through the lighted groves, was striking in the extreme. Beautiful flowering exotics decorated the pavilion of Elvira, and the balmy air that fanned their blossoms, seemed loaded with sweets; whilst the richly illuminated castle, rearing its lofty towers in awful grandeur in the distance, had the appearance of a fairy palace.

Elvira listlessly gazed upon the magic scene, till she felt almost fainting with the fatigue her situation as hostess imposed upon her; and she looked with a languid and almost despairing eye upon the crowds that came still pouring into the gardens. The throng, however, now opened, and a tall and dignified figure found its way through the mass. It was Lord Edmund: he approached rapidly, and threw himself at Elvira's feet: "My adored Elvira!" exclaimed he.

"You here, my Lord?" cried the princess; whose eyes, enfeebled by exhaustion, had not permitted her to recognise him till he was immediately before her: "I did not expect to see you here to-night!"

"Does my presence pain you then?" said Lord Edmund, looking at her attentively. "They told me you were ill, and I do indeed find you changed."

"I am better now," returned Elvira faintly.

"Do not deceive yourself," cried he, with the most intense anxiety. "You are ill — you are not equal to this fatigue. Retire from this scene, it will destroy you."

"I dare not," replied Elvira, still more feebly, "without permission from my father; though, I own, I do feel exhausted!"

Lord Edmund waited for no more; but darted to find the duke, and obtain his wished for sanction. The next instant, his place was supplied by Prince Ferdinand, who had been invited into the country a few days before by the duke; and who, with the inconstancy natural to his disposition, had now become as deeply smitten with Elvira, as he had before been with Rosabella. Elvira, however, saw him not; and, looking gratefully after Lord Edmund, sighed profoundly as she lost sight of him among the crowd.

"Happy Edmund!" said the prince; "what would I not give to create a feeling in that lovely bosom, like that caused by thy absence!"

Elvira blushed at the earnest gaze of the youthful German, as she replied, without exactly knowing what she said, "Do you suppose, then, that the absence of Lord Edmund gave me pain?"

"What other cause can I divine for your melancholy?" said Ferdinand. "Adored by every heart, admired by every eye, and blest at once with rank, beauty, and affection, what can Elvira wish? — and what can cloud her brow with sorrow, or heave her lovely bosom with a sigh, unless it be the loss of the favoured lover whom ambition bids her sacrifice?"

"And think you so poorly of me," returned Elvira indignantly, "as to suppose, if I really loved Lord Edmund, that ambition would tempt me to sacrifice him?"

"Can a heart like yours then be really dead to love?" said the prince, gazing upon her earnestly. "Can Nature have formed such exquisite beauty, and forgotten to give a soul to pity the wretches it must make?"

Elvira blushed deeply as he spoke, for his ardent look embarrassed her; and her eyes having been modestly withdrawn, again met those of Lord Edmund, who had returned without her perceiving him. 'Twas but for a moment, however, that she gazed upon him, for she shrank aghast from his withering glance. Jealousy and hatred curled his lips, and darkened upon his brow; whilst his features seemed so changed, that Elvira could scarcely believe he was indeed the same she had so lately spoken with.

"I beg your Highness's pardon," said he haughtily; "I would not have presumed to intrude, if I had known you were engaged. I fancied that you wished to retire, and had obtained the duke's permission for your doing so; but—"

"Oh, thank you! thank you, Edmund!" cried Elvira; "most gladly will I seek my chamber." Then marking a slight smile upon Prince Ferdinand's face, she hesitated, for she recollected the interpretation he had put upon her melancholy and indifference. Lord Edmund's agony was beyond description: he saw her hesitation; he saw her look at Ferdinand, and fancying she sought his approval before she would retire, his jealous rage was unbounded, and, darting at her a look of ungovernable passion, he sprang from the pavilion, and was out of sight in an instant. Elvira could not bear his look, nor his unreasonable jealousy; and, exhausted by her previous fatigue, she fainted. A crowd soon gathered round her, and she was carried to her chamber in a state of insensibility.

"Mark me!" said a figure muffled in a thick cloak, speaking in a deep, low whisper, as he laid his hand upon the arm of Father Morris, who stood gazing after Elvira, with a look of intense anxiety; "she must not die; for if she does, I swear by the holy tomb of Osiris at Philæ, Rosabella never shall be Queen!"

From that hour, Elvira recovered; and the consumptive symptoms, that had so strongly excited the alarm of her friends, entirely disappeared.

Lord Edmund was conversing earnestly with one of the deputies, and, notwithstanding his jealousy, advocating the cause of Elvira with vehemence, when he was informed that she had fainted: his first impulse was to fly to her assistance; and when he found she had been removed to her chamber, his heart smote him for the cruel manner in which he had left her.

"She was really ill," thought he; "and, in her feeble state, my harshness overpowered her. But never again shall my foolish jealousy disturb her peace. No! let her scorn me—hate me, if she will. I will bear all the tortures she can inflict, rather than again hazard wounding that gentle bosom. Let her smile on whom she lists, even upon that hated German, I will not repine: if she be happy, I will ask no more."

Thus thought Edmund, and he knew not that he deceived himself, till he saw Prince Ferdinand, who, with the happy elasticity of youth, was chatting gaily with one of the beauties of the court. "Love him!" thought he, as a scornful smile passed over his features—"love him, did I say? Oh, no! it is impossible; I could not endure to see her love that coxcomb:" and, shuddering with the torments of jealousy, he turned away.

Cheops was near him, muffled in a thick cloak that shrouded him from observation; the Mummy marked the changes in Lord Edmund's countenance, and read well the feelings they betrayed.

"Yes, even he," said he, with one of his fearful laughs, "will soon be mine; for never yet did man trust in his own strength, that did not fall."

CHAPTER XVIII.

The day of election now rapidly approached. The duke, Sir Ambrose, the rival candidates, and the opposition lords, were all in London. The deputies were also assembled; and though it was forbidden to declare publicly for whom they intended to vote, till the decisive moment arrived; yet the popular feeling seemed so strongly in favour of Rosabella, that there appeared scarcely a chance for her rival.

Exulting in her expected triumph, and confident of success, Rosabella sate in the splendid boudoir allotted to her use in Lord Gustavus's house, musing on her hoped-for grandeur. A large mirror was opposite to her; and as Rosabella saw her own fine figure reflected in it, joy sparkled in her eyes, and her mind wandered enraptured through scenes of future glory. Thus, completely absorbed in pleasing meditations, Rosabella was not aware that Cheops stood before her, till she heard his full, deep-toned voice repeating her name.

"Rosabella!" said he—"Rosabella! Queen of England! hail!"

"Cheops!" exclaimed she.

"Hail to the Queen of England!" resumed he: "no longer need you stoop to solicit suffrages: your fate is sealed!"

"Think you that I am quite safe?" asked the princess; her eyes sparkling, and her cheeks glowing.

"Certainly—there cannot be a doubt."

"Then I may bid defiance to these wretches, and need no longer submit to their caprices, or be subservient to their humours."

"Not unless you like it."

"Like it!" exclaimed Rosabella, her eyes flashing fire; "can you suppose I like to practise meanness?"

"Policy, indeed, recommends a contrary course," continued the Mummy; "as, if you do not assert your own independence, they will encroach upon your condescension, and treat you as a slave."

Rosabella bit her lips, and her bosom swelled with indignation.

The Mummy took no notice of her agitation, but went on. "Let them not bind you by any promises. Prove yourself a free and independent sovereign. Trample upon them, and they will crouch at your feet: but crouch to them, and they will trample upon you!"

"You say right," said Rosabella proudly; "and my would-be masters shall soon find their error. They think weakness has made me submit to their arrogance; but they shall see their folly."

The influence the Mummy exercised over the minds of all those he came in contact with was astonishing; and, in pursuance of his advice, Rosabella, from this moment, resumed her usual imperious manner; and received the compliments paid to her with the air rather of an empress long seated upon the throne, than that of an aspiring candidate for regal honours, dependant only upon the favour of the people. This excessive confidence, however, displeased the deputies.

"She hardly leaves us a choice," said they; "for she seems to command us to choose her. Notwithstanding the strength of her party, and the weakness of her rival, we don't think she should take the thing quite in her own hands: the old Queen ordered that the people should choose her successor; but this princess seems to have chosen herself. It is very kind of her to wish to save us the trouble; but, with her good leave, we think we might have managed to go through it without her help."

These murmurs, however, though deep, were not loud; the party of Rosabella being too firmly established for any one to dare openly to oppose it. The opposition lords had all returned to town, and, though they had not completely succeeded in the object of their journey to the country, they had at least satisfied themselves; and by the activity they had displayed, given themselves, as they imagined, a just title to the gratitude of their future Queen.

In the mean time, the friends of Elvira almost despaired; few persons of note declared themselves her advocates; and though the favourable impression she had made upon the deputies still faintly operated, the feeling was fast fading away. An invincible repugnance to appear as the leader of a party, oppressed her; and she shrank from the public gaze with a sensation little short of horror. Lord Edmund, however, still remained her firm and almost her only friend. Yet, though he exerted every nerve on her behalf, even he despaired of obtaining her election. Sometimes, indeed, as he gazed upon her beauty, a selfish feeling crept over his soul, and he could scarcely repress an emotion of joy, as he thought of the possibility that she might still be his; for the very qualities that impeded her success, only endeared her yet more fondly to his heart. The next instant, however, his nobler feelings would reproach this selfish joy, and with a kind of penitential sorrow, he would strive by fresh efforts to destroy the hopes, for the gratification of which his very soul panted.

"I presume," said Lord Gustavus de Montfort to Rosabella, the day before that appointed for the election, "your Highness does not intend to make Lord Maysworth a minister as well as a general; for, thinking as I think, and as I am confident every one else must think, I feel assured he has no talents for the cabinet."

"As Queen of England, my Lord," returned Rosabella proudly, "I will not be dictated to; though I will do my best to choose such ministers as may, in my judgment, be most likely to promote the welfare of my country."

Lord Gustavus was thunderstruck, and he gazed after her, as she retired, with mingled feelings of astonishment and indignation. "You are not Queen of England yet, however," said he to himself, "and it is possible you never may be. What pride! what haughtiness! If I had been a slave, she could not have shown more contempt. 'When I am Queen of England,' said she, I 'will not be dictated to.' 'Queen of England,' said she? Humph! thinking as I think, and as I am sure every one else must think, it is possible, that that is a contingency that may never arrive. Humph! 'I will not be dictated to'—Humph! Well, certainly I must confess I never heard a more dignified 'will not' in my life."

It was the hour when Lord Gustavus was accustomed to hold a kind of levee where the partizans of the princess had been in the habit of assembling, under the guise of casual visitors; and as he thus cogitated, Lord Maysworth and Dr. Hardman were announced.

"My dear Lord Gustavus," cried the former, "you cannot imagine how impatient I feel to have to-morrow over. The uniform of the household-troops is horrible: I have determined to change it the very instant I am appointed commander-in-chief."

"If you should obtain that situation," replied Lord Gustavus doubtingly.

"What do you mean?" asked his friend, in astonishment. "I thought the means we had taken must infallibly ensure success."

"They must ensure the election of Rosabella," replied Lord Gustavus.

"And is not that all we wish?"

"Not quite," returned Lord Gustavus dryly.

"I do not understand you," said Lord Maysworth.

"What can you mean?" demanded Dr. Hardman.

"I mean," replied Lord Gustavus, in his usual cold, precise manner, "that, thinking as I think, and as I am sure every one else must think, from the conversation that has just taken place between the princess and myself, I am convinced that our possession of the places she has promised to us, is by no means the necessary consequence of her accession to the throne."

"Oh!" cried his auditors, looking perfectly aghast: a farther explanation confirmed their fears. "I could not have believed it!" exclaimed both; and as the partizans of Rosabella continued to arrive, they were successively apprized of and paralyzed by the appalling news. Divers were the sensations thus excited: but amongst all, notwithstanding their professed disinterestedness, there was not one whose sentiments remained unchanged by the intelligence.

In the mean time, Rosabella, in the solitude of her own chamber, became aware of the imprudence she had committed, though she brooded in secret over her uneasiness, and felt too proud to avow it even to Marianne; whilst that faithful confidant, quite unsuspicious of the error of her mistress, exulted in her expected triumph with as much transport as though it had been her own.

"To-morrow," said she, "I shall have to do homage to my Queen, and I shall have the rapture of seeing crowds kneel humbly at her feet. Oh, would the happy day were come! how tedious will seem this long, long night! how wearisome will be the hours! Does not your heart also throb, my princess? To-morrow I shall see my Queen. To-morrow! oh, would it were to-day!"

The important day at last arrived, and the delegates,

The Mummy!

assembled in Blackheath Square, awaited with impatience the arrival of the princesses. Each was to deliver a speech; after which, a nobleman was to be permitted to address the mob on her behalf, and then the majority of their votes was to decide.

The rival princesses appeared, and were hailed with enthusiasm. They were dressed with the utmost simplicity, in the purest white; whilst from their heads hung long veils of gossamer web, the ample folds of which effectually shielded their persons from observation. They were followed by their respective suites; Lord Gustavus and the opposition lords being most conspicuous in that of Rosabella; and Lord Edmund in that of Elvira. The Duke and Sir Ambrose, attended by the reverend fathers Morris and Murphy, were amongst the number of spectators: the two former feeling too much agitated to allow of their appearing as actors in the scene; and the others being, from different reasons, equally disqualified from taking a part in it.

All now was silent—the tumultuous, wave-like heaving of the multitude ceased; and every one listened in breathless expectation—for the princesses were about to speak. It was an awful moment: the poor old duke's heart beat almost audibly; he sate, his eyes fixed upon the ground, not daring to look up, and holding the hand of his friend, Sir Ambrose, firmly in his own. It was Rosabella who was to speak first: she advanced with a firm, decided step; and when the attendants drew back the veil that covered her, the assembled multitude uttered a shout of admiration at her beauty. Her dark eyes flashed fire, as she proudly surveyed the crowd; and anticipated triumph gave an animated glow to her fine features. She looked, indeed, already a Queen, and seemed born only to command, and be obeyed. The multitude were awed by her presence; and listened with uplifted eyes, and the most profound silence, whilst she thus addressed them:

"My Lords and Gentlemen,

"I feel the presumption I am guilty of, in thus venturing to address so august an assembly; but I trust the magnitude of the occasion that calls me forward may afford an excuse for my temerity. I come, gentlemen, to offer myself to you as your Sovereign, and the exalted nature of the trust I wish you to repose in me, inspires me with courage to deserve it. Yes, gentlemen, I say to deserve it; for I should consider myself unworthy to be appointed your Queen, if I were to shrink from performing any of the duties attendant upon the station; and one of the most arduous of these do I consider that of thus addressing you. I am aware, that, upon occasions like the present, it is usual for the aspiring candidate to promise miracles of reformation, that are to be effected upon the obtaining of power; I promise nothing of the kind, for I will tie myself to no promises. Elect me for your Queen, and I will fulfil the duties of my rank, according to the best of my own judgment. I will not submit to dictation; neither will I be censured by my subjects. I will be a free, independent Sovereign, or I will remain a subject. I scorn to attempt to practise any deception upon you. I wish you to see me as I really am; and then, if you think me worthy of the high office I aspire to, then, at least, I may assure you, you shall never have reason to blush for your choice; nor shall the proud character which England has so long maintained, ever suffer a stain upon its glory at my hands. No, my countrymen, haughty as I may be deemed, I assure you, with sincerity, that I have ever held the name of Englishwoman as my noblest boast; and that I would not relinquish my title to it, were kingdoms offered in exchange. I can say no more. If you approve me as your Sovereign, your voices will obtain the fulfilment of your wishes; if you do not, worlds would not tempt me to accept the throne."

Rosabella now sate down amidst thunders of applause, whilst acclamations of "Long live Rosabella!" rent the air. These symptoms of approbation were, however, only produced by her beauty and her commanding manner; for when men came to analyze her speech, they found much in it to disapprove. The haughty manner in which she had disavowed control, indeed was neither calculated to win new friends, nor secure those she already had: as the counsellors who had so warmly supported her cause, had certainly not imagined, that by so doing, they should shut the door of preferment against themselves; and what hope of promotion or power could remain during the reign of a Queen who had thus openly announced her intention of acting entirely for herself?

The prejudices of the people, too, were wounded; they had been so accustomed to promises of reformation and relief from taxation, upon the accession of a new Sovereign, that they were disappointed at not receiving them, although they knew from experience, that they meant nothing: just as persons fond of flattery cannot live without it, though they are well acquainted with its fallacy. Besides, even experience cannot make some people wise; and though the hopes of the English had been so often disappointed, it was pleasant still to have something held out to them to hope for. These thoughts soon arose in the breasts of the multitude; and a rising murmur was beginning to swell upon the ear, when the assembly was hushed to silence by perceiving Lord Noodle had risen, and was about to address them.

"My lords and gentlemen," said he, "it is with feelings of considerable embarrassment that I rise to address you. Every thing that can be said, has been said; and every thing that has been said, ought to have been said; and every thing that ought to have been said, has been said. What, then, can there possibly be left for me to say?

"Let it not be supposed, however, by my saying this, that I have nothing to say for myself; on the contrary, I think every body must allow I have said a great deal upon the said subject;" (here the noble lord tittered at his own wit, and well it was that he did so; as, if he had not, perhaps nobody might have found it out;) "say what I will, however, one thing must be clear, and that is, (if I was to speak for an hour I could say no more;) — that is, that you must have a Queen; and that you cannot choose a better one than the noble lady who has just sat down! — and so, gentlemen, she having finished, I think I cannot do better than follow her example!"

Shouts and roars of laughter followed this speech, to the infinite delight of the enlightened orator; and he bowed and bowed on all sides, till his little head and bobbing periwig seemed to have acquired the gift of perpetual motion.

No sooner was the tumult a little subsided, than Elvira came forward to address the people. When her veil was removed, her agitation was extreme. Elvira was delicately fair, and the "eloquent blood spoke in her cheeks" in a thousand varying tints; for a few seconds she stood, her eyes fixed upon the ground, apparently endeavouring to collect herself: then raising her eyes, she seemed on the point of speaking, but her courage failing as she surveyed the immense multitude, every eye fixed upon her, and every ear listening for her words, the sounds died upon her lips, and after a few ineffectual attempts to speak, she buried her face in her veil, and sobbed aloud.

Who can describe the agitation of her aged father at this moment! When she appeared, he had risen, and, leaning forward, listened with a fearful eagerness, as though his ear would drink in every syllable, and as though his own death-warrant hung upon her words. He became pale as he saw her agitation, and his countenance varied with every variation of hers; till, when he saw her total inability to speak, his lips became of livid whiteness, he uttered a piercing shriek, and fell senseless to the ground!

A bustle immediately took place; the duke was carried off; and Elvira remained pale, trembling, and almost fainting, leaning against one of the pillars that supported the canopy over the platform upon which she stood. An awful pause ensued, which was at last broken by Lord Edmund rushing forward, and eagerly addressing the crowd in the following words:

"My friends and countrymen,

"If one spark of kindness and compassion dwell in your breasts; if your hearts are open to noble feelings; if you can pity defenceless age and helpless womanhood, listen to me now! Hear me whilst I plead the cause of the timid female now before you; who, agitated by the solemn occasion for which you are convened, and awed by the august majesty of this assembly, finds it impossible to give vent to her feelings in words; for difficult, indeed, is it to express by words the strong emotions of the heart. Oh! would to Heaven, my friends, that I could lay her heart open before you, that you might there read the love of her country—the devotion to your dearest interests—and the generous wish to sacrifice her domestic happiness to secure yours, that prompt her this day to appear before you. Do you fear tyranny? Is this trembling woman likely to impose it? Do you wish remission from oppression? Is not she who evidently possesses such extreme sensibility likely to relieve your cares? Can her breast, which now throbs with emotion, ever be deaf to the cry of misery? No, no; that gentle spirit which shrinks from exposure in the garish light of day, will devote itself to soothing your woes, and lightening your burdens. Do you wish for victory? Has not my arm been hitherto successful, and am I not devoted to Elvira?

"My countrymen, I plead not from interested motives, God knows I do not! Nay, there may be some among you who know I now plead for the destruction of my dearest hopes: but the welfare of my country is more to me than my own. I give my country the treasure that might have been mine: contented, if by the sacrifice of my own happiness, I can secure that of thousands.

"My countrymen, I cannot more strongly prove my devotion to your interests, for if you choose Elvira for your Queen, my widowed heart will have no bride but glory. Take, however, the treasure I resign to you. Prize her as she deserves, and Heaven in its mercy grant that prudent counsellors and sagacious statesmen may so direct her steps, that victory may shine on her banners, wisdom in her counsels, and happiness in her kingdom!"

Lord Edmund stopped, overpowered by his own emotions; and his agitation found an echo in the bosom of every auditor. The effect of his speech was instantaneous: cries of "Elvira shall be our Queen!" "Elvira for ever!" rose in deafening tumult from the crowd, nor did there appear a single dissentient voice. In fact, after all that can be said upon the subject, feeling is the only true eloquence. The passions of the crowd were strongly excited: the fainting of the duke; the agitation of Elvira; and the speech of Lord Edmund, who was the hero of the day, absolutely had driven them distracted. They shouted again and again that Elvira, and Elvira alone, should be Queen, and, forming a triumphal car, placed her in it, and dragged her along to Westminster Abbey, where the ceremony of the coronation was appointed to take place. This venerable pile, which had stood for centuries, and resisted alike the war of nature, and the destroying hand of innovation, with which the barbarous taste of the middle ages had endeavoured to destroy its grandeur, shone forth in all its original splendour, and afforded another magnificent proof of the length of time the labours of man survive the term of his fragile existence.

It had been a brilliant sight, when Westminster Hall was crowded with the nobles of the land, to choose the council of state; but far more splendid was it now, when, after the religious part of the ceremony of the coronation had been performed in the Abbey, the trembling and beautiful Queen entered its sumptuous walls, surrounded by her counsellors, and welcomed with transport by her kneeling subjects. All had been previously prepared for the ceremony, as the ordinance of the old Queen had directed the coronation to take place immediately after the election; and the venerable Hall was now crowded with the nobles and ladies of Claudia's court, splendidly attired, waiting for the Queen, whom the choice of the deputies might give them, with the most eager impatience. Elvira was received with transports; and though, perhaps, under different circumstances, her rival might have been honoured with equal rapture, yet, as Elvira knew it not, the thought did not damp her pleasure.

In the mean time Father Morris had remained aghast, a prey to the combined tortures of grief, rage, and disappointment. The crowd had disappeared, yet still he stood gazing upon the platform, the speechless image of despair.

"For Heaven's sake, do not remain here," cried a voice he knew only too well; and, obeying the impulse of Marianne's arm, he suffered himself to be led from the scaffold, where all his hopes had perished. There was a small house, at no great distance from the spot, where the partizans of Rosabella had held frequent conferences respecting their plans for securing her election; and to this place Marianne led the disappointed friar.

"Curses on the fiend that has betrayed me to my ruin!" said he, as he threw himself upon a sofa in this abode: "may demons haunt him here, and eternal misery be his portion hereafter!"

The fiendish laugh of Cheops rang in the father's ears as he pronounced these words; and ere he finished, the hated form of the Mummy stood before him.

"What, Father Morris!" cried the Egyptian, "is this your treatment of your friends? Fie! fie! is this your strength of mind? I am ashamed of you. Is it the part of a man of courage to shrink from such a slight reverse? However, I am still your friend, and if you will follow my advice—"

"Avaunt! demon!" cried Father Morris; "tempt me no more! Ruin hangs upon thy words, and it is thy advice that has destroyed me."

"Say rather, your own evil passions," returned the Mummy.

"Fiend!" exclaimed the monk; "was it not by thy advice Rosabella rejected the address I had prepared for her, and determined to deliver her own sentiments extempore."

"Such an expression of her genuine feelings was likely to produce ten times the effect of a studied address. The oration of Lord Edmund was from the feeling of the moment, and you saw its power was magical."

"And it was not by your desire that the fool Lord Noodle seconded her, instead of Lord Gustavus, as I had intended?"

"A ridiculous fool was more likely to put the people in good-humour than a prosing one."

"Yes, yes, I know; it was thus you made your plans seem feasible, but how have they succeeded?"

"Success is not always the test of merit. How could I foresee the fainting of the duke, and the agitation of Elvira? That timid silence said far more for her than words: if she had spoken, she would have had no chance."

"Would she were dead!" said Father Morris, grinding his teeth.

"So would you seal your ruin. Rosabella would be suspected, and her chance of reigning destroyed—destroyed for ever."

"What shall I do?"

"Let Elvira reign!—Nay, start not! for it is but for a time: she will naturally make Edmund her first counsellor from gratitude for the service he has rendered her; and, as he has sense and talent, he will as naturally either reject employing the noble lords who were your friends entirely; or, at best, give them but subordinate situations. Their hopes having been previously raised, they will feel this disappointment bitterly, and look back with longing eyes to Rosabella, by whom they were promised place and power. That princess must moderate her natural haughtiness: if she wish to reign, she must submit to bend before she rise; for, though ambition be the most lofty of all passions, perhaps no one makes its votaries occasionally condescend to greater meanness. At present patience alone is required. Novelty is always delightful; but the pleasure it produces can never be lasting: and the expectations of men having been raised too high by the brilliancy with which a new government is certain to commence, they will soon be disposed to quarrel with every thing that may chance to fall short of the standard they will then propose to themselves: though this same standard, if they give themselves time to consider, they would find far too exalted for mortals to have ever any hopes of reaching. Their extravagant expectations not being realized, they will then plunge into the opposite extreme; they will see every thing with a jaundiced eye; and, not liking to own they find themselves deceived, they will overturn the government of Elvira to conceal for ever the folly they have been guilty of."

"But will not the government of Rosabella afterwards share the same fate?"

"No: for they will have learnt wisdom by experience; and having just suffered from the inconveniences inseparable from a revolution, they will idolize every word and action of Rosabella, to spare themselves the necessity of again undergoing the same horrors, and yet avoid the charge of inconsistency. They will thus fear even to censure, and will gloss over any thing that may not quite please them, rather than run the risk of again interrupting that tranquillity which the late disturbance has made them taste the sweets of."

The sophistry of Cheops was well suited to the feelings of his hearers; and well did he know how to work upon the passions of those he conversed with. The indignation of Father Morris and Marianne subsided, and they again became the Egyptian's devoted slaves. Cheops watched them as they retired; a smile of derision curling his haughty lip.

"Fools that they are!" said he, as again a fearful expression flashed across his saturnine countenance: "by Typhon! they are scarcely worth deceiving, for they rush blindfold into the net."

In the mean time, nothing could exceed the grandeur of the scene exhibiting in Westminster Hall. The ceremony was finished; for the Queen had taken oaths of fidelity to the interests of her new subjects, and had received their humblest homage in return. A sumptuous banquet was now served, where all that could please the eye mingled in luxuriant profusion with all that could tempt the appetite. Music completed the charm; and as the harmonious notes swelled through the lofty dome, it seemed a choir of angels rejoicing from on high. Thus, whilst all that could gratify the senses was combined, the fairy loveliness of Elvira seemed to fit her well to be the goddess of the scene; and the figure of the poor old duke, her father, gazing at her with indescribable rapture—the tears trickling down his furrowed cheeks, and his long white hair hanging loose upon his shoulders, completed the interest of the picture.

Great and glorious was the triumph of Elvira: but, whilst the nation rang with acclamations of joy, and bonfires and illuminations proclaimed the transport of the people, who shall paint the despair, the desolation, of the unfortunate Rosabella? Forlorn and deserted by her friends; despised and injured by him she loved; disappointed in the fairy dreams of her ambition; and disgusted with a world that had rejected her— what could she do? where find a refuge from her woes?

Rosabella sought no refuge: wretched as she was, her proud spirit still supported her: she neither retired from society, nor gave herself up to the paroxysms of despair. Hers was not a mind to brood over useless grief. She felt her wrongs, it is true, and most keenly did she feel them, but she wasted not her time in lamentation, and burnt only to avenge them. Marianne had communicated to her the advice of Cheops, and her whole soul was now devoted to revenge. For this, she determined to obey his injunctions; to bend her haughty spirit to his wishes; to conciliate the friends that had deserted her; and to submit to any meanness to keep up a party in the state. This done, she resolved to watch for the errors unavoidable in a new government; to take advantage of every weakness, and foment every discontent; in short, to open a chasm under her rival's feet, and then, like the lion pismire on the brink of his sandy trap, to rest concealed until the entanglement of the expected prey enabled her to rush upon and destroy it.

Elvira's disposition was naturally noble; and, satisfied with the possession of the throne, she sought no farther triumph. Her generous soul was touched by the apparent resignation of her rival, and she endeavoured, by every means in her power, to console her for her disappointment. The duke had quitted the country, and now resided entirely with his daughter; whilst upon Rosabella, Elvira, with the utmost delicacy, conferred a palace and a separate establishment.

Notwithstanding, however, the delicacy with which Elvira's favours were conferred, Rosabella could not forget that they were favours, and hers was not a mind to brook dependence. Her hatred for her cousin thus increased with the weight of her obligations, whilst that of Elvira had vanished with the occasion that gave it birth. It is, indeed, scarcely possible for a proud, haughty temper, like that of Rosabella, to love the person to whom it owes every thing. Such dispositions find infinitely more pleasure in obliging, than in being obliged — pride being gratified in one case and humbled in the other. People are thus often devotedly attached to their protégées, as they seem, in some measure, creations of their own, and lavish favours upon them with a profuse hand; but they often expect such devotion in return, that love withers into slavery, or changes into hatred, and what was once gratitude, soon becomes mortification.

Elvira had an arduous part to sustain. It was difficult to find the medium between giving too much or too little; and more difficult still, to discover a means of giving at all, without hurting the feelings of Rosabella. The sense she had of this, rendered the manner of Elvira towards her cousin, occasionally, cold and restrained, and Rosabella felt acutely the slightest change. She, indeed, saw every thing with a jaundiced eye: she imagined insults, where none were intended; she shrank from the slightest observation, that could be supposed to allude to her present situation; and she appeared to feel so much pain whenever she was in the society of Elvira, that the intercourse between the cousins gradually dwindled to a mere formal interchange of visits, and the customary ceremonials of court etiquette.

The cousins thus completely estranged from each other,

Rosabella's palace became the resort of the discontented. The King of Ireland had died soon after the departure of the Duke of Cornwall for the country, and those malcontents, formerly in his pay, being repulsed by his son, now crowded round Rosabella. Men of talents, but of dissolute habits; daring spirits that preyed upon themselves for want of employment; and desperate characters, to whom every change was agreeable, as they had nothing to lose, and every thing to hope for by a revolution, vied with each other in devoting themselves to her service. It was often grating to Rosabella's feelings to associate with wretches such as these; but to what cannot proud spirits sometimes submit, to gain the determined purpose of their souls! Every thing is swallowed up in one vast overwhelming passion, and minor difficulties are neither seen, thought of, nor felt.

Thus, Rosabella scrupled not to waste her time in the society of such beings as Lord Noodle and his friend Lord Doodle; she even stooped to flatter them, and occasionally to ask, and appear to follow their advice: she endured patiently the dictatorial prosing of Lord Gustavus, and listened with an appearance of interest to the wearisome pettinesses of Lord Maysworth. All she thought of, was whether any particular line of conduct were likely to conduce to placing her on the throne; and if it were, be it what it might, the haughty Rosabella instantly condescended to practise it. Taught by the late events not to rely too confidently upon her own strength, she rushed into the opposite extreme, and descended even unto servility.

In the mean time, the attention of Elvira was completely devoted to the establishment of her government. She had many qualities worthy of her rank; and some of the most conspicuous were her nobleness in forgetting injuries, and her inflexible sense of justice: thus, though she had made no promises herself to her people on the day of her election, she justly considered those made by Edmund on her part as equally binding, and endeavoured by every means in her power to redeem the pledges he had given. Cheops had judged rightly in supposing she would make Edmund her prime minister—her gratitude to him, indeed, was unbounded; and though her noble and generous disposition prevented her depriving the lords who had voted against her of their dignities, yet that the strong mind, and commanding genius of Edmund would make them dwindle into nonentities, he had also been equally correct in predicting. The noble lords, quite unconscious of their own inefficiency, were indignant at finding themselves subalterns where they had hoped to be commanders, and rallied round the standard of Rosabella, who, on her part, received them so graciously, that her former haughtiness was forgotten.

Elvira was not aware of their defection, or if she were, she thought them too insignificant to merit notice, her attention being entirely occupied in affairs which she considered of infinitely more importance. Though the laws of the old Queen had been excellent, many abuses had crept into the manner of putting them into execution; and these Elvira now, with the aid of Edmund, set herself diligently to work to discover and correct. She could not, indeed, have chosen an assistant more competent to the task. The penetrating mind and commanding genius of Edmund were unequalled. With a single glance, he saw where errors had been committed, and how they ought to be amended. Whilst under his auspices, vice was punished and virtue rewarded, goodness, though in rags, was raised to affluence, and villainy compelled to disgorge its ill-gotten wealth. Justice was impartially dispensed to all, and the first Monday in every month, the Queen proceeded in solemn state to the grand square at Blackheath, to receive there, in person, the petitions of her subjects.

The crowd assembled upon these occasions was immense. However well a constitution may be organized, it is impossible to give satisfaction to every one; and even under the best-regulated governments there will be always some who fancy themselves aggrieved. Besides, as free access was allowed on these occasions to every one, numbers went merely to see the Queen; and nothing could be better contrived for letting her Majesty know the real feelings of her subjects, than this arrangement; as, from the people being placed in lines, along each of which the Queen walked, she became alternately in personal contact with every separate individual. Like every thing else, however, that sounds perfect in theory, difficulties arose when this plan came to be put in practice: it was originally intended that the Queen should receive, with her own hands, and read herself, all the petitions that might be presented; but when it was found their numbers frequently amounted to some thousands, this scheme was abandoned as impracticable, and the Lords Noodle and Doodle were appointed to the important office of walking behind the Queen, carrying large bags, in which the petitions were deposited, and from which they would probably never again have emerged, if they had not been dragged to light by the persevering and indefatigable exertions of Lord Edmund.

The people, however, were not aware of this, and there was something in the show that delighted them. It was indeed a fine sight, to behold so many hundreds of human beings anxiously watching the movements of their beautiful Queen, as she glided along their ranks, smiling graciously upon all, and looking like an angel sent upon earth to dispense blessings to mankind: ladies of honour walking behind her, with pages bearing their train, and the two aged counsellors of state, bending beneath the weight of their ponderous bags, bringing up the rear.

Thus gloriously commenced Elvira's reign. The people, delighted with the attention paid to their wishes, and struck by some instances of the Queen's love of justice and hatred of oppression, lauded her to the skies; the nobility, hoping riches and power from her liberality, almost worshipped her; and the ambassadors of foreign powers, dreading the valour of Lord Edmund and his soldiers, offered the humblest homage at her feet. In short, all seemed to smile upon her, and the kingdom to bid fair shortly to rival even the imagined happiness of Utopia itself.

CHAPTER XIX.

In the mean time, what had become of Edric and Dr. Entwerfen? Gloomy indeed were the reflections of our travellers when they found themselves immured in a dungeon, so far from all they loved or reverenced, without friends, and accused of a horrible crime, from the guilt of which they felt it would be vain for them to attempt to free themselves. Days and weeks rolled on, yet no change took place in their destiny. Every night the grating of a rusty key in the lock announced the arrival of the gaoler, bringing their daily pittance of bread and water, but he never spoke, nor could the most earnest entreaties of the doctor and Edric bring one word from his lips.

Despair at length began to invade the bosoms of the travellers; till one day, as they were examining, for the thousandth time, the hieroglyphics on the stones in the wall, Edric perceived that one of them was loose. With infinite difficulty they removed the stone, and found a long vaulted passage, dimly lighted by an opening at the farther extremity. The transport of the prisoners, on making this discovery, was unbounded, and can only be imagined by those who have felt the loss of liberty, and rejoiced at its recovery.

When their first raptures had a little abated, they began to consult upon the best means of availing themselves of their good fortune, and preventing pursuit. The doctor had luckily several chemical preparations in his walking-stick; with one of these he dissolved the iron of their chains, so as to free Edric and himself from their weight, and then, smearing them over with the remainder of the composition, he laid them in a heap, exclaiming with a laugh, "The jailors will be dreadfully frightened when they find these fetters; for though they look perfect to the eye, they will crumble to pieces at the slightest touch."

Edric was too anxious to effect his escape, to listen to his tutor's exultation; and his arrangements being made, the travellers, with trembling steps and throbbing hearts, explored the vaulted passage, and found, to their infinite delight, that it had led them to the borders of the Nile. A small boat was anchored to the shore, and its crew, an old man and his son, who gained their living by conveying goods up the Nile, were peaceably taking their supper on the bank.

Edric and the doctor had taken the precaution to replace the stone that had concealed the vaulted passage, and having smeared the opposite wall with phosphorus, they had no doubt that when the jailor entered the prison, which he generally did in darkness, he would be too much alarmed to take any effectual means for pursuing them till it should be too late. Having luckily also plenty of money, that certain road to the human heart, they easily persuaded the old man to take them on board, and in a short time they embarked in his fragile vessel and set sail.

Slowly and silently they floated along the majestic river, which rolled in solemn waves like an inland sea, and swept proudly on to the ocean, seeming to scorn the degenerate land it left behind; and without one pang did our travellers quit for ever the fertile plains and gorgeous cities of Egypt. One only thought swelled in their bosoms, and that was joy at their escape. Offering up silent prayers of thanksgiving, our travellers continued their progress down the river, and, when morning dawned, and the enormous forms of the Pyramids were seen grimly frowning through the mist, they shuddered involuntarily, and, devoutly crossing themselves, muttered new prayers for protection and deliverance.

After a long and tedious voyage, our travellers at length reached the sea in safety. The mouths of the Delta were at that time the seat of extensive, and almost universal commerce; and our travellers trembled lest they should here encounter some emissary of their enemies, who might re-convey them to the prison from which they had so miraculously escaped. They found, however, the belief of their supernatural disappearance too strongly impressed upon the minds of the multitude for even a suspicion of their existence to remain; and they stood upon that sumptuous quay, surrounded by Greeks, Russians, Egyptians, Arabs, and Turks, without exciting a single remark, or obtaining the slightest attention. They wished to proceed to Constantinople, then the capital of the powerful empire of Greece, and entered into conversation with the master of a felucca, for that purpose.

"I will attend to you directly, gentlemen," said the sailor, leaving some persons with whom he had been previously talking: "but I have been listening to such a horrid tale!"

"What was it?" asked Edric, suspecting the subject, but aware that to seem incurious upon such an occasion, might betray that they were already only too well informed.

"Two sorcerers," returned the man, "have been taken into custody, for blowing up the Pyramids and bewitching the mummies!"

"And how were they punished?" asked Edric.

"Oh, you haven't heard half they did yet!" said the man. "When they were put in prison for their pranks, the Old One came to their help, and carried them off in a flame of fire, leaving a long train of light after them in the sky, like the tail of a blazing comet. Dick Jones, who was telling me, swears he saw them all going off together. The old one hanging by the Devil's horn, and the young one keeping fast hold of his tail!"

"Shocking!" said Edric; scarcely able, however, to repress a smile at this proof of the vividness of Dick Jones's imagination.

"I haven't told you half," resumed the man. "All Sumatra rings with it; several have gone mad, and others died with fear; and the man who was with Dick Jones, and who was one of the soldiers of the guard set over them, assured me as a positive fact, that the chains they had had on, and left behind them, crumbled between his fingers like a bit of rotten wood."

"It is very awful!" said Edric.

"Ay, is it not?" rejoined the man; "thank God I was not there to see! I am sure the very look of one of those conjurors would have driven me mad! I never could abide such things."

Edric now, with some difficulty, persuaded the man to return to the subject of their transit.

"I am very sorry, Sir," said he; "but I don't think there'll be a vessel going out to Constantinople for this week at least; for they've got the plague there, and our magistrates won't let a ship that has been there, return to our harbour again without performing quarantine; and that is such a hindrance to trade that our folks don't like it. But perhaps you're in no hurry, and can wait?"

"Oh yes, we can wait quite well!" said the doctor, trembling with anxiety to be off.

The sailor, however, had no occasion to say more; for the bare mention of the plague was quite sufficient to deter our travellers from visiting Constantinople; and finding he was bound for Malta, and that no other vessel would quit the harbour that day, they hastily embarked, notwithstanding his vessel was old and inconvenient, and not forwarded by steam, and though the superior certainty of the steam-packets was now so generally felt and acknowledged by all, that perhaps this was the only common sailing-boat in the harbour. The joy of our travellers at their deliverance was, however, too great to permit them to dwell upon trifles; and as the cabin was scarcely habitable, they resolved to remain on deck the whole of the voyage, being determined to submit to any thing sooner than delay their departure. Accordingly they stretched themselves upon their cloaks, and, reclining against some ropes, watched attentively the lovely scene around them. The evening was beautiful, and, as the shores of Egypt swiftly receded from their view, they felt their minds soothed by the contemplation of the grand scene that presented itself. There is, indeed, something in the awful majesty of the world of waters, which, like the gigantic monuments of Egypt, powerfully affects the mind by its very simplicity, and, by raising the soul far above the common trifling occurrences of life, soothes it to tranquillity.

The voyage was long, for contrary winds impeded their progress; and one evening, after Dr. Entwerfen had remained for some time gazing steadfastly on the water, with a look of deep abstraction, he exclaimed suddenly, "There will be a storm!"

"Impossible!" returned Edric. "The sun set in unwonted splendour, spreading its rays of purple and gold through the waters like a jewelled diadem; and the wind is even now dying away to a gentle breeze, which scarcely curls the surface of the ocean as our bark dances gaily over it."

"That is a bad sign," said the doctor. "Have you not often heard that a storm is generally preceded by a calm? You will find it no metaphor now."

The moon soon shone brightly; and as the ship ploughed her way slowly through the almost motionless waves, its beams sparkled through the spray, which fell in silvery showers over the prow. All now was still, except the heaving of the vessel, and the monotonous splashing of the waters as she slowly worked her way through them. The wind gradually sunk, and the sails only feebly flapped in the breeze that could no longer inflate them, till at last even that failed, and the vessel, completely becalmed, lay like a log upon the water, which spread like a vast and tranquil mirror around her.

Bitterly now did our travellers regret the precipitate haste that had made them embark in such a frail, unmanageable boat; and they regarded with longing eyes the compact steam-packets that glided past them; their black smoke curling in the air as they were wafted swiftly along. It was too late, however, to repent; and the doctor consoled himself by taking advantage of the effect produced by the thick black smoke, as they saw it rising in the distance, to illustrate the lecture he had formerly given his pupil, on the theory of combustion and decomposition of amphlites, till he fairly lulled him to sleep.

Morning came, but brought not with it the wished-for breeze. Edric rose, and walking upon deck, encountered the doctor. "How still all seems!" said he; "Nature seems to sleep: but 'tis an awful stillness, such as falls upon a dying patient, prophetic of his end. Nature seems exhausted, and I could fancy is seeking a short repose to rally her energies for some decisive blow."

"You are fanciful, Edric," said the doctor; "you alarm yourself unnecessarily. The violent shock your nerves have sustained, unfits you for exertion, and renders you disposed to see every thing in a gloomy light."

"I beg your pardon, Sir," said a ragged English sailor, who happened to be on board; "in my opinion the gentleman is right, for every thing portends a storm. Cirro-strati streak the sky, and as they join with the fleecy cumuli below them in cumulus-strati, nothing can more clearly indicate wind and rain, and probably thunder. And see, too, how the dark, frowning nimbus spreads its black shade along the edge of the horizon, and how the birds fly cowering, almost touching the waters with their wings as they flit along. Now it begins, hark!"

Whilst the sailor had been speaking, the clouds had thickened gradually, and the sky had grown dark as night. A hollow murmuring was heard, which seemed to gather fury as it came, till it burst over the devoted vessel with terrific violence, and rent the sails to atoms, whistling round in fearful gusts, as though mocking the mischief it had done. The sea now heaved mountains high. The forked lightning played like writhing serpents along the deep black sky; now streaming like floating ribands in the air, and then darting downwards like fiery arrows. Thunder rolled heavily in the distance, approaching however nearer and nearer, every peal reverberating through the sky, as though echoed back by unseen rocks, till at last a tremendous crash announced the fall of the electric fluid. Our travellers were preparing to retire below, when, just as they reached the cabin stairs, the heavens seemed to open, and a ball of light-blue fire, of a most vivid brightness, shot downwards from the chasm, and struck the mast of the labouring ship. Immediately after, a loud crackling noise rattled over their heads, and then all again was still, save the howling winds, and the groans of some prostrate seamen, wounded by the scattered fragments of the splintered mast.

The rain now descended in torrents, and the feeble vessel, at one moment raised to a fearful height, then dashed down, and apparently engulphed by the heavy seas that washed over her, seemed every instant doomed to destruction, and to escape only by a miracle. The shouts of the seamen, and creaking of the strained timbers of the ship, mingled horribly with the howling of the wind, and roar of the billows. Every instant it was expected she must go to pieces; for she had sprung a leak, and the water rose so fast as to baffle every attempt made to check its progress. The seamen were now in despair: they broke open their trunks, and dressing themselves in their best clothes, they filled their pockets with all the valuables they could find: then, whilst some went to prayers, others broke open the captain's spirit-chest, and many rolled overboard in a state of intoxication, whilst the ship, now become a perfect wreck, drifted before the wind, and was rapidly sinking. The storm, however, seeming to abate, the master ordered out the boat, and all the seamen who retained their senses, eagerly sprang on board. Our travellers attempted to follow, but the seamen pushed them back, and exclaiming the boat was full, rowed off, leaving them to their fate.

The English sailor had been in the act of stepping on board the boat, the very moment she pushed off, and the sudden shock precipitated him into the sea. A piercing scream burst from his lips, as his body, with a dying effort, sprang from the waves, which seemed to rise after him and suck him back into their gulph. Our friends heard the cry, and rushed to the side of the vessel, but alas! they were powerless to save him: the ship drifted rapidly by, they saw his hands gleam for a moment through the waves, as he raised them in agony, and then the roaring billows rolled on, deep, black, and gloomy as before.

The horror of Edric and the doctor was excessive; but the impending terrors of their own fate prevented the possibility of their minds dwelling long upon his. The storm, however, visibly abated, and the dismantled hulk they were upon, lightened by the desertion of the sailors, still swam: light, fleecy clouds now scudded rapidly along the skies, and the moon, struggling to break forth from behind them, shed a faint and watery gleam upon the scene.

Our travellers now, by the feeble light afforded by the moonbeams, perceived the boat labouring heavily through the dark-grey sea, and struggling to reach a long black line of rocks, distinctly marked in the distance, against which the still boiling waters broke with tremendous roar, curling in whitened foam as they laved their craggy sides; whilst the wreck our travellers were upon, seemed rapidly drifting upon the same point. Death now appeared inevitable, as it was impossible their shattered bark could resist the shock, if it should be tossed against these jagged crags; and every moment she seemed rising upon a wave that must dash her upon them, and floating back to escape only by a miracle. The doctor and Edric became giddy with these repeated shocks, and in despair fancied themselves resigned; or rather, stunned by the misfortunes which had followed each other with such overwhelming rapidity upon their devoted heads, they awaited their fate with an apathy which they mistook for resignation.

The seamen in the boat still continued labouring on, straining every nerve to reach the shore, though ineffectually; for the foaming surge beat them back with repeated, with resistless violence. With anxious eyes and beating hearts, our friends marked the progress of the boat; till, giddy with watching, and feeling their spirits exhausted as they surveyed the fruitless struggle of the toiling boatmen, they hid their faces with their hands, and shut it from their sight.

At this instant a wild and piercing cry rang in their ears: — 'twas from the boat. She had swamped; the human beings she contained were all swallowed up in the boiling waves, and that shriek of agony was their funeral knell. A horrid silence followed this appalling scream, unbroken save by the lashing of the billows against the rocks, and the low, half-suppressed moaning of the winds, — till the senses of the travellers became bewildered, and they shrieked in agony. Their peril indeed grew every moment more intense, for every wave carried them nearer and nearer to those frowning crags, whilst their dark sides, rearing themselves in awful majesty, seemed mustering their strength to repel the insolent intruders that sought to invade their territory. The doctor and Edric, in the mean time, suffering a thousand deaths in the protracted horrors they were compelled to endure, and which they could neither mitigate nor evade, shrank back with the shivering of affrighted nature trembling at dissolution, every time the wave on which their vessel floated seemed to dash against the shore.

At length, however, the fate they had so long dreaded arrived. Their shattered hulk was raised on a tremendous billow, and thrown with fearful violence upon the rocks, with a force that shivered it to atoms, and engulphed the doctor and Edric in the boiling surge. The next wave, however, returning, swept them along in its bosom, and threw them, perfectly insensible, though locked in each other's arms, upon the shore.

CHAPTER XX.

It was morning, and the glowing sunbeams danced gaily on the sparkling waters of the dark blue deep, as, gently rippling, it laved the rocky shore on which Edric and his tutor had been thrown; and seemed to smile, as if in mockery of the mischiefs it had wrought. There, sheltered by a rock, whose jutting crag had saved them from being carried back into the devouring ocean, lay our travellers, apparently buried in sleep; returning consciousness not having yet dispelled the torpor produced by the fearful terrors of the night. The sun now shone brightly, and its glowing heat revived Edric from his trance. Slowly and heavily he unclosed his languid eyes, and, forgetting where he was, attempted to rise. He succeeded; but weak and dizzy, he only staggered a few paces ere he again fell: the roaring of the ocean still sounded in his ears, his senses swam, and, giddy and enfeebled by his previous exhaustion, he fancied himself still tossed upon the foaming billows. For some time, he lay in a state of torture, the thrill of returning circulation tingling through his veins, till the recollection of what had passed flashing across his mind, he again endeavoured to rouse himself, and seek his tutor. The unfortunate doctor, however, appeared to be no more, and as Edric gazed upon his inanimate form, he might have exclaimed with Prince Henry, "I could have better spared a better man."

At this moment, Edric recollected the strong chemical preparations the doctor generally carried about him, and, searching his pockets, found a potent elixir. With some difficulty, he forced a few drops down his throat, taking a dose also himself. The effects of the medicine were soon visible: the doctor heaved a deep sigh, and, opening his eyes, gazed vacantly around, whilst Edric himself felt perfectly restored.

"Where am I?" cried Doctor Entwerfen, as soon as he was sufficiently recovered to speak, and then, as some of the horrors he had so lately witnessed recurred to his mind, he exclaimed: —"I will never disclose it—no torture shall compel me; where is the justice? He fled away in a flame of fire hanging to the Devil's horn. Ah, Edric! where are we? Ah! I have had such a horrid dream."

"Alas!" returned Edric, "it is but too real!"

"What! what!" cried the doctor, getting up and staring wildly around him; "I remember now, we were drowned—but where—where are we?"

"I know not," replied his pupil mournfully. "You forget I have been exposed to the same perils as yourself, and that I am equally ignorant where fate has thrown us. I should think, however, from the position we were in when the storm began, that we are somewhere on the shores of the Mediterranean; but whether in Europe or Africa, I have as yet had no means of ascertaining."

"We must explore," said the doctor solemnly; "we ought not to remain in doubt another instant upon so important a subject. Follow me!"

They now quitted the rocky beach on which they had so long lain, and advanced towards some cliffs which shut them out from the view of the surrounding country. When they had surmounted this natural barrier, they found the prospect that presented itself superb; and their eyes wandered with delight over orange groves and forests of cork-trees; whilst the green shining leaves, and rich scarlet blossoms of the pomegranates, and light tender waving foliage of the olive, afforded variety to the scene. The burning heat of the sun's rays felt softened by the breezes from the sea; a balmy fragrance seemed to pervade the air; birds flew twittering around them, or, perched upon the branches of the trees, made the groves resound with melodious harmony; whilst butterflies of the most brilliant colours fluttered from flower to flower, and innumerable buzzing insects seemed to fill the air with motion.

"What a lovely country!" said the doctor, as he and Edric penetrated into the deep recesses of a shady grove; "and how delightful is this sensation of refreshing coolness, after having been exposed to the burning rays of the sun! It is yet early, for the sun has not yet reached far above the horizon, and the dew-drops still glisten in his rays like diamonds hanging from every leaf. Where can we be? Surely we are not dead, and now in Paradise!"

Edric smiled: "I rather think," said he, "that we are in Andalusia. I have often read of the exquisite beauty of some of the southern provinces of Spain, and this seems well to accord with the ideas I have always entertained of that country."

They now approached what appeared to be a cemetery, and which was tastefully adorned with weeping willows hanging over the graves; whilst roses, and a thousand beautiful flowering shrubs, flourishing in wild luxuriance from the genial nature of the climate, spread around, and gave this receptacle of the mouldering remains of mortality the aspect of a blooming garden.

"How different from the Pyramids!" exclaimed the doctor and Edric at the same moment.

"The tomb-stones seem to have inscriptions upon them," continued the former, after a short pause; "let us approach and examine them: they will at least declare the country we are in, by the language in which they may be written."

The idea struck Edric as feasible, and they entered the cemetery. "You are right, Edric," said the doctor; "we are in Spain, for here lie the mortal remains of Don Alfonso, that mighty hero of the Bourbon race, who, you doubtless remember, was the first that conquered the northern part of Africa, and by transferring the seat of the Spanish empire to Fez, contributed so powerfully to the civilization and conversion to Christianity of all that vast territory."

"And who destroyed Spain as a monarchy, by so doing," added Edric.

"It is true," replied the doctor, "that Spain, finding itself too mighty for a province, shook off in consequence the yoke of his descendants, and erected its present republic, which it most probably would never have done if the seat of government had remained at Madrid. But that is trifling compared with the inestimable benefits produced to the world at large, by the civilization and reduction to a Christian state, of such a mighty empire as that of Morocco. Had it not been for that, we might still have remained in the degrading ignorance in which mankind were immersed for so many centuries respecting the interior of Africa:—Timbuctoo would never have risen to its present eminence in science and commerce; the real course of the Niger would never have been discovered: and the sources of the Nile still remained wrapped in oblivion. Yes, mighty shade! thou wert indeed a hero! Calumny may assail thy fame, and unenlightened minds cavil at the wonders of thy glory; but one firm and attached votary still remains to thee, and thus he humbly bends to do thee homage."

So saying, the doctor prostrated himself upon the tomb, and reverentially kissed the cold marble inscribed with the hero's name.—"Hold! hold!" cried a man, rushing from behind a small temple, and seizing him, whilst in an instant Edric and his tutor found themselves surrounded by soldiers, whose grim visages spoke them inured to blood and warfare.—"Wretch!" exclaimed the leader, apostrophizing the terrified doctor; "but thy life shall soon pay the forfeit of thy crimes. Away with him!" continued he, addressing his soldiers; "bear him before the next alcaide, and let him there suffer the punishment the law enacts against all those who dare to praise the actions or worship the memory of the tyrannic Alfonso—Away with him, I say."

"Mercy! mercy!" implored the doctor.

"Impossible!" said the leader sternly; "do you not know that this is a land of liberty, and that we abhor the very name of tyranny and oppression? How then can the admirer of a tyrant hope for mercy at our hands? Away with him, I say, and with his companion too; for as they appear to be associates, no doubt their principles are the same."

"And do you call this a land of liberty?" asked Edric reproachfully.

"Hear him! he blasphemes!" cried the soldiers; "gag him if he dare again to breathe such impiety!" and amidst their shouts and execrations, Edric and his tutor were dragged away. Taught by this lesson that the liberty of the republican Spaniards did not extend to the tolerance of any opinions except their own, Edric and the doctor did not again venture to speak; and they soon, to their infinite dismay, found themselves in the presence of the alcaide; who, however, luckily for our travellers, happened to be a man of some sense and liberality. He smiled when he heard the substance of the facts gravely stated against the prisoners. "This case requires a private hearing," said he: "Velasquez, conduct the prisoners to my own apartment."

"We will have no private hearing," clamoured the people and the soldiers. "The crime was public, and the punishment should be so too; we will not be gulled."

"But, gentlemen," said the magistrate, "supposing these prisoners to be part of a gang of conspirators who have been plotting against the state, it might defeat the ends of justice to have them examined publicly; as it is possible—mind, gentlemen, I only say, as it is possible—some traitors may lurk even among the crowd before me, who might give intelligence to other parties interested, who might be thus enabled to make their escape."

"Ay, now you speak reason," said the mob; "we are always willing to listen to reason;" and without farther remonstrance they permitted the alcaide and the prisoners to retire.

The Mummy!

"You see, gentlemen," said the alcaide, shutting the door of the room carefully, and placing chairs, in which he invited his prisoners to sit down, "that all is not liberty which is called so, and that a mob can occasionally be as tyrannical as an emperor. I know that in reality there is not a shadow of complaint against you; yet I dare not release you, as my own life would be the forfeit if I did. You must thus submit to a temporary restraint, which you may rest assured I shall not only endeavour to shorten, but shall render as light as possible whilst I am compelled to inflict it."

"My dear sir," said the doctor, "we are exceedingly obliged by your kindness. If we had not met with you, I do not know what would have become of us. I could not have believed people were in existence so illiberal as these Spaniards, or that any human beings could be so weak as to fancy themselves in a land of liberty whilst they are practising the most refined tyranny."

"And yet my countrymen are neither fools nor hypocrites," returned the alcaide; "but, like many other people, they deceive themselves, and talk about freedom till they fancy they possess it. Their great fault, however, has been, that they did not know where to stop; and as even virtue becomes vice when carried to the extreme, so have the most sublime principles of liberty and patriotism become degraded in their hands, by being attempted to be carried to an exaggerated degree of perfection!"

"Oh, England! England!" sighed the doctor; "would to Heaven I had never left thy happy shores! Alas! alas! what a crowd of horrible events have occupied the last few months!"

"Why did you leave your country, since you so bitterly regret it?" demanded the alcaide.

"Because we could not be contented," replied Edric. "Devoted from my earliest youth to the pursuits of science, I craved ardently for knowledge denied to mortals; I aspired to penetrate into the profoundest secrets of Nature, and burnt to accomplish wishes destined never to be realized. The desire of seeing foreign countries also filled my soul: I longed to travel, to acquire new ideas and meet with strange and wonderful adventures; I sickened of the quiet and tranquillity of home. 'Give me change,' cried I in my madness, 'give me variety, and I ask no more; for even wretchedness itself were better to bear than this tiresome unvarying uniformity.' The unreasonableness of my wishes deserved punishment, and I have been curst with the very fulfilment of my wishes."

"Is this gentleman also a votary of science?" asked the alcaide, who had appeared musing whilst Edric spoke.

"What a question!" exclaimed the doctor, in a transport of indignation. "What! has my whole life been devoted to scientific pursuits! have I deprived myself of rest and almost of food! and wasted the midnight lamp in bringing to perfection some of the most sublime discoveries ever vouchsafed to man, to be insulted suited with such a doubt as that? Know, sir, that you see before you Doctor Entwerfen, the fortunate inventor of the immortalizing snuff, one single pinch of which cures all diseases by the smell; the discoverer of the capability of caoutchouc being applied to aërial purposes; and the maker of the most compendious and powerful galvanic battery ever yet beheld by mortal!"

"Then you are the very man I want," said the alcaide; "go to prison contentedly, and rest satisfied that your confinement will be of very short duration. In a day or two I will see you, and explain the project I have conceived for your deliverance."

So saying, he summoned his guards, and, ordering them to convey the travellers to prison, the doctor and Edric were dragged away, and, being immured in separate dungeons, were left there to ruminate upon the varied and busy scenes in which they had been so lately engaged. Sadly and heavily passed the time; yet days and weeks rolled on ere they again saw the alcaide. At length, when they had begun almost to despair, they were reconducted to his presence.

"Do you understand the management of an electrical machine?" asked he abruptly.

"Certainly!" cried the doctor, transported with joy at the question, before Edric, who was half blinded by the sudden change from his gloomy prison to the broad light of day, had sufficiently recovered himself to reply.

"Then it is in your own power to set yourselves free," continued the alcaide. "The principal general of the army stationed here is ill; a powerful party exists against him who wish his death, at the head of whom stands the leader who was the cause of your being taken into custody. The general himself is a mere nonentity; but the opposite party, to which I belong, wish to save his life, as his name affords a sanction under which they can act. He is now ill of a palsy, and has been recommended to try the effects of an electrical shock. A machine has been with difficulty procured in this remote district; but the

The Mummy!

philosopher of the army being lately dead, and another not having been yet appointed, no one here knows how to apply it. Now, if you—"

"Say no more!" cried the doctor, interrupting him, in a transport of delight; "say no more—I see, I comprehend the whole! I shall restore him, and receive my liberty as the reward. Nay more, I shall obtain immortality amongst the Spaniards by the deed; their poets will sing my fame, and their historians will pause upon the fact!"

"You will undertake it then?" said the alcaide, and, reading an indignant affirmative in the doctor's looks, he led the way to a camp, at a short distance from the village, where the paralytic general was sitting in a kind of throne, placed without his tent, and surrounded by the principal officers of his staff; the electrical machine, a large, clumsy, heavy-looking thing, standing before him. The doctor looked with dismay at this unwieldy apparatus, so different from his own neat, powerful compendium of science, as he was wont to call it; and saw with infinite horror that even its construction was totally different from those he had been accustomed to. His natural vanity and presumption, however, revolted from making this mortifying acknowledgment, particularly after the boasts he had been indulging in to the alcaide; and, relying upon his general knowledge of the principles of science, he walked boldly up to the machine, with as much composure and self-confidence as though he had been accustomed to the management of it all his life.

A considerable trepidation, however, crept over him as he examined it and found its movements intricate and complicated in the extreme; and his hands trembled, and a thick film came over his eyes, as he attempted to charge and adjust the cylinder. No time, however, was allowed for deliberation; he was ordered to apply it instantly; and, terrified by the recollection of the prompt manner in which the Spaniards were accustomed to make themselves obeyed, and the already long and severe imprisonment he had undergone, he set it in motion: an unlucky wire, however, which he did not quite understand, pointed upwards, and he tried in vain to arrange it; he tried again, but was instantly felled to the ground by a tremendous shock, whilst a loud crash of thunder burst with violence over his head, and a vivid flash of lightning proclaimed that the ill-managed machine had drawn down the electric fluid from a heavy cloud, that happened unfortunately to be just above them, upon the head of the unfortunate general, whom it scorched to a cinder, levelling some of his officers to the earth, and scattering the rest in all directions. For the moment, the doctor himself was blinded by the sudden light, and, when he recovered his sight, the first thing that met his eyes was his friend the alcaide sticking fast by the skirts of his coat in a hedge.

Terrified at the mischief he had done, the first impulse of the learned doctor was to run away; but, notwithstanding the general confusion and dismay, the first intimation he showed of his design, drew around him a crowd of soldiers, like peasants round a mad dog, who seemed to think him as little entitled to mercy as though he had really been one of those unfortunate animals. "Cut him down!" cried one—"blow his brains out!" shouted another—"chop his head off!" screamed a third; and summary punishment would instantly have been inflicted, if the alcaide, who in the mean time had contrived to extricate himself from his uncomfortable situation, had not interfered. "Villain!" cried he, as soon as he had recovered his breath—for being rather fat, he found flying exercise rather too violent to suit his taste; "is this the manner in which you treat me? Was it for this I brought you to the camp, and would have made your fortune? Wretch that you are! hanging is too good for you, and impaling alive mercy to what you deserve.—Away to prison with him! he merits not a death so easy as you would give him; carry him back to his dungeon, and let him there await what punishment the council of state may judge fit for killing a general and frightening an alcaide out of his senses."

"Mercy! mercy!" screamed the doctor; but his cries were disregarded, and he and Edric were dragged back to prison, deprived of every hope of obtaining forgiveness. Sadly and silently passed the hours in this gloomy abode; for, though the doctor and his pupil were now permitted to be together, little communication took place between them, as, though Edric was too good-natured to upbraid his unfortunate companion, yet it was past the power of human nature not to feel enraged at the folly that had drawn them into so disagreeable a situation.

The poor doctor, however, needed not to be upbraided; for the reproaches of his own conscience were more bitter than any Edric could have lavished on him. "I am lost!" cried he; "ruined, and utterly undone! Not only my body will perish miserably, but my fame, my immortal fame is destroyed—oh! I shall go distracted!"

In this manner he lamented; wringing his hands and tearing his hair, whilst Edric felt too angry to attempt to console him.

The Mummy!

"Speak to me, Edric, dear," cried the poor doctor at last, quite in despair at his silence; "for Heaven's sake, speak to me! Do let me hear the sound of some voice, besides my own and that of those cursed Spaniards. Oh, Edric! Edric! solitary confinement is quite enough to drive a man distracted; but to have a companion in such a place as this, and he to refuse to speak — Oh, Edric! Edric! your heart must be turned to stone, if you can resolve to use me so cruelly."

Edric was moved by the doctor's sorrow.

"What do you wish me to say?" asked he, smiling.

"Oh, now that's like yourself," cried the poor doctor, bursting into tears, and throwing his arms round Edric's neck, whilst he sobbed upon his shoulder like a child. "Now I shall die happy! I don't care what they do to me; I am quite ready for any thing that may happen."

Edric was affected by the doctor's manner, and returning his embrace warmly, he could not restrain his own tears.

"Oh! my dear, dear Edric!" cried the doctor; "how I love you! would to Heaven I could save you! I would not care for myself."

"And I would not accept of liberty without you, my dear tutor, I assure you!" returned Edric. "No, no! the perils we have undergone together have added new force to the ties that formerly united us; and our fate now, be it good or ill, shall be the same. It is possible, however, that there may be some means of escape."

"Alas! no!" said the doctor mournfully; seeing Edric look round at the walls and windows: "this is the same dungeon I have been so long confined in, and not even a mouse could get out of it without the keeper's permission."

"What is to be done, then?" cried Edric.

"Ay," returned the doctor; "what, indeed! However, it is certainly a great comfort to have a companion in one's misery; and though my prospects are certainly not much improved since you joined me, my cares are lessened at least one-half."

"Oh! my poor father!" exclaimed Edric. "The hardest part of my fate seems to die without obtaining his forgiveness! Alas! if he could see me now, he would surely repent his ill-timed severity. Fain would I also know what has passed in England since we left it: if Edmund be married, and if Claudia still reigns. It was spring when we left England, it is now winter: alas! alas! how many changes this brief space of time may have produced. If, however, my father's life has been spared, I care not for the rest."

"How little did we anticipate," said the doctor, "when we first proposed to travel, the misfortunes that were to attend us! Alas! they seem a just punishment for our crime, in presuming to wish to pry into secrets never intended to be revealed to man."

"Can you believe it," returned Edric, "but in spite of all the misfortunes I have suffered, a restless curiosity to know the fate of the Mummy we so strangely resuscitated, is one of the strongest feelings in my bosom."

"I can readily credit it," said the doctor; "for the same feeling operates upon me! It is, however, vain to indulge in useless regrets: we must die; and all we have to do, is to endeavour to become resigned to our fate."

CHAPTER XXI.

A few days after this, the prisoners were honoured by another visit from the alcaide.

"Thank God!" cried Edric involuntarily, as soon as he saw him; for, as he felt confident that the anger he had expressed against them, had been assumed, he hoped he was now come to save them.

"Alas!" returned the worthy magistrate, "I fear you have little reason to be thankful. All my endeavours to save you have only succeeded in obtaining a few hours respite, and to-morrow morning you are condemned to be burnt alive."

"Oh!" shrieked the doctor; whilst even Edric's courage could not prevent his turning deathly pale. "It is dreadful," said he, "to die thus so young in a foreign country, and by such fearful means."

"Oh! don't talk of it," sobbed the doctor. "My poor dear, dear Edric! Save him, sir! in mercy, save him! Though I may be doomed to pay the penalty of my folly, it is very hard he should suffer."

"It is, indeed," returned the alcaide; "and my wish to save him, joined to the hatred I bear the present general, has made me a traitor to my country. I see you look astonished, but to explain what I mean, it will be necessary to give you a short sketch of the present state of this country, which I will endeavour to do in as few words as possible. You know, no doubt, that Spain was once a powerful empire, till the ill-judged policy of one of her monarchs, in removing the seat of government to Africa, occasioned her fall: for the tree of majesty becoming too widely extended, it was but natural that some of its branches should strike root for themselves, and detach themselves entirely from the parent stem.

"This was the case with Spain; and her first directors as a republic happening to be intelligent men, the infant state grew and flourished, exciting the admiration of its neighbours, and the envy of its mother country. Unfortunately, however, the wheel of fortune is always turning, and Spaniards, as I before said, not knowing where to stop, have gone on, getting worse and worse by degrees, till they have become the bigoted and intolerant wretches you have found them. In fact, the army now rules the state, and the people, finding the tyranny of the soldiers insupportable, have been for some time attempting to throw off the yoke. They were long unsuccessful, as they found the discipline of the soldiers far outweighed all their bravery and self-devotion. In their distress, however, they called in the aid of Roderick the Second, the young and warlike King of Ireland. This powerful monarch, who realizes in himself all the romantic qualities of the ancient knights of chivalry, hastened instantly to their assistance, and they are now combating under his auspices with every prospect of success. His progress has been magical; success has followed wherever he has gone, and his army now lies at a little distance, though he landed in the north of Spain. It is to him, therefore, that I have sent secretly, giving him (in the hope of saving you) instructions, by which, if he follows them, he cannot fail of surprising the camp."

The doctor and Edric, though they were fully aware that they were principally indebted to the hatred the alcaide bore the present general for the steps he had taken in their behalf, yet felt and expressed themselves properly grateful; and the alcaide quitted the prison, leaving the flatterer Hope behind to console them for his absence, mingled, however, with the natural anxiety, which they could not help feeling, lest the well-arranged plan laid for their escape should fail. Morning had just dawned, after a tedious and miserable night, and the doctor and Edric were yet shivering from the damp cold which often precedes the break of day, and which now seemed to have struck a chill to their inmost souls, when the door of the prison opened, and a file of soldiers appeared, ready to conduct them to the place of execution. The doctor's heart beat thick, so as almost to impede respiration, and a heavy film spread before his eyes; whilst the agitation of Edric, who had, however, now quite forgiven him, was scarcely inferior to his own. Fervently they embraced, and then submitting to be pinioned, they were forced to march to the spot appointed for their sacrifice, where an immense crowd awaited their approach.

The doctor's heart sunk within him as he looked down from the kind of terrace upon which the ceremony was to take place, upon the mass of human heads jammed together below, every face regarding him with a gaze of anxious expectation; and as he turned from these eager looks with a thrill of horror, his feelings were yet more forcibly harrowed up by the sight behind him. This was composed of two iron stakes fixed firmly in the ground, and provided with ponderous chains so as to prevent the remotest possibility of escape, whilst the enormous heaps of green wood piled round each, gave a frightful idea of the intensity of the lingering torments the unfortunate prisoners were condemned to suffer. The mind of Edric, in the mean time, was not much more composed than that of his friend. He also had looked round, and whilst nature shuddered at the thought of the horrid death awaiting them, the immensity and compactness of the crowd seemed to destroy all probability of a rescue, and the hope which had till then supported him, fled from his breast; whilst, as his eyes again met those of the poor doctor, mournful, indeed, was the glance that they exchanged.

It is an awful thing to die! and though there are occasions when death may be braved, or at least met with unabated courage; yet when it comes on thus slowly and deliberately, seen from afar off, and yet impossible to be avoided, the firmest mind will find it difficult to bear its approach unmoved. That of Edric, however, notwithstanding it had been weakened by his long confinement, and by the delusive flattery of hope, did not shrink from the trial: and calmly he even saw the crowd divide, to make way for the executioner, who slowly advanced, preceded by a band of martial music, playing a mournful air, the drums being covered with black crape, and followed by a long train of soldiers, in mourning cloaks, with their arms reversed. Nothing could be more appalling than this lugubrious procession: the executioner, musicians, and soldiers, being all shrouded in their gloomy cloaks, (the very hoods of which were drawn over their heads,) had the air of demons coming to bear away the miserable victims to everlasting perdition; and the mind of the unhappy doctor not being able to endure such accumulated horrors, he sunk upon his knees, uttering shrieks of anguish, whilst the cold sweat ran in large drops from his forehead, and every nerve quivered with agony.

The procession had now nearly reached the prisoners, and even Edric's firmness gave way, as he saw the executioner spring upon the terrace, and advance towards him. A convulsive throb of anguish seemed to rend his heart, and his lips and cheeks turned of a livid paleness. But how was he surprised, and what a sudden revulsion of feeling did he not experience, when the supposed executioner, after having unbound his arms, put a sword into his hands, and whispering, — "Now is the time, defend yourself! — our soldiers are in green," left him completely free.

Completely overcome, Edric stood for a moment lost in amazement, unable to credit the evidence of his senses, and gazing after his deliverer, who, the moment he had also unbound the doctor, threw off his disguise, and shouting "Roderick for ever!" disclosed to the multitude below the dreaded form of the Irish hero himself. Shouts of "Roderick for ever!" now rent the skies; the soldiers who had followed their monarch, and several others who had lurked concealed amongst the crowd, threw off their disguises at the same moment, and formed round the leader; whilst the main body of his troops, left behind in the care of experienced generals, tutored for the purpose, charged the affrighted Spaniards in the rear.

The confusion and dismay that now prevailed were quite beyond description. The terrified Spaniards, who, naturally superstitious, had long fancied the wonderful acts of heroic valour attributed to Roderick could only be performed by magic, were now firmly convinced that his sudden appearance amongst them was an act of especial favour from his Infernal Majesty himself! and finding themselves attacked on all sides, imagined their enemies multiplied by the powers of darkness, and fled without striking a blow. Roderick and his soldiers returned laughing, after they had pursued them a little way, to ransack and burn their camp; which when they had done, they retired to their former station; having previously promised the alcaide to spare the town, and not to push the consequences of their victory farther.

The doctor and Edric, who had been too much agitated to take any very active part in the combat, had been conveyed by the guards of Roderick to their master's camp, to await there the return of the monarch, in whose hands destiny had now placed them. Neither of our travellers had noticed the person of the Irish king in the bustling moment of their deliverance; but the almost magical celerity with which he had contrived to disperse their enemies; the evident terror with which his very name seemed to inspire the Spaniards; and the wondrous feats the guards around them seemed to delight in attributing to him, made them now almost tremble at the thought of being presented to so tremendous a personage; whom they amused themselves in picturing as a stern, fearful tyrant, breathing nothing but war and desolation.

Roderick the Second, surnamed the Great, was then in the flower of his age. He had not long ascended his throne; and his father, who had been a prudent prince, having left behind him a well-established government, able statesmen, and a considerable sum in the treasury, Roderick had little to employ his mind at home. Brave, ardent, and enterprising, burning for conquest, and spurning the quiet of domestic peace, the overtures of the Spaniards had met his most ardent wishes; and he had embraced their cause with an eagerness and impetuosity that had hitherto carried every thing before it. The greatest part of Spain lay at his feet. Even Madrid was his! but it was to attack Seville, that queen of cities, that he was now in

Andalusia. This city was still in the power of his enemies, and Roderick, having made Cadiz his head-quarters, was about removing thither, when the message of the Alcaide, had induced to undertake the romantic enterprize he had just so successfully accomplished. Romance was, indeed, a leading feature in Roderick's character: it had been the policy of his father, the late King, to foment secretly the discontents nourished amongst the English; but the spirit of Roderick revolted at conduct he considered so mean and base. The Spanish war, on the contrary, exactly suited his disposition: to aid an oppressed people—to throw off the yoke of their oppressors, seemed noble and generous; and he engaged in the enterprize with all the energy of his bold and daring temper. His soldiers adored him, and his people warmly seconded his efforts; for, as the seat of war was far removed from them, and as the treasury of the late King defrayed the expenses, they felt none of the inconveniences of war, and gloried in the triumphs of their Sovereign. Thus, Roderick's praise was the theme of every tongue: even the Spaniards worshipped him almost as a god, and their active imaginations magnified his exploits, till both friends and foes alike regarded him as a being who had only to will to conquer! and whose prowess it was perfect madness even to struggle to resist.

Such was the monarch our travellers now anxiously awaited, till suspense became almost agony. At last the joyful sounds of "He comes! he comes! Long live the mighty Roderick!" burst upon their ears, and the travellers bent forwards, eagerly expecting, yet dreading to see, a countenance stern and fearful as that of Cheops in his tomb: but how were they astonished to behold, in the redoubtable Roderick, only a tall handsome young man, riding carelessly upon a beautiful Barbary charger, and laughing and talking gaily with his officers as he came along.

"What!" cried the doctor indignantly, "would you attempt to make me believe that slight blooming boy a conqueror? the thing is impossible! It is quite ridiculous to mention it. Those laughing eyes, smooth down-like cheeks, and white teeth, may be well adapted to win a lady's heart, but I am sure they never can belong to a hero!"

The King, in the mean time, was equally struck with the doctor; and seeing something peculiarly honest and simple in his fat, round, oily face, he felt a lively interest for him, and an excessive curiosity to know what could possibly have brought a man, apparently so harmless and inoffensive, into so perilous a situation. The fine person of Edric, disfigured as it was by the troubles he had undergone, also attracted his attention; and as he rode up to his guests to question them as to their adventures, (the noble barb that carried him, pacing proudly along, as though conscious of the illustrious burthen he bore,) even the doctor was compelled to admit, the face and figure of his rider bespoke firmness, intellect, and dignity.

"What crime had you committed amongst the Spaniards?" asked he, as he approached, addressing himself to the doctor in a full, mellow, yet commanding tone. "It must have been of the blackest dye, if we are to judge by the enormity of the punishment."

"I am innocent!" cried the doctor, "an' it may please your Majesty! I am quite innocent."

"It will please me very much to find you so," said Roderick, smiling; "but assertion is nothing—what proof have you?"

"My friend here will bear witness in my behalf," said the doctor solemnly, not feeling at all pleased with what he thought the King's unseasonable disposition for merriment; whilst as he stood looking very cross, his red face and bald head streaming with perspiration from anger and vexation, his clothes having been torn to rags, and his hat and wig lost in his late troubles, he struck Roderick as presenting so very whimsical and ridiculous a figure, that after looking at him a few minutes, the Merry Monarch burst out into a violent and almost convulsive fit of laughter.

"Well!" said the doctor, still more gravely, "I am glad your Majesty seems so well amused; but for my part, I don't see any thing at all agreeable or entertaining in being about to be burned alive."

The doctor's solemn look and lengthened face, as he made this naïve remonstrance, only increased Roderick's peals of laughter. "I beg your pardon, Sir," said he, addressing Edric, as soon as he was able to speak; "I really beg your pardon; but your friend here is so exceedingly amusing, that I am really under infinite obligations to him, and know not how I shall ever be able to repay him."

"It is we who are under obligations to your Majesty, for which we can never be sufficiently grateful," said Edric gravely; for he also was not very well pleased at seeing his friend so openly ridiculed; as, though he did sometimes take the liberty of smiling at the learned doctor's innocent follies himself, he did not like to see him made the laughing stock of another. Roderick, however, saw and instantly understood the ill-humour of Edric; and as he applauded its motive, he endeavoured to divert it by every means in his power, and soon completely succeeded. Few people, indeed, knew so well how to make themselves agreeable as Roderick; and though Edric, at first, felt indignant that the King should treat him so much like a child, as to suppose his displeasure could be easily joked away, yet this feeling insensibly wore off, and he soon thought Roderick the most fascinating of human beings. Indeed, that heart must have been hard that could have withstood unmoved the fascinations of Roderick when he wished to please. His bright laughing eyes that looked the very colour of gladness, and his arch smile, might have subdued the melancholy of a stoic; whilst his character had something bewitching in its very failings. He had been all his life the spoiled child of fortune, and though his rashness and impetuosity, his pettishness and his caressing manners, his bravery, haughtiness, and obstinacy; his fondness for any thing that promised a frolic, and his chivalrous devotion to noble and grand enterprizes, formed a singular melange, he was, perhaps, more beloved than he would have been if his character had been more perfect; and it was this very inconsistency that made him so completely the idol of his soldiers.

"Believe me," said he, addressing Edric, "that it is impossible for me to describe the pleasure I feel in having had it in my power to be of service to you; and though I should have been happy to relieve any of my fellow-creatures in distress, yet I must own I am glad you are Englishmen. It was the policy of my late father to act as the enemy of England; but I have always been her friend. I am sure that Nature intended the English and Irish for brethren; and I am too sincere a votary of the goddess to wish, even in the slightest degree, to counteract her designs."

"Your sentiments perfectly coincide with mine," said Edric; "and as it has been my fate to live in habits of intimacy for several years with a very worthy countryman of yours, Father Murphy, confessor of the Duke of Cornwall, who was the most intimate friend of my father—"

"Father Murphy!" interrupted Roderick.

"Yes," returned Edric, surprised at the wonder expressed by the King. "Is it possible you can know him?"

"The name appeared familiar to me, that was all," replied Roderick, evidently finding it difficult to repress a strong inclination to laugh. Edric looked at him with still increasing astonishment, not being able to discover any thing in the slightest degree ridiculous in what he had said; and Roderick's disposition to mirth seemed to increase in exact proportion to Edric's gravity. At length, perceiving he remained silent, Roderick with infinite difficulty contrived to say,—

"Go on, my dear Mr. Montagu, I entreat you to go on; never mind me; it is a strange thought that has just entered my head."

"Mr. Montagu!" exclaimed Edric. "I was not aware that your Majesty was acquainted with my name; I do not recollect having mentioned it."

"Perhaps, however, the doctor did," returned the King; "or the alcaide might have told me, or my servants may have seen it marked upon your trunks or your linen, or—"

"Your Majesty need not give yourself so much trouble to explain a circumstance in itself perfectly immaterial," replied Edric. "I have no wish to conceal my name; I was only astonished to find your Majesty so well acquainted with it."

"Well, well," cried Roderick, somewhat impatiently, "the circumstance is, as you say, quite immaterial, so pray go on with what you were saying of Father Murphy."

"I was simply observing that the excellence of his disposition had given me a favourable opinion of your Majesty's countrymen."

"Which I hope the thoughtlessness of their King will not induce you to change. I trust you have too much good sense, Mr. Montagu, to feel offended with what you may call the frivolity of my manner. My heart, I hope, is good, though I own even I cannot say much in favour of my head. I am a laughing philosopher however, a sort of Democritus the second; and finding it more agreeable to laugh than cry, I generally try to extract amusement from every thing that happens to fall in my way. We shall soon know each other better, and so now, as doubtless you may wish for repose after the fatigues you have undergone, you will perhaps like to retire to the tent prepared for you."

The doctor and Edric willingly assented and repaired to their new abode, completely puzzled by what seemed to them the extraordinary and inconsistent character of the King.

Under this gay, laughing exterior, however, Roderic hid a sound penetrating mind, and a firm determined spirit; whilst, though no one enjoyed more to ridicule occasionally the foibles of his subjects, no one knew better how to check them, and bring them back instantly to their proper stations, if they ventured a hair's breadth beyond the limits he prescribed to them. He had thus the art to make himself feared as well as loved, and to rule his subjects despotically, though he never spoke to them without a smile.

Such as I have described him, it may be easily imagined Roderick was not long in winning the affections of his new friends, and he, in his turn, was equally delighted with them. The noble, generous, and inquiring spirit of Edric exactly accorded with his own; and the follies of the learned doctor afforded him never-ceasing amusement, whilst Edric, delighted to meet with a companion who could understand and sympathize with his feelings, felt happier than he had been for years; and the learned doctor, proud of being admitted to the intimacy of such a man as Roderick, declared all his troubles were repaid, and that he now considered himself as the most fortunate of mortals.

CHAPTER XXII.

The Spanish nobility were daily collecting round the Irish King. To one of the most distinguished of these, the Duke of Medina Celina, Roderick was particularly anxious to introduce Edric. For this purpose, therefore, as soon as the army of Roderick returned to his head quarters at Cadiz, where the duke had remained, the friends went together to pay him a visit.

Edric was exceedingly interested by this call. The duke's family consisted only of himself and his grand-daughter, the Princess Zoe, but the appearance of both was excessively striking. The duke was a blind old man with white flowing hair and a long silvery beard, clad with almost patriarchal simplicity; whilst Zoe, who sate closely by his side, and seemed devoted to his comfort, was beauty itself. Exquisitely lovely, however, as her features were, they excited rather pain than pleasure in the mind of the beholder, from their excessive paleness. Her dress was simple: a robe of black silk fitted tight to her slender shape, and her jet black hair was simply braided on her forehead, and confined in a net behind.

When she saw the strangers, a slight blush stained the usual alabaster fairness of her complexion, and a trifling agitation was visible in her manner. It was but for an instant, however, that this glowing tint suffused her pallid cheeks, or that her fine features betrayed agitation. Her usual calm dignity of expression was immediately re-assumed, and her countenance regained its marble whiteness. There was, indeed, something very singular in the whole countenance of this young beauty, for, notwithstanding the exquisite loveliness of her features, her charms were rather those of a statue than of a human being. Her fine features were strictly Grecian and perfectly regular, but they were always fixed in one unvarying expression; whilst her large black eyes fringed with long silken eyelashes, and her glossy raven hair, contrasted strangely with the spotless fairness of her complexion; the whole gave her the air of some unearthly visitant from the tomb.

Zoe had been unfortunate from her birth. Her mother having accompanied the old duke upon an embassy to Constantinople, had happened to please the fancy of the reigning Emperor so forcibly, that, contrary to the advice of his counsellors, he had married her. Disproportioned marriages, however, are seldom happy ones: and that of the parents of Zoe formed no exception to the general rule. The Emperor soon repented his rashness, and, becoming tired of his wife, treated her with coldness and neglect; whilst she, far removed from all her former friends, and finding herself despised by the man for whose sake she had sacrificed every thing, lingered a few years and then died unheeded and forlorn, leaving only the hapless Zoe to lament her fate.

The Emperor married again; and Zoe had dragged on a miserable existence, till in an insurrection of the Greeks, her father had been murdered, and she herself compelled to fly from Constantinople. She had repaired first to Africa; but finding her grandfather was in Spain, she had followed him thither, and still remained with him, under the protection of Roderick.

It was, indeed, the aristocracy of Spain for which the Irish hero was now principally fighting; for they had suffered most severely from the licentious conduct of the soldiers, and were most earnest in imploring his assistance. When the seat of the Spanish monarchy had been removed to Africa, most of the nobles had followed in its train, whilst those that remained had become objects of hate and suspicion to the republican governments that ensued. Still, however, the amor patriæ glowed strongly in their breasts, and chained them to their country; they submitted patiently to innumerable grievances, till, a few months before they applied to Roderick, finding the insolence of the soldiers become insupportable, they determined to throw off the yoke, and re-establish a monarchy in Spain.

For this purpose, they had invited Don Pedro, a younger branch of their former Royal family to come over from Africa to accept their throne. He complied, and had brought in his train many of the old nobility; and amongst the rest the venerable Duke of Medina Celina, whose most passionate wish it was, that he might die and be entombed in Spain. Don Pedro had been unsuccessful, and had fled; but many of those who had accompanied him remained, and with the resident Spanish nobility now formed the splendid Court of Roderick at Cadiz.

The duke received Edric kindly, and treated Roderick with that enthusiastic devotion, which is, beyond all other praise, flattering to the mind of man. Zoe never spoke, nor did her features betray that she took the slightest interest in the scene before her. It has been before observed, that education was carried to such a pitch in England, that all, even the common people, were universal linguists. Instruction indeed, in that respect, was imparted in many brief and ingenious modes; and knowledge being thus rendered so cheap and easy, as to be à la portée de tout le monde, it of course was going partially out of fashion with the higher classes; but as Sir Ambrose piqued himself on his devotion to all the old customs, he would not swerve from them in the education of his sons; and in consequence, Edric was almost as learned in this respect as a servant or a labourer.

This had often been a source of chagrin to him at home, as it prevented his feeling upon equal terms with those in the same situation of life as himself, and had contributed greatly to give him those shy and reserved manners we have noticed. On the present occasion, however, Edric found his learning advantageous, as it enabled him to enjoy thoroughly the animated and entertaining conversation of the old duke. After a lively and spirited discussion of the manners of the age generally, and the state of Spain in particular, the friends retired, having first obtained a promise from the duke and Zoe to be present at a grand tournament Roderick intended giving on the following day.

"Well, Edric!" said Roderick, "what think you of the Princess Zoe?"

"That she would be a Venus de Medicis, if she had a little more soul."

"Oh come! Edric," said Roderick, laughing; "that is really too bad. I'll allow that Zoe wants animation; but she has at least as much as a statue. Besides I thought you were fond of still life, or you would not feel so anxious about your Mummy."

"Oh, for God's sake!" said Edric, "do not joke me upon that subject; it is too solemn, too awful!"

"At least, your doubts are now satisfied," said the King.

"Not at all," returned Edric; "for I cannot help imagining it was only permitted to appear resuscitated to punish my presumptuous daring; and its mysterious disappearance, added to the strange and fearful adventures that have since attended us, only confirm my opinion."

"It must have been a horrible feeling when you first saw it stir," observed Roderick.

"Words cannot express the agony of that moment," replied Edric, "when I saw my strange unearthly wishes gratified, and felt the impiety I had been guilty of in having formed them; and I would have given worlds to restore the Mummy to the deep sleep I had disturbed. It was, however, then too late."

The Mummy!

"Can you form any idea of what has become of it?"

"None. If the Egyptian's story be correct, it contrived to re-inflate the balloon, and that carried it away, though it is quite impossible to say how far it might go, as the Mummy could not possibly understand the management of the machine, though he might accidentally fill it."

"Would it relieve you to think the Mummy safe in England?"

"Oh no! I shudder at the thought."

"Well, well, then it is useless to make yourself unhappy about the subject. Depend upon it, all is for the best. I am sure, for my part, I am very much obliged to the resuscitated gentleman; as, if it had not been for his freak of flying away with your balloon, you would not have been here at the present moment, and I might never have even known that such a person was in existence. However, now you are here, you must not leave me; and when we have finished our campaign, we will return to Ireland together, and pass the remainder of our lives in peace and tranquillity."

Edric smiled, for the very idea of peace and Roderick seemed incongruous.

The tournament was held on a fine plain on the mainland, a few miles from Cadiz, and nothing could exceed the brilliancy of the show. "The sun shone o'er fair women and brave men," for even in winter, the bright beams of an Andalusian sun give a glowing animation to the scene. The busy murmurs of the crowd, the prancing of the horses, and the gay laugh of the light-hearted Irishmen, as they paid their highflown compliments to the Spanish beauties, were, however, soon interrupted by the firing of cannon, and a pause ensued, which was at length broken by loud shouts of "Roderick! Roderick, for ever! Long live the Conqueror of Spain!" And immediately, the pressure and bustle of the people, and the sound of warlike music which gradually swelled upon the ear, announced the arrival of that illustrious Sovereign upon the field.

Roderick was, as usual, riding upon Champion, his noble barb, and surrounded by the officers of his staff; but he was not talking to them with his accustomed familiarity; his countenance even wore an air of sadness and reflection, very unusual to it. However, as he rode along, his fine horse tossing his head and spurning the ground as he advanced, he looked completely the powerful Sovereign that he really was.

His dress was exceedingly becoming. Roderick knew mankind too well not to appear to adopt, in some measure, even the prejudices of those he associated with; and knowing the partiality of the Spaniards for dress and appearance, his own was magnificent. A tight vest and pantaloons of black satin displayed the elegance of his figure to the best advantage, whilst a short cloak of the same material, hung from his shoulders in graceful negligence, and his head was covered with a large Spanish hat of black velvet, having a magnificent plume of ostrich feathers, secured by a diamond aigrette in front. A superb collar of diamonds also adorned his breast, and a deep frill of vandyk lace was fastened round his neck.

Splendid, however, as was the attire of Roderick, it was far exceeded by his personal advantages; and no one could look upon that fair, open brow, those bright blue eyes, that manly, though youthful form, that glossy chestnut hair and curling mustachios, or, what was more than all, upon the fascinating smile of the mouth they decorated, without feeling deeply interested for their possessor.

The fascinating manners of Roderick have been already mentioned; but, upon the present occasion, his usual gaité de cœur was tempered by an air of dignity and command which became him equally well, and which powerfully told, that though he might sometimes condescend to seem amused with trifles, he could, when he pleased, be indeed a king.

The affairs of Spain were now beginning to assume a favourable appearance, and, consequently, the people were better disposed to be amused; whilst, as a truce had been granted for some weeks, during a negotiation for peace which was carrying on, the combined Spanish and Irish soldiers shut up in the Isle of Leon, and thrown entirely upon their own resources for amusement, like most persons in similar situations, grasped eagerly at every trifle that seemed to promise variety and amusement.

Roderick was perfectly aware of this; and it was partly to afford employment for his officers, and partly to gratify his own taste for the pursuits of chivalry, that he had proposed the present tournament. The lists were marked out, and a flourish of trumpets summoned the combatants to the field. Two of the Irish officers were the first who engaged, and whilst every eye was occupied in watching their movements with the most intense anxiety, Roderick took an opportunity of whispering to Edric that he had just received news from England.

"Well!" cried Edric, his eyes sparkling with impatience.

"Elvira is elected; but I am afraid there is a strong party in the state against her."

"And my father?"

"He is well, and Edmund is prime minister!"

"What says Rosabella?"

"She is silent; and, therefore, I fear —"

"You are right. In such a case, Rosabella's silence can only portend a storm."

"The duke has left the country, and now resides entirely in town."

"What a change," said Edric, "a few short months has produced! all is altered. I was excessively shocked when you informed me of the death of Claudia; but this news, though it surprises, does not displease me; and, thank God! my father is well."

The defeat of one of the combatants, and the shouts and triumph attending the success of the other, now interrupted the conference; and the rush of all parties towards the King separated him from Edric, who walked quietly away from the crowd to meditate upon the news he had received. The train of thought thus conjured up was so pleasing, that he was soon completely lost in it. His father, his brother, and all the scenes of his childhood, those early recollections so dear to every heart, seemed to rise before him, and he had forgotten Spain and all that it contained, when he was roused from his reverie by a piercing scream; and, looking round, he saw the Princess Zoe, near whose palanquin he had accidentally placed himself, attempting to break from her carriage in a state of the most violent agitation.

Astonished beyond the power of expression at her emotion, Edric hastily assisted her to unfasten the door of her palanquin, and offered her his arm: Zoe took it without speaking, and with trembling steps hurried across the plain. In a few minutes, however, the cause of the princess's agitation was explained; for, as they approached the spot she evidently wished to reach, Edric saw the body of Roderick extended upon the ground, apparently without life or motion. Uttering an exclamation of horror, he attempted to rush towards him, but the princess held his arm firmly, and prevented him. Quite astonished, he looked up in her face; she was still dreadfully agitated, but she did not speak, and only pressed her finger against her lips.

In a few minutes, Roderick opened his eyes, and the princess again pressing Edric's arm, said in a hurried, though low tone, "Let us go!" Edric obeyed; and they walked hastily back to the palanquin in perfect silence. When Edric had assisted the princess into her carriage however, and was about to retire, she pressed his hand, and said again in her peculiarly low soft voice, "Do not speak of this!"

"I will not," said Edric; and bowing respectfully as he pressed her hand to his lips, he walked away excessively surprised at the scene he had witnessed. Upon reaching the King, he found he had been thrown from his horse, and so slightly hurt as not to think it necessary to interrupt the amusements of the day; which concluded after a brilliant display of Irish and Spanish valour, without any other incident worthy of notice.

A few days after this adventure, as Edric was sitting, lost in thought, in his own apartment, musing, as was his custom whenever he was alone, upon the strange adventure of the Mummy, and endeavouring in vain to imagine what might be its probable fate, he was startled by the door of his room flying suddenly open, and Roderick's rushing in pale and in violent agitation.

"Oh, Edric!" cried he, "I am ruined! my fame is lost for ever! whilst I have been loitering away my time here, the enemy has obtained the assistance of the French: they have taken Madrid, and almost all the towns between that and the frontier! An immense army is marching upon Seville, and they intended to have blocked me up here, amusing me with their pretended treaties, till they had caught me in their snare."

"And how has their plot been discovered?"

"The Princess Zoe—yes! I know what you would say—she loves me, and though I love her not, nay, though I am devoted to another, if I reconquer Spain, myself and crown shall be thrown at her feet;—but, if I fail, I will never live to be the herald of my disgrace."

"It is unworthy of Roderick to despair: it will be by treachery, if you are vanquished."

"Hold!" cried Roderick, driven almost to frenzy at the thought. "For mercy's sake, talk not so calmly of my being vanquished. I will conquer—I will redeem my name, or perish in the attempt; and if they do vanquish me, it shall be my corpse alone that they shall conquer, for the immortal spirit shall escape their fury."

"Alas! alas!" said Edric; "your words have again conjured up the fiend that so long has haunted me:—does the immortal spirit escape?"

"Edric," returned the King, "this is not a moment for metaphysical subtleties; we must act, and that immediately and decisively. We must advance upon Seville, and, if possible, get possession of that city before the army of the enemy shall reach it: this blow will strike the Spaniards with awe, and before they have recovered themselves, I shall have made myself master of half Spain. I know the character of the people I have to combat; I must carry every thing by a coup de main, or I shall fail."

It was impossible to deny the justice of this observation, and Edric warmly seconded the preparations of Roderick to march immediately upon Seville. These preparations were soon made; for Roderick was so completely idolized by his soldiers, that they regarded his will as law, and were ready to march at an hour's notice, though they knew not where they were going. Dr. Entwerfen was excessively agitated when he found he was going now really to engage in war; not that the base emotion of fear took possession of his soul, but a slight trepidation, such as that which scandal says even heroes feel at their first battle, crept over his nerves, and gave him an odd kind of sensation, which, he said, was only anxiety to engage.

No one knew where they were going; it was only rumoured, indeed, that hostilities were about to recommence, and, as the doctor said, it was very disagreeable to be unacquainted with the theatre of their future glory. Roderick was amused, notwithstanding even the agitation of the moment, with the efforts of the doctor to discover the secret, and told him, as though in confidence, that they were going to attack Lisbon. Delighted with this news, which he firmly believed, the doctor strutted about with indescribable dignity, walking upon the tips of his toes, pressing his lips together, and swelling out his cheeks like a cherub in a country church-yard, whilst he seemed absolutely bursting with the importance of the secret he carried. All was now ready; but before Roderick quitted Cadiz, he took leave of the Princess Zoe.

"It would be unjust to your merit, and my gratitude," said he, "to insult you with words; but if I survive, the devotion of my whole life—"

"Stay!" interrupted Zoe, "nor overrate so strangely the value of the service I have been so fortunate as to render you. Besides, even if your estimate were just, know that the services of Zoe are not to be purchased. No, prince, judge me not so meanly. Had I not determined that we should never meet again, the intelligence you so highly value would never have reached your ears. My greatest enemy is dead; and to-morrow I return to my native land, where the rebels have no longer the power to injure me. Demetrius, the ancient minister of my father, arrived yesterday, with the permission for my return, and I do not hesitate an instant—yet, before I go—"

"Speak," cried Roderick hastily; "command my life! my throne! my fortune!"

Zoe smiled. "The favour I have to request is trifling. I have a favourite page, who dreads to return to Greece, and I would willingly place him under your care."

"He shall be my brother!" exclaimed Roderick enthusiastically; "my friend! my companion in arms! He shall live with me, fight with me, and—"

Again a faint smile played on Zoe's marble features, like the ghost of departed joys; it was but for an instant, however, and it added fresh darkness to the succeeding gloom. "I wish no privileges for my page," said she gravely, "beyond those usually bestowed upon his class. Treat him kindly, but promise me you will not over-indulge him, or I will not leave him with you."

"You have only to command," said Roderick, "and you may rely upon obedience."

"Adieu! then," exclaimed the princess, extending her hand, whilst a slight blush stained her alabaster complexion. "God bless you!—we may meet again."

Roderick kissed her hand as he would have done that of an empress. "Heaven grant we may!" exclaimed he, "for, rest assured, no earthly pleasure could afford me half the joy."

"None?" asked Zoe incredulously.

"None!" repeated he firmly; "unless, perhaps," added he with

The Mummy!

a smile, "the re-conquering of Spain."

"Then you will accept my page?"

"As a gift from Heaven!"

"He shall join you ere you cross the bridge: once more, adieu!"

"Adieu!" cried Roderick, and Zoe vanished. In half an hour the troops were under arms, and had quitted Cadiz; but Roderick, in the bustle and confusion attendant upon the removal of so large a body of men so suddenly, had quite forgotten the Greek page. As he was crossing the bridge, however, his noble barb started, and Roderick, looking for the cause, saw a slight, graceful boy, who, kneeling, presented him with a letter; it was from Zoe.

"I forgot to tell you," wrote she, "that my page is dumb. As his loss of speech, however, was accidental, he is, notwithstanding, perfectly intelligent, and will obey your slightest gesture."

Ordering some of his attendants to provide a horse, Roderick desired the page to mount it, and ride by his side: the boy crossed his arms upon his breast, and bowed his head in token of obedience, and then lightly vaulted into the saddle.

CHAPTER XXIII.

The army of Roderick advanced rapidly through a lovely country richly tinted by the rays of a southern sun. Nothing, indeed, could be more beautiful than the scene. Though spring was only just bursting from the icy chains of winter, vine-covered cottages peeped through orange groves loaded with their fragrant flowers; whilst behind, the dark foliage of the lofty palm-trees gave depth and richness to the landscape. Innumerable flowers perfumed the air, and the sky glowed with azure and gold.

Under these circumstances, the advance of Roderick's army, though rapid, resembled rather the journey of a party of pleasure than a fatiguing and toilsome march; and when, just as the sun was setting, they approached a small village, Edric paused on the summit of a hill, to survey with delighted admiration the lovely scene below. A white church peeped from between a thick cluster of trees, and romantic cottages covered with wild festoons of luxuriant plants, were scattered about at intervals; whilst sitting before the doors, were placed groups of peasant girls, singing patriotic airs to their mandolines or lutes, and others were dancing gaily beneath the shade of some widely spreading trees. Neat dresses of black serge fitted tightly to the shape of these girls, and displayed the graceful elegance of their figures to the utmost advantage. Their long dark hair was bound in a simple net; and their sparkling eyes beamed with animation and love, whilst the clear dark complexion, well proportioned forms, jet black hair, and aquiline noses of their male partners, still, notwithstanding the lapse of so many centuries, strongly marked their Moorish origin. Songs of joy and lively music swelled upon the gale; but these sounds of peace and happiness were soon changed to shrieks of terror, as the unfortunate peasants saw the army of Roderick wind slowly through the trees, and they fled screaming for mercy, whilst all their little store of wealth fell an easy prey to the foe they left behind.

Edric shuddered at the pillage that ensued, and warmly remonstrated with his friend.

"My dear Edric," said Roderick, "these things are inevitable; though what you see here can give you but a very faint idea of the dreadful havoc and devastation of war. My soldiers destroy nothing, and generally even pay for what they take: but commonly in an enemy's country, men burn what they cannot make use of, and treat the unfortunate inhabitants with the most appalling cruelty. However these are things we cannot reason about."

"I think not," returned Edric; and finding his remonstrances unavailing, he had the discretion not again to allude to the subject, till the army approached Seville. The first view of this splendid city, illumined by the glowing rays of the setting sun, struck our young philosopher most forcibly. "Oh, Roderick!" cried he, "look at that long line of sumptuous palaces, adorned with marble pillars, and the finest statues; those lovely gardens—those bowers of roses; and those crystal fountains, whose sparkling spray looks dazzling in the sunbeams."

"Well," said Roderick, "I see them all, and more, the lofty spires of the town rising beyond, their gilded vanes glittering in the sun."

"And can you look upon this fair scene?" asked Edric, "and not feel compunction? Alas! alas! that the cruel hand of man should dare to destroy so lovely a picture!"

"My dear Edric," returned Roderick, smiling, "you would never do for a conqueror. If you make war a profession, Glory must be your mistress, and to obtain her, you must sacrifice all your better feelings. But, ah! what is that? look yonder, Edric!"

"I see nothing but a volume of fleecy smoke curling up between the trees," said Edric; "which harmonizes well with the lovely scene around—that scene which the grim hand of War is destined so soon to desolate. Oh, Roderick, can it be possible, that you, whose kind and charitable nature would not crush a worm to death unnecessarily, should—"

"They have fired the suburbs!" cried Roderick, interrupting him; and clapping spurs to his horse, he darted forward like an arrow discharged from a bow. His suspicions were correct. Light clouds of white vapour hung high in the clear blue heavens; whilst below, a thick yellow smoke, mingled with flames, spread wide ruin and devastation. Crackling pieces of wood, sparkling like a feu d'artifice, were thrown up with violence at intervals, and the scorching heat felt intolerable, as showers of sparks, and pieces of ignited matter, rained thick and fast upon the plain.

Edric and Roderick were on a gentle eminence when they first saw the city; and, deceived by the remarkable optical delusion often observable in similar situations, they had fancied it very near them. When they plunged into the valley, however, they soon discovered that this was of very considerable extent;

and their horses, weary with their toilsome march, with difficulty made their way through the thick underwood and tangled grass that every moment threatened to impede their progress. At length, they entered into the mazes of a wood, that quite obscured the city from their sight; and when fair Seville again broke upon them through an opening in the trees, she appeared one vast mass of flame.

"Good Heavens!" cried Edric, "surely they will not burn the city! What a multitude of human beings will be sacrificed if they do!"

"I hope they will not be so foolish," said Roderick, "yet I own I fear; no — no — " cried he, after a moment's pause; "see, see! the smoke divides, and as the wind bears the rolling volumes asunder, the city's walls still stand: no fire as yet has touched the glory and the bulwark of proud yet fair Seville."

The glowing embers still crackled as they approached, and still threw up occasional showers of sparks fearfully glaring amidst the darkness of the night, which now closed in upon them with a thick gloom very unusual to that climate. The flames had caught the bridge ere the army of Roderick reached the banks of the river; and the fiery bow, glowing through the surrounding darkness, looked like the fabled arch over which the Mahometans believe the souls of the dead are destined to skait into Paradise.

At length the army of Roderick found their progress stopped by the deep and rapid waters of the Guadalquiver; the black smoking remains of the bridge which had once stretched across the river, seeming to forbid their farther progress. Magnificent palaces lay around them, crumbling into ruins, whilst their half-burnt roofs fell occasionally with a tremendous crash. Fearful indeed was the spectacle that presented itself, and the once superb suburb seemed the very temple of Desolation. Vases and statues lay overturned, and blackened by the smoke. Majestic trees, scorched by the flames, and their shrivelled leaves stripped from their withered branches, stretched forth their bare arms forlorn and desolate, like bereaved mothers mourning over their murdered children. A chill drizzling mist began to fall, and all looked dreary and uncomfortable.

Roderick stood upon the banks of the river and marked its dark rolling waters, in which the fire that still crept amongst the ruins on the other side reflected its red lurid glare. "We must pass the river," said he; "these Andalusians are too crafty to have destroyed this fine suburb, in itself a town, had not some imperious reason urged them to it. They want to gain time; but we must show them that we dare brave the combined terrors of flames and water, when Glory gives the word."

"And what is this Glory you pursue so madly?" asked Edric. "May not Prudence be admitted to its councils? And will it not be more certain if we wait till morning to seize it? The night is dark and gloomy; I think it forbodes a tempest; and at any rate it will be difficult to ford this black rolling stream in the obscurity. To-morrow with the dawn we will effect a passage; our troops will be then refreshed with rest, and we shall be ready to encounter with vigour the dangers that may oppose us."

Roderick smiled sadly. "To-morrow, Edric," said he, "it may be too late. To-morrow, the army our enemies expect may advance upon us, and either obtain possession of the town, or cut off our retreat. We have traitors amongst us; for even now, secret as our movements have been, you see the enemy has had notice of our approach."

"Why should we pause?" cried Lord Arthur O'Neil, one of the Irish lords who had followed his Sovereign to the field. "Your Majesty may confide in your soldiers.—Tired! An Irishman knows not the meaning of the word. Shall the heroes of Burgos, Valladolid, and Salamanca, complain of fatigue? Have you forgotten how they fought and conquered? Have you forgotten the proud day before Madrid, when a handful of Irish fought and defeated a whole legion of Spaniards? Can we think of these things, and yet talk of fear? Oh no, surely not! Surely if we did, every warm drop of blood in our veins, every spark of enthusiasm in our hearts, would give the lie to the assertion. Lead us on, brave Roderick! Damp not the spirit of your troops by unnecessary delays, but lead us forward to victory."

"Lead us to victory!" shouted the officers and troops; and Roderick, animated by their cries, gave orders for the instant fording of the river. The evening had now quite closed in; not a star broke the thick dull grey of the heavens, and the sky began to look dark and threatening. The lowering clouds grew gradually darker and darker; whilst a dusky veil seemed to fall over the distant turrets of the town, and to envelope them in gloom.

The fire that still raged in the suburbs, had now seized an ancient castle, and a thick yellow smoke burst from its embrasures: it seemed like a huge giant vomiting forth flames. In the mean time, heavy clouds that had gathered over their heads, seemed big with destruction, and a low moaning sound was heard at a distance as though the winds were sighing over the fate of the unhappy wretches, who were soon to fall victims to their fury! The hollow murmuring continued; it grew gradually louder and louder; and at length, burst with tremendous violence in fearful blasts over the heads of the army. It was now as dark as night, and the thunder rolled with awful grandeur; the rain descended in torrents, and the flashes of lightning showed by glimpses the pouring vengeance of the clouds, and the still smoking fragments of the ruined bridge.

It seemed madness to attempt the passage of the river at such a moment; but the determined spirit of Roderick, when once resolved, was not easily to be shaken, and crying out, "Glory and Roderick for ever!" he attempted to plunge into the boiling flood. At this instant the heavens seemed to open, and a vivid ball of bright blue fire to dart from them. The lightning had struck a tree, beneath which a group of soldiers had taken shelter, splitting it asunder and scattering the branches in all directions; whilst the groans of the unhappy wretches, crushed by its fall, mingled horribly with the howling wind and crashing thunder. Nothing, however, could intimidate the daring spirit of Roderick, and calling upon his soldiers to follow him, he struck his spurs into Champion, his faithful barb, and the noble animal plunged with him into the stream. The river, swollen by the torrents of rain, now rushed along in roaring waves like the sea. Champion, and the horses of those who had followed the example of their Sovereign, were soon obliged to try to swim, and struggled in vain to reach the opposite shore. The impetuous current, however, swept them down the river, and soon the cries of the drowning men, and the plunging of the horses, added fresh horror to the roar of the raging waters.

Fearful was the struggle, till, after a few horrible moments of almost supernatural exertions, the storm partly ceased; and though the wind still continued to howl at intervals, and the thunder to roll, its growl became fainter and fainter; and soon nothing was heard but the splashing of the waves, and the struggles of the swimming animals who tried in vain to stem the boiling current.

Champion had made most violent efforts to save his master, but he strove in vain! he only floated upon the waves. No longer could he toss his head and proudly champ his bit; his strength was fast leaving him: his long thick mane and heavy armour weighed him down. His feeble eyes, however, caught a glimpse of the opposite shore; they had almost reached it, and the noble animal, collecting all his strength for one attempt, sprang

The Mummy!

forward: but, alas! his heart broke in the effort; his strength failed; the slippery clay slided from beneath his feet, and the lifeless body of poor Champion fell back into the river, dragging his illustrious master with him. Roderick was too much exhausted to swim; and, encumbered by the dead body of the horse, he was fast sinking to rise no more, when a powerful arm caught hold of him: —

"Take this knife!" cried a voice that he knew to be Edric's: "disentangle yourself from the horse, and I can save you!"

His words recalled the fleeting spirit of Roderick; he grasped the knife and hastily cut asunder the cord that confined his cloak round his neck. It was this cloak which had become entangled in the saddle, and the moment it was released from the neck of Roderick, it floated down the stream with the body of poor Champion, whilst the fainting Monarch was dragged on shore by his friend Edric. The storm had now entirely ceased; the water began to get more tranquil, and the moon, breaking from the clouds that drifted rapidly across the skies, showed the opposite bank so plainly that the rest of the army passed with little difficulty. In the mean time, restoratives had been applied to Roderick, and he opened his eyes. A slight shudder, however, ran through his frame, as he looked, around, and, heaving a deep sigh, he hastily reclosed them, as though he wished to shut out for ever the recollection of what had just passed. 'Twas but for an instant, however, that the manly mind of the Irish hero indulged in this overwhelming sorrow; the next, smiling though mournfully, he took the hand of Edric, and looking at him with affection, he said, "I owe my life to you. God only knows whether the boon be worth the meed of thanks, or whether you have not been cruel to my people in saving me. They have small reason to wish my life, if I am often to be seized with such freaks as these. Good God! I shudder when I consider that the lives of several of my fellow-creatures have been sacrificed to my misguided folly. Poor Champion too," drawing his hand across his eyes to wipe away his tears, and then again trying to smile. "You will laugh at me, Edric, but you don't know how much I feel the loss of that horse. Poor fellow! how nobly he breasted the tide, and struggled on. But he is gone, and it's of no use thinking of him."

And as he spoke, he resolutely started from the bed upon which he had been laid, and again dashed the tears from his eyes. "I have other things to think of that are of far more importance than poor Champion; and yet, poor fellow, I can't forget it was his obedience to me that destroyed him! Poor fellow! You would have been sorry for him, Edric, if you had heard how deeply he sighed when we were in the middle of the water, and I forced him to go on. But I will think no more of him. Summon my officers, and let us hold a council as to our future proceedings."

The council was called, and it was soon ascertained that the army had sustained no other loss than poor Champion, a few other horses, and about eight or ten of the King's bodyguard, who had thrown themselves into the river the moment they had seen their master do so. Roderick felt keenly the folly that had occasioned the loss of these brave men and useful animals; but as he was aware that he was now surrounded by his soldiers and the allied Spaniards, and that it is always necessary for a Monarch to seem great, whether he be so or not, if he wish to be obeyed, he had too much self-command to show any signs of weakness, and gave orders for the commencement of the siege of the town with as much coolness as though he had merely quietly marched up to its walls.

In the mean time, Dr. Entwerfen had safely floated over the stream, riding astride upon one of the ammunition waggons, which were contrived of cork, and supported by bladders, or rather balloons, filled with gas upon each side; whilst the middle part, upon which the doctor rode, being nearly in the form of a barrel, the worthy gentleman had formed no bad representation of Bacchus as he swam merrily across; for the learned doctor, having wisely considered how much the interests of science would suffer if any accident befell his precious person, had waited till the river was as smooth as glass, before he would venture to traverse it.

It was perhaps also well for Roderick, that he now found himself upon the theatre of war: that he had orders to give — decisions to make; in short, that he had sufficient to occupy his mind, and prevent its dwelling upon the unpleasant circumstances that had just passed. Occupation, indeed, is the only sure remedy for grief. The consolations of friends and hopes of religion may do much; but constant employment is the most effectual medicine for woe that the skill of man has yet been able to discover.

Roderick now enjoyed the benefit of this invaluable panacea in its fullest extent; for he had much to do. Notwithstanding all their affection for him, his army could not conceal from themselves, that he had sacrificed several valuable lives unnecessarily by his rashness, and their confidence in his prudence was proportionably diminished. Roderick saw, and was mortified by this; the more so, as he felt it was occasioned by his own folly; and he struggled to do something to retrieve the confidence he had lost. There is, perhaps, no situation more painful to a noble, high-spirited mind, than the consciousness of error; and the feelings of Roderick upon this occasion were an ample penance for his faults.

During the whole of the passage of the river, and the encampment of the army upon the opposite side, under the very walls of the city, not a single soldier of the enemy had been seen: but when that was completed, and the harassed host of Irish had stretched their weary limbs upon the earth, to seek a few minutes' repose before the attack that was ordered at daybreak, lights could be plainly seen moving to and fro in the city, and the heavy tramp of the soldiers heard as they paraded the walls. All now was still; a calm seemed to have succeeded a mighty tempest.

A tent had been erected for Roderick and his chief officers; and there the Monarch now sate gloomily musing, whilst his officers were scattered, in various attitudes of repose and thought, around him. Alexis, the Greek page, who had with difficulty passed the river, lay at his feet. At length, all slept but Edric and Roderick. After a long pause, the Irish hero looked at his friend, and seeing him gazing at him with a look of the tenderest concern—"Edric," said he; "I suffocate here; will you walk forth?" Edric willingly consented, and they sallied from the tent.

The moon now shone brightly, and the night was calm and still. They walked together towards the banks of the river. Those waters, which so lately had raged like a roaring lion seeking to devour, now rippled gently along, dancing in the sunbeams, and seeming almost to smile at the mischief they had done.

Roderick could not bear the sight; remorse for his impatience struck like a barbed arrow through his heart, and he turned hastily away. He now looked at the scene that lay before him towards the town. The moon shone brightly upon the tents of his soldiers, which contrasted strongly with the black and disfigured ruins of the suburbs, amongst which they had been hastily pitched; whilst the lights in the city, seen only from the summit of the walls, made it look almost like an eagle's nest suspended between heaven and earth. Roderick grasped Edric's hand. "How calm," cried he, "how peaceful seems the scene before us! Alas! how different from that which so lately—but ah! what's that?" exclaimed he, suddenly interrupting himself; "surely I heard a groan."

Edric listened, and distinctly heard the feeble moaning of a human voice. Neither Roderick nor himself uttered a syllable; but both darted to the spot from whence the sounds proceeded. Just at a bend in the river, surrounded by lofty trees, now scorched and half destroyed by the fire, had stood the maison de plaisance of one of the Spanish nobles. It had been built in the Italian style; hedges of myrtle and pomegranates had bloomed in the garden, and a raised terrace had surrounded the house, ornamented by statues. Now, however, this terrace was covered with fallen pillars and broken vases—ruin and desolation spread around. The trellis-work, against which, different creeping shrubs had been trained, hung in wild disorder, torn from the walls, and crushing with its weight the shrubs to which it had once served as a support.

Edric and Roderick entered the dwelling, for the cry seemed to proceed from its ruins. With hasty steps they traversed the deserted chambers, in which magnificent tapestry hung in tatters from the walls, whilst shattered remnants of valuable pictures and shivered mirrors showed the grandeur that had once been there. All now, however, was desolation! the gilded walls and ceilings looked black with the smoke, and the splendid furniture lay half-burnt and half-destroyed upon the ground. Roderick and Edric, however, did not stop long to survey the misery around them, for they hurried hastily forward to the place from which the cries had proceeded. As they approached, they found they were the accents of a female voice that had attracted them; and advancing a few steps farther, they beheld a sight that filled them with pity.

Beneath a fallen column, in the ruins of which she was so entangled that she could not move, lay, or rather stooped, a beautiful female, bending over the apparently lifeless body of an old man, whose fine features and venerable appearance were sufficient of themselves to create a deep interest in his behalf, but which interest was trebly increased by the evident anxiety painted upon the beautiful face of the female.

"Oh, Heavens!" cried she, as soon as they approached; "if you have any mercy or Christian charity in your disposition, succour this poor old man. Those cruel wretches have left him to perish miserably: though we are strangers, we are human beings, and have committed no crime."

By this time, Edric and Roderick had arrived near enough to draw her from the column, when they perceived, to their infinite horror, that her arm was broken, and that she was otherwise seriously hurt. "Oh, think not of me," cried she, finding they wished to succour her before they attended to the old man, who appeared to be dead; "save my father, I am quite well—can I help you?" and heedless of her own pain, the heroic girl assisted in dragging her father from his dangerous situation.

"I fear he is dead," whispered Roderick.

"Oh! say not so," shrieked Pauline, for that was her name; "he must, he shall recover. Give him air," continued she, endeavouring with the one trembling hand, the use of which remained to her, to unfasten his collar. Edric gazed at her with admiration, and, struck with her filial piety and generous self-forgetfulness, he felt an interest for her that he had never before experienced for woman. He assisted her pious cares, and finding the old man still insensible, he bore him in his arms to the banks of the river, and sprinkled him with its waters.

Whilst he was thus engaged, the little fat Dr. Entwerfen, quite out of breath with his exertions, came puffing up, in something between a run and a trot. "Oh! Edric dear!" cried he, gasping for breath, "I've found you, have I; but, heyday! what's the matter? You haven't been killing any body, have you?"

"Doctor!" exclaimed Edric, "I am rejoiced to see you; this gentleman has been hurt by some falling ruins—will you bleed him?"

The doctor had studied surgery in his youth, and had since practised frequently for charity; and, being in all things in which his particular foibles were not concerned, a man of sense and feeling, he instantly comprehended the importance of the case, and drawing forth his lancet, after having first bared and bound up the arm of his patient, he bled him. At first the blood dropped slowly, drop by drop; but it soon began to flow more freely, and then the patient, heaving a deep sigh, opened his eyes.

Pauline had been bending over her father with an intenseness of anxiety that repressed every personal feeling; but the moment she heard him sigh, the unnatural strength that had supported her gave way; nature could bear no more, and she fell senseless to the ground.

Every one flew to her assistance, and Dr. Entwerfen, in particular, was quite in agony. "Dear, pretty creature!" cried he, pushing his wig on one side, in his hurry to raise her up—"Pretty dear! I do declare her arm is broken, and her shoulder dreadfully lacerated! Poor thing! I wonder how she could contrive to hold up so long."

"It is wonderful!" repeated Edric. "It is the triumph of mental energy over bodily suffering."

"See! she opens her eyes! she survives!" exclaimed Roderick. "Had I not better return to my tent for assistance?"

"There are some soldiers just there," replied the doctor, pointing to a group of men a few paces distant; "they came with me to protect me, but I outran them when I saw Edric."

The soldiers soon formed a litter, upon which M. de Mallet, for that was the name of the old man, and his daughter were conveyed to the tent of Roderick, where proper surgical aid was afforded them. And whilst they are recovering from the injuries they had received, we will take the opportunity of informing our readers of the circumstances that had placed them in so unpleasant a situation.

M. de Mallet was a Swiss noble; and upon the usurpation of the then despot of Switzerland, he had vehemently defended the liberty of his country. The tyrant had imprisoned him, and he had with difficulty made his escape, followed by his only daughter, who was devotedly attached to him, and who, in all his dangers, had never quitted his side. She had lost her mother in her earliest youth, and since that period, all her thoughts and cares had been devoted to her father.

To comfort him, had formed the sole occupation of her life; and self was quite forgotten in her anxiety for his welfare. After escaping from Switzerland, they had taken refuge in Spain, flattering themselves, that, as it was a free country, they should there be safe and happy. But, alas! they soon found the charms of freedom were more ideal than real; and M. de Mallet, though he had been an enthusiast for liberty under the despotic government of Switzerland, found the sweets of freedom not quite so great as he had imagined amongst the Republicans of Spain; the pride of the nobles, and the conceited ignorance and insubordination of the people, being, as he found by sad experience, things much more agreeable to talk about than endure. In Switzerland, he had called the one, proud independence, and the other manly daring; but he now discovered nobles and democratic chiefs can be tyrants as well as kings; and that the mob is a many-headed monster most exceedingly difficult to manage.

The Mummy!

At first, M. de Mallet and his daughter were rapturously received in Spain. No human beings could be more interesting: applauses filled the air whenever they appeared; addresses were presented to them from all quarters; the people crowded to see them, and the Spanish nobles vied with each other in offering them an asylum. All this was very fine; but, unfortunately, it was too charming to be lasting. As M. de Mallet and his lovely daughter had been often seen, congratulated, and condoled with, there was nothing now to be done, and the enthusiasm of the Spaniards began rapidly to abate. In the first moment of triumph, M. de Mallet had blindly believed every thing the people had advanced, and had fancied himself, really as they called him, a hero and a martyr. He thus felt sensibly the change of feeling they so soon evinced; he became disgusted with a people so fickle; and, being too candid to conceal his sentiments, he suffered the Spaniards to perceive his disgust. The total alienation of the remaining interest they felt for him, was the natural consequence.

In the heat of enthusiasm, M. de Mallet had accepted freely the offer of a Spanish nobleman to make his house his home; but, with the usual tenacity of a generous mind in a state of dependence, as soon as he fancied he saw a coldness on the part of his host, he left him instantly, and hastened to the house of another, who had been still more warm in his offers of friendship. He, too, soon became cold; and M. de Mallet, like the hare with many friends, though overloaded with professions, found himself completely desolate when he really wanted protection.

M. de Mallet had provided no funds when he left his native country, and his estates having been confiscated, he was thus thrown entirely upon the bounty of strangers. Too high-minded to endure dependence, and too proud to humble himself to labour, M. de Mallet had solicited and obtained the promise of a post in the Spanish army; and the directors of the government having promised him a place in the garrison of Seville, he had proceeded a few weeks before to the house of the Duke of Sidonia, the governor of that city, for the purpose of taking possession. The duke, however, received him coldly, amusing him with procrastinating promises, till M. de Mallet found too late he had been duped by the directors; who, to rid themselves of his importunities, had sent him to Seville, merely on account of its distance from Madrid, and the difficulty he would have in returning to torment them, instead of having any real intention of complying with his wishes.

Indignant at the treatment he had met with, M. de Mallet

expostulated warmly with the duke; and the violence of his feelings produced an apoplectic seizure. The duke, though indifferent to the suit of M. de Mallet, was not destitute of the common feelings of humanity; he had him, therefore, carried to a chamber, where proper surgical assistance was afforded him. This scene took place at the duke's country-seat, upon the banks of the river; and M. de Mallet had remained there till, aided by a strong constitution and the vigilant attention of his daughter, he was fast recovering. When, however, intelligence being received of the rapid approach of the army of Roderick, the duke ordered the suburbs to be burnt, including his country-house; his unfortunate guests had entirely escaped his recollection; and the Spaniards appointed to destroy the suburbs, having performed their task with the utmost barbarity, tearing to pieces and destroying what they could not burn; the servants had flown at their approach, entirely forgetting M. de Mallet and his daughter; who, being in a distant quarter of the mansion, knew nothing of what was passing, till they were roused to a sense of their situation by the flames attacking their apartment. With piercing screams Pauline succeeded in rousing her father, and forcing him from the chamber; but they knew not where to fly. The crackling flames seemed to pursue them wherever they went, and the falling timbers threatened every instant to destroy them. At last they reached the hall, and Pauline's beautiful features beamed with joy at their approaching deliverance, when the tottering roof gave way, rocking a few moments with a fearful cracking noise, and then falling with a tremendous crash. Pauline saw it coming; but there was not time to escape; and uttering a faint cry, she threw herself before her father, striving to shield him with her delicate body from the coming danger.

Feeble, however, would have proved this slight and fragile barrier to ward off the impending peril, had not fortunately one of the descending rafters struck against a projecting pillar, and thus formed a kind of arch, which served to protect them from farther injury; the falling of the roof having also nearly extinguished the fire. Pauline's arm had been broken with the blow, and her shoulder dreadfully lacerated; yet still the heroic girl supported herself; and, sustaining with her remaining arm the apparently lifeless body of her father, who, stunned with so many misfortunes, lay insensible at her feet, she endeavoured by her cries to draw the attention of some one to the spot; as she found her father and herself were so entangled in the ruins, that it was impossible they could be extricated without powerful assistance.

The keenest interest was excited by Pauline and her father in the breasts of Edric and Roderick; but, powerful as it was, it was destined soon to give way to yet more painful sensations; for scarcely had they been removed to the tent, when Roderick, perceiving the first feeble tints of day streak the horizon, gave orders for the assault. The city was strongly fortified, and even where the ancient bulwarks had decayed, the governor had hastily supplied their place with wood so skilfully painted to resemble stone, as quite to deceive the eyes of his opponents. Thirty towers were ranged at intervals along this formidable-looking wall; and on one side appeared a citadel strongly garrisoned, which commanded that space between the river and the city where the army of Roderick was now encamped, and which was aided by a kind of ditch which served occasionally as a covered way.

The sun now rose in all its splendour, spreading its rich tints of purple and gold over the scene, and sweeping away before it the mists of morning. Soon, however, was its brilliancy to be obscured, and the savage rage of man to deface the beauty of nature; soon did roaring cannon and flashing weapons imitate a contention of the elements; and soon did the gashed and bleeding forms of the assailants strew the ground, rendered slippery by their blood. The besieged defended themselves vigorously; three times did Roderick and his followers attempt to scale the walls, and three times were they repulsed; but at length a breach was made, and Roderick, transported with joy, threw himself into it, shouting to his soldiers to follow him. They obeyed; and the siege would have been at once terminated, had not a cloud of dust, rising in long black columns in the distance, through which the reflection of arms shone dazzling in the sun, given new spirits to the besieged, and discouraged the besiegers.

Deep masses, half hidden by this heavy cloud, and appearing only more vast from the obscurity thrown over them, advanced rapidly, seeming to come on with the mighty force of the raging sea when it rushes along with irresistible violence and sweeps before it every thing that dare oppose its fury.

The garrison of the town, animated at the sight, rallied their half-exhausted forces, and drove back the assailants with such carnage that the line of their retreat was marked by a long stream of blood and expiring bodies. Roderick, for the first time in his life, refrained from renewing the attack, for, as he feared being surrounded, he determined to draw off his forces, and give battle to the combined French and Spanish army that was now fast approaching.

CHAPTER XXIV.

Notwithstanding the danger of his situation, Roderick was delighted at the sight of the allied army. "Now we shall fight," cried he, "and not be thrown down like dogs from the walls to perish. I could not bear to see my brave soldiers so sacrificed. But now that we shall meet fairly upon the open field, and struggle hand to hand, and man to man, we cannot fail to conquer!"

"Heaven grant us victory!" said Edric, sighing.

"Why, and so it will, man!" repeated Roderick gaily. "Come, come! rouse, and cheer thy spirits, for the moment of glory ought not surely to be that of gloom!"

The force of the enemy had, in the mean time, rapidly advanced, and the two armies were now opposite to each other; the river curving round that of Roderick like a silver band. The situation of the Irish hero was, indeed, now become hazardous in the extreme; and, if defeated, he could neither retreat nor advance without being exposed to imminent peril, as the river lay before him, and his rear was open to attacks from the town. But neither Roderick nor his soldiers ever contemplated the possibility of defeat; they breathed nothing but victory; and, as the confidence of success often ensures it, they had hitherto found themselves invincible, principally from the firm belief they entertained that they really were so. Roderick divided his army into three parts, and, determining to lead the van himself, he gave the command of one of the other divisions to Lord Arthur O'Neil, son of the Earl of Tyrone; and confided the other, which consisted entirely of Spaniards, to the conduct of the Spanish general, Don Alvarez Ripparda, upon whose prudence he knew he might confidently rely: whilst he retained Edric, the doctor, and Alexis, the Greek page of Zoe, immediately about his own person.

The battle soon raged with terrific grandeur; the shouts and cries of the combatants, mingling horribly with the roar of the cannon, which echoed from the walls of the town, seemed to leap from hill to hill, and reverberate in the distance like peals of rolling thunder. Roderick, in the mean time, performed prodigies of valour. Not satisfied with directing the movements of his troops, he fought bravely, sword in hand, like a common soldier, with all that prodigious energy and unexampled good fortune, which had previously induced the belief amongst the lower classes of Spaniards, of his being assisted by supernatural agency. A square was attacked and seemed upon the point of giving way; but when Roderick saw its danger and threw himself into the centre, the soldiers were inspired with unwonted courage, and, fighting like lions about to be despoiled of their prey, repulsed the enemy with tremendous slaughter. In fact, nothing could resist the valour of Roderick's arm; like Homer's Achilles, he seemed ready to triumph even over Fate herself.

An unexpected occurrence, however, notwithstanding his prowess, was very near turning the tide of the battle against him. Lord Arthur O'Neil, whom he had placed at the head of one of the divisions, though brave as an individual, was nothing as a chief; and, unequal to the responsibility of the task he had undertaken, stood hesitating and uncertain what to do, whilst the moment for action passed away. His division had been sent round to attack the enemy in the rear; and Roderick having advanced farther than he would have done, had he not depended upon their assistance, their inaction seemed likely to produce the most fatal consequences. Edric saw Lord Arthur's uncertainty; and, comprehending in an instant both the cause and its effects, he put himself at the head of a few men and galloped to his relief. Arthur, bewildered and overwhelmed, willingly resigned his command; and Edric, leading his division to the charge, changed instantly the fortune of the day. The victory that followed was decisive. Those combating in front against Roderick, astonished at hearing the din of battle in their rear, wavered and became irresolute; whilst disorder being once thrown amongst such a mass of men, horses, and ammunition-wagons, its consequences were irreparable. The rout soon became general. The French and Spaniards fell over each other in dismay; whilst, in some instances, their confusion was so excessive, that they turned their arms upon their own troops, mistaking them for those of their opponents.

The pursuit of the flying foe being confided to the Spanish division of Roderick's army, that victorious monarch returned himself in triumph to his camp before the city. Gloom hung over the walls of Seville, as that proud city expected to become instantly the prey of the conqueror. Roderick, however, finding the garrison were still determined to resist, and that his own soldiers were exhausted by the fatigue they had undergone, resolved to defer the attack till the next day. Then retiring to his tent, he ordered his officers and nobles to be summoned to hold a council of war as to their future proceedings. A crowd had, in consequence of this summons, already collected round the Monarch when Edric appeared amongst them. Roderick saw him, and hastily rushing forward, clasped him in his arms. "My dearest friend!" cried he; "yesterday you saved my life, but to-day you have preserved my honour. I do not attempt to thank you, for I feel the utter incompetency of words to express my feelings. Do not, however, look miserable, Arthur," continued he, addressing the unfortunate general; "for I do not blame you. It was my fault for putting you in a situation you were not competent to fill. For the future, you and Edric shall change places; and then I trust, whilst I have still the pleasure of employing my friends, the interests of the state will not suffer."

A page now appeared, bearing a ribband, attached to which, were fastened some glittering crosses. "It is well," said Roderick, taking the ribband in his hand. "Edric," continued he, "I hope you will oblige your friend by accepting these splendid baubles from his hand. They can confer no additional honour upon you in his sight, but they may aid in establishing your authority amongst the soldiers you in future will command, who regard these trinkets with respect."

Edric gracefully bowed assent, and kneeling before the Monarch, received his new honours with as much grace as Roderick bestowed them; the assembled officers and nobles pressing round, and offering their congratulations. Whatever they might say, however, no one present really felt a tenth part of the delight experienced by Dr. Entwerfen upon the occasion. His transport, indeed, quite defies description; for he danced, sang, jumped, nay, absolutely screamed with rapture; till at last, quite unable otherwise to give vent to the violence of his emotions, he sprang to the pillar of the tent, and clinging round it, embraced it with all his strength. All these antics had been slyly watched and enjoyed by Roderick, even through the circle that surrounded him: he lost sight of the doctor, however, when he darted away; and it was not till the officers and nobles dispersed, that the King discovered his learned friend, to his infinite amusement, still hugging the post.

It has been already observed, that an unconquerable love of mischief mingled with the thousand good qualities that formed the composition of Roderick, and that he was continually getting into scrapes, and playing tricks upon all the unhappy personages who happened to fall in his way; though his invincible good-humour, and a certain indescribable degree of the bon enfant peculiar to his character, rendered it quite impossible for any one seriously to resent his pranks.

It was not, indeed, in nature, for any human creature to be long angry with Roderick; and thus being certain of not giving lasting offence, whenever he was not positively engaged in war, the restless activity of his disposition made him frolic about, like

The Mummy!

a spoiled and petted child, who, even at the very moment of his sins being forgiven, is entirely occupied in plotting some new exploit.

Under these circumstances, it may be easily imagined what an infinite fund of amusement the confiding simplicity of Dr. Entwerfen had proved to Roderick, and innumerable had been the tricks he had played off upon him during their long and tedious sojourn in the Isle of Leon. The important events that had since occurred had, however, entirely occupied the monarch's attention, and the poor doctor had been suffered to enjoy a long respite, till this sudden view of his unabated enthusiasm presented an opportunity too tempting for the laughter-loving Monarch to resist.

Accordingly that evening, one of Roderick's pages, affecting an air of profound secrecy, presented the doctor with a mysterious bag, containing several small balls of dough, and a billet from the King, in which he informed the doctor, that these balls when boiled would be converted into a gunpowder of such amazing strength and efficacy, that ten grains of it would be sufficient to blow up a whole city; and that having become possessed by accident of the invaluable secret of their composition, he wished to use them for the destruction of Seville; and not having in his whole camp so skilful an experimental philosopher as the doctor, he had determined to confide their preparation exclusively to his care.

It is impossible for words to do justice to the importance that swelled in the breast of the doctor as he perused this epistle. He strutted, puffed himself out, and did his very utmost to look big—a feat he doubtless might have contrived to accomplish, had not Nature perversely determined to counteract his endeavours, and confined his stature to about four feet eleven. As it was, however, he certainly did make the most of himself, and being firmly resolved not to lose a single instant in putting the designs of the King into execution, he hastened to a vacant place between the camp and the city, where some cauldrons had been hastily erected for cooking the soldiers' food, and there commenced his operations.

In the mean time, Roderick, who had no idea the doctor would be so expeditious in his movements, was busily engaged in superintending the removal of the wounded, and in giving orders of the assault which was to take place upon the following day. He had indeed much to do; for awfully heavy is the responsibility of a general who is not entirely divested of feeling for his men; and the heart of Roderick, though a mistaken thirst for glory had made him a conqueror, was kind and generous, nay even tender in the extreme.

Urged by his compassion, he thus could not rest satisfied, after the more arduous labours of the day were over, without visiting himself the hospitals of the sick. He saw their wounds dressed, and tried to soften their pains, whilst he spoke kindly to them, and praised their valour. Thus employed, as he passed from tent to tent, the eyes of his soldiers beamed with rapture at his approach; and even in the agonies of death, they raised their feeble voices to call down blessings upon his head. Alexis followed his master in this excursion, and his fine eyes sparkled with pleasure as they followed the god-like form of Roderick through the crowd. The Monarch, indeed, himself, started with amazement as, turning suddenly, he accidentally met their gaze. "This page," said he to Edric, who happened to be near, "possesses a glance of fire—I really never saw more expressive features."

"It is often the case," returned Edric calmly, as he assisted one of the surgeons to bind the arm of a wounded soldier. "The dumb frequently employ gestures to make themselves understood, and their features insensibly become more expressive from the muscles being more frequently brought into play."

"You fought like a hero, my brave fellow!" said Roderick to the poor man Edric had been assisting. "I hope your hurt is not serious!"

"And if it were through my heart," said the man, "it's no more than I'd be proud to bear for your Majesty, any day of my life."

"Oh, these Irish!" sighed an old Andalusian soldier, who lay near, and happened to understand them. "They are brave as lions in the field, but gentle as doves when they are in a chamber."

"Have your wants also been attended to?" asked Roderick.

"Yes, God bless your Majesty!" returned the soldier. "If the devil does help you when you are fighting, I am sure it is God's own spirit makes you so good to your soldiers afterwards."

"If the devil helped me to-day," said Roderick, laughing, "I am sure I am very much obliged to his Satanic Majesty, for I never was in greater peril. Do not look so grave, Edric, you know I am only joking; and that whatever my tongue may say, my heart only feels gratitude where it is really due:" and as he spoke, he devoutly crossed himself.

"I know," said Edric gravely, "that your heart is infinitely better than your head."

"The fault of my countrymen," cried Roderick, again smiling, "or rather the fault of nature, for they, poor souls, can't help it. Our imaginations are so vivid that, like a restive horse, they are apt to take the bit in their teeth and gallop away at full speed, in spite of all that the sage Dame Reason, who still keeps uselessly pulling the rein, can do to prevent them."

As soon as the more important duties of his station were fulfilled, Roderick intended paying a visit to Doctor Entwerfen, to discover what effect had been produced upon the doctor's mind by his treacherous letter; but Edric proposing that they should see the fair Swiss, as common politeness required they should inquire after her arm, the poor doctor was driven entirely from his thoughts.

A separate tent had been pitched for the reception of M. de Mallet and his daughter; and when our friends entered it, they found that worthy gentleman quite recovered, and his lovely daughter reclining upon a kind of couch, and looking more beautiful than ever. Her angelic features had, it is true, lost the animation they before expressed, but their present languor made them infinitely more interesting than their former energy. Softness was indeed the characteristic of Pauline's beauty. Her figure, though slight and sylphic, was yet round and full enough to please a voluptuary. Her complexion was exquisitely fair, but a beautiful rosy tint glowed on her cheeks, whilst her clear blue eyes and golden hair gave her the look of a seraph; and when she raised those bright blue eyes in gratitude to Edric, her look sank deep into his soul, and he thought he had never before seen beauty.

Such was Pauline; and when she spoke, Edric, as he listened in rapture to the soft melting tones of her melodious voice, felt he could no longer resist, but yielded up his heart a willing captive to her charms. Yes; the calm, the reasoning, the philosophic Edric was actually in love. He, who had so despised and ridiculed the passion, and who had affected to doubt its very existence, was now become one of its most devoted victims.

Roderick was almost as much charmed as Edric with the

beauty of Pauline, and as the circumstance that had at first introduced her to their notice formed so striking a contrast to the softness and delicacy of her present appearance, that it was scarcely possible to suppose her the same person, a feeling of curiosity mingled with the interest she excited. When our friends entered the room, M. de Mallet rose to receive them: "I know not how to thank you," said he; his voice almost stifled with emotion: "my own life was of little value; but for that of this dear child—" he could not proceed.

Roderick took his offered hand. "My dear Sir," cried he, "talk not of thanks; Edric and myself are but too well repaid in seeing you thus recovered; and I am sure we shall ever esteem the day when we were so fortunate as to be of service to you, as the happiest of our lives!"

"You are too good," exclaimed M. de Mallet—"too good!" and he could no longer restrain his tears.

Roderick was deeply affected; he could not bear to see an old man weep; and he again took M. de Mallet's hand, pressing it respectfully to his lips: "My dear Sir," exclaimed he, "what I have as yet been able to do for you is nothing; but if you will return with me to Ireland, I may be able—"

"Hush! my good friend," replied M. de Mallet; "I do not doubt your kindness nor your power; but I have had too much of professions!"

"My father," said Pauline, interposing her soft sweet voice, "has suffered much; forgive him if he seem ungrateful for your kindness; but repeated disappointments sour the spirit. We have seen much trouble!" and her voice trembled as she spoke.

"Alas! if you have not been exempt from trouble, who shall dare complain?" exclaimed Edric, in a voice as soft and tremulous as her own.

Pauline turned her beautiful eyes upon him: "Pardon me, Sir," said she, "that I have not before thanked you! be assured it has not been for want of feeling your kindness; but sometimes the heart is too full for utterance."

"Thanks from your lips, madam," returned Roderick, "would be a reward for any service."

Pauline blushed: "You too, Sir, were kindness itself," rejoined she: "think not I am insensible to your favours; but I am a

The Mummy!

bankrupt even in thanks. Alas! fate destines us to incur continually obligations which we can never repay."

"A grateful heart is more than words," said her father; "and in that, my child, I know, you will never be deficient; but to whom are we indebted for such kindness?"

"I am the King of Ireland," said Roderick, smiling; "surnamed the devil's favourite here in Spain."

"Is it possible?" cried M. de Mallet; "do I, indeed, see the illustrious Roderick?"

"And this," continued Roderick, without noticing his exclamation, "is my friend, Mr. Montagu, an Englishman; who, like many of his countrymen, not contented with enjoying every luxury at home, rambles into foreign climes, to grumble and find fault with every thing he may chance to meet."

"Do not believe him, madam," cried Edric; "my countrymen are fond of travelling, it is true; and may find fault occasionally with what they think deficient in a strange land; but I assure you, we travel from a desire of improving ourselves and acquiring knowledge, whilst we only find fault in the charitable hope that our censures may produce amendment."

"That is, supposing your censures are just," replied Roderic; "but that we sometimes take the liberty to doubt."

"I think nothing more unreasonable than to censure customs merely because we are not used to them," said M. de Mallet; "for my part, when I travel, I make up my mind to be satisfied with every thing, as I think I have no right to quarrel with inconveniences I have sought myself."

"It would be well," rejoined Roderick, "if all were of your opinion, and if those who cannot be contented abroad would try to rest contented at home. But you speak as though you had travelled, and I think your daughter mentioned yesterday that you were strangers in Spain."

"We are Swiss," replied M. de Mallet; "my name is de Mallet, a name which you may have heard as belonging to a champion of liberty. Powerless as my efforts have been, I was that champion, and the reward of my labours is poverty and disgrace in a foreign land."

"But surely," said Roderick, "the Spaniards as a nation of

freemen would receive a martyr for liberty with open arms, and would treat him as a brother."

"Yes, yes," replied M. de Mallet bitterly; "I have had a tolerable specimen of their fraternal affection: they received me with protestations, fed me with delusive promises, and then left me to perish miserably."

"Not designedly, my dear father," said Pauline; "I cannot suppose they left us to perish designedly."

"Oh, no!" cried Roderick; "that must have been impossible: tigers must have been moved to pity by that voice. They never could have intended to leave you to perish."

"Sire," replied M. de Mallet gravely, "you forget my daughter and I are but plain simple Swiss; we are unused to flattery and to the language of Courts; do not then address expressions to us above our comprehension, which may lead us to forget the distance fortune has placed between us."

"Speak not of the difference of rank," interrupted Roderick impatiently; "beauty and merit, like that of your daughter, place her upon a level with a throne."

"Pardon me, Sire," replied Pauline, blushing, and casting her eyes upon the ground; "I am perfectly aware of the humility of my station. I am aware that I was not born to be a companion of kings and princes, nor have I any wish to exalt myself above the situation in which nature has placed me. My duty to my father led me to follow him to the Spanish Court. It was the first that I had seen; and, forgive me, Sire, if I say I sincerely hope it may be the last."

"But you must not judge of us by the Spaniards."

"I know it well, Sire; report has always spoken of the Irish hero as noble, generous, and kind: even his enemies have done justice to his merits, and the fame of Roderick has spread to every corner of the globe. I know that he is incapable of treating my father as he has been treated by the directors of Spain; but I know also, that he is so far superior to myself as to make his notice a condescension which I dare not flatter myself will continue, and of which I know myself perfectly undeserving."

Edric's eyes expressed his admiration, and Pauline's glowing cheeks proved she saw and understood their meaning. Roderick, however, was not quite so well pleased; he felt himself rebuked, and Roderick did not like to feel himself in the wrong.

"You are too modest," said he; then turning to Edric, "Edric," continued he, "have you any idea what is become of Dr. Entwerfen?"—then again addressing himself to Pauline, he added, "Apropos—you will be very much amused with the learned doctor, Mademoiselle de Mallet; but I give you fair notice before you see him, that you must not laugh at him before his face, for Edric is as tenacious of the feelings of his tutor as of his own."

Pauline's eyes expressed her approbation of Edric's delicacy upon this point; and, as they met his, they conveyed more pleasure to his heart than language could express. From this moment, Pauline and Edric seemed to understand each other, for they felt there was a community of feeling between them. The mute intelligence of the eyes sometimes says more than whole years of common-place intercourse; and thus Pauline and Edric felt like old friends, though they had scarcely exchanged half a dozen sentences.

"Was not that the gentleman that relieved me from my swoon?" asked M. de Mallet.

Before Roderick had time to answer, an officer rushed into the room, looking the very image of despair, and, approaching Roderick, bent his knee before him.

"What is the matter?" cried the Monarch sternly. "Speak! If you have committed a fault, you have less to fear from my justice than my mercy, for misplaced lenity only encourages crime."

"Pardon, Sire!" exclaimed the officer, still kneeling; "but—but—"

"Speak!—no evasion."

"Your Majesty commanded that we should watch that no harm happened to Dr. Entwerfen, and—and he has been taken by the enemy."

"Fool! dolt, blockhead!" cried Roderick; and, taking leave of M. de Mallet and his daughter, he and Edric hastily quitted the tent.

The balls the Irish King had given the doctor were simply

formed of dough, the same as that used in the making of bread, with only the addition of a little bit of quicksilver rolled up in the centre of each. This, the merry Monarch knew, as soon as it was exposed to the action of heat, would make the dumplings dance about, as though they were bewitched; and he anticipated great amusement from seeing the doctor's exertions to keep them in the pot, and his despair at not being able to do so. To prevent the possibility of mischief, however, he had desired a select guard to keep watch over the unfortunate philosopher, and never to lose sight of him, taking care to prevent, if possible, his being exposed to any danger. These fellows, however, did not perform their duty, and it was to their negligence that the unhappy fate of the doctor was owing.

The moment the doctor had received the fatal balls, he hastened to the cauldron, and, hastily kindling a fire, began to try the experiment. The balls more than answered Roderick's expectations, for, as soon as they were affected by the heat, they began to jump out of the pot, one after the other, with the most determined perseverance. The doctor was in a violent heat from being exposed to the steam of the cauldron; and he threw off his coat to cool himself; his wig also slipped off, in his exertions to recover the provoking balls, he being obliged to skip after them with the utmost agility as they rolled bounding along; and no sooner had he caught one and put it back into the pot, than another would jump out and begin a new set of vagaries. The doctor, though tired and provoked, did not however relax his labours even for an instant, and he was running, panting and out of breath, after one of these mercurial harlequins, when he was stopped by a rough arm, whilst a man in a gruff voice demanded what he was doing there?

The doctor looked up, and finding with horror that he was surrounded by eight or ten armed Spaniards, answered, in trembling accents, "that he was making gunpowder."

"Gunpowder!" exclaimed one of the men. "But what were you doing with those balls?"

"I was boiling them," replied the doctor, with great awe.

"You seemed to be playing with them, I think," resumed the man. "Were you running after them to make gunpowder?"

"Yes, they wouldn't stay in the pot; and I was obliged to run after them, to catch them."

The soldiers burst into a horse laugh at this naïve reply, and their merriment offered a ridiculous contrast to the doctor's woeful visage. They now prepared to retire, dragging the doctor with them, totally heedless of his supplications for pardon and declarations of innocence. They declared him to be a spy, and swore that they would hang him as such as soon as they should get within the town. The soldiers who were appointed to guard the doctor, and who, by indulging in a comfortable game at piquet, had neglected their charge, now came up, and, dismayed at seeing the doctor in custody of a force too considerable for them to engage with, fled to inform their Sovereign, trembling, however, all the time at the consequences of their disobedience.

When Roderick and Edric reached the plain, the group of soldiers, with the poor doctor in the midst of them, were just entering one of the gates of the town through which they had made their sally. The rays of the setting sun fell full upon the poor doctor's bald head and shining face; and these, and his white shirt sleeves, as he raised his hands in a supplicating manner towards Heaven, made him a conspicuous object even at a distance, till he was hidden from the sight of his friends by the heavy gates closing upon him. Roderick and Edric were in despair at the loss of their favourite; and to see him dragged away so barbarously, without having the power to assist him, was enough to try the philosophy of a stoic. It was no wonder, therefore, that it was too much for the patience of the Irish hero, who had rarely known disappointment or control: he raved, stamped, and, unable to contain his rage, ordered an instant attack of the place.

The enemy, imagining the Irish too much fatigued with the battle they had just fought, to assault the town that night, were far from expecting an attack; but, encouraged by the successful opposition they had before made, they received the assault with firmness, and repulsed it with vigour. The cannon roared with tremendous fury on both sides, and whole columns of men were swept away as grass falls before the scythe. The impatience of Roderick increased every moment, and the discharge from a petard having set fire to the wooden bulwarks of the town, he threw himself upon the blazing breach, sword in hand, heedless of the crackling timbers and fast spreading flames, whilst Edric and some of his most devoted soldiers followed him, and they were all soon warmly engaged with the Spaniards who opposed their entrance upon the walls. A loud shout from below, however, soon engaged their attention; the besieged had made a sortie by means of the covered way; and Edric and his royal friend, finding their retreat would be cut off if they stayed, were reluctantly compelled to retire with their followers. Roderick, indeed, was struck down by a Spanish soldier, whilst in the act of leaping from the walls. The soldier, seeing the effect he had produced, was about to repeat his blow, and the Irish hero must have perished before he could have recovered himself, if Edric had not interposed, and received the gash instead of his friend; then instantly turning round, he cut down the soldier. In the mean time, Roderick had revived, and he and Edric fought their way back to the rest of the army. It was now getting quite dark, and the besieged falling back within the town, the army of the Irish Monarch returned once more to their camp.

"How provoking!" cried Roderick, the moment they entered his tent, taking off his helmet, and giving it to Alexis the Greek page: "I shall never be happy again, if they hurt the doctor. Take my sword also, Alexis: but what is the matter with the boy? methinks he looks wondrous pale. Does he not, Edric?" Then turning to Edric, he was excessively shocked at the change in his appearance. It has been before stated, that Edric received the blow the Spanish soldier intended for Roderick. The wound had bled profusely, but the blood having congealed, the flow had stopped, and Edric, aided by his own courage, presence of mind, and firmness, had been enabled to sustain himself till he had reached the tent. Now, however, that the necessity for exertion had ceased, his pallid looks and ghastly countenance bespoke what he had suffered. He had received one horrid gash upon the temple, and the coagulated blood upon his face and hair contrasted frightfully with the whiteness of the rest of his face. In fact, he looked like the ghost of some poor murdered wretch appearing to implore vengeance upon his destroyer.

He had seated himself at a table, resting his arms upon it, and supporting his head with his hands. He attempted to smile in answer to Roderick's inquiries; but the effort was too much for his already exhausted strength, and his head fell heavily upon the table. Roderick flew to support him, and despatched Alexis for a surgeon. "My dear! dear Edric!" cried he, "speak to me! for God's sake, speak to me! Do not let me think that I have destroyed my friend. Oh, Edric! 'tis Roderick calls. Speak! speak, for God's sake, speak!"

Edric was, however, incapable of speaking; and the torture of the Irish King, when he found his friend could not answer him, was beyond description.

"My beloved Edric!" exclaimed he, wringing his hands in an agony of grief, "I implore you to answer me. Alas! he cannot: he is no more. Curses on my folly! I might have been blest and happy: but, in pursuit of the phantom Glory, I have sacrificed all I ever loved on earth. Oh! would to God that I had never visited Spain!"

A heavy groan behind him startled Roderick as he finished speaking; and turning round he beheld Alexis, who had now returned with the surgeon. The boy's appearance was singular; his complexion was usually a clear dark brown, with a rich glow of colour, and remarkably full rosy lips; now the deep colour on his cheeks remained unfaded; but his lips had assumed a ghastly livid hue, his limbs trembled with agitation, and a dark mysterious expression seemed to sit upon his features. Roderick looked at him with amazement and almost horror, as strange suspicions arose in his mind respecting him.

Before the Irish army had left Cadiz, it had been whispered that the Duke of Medina Celina's claim to the throne was at least equal to that of the Prince whom Roderick was fighting to establish. The duke, indeed, had many partizans, but his age and blindness enfeebled their efforts. An express from Cadiz had just brought intelligence that the duke was dead; and as Zoe was his sole heiress, this extraordinary agitation in her page looked at least suspicious.

"I must beware of him," thought Roderick, regarding him attentively; "for as Zoe knows that, notwithstanding my obligations to her, I shall never permit any monarch to reign in Spain but Don Pedro whilst I live, my life will be the first sacrifice required in her cause."

Thus mused Roderick, though it was but for an instant, that even the dread of personal danger could divert his thoughts from his friend.

The surgeon, when he probed Edric's wounds, however, declared to the great joy of the King that they were not dangerous, and that he had only fainted from loss of blood. He was now placed upon a couch in the same tent with that of the King; and Roderick, soon after stretching his fur mantle under him, threw himself upon his bed; if not to sleep, at least to muse upon the eventful occurrences of the day.

In the mean time, Dr. Entwerfen was forcibly dragged by the Spanish soldiers towards a kind of town-hall, in one of the principal squares of Seville, where, on a platform or dais, raised a little above the floor, sate the sapient magistrates of the town. When the prisoner was brought before them, they all put on their spectacles and surveyed him attentively, examining his bald head with the most scrupulous exactness.

"Here is the lump of a spy," said one.

"And here that of a rogue," rejoined another.

"Yes, the organs of observation and self-appropriation," resumed the first, "are strongly developed. That head is enough to hang an angel!"

"Alas! alas!" cried the poor doctor; "would to Heaven that I had not lost my wig!"

"It would have been of no avail, if you had retained it," said one of the judges gravely, "as it would have been forcibly removed; and even if you had worn your own hair, you must have had your head shaved; for, knowing the general corruption and inaccuracy of witnesses, the judges of this enlightened court reject verbal testimony altogether, and form their correct and infallible judgments upon the sure and undeviating basis of that most profound and useful of all sciences—craniology."

"And happy are the prisoners judged by so wise a rule," said another.

"Yes," rejoined a third; "for, though the minds of men are weak, and their judgments liable to err, the broad and general principles of science must ever remain unchangeably the same."

In this manner they went on, whilst the poor doctor, looking ruefully from one to another, as they severally pronounced their opinions, stood the very image of despair.

"Let us question him," resumed the first magistrate: "what were you doing when you were taken?"

"I was making gunpowder," sighed Dr. Entwerfen.

"The wretch!" exclaimed all his judges together; "he acknowledges he was manufacturing weapons for our destruction."

"And how were you making this gunpowder," resumed the judge.

"I was boiling it," moaned the doctor.

The Mummy!

"Boiling it!" exclaimed the judges; "what a villain!" and they all shook their wise heads in concert. The poor doctor could not bear this; and throwing himself upon his knees begged stoutly for mercy.

"In my opinion," said one, "we should be guilty of a crime in letting him escape."

"I think so too," cried another.

"I would not have such a sin upon my conscience for the world," exclaimed a third.

Whilst the unfortunate doctor, reading his condemnation in their countenances, groaned aloud in the agony of his spirit.

At this moment, the deep awful roar of a cannon was heard, and Dr. Entwerfen leaped from his knees. "Thank God! thank God!" cried he, strutting up and down, and wiping his forehead with his pocket handkerchief, as the continued roar of the cannon rolled awfully along, rebounding from house to house, and shaking the very court in which they stood. The magistrates looked aghast, whilst their pallid lips and trembling limbs told that, however great they might be in the council, their courage was not particularly conspicuous in the field.

The doctor, in the mean time, kept ejaculating, "I'm safe! I'm safe! See what a thing it is to have a friend for a sovereign: no, no! what did I say? a sovereign for a friend, I mean. Ay, ay! that's it! that's it!"

Thus did the doctor exult, whilst the citizens crowded round their chiefs, begging for directions, and not knowing whither to fly for safety. In this dilemma, the exclamations of the doctor attracted their attention; and, enraged to see him rejoice at their misery, the magistrates ordered him to prison, whilst they consulted as to what steps it was most advisable to take.

The poor doctor's joy was thus quickly changed to grief; and he lamented loudly his foolish transports of delight, without which, he might perhaps have passed unnoticed in the crowd. It was too late, however, for repentance; the command had gone forth, and the unfortunate doctor was dragged away to a loathsome dungeon. The assault was, as we have seen, repulsed, and it being too late, when it was over, to think of hanging Dr. Entwerfen that night, the magistrates retired to their beds, determined to have him executed the first thing in the morning.

All was now still; the plain between the camp and the city, which had so lately echoed with the heavy tramp of horses and human beings, now slept tranquilly in the moonlight; undisturbed, save by the groans of some expiring wretch, or by the busy labours of those employed to remove the dead and relieve the wounded. Roderick had thrown himself upon his couch, and dozed, but in a disturbed slumber; whilst Alexis, placed at a table, was writing dispatches from the dictation of Don Alvarez de Ripparda, who had returned from the pursuit, and sate opposite to him; whilst Lord Arthur O'Neil nodded at his side, and Edric lay reclined on another couch, at a little distance, near the opening of the tent.

All was silent, save the whispered voice of the Spanish general, the heavy breathing of Lord Arthur, and the measured steps of the sentinel, as he paced his weary round. Edric listened till he grew tired of the same sounds falling uninterruptedly upon his ear, and turning on his couch, tried to divert his attention by gazing upon the objects before him. The strong light from the lamp placed upon the table, fell upon the fine features of Alexis, as he looked up to the Spaniard; and Edric thought, as he gazed upon them, that he had certainly seen those features before, though where he could not remember; and fatigued with the effort of trying to recollect, he turned to survey the noble Roderick, as he lay gracefully stretched upon his couch. One arm was raised above his pillow, and the other fell carelessly by his side, whilst the fine contour of his head and neck was fully displayed, the rich, thick, glossy curls that generally hid his forehead being thrown back. His coral lips were half open, and his long black eyelashes fringed his closed eyelids; whilst his dark whiskers and mustachios, with the rich brown tint that glowed upon his cheek, contrasted finely with the whiteness of his throat. "God bless him!" thought Edric, "and send him all the happiness he deserves!" And then seeming fearful to disturb him, he looked again towards the town. The curtain of the tent was partly looped up, and Edric watched, with interest, the lights of those still employed in their several duties of burying the dead, and relieving the wounded. The figures of the persons engaged in these painful duties were frequently imperceptible; and the lights gliding to and fro, apparently without any human means, looked like ignes fatui, or an assemblage of ghosts at their infernal revels.

Edric sighed as he surveyed them, and: his thoughts flew back, he knew not by what connection of ideas, to his native land. He thought of his father, his brother—of the good old Duke of Cornwall—of Rosabella and Elvira, till, one by one, the lights appeared to die away; the images that floated before his fancy became gradually fainter and fainter; his thoughts more confused: the scene before him faded rapidly from his sight, and, in short, he was fast sinking into repose, when he was roused by a slight sound, and looking up, saw the Spanish general and the Greek page standing by his bed-side.

Edric roused himself immediately, though he still pretended to slumber. The recollection of all he had heard respecting the Duke of Medina, Pedro, and the Princess Zoe, mingled with the suspicions that had been breathed of the mysterious page, flashed across his mind, and effectually destroyed all inclination to sleeping: indeed, a cold shudder ran through his frame, as he remembered, with horror, that if any thing were designed against Roderick, the first step of the conspirators would be to destroy him, from his known devotion to the Irish monarch, and that, in his present enfeebled state, he was quite incapable of resistance. His blood seemed to run more feebly through his veins, and he panted for breath, whilst he listened attentively, and heard the Spanish general whisper, "He sleeps, but not soundly enough for our purpose."

An icy thrill seemed to chill Edric's heart, and involuntarily he heaved a deep sigh. The supposed conspirators started, and retired. Edric, now completely roused from his slumber, gazed after them, as, with creeping, stealthy steps, they glided across the plain. Astonished at what he had seen and heard, Edric lay lost in bewildering speculations; but soon a new object caught his attention. Thick, black, pointed columns of smoke arose from the town through which, first a red glow, and afterwards sparks, appeared at intervals. At first, Edric could not imagine what it was; he rubbed his eyes, and almost fancied it was a display of fireworks; but, presently, long spiral columns of flame burst through the smoke, and, uniting in one immense body of fire, rose up to heaven, and seemed to swallow up the devoted city.

The moment the flames broke forth, Alexis and the Spanish general hurried back to the tent, and Roderick sprang from his couch, when he heard their hurried footsteps. "What is the matter?" cried he, rubbing his eyes, and half blinded by the sudden glare of light.

"The city is on fire!" exclaimed a thousand voices at once, and Roderick rushed forth upon the plain. The air felt hot and scorching: "Save them! save the inhabitants!" cried Roderick; "promise them quarter—peace! any thing to save them! Let all the soldiers fetch water from the river! I will have no plunder. He dies who touches an article belonging to the town, or injures a single creature escaping from it. Let us fight like men! It is beneath us to take advantage of misfortune!"

The orders of Roderick were as promptly obeyed as given; the monarch himself leading the way to the town, and assisting in endeavouring to quench the flames. The gates were thrown open, and men, women, and children rushed forth half naked, and were received and supplied with food and shelter by the army of the Irish hero. The Irish adored their sovereign; his valour, his rashness, and his romantic generosity, won their hearts; and even his most discontented soldiers loved whilst they blamed him: thus his will was law—nay, there was something so noble in his orders, that his soldiers were proud of implicitly obeying them, and not the meanest slave of the camp would have presumed to violate them in the slightest instance. The flames had now caught some cotton-mills on the river, which had been spared in the previous conflagration, and they burst forth in fresh volumes of fire, as the light materials they contained added fuel to the flames. The buildings in the town were mostly old, many of them wood, and some were large warehouses filled with the most combustible substances, which burnt with added fury as the long pointed flames lapped them into their devouring vortex; curling round them, and wrapping them in columns of fire as they, one by one, fell victims to their rage. The town was now half destroyed, and the flames were fast approaching the citadel; the governors of the city had been roused from their beds, and had taken refuge, half naked, in the camp of Roderick; but the prisoners yet remained in the citadel, shut up, however, in dungeons below the surface of the earth. Roderick had anxiously inquired of every one for Dr. Entwerfen, and at last, to his infinite horror, he learnt he was in this fated citadel; he rushed forward in agony to save him, for he knew that the powder was kept there. He was aware too, that the flames had already seized the fortress: long ere he could reach it, indeed, a tremendous explosion took place—a vast burst of fire rushed forth, scattering red flaming furniture, bricks, pillars, and every kind of rubbish in all directions, and then all sank to comparative darkness. The fire seemed to have spent its fury in that last effort, and, though it still feebly crept along in a half-smothered flame, its violence was passed. Dreadful, however, was the scene that now presented itself, for Seville was levelled with the dust. Black disfigured smoky ruins supplied the place of what had once been lofty towers and sumptuous palaces; the splendid cathedral, that had withstood the rage of centuries, was now no more; and human bodies lay in the streets, thrown in fearful heaps, some half burnt, and others blackened and dried by the scorching fury of the flames.

Roderick, however, stayed not to examine the effects of the fire; he rushed over heaps of yet hot ashes, and threw himself amongst the still smoking ruins of the citadel. A Spanish soldier, whom he had saved from destruction a few minutes before, was his guide, and, under his directions, Roderick hastened to the dungeons: he hurried from one to the other, releasing the unhappy wretches confined there, searching everywhere for the doctor, but in vain: at last he heard his well-known voice—the dungeon door was thick, but it could not resist the impatience of Roderick—he could not wait for the soldier to assist him to open it—he burst the fastenings asunder, and in an instant the poor doctor, sobbing with joy, was locked in the monarch's arms. Some of the soldiers of Roderick had followed him to the citadel, and he left it to them and the Spaniard to release the other prisoners, whilst he returned with his dear doctor in triumph back to the camp.

END OF VOL. II.

CHAPTER XXV.

When Roderick and Dr. Entwerfen returned to the camp, they found Edric most impatiently awaiting their arrival. He was too much agitated to speak; and the worthy doctor found all his troubles amply repaid by the interest his friends took in his welfare.

Whilst Dr. Entwerfen was employed in relating his adventures to Edric, Roderick was occupied by a task far more difficult and important than any he had yet undertaken, viz. that of organizing and of providing for the disorderly multitude that had thronged into his camp from the city: their number was immense; men, women, and children, crowded round their deliverer, falling upon their knees, blessing him and kissing the edge of his garments. Roderick was affected even to tears: "For Heaven's sake, my good friends," said he, "spare me; I have done but my duty; I have been but an humble instrument in the hands of Providence; address your thanks to him: there they are due."

Roderick, however, was quite aware it was not enough to have saved these people: he knew he must do something to provide them with food and lodging; and that if he did not, when the first moment of enthusiasm should be passed, unpleasant scenes must inevitably take place. He accordingly made dispositions to this effect, with a prudence and sagacity that would have done credit to far more advanced years. Temporary huts were erected, till the streets of Seville could be cleared of the ruins that encumbered them, and the houses in some measure repaired. Shelter for the inhabitants being thus provided, Roderick harangued the magistrates, directing them to take the people under their direction. These sapient ministers of justice gladly gave him possession of the town, which Roderick was too generous to assume without their permission, and acknowledged themselves and the garrison prisoners of war. The peasants, when they found the kindness with which the citizens had been treated, flocked in with provisions, and the camp of the Irish monarch soon resembled an immense fair.

Alexis had followed his master during the whole of these arrangements, and had frequently sighed deeply as they proceeded. "What is the matter with the boy?" said Roderick in one of these moments: "I cannot imagine why he looks so melancholy!"

The boy enthusiastically clasped his hands together, looking up to Heaven, as though murmuring an inward prayer.

"What can this mean?" exclaimed Roderick with astonishment.

The boy took his master's hand, pressing it first to his lips, and then vehemently to his heart, and knelt before him, reverentially bending his forehead to the earth. The next moment, however, officers entering for directions, the attention of Roderick was diverted and Alexis forgotten.

In the mean time, M. de Mallet and his daughter, who had been exceedingly agitated by the events of the day, thought not of repose, but sat in the tent prepared for them, conversing upon the merits of their deliverers.

"I never saw a finer countenance," said M. de Mallet, "so noble, so animated, and yet so good."

"Good indeed," ejaculated his daughter; "surely if we could believe a superior spirit would ever descend upon earth, such would be the form he would assume!"

"How kindly he spoke, and how considerately!" exclaimed the father.

"How attentive he seemed, and how delicate!" rejoined the daughter.

"Such a majestic figure!"

"Such a graceful manner!"

"It is so rare to find such condescension in so great a monarch."

"Monarch!" cried Pauline: "were you speaking of Roderick, father?"

"And of whom were you speaking, child?" returned her father, turning quickly round, and fixing his eyes upon her.

"Of—of—Mr. Montagu, father," replied Pauline, casting down her eyes and deeply blushing.

"Pauline!" said M. de Mallet. She started at the sound of her father's voice, and looked timidly up in his face. "Pauline," repeated he, "my dear child, beware!"

At this moment a roar of cannon shook the tent; the sound

echoed by the walls of the town, and leaping from hill to hill in lengthened peals, Pauline sunk upon her knees, hiding her face in her father's lap. "My child! my beloved child!" cried M. de Mallet, bending over her as though to shield her from danger, "Heaven defend thee!"

In this painful situation, the father and daughter continued till the cannonading ceased. All was now still; and awful was the calm that succeeded such a tumult. Pauline raised her head, and looked fearfully around. "Come, my child," said her father, "let us endeavour to ascertain who are victors."

Pauline rose from her knees, and, leaning upon her father's arm, accompanied him to the opening of the tent; but she shrunk back, shuddering at the horrid scene that presented itself. Their tent was situated at the extreme edge of the camp, and commanded a view of the whole field of battle where the combat of the morning had taken place. The plain that stretched to their left, lay covered with the bodies of the dying and the dead, whilst a multitude of horses broken loose, galloped over the field, plunging, snorting, and crushing beneath their hoofs, the bodies of their fallen riders.

In some places, the branches of half broken trees strewed the ground, whilst their mutilated trunks, perforated with shot, remained as melancholy relics of their former beauty. Swords and helmets, mingled with overturned waggons and military utensils of all kinds, were scattered in wild disorder around. The earth, ploughed up by the cannon balls in deep furrows, save where the ridges had been beaten flat by the feet of the combatants, looked wild and uneven as the waves of the mighty ocean arrested in the moment of tempest. Blood lay in pools upon the ground; and clotted gore, mingled horribly with remnants of human bones and brains, hung to the still standing bushes, disfiguring the fair face of nature.

Pauline shuddered, and turned eagerly to the other side of the landscape, which commanded a view of the town. Here still, however, she found nothing but death and war. It was the moment when the explosion of the petard set fire to the wooden bulwark; and Roderick and Edric leaped through the flames upon the beach. The bright glare of the blazing bulwarks relieved strongly their dark figures, and Pauline distinctly saw and recognized them for a moment, though the next they were lost in a cloud of smoke. She screamed, and grasped her father's arm in convulsive agony. M. de Mallet was scarcely less agitated than herself; and, as the smoke cleared away, they saw distinctly through its flaming volumes, Roderick and Edric upon the breach, opposed by a crowd of Spaniards, and fighting with inveterate fury. "Roderick is on his knees," cried M. de Mallet. "But see! he rises suddenly, and plunges the Spaniard, who had raised his sword to cut him down, into the flames." Pauline did not speak; but she gasped for breath, and held her father's arm yet more tightly than before. Edric was now seen grappling hand to hand with a Spaniard, when the fire and smoke closed upon him and hid him from their view. The next instant, a tremendous crash was heard, and loud shouts, followed by a rush of men; it was the sortie of the besieged.

"Oh, heavens!" cried Pauline, turning pale, and resting her head upon her father's shoulder, "war is a dreadful thing."

"You are faint, my child," replied M. de Mallet; "this is no fitting scene for you. Shall we go in?"

"Oh, no, no!" cried Pauline feebly; "I cannot leave the spot." Here shouts of "Roderick! Roderick for ever! Roderick and glory!" rung in their ears. Pauline shuddered; a faint sickness crept over her; the scene seemed to swim before her eyes; and she would have fallen, but for the supporting arm of her father. At this moment, some soldiers, carrying a bier, passed at a little distance from the tent. Upon it lay the body of an officer; his head hung back, his long thick hair was matted with gore, and a ghastly wound gaped on his uncovered breast. Pauline could bear no more—she thought it was Edric, and she fell fainting into her father's arms.

M. de Mallet bore her back into the tent, and as soon as she was sufficiently recovered to enable him to think of any thing but herself, he dispatched one of the soldiers, appointed to attend them, to ascertain if the Irish monarch had escaped. The soldier did not return; and M. de Mallet, too impatient to remain in his tent, sallied forth to learn the news himself. Scarcely was he gone, however, when the soldier's wife, whom he had called to the assistance of Pauline, perceived the town was on fire. Pauline's agitation now became excessive; she trembled in every limb, and listened till the sense of hearing seemed agony. She could not comprehend the cause of the noise and bustle made by the citizens, as they came crowding into the camp; she looked forth, but the throng of half naked men, women, and children, that came hurrying along, seemed inexplicable; she stopped a woman, who, half dressed, had her clothes tucked up in one hand, whilst with the other she led two half naked children—"What is the matter?" asked she. "Roderick," cried the woman bewildered in her grief, "God bless the noble Roderick!"

"Where are you going?" demanded Pauline of two young men, bearing between them a bed containing their sick father.

"Roderick!" shouted the pious Spaniards. "Heaven, in its mercy, bless Roderick!" Pauline was proceeding in her inquiries, though without the smallest hope of receiving a direct reply, the hearts and minds of Spaniards being so full of Roderick, that no other name could find utterance from their lips, when she perceived her father.

"My dearest father!" cried she, running to him; "now I shall know all! What is the matter?"

"Roderick, the noble Roderick is safe!" repeated M. de Mallet. Pauline was chagrined — she longed to hear of Edric, and she envied, for his sake, the renown of the Irish hero. "Can you, too, speak of nothing but Roderick?" said she, somewhat reproachfully.

"And of whom else should I speak?" replied her father. "Who else deserves to be spoken of? for surely he is the bravest! the noblest of men!"

"I do not doubt it," observed Pauline coldly. "Every tongue utters his praise — every breast swells with gratitude at his goodness — and every hand is raised to Heaven in prayers on his behalf.

"Have there been many persons killed?" asked Pauline.

"How can you ask so foolish a question?" replied her father. "Do you not see the ground heaped with slain?"

"But persons of note, I mean?"

"Let me see; I think they said there were the Generals H— — and M— —, and Counts L— —, P— — and T— —."

"Oh!" groaned Pauline, impatiently.

"And besides, I think they say Mr. Montagu is seriously wounded."

"I feared so!" sighed Pauline, "he is so brave."

"Yes — every one says he is brave, and implores blessings upon his name — for he saved the life of Roderick!"

Pauline's countenance had beamed with triumph at the commencement of this sentence; but it rather fell at the conclusion. She did not quite like her hero to owe his glory to any one but himself.

M. de Mallet continued: "His bravery and nobleness of spirit were unequalled. Every one praises him. There is certainly something very extraordinary in the character of the English. Their daring tempers and love of adventure lead them to quit peace and riches in their native country, to seek glory and distinction elsewhere. This Mr. Montagu is really an exalted young man."

Pauline's eyes flashed joy—she felt she loved her father better than ever—she could have embraced him as he spoke, for the praise of Edric sounded as the sweetest music in her ears. Strange that so slight an acquaintance should have produced so strong a passion! but such and so inexplicable is love.

Pauline had now patience to hear the explanation of her father respecting Roderick. She even felt pleasure in the repetition of his exploits, for he was the friend of Edric; and she retired to rest—happy in herself, and contented with all the world; having been first assured by her father that the surgeon confidently expected Edric would soon recover. Pauline, however, would have been very much puzzled to explain the cause of the excessive contentment that she felt. The situation of herself and father was as hopeless as ever. They were still prisoners in a strange land, without fortune, without friends; but so little does happiness depend upon external circumstances, that the breast of Pauline seemed to have been a stranger to it till now.

After arranging every thing for the comfort of the refugees and his own soldiers, Roderick took a few hours of hurried repose. When he rose in the morning, he sent his compliments to M. de Mallet and his daughter to demand permission to wait upon them. This was instantly and gladly accorded, and in a few minutes the Irish hero was in their tent.

"I condole with your Majesty upon the situation of your friend," said M. de Mallet, the moment he saw him: "I hope he is better."

The monarch smiled; he forgave the abruptness of the question, in favour of the excellence of the motive, and he replied that Mr. Montagu was fast recovering. "He regrets exceedingly," added he, "that it is not in his power to pay his devoirs here"—bowing to Pauline, "and well can I sympathize with him, as I know what he loses."

Pauline inquired modestly the particulars of the combat. "Upon my word, Madam," replied Roderick, "I know very little about it."

"I thought your Majesty had been engaged."

"That is the very reason. If I had not, the case might have been different; but as it was, I only just saw a great many people that tried to kill me, and a great many that I tried to kill, and the smoke hid all the rest."

"A very satisfactory account of a battle, upon my word," cried M. de Mallet, smiling; "but other people saw more of your Majesty's acts than you did yourself; and they say, you performed prodigies of valour."

"It is very kind of them to say so," said Roderick, "for I am sure it is more than they know."

"Your Majesty's modesty wishes to throw a veil over your valour," observed Pauline, "but luckily it cannot be concealed."

"Your praises, Madam, would make any man a coxcomb," returned the Monarch: "I own I have not the courage to refuse commendations from your lips."

Pauline blushed—she fancied she had said too much, and now remained silent.

"I cannot describe how much I admire your Majesty's leniency to the inhabitants of the city," said M. de Mallet: "it proves your benevolence is equal to your valour, though indeed it was sound policy to act as you have done; for by this you have conciliated the hearts of the Spaniards; whereas, if you had exercised any cruelty, they would have risen against you en masse; but this, I dare say, your Majesty considered."

"Indeed," replied Roderick smiling, "my Majesty considered no such thing; I only thought as a man: I did not like to see my fellow-creatures burnt to death, or poniarded if they attempted to escape; I should not have liked it at all, if I had been in a similar situation, and so I did all in my power to save them—that is all I know about the matter. But to change the subject, I have a great favour to beg of you, Mademoiselle de Mallet."

The Mummy!

"What is it?" asked Pauline: "your Majesty has only to speak to be obeyed."

"Oh! for Heaven's sake do not talk of obedience—it is I who should obey—I only ask a favour, and that is, that you will permit me to bring Dr. Entwerfen to kneel at your feet and kiss your fair hand, in token of his homage."

"I would not advise Pauline to let him kneel," said M. de Mallet laughing, "as I fear, if she does, there will be some difficulty in getting him up again."

"Your Majesty's commands,—" said Pauline.

"Do not talk of commands," interrupted Roderick; "I hate the word."

"Your Majesty's wishes, then," continued Pauline smiling, "shall be complied with."

"This evening, then," cried the gay monarch, "the doctor shall make his appearance. Till then, adieu!"

"Will your Majesty have the kindness to present my best wishes to Mr. Montagu for his recovery," requested M. de Mallet.

"Certainly," replied Roderick; "but am I to tell Edric that Mademoiselle de Mallet has no wishes for his welfare?"

"I wish—I hope—that is, I think——" stammered Pauline.

"My daughter means her sentiments are exactly similar to my own upon the subject," said M. de Mallet gravely; for he was not at all pleased with the interpretation he thought the King might put upon the embarrassment of his daughter.

"Very well!" repeated Roderick provokingly: "I shall tell Edric, that M. de Mallet and his daughter think exactly alike of him.—That is it, is it not?"

M. de Mallet was about to reply, when the King, nodding and waving his hand, bade them adieu, and hurried away. "I don't know what to make of the Irish hero," said M. de Mallet, the moment he had left them. "With all his good qualities, there is something very strange about him: I don't know what to make of him!"

Pauline sighed assent; though she did know what to make of him very well, for she fancied he saw, and ridiculed her partiality for Edric. This idea roused every spark of pride in her nature; she could not bear the thought of being supposed to give her love unsought, and she determined when she next saw Roderick to show by her coldness and indifference, when Edric was mentioned, how completely he had been deceived.

When Roderick left the tent of M. de Mallet, he returned to Edric, whom he found pale and feeble.

"You are the happiest fellow in existence, Edric!" said he: "I would willingly give all my glory, and even my demoniacal renown, that the Spaniards talk so much about, to be able to call up such blushes to the cheek of beauty as your name can raise. Oh! if you had seen Pauline. By Heaven! she is the loveliest creature I ever beheld in my life!"

As he spoke, Alexis, the Greek page, who had been crouching rather than sitting at the foot of Edric's couch, resting his head upon his hands, and looking absorbed in grief, uttered a faint cry, and rushed out of the tent.

"There is something very extraordinary about that boy," said Roderick, looking after him.

"There is, indeed," replied Edric, "and I have something that I wish to communicate to you respecting him:" and in a few words he related what had passed the preceding night in the tent.

"Impossible!" cried Roderick, "you must have been dreaming, Edric! What communication would the boy hold with Alvarez? You know he is dumb. Besides, even if Alvarez were inclined to plot against me, he is too prudent and reserved to make a confidant of a beardless boy!"

"I simply relate the facts as they occurred," said Edric; "I do not pretend to explain them. But I can assure you, I was neither dreaming nor delirious."

"It is very strange!" repeated Roderick musing, "and it corresponds remarkably with what I have observed myself." For some moments he remained lost in thought; but it was not in his gay and joyous nature to suffer anything to depress him long; and the next instant, Alexis was forgotten.

The fall of Seville, and the destruction of the army sent to defend it, produced a powerful effect upon the destinies of Spain. The Cortes again sent ambassadors to negotiate with the Irish hero; but, taught by experience, he now received them haughtily, refusing to treat with them but as a conqueror; and to put his threats in execution he determined to advance immediately upon Madrid.

"We must follow up our victory," said he to Edric, after he had somewhat contemptuously dismissed the deputies from the shattered remnant of their allied army, who came to sue humbly at his feet for peace. "These people are treacherous beyond description. They do not understand leniency, and they must be treated with sword in hand. I am thoroughly tired of them; their fickleness and uncertainty have quite disgusted me; I will therefore march to Madrid, establish Don Pedro as their sovereign, and take my leave of them for ever."

"I am rejoiced to hear it!" exclaimed Edric. "You will then return to Ireland, and devote your time to your own subjects."

"I will try to satisfy them as well as I can; but as perfection cannot be expected all at once, you must not be surprised if some day I should fly off in a tangent, and take it into my head to colonize the moon."

Edric laughed: "If you promise to wait till then," said he, "I shall be satisfied."

"You may not find my project so wild as it appears," rejoined Roderick. "The moon is a very pretty, mild, modest-looking planet, and I must own I should like amazingly to see what kind of inhabitants she contains; and if I should determine to go there, here is a gentleman who I am sure will be quite ready to accompany me."

Dr. Entwerfen entered the tent as he spoke. "Of what was your Majesty speaking?" asked he.

"Of a voyage to the moon," said Roderick. "Will you go with me?"

"With all my heart," cried the little doctor, rubbing his hands and looking all glee at the thought.

"There, I told you so," said Roderick, laughing.

"I should have thought the many adventures you have met with had cured your passion for travelling," rejoined Edric.

"Cured him! Given him a zest for it, you mean," replied Roderick. "The appetite for travelling always grows with what it feeds upon; and though the doctor may boast

'That he has fair Seville seen.

So is a traveller, I ween,'

yet I do not doubt but that he is just as eager to explore new places as ever."

"Yes," returned the doctor, "I certainly did see Seville."

"Every part of it, my dear fellow, from its palaces to its dungeons," resumed Roderick; "nay, I believe you were very near being indulged with a view of its ropes."

The doctor did not quite relish this raillery. "I can assure your Majesty—"

"Apropos de bottes," cried Roderick, interrupting him, "I had entirely forgotten I promised to introduce you to Mademoiselle de Mallet. We will go now. Will you accompany us, Edric? I am sorry to ask you to do any thing so disagreeable; but I think it will be but decent to kiss hands, take leave, and all that sort of thing, before we set out for Madrid: besides, it may be as well to make some kind of provision as to what is to become of them in our absence."

"Then you will not take them with you?" said Edric, despondingly.

"Who ever heard of such a thing?" cried Roderick; "How could I possibly ask the lovely Pauline to endure the inconveniences of travelling with a camp? I really have not the assurance to attempt it."

Edric sighed deeply; and his countenance assumed an expression of so much melancholy that Roderick laughed immoderately: "I could not have believed it possible," cried he, "that you could ever become such a sighing Strephon; the thing's incredible!"

"The pain of my wounds," said Edric, blushing; for even philosophers don't like to be laughed at.

"The pain in your heart!" repeated Roderick, mimicking him. "But, come! come! I can pity you. I have been in love at least fifty times myself—so I know what it is."

"But I am not in love," remonstrated Edric.

"Denial is one of the most dangerous symptoms," resumed Roderick, gravely. "Experienced physicians rarely think their patients really ill, till they are not conscious of it themselves. Let me feel your pulse."

"Psha," said Edric, impatiently.

"Will you go then!" asked Roderick, laughing; and to avoid being farther tormented by his raillery, Edric hastily rose from his couch, and declared himself ready to attend him. The injuries he had received, having been only flesh wounds inflicted with a sabre, had now nearly healed; and the only change they had produced in his appearance, had been to make him look more pale and interesting, one arm being supported by a sling, and a bandeau bound round his forehead. Pauline's eyes sparkled when she saw him, in spite of her intended indifference; and she could not command her voice so entirely, but that its tremulous tone betrayed her inward agitation.

Edric's eyes also involuntarily expressed his pleasure; whilst the gay laugh and arch look of Roderick told that he was perfectly aware of what was passing in the mind of each. Doctor Entwerfen, however, saw nothing of the kind, his mind being quite absorbed in the delightful contemplation of his own glory. He had been presented to M. de Mallet by Roderick, as "his friend and counsellor, the learned and justly celebrated Dr. Entwerfen;" and that moment seemed a sufficient reward for a whole life of misery, the doctor's ecstasy upon the occasion being so unbounded, that he neither knew what he did nor what he said. Whilst Roderick had been speaking, indeed, he had been in perfect agony; stretching himself out on tiptoe, opening his hands and closing them again with every sentence, as though bursting with impatience to speak, that he might by his eloquence confirm the monarch's eulogium, yet trembling every instant lest he should interrupt it.

M. de Mallet had been a dabbler in scientific experiments in his youth, and, pleased to find a person who could talk to him, and understand his ideas upon the subject, he soon drew the doctor on one side, leaving his younger friends to be entertained by his daughter.

"I am glad, very glad, to see you so soon recovered," said Pauline, addressing Edric in a gentle tone; "I feared, that is, my father feared, your wounds were more serious."

"You see, Edric," cried Roderick archly, "it is as I said — Mademoiselle de Mallet feels for you exactly the same interest as her father does."

"I should be flattered by exciting any interest in so gentle a bosom," sighed Edric, looking at her tenderly.

Pauline sighed too — involuntarily, but remained silent.

"Do you then feel no interest in my behalf?" continued Edric; "not even the cold, chilling feeling sanctioned by your father?"

"Oh! call not the interest my father feels for you cold or chilling!" exclaimed Pauline with energy, "I am sure — that is, I think — " and here, fearing she had said too much, she stopped abruptly, totally unable to proceed.

"Oh, go on!" exclaimed Edric, gazing earnestly upon her blushing face — "go on, I could listen to you for ever!"

Pauline trembled, blushed, and hesitated. "I — I — I think I had better go to my father," stammered she after a short pause.

Roderick smiled: "By all means!" said he. "Don't you think so, Edric?"

Edric did not reply; for in fact he did not hear the question; whilst poor Pauline's agitation increased, and her colour changed rapidly every moment: she dreaded Roderick's raillery, and trembled so violently that she could scarcely stand.

At this moment her father returned; he looked at his daughter with some surprise, and then, turning to his guests, he apologized for her abstraction. "My daughter is unused to camps," said he, "and the scenes she has lately gone through have been too much for her nerves."

"She will now have an opportunity of recovering herself," replied Roderick; "my army will move forward to-morrow, and if you will accept the post, I will leave you governor of this city, with a sufficient garrison to keep it on my behalf."

Pauline turned deathly pale as he spoke, and every hope of happiness seemed to fly from her breast for ever.

M. de Mallet, however, was not at all aware of his daughter's anguish; and, thanking the king gratefully for the high honour conferred upon him, his fancy began to revel by anticipation in the delights of governorship; and in ten minutes he had arranged in his mind as many improvements and alterations as it would take fifty years to accomplish.

"Farewell," continued Roderick, "I trust we shall meet again, if not here, at least in another and a better world. Permit me, lady!" continued he, slightly touching with his lips the pallid cheek of Pauline. "To-morrow with the dawn we advance, and we have so much to do ere then, that we must deny ourselves the pleasure of again enjoying your society. Farewell, Governor, you will find the necessary papers to install you here," (giving him a packet) "and the soldiers have orders to obey you as myself. Come, Edric."

Edric advanced, and bowing, took the hand of Pauline and pressed it respectfully to his lips;—his heart was too full to speak. Pauline could scarcely restrain her tears, and shaking hands with the doctor, she hastily retired to a part of the tent enclosed for her use.

"My daughter is not well," said M. de Mallet, "these scenes of blood and war are too much for her nerves; but she will soon recover when you have left us."

"I doubt that," murmured Roderick in a half whisper; and soon after the friends retired. Edric was not insensible to Pauline's emotion; and as he more than suspected the cause, a pleasure, unknown before, throbbed in his bosom. His eyes sparkled, and his whole appearance presented so complete a contrast to his usual depression, that Roderick could not resist the temptation of again rallying him most unmercifully upon it. "Talk of medicine," cried he, "there is no elixir like the magic of a pair of bright eyes. All the physicians in my camp can effect nothing like it. Nay, you need not blush so, Edric! I did not imagine you were so far gone as that."

"I do not blush, that I am aware of," returned Edric, somewhat peevishly; for he did not relish being teased; "at least, I am sure I have no occasion for blushing."

"Well, then, don't look so like a bashful maiden, disavowing her first attachment, with a 'La, Pa! how can you think so!'—I did not suppose you were capable of such affectation."

"I am not aware that I have been guilty of any."

"Come, then, own the truth candidly—you love Mademoiselle de Mallet?"

"How can you think so?" replied Edric, blushing deeply in spite of his efforts to look composed.

"You are indifferent to her, then? Dear me, I had no idea of it, I never was more completely deceived in my life! Well, if that's the case, I will resume my first design of trying my own fortune."

"How can you be so provoking?"

"Why it is very hard, if you are not in love with her yourself, that you should wish to prevent every one else from being so."

"Your Majesty's rank, I should think, would prevent your even thinking of Mademoiselle de Mallet."

"Why should my rank prevent the possibility of my being happy?"

"Your Majesty's rank prevents the possibility of your marrying Pauline; and I should hope you would not dare to entertain dishonourable views respecting her."

"Dare! dishonour! Do you remember whom you are speaking to, Edric?"

"Perfectly; for I have not forgotten Roderick, though he appears to have forgotten himself."

"Edric! But I won't be angry with you. When people are in love, they never mean what they say; in fact, they very seldom know what they are talking about. I remember once when I was in love myself—"

Alexis, who had waited at the entrance of the tent during the visit his master had paid to M. de Mallet, and was now following them, sighed heavily at this remark. Roderick heard him;—"What is the matter with the boy?" said he: "Were you ever in love, Alexis?" The page sighed yet more deeply than before, and, crossing his arms upon his breast, bent his head in token of assent.

"It is to be much lamented you cannot tell us all about it," continued Roderick; "for you could never choose a more fitting moment for such a tale; as you may depend upon the sympathy of Mr. Montagu, even if I should be so barbarous as to refuse you mine:—

'We pity faults to which we feel inclined,

And to our proper failings can be kind;'

as one of your own poets says. Eh, Edric! Don't you think he's right?"

"I think you are very provoking."

"That is because I am touching upon a string that happens to be not quite in tune; so no wonder it jars a little. Do you not remember the old proverb?

'Touch a man whose skin is sound,

He will stand, and fear no wound:

Touch a man when he is sore,

He will start, and bear no more.'"

"How can you condescend to repeat such nonsense?" cried Edric, indignantly. "It is unworthy the poorest beggar in your dominions!"

"And how can you condescend to be moved at such nonsense, Edric?" replied Roderick, laughing. "Come, come! own the truth, for it is useless to attempt any longer to deny it. Say, candidly, that you are in love with Mademoiselle de Mallet, and I will tease you no longer."

"In love is too strong a term. I admire, esteem, and respect Mademoiselle de Mallet. I even think her possessed of a thousand charms and a thousand virtues; but as to being in love——"

"Well, well! we will not quarrel about words. I do not think you will ever make a romantic lover. You Englishmen are too reasoning and prudent ever to fall violently in love. Your blood is as cold as your climate. Now we take the thing quite differently; with us love is a devouring flame! a fire that absorbs our whole being—a stream that sweeps every thing before it—a madness—a delirium! In short, I don't know what it is!"

"I think not," said Edric, dryly.

"Psha, psha!" continued Roderick; "if it could be described, it would not be worth feeling. It is all spirit! all soul! if you tie it down to rules, it evaporates. Don't you think so in Greece, Alexis?"

The page bowed, and shaking his head, pressed his finger upon his lips.

"True," returned his master; "I had forgotten: but if you cannot speak, you can write. Take these tablets, I should like to know your opinion."

The page took the tablets, and wrote with astonishing rapidity — "Since your Majesty condescends to ask my opinion, I think that the love which can stay to reason, or hesitates to sacrifice every thing to the beloved object, does not deserve the name."

"Bravo, my little hero!" cried Roderick, tapping him upon the shoulder; "spoken like a true Greek. An Irishman, however, would have said nearly the same."

The boy's slender figure trembled in every nerve at his master's touch, and his cheeks were flushed with unwonted passion, though his eyes remained fixed upon the ground, from which indeed he rarely raised them. Roderick gazed upon him a few minutes in silence, as though he wished to read his inmost soul. Then turning abruptly to Dr. Entwerfen, who had taken no part in the last conversation, he demanded gaily what he was thinking of.

"I was thinking, your Majesty," said the doctor, gravely, "that it is a long way from hence to Madrid, and that it will be very fatiguing for your men to march so far."

"Upon my word, doctor," said Roderick, laughing, "you have really made a most sublime discovery, and I perfectly agree with you in the justice of your conclusions."

"That being granted," continued the doctor, "if any means could be devised by which your army could be transported to the gates of the city without the trouble of walking there, it would be a good thing."

"Certainly," said the King; "the fact does not admit of a dispute."

"The only difficulty is to contrive how it is to be done," resumed the doctor, musing.

The Mummy!

"Ay, there's the rub," cried Roderick, laughing immoderately; "however, if any one can do it, I'm sure you can, my dear doctor. So rally your energies and consider the best means of commencing operations: I am sure, if you exert yourself, you cannot fail of success."

"Your Majesty does me honour, and I will endeavour to prove I am not undeserving of the confidence you repose in me," said the little doctor, drawing up himself to his full height, and puffing out his cheeks as he walked on absorbed in meditation. "I have it," cried he, suddenly stopping short; "what does your Majesty think of an immense raft?"

"Excellent, my dear doctor! I see but three objections to making one large enough to convey the whole army:—First, that we have no timber to make it of;—secondly, we have no horses to draw it;—and thirdly, the roads are not wide enough to admit it."

"Balloons would do, but we have them not," resumed the doctor, still profoundly cogitating, with his eyes fixed upon the ground, and his hands in his breeches-pockets.

"What think you of packing the soldiers up in bombs, and shooting them out of mortars?" asked Roderick.

"Your Majesty is pleased to jest," observed the doctor, gravely; "but ridicule is not argument."

"Certainly not," replied the King; "and you mistake me greatly if you thought I meant to ridicule your plan. I only wished to remark that I feared it would be rather difficult to put it in execution."

"That which can be accomplished without difficulty," said the doctor, solemnly, "is scarcely worth the trouble of undertaking, and quite below the consideration of a man of genius. Difficulties to a man of science are but incentives to action."

"Most sensibly observed, my dear doctor," cried Roderick; "however, as we have now reached our tent, I must leave you to contrive some plan to bring us back from Madrid, as I am afraid we cannot wait now to put your designs in practice to enable us to get there: we must march with the dawn. Of course you will accompany us."

"Certainly!" returned the doctor, still musing; then muttering to himself—"I don't much like the plan of shooting off the soldiers, it would take such large mortars and so much gunpowder:—however, there is no knowing what might be done: I will think of it:"—he retired to his tent, though no sleep visited his eyes that night, so completely had the idea of packing up the soldiers in bombs taken possession of his imagination.

Roderick's arrangements were soon made, for Nature had certainly intended him for a general. His intelligent mind foresaw every thing, and provided against every contingency. Brave in the field, and prudent in council, the only fault of Roderick as a soldier was that he sometimes suffered himself to be carried away by his ardour when it would have been wiser to delay. But this very impetuosity had its charms in the eyes of his soldiers, as he never hesitated to expose himself to the same dangers or to undergo the same privations as themselves, and they would all have followed him willingly into the very jaws of destruction.

After arranging every thing for the morning's march, the Irish hero snatched a few hours of repose. With the dawn, however, the drums beat the reveillée, and the Irish army left Andalusia to advance by rapid marches upon Madrid.

CHAPTER XXVI.

Whilst these scenes were taking place in Spain, Elvira was beginning to discover, in England, that it was not quite so delightful to be a Queen as she had previously imagined. The contending parties in the state had been roused into action by the late struggle, and party spirit is of all others the most difficult to conquer. Besides this, the choice of Elvira having been rather a matter of feeling than of judgment, men felt dissatisfied at having suffered themselves to be hurried away by their passions, and, as is usual in such cases, they were disposed to vent the ill-humour they felt at their own conduct upon every thing which chanced to fall in their way. Thus, even the best measures of Elvira's government were warmly criticised; and as she unfortunately altered some of her laws in consequence of these objections, the critics were encouraged to proceed; and fancying her plans to be the result of weakness, when they were in fact only produced by her natural candour and love of justice, the people became more outrageous and troublesome with every concession that was made to them.

Elvira's intentions were excellent, but by unfortunately wishing to please every one, she destroyed their effect. This made her councils vacillating, and her measures uncertain: nothing indeed but the strength of mind and commanding genius of Edmund, joined to his complete devotion to her cause, could have prevented the ruin of her government almost in the moment of its formation. From a mistaken motive of generosity, she had retained in her council those lords who had most vehemently opposed her, though, in compliance with the wishes of Edmund, they were shorn of their beams. This was a fatal error; half measures are always dangerous: the lords in question should have been discarded altogether, or retained in their former seats; as it was, Elvira had made them enemies, and yet left them the power to sting her.

The emissaries of Rosabella were also very active, and the ferment of the public mind excessive. The taste the people had just enjoyed of power, had only been enough to make them long for more. They had only just began to relish its sweets, when the dish was snatched away from them, with which, if it had been left them to devour, they would have soon been cloyed. Discontents became general, disturbances arose, which were no sooner quelled in one quarter than they broke out in another, and these petty insurrections, though almost too trivial to mention, were excessively annoying. For trifling inconveniences, like a host of flies buzzing round a nervous man on a sultry day, are often more irritating to the temper, than serious grievances; and the noble mind of Edmund was wearied by subduing such paltry enemies.

"They want employment," said he one day to the Queen, after reading a dispatch containing an account of one of the most vexatious of these tumults; "you must build bridges and cut canals to amuse them."

The active mind of Elvira caught eagerly at the idea, and she vainly fancied her name would be handed down to posterity as one of the greatest of Queens, who, though in the bloom of youth and pride of beauty, did not hesitate to sacrifice herself for the good of her people, and to devote that time to their welfare and the improvement of her kingdom, which others of her age and rank wasted in mere amusements.

Delighted with the thought, Elvira did not delay a moment before she prepared to put it in practice; and she was found for several days together constantly surrounded by her counsellors, and seated at a table absolutely loaded with papers, which she was busily employed in inspecting and arranging.

Plans for the erection of public buildings, for hospitals, bridges, museums, and churches, schemes for new manufactories, hints for new establishments conducive to the public good, and sketches of new discoveries, lay in heaps before her; mixed with addresses of compliments, votes of thanks, complaints of grievances, petitions, secret informations; and in short all that multifarious collection of paper, with which a monarch is sure to be surrounded who is said to be anxious to ameliorate the condition of his people, or who is unhappily reported to possess a genius for improvement.

Unfortunate is the man possessed of power, of whom such reports are current. He is directly surrounded by projectors, each presenting a scheme more futile than that of his predecessor; and discontented dependants, each bringing a long list of grievances, half of which are imaginary, but which have been conjured up by the complainants that they may not lose the precious right they enjoy of complaining.

Unhappy he whose fate obliges him to decide between the rival claimants! certain alike to be blamed, if he give or refuse; if he accept, or if he reject!

Elvira had not yet found the evils of power; but she now tasted of its sweets, and was enchanted. It seemed to her the most delightful thing in the world to hold in her hands the destinies of thousands of her fellow-creatures; and she thought not of the heavy responsibility it entailed, nor how often her path would be followed by curses instead of blessings. Some one has said that every time a sovereign confers a favour, he makes one ungrateful subject and nine discontented ones; but Elvira and Edmund as yet had not discovered the truth of this maxim. Since their present plan had been suggested, every thing with them had been the couleur de rose. I say, them, for Edmund was associated with Elvira in all these gigantic schemes of improvement; and as he had conceived the first idea of them, so it was he only who could carry them into execution. His active mind required something to employ it; and the same strong feelings which had formerly been devoted to love and glory, were now turned into another channel.

The energies of Elvira's mind had also been awakened by the struggle for the crown, and the passion awakened in her breast by the youthful stranger; and she now felt that she could not quietly return again to the commonplace stillness of every-day life. The passions when once roused from their dormant state, must have something to occupy them, or they will prey upon themselves. Thus we generally see great warriors, or statesmen, or in fact any class of men who have passed their lives in activity, wither away when forced to the dullness of an obscure retirement: their minds and bodies decay alike from want of stimulants to call them into action.

The improvement of her people supplied this stimulus to the mind of Elvira,—but alas! she entered upon it rather with passion than judgment, and had not patience to wait to see her plans gradually carried into effect: No—no—she could not endure any thing slow: with her every thing must be done by a coup de main; and as the people and the buildings were so stupid as not to be made perfect by the first attempt, she was continually disappointed and discouraged. In fact, by attempting to do too much, she did nothing.

When Elvira ascended the throne, she determined no public act should take place without the approbation of her council; and these noble lords were one day debating upon the propriety of a new road, that was proposed to intersect the entire kingdom at right angles, when Lord Gustavus de Montfort rose to oppose it, upon the ground of the injury it would do to private property if carried into effect.

Elvira could not endure Lord Gustavus: his cold, prudent, calculating manner, without a single spark of imagination, disgusted her beyond description; and the only good quality he possessed, that of being indefatigable in following up his point, completed her abhorrence. Wit and eloquence were quite thrown away upon him, for he understood neither the one nor the other; and when any new or brilliant scheme crossed Elvira's imagination, and she described it to her council with all the fire of genius and animation, there he sate with his calm, cold unvarying countenance, ready to damp it with a doubt. Lord Maysworth also was her aversion; his narrow mind, which could only take in such trifles as escape the observation of men of genius; his mean and paltry spirit, and his grovelling ambition, were all her detestation; whilst Lord Noodle and Lord Doodle, who, though ciphers in themselves, yet, like their prototypes, prodigiously increased the weight of the figures placed before them, completed the group.

Much, however, as Elvira disliked these members of her council, she felt unequal to resist their combined influence; and she was just upon the point of being teased into their opinions contrary to her own judgment, when Lord Edmund entered the room. Indescribable was the effect produced by his presence; for indeed his commanding talents swayed all before them; and Elvira could not help smiling when she saw her counsellors of state shake their wise heads, and imagine they were assisting the debate with their wisdom, whilst, in fact, they were mere tools in his powerful hands. It is true they were the agents that produced the intended effect; but his was the master spirit that set them in motion, and taught them where to go. His powerful intellect caught in an instant the comparative merits and disadvantages of the plan now in discussion, and his nod decided its fate.

The council, however, though they implicitly obeyed his will, had not the least idea that they were doing so; as he had the address so to form his opinions as to let each person imagine them the suggestions of his own breast.

Whilst the principal personages in the cabinet, fancying they were leading, were thus blindly led, the nonentities of course followed in their train, and our old friends the lords of ancient family were perfectly astonished when they heard the magnificent plans and sagacious councils attributed to them, and sate quite lost in admiration of their own wisdom, whilst their little heads and enormous periwigs kept bobbing with at least threefold their accustomed rapidity.

Elvira's accession to the throne had induced both her father and Sir Ambrose to leave the country; the duke inhabiting his former palace, and Sir Ambrose taking possession of a

The Mummy!

moveable house in one of the streets upon the banks of the Thames. Here the worthy Baronet found himself perfectly happy in the society of his niece Clara, (whom her parents permitted to keep his house,) and that of his old friend the duke.

"I begin to repent that my daughter is a Queen," said the duke to Sir Ambrose, one night after supper, when the whole party were sitting cosily round the fire in Sir Ambrose's library. "I have not half the enjoyments I used to have when I could have more of her society. Now when I see her, it is but for an instant, and she can scarcely stay to ask me how I do, before she flies off to some of her new plans of improvement."

"The face of the country will be quite changed in a few years, if all the plans of the Queen prosper," said Father Morris in his usual smooth hypocritical manner.

"I hope not!" cried Sir Ambrose; "I hope it's no treason, duke—but I must confess I wish your daughter had never been Queen, if she can't leave things as they are."

"They are such wildgoose schemes too that she takes into her head," said the duke piteously. "Only imagine, Sir Ambrose, she showed me this morning a plan for making aërial bridges to convey heavy weights from one steeple to another; a machine for stamping shoes and boots at one blow out of a solid piece of leather; a steam-engine for milking cows; and an elastic summer-house that might be folded up so as to be put into a man's pocket!"

"It is really provoking; and Edward is quite as scheming and visionary. I absolutely think, if we were both to die, they would not feel more than a temporary uneasiness at our loss, their minds are so completely occupied in these gigantic projects."

Whilst these two old men were sitting comfortably over the fire, commenting on the glorious days when they were young, and when all went right, or, what was nearly the same thing, when all appeared to them to do so (quite forgetting that age has other eyes than youth, and that the change was in themselves, not the times), Clara was at a splendid party given by Elvira, and Father Morris soon left the duke's library to join her.

It was a ball; and the splendid court of Claudia seemed yet more brilliant under the reign of her successor. It was the first time Clara had ever been at court, and the effect the gorgeous magnificence of the scene had upon her was powerful in the extreme. She forgot her cares, her sadness, and her love—all seemed enchantment; and the old lady, who acted as her chaperon, was quite horrorized at her gaucherie.

Brilliant as all was, however, the lovely goddess of the temple far exceeded even the splendour of the shrine; and the beholders gazed upon her with indescribable rapture. Beautiful as the fairy image of a dream; kind, affable, and condescending to all, Elvira glided through the crowd, followed by her suite to the concert-room. Here, all that the imagination of man could devise of harmony, enchanted the ears. But harsh was every other sound to that which stole upon the senses when Elvira was induced to forget her rank and mingle her voice with the music.

Elvira's singing was perfection: "clear as a trumpet with a silver sound;" the round full notes now swelled upon the ear in liquid melody, and then died away, soft and sweet, yet distinct even in their faintest strains. Prince Ferdinand was at her side, and his ardent gaze bespoke the intenseness of his admiration. Elvira had not before seen him since the night when her conversation with him had so powerfully excited the jealousy of Edmund; and as she now observed his manner had again attracted Edmund's attention, she blushed yet more deeply than before.

Edmund saw her blushes; and, stung almost to madness by the sight, rushed violently out of the room.

The night was cold and damp, a drizzling mist fell fast, and that peculiar chill that marks the first approaches of winter, hung in the air; but Lord Edmund thought not of the weather, and he strode bareheaded through the palace-gardens with hurried steps and the actions of a maniac; whilst the thick gloom that pervaded the sky, contrasted fearfully with the brilliantly illuminated apartment he had just quitted. The gloominess of the scene, however, harmonized well with Edmund's feelings; he felt soothed insensibly; and though he still stalked moodily backwards and forwards, he became gradually more calm.

"Ungrateful woman," thought he, "to treat me thus! Does she not owe every thing to me? I could bear her coldness; I could resign her to a throne; but the idea of her loving another drives me to distraction!—Curses on that fiend! It must be by his infernal arts that Ferdinand has triumphed. The cold, the chaste Elvira could never give her love thus—thus almost unsolicited,

The Mummy!

and at first sight if it were not the work of magic. By Heaven, I would risk my soul for vengeance on that demon!"

As he spoke, his eyes fell upon a thicket near him, and he fancied he saw the figure of a man, half obscured however by the mist, emerge from its gloomy recesses. He gazed intently, and the figure glided slowly on with catlike, creeping steps. The mind of Edmund was worked up to frenzy—he almost fancied a demon had appeared obedient to his wish, to receive his pledge, and work his bidding. "Speak!" cried he, in a voice that sounded fearfully amidst the surrounding stillness—"Speak! art thou a demon, or a mortal?"

All was silent: the figure glided on; and Lord Edmund, oppressed by supernatural terrors, and shuddering at the sound of his own voice, could bear no more; he darted upon the figure, and grasping it roughly, he exclaimed, "Man or devil, I fear thee not, and thus will I grapple with thee."

"Gently, my son," replied the well-known voice of Father Morris; "in what have I offended you?"

"Pardon, holy father," returned Edmund "I knew you not—I knew not what I did—my passion blinded me."

"And what has caused this passion? The mind of Edmund is too noble to be lightly moved."

"Oh! talk not of the nobleness of my mind, father; I feel I am but a poor weak worm. Nobleness belongs to God alone; 'tis blasphemy to apply the term to man."

"Tell me your grievances. They must, I am sure, be great, or they would not thus affect you. It is my holy office to console affliction. Speak then, my son; for, remember, that though joy is doubled by being partaken, grief is lessened by being shared—and woe robbed of half its bitterness."

"I have little to confess, father. I was weak and foolish; but Elvira—"

"And are you astonished at a woman's fickleness? Light as the eider down, and unstable as the changing wind, inconstancy is natural to the sex—they crave incessantly for novelty;—and as vanity is their only real passion, if that be gratified they ask no more."

"And has not Elvira's vanity been gratified even to satiety?

Have I not idolized, worshipped her? Was it not my power that made her what she is? And is this my reward? To be scorned, deserted, laughed at, and for what? A stranger!—a boy!—my prisoner!"

"Whom do you mean?" asked the friar.

"Prince Ferdinand," returned Edmund.

"Impossible!" cried Father Morris, starting with well-feigned astonishment. "Elvira cannot, surely, love Prince Ferdinand! And yet, now I recollect, I saw her talking to him, even now, with an appearance of deep interest, when I passed through her splendid chambers."

"Damnation!" exclaimed Lord Edmund vehemently, driven to distraction by this speech; for, strange to tell, though we may be certain of the reality of our own sufferings, they always seem to come with double poignancy when we hear them related by another.

"Calm yourself, my son," said Father Morris in his silky tones, eyeing him with about as much compassion as an angler feels for the writhing of a worm upon his hook. "These bursts of passion are unworthy of you."

"Oh, father!" cried Edmund, softened almost into tears, "you know not how I loved that woman. Your grave, serious feelings, disciplined by the restraint of a cloister, mortified by your renunciation of all earthly pleasures, can form no idea of the depth and fierceness of mine. Your passions, father, are dead within you; subdued by holy penitence to calmness; but mine rage with the fury of a volcano, and destroy me! O that my fond attachment, my long devoted services, my adoration, should be thus rewarded. Yes—my adoration, for I have adored her, father! I worshipped her like a goddess; and though I doted on her charms, and would have endured unheard-of torments to have been blest with their possession, yet, did I not sacrifice my hopes?—did I not relinquish the treasure when just within my grasp, because her happiness was dearer to me than my own? And now to see her lavish her favours on that boy! She smiled upon him, father, and he dared to take her hand and press it to his lips. I saw him kiss it, not with the calm respect of a kneeling subject, but with the fervour, the impassioned ardour of a lover; and then he looked at her—curses on the thought!—and she did not reprove; but, casting down her eyes, softly blushed consent. Damnation! I cannot endure it."

"Passion, my son, entails its own punishment. You see every thing with a jaundiced eye. Elvira's nature is gentle and yielding; she feared to hurt his feelings by her harshness. 'Tis but the natural consequence of that very softness you so often have admired. Why should you quarrel with it now? 'tis still the same that charmed you, save that now it is extended to another, and will be soon, no doubt, to all the world. Elvira has been educated in retirement, and, seeing only yourself and Edric, you thought her conduct was the effect of partiality for you, when it was in fact but her natural manner. She is now upon a larger theatre; and you must expect to see myriads of kneeling victims worship her beauty, and pay homage at her feet! And do you suppose she will be displeased at their attention? No; she is far too gentle; she has no firmness; and the same submission she now pays to you, she will, if you offend her, easily transfer to another. She is not formed to govern; she would obey and be happy; but the weight of government would overwhelm her if she were left alone to sustain it. Shake off, then, these selfish feelings, and be again yourself. You have often said, you only wished her happiness; and if that be the case, even if she should really love Prince Ferdinand, you ought to rejoice to see her in his arms."

"Sooner would I perish, sooner would I involve all in one universal ruin! But it is impossible; she scarcely knows him."

"And if it were so, still you would be wrong to blame Elvira for what, in fact, she cannot help. Her yielding softness is the defect of her character."

"Fool that I was, that very softness caught me, and my fond heart fell captive to its chains. But it was folly, infatuation! I see my error; Rosabella has more character. She can love."

Lord Edmund crossed his arms upon his breast and was soon lost in a reverie, which Father Morris was careful not to interrupt, but which was broken by the approach of Trevors, his lordship's aide-de-camp and secretary.

"What do you want?" asked Lord Edmund sternly.

"I came to seek your Lordship. I feared you were unwell, as I missed your Lordship from the party."

"You missed me!" repeated Lord Edmund bitterly. "You missed me! and did no one else discover my absence? Was it so marked that my servant could observe it, and yet no one else?"

"Did not the Queen inquire for Lord Edmund?" asked Father Morris.

"I did not hear her Majesty," replied Trevors.

"How was she engaged? what was she doing?" demanded Lord Edmund.

"She was sitting, talking to Prince Ferdinand, my Lord."

Lord Edmund gnashed his teeth together, grinding them with fury, and rushed back to the house without speaking, whilst Trevors followed at an humble distance.

"He has it," cried Father Morris triumphantly—"he has it, and he is mine for ever."

Several days elapsed from this period before Elvira again saw Lord Edmund. She was surprised at his absence; as indeed he was so interwoven in her schemes and plans, that nothing went on well without him.

"Will your Majesty have the goodness to affix the royal seal to this ordinance?" asked Lord Gustavus one morning.

"I don't know," replied Elvira. "I can't tell what to do. I wish Lord Edmund were here."

"He may soon be sent for," said Lord Gustavus pompously. "Though, with all due deference to your Majesty's better judgment, it does not appear to me that his presence is exactly requisite."

Lord Edmund, however, was summoned, and he came. But oh! how changed since Elvira had seen him last! His face looked pale and thin, his cheeks were sunken, and his eyes hollow and heavy, whilst his deep voice sounded hoarse and unnatural. Passion had passed through his soul, and withered as it went. Elvira's heart smote her as she gazed upon him.

"You have been ill, Edmund!" said she, in tones of melting softness. "Why was I not informed? Surely you could not think I would willingly neglect you? Could you judge so harshly of me?"

The firm breast of Edmund softened as she spoke, and tears swam in his eyes as he struggled to reply with calmness—yes, tears; the brave, the warlike Edmund, whose strength of mind and firmness had resisted unequalled dangers, now trembled before a woman.

"You must have some advice," continued Elvira. "Dr. Coleman, Dr. Hardman, can you not prescribe for your patient?"

"His Lordship appears feverish," said Dr. Coleman. "No doubt he has rested ill."

"Yes — yes," rejoined Dr. Hardman, with a malignant smile. "His Lordship's eyes betray his want of rest."

"I have been slightly indisposed," said Lord Edmund, rallying his spirits to speak: "but I am better. Is there any thing in which my services can be useful to your Majesty?"

"Her Majesty wishes you to inspect this bill," replied Lord Gustavus solemnly, "before she gives it her royal assent."

Lord Edmund's eyes sparkled. "Then she still thinks my opinion of importance," thought he.

"Lord Edmund's illness, I hope, is passed," said Dr. Hardman maliciously; "for he certainly looks better even since he came into the room."

Lord Edmund was better; a sudden revulsion of feeling had taken place within him, and hope was again illumined in his bosom. Passion again rushed through his soul. "She must, she shall, be mine," thought he, whilst fire flashed from his eyes. "The hated law shall be repealed. Difficulties only increase the value of the prize, and they vanish before a determined spirit. What! shall I, before whose arm whole nations have fallen vanquished, shrink like a coward from the first trouble that assails me! Oh, no! I will not be so weak; opposition shall only animate my courage. Treasures would be scarcely worth acceptance if they lay beneath one's feet — a brave man spurns an easy victory! I will exert my powers, and Elvira shall be mine."

Father Morris was at the levee, and he watched with anxious eyes the fluctuations in Edmund's expressive countenance. "Perdition seize her beauty!" muttered he; "with one look she undoes whole months of labour. But he shall yet be mine — Cheops has sworn he shall, — and Rosabella shall be Queen. Be the Mummy mortal or fiend, he is resistless; he has unbounded power over the human heart, and what he wills must be accomplished."

Some weeks elapsed, during which Lord Edmund, restored to his former influence in the government, laboured assiduously to prepare the minds of the people for abolishing the law that prevented the marriage of the Queen. With the greatest care he endeavoured to make Elvira popular. For this purpose he persuaded her to remit those burthens that weighed most heavily upon the people, replacing them by taxes levied in a more indirect way; for the mass of a population seldom grumbles at taxation, unless it see the trifles for which it pays: men do not regard the giving double the real value of a commodity, a tenth part so much, as paying even a small direct sum for the use of any of the common necessaries of life.

By judiciously acting upon this principle, Edmund made himself adored; and whispers even were buzzed about, lamenting that he was not King. This was the point to which Edmund had wished to bring the people; and he pursued his plan by supporting the poor against the rich, and rigorously punishing the magistrates or officers of justice who attempted to oppress the people. The multitude generally hate those entrusted with the execution of the laws, perhaps upon the same principle as the bleeding culprit abhors the sight of the whip that has flogged him; and their natural conceit and presumption were flattered by the attention paid to their complaints; till, by his judicious management, Lord Edmund found that he had obtained the entire devotion of the mob, and could wield them at his pleasure.

Time rolled on, and winter had already wrapped its frozen mantle round the world, when one day Father Morris abruptly entered the apartment of Rosabella. "It is all over," cried he, as he threw himself in despair upon a couch. "Edmund has obtained the consent of the people for the Queen to marry, and no doubt in a few weeks he will be the husband of Elvira!"

"The husband of Elvira!" cried Rosabella, her eyes flashing fire, and her cheeks glowing, whilst every fibre quivered with agitation, and her fine features bespoke the tremendous passions of a demon. "Then may everlasting misery attend the fiend that has deceived us; that has led us on step by step to our destruction, and is perhaps even now mocking our despair! Yes, yes," continued she, as the fiendish laugh of Cheops rang in her ears, and his detested form stood again before her,—"I expected this; you come to enjoy your triumph and mock our credulity; but know, this arm is yet powerful enough to revenge my wrongs; it shall annihilate my rival; and thou, wretch! detested

The Mummy!

hideous wretch! thou too shalt feel its vengeance!"

"This to your friend!" said Cheops with a bitter smile: "fie! fie! How blind is human reason when the passions intervene!—all is for the best—have patience; wait a little, and my promises will yet be accomplished."

"If Elvira had died," murmured Father Morris, a dark frown gathering upon his brow.

"You would not be now alive," said the Mummy. "But fear not, all is as you can wish."

"As we can wish?" cried Rosabella indignantly.

"Yes, as you can wish," returned Cheops firmly. "Edmund has obtained permission for Elvira to marry any natural born subject of the realm; but she will not wed him, for she loves another, and that other is a foreigner. He will be enraged at her refusal, and jealousy will alienate him from her cause. He will then naturally espouse that of her rival from ambition and revenge. Rosabella will be Queen, and the law which prevented the marriage of the Sovereign being abolished, Edmund will become her husband—if not from love, at least from ambition."

"O Cheops! 'tis useless to resist—we are thy slaves,—do with us as thou wilt."

"Say rather you are slaves of your own passions," murmured the Mummy; and they parted.

It was a clear frosty day in November, when Elvira, scarcely knowing why, wandered into the garden belonging to her splendid palace of Somerset House; and, entering a pavilion, reclined upon a couch placed opposite to a window that commanded a view of the river. The pavilion was decorated with the utmost taste. Its windows, opening to the ground, were shaded with curtains of gossamer net, lined with pink; the walls were beautifully painted, and divided into panels by highly ornamented columns; books, drawings, and musical instruments, were scattered around; whilst tripods, supporting vases filled with the rarest exotic flowers, shed sweet fragrance through the air; and the carpet was so soft and thick, that it felt like moss beneath the feet.

Even in this temple of luxury, however, its fair possessor was not happy. She sighed as she surveyed the gorgeous refinement around her, and felt forcibly the insufficiency of greatness. Listlessly she turned her eyes upon the figures painted upon the walls: they represented the loves of Mars and Venus: they were exquisitely painted: the artist had given to the life the tender modesty of the goddess, and the ardent passion of her lover. Elvira gazed upon his glowing countenance and sparkling eyes; and then, looking down, sighed yet more heavily than before.

She dismissed her attendants, retaining only Emma; and long her eyes were fixed on vacancy, and her mind absorbed in mournful contemplations; when suddenly she was startled by the entrance of a page, and the appearance of Lord Edmund Montagu, who followed almost at the moment of the page's repeating his name: his countenance beaming joy, and hope dancing in his eyes.

"Oh, Elvira!" he cried, "you are now mine — mine for ever! The people permit you to marry. The lords in council have signed the law; the people have proclaimed it with acclamations. You are free! you are no longer debarred from the inestimable pleasures of domestic life — you are independent — you may marry any natural born subject of the realm, and will you now be mine?"

"And so relinquish my independence the moment I obtain it," said Elvira, smiling.

"Oh, my loved! my adored Elvira! consent to make me happy! Believe me you shall be free, and still as much a Queen as at this moment."

"Edmund!" said Elvira seriously, "you deserve more than I can give you; for I will not insult you by supposing you would be satisfied with the possession of my crown without my heart; — and that it is not in my power to bestow."

"My dearest Elvira, you but fancy this. I know your feelings are warm, your sensibility acute, and your generosity unbounded — can you then want a heart?"

"Alas, no! but I have discovered I possess one, only in time to know also that I have given it to another."

"And is that other a youth and a stranger?" asked her lover, gasping for breath.

"He is," replied Elvira, blushing, and looking down.

"Then, indeed, I am wretched!" cried Lord Edmund; and, striking his clenched hand vehemently against his forehead, he darted out of the room.

Elvira gazed after him with a feeling almost amounting to horror. Terrified at the strength of the passions she had awakened, she appeared stupefied, and stood looking like a child who had accidentally cut the string which confined the wheels of some powerful machinery, on hearing its fearful clatter above its head.

"Oh, madam, madam!" cried Emma, wringing her hands, "what will become of us? Your Majesty has offended Lord Edmund for ever, and for that wretch, who, I am certain, is a fiend incarnate!"

"Peace, Emma!" said Elvira, "you forget my rank—I will not be dictated to."

"Pardon me, dear madam, you know I love you, and—"

"I know, also, that you presume upon my love. Begone!"

Emma obeyed, and Elvira was left alone.

Dreadfully agitated, and quite unable to compose herself or arrange the chaos of her thoughts, she walked to the windows of the pavilion, and, opening one of them, looked out upon the gardens. It is already said that these delightful grounds were thrown open to the public; but, in consequence of the ease with which they might be enjoyed, a few half-pay officers, attorneys without clients, physicians without patients, clergymen looking out for livings, hissed players, disappointed authors and discarded servants, alone strolled through their romantic walks, and paused occasionally to gaze upon the beautiful works of art with which they were decorated. The English were now decidedly the first sculptors in the world. Chemical preparations alone being used to supply light and heat, smoke was unknown, and the atmosphere being no longer thick and cloudy, marble bore exposure to it without material injury. Besides this, perhaps no nation in the world produced more beautiful models of male and female beauty than England; and now that the women had long thrown off those deformers of the human shape ycleped stays, their forms developed themselves into perfect symmetry. Elvira, however, thought not of the gardens, nor of the works of art they contained; yet as she stood at the window, though absorbed in her own reflections, her eyes rested upon the exquisite statues before her. The inanimate marble seemed endowed with soul and spirit, whilst the graceful forms it represented seemed to pause only for a moment, and to be ready to start again into life and action after a short repose—in short, they appeared to breathe; and the spectator felt almost surprised, when his eye had turned from them, to find them still in the same attitude when he looked again.

The river was frozen, and persons glided along it in glittering traineaux, or skated gracefully with infinite variety of movement; whilst, every now and then, a steam-percussion-moveable bridge shot across the stream, loaded with goods and passengers, collapsing again the instant its burthen was safely landed on the other side.

Pleased with the busy scene around her, Elvira stood and gazed, till half her troubles seemed to vanish, and a pleasing train of thought crept over her mind. "What have I done?" thought she,—"and yet I do not repent.—No, no! I could not act otherwise. The noble and devoted love of Edmund deserved my warmest gratitude, and I have done right to own the truth to him, painful as it has been to me to do so, rather than torture his generous bosom by exciting hopes I never meant to realize. Yes, I have done right," repeated she aloud; "and I am perfectly satisfied with my conduct."

"Then you have reason to be contented," said the deep voice of Cheops, immediately behind her; "for few indeed are the mortals that can say so with justice!"

The solemn tones of the Mummy sank like a foreboding of evil upon the heart of Elvira, and she shuddered involuntarily.

"You think I have done wrong then?" said she.

"I did not say that," returned he calmly.—"But had I not known the sex, I might perchance have felt surprised that you should avow, unasked for, a secret to Lord Edmund, which you have sedulously endeavoured to keep concealed even from me."

"Alas," cried Elvira, "my motives—"

"Were those of a woman," interrupted Cheops; "a being fated to work mischief. I do not blame you; for you have only acted according to your natural instinct."

"What do you mean?" asked Elvira, turning pale and trembling, for the words of the Mummy created an undefinable dread upon her mind.

"Listen!" said Cheops, "and I will tell you.—If you had confided your secret to me, it would have produced good, for I should have aided your passions, and I cannot give assistance unless it be required;—but by telling it to Lord Edmund you have produced evil, for he mistakes your lover for another, and the consequences may be fatal. Thus, it is clear that you could not have done otherwise than as you have; for when was a woman known to hesitate between good and evil, and not choose the latter?"

"Mistakes my lover for another!" exclaimed Elvira. "For God's sake, explain yourself!"

"He thinks you meant Prince Ferdinand," said the Mummy coldly, "and he is now seeking him in order to destroy him."

"Oh, God!—Oh, God!" cried Elvira in the bitterest agony: "what will become of me? where is Edmund! Let me fly to implore him to spare the prince!"

"It does not appear to me," said Cheops still more calmly, "that your endeavours to preserve him are at all likely to produce the effect you wish; for, as Lord Edmund already believes you love the prince, and as that belief is the reason of his hatred, your showing a violent anxiety for his welfare does not appear to me exactly the mode most calculated to destroy his suspicions."

"True! true!" cried Elvira, wringing her hands. "Alas! alas! what will become of me?" whilst, as she spoke, a piercing cry rang in her ears, and a sudden rush of all the persons in the gardens took place towards one particular spot. Scarcely knowing what she did, Elvira followed the crowd, and shrieked with indescribable terror as she heard the clashing of swords. Pale and trembling, she hurried forward, and arrived just as Prince Ferdinand, uttering a deep groan, fell beneath the sword of Lord Edmund. Elvira screamed, and throwing herself upon the body, endeavoured in vain to revive it, quite forgetting in the excess of her agitation the crowd that surrounded her, and the interpretation that might be put upon her behaviour. One sole idea occupied her mind, and chilled it with horror: it was, that her imprudence had most probably deprived a fellow-creature of existence.

Lord Edmund in the mean time stood in statue-like insensibility, gazing upon her with feelings of unutterable anguish. Her grief, her violent emotion, seemed to confirm the passion she had avowed; and if she loved, his exertions had only paved the way for the success of his rival. The thought was madness. Lord Edmund gnashed his teeth, his countenance changed, blood gushed in torrents from his side, for he too was wounded, and he leant fainting against a tree.

The confusion that now prevailed was indescribable. It was high treason to draw a sword in the precincts of the royal palace; and the guards, who were instantly assembled, took the offenders into custody. They were both incapable of offering any resistance, and they were hurried away to prison amidst the exclamations of the mob. Elvira had fainted, and she was carried back to the palace; whilst the whispered speculations of the crowd, upon the strangeness of the scene, arose in half-stifled murmurs like the distant roar of ocean. The attention of the spectators, however, was soon fixed upon the poor old Duke of Cornwall. He had stood bending forwards—his hands clasped, and his eyes riveted upon his daughter during the whole of her ineffectual attempts to revive the prince. The old man seemed turned to stone: he neither moved, nor spoke; his glassy eyes were set, and his livid lips slightly quivered; at last he uttered a faint groan, and fell senseless into the arms of his attendants in a fit of apoplexy. The spectators thought him dead, and fancied his heart had broken, on discovering this unexpected weakness on the part of his adored daughter.

Every one was powerfully affected, and every one seemed bursting to speak; though no one knew exactly what he might venture to say. Lord Gustavus looked stern, Lord Maysworth important, and Dr. Hardman sly; whilst the Lords Noodle and Doodle shook their little heads, till they seemed in imminent danger of becoming separated from their bodies. Rosabella's heart alone swelled with rapture, and her eyes beamed with ill-concealed triumph.

"The Mummy was right," thought she;—"Elvira must fall, and Edmund will be mine."

CHAPTER XXVII.

The evening of the day on which Prince Ferdinand and Lord Edmund were committed to prison, Sir Ambrose, as he was writing in his study, was startled by a loud scream; and flying to the spot from whence it proceeded, he found Clara lying upon the ground insensible, whilst Abelard was stooping over her, and endeavouring to render her some assistance.

"Good God!" cried Sir Ambrose, "what is the matter?"

"It is all owing to the carelessness of the domestic assistants at the next door," replied Abelard. "No. 7, is just come back from Brighton; and one of the assistants being occupied in making observations on the sky, instead of minding what he was doing, pushed the house a little on one side as it was slipping into the sockets; and poking their horizontal spout through our library window, they have knocked down this shelf of books, and frightened poor Miss Clara out of her wits."

"Stupid idiots," said the baronet; "they might have killed her if the books had fallen upon her."

"I beg your pardon, Sir Ambrose," said the culprit, putting his head through the window; "I do not conceive Miss Montagu would have been injured even if the books had fallen upon her. The weight of her body, I should apprehend, must be nearly equivalent to that of the books; consequently, the resistance she was capable of opposing, being fully equal to the blow she would have received, the effect must have been neutralized."

"Confound your explanations!" said Sir Ambrose, whose anger was increased tenfold by this speech; "you've killed my niece, and now you want to drive me distracted. Clara, my dear Clara! open your eyes, my love; are you hurt?"

"Oh, my dear uncle!" sighed Clara, "Edmund is in prison, and he certainly will be beheaded."

"In prison, child! you must be dreaming."

"Indeed I am not, uncle: I heard the men who are placing the adjoining house say so. He has fought with Prince Ferdinand in the palace garden."

"My boy, my darling boy!" cried Sir Ambrose, and rushed out of the room in despair.

"Follow him, for Heaven's sake, follow him, Abelard," said Clara. The worthy butler obeyed, wringing his hands, and lifting his eyes up to heaven; whilst Clara remained perfectly motionless, and apparently absorbed in thought.

"I will save him," said she after a short pause, "or perish in the attempt."

In the bitterest anguish of mind, Sir Ambrose hastened to the palace; but he was refused admittance, as he was informed the Queen was in a high fever. He inquired for his friend the duke: he too was invisible, his late attack having placed his life in imminent danger. Dr. Coleman was in attendance on the Queen; and the lords of the council, though they affected to sympathize with the unfortunate father, evidently, though covertly, rejoiced at the disgrace of their most powerful rival. Repulsed on every side, Sir Ambrose now proceeded to the prison; but here also he was refused admittance, and sadly and slowly he returned home in despair, resting his sole remaining hopes upon the advice and assistance of Father Morris, upon whose gigantic strength of mind he was accustomed implicitly to rely in all the impotency of age and misery.

The prison to which Ferdinand and Lord Edmund had been conveyed was situated in a close disagreeable part of the city of London, called Kensington. It had been formerly a palace, and had been surrounded by a noble park miscalled a garden. The devastating hand of improvement had however, as usual, waged war against all the sublimer charms of nature, and the majestic beauties of Kensington fell victims to its fury. Narrow, unwholesome streets now rose where spreading oaks had once stretched forth their venerable arms, and verdant lawns had become dirty causeways; whilst ponds were turned to water pipes, and Jacob's well kept clean a common sewer. As Ferdinand and Edmund, however, had never seen Kensington in its pristine glories, they could not now regret the change: and it was to them neither more nor less than a place of confinement, a spot very few people show any manifest relish for.

Immediately upon their arrival, Prince Ferdinand and Lord Edmund had their wounds dressed by the automaton steam surgeon belonging to the prison, which, being properly arranged and wound up, staunched the blood, spread the plasters, and affixed the bandages with as much skill as though it had done nothing but walk a hospital all its life. As soon as these operations were performed, the prisoners were locked up in separate cells, and left to meditate upon their situations.

The Mummy!

"Good Heavens!" cried Ferdinand, looking round with astonishment at the elegant apartment he was shown into, adorned with a painted velvet carpet, silk curtains, and chairs and tables inlaid with brass and ivory; whilst a sumptuous canopy hung over a bed of down on one side, and divers little Cupids supported lights, held back curtains, and performed numerous other useful offices in different corners. "Can this be a prison? Neither Paris nor Vienna possess palaces half so splendid!"

The surprise of Ferdinand was natural, as he was still almost a stranger in England, and did not know that our happy island had been long blest with a race of people who thought prisons should be made agreeable residences, and had gone on improving them till they had ended in making them temples of luxury. In spite of all the conveniences of his prison, however, Ferdinand was perfectly wretched. He could not imagine what reason Lord Edmund had had for fastening a quarrel upon him; for, as his passion for Elvira, though violent, had been quite as evanescent as that he had formerly entertained for Rosabella, he had not the least idea of having excited Lord Edmund's jealousy. Fatigued at length with forming fruitless conjectures, he threw himself upon his bed of down, and soon lost the remembrance of his cares in a refreshing slumber.

In the mean time, Clara was revolving in her mind the best method of putting in practice a wild scheme that she had formed, of visiting Prince Ferdinand in prison. She did not dare confide her plan to any one, for she feared that anybody she might consult would either laugh at her folly or betray her secret. Besides, to obtain any assistance, she must give some motive for her conduct; and as Clara did not exactly know her own reasons for thus acting, it was quite impossible she could make out a case to satisfy another. To go, however, she was determined; and when the family of her uncle were all retired, she wrapped herself in a large mantle, and with some difficulty contrived to reach the street. The night was cold and dark; a thick mist fell, and Clara seemed chilled to the heart; yet a feeling she could not account for, urged her on. Clara was young and romantic; she loved Prince Ferdinand, and she fancied him in danger. How she was to save him she knew not, and yet it was solely the hope of saving him that urged her forward.

She had discovered he was confined at Kensington, and thither she bent her steps:—but as she passed the palace, she found a crowd of balloons floating around it, laden with persons whose anxiety respecting the Queen had kept them waiting, and induced them to besiege her door personally with their inquiries; whilst the lighted flambeaux, belonging to these aërial vehicles, flashed brightly in the air, and looked like a multitude of dancing stars, as they rapidly crossed and recrossed each other above her head.

This little incident completed poor Clara's bewilderment; and, terrified lest she should be seen and recognized, she hurried on without exactly knowing where she was going, till, perplexed by the different appearance the streets seemed to assume in the darkness, and her own fears, she found to her unspeakable dismay that she had lost her road. In the greatest agitation and distress, she now wandered to and fro, whilst her embarrassment was increased every moment by the ill-timed raillery of the passers by. At last, she became quite surrounded by a group of people, who assailed her with so many questions and jokes, that the poor girl, quite overpowered, stopped short, and burst into tears.

"Och! and what are ye about to be after disturbing a poor young cratur like that," cried the well-known voice of Father Murphy, as the friar's portly figure was seen bustling through the mob. "What are ye after there? Don't you see the poor thing has lost her way in the darkness; and if ye bother her so, how d'ye think she'll ever be able to find it?"

Never did any music sound so harmoniously in Clara's ears, as the father's rich deep brogue; and darting forwards she threw herself at his feet, and, clasping her arms round his knees, she exclaimed—"Oh! save me! I am Clara! Clara Montagu!"

"Clara!" cried Father Murphy, in the utmost astonishment. "Clara! why, what in the name of Heaven brings you out, child, at this hour of the night?"

"Oh! don't ask me, father," returned Clara, gasping for breath; "that is, I will tell you presently. But take me away; for the love of the blessed Virgin, save me from these men!"

"Come here, my child," said the Father, drawing her arm within his own, and walking away with her; "let us lave these people. And now," continued he, when they were already at some distance from the crowd, "you must tell me, child, what brings ye here?"

This question, though it was a very natural one for the friar to ask, was beyond Clara's power to answer. In fact, she trembled so dreadfully that she could scarcely stand; and when she attempted to speak, her teeth chattered in her head so violently, that she could not articulate a syllable. "Poor thing," muttered the compassionate priest, after waiting a few minutes in vain for an answer, "she'll be better presently."

All now was dark, and they walked slowly on some paces without speaking, when four bright flashes from a neighbouring clock announced the completion of some hour, and the next instant the solemn deep-toned bell distinctly pronounced the word "one," and then all again was silent.

"I had no fancy it was so late," said the father, whose disposition was naturally too cheerful to let him ever remain long silent.

"Did you think it was one o'clock, Clara? I little thought I should ever be wandering with you, dear, in the streets at such a time of night. I can't help fancying it's all a dream, any how: so speak, darling, if you can, and tell me all about it."

Clara felt still more faint, and only replied by clinging yet more firmly to the friar's arm. Father Murphy was frightened and thought she was going to die. — "Oh murther!" cried he, "what will I do? she brathing her last, sweet cratur, and nobody by to help her, and I not knowing how to comfort her."

The delicate form of Clara seemed every instant to become more heavy, as she still clung almost unconsciously to the friar's arm, and gasped feebly for breath.

"Oh! what will I do? what will I do?" repeated the poor father, looking eagerly around for aid: all however was dark, and gloomy and silent as the grave. Suddenly, however, a bright meteor-like substance appeared at the edge of the horizon, and the friar, to his unspeakable transport, discovered it to be a patent night fire-stage balloon. He hailed it, and in a few moments it was hovering over their heads; the accommodation ladder was let down, and Clara and her companion having ascended to the car, the balloon again rapidly sailed along.

"Where are we going?" asked Clara faintly.

"Och!" returned the friar, "and that's what I never thought of asking, darling; but Heaven be praised that ye are so much better as to be able to bother yourself about it."

"We are going to Kensington, miss," said the balloon

conductor.

"Kensington!" repeated Clara, clapping her hands together in transport—"thank God!"

"It's a very good thing to be thankful any how," said the father; "but I own I don't see why you should cry out in such rapture, when you find we are going the wrong road."

"Oh! no, no, father," returned Clara, "not the wrong road; for Kensington is the goal of all my wishes."

"Poor thing! she is certainly distracted," thought Father Murphy. "The loss of her cousin has deprived her of her senses; but I will let her take her own way; perhaps she'll be better presently."

"Where will you like to be set down?" asked the man.

"Near the prison," cried Clara eagerly.

"Near the prison!" repeated Father Murphy, shrugging his shoulders. "Ay, ay, I was right."

Not another word was spoken till the balloon stopped and the passengers were set down: all still was dark, save a land-light that gleamed from the battlements of the prison, and showed a tall, clumsy-looking figure that marched with heavy, measured steps to and fro before the gates, whilst at a little distance lay a party of soldiers bivouacking. Clara shuddered as she looked at them, and hastily turning away, timidly approached the figure, and begged it to let her into the prison. It continued its march, but as it did not speak, she attempted to pass by it.

"No admittance," said the figure, as she touched it, in trying to reach the door.

"I implore you," cried Clara, wringing her hands in agony.

The figure did not reply, but continued its solemn tramp unmoved; its hollow steps falling heavily upon the ear at regular intervals. Driven to despair, Clara again endeavoured to rush past it; but she was again repulsed as the figure reiterated its monotonous "No admittance!" Clara threw herself upon her knees before it in agony.

"Clara! Clara dear!" cried Father Murphy, attempting to raise

The Mummy!

her, "you are certainly quite beside yourself; don't you see it is an automaton? nothing can stop it but the proper check-string, and that is in that little guard house, round which you see the soldiers lying."

"Then they can admit me," cried Clara wildly, "they are men, and will surely listen to me:" then before the father could stop her, she flew towards them, and throwing herself at the feet of the commanding officer, implored his pity. The officer was a man of feeling, and, touched with compassion at her evident anguish, had promised to grant her petition ere Father Murphy, who was too fat to move with much agility, could reach them. "Thank you! thank you!" cried Clara, kissing the officer's hand. "God bless you!"

The officer smiled at her warmth. "Wait here a little," said he: "I will soon return and admit you, if I obtain permission; but State Prisoners are ordered to be guarded so closely, that I dare not take any step respecting them, without consulting the governor."

"So then you'll get in after all," said Father Murphy, who had approached near enough to hear this last speech. "Well, well, what a world this is we live in! Here have been dukes and princes begging for admission unsuccessfully, and yet a little saucy girl, only because she happens to be half distracted, is let in at the very first word."

Clara did not reply; but wrapping herself in her cloak, sate down on a large stone near the gates to wait the officer's return. The solemn automaton had been stopped for a moment to allow him to pass, but it had now resumed its slow measured step, and Clara's heart sickened at the sound. The mist cleared away, and the night became fine, though cold, whilst the moon having struggled through the clouds that rapidly scudded across the sky, shed her pale feeble light upon the scene. Clara shuddered as she looked at the dark heavy building behind her, and, wrapping her cloak tighter round her, fixed her eyes anxiously upon the sky, watching the varied shapes assumed by the clouds as they drifted along, and sighing heavily as they passed.

"Now tell me, dear," said Father Murphy, seating himself beside her, "what ye mane to say to yere cousin when ye get in to see him. Spake freely, for the devil a word the spalpeens yonder shall hear of what ye're going to say, by rason of their being all fast asleep."

"My cousin!" exclaimed Clara. "Who? what?"

"Your cousin Edmund, that ye're come so far to see," resumed the father.

"My cousin!" replied Clara; "Oh! ay, true. It was my cousin that fought with him, you know. But I don't want to see my cousin."

"Not want to see your cousin!" reiterated Father Murphy, his eyes almost starting from his head in the excess of his astonishment. "Why did you come here then?"

"To—to see Prince Ferdinand," said Clara in a faltering voice, looking down, and blushing.

Father Murphy's astonishment was now far too great for words, and he could only look at her in speechless horror as he revolved some plan in his mind for getting her quietly back to her friends.

"How wild she looks!" thought he: "she must be put in confinement; there is no saying to what lengths, so strange a delusion may carry her."

Whilst the poor father was thus cogitating and repeating to himself divers coaxing forms of words, by the help of which he hoped to persuade her to return, the automaton again stopped, and, the prison door flying open, the officer beckoned Clara to advance. She flew towards him. "Clara! Clara dear!" said Father Murphy, "had you not better go home?" But Clara heard him not; she was already in the prison; the doors had closed, and the automaton sentinel had again resumed his measured, beaten track.

"Oh dear! oh dear!" cried the unhappy Father Murphy, "what will I do? How will I get her out? Poor Sir Ambrose—he will break his heart. I dare say he knows nothing about it. These kind of fits always come on suddenly."

Thus lamenting, the worthy father walked up and down before the prison in a state of pitiable distress, till a bright thought flashed across his mind, and he set off as fast as his trembling limbs could carry him to put it in execution.

In the mean time Clara had followed the officer into the prison, and her heart beat faster as she advanced, for her undertaking now appeared to her in a new light, and she trembled as she thought of the interpretation the Prince might put upon her boldness. It was, however, too late to repent; she had not even time for hesitation. The officer is already at the door, the bolts are withdrawn, and Clara finds herself in the presence of Ferdinand. Confused and horror-struck at what she had done, she, however, scarcely knew where she was, every thing seemed to swim before her eyes, and, gasping for breath, she caught firm hold of the door-way for support.

For some moments, Ferdinand was not aware of her presence, as he sat gloomily resting his head upon his hand, his elbow supported by a table, upon which lay a variety of papers, whilst Hans, a favourite servant, who had followed him from Germany, stood beside him.

Awed by his abstraction, and abashed by the presumption she had been guilty of, in intruding, unsolicited, upon his presence, Clara still stood irresolute, fearing alike to advance or to recede, till the officer, impatient at her delay, cried, in a loud voice—

"Walk in, if you please, Ma'am, that I may re-lock the door. I shall return to let you out in an hour."

The sound of the officer's voice caught the attention of Ferdinand, and he looked towards the door-way, from the shade of which the trembling Clara was now forced to advance.

"Miss Montagu," cried Prince Ferdinand, who had seen her at one of Elvira's parties, and had thought her so pretty as to inquire her name,—"this is an unhoped-for pleasure; I did not expect this."

"I came—I came—" stammered Clara: and here she stopped short, for upon recollection she really could not tell why she did come.

"I am delighted to see you," said the prince, smiling, and taking her hand, "whatever may be the cause that has procured me this honour."

"I—I—I—had—rather—sit—down," stammered Clara, without having the least idea what she was talking about.

"Well then, we will sit down," said Ferdinand: and, gently placing her upon a chair, he drew one to her side, and again took her hand. His touch thrilled through Clara's whole frame. She felt his ardent gaze upon her face, and dreadfully agitated, fearing she knew not what, she turned away from him, and tried to withdraw her hand.

"I — I — I — believe — I must go," said she.

"So soon," cried Ferdinand, again smiling, for it was impossible to mistake the cause of her confusion. "I thought the gaoler said he should not come again for you in less than an hour."

"Did he!" repeated Clara, quite unconscious of what she said, and without daring to look at him.

"My dear Miss Montagu, will you not bestow one look upon me?" cried Ferdinand, in his most insinuating tone, sinking upon one knee before her, and gently encircling her slender waist with his arm, as he turned her towards him. Clara could not resist his imploring eyes; her heart beat, she blushed, she trembled, she looked upon the ground; when suddenly Ferdinand uttered a faint cry, and started upon his feet. Clara gazed at him with wonder, for that countenance, so lately beaming with love and tenderness, now seemed aghast with horror. She followed the direction of his eyes, and beheld in the door-way the giant form of Cheops; whilst the Mummy's appalling laugh resounded in his ears. Involuntarily Clara shuddered, and hid her face in her hands.

"By the silver bow of Isis!" cried Cheops tauntingly, "I admire your charity, Miss Montagu. Why do you hide your face? But so it is, true merit is always bashful, and the beneficent spirit that prompted Clara Montagu to visit the distressed, and even prefer a stranger to her own cousin, makes her blush to avow her goodness."

"Mercy! mercy!" cried Clara, falling at his feet. "You know my heart, and I implore your assistance."

"And you shall have it," returned Cheops. "As for you," continued he, addressing the prince; "what is your wish?"

"Deliver me from this prison, and make Clara mine, and I will be your slave."

"It is well," said the Mummy. "Clara, you must retire with me; this is no place for you. As for you, prince, Lord Maysworth and Father Murphy will be admitted to your presence in the course of a few hours, to consult with you respecting your defence. Follow their advice, and fear nothing. Rely upon me, and you shall be safe. Come, Clara! you must return to the house of your uncle. He is prepared to receive you, and will forgive your absence, as Father Murphy will, ere we reach him, have fully explained its cause: and Sir Ambrose will overlook your folly, in consideration of your youth. Adieu, Prince! we shall meet again!"

The Mummy and Clara now withdrew, leaving the prince's mind much relieved, as his confidence in his new friend was unbounded; whilst the discovery he had made of the devoted love of Clara soothed his troubled spirit, and robbed his confinement of half its bitterness.

CHAPTER XXVIII.

In the mean time, Lord Edmund's mind had been tortured by the bitterest anguish, and his agitation, added to the pain of his wounds, had produced a considerable degree of fever. The conduct of Elvira, and the anxiety she had evinced respecting the prince, seemed to confirm his worst suspicions. "O God! O God!" cried he, as he paced his prison in agony; "I could have borne any thing but this—it is too, too much. By Heaven! I could sell myself to everlasting perdition to be revenged."

As he spoke, he heard the key of his dungeon door grate in the lock, and he shuddered, for he almost fancied some hideous spectre would appear in answer to his call, and he felt indescribably relieved when he heard the gentle, insinuating tones of Father Morris. Sweet is the voice of friendship to the disappointed spirit, and soft falls the balm of consolation from those we love, upon the wounded heart. Edmund's bosom thus throbbed with transport when he saw the reverend father, and, throwing his arms round his neck, he sobbed like a child.

"My dear Edmund," said the priest, also excessively affected, for he really loved Edmund, "it breaks my heart to see you thus—cruel Elvira!"

"Oh, blame her not, father!" exclaimed Edmund; "I cannot bear that even you should blame her. She is deceived—she is under the influence of infatuation. We cannot control our hearts, you know, father."

"But that she should be capable of loving another, when your services, your devoted affection—"

"Alas! alas! father, love is not to be bought by services. All she could give she has given; I possess her friendship and esteem."

"And are you satisfied with those?"

"Satisfied! Oh heavens!"

"At any rate, I suppose you could bear to see her married to Prince Ferdinand, if you thought it would contribute to her happiness."

"Married to him!" cried Edmund, gnashing his teeth in agony—"married to him! Oh any thing but that: but I will never live to see it."

The Mummy!

"You are not likely," calmly returned the priest; "for, as the state requires a victim, and Elvira will certainly not resign her Endymion, you will doubtless be sacrificed to save him."

"Hold, hold!" cried Edmund, driven to madness by the thought; "do not dare to repeat those cursed words; I could die to serve her, but I will not be sacrificed. What! am I to be made a tool, a child, an idiot?—destined to labour for my rival, and denied even the poor satisfaction of showing the extent of my devotion? But I will not die so calmly; Elvira shall not forget me—I will see her—she shall at least know my sentiments; and if she treats me with scorn, I will die, it is true, but it shall be by my own hand, and at her feet. I will not be sacrificed—I will not steal out of life like a common criminal.—No; the world shall know my wrongs—I will be heard, I will not fall unnoticed and unknown. Take this chain, Father Morris; give it to her, and tell her I implore, by the recollection of the moment when she bestowed it upon me, that she will grant me an interview. If she refuse me—but no, no, she cannot."

Father Morris took the chain, and, promising to see the Queen, withdrew, leaving Lord Edmund in a state of indescribable agitation. He was not left long, however, to his solitary reflections, for, as he paced with hasty strides his prison, and turned as he reached the wall, the Mummy, Cheops, stood before him.

"Ah, wretch!" cried Edmund, "what brings you here? Came you to torment your victims?"

"I came to help and comfort the unfortunate," said the Mummy.

"Begone!" cried Lord Edmund, "I do not want your pity, and your proffered help I scorn."

"Spare your scorn, proud Lord," returned Cheops, "it will not aid you, though I might."

"I want no aid!" exclaimed Lord Edmund, "and, least of all, such help as you can give me. I despise alike your pity and your vengeance. Come what will, I rely upon myself. Conscious of my own integrity, I do not fear to fall, though demons should assail me. Avaunt then, fiend, for over me thou hast no power!"

Cheops burst into one of his fiendish laughs, and exclaiming, "That time will show," disappeared.

Edmund felt relieved by his absence, though, in spite of his boasted firmness, and the sovereign contempt he expressed for the Mummy, he could not prevent his mind from dwelling upon the circumstance. The appearance of Cheops, indeed, never failed to excite a deep and powerful interest in the minds of all who conversed with him, whilst his appalling laugh struck terror to the firmest breast, and even those who affected to despise his menaces could not prevent their minds from dwelling upon his words. This irresistible power had its full effect upon the mind of Edmund, and, though he endeavoured in vain to shake it off and rouse his mind to think of other things, still the gigantic Mummy seemed to stalk before him. In vain did he strive to picture to himself his interview with the Queen; the hideous features of the Mummy rose in his imagination instead of the lovely form of Elvira, till at length, fatigued and exhausted, he threw himself upon his couch: yet even in his dreams the same image haunted him, and the same words rang in his ears.

Whilst these scenes were taking place in the prison, Elvira was suffering all the torments of a burning fever; she was, indeed, seriously ill: the excessive agitation of her mind, and the horror she felt at the idea of being the murderer of Ferdinand, had overpowered her reason; and by the time Dr. Coleman arrived, (he having been sent for on the first alarm,) she was quite delirious. The thought that she alone had caused the danger of Ferdinand, occupied her mind; and, not being able to bear the idea that her folly might occasion the destruction of a human being, she raved of him incessantly, and repeatedly offered to sacrifice her life to preserve his.

Her ravings were heard by her domestics, and being neither exactly understood, nor correctly repeated, their reports, aided by the artful insinuations of Father Morris, soon produced rumours throughout the city, that the Queen was violently in love with Prince Ferdinand, and had gone mad because the law did not permit her to marry him. The effect this idea produced was prodigious; it was implicitly believed, for the lower classes are naturally fond of the marvellous, and, when there are two sides to a question, are very seldom disposed to err by judging too favourably; whilst the indignation it excited was unbounded. In some cases, men are more tenacious of their prejudices than of their rights. Thus, then, though the English, by consenting to the marriage of their Queen, had deprived themselves of the important right of electing their own Sovereign; they considered what they had done as trifling, when compared with the horror they felt at the thought of submitting to a foreign King: whilst the emissaries of Rosabella, taking advantage of this feeling, by alternately playing upon their fears, and magnifying their terrors, worked them up almost to a state of desperation.

The party of Elvira, in the mean time, was quite unable to stem the torrent opposed to it. The Queen and her father were both too ill to leave their beds, and Lord Edmund was in prison.

"What will become of us?" whispered Emma to Dr. Coleman, one day in the chamber of Elvira, when she fancied the Queen to be asleep. "To-morrow Prince Ferdinand and Lord Edmund are to be tried, and, they say, not even the Queen has power to pardon them if they are convicted."

"It is but too true," returned Dr. Coleman; "they must die, and the punishment is horrid. The criminal is doomed to be burned by a slow fire."

"Horrible!" cried Emma; "and this only for drawing a sword in the vicinity of a royal palace."

"Alas! that is not all! Ferdinand is accused of wishing to marry the Queen; and the laws that devote to a horrid death the man who shall presume to address her in the language of love, yet hold good against foreigners."

"I cannot believe Prince Ferdinand ever dared even think of the Queen," said Emma.

"God only can judge the heart," observed Dr. Coleman; "but, I am sorry to say, the proofs are very strong against him: I have heard, from undoubted authority, that persons will swear they heard him absolutely make love to the Queen; and that she promised to marry him if she could obtain the consent of her people."

"It is false!" cried Elvira, starting from her bed, and standing suddenly between them—"false as hell! Prince Ferdinand never addressed a single syllable breathing of love to me in his existence. He is the victim of a mistake, or rather of my folly; but he shall not die—I will save him, or perish in the attempt!"

The calm, decided tone in which Elvira spoke, and her spectral appearance, produced an almost magical effect upon her auditors, and they stood awestruck and aghast, whilst Elvira continued:—

"Dress me, Emma; I will see my people; I will appeal to them myself. It is the day for receiving petitions in Blackheath Square: there will be a multitude assembled. I will go there in person, and address them."

"It is the raving of delirium," whispered Emma to Dr. Coleman; "what shall I do?"

"Do you dare to hesitate?" said Elvira, whose sense of hearing, sharpened by her recent illness, enabled her to catch distinctly the words of her favourite.

"Humour her," returned Dr. Coleman; "in her present state, opposition would be fatal."

"It would indeed be fatal," said Elvira, seating herself in a large arm-chair, whilst the temporary colour her previous exertion had given her, faded from her cheeks, and she looked the image of death.

"She will faint!" cried Emma, flying for aid.

"It is impossible for her to go in this state!" said the doctor.

"Impossible!" cried Elvira, starting up wildly, and her cheeks again glowing with the deepest crimson, whilst her eyes sparkled with superhuman fire; "what is impossible to a determined spirit? Haste! haste! Emma, and let me go, whilst I have yet strength; for go I will, though death await me there. My rashness has endangered the life of Prince Ferdinand, and I will die to save him!"

Farther opposition was useless, and the doctor retiring, Emma hastily attired her mistress. The people were expected to assemble as usual in the Square, though, from the illness of the Queen, a deputation of nobles had been appointed to receive the petitions. The feelings of Elvira were wrought up to an unnatural energy: every limb trembled with agitation, and every nerve thrilled with impatience, whilst she was dressing; and when she was ready, she descended the staircase, leaning upon the arm of Emma, her cheeks flushed with a hectic glow, her lips quivering, and her eyes shining with unusual brightness.

At the foot of the staircase they met Cheops. He stedfastly regarded the Queen, and smiled at her agitated appearance with his usual calm scorn.

"Oh!" cried Elvira, the moment she beheld him, "my pride is

The Mummy!

humbled. I own I love Seymour. Aid me to save Ferdinand, and I am thy slave."

"Appeal to your people," said Cheops, his eyes flashing with proud triumph; "your feelings will give you eloquence. But do not confine yourself to obtaining the power to pardon Ferdinand. Demand to be free; the people will refuse you nothing. Tell them, first, that they have insulted you by giving you permission to marry, and then dictating whom you shall choose. Require perfect freedom. They will comply, and bow their necks beneath your footstool. But rest not satisfied with any thing short of actual submission. Endure no conditions. This is the moment to decide your future destiny. Act with energy, and you will be happy. But if you falter, destruction is your portion."

"I will obey you to the letter," said Elvira, as she walked with a firm step past him, and sprang into her balloon, followed by Emma.

"Oh, my dear, dear mistress!" said that faithful confidant, "do not listen to that wretch; he is a serpent sent to wile you to destruction. Do be advised; do return and relinquish this mad enterprize."

Elvira did not reply. Her feelings were too highly wrought to permit her to speak, and bending eagerly forward, she watched, with an impatient eye, the streets and houses they flitted over, scarcely able to bear the agony of suspense during the time necessarily lost in the transit, and seeming every instant to long to precipitate herself forward to the goal of her wishes.

The balloon now rose unusually high, whilst masses of fleecy clouds hid the town from their view, and looked like flocks of sheep beneath their feet.

"We are going wrong!" cried Elvira, in agony; "we shall be too late."

"No, no," said Emma, "I feel we descend again—we are arrived."

And as she spoke, the balloon sank rapidly, whilst the clouds opening, discovered the immense Square below them, apparently paved with human heads.

"Thank God! we are not too late!" cried Elvira, clasping her hands together, and sinking back upon her seat; whilst the balloon-conductor directed the machine to the palace usually appointed for the reception of the Queen. Elvira did not wait to arrange her dress; she did not wait to take refreshment, or even to rest a single moment from her fatigue, but she rushed upon the terrace the instant she quitted the balloon, and presented herself before her astonished people, every limb quivering from the violence of her agitation.

The crowd was immense. The extensive space looked one compact mass of human heads; but Elvira's courage did not fail her. Though she had now no Lord Edmund to support her, and no father or applauding friends to listen as she spoke, yet the enthusiasm of the moment gave her strength. She forgot every thing but the cause that brought her there; and her mind, thrown back upon its own resources, rallied its energies, and seemed to gather courage from the thought; whilst her sylphic figure appeared to dilate in size, and assume an almost awful dignity from the grandeur of the spirit that animated it, as she thus stood before her subjects, her life or death hanging upon their will.

Her arrival had been hailed by the loudest shouts of wonder and of joy; but when the multitude saw she wished to address them, the tumult was hushed, and they waited in breathless silence for her speech. The deep stillness that prevailed amongst this so lately bustling crowd of human beings, and the thought that every ear and every eye were turned towards her, slightly affected the nerves of Elvira, and her lips trembled as she began to speak; but as she became warmed with her subject, her voice gradually assumed its natural depth, melody, and sweetness; whilst its full tones sank deep into the hearts of her auditors, and carried conviction as she went on.

She first appealed to their gratitude; and, after alluding to all she had done to secure peace and plenty to their domestic firesides, she reverted to the misery of her own situation, before the laws had been revoked that had condemned her to celibacy. She powerfully painted the harshness of the destiny that debarred her from the blessings she had so lavishly bestowed upon others. She alone, of all her subjects, had been destined to the wretchedness of a solitary life, unsoothed by the tender cares of a husband, uncheered by the affection of children. She alone had been doomed to wither away her youth in cheerless widowhood. Their fiat had changed her destiny; but was it the part of a noble and generous people, whilst they conferred a benefit to encumber it with restrictions? No; she was confident the liberal spirit of the English would spurn the sordid thought,

The Mummy!

and shrink from such a manner of obliging. "Make me free!" said she, "really, absolutely free, and I promise solemnly you shall never have occasion to blush for your Queen."

As she spoke, her cheeks glowed, and her eyes sparkled with unwonted fire; whilst the people, struck by the suddenness of her appearance, and her enthusiasm, and carried away by the force of the sentiment that could metamorphose the tender, gentle Elvira into the exalted being before them, shouted applause; whilst cries rang loudly through the air of "Long live Elvira!" "Marry whom you list, we shall still be your slaves! Still be our Queen, and let your children and children's children reign over us, when you shall be no more."

Delight danced in the bright eyes of Elvira, and a blush of pleasure mantled on her cheek, as she gracefully thanked them. "And yet, my friends," continued she, in a fainter voice, "there is another privilege I would demand at your hands. I am called free and absolute, yet I am chained by the laws. Unloose these bands; give me at least the power to pardon. I know, that if I wished it, I might reverse these laws at my will, as the power of the Queen that made them was not greater than that which you have bestowed upon me. But I wish not to do so: I would rather accept that from your hands as a favour which I might exact as a right. Give me then, my people, the most blessed attribute of royalty. Let me pardon. Can you refuse me this?"

"No, no!" shouted the people with enthusiasm; "we are your slaves! Do with us as you list. The laws are yours; and though you change them at your pleasure, we will obey! Long live Elvira! Elvira for ever! From henceforth we own no law but her will!"

Elvira's rapture was unbounded; she forgot the unstable nature of the vox populi, and triumphed in the devotion of her people; whilst they, in return, shouted forth her praise, as she warmly expressed her gratitude, in tumultuous transports. The air rang with acclamations; and Elvira, looking proudly round upon her obsequious subjects, felt herself indeed a Queen. There is perhaps no sensation in the world more delightful than thus to feel oneself the idol of the multitude, to see every eye beaming with admiration, to hear every voice resounding praise, and to know every heart is devoted to one object. The human mind cannot enjoy a higher gratification than in the consciousness of power; whilst the man thus exalted, seems raised to the level of a divinity, and triumphs in the worship of his fellow-creatures: but, alas! such glory is too much for mortals, and nothing can be more evanescent, or rather, nothing a more certain prelude to disgrace.

Elvira, however, knew not that her popularity was too great to be lasting. She implicitly believed her people would continue to feel what they now expressed, and, catching the spirit of the moment, she persuaded them to sign an abolition of the laws, and a confirmation of her absolute power. The people obeyed with rapture; the enthusiasm that animated them had not yet abated; and even if Elvira had desired their lives, they would have obeyed. They considered her inspired, and it seemed sacrilege even to hesitate to comply with her commands.

So powerful was the energy of a woman's will, and so sure it is that a determined spirit may overcome any difficulties when once roused resolutely to exert itself. Such also is the influence of beauty and eloquence upon the human mind, and so weak is judgment when attacked through the medium of the senses.

In the mean time, the council of Elvira had met in their usual apartment, and were holding a solemn consultation, previous to going to receive the petitions, on the propriety of addressing the people whom they might find assembled in the Square, respecting the illness and consequent incapacity for reigning of the Queen.

"Thinking as I think, and as I am confident every one here must think," said Lord Gustavus de Montfort, "there is no middle course to be pursued: a regency must be appointed, or the government will be overturned."

"Oh! there is no doubt, we cannot exist without a regency," said Lord Noodle.

"Yes, yes! we must have a regency!" cried Lord Doodle.

"It appears to me, to say the least of it, premature," observed the Duke of Essex, a highly respectable nobleman, who had hitherto observed a cautious neutrality; "I think, before deciding upon so important a question, we should at least examine her Majesty's physicians, and be guided by their report."

"His Grace is quite right," said Lord Noodle.

"We ought to examine the physicians," said Lord Doodle.

"One of them has just entered the council-chamber," observed Lord Gustavus; "I presume he brings the usual daily bulletin of her Majesty's health: is it your pleasure, my lords, that he be examined?"

"By all means!" cried all the noble lords simultaneously, and Dr. Hardman advanced.

"How is her most gracious Majesty?" asked Lord Gustavus, with his usual solemnity.

"Alas! my lord," said Dr. Hardman, "her Majesty has slept badly, and is much worse this morning."

"Is she still delirious?" asked the Duke of Essex.

"Quite, your Grace," returned the doctor, shaking his head.

"Then I fear there is no hope?" said the duke.

"None!" said Lord Noodle, shaking his head.

"None!" echoed Lord Doodle, shaking his.

"Thinking as I think, and as I am sure every one here must think," said Lord Gustavus, "we must not suffer the interests of the people to be invaded with impunity. The constitution requires watching over, and I consider this a matter that ought to be inquired into."

"Then you think the senses of the Queen irrecoverable?" asked the Duke of Essex, addressing Dr. Hardman.

"Not irrecoverable, I hope, my lord duke," replied the doctor; "though I own her delirium is alarming."

"What does she rave about," asked Lord Doodle; curiosity being the only mark he ever gave of his being a rational animal.

"It is a delicate subject," returned the doctor; "and if your lordships will excuse me—"

"Oh, no! you must tell us," said Lord Doodle.

"Thinking as I think, and as I am sure every one else ought to think," said Lord Gustavus; "concealment in this case would be a crime."

"Since your lordships command me," replied the doctor, "however reluctant I may be to betray her Majesty's secrets, it is my duty to obey. The Queen raves incessantly of Prince

Ferdinand."

"I feared as much," said the Duke of Essex.

"And do you think if she recovers she'll want to marry him?" asked Lord Doodle.

"I fear it cannot be doubted, my Lord:" returned the doctor.

"Then, thinking as I think, and as every free-born Englishman ought to think," said Lord Gustavus, "she will forfeit her crown."

A deep silence followed this daring speech, yet, though no one assented to it, no one attempted to contradict it. In fact, every man seemed afraid of committing himself; for, though every one thought Lord Gustavus would not have ventured so far, had he not felt assured the party against the Queen was strong, yet no one liked to be the first to declare himself her opponent. This awkward pause was broken by the entrance of Sir Ambrose and Father Morris, who came with a message from the Duke of Cornwall, imploring them not to decide upon any measure hastily, and informing them that on the following day his physicians assured him he would be able to assist their deliberations in person.

"We all esteem and respect the duke," said Lord Gustavus. "But, thinking as I think, and as I am confident every one who hears me must think, not even our respect for him ought to induce us to consent that the Queen should marry a foreigner! No, no, we must not let private feelings make us risk the interests of the people."

"I dare say they will not be in any danger," murmured the soft, insinuating voice of Father Morris—"I dare say they will run no risk. Foreigners have sometimes been known to respect the interests of a people, and reign as gloriously as native-born monarchs."

"Not often, I believe, father," said Sir Ambrose. "At any rate, I am sure it would break the duke's heart to see his daughter married to Prince Ferdinand, and I am sure it would break mine to see him King of England. Weak, silly Elvira! I cannot account for her infatuation; and I have no patience with her, for causing all this misery solely by her folly."

"You use strong language, Sir Ambrose," said the Duke of Essex.

"Not stronger than the occasion requires, my lord duke," returned the worthy baronet. "I have known the Queen from her childhood, and loved her as a daughter; but now—"

"The matter must certainly be inquired into," said Lord Gustavus. "It is the duty of every well-disposed patriotic Englishman not to suffer the slightest invasion of the constitution. Our laws are our bulwarks; we ought to die to defend our laws; and if the Queen be no longer in a fit state to administer them, or if she even contemplate the design of putting the administration of them into hands in which their purity will be contaminated, then, thinking as I think, and as I feel confident every individual who hears me must think, or, at least, ought to think, there can remain only one course for us to pursue."

"Perhaps," said Father Morris, "we may be deceived, and the delirium of the Queen may be transient, or, at least, her mentioning the name of Prince Ferdinand in her ravings quite accidental. It is not well to be too rash—"

"Oh, no, reverend father," replied Lord Gustavus; "you deceive yourself. Your abstraction from the world, and the goodness of your heart, lead you to judge too favourably of others. But we, who know the world, see deeper. You, holy father, can form no idea of the folly of human passions; you are above their weaknesses, and cannot suspect that in another which you are incapable of feeling yourself: but, as I said before, we, that know the world, see deeper. Elvira is in love with Prince Ferdinand, and is quite capable of sacrificing her throne and people to the caprices of a romantic passion."

"Impossible!" cried Father Morris, with well-acted astonishment.

"Is is very true, notwithstanding," said Lord Gustavus, shaking his head sagaciously; whilst his attendant satellites, the Lords Noodle and Doodle, shook theirs for sympathy.

"Impossible!" cried Sir Ambrose; "she cannot surely carry her infatuation to such a height: she is too noble: but even if she be so mad, will no one step forward and save her from destruction?"

"I do not see how any one can save her, if such be her intentions," said the Duke of Essex. "Women are proverbially self-willed; and, now that the people have put the laws into her own hands—"

"The people were cajoled into consent," exclaimed Lord Gustavus; "but if the Queen be so mad as to intend to marry the prince, she must lose her throne and suffer death, for the laws against foreigners remain inexorable."

"Yes, the laws are inexorable!" echoed the Lords Noodle and Doodle.

"Good Heaven!" cried Sir Ambrose, "is it possible I am in England, and yet hear such barbarous sentiments openly avowed? No one has more right to feel anger at the folly of Elvira than myself; but even I cannot bear such cruelty. What! is a young and beautiful woman, in the very flower of her age, to be doomed to destruction, merely for having shown a susceptible heart? Forbid it, Heaven! And what are we that we should dare to judge so harshly and refuse mercy to a fellow-creature? Are we not all feeble? Do we not all err? And if we show such cruelty in judging such a trifling offence, how shall we expect mercy for our own more weighty ones? Have mercy, then. Let us show ourselves men! Let us dare to exert our reason and throw off the shackles of prejudice. We boast that the law in this case makes us free, and arms us with power against our Sovereign. Let us use that power, then, and show that we are really free by daring to act justly. If we do not, we are slaves!"

"It cannot be," said Lord Gustavus; "you talk well, Sir Ambrose, but words are nothing against facts. If the Queen intend to marry Prince Ferdinand, she must either be insane or intend to subvert the constitution; and, in either case, thinking as I think, and as I am sure every reasonable person in the kingdom must think, she is no longer competent to reign, and is no longer worthy to live. Eloquence is a fine thing, and I do not deny that the worthy baronet speaks fluently; yet, notwithstanding all he can say, or indeed all that can be said, upon the subject, law is law."

"Yes, law is law!" echoed the repeating lords.

"Sir Ambrose, I thank you from my soul!" cried the old Duke of Cornwall, starting from the midst of the crowd. "You have, indeed, proved yourself my friend; but I should blush to think that my daughter was slandered in my presence, and that I left it to another to undertake her defence. Yes, gentlemen, Elvira is slandered—I will venture my life upon her innocence. Her heart is English, my lords, thoroughly English; she will marry no German; no—no, my poor, dear Elvira never dreamed of such a thing; she is innocent." And here the poor old man, overpowered by his emotions, could not proceed, but, leaning

The Mummy!

upon the shoulder of his friend Sir Ambrose, wept bitterly. It is hard to see the tears of aged men; and every one was affected: they had started at the sudden appearance of the duke amongst them; for his gaunt looks and wasted form, aided by the belief of his serious illness, gave him more the aspect of a spectre than a man: and now his trembling voice, and grey hairs, as he attempted to vindicate his child, came home to the hearts of his auditors.

"Alas! why is not Edmund here?" sighed Sir Ambrose; "he would not have left the cause of Elvira to such feeble hands. But he is gone, and, wretched father that I am! I may soon no longer possess my darling boy. Six months ago, two brave sons were the pride of my heart, and the admiration of every eye. Where are they now? the one wandering in foreign climes, exposed to every misery of want, and the other confined in a prison and doomed to suffer an ignominious death. Alas! alas! why has my life been spared to endure such misery?"

Whilst the old man thus lamented, a bustle was heard amongst the crowd, and the noble lords of whom it was composed, dividing, made way for Elvira! With glowing cheeks and sparkling eyes, the Queen walked proudly along the lane made for her, having a roll of parchment in her hand, and with dignity took her seat upon the vacant throne. A solemn silence prevailed: the conspirators were awed by the sudden appearance of their Sovereign; and those who had hitherto remained neutral, surprised, stood hesitating, unknowing how to act. Elvira paused a few seconds, sternly surveying the crowd, and finding that no one attempted to speak, she exclaimed, "How now, my Lords? what means this silence? I came to assist your councils, not to interrupt them. Go on, I pray you; for surely such enlightened senators can have no sentiments they fear to breathe before their Queen."

"We were surprised at the sudden appearance of your Majesty," said the Duke of Essex, "as, from the report of your Majesty's physicians, we had feared your Majesty's illness—"

"My illness was of the mind, my Lord Duke!" said Elvira, "and this is the medicine that has cured it. Look, my lords," continued she, unrolling the parchment she carried, and suddenly flashing it before their eyes—"behold my panacea! Now I am, indeed, a Queen; for my people have made me absolute, and, abolishing all laws, have placed their lives and fortunes at my feet."

Lord Gustavus and his adherents stood aghast, gazing upon

the Queen and the parchment she held so triumphantly, without the power of uttering a word.

"Ere this," continued the Queen, "the purport of this parchment has received some thousand signatures; yet I do not wish to abuse my power. Go, my lords; I have no longer occasion for your counsels; when I have, I will summon you."

The dignified manner in which Elvira waved her hand as she said this, prevented reply; and the lords of the council dispersed, without daring to utter a single syllable. The duke and Sir Ambrose alone remained. "My dear father," cried Elvira, throwing her arms round his neck, whilst the overstrained feelings that had so long supported her gave way, and she sobbed in agony upon his shoulder.

"Remove her to her chamber," said Dr. Coleman, who now appeared; "this agitation will destroy her—her exhausted frame is not able to endure it."

In fact, the Queen was now completely overpowered, and was carried off by Emma and her attendants in violent hysterics.

Lord Maysworth had not been present at this scene, for his time had been otherwise engaged; and, to explain what occupied him, it will be necessary to go back to the prison of Prince Ferdinand. It may be recollected, when Cheops removed Clara, he had informed the prince that Lord Maysworth and Father Murphy would be with him in a few hours. The Mummy's information was correct, for at the appointed time they came.

"Och!" said Father Murphy, "and where's Clara? So they've let me in after all, ye see; for, knowing Lord Maysworth was your friend, I went to consult him, and he talked to them and tould them how barbarous it was to deny a poor fellow that was just going to be burnt alive, the consolations of religion;—they hadn't the heart to refuse me."

"Oh!" groaned Prince Ferdinand; "is there no hope of escape?"

"I fear not," said Lord Maysworth; "for, notwithstanding the enormous expense attending public executions, the people are so fond of them, that it is necessary to indulge them now and then; and they are so devoted to Lord Edmund that his adversary has no chance. Besides, they say there are plenty of witnesses to prove that you have addressed the most impassioned language to the Queen; your enthusiasm one night at her singing—"

"I remember," cried Prince Ferdinand; "idiot that I was—oh! curses on my folly."

"Ah, that's right," exclaimed Father Murphy; "indulge yerself a little, my honey, and it will do ye good. I don't know a prettier amusement than cursing and swearing, and finding fault when one's in trouble; and I'd be far from denying ye a little harmless indulgence; for, as ye're to die so soon, it would be cruel, ye know, not to let ye have all the consolation ye can get hold of."

"Oh!" exclaimed Prince Ferdinand, "I am the most wretched of human beings."

"And ye may say that, for I don't see any great hope ye have, in respect that the people must have a victim, and they'd like you better than Lord Edmund. But never mind that, for the worst that can happen at all, is that ye'll be roasted alive!"

"Oh!" groaned Prince Ferdinand, not much consoled by this encouraging speech.

"Wehe mir!" exclaimed Hans; "and can nothing be done?—for though roasting alive may be the worst that can happen, I don't think my master such an amateur in cookery as to wish to try the experiment."

"Och!" cried Father Murphy, "and I'm quite of your opinion; and so, if the prince would just try, and get ready a word or two of defence—or if some clever person that knows the world like yere lordship, for instance, would just give him a word or two of advice—the thing would be entirely done, and all right."

"Oh!" cried the prince, clasping his hands together, "save me! I implore you to save me!"

"I will do all I can," said Lord Maysworth, smiling most graciously; "rely upon me, prince; the suggestion of the holy father shall be attended to. The gratitude I owe your father, demands my greatest exertions—and I am most happy to have an opportunity of serving his son. This worthy father's plan is excellent: I wonder it did not strike me before. Confide securely in me, prince; a proper defence shall be prepared, and I think by it you may escape."

So saying he retired, leaving Prince Ferdinand somewhat

consoled by his assurances, but by no means reconciled even to the possibility of being roasted alive. The intermediate time between this conversation and the day fixed for the trial of the prince, was spent by Lord Maysworth in preparing, with the assistance of those "learned in the law," this defence: and when it was finished, his rapture was beyond description. Three times did he read it over with still increasing satisfaction, for, as he considered it as his own production, he regarded it with all the true, yet indescribable rapture of a doting parent. We are all so fond of our own children, whether of the mind or of the body, regarding them as emanations from ourselves, upon which we may indulge our self-love without the grossness of undisguised vanity, that the transport of Lord Maysworth is not surprising; though he actually carried it so far, that, notwithstanding his professed attachment and gratitude to the German Emperor, I believe if the means of procuring the prince's escape had been offered to him, he would rather have let him stay at the risk of being burned alive, than have lost the pleasure he anticipated on hearing the delivery of his speech.

The important day arrived, and the prince, accompanied by his faithful Hans and Lord Maysworth, proceeded to the court; the latter carrying his beloved brief in his own pocket, rightly considering it far too estimable to be entrusted into any other hands than his.

The court was crowded to an excess—for strange tales of the passion and illness of the Queen had gone forth into the world, each edition more wonderful than that which went before it, and the people now thronged to see the prince with that extraordinary feeling, so common amongst the English, which makes them stare at a great man in much the same way as they would at a wild beast.

An automaton judge sat with great dignity upon a magnificent throne, looking, though a little heavy, quite as wise and sagacious as judges are wont to look. A real jury (that is, a jury of flesh and blood,) was ranged upon one side of him, and some automaton counsel sate in front, their briefs lying upon the table before them, and having behind each a clerk ready to wind him up when he should be wanted to speak; it being found that the profession of the law gives such an amazing volubility of words, that it was dangerous to wind up the counsel too soon, lest they should go off in the wrong place, and so disturb the silence of the court. In different parts of these counsel were holes, into which briefs being put they were gradually ground to pieces as the counsel were being wound up, till they came forth in words at the mouth: whilst the language in which the counsel pleaded, depended entirely upon the hole into which the brief was put, there being a different one for every possible tongue.

All now was ready; the prisoner with his friends placed themselves at the bar, and the judge and jury prepared to hear and decide with all due decorum. The signal to begin was given, and the brief for the crown being put into the English department of the counsel appointed to conduct the prosecution, the clerk began to wind away, and in a few minutes the counsel burst forth in the following impassioned strain of eloquence:—

"My Lord, and Gentlemen of the Jury,

"It is with feelings of the most unfeigned regret that I now rise to address you. Sensible—oh! how deeply sensible, of my insufficiency! and of the much greater competency of any one of my learned brethren at the bar; how willingly would I resign the task to any one of those eloquent gentlemen, feeling so indisputably convinced as I do, of their eminent talents and of their merit; and of their great, oh! how much greater fitness for an undertaking of this magnitude than myself!"

"Ach! Es ist aus mit uns! wir sind verlohren!" cried Hans; "if thou art so unfit for the task, I wonder why the deuce they employed thee!"

"Peace, fool!" said the prince; "do you not see that this is only the exordium—these are words of course."

The orator had paused for an instant from some error of his machinery; but his clerk setting him in motion again, he went on as follows:—

"But having being deputed to act, I will not shrink from the arduous duty imposed upon me; I will, therefore, state the principal points of the case; prove my facts by witnesses; and then leave the decision to the well-known judgment and penetration of the enlightened and intelligent tribunal before me!"

It was here intended the counsel should bow to the court, but, owing to his defective machinery, he only gave a kind of jerk, and then continued:—

"My Lord, and Gentlemen,

The Mummy!

"It sometimes falls to the lot of members of my profession to relate astounding circumstances and soul-harrowing facts!—facts that pierce into the inmost souls of their auditors, and rend their tortured spirits by their iron fangs! as the teeth of the tangible harrow pierce into and rend asunder the clods of inanimate earth over which it is dragged! But what I shall have to tell you, gentlemen, will make even facts like these hide their diminished heads, and run skulking into corners like owls trembling, and flying hooting away on being exposed to the scorching glare of the noon-day sun.

"Do you not tremble, gentlemen?—do not your hearts pant in breathless expectation of what is coming? Indulge your anticipations—bid fancy take her wildest flight, and let imagination conjure up all the horrors of the infernal regions. Paint the angel of death hovering upon leathern wings over a devoted city—and shrieking mothers imploring mercy in vain for their murdered children! Paint all the multiplied horrors of famine, fire, and carnage!—paint miserable starving wretches screaming wildly for food, and, in the agonies of despair gnawing the flesh from their own withering bones!—Paint flames surrounding with their pointed arms an helpless family crying in bitter anguish for the aid that cannot be afforded them!—paint witches celebrating their detested sabaoth! Imagine demons indulging in their infernal revels! Yes, paint and picture to yourself all these, and ten thousand other horrors, each more frightful than the last;—dwell upon them—let them haunt your imaginations; but whatever you may fancy, picture, or paint, nothing can ever equal the horror you will feel when you learn the crime of which the prisoner at the bar stands accused. Know then—my tongue falters as I speak, and my quivering lips almost refuse to give utterance to the appalling sounds—know that he has dared, impiously and presumptuously dared, to fall in love with the Queen!

"I see your indignation at such baseness—I feel the virtuous shame that burns upon every cheek—yes, yes, my friends, I too am an Englishman, and I, like you, spurn with disdain the thought of submitting to a stranger. What do we want with a King? Has not the country been happy, prosperous, flourishing—respected at home, and honoured abroad, under the dominion of a Queen?—Yes, yes, my friends, it has, and, under her gentle sway, the murderous weapon of war has been converted into a ploughshare; the nodding helmet and ponderous corslet into the peaceful wig and graceful gown; and the grim aspect of frowning ruin and grinning desolation into the gentle smiles of benignant peace and overwhelming plenty. Long, long may gentle peace continue to shed her benignant

The Mummy!

smiles upon us.—Long, long may we sit beneath the grateful shade of her olive branches; and long, long may their feathery foliage hang in graceful festoons above our heads, and their pale green wreaths encircle our brows; for in the arms of peace lie joy, ease, and happiness—her smile gives health and contentment, and her blessing wealth.

"And what threatens to affright this bewitching deity from our shores? 'Tis this audacious stranger, who deserves the bitterest punishment for his unparalleled atrocity. But this is not all;—not satisfied with endeavouring to destroy the happiness of the Queendom, and overturn the laws enacted by the wisdom of our ancestors, he has done more: yes, intolerable as his crimes have been, there is still one more deadly behind. Shudder, my friends, and turn away your eyes as the fear-inspiring words drop from my tongue.—He has dared to draw arms within the precincts of the reginal palace.

"Insufferable audacity! Hear this, ye shades of former royalty, and tremble in your Elysian groves, at the profane hand that has dared thus to invade your august privileges. Can it be believed? Will after-ages credit the report? Oh no, no! the fact will appear too monstrous for even credulity itself to swallow!

"When the crime, the fatal crime was committed, earth trembled beneath his feet: the winds hushed their murmurs, and all nature stood aghast. The frightened ocean receded from its rocky bed. Pluto rushed shivering from his nether throne, and Neptune waved in vain his tranquillizing trident. The elements were convulsed; lightning streamed from the swords of the combatants, and thunder rolled above their heads as they stood like two heroes of Arabian fiction wielding the elements in their wrath!

"But I have done, my lord and gentlemen. I say no more; for I scorn to prejudice your minds against the prisoner, or make the slightest appeal to your feelings to condemn him. However, this I must say, that if ever a case could rouse every nerve of a true-born Englishman against it, it is this. Does any man dread to be torn from the calm delights of his comfortable fireside, where he was surrounded by his adoring wife and attentive children, and doomed to incur all the wretchedness of misery and want?—let him condemn the prisoner. Does any man dread being dragged across burning sands, or forced to wade up to the knees in water through marshy deserts?—let him condemn the prisoner. Would any man shudder to be obliged to sleep upon the hard cold ground, his limbs racked with rheumatism, and his body exposed to all the vicissitudes of hunger, thirst, and inclement seasons, whilst his life is endangered every instant? — let him condemn the prisoner; — but if he prefer these horrors to the comforts of a warm down bed, or if he enjoy the prospect of having his substance devoured by tax gatherers, to support the expenses of a foreign war, then let the prisoner be acquitted. But — unless — he — can — make — up — his — mind to — undergo — privations — like — these — let — him — aid — by — his — vote — to condemn — the — wretch — who — "

And here the orator stopt abruptly, being quite gone down. He had indeed uttered the last words gradually slower and slower, and at lengthened intervals, because the attendant clerk had unfortunately given him a turn too little, and had not screwed him up quite tight enough. The witnesses were now called. Several spoke to the circumstance of the extravagant admiration expressed by the prince of Elvira's singing; others deposed to the fact of the combat, and others mentioned the Queen's sighing and abstraction; but the principal one distinctly stated, that he had heard the prince make the Queen an offer of his hand in the gardens of the Somerset House, and that she had consented to marry him if she could obtain the consent of her people. A general thrill of indignation ran through the Court at this evidence, and it was with difficulty that silence was obtained for the pleading of the defendant. At last all was still, and the attendant clerk began to wind up the counsel for the prince. Lord Maysworth watched the moment; but being afraid to trust his beloved brief into any hands but his own, unfortunately in his agitation, he popt it into the wrong hole, and when the counsel began to speak, he burst forth in French! Words are wanting to express Lord Maysworth's unutterable consternation at this unfortunate accident.

"Stop! stop!" cried he, "Hush! hush! Can nobody stop him?" but the inexorable counsel would not stop: — for once wound up, and properly set in motion, not all the powers of Heaven and earth combined could stop him till he had fairly run down.

"What shall I do?" cried Lord Maysworth, in an agony of despair; "for, if the judge and jury don't understand French, my fine oration will be utterly lost."

"Oh, if that be all," said the clerk, "your lordship need not distress yourself, for as soon as I found what was going on, I ran up to the judge and pulled out his lordship's French stop!"

"And the gentlemen of the jury?"

"O, they all understand French."

The Mummy!

"It is well," said Lord Maysworth, "though I am still sorry the hole happened to be French, as I am afraid the verbosity of the language may deteriorate the strength of my expressions."

Thus muttered the noble lord, not sorry, however, I believe, if the whole truth were to be openly declared, that he had an excuse in the change of languages for the failure of his speech, if it should not happen to meet with that brilliant success that he felt so perfectly confident it deserved.

The counsel, in the mean time, went on. The following is a translation of his speech:—

"My lord, and gentlemen of the jury.

"It is with feelings of considerable diffidence and hesitation, that I rise to address you, after the flood of eloquence that has poured from my learned brother. I, gentlemen, am not gifted with such an enviable facility of speech; nor is my imagination endowed with that creative power he has so forcibly displayed. I cannot, gentlemen, like him

Uprear the club of Hercules—For what?

To crush a butterfly, or brain a gnat.

Nor have I the least intention of drawing either Neptune or Pluto from the quiet nap they have been taking for so many centuries—to assist in our debate. I assure you, also, gentlemen, that I shall neither disturb the ocean from its rocky bed, nor make Nature stand aghast.—No, my lord and gentlemen, my intentions are perfectly pacific, and your harassed imaginations may repose tranquilly upon my speech, after the tumultuous one of my learned brother, as the way-worn traveller rests peaceably upon the soft green turf, after having been tossed about upon the heaving billows of the tempestuous ocean.

'Tis sweet to rest from dread of danger free,

And mark the billows of the foaming sea;

'Tis sweet, a little skiff to safely urge

Through the tempestuous ocean's boiling surge;

To hear the pattering rains against the roof,

And feel your hospitable mansion proof.

But sweeter far the troubled mind's repose

When of a speech like this, it hears the close.

When I listened to the powerful exordium of my learned friend—and I did listen to him with the most profound attention—I confess my imagination was too highly excited to be satisfied with so lame and impotent a conclusion.—'What!' cried I, 'have the laws of nature been reversed—have demons been disturbed in their infernal revels, and witches called from their dusky caverns, merely because a beautiful woman has excited a tender passion in the breast of a youthful stranger? Is this so extraordinary an occurrence that it should create such excessive wonder? Are our hearts so dead to beauty that such a catastrophe should occasion surprise? Forbid it, Heaven! No! whilst our hearts still throb in our bosoms, may they ever beat responsive to the attractions of the fair! May we never become insensible to the charms of the loveliest objects of creation! May we ever own their witchery, and bend beneath their magic sway! Or man, degraded man! would soon sink below the level of the brutes. View man as he degenerates when secluded from the influence of female society;—is he not rough, brutal, and unpolished? Does he not want all those winning graces and those delicate attentions that form so undeniably the charm and solace of life? In proportion as our sensibility, as our goodness, and all the best feelings of our nature are awakened, we become susceptible of love. It is indeed, excessive sensibility, and a kindly feeling to our fellow-creatures, that creates it. Does there exist a generous or noble mind that has not felt this passion? No, not one! there is, indeed, something generous and ennobling in it. We cannot prefer the welfare of another to our own, nor be completely absorbed in another's being, with the devotedness of true love, without becoming purified in our ideas, and raised from that disgusting selfishness which is ever the inspirer of base and mean actions.

Yes, love indeed is light from Heaven,

A spark of that immortal fire,

With angels shared, by Alla given,

To lift from earth our low desire.

Devotion wafts the mind above,

But Heaven itself descends in love.

And from this heavenly, this inspiring feeling, shall my unfortunate client be debarred? Hear me, ye shades of heroic lovers, who, though dying for the hopeless object of your passion, have still exclaimed, with the enthusiastic devotion of a

The Mummy!

modern poet—

> Lead on, lead on, though horrors wait
>
> In awful fury round thy gate!
>
> And danger, death, and grim despair,
>
> Forbid my hopeless passage there!
>
> If love, still smiling, beckon on,
>
> The path is passed, the gate is won!

And ye poets and philosophers, who have painted love as the oasis of the Desert, the green spot in memory's waste, where affection still lingers even when hope decays; have you no compassion for my unhappy client, whose only fault was 'that she was beautiful, and he not blind?' And is this an offence for which a man deserves to be burnt alive? Forbid it, humanity! forbid it, mercy! No, no! such inhuman cruelty exists not in the breasts of Englishmen. I know, I feel that you must acquit my client on this head. But this is not the only charge brought against him; he is accused of having violated the sanctity of a royal palace, by drawing his sword within its precincts. To describe the enormity of this crime, my learned friend has brought forward such an overwhelming torrent of eloquence, that unhappily his meaning was swept away in the current of his words. At least I suppose so, as, with all my industry, I have been totally unable to find it. As, however, I cannot imagine my learned friend could have harangued so long without having some meaning in what he said, I suppose it has slipped undiscovered into some sly corner, where it lies, poor thing! quite concealed, and almost crushed to death by the ponderous weight of metaphors heaped upon it. Gentlemen, my client drew his sword in the Royal Garden. This is the plain statement of the fact, when stripped of the load of ornaments with which my learned friend has encumbered it. My client, a stranger to the English laws and customs, chanced to be walking in the public garden belonging to a Royal palace. He there met a noblemen of the court; from causes irrelevant to the question before us, high words took place between them. My client was grossly insulted in a manner impossible to be borne by a man calling himself a gentleman, or making the least pretensions to honour. He drew his sword to defend himself. Can any thing be more simple? And yet for this, all created nature is thrown into confusion, and Neptune and Pluto called shivering from their beds. Gentlemen, my learned friend's brain was teeming with a monstrous conception, and longing to be delivered; he dragged it into the speech with which we have just been favoured. Not satisfied with piercing us through with the fangs of a mental arrow; plunging us into all the disasters of war, and distracting our imaginations by exhibiting the combined effects of plague, pestilence, and famine—he has entangled, in his snares, these unfortunate deities, whom he has forced to upper earth to bear witness on his behalf, I am afraid, very much against their wills. Nothing, indeed, can be more distressing than to see an unfortunate thought thus hunted through the meandering of a sentence; a crowd of unmeaning words, like a pack of hungry dogs pressing close at its back, till at last worn out and completely exhausted, it sinks feebly away, and gives up the ghost so quietly, that no one can reasonably imagine what can possibly have become of it.

"Thus it was with the argument of my learned friend, it has vanished amidst the bustle he created around it. One thing more, my Lord and Gentlemen, and I have done; for I shall not, like my learned friend, after disclaiming all intentions of appealing to your feelings, endeavour by an artful peroration to come home to your inmost souls. It is simply this, that my client is a stranger, the son of a powerful foreign monarch, and, of course, as he has never taken any oath of allegiance to the English government, he is not amenable to the English laws. After stating this fact, I sit down, confidently assured that your verdict will be in my favour, and that, by it, you will again vindicate that proud right you have so long and gloriously maintained of acting always as enlightened and free-born Englishmen."

As the orator sat down, a tumult of applause rang through the hall, and the delight of Lord Maysworth can be only justly appreciated by an author who recollects what he felt when he first heard of the success of a favourite work. But he had little time for exultation, as the Judge, having been wound up in his turn, now began to sum up the evidence. Slowly and heavily did he go on, the machinery that composed him wanting oil, and creaking ominously as it moved, whilst, ere he had half finished, a cry was heard through the outer court, and instantly a rush of people announced the arrival of the Queen.

After the exertions made by Elvira the previous day, her fever returned, and she lay insensible to every thing that passed till she was restored to recollection by the tolling of a deep-toned bell, which was always set in motion the moment a prisoner was put upon his defence. She heard the solemn sound distinctly; the court where state criminals were tried, adjoined the palace, in order that the Queen might have an opportunity of hearing appeals, or deciding on any difficult case that might arise; though as offences against the state had been very rare in the female dynasty, (whether from the goodness of the people or the severity of the punishment, I leave it for my readers to determine,) the privilege had been seldom called in action, and the bell now grated harshly as it tolled. Elvira, however, had heard of the custom, and its cause flashed instantly upon her mind, as she started from her bed, and listened to the solemn sound as it fell slowly and heavily upon her ear, every knell seeming to strike upon the naked nerve.

"Emma!" cried she, "let me go—quick, let me save him, or I shall be too late." Emma obeyed; but whilst she was attiring her mistress every moment seemed an age, and Elvira listened to the heavy tolling bell till the sense of hearing became agony; and, unable to endure any more, she pressed her hands firmly against her ears to shut out the dreaded sound. At length she was ready, and hurrying to the court, arrived just at the critical moment I have mentioned.

"Stop!" cried she, "I command you to stop proceedings. The prisoner is free. My people have given me a right to pardon all offences, and I thus first exercise it. Set him free!"

The guards obeyed; and it not being possible to stop the automaton judge till he had run down, he was carried out of court, repeating, (for it happened he was summing up the evidence at that moment,) "And the Queen said she loved him, and would sacrifice even her life for his sake."

"You are free, Sir," said Elvira to the prince. "I only blush that a stranger should have been so inhospitably treated in my court. My illness, however, must plead my excuse; and I can only now show my sorrow by releasing you from the parole of honour you have given. You are absolutely free, prince, not only from these chains, but also to leave the kingdom whenever you shall think fit."

The prince, in a transport of gratitude, knelt and kissed her hand; and then retired with his friends to the house of Lord Maysworth; whilst Elvira, satisfied with herself, and hoping she had disarmed scandal by desiring the prince to quit the kingdom, returned to her palace more happy than she had before felt since the fatal combat in the garden.

CHAPTER XXIX.

The effect produced by the scene just described upon the minds of the multitude was magical. It seemed a confirmation "strong as proofs of holy writ" of all that had been urged against the Queen, and alienated from her side even those who had remained neutral.

"I really could not have believed it possible," said the Duke of Essex, as he retired slowly from the court.

"Thinking as I think, and as I am confident every one else must think," said Lord Gustavus, "she seems to have lost all sense even of common decency."

"What do you say to this, Sir Ambrose?" asked Dr. Hardman triumphantly.

"Nothing," replied Sir Ambrose, sighing.

"Then the case is hopeless," said the Duke of Essex; "for I know Sir Ambrose so well, that I am certain if a single word could be said in the Queen's behalf, he would not remain silent."

"Your grace judges me too favourably," returned Sir Ambrose; "for there is, on the contrary, much to be said for the Queen, if I had been disposed to say it. You see the story of her wishing to marry Ferdinand was evidently false, for she desired him in plain terms to quit the kingdom."

"A mere blind," cried Lord Gustavus, who felt he had now gone too far to recede; "an absolute farce; and I am only astonished a man of your penetration, Sir Ambrose, could have been deceived by it."

"It has long been the proudest boast of the English law," said Sir Ambrose, "that every one is presumed innocent till he be proved guilty; and I confess I do not see why the Queen should alone be made an exception to the rule."

Lord Gustavus made no reply, and the party proceeded to their several homes. The following day was appointed for the trial of Lord Edmund, and the court was, if possible, yet more crowded than before; for the singular termination of Prince Ferdinand's trial had created the most intense anxiety upon the part of the mob to know what would be the result of that of Lord Edmund. It has been already stated that he was the idol of the people, and now thousands of human voices shouted his praises to the sky, and heaped curses and execrations upon his enemies.

The tumult, however, was hushed to breathless expectation when it was announced that the officers of justice were gone in search of the prisoner; and innumerable human beings stood craning their necks over the lane made for his approach through the crowd, all eager to catch the first glimpse of him. But what language can express their disappointment and surprise when they saw the officers return, pale and trembling, fear painted upon their countenances, and their teeth chattering in their heads!

"He is gone," they cried: "the prison door was locked, and the windows fast, but he is gone; and doubtless some evil spirit has carried him off."

Great was the consternation excited by this unexpected news; every one rushed to the prison, and each in turn was struck with horror on finding it exactly in the state the officers had described. — "It is the Mummy that has done this," said the people, whispering amongst themselves: "some horrible event certainly hangs over us; and it is in vain to attempt to resist our destiny! All is supernatural, and we are merely blind instruments in the hands of Fate."

The disappearance of Lord Edmund had, however, nothing supernatural in it; and, indeed was effected by very simple means, and mere mortal agents. The agitation of his mind after his interview with Cheops became excessive, and every hour seemed stretched to an unnatural length as he anxiously awaited Father Morris's return; but the monk came not. Lord Edmund's impatience increased every instant, till it became absolute agony; yet still he was alone. He paced his chamber with uncertain steps—his brain burning with incipient madness, till, no longer knowing what he did, he dashed his head against the walls, and tore off his hair by handfuls. In this state the gaoler found him; and reporting his condition, his trial, which was to have taken place previously to that of Ferdinand, was postponed a few days to allow time for his recovery.

Bleeding and blistering reduced Lord Edmund's fever; but his soul was still on fire. In the paroxysms of his disorder, no less than in his lucid intervals, one sole idea seemed to have taken possession of his fancy; and he inquired incessantly if Father Morris were returned? No, no, was the continual answer to his queries; till the heart of the poor prisoner sickened within him at the sound. At length, he appeared well enough to take his trial, and the day was fixed, as we have already stated. The mind of Edmund now seemed tolerably composed; but it was the stillness of apathy, rather than that of resignation; and on the night preceding the day fixed for his trial, some of his former anxious and tormenting fantasies returned.

"I will shake off this weakness," said he; "I will read;" and, drawing his chair near the fire, he took up a book: it was in vain, however; for though he read over the same page repeatedly, he could not compose his mind sufficiently to comprehend its meaning. He threw his book aside, and, fixing his eyes upon the fire, was soon lost in gloomy meditations: when a slight noise attracted his attention; and, looking round, he saw a panel in the wall slowly detach itself, and Father Morris appear in the aperture, followed by another figure, closely wrapped in a large black cloak.

"Father Morris!" cried Edmund; "is it indeed Father Morris; or some kind spirit that has assumed his shape?"

"It is indeed I, my son!" returned the priest; "and I come to rescue and console you."

"Methinks you come somewhat late, father," said Edmund, rather coldly; "for I have suffered much since I saw you!"

"Others have suffered also," resumed the monk, "and for your sake! Notwithstanding you have fancied yourself neglected and forgotten by all the world, there is one human being who has never ceased to watch over you; who thinks only of you; who makes your happiness her only care; and who would sacrifice her life to preserve yours!"

Edmund's heart beat, and his cheeks glowed as he exclaimed, "And this kind friend is?"

"Now before you!" interrupted the monk; tearing aside the cloak that shrouded his companion, and discovering Rosabella!

"Rosabella!" exclaimed Edmund; a slight shade of disappointment passing over his features.

"Oh Edmund!" cried Rosabella, throwing herself at his feet, "can you forget that I have overstepped the bounds prescribed to my sex: will you not hate me?"

"I do not blame you. I were unworthy of the name of man if I could. But father, what says Elvira? Have you delivered the chain?"

"She refuses either to see or hear from you."

"Cruel woman! But perhaps she dreads to see me?"

"I know not; but she treated your petition with contempt. 'Tell him,' said she, 'it is not possible he can have aught to say that can interest me. I will not hear his suit.'"

"Proud, haughty princess! But was this all?"

"No: I again entreated her to see you, when she turned from me in scorn, and bade me leave her. 'Talk not to me of Edmund,' cried she, with a look of ineffable contempt. 'Has he not wounded Ferdinand, and would you have me forgive him? — a thousand deaths are not sufficient to punish such a crime!'"

"What strange infatuation!"

"Strange, indeed — for she has interrupted his trial and set him free; besides which, they say she has actually offered her hand and he has refused it; yet still she dotes upon him to distraction. 'Go,' continued she, when I had finished all I had to say, 'and tell Edmund, that I neither hate nor despise him; for he is incapable of exciting any emotion in my breast; however, if he wishes to make amends for his past conduct, and be restored to my favour, his first step must be, humbly to beg pardon of the prince.'"

"Damnation!" cried Edmund, starting up fiercely: "she did not, surely she could not, say that?"

"Indeed she did, my lord."

"Then may ten thousand curses light upon me if I forgive her! Pardon of that wretch! my slave! my prisoner! no, sooner would I expire in horrid torments — sooner be torn asunder by wild beasts. — Pardon of that boy! — oh! she could not mean it."

Whilst Edmund thus raved, Father Morris and Rosabella watched his torments with much of the same coolness, as a French philosopher would those of an unfortunate animal upon which he was trying experiments. No feeling of compassion entered their souls, and they only waited to see the effect their words would produce. It may easily be perceived that the whole scene which Father Morris related as having passed between him and Elvira, was a fabrication; but Lord Edmund saw not this, for jealousy often throws a veil over the eyes of its victims, which gives a delusive colouring to every thing they see. Thus, Lord Edmund believed every word the father uttered, and his whole frame trembled with agitation as he paced the room with hasty strides. At last, he threw himself upon a chair—"Beg his pardon!" exclaimed he: "Oh Elvira! Elvira!" and he hid his face in his hands, whilst the big tears trickled through his fingers, and Lord Edmund, the stern, courageous soldier, the philosopher, the hero, and the statesman, wept, actually wept, like a feeble child.

"Oh Edmund!" exclaimed Rosabella, approaching him, and taking his hand—"I cannot bear to see you in distress. Would to Heaven that by the sacrifice even of my life I could relieve you!"

"Rosabella, you will drive me to distraction."

"Not for worlds, Edmund; on the contrary, were I mistress of worlds, I would cast them at your feet."

"I know it—I know it; but spare me now."

"Spare you, Edmund! Spare what? spare my reproaches, mean you? Alas! you need not fear them. Am I not devoted to you? Is it not for your sake that I have thus passed the boundaries of my sex? Are you disgusted with my boldness? But no: you will surely forgive me, for my only motive has been to save you, and my only hope of happiness is bound up in yours."

"Rosabella!" repeated Edmund, "I believe that you love me."

"Love you! Oh heavens! can you doubt my love?"

"I do not doubt it, and this last action proves it more than words. I have long done you injustice; can you forgive me, Rosabella?"

"Oh Edmund!" exclaimed the princess, whilst her full heart heaved almost to bursting and the tears streamed down her face.

"I have been the victim of infatuation," continued Edmund; "I have loved a false, ungrateful woman, who has betrayed me. But I see my folly; and if tears of penitence shed at your feet can earn my pardon—if you will accept a broken, bleeding heart—"

"Oh Edmund!" interrupted Rosabella, throwing herself into

his arms, "say no more—I am yours—yours for ever—your devoted slave—"

"Not my slave, Rosabella," said Edmund, gently disengaging her from him, and placing her upon a chair, "but my wife, my beloved wife."

"Your wife!" exclaimed Rosabella, "Edmund's wife! am I indeed so blest? Oh no! surely it is a dream, a fond delusive dream! You cannot surely be serious."

"Is this a moment for jest?" asked Edmund calmly.

"It certainly is not," said Father Morris, whose agitation had been nearly equal to their own, and who had stood gazing upon them with looks of the fondest affection. "We must immediately escape, or it will be too late; it wants but two hours of daybreak, and, with the dawn, Lord Edmund's trial will commence."

"True, true!" cried Rosabella, "I had forgotten. Dearest Edmund, you must condescend to fly, or your precious life will be sacrificed."

"But how shall I escape?"

"Through this panel. A balloon waits at a little distance, and this cloak will conceal your person from observation."

"Dear Rosabella!"

"Come, come," cried Father Morris, "we have no time to lose. Though Ferdinand was acquitted you must fall, for the state requires a victim."

Lord Edmund waited for no more; the name of Ferdinand was torture to him; and, hastily disencumbering himself of his chains, he followed the father and Rosabella from the prison. He sighed, however, and looked back for a moment with regret ere he quitted the outer walls, for he thought of Elvira. Rosabella's quick ear caught the sigh and her subtle spirit divined its meaning; but this was not a moment to complain, and stepping into their balloon they were soon out of sight of London. They proceeded to a palace of Rosabella's, a few miles out of town, and there, the following day, Edmund became her husband.

In the mean time, the excessive agitation Elvira experienced on the day of Prince Ferdinand's trial brought on a return of her fever, and it was several weeks ere she was sufficiently recovered to leave her bed. When she did so, however, she was really shocked at the state in which she found her kingdom. When she first began to reign, carried away by the enthusiasm of the moment, she had taken too much of the executive part of the government upon herself; and as her illness had been too sudden to allow her to appoint a regency, no one knew who ought to supply her place. All therefore was confusion and disorder, and Elvira shrunk disgusted from the chaos before her. She had now no Edmund to smooth the way for her, and the native energy of her mind was gone. Pale, heart-broken, and dispirited, she felt languid and incapable of the slightest exertion. What had formerly been a pleasure, was now become an overwhelming burthen, and the weight of life seemed insupportable.

She was now weary also of the fatigue necessary to carry on the plans she had projected for the benefit of her people. At first, when all seemed new and delightful, she had devoted herself entirely to their interests: she had denied herself even the most trifling pleasures, and scarcely allowed herself the time absolutely necessary for food and rest. This was all very well, whilst her plans had the charm of novelty, and were supported by passion. But now that novelty had worn off, and they had assumed the dull wearisome appearance of duties—when repeated disappointments had extinguished almost the hope of success, and when she found her people expected, nay, demanded as a right, that which she had originally granted them only as an especial mark of favour, she discovered, though too late, the folly of the toil she had imposed upon herself.

She now also discovered that improvement to be effectual must be slow: that people don't like to be forced out of old habits, till they have seen the effect of new ones proved by experience, and that nothing is so difficult as to improve people against their wills. Increase the resources of a country, throw money into the hands of the middling and lower classes, and they will improve themselves; but, at least, nine-tenths of a population will never suffer themselves to be improved. Those only who have attempted this thankless and painful office can fully estimate the sufferings of the unfortunate Elvira, who, disappointed in all she undertook, found life become tasteless and insipid, and was completely wretched,—though surrounded by all the gifts of beauty, power, and fortune.

Every thing seemed to conspire to increase her misery. Those whom she raised from indigence to affluence treated her with the most provoking insolence and discontent. A plan which had been opposed by the lords Gustavus de Montfort

The Mummy!

and Maysworth, and which she had persisted in having tried, had completely failed, and the noble Lords had triumphed in the most provoking manner in her disappointment. In short, every thing went wrong; and Elvira, disgusted with the world, felt mortified and disgusted with herself.

"How hard it is," thought she, frequently, as she tossed upon her sleepless couch, "that I who, since my accession to the throne, have devoted myself entirely to the interests of my subjects, should be thus wretched; whilst tyrants, who live but to oppress, sleep quietly upon their beds of down. Alas! why cannot I be as they are? Why cannot I divest myself of reflection, and enjoy the pleasures that surround me? But what pleasures can I enjoy? alas! the world presents nothing that can interest me; an insipid vacuum spreads through creation; my heart is cold and desolate; my affections are thrown back upon myself, and I am miserable."

Thus raved Elvira, and, absorbed in painful meditations, she neglected the duties of her station, and resigned herself to despair, whilst the people, attributing her evident wretchedness to her grief for the absence of Prince Ferdinand, who had left London immediately after his trial, and had not since been heard of, became every hour more and more discontented with their Queen.

In the mean time, the marriage of Lord Edmund, though not openly avowed, was generally suspected; and the party of Rosabella gained strength every day, whilst mysterious rumours were whispered from mouth to mouth, and divers hints given that many knew more than they chose to say; though from the immense number of these mystery-mongers it seemed, as in the celebrated scene in the Barber of Seville, that every one was in the secret, though nobody was to divulge it. The listlessness of Elvira soon produced the most serious effects. A kingdom without a government, or rather a government without a chief, cannot long go on well. It is like a ship at sea without a pilot, and it must founder upon the first rock that impedes its course.

When the vigour of government is from any cause relaxed, there are always plenty of persons ready to take advantage of the opportunity afforded them to commit evil with impunity; and crimes of every description multiplied so fast under the negligent sway of Elvira, that the people became clamorous in their complaints. But to whom could they address themselves? The Queen was rarely visible—Lord Edmund was gone, and the lords of the council were too busy talking about the interests of the people to think of really attending to them; whilst the duke and Sir Ambrose seemed too old to be likely to trouble themselves by intermeddling with an affair of state. To them, however, the people looked as a dernier resort; and as it seemed indelicate to apply to the duke when the person they complained of was his own daughter, they entreated Sir Ambrose to present a petition to the Queen in their behalf.

The worthy baronet acceded to their request, and though almost bent to the earth by age and misery, prepared once more to appear at court. The loss of his beloved Edmund had affected the old man deeply: he considered his flight before trial as a confession of guilt, and the thought of disgrace weighed down his grey hairs with sorrow to the grave. The distress of the people, however, roused him from the apathy into which he was fast falling; and when he waited upon the Queen, it was with all the energy of his former years.

The Queen received him sullenly. "I cannot help it Sir Ambrose," said she; "I am sorry for my people, but I cannot do any thing to relieve them. I feel that I am fast sinking into the tomb; do not then disturb my last moments by fruitless solicitations."

"Last moments!" cried Sir Ambrose, indignantly; "rally your energies, and you may live half a century. You give way to a morbid sensibility that oppresses you; and, because some of your hopes have been disappointed, you shrink from the duties that you have imposed upon yourself, and talk of your last moments. Shame! shame! Elvira! rouse yourself from this lethargy, and be indeed a Queen. Remember, that though Nature has ordinarily denied your sex the power of triumphing in the field, she has yet left a far greater conquest for you to achieve — the conquest of yourself; for it is far more glorious to subdue the wayward desires of the human heart, than to lead scores of monarchs captives in your chains. Struggle then with your feelings: conquer those fatal passions that threaten to destroy you; show yourself worthy of your crown, and be again the Elvira for whom even in her childhood, I anticipated greatness."

"It is too late," interrupted the Queen impatiently — "it is now too late. Urge me no more, Sir Ambrose, or you will drive me to despair."

Sir Ambrose was provoked at her obstinacy, and a pause ensued, which was broken by a tumultuous noise and shouting. It was the people at the gates of the palace, who, impatient at the length of Sir Ambrose's stay, were now becoming clamorous for an answer.

"What shall I say to them?" asked the baronet.

"Tell them I deny their suit!" replied the Queen. "Away, away, away! I would be quiet; go without reply; I will hear no more; I will not be tormented:" and waving her hand for him to depart, she hurried to her chamber. Finding there was no alternative, Sir Ambrose was compelled to appear before the people and acquaint them with the will of their Sovereign. The tumult became more violent as he spoke. An English mob is proverbially impetuous; and now their rage rose beyond control. "The Queen! the Queen!" they shouted; "we will see the Queen!" The crowd increased every moment—the multitude heaved in tremendous waves like the rolling billows of the sea, and the hum of thousands of human voices filled the air. They threatened to storm the palace. A man in complete armour, his face entirely concealed by his vizor, headed their attempts; the outer gates were forced, and the throng rushed tumultuously into the court of the palace.

All there was confusion: soldiers might have been summoned, and the place defended; but there was no one to give orders; and the servants ran to and fro in the greatest possible distress, without knowing either where they were going, or what they intended doing. In the midst of this bustle, Elvira sate burying her face in her hands, and obstinately refusing to take the slightest interest in the scene. The door opened violently, and Sir Ambrose and some of her principal servants rushed in. "For God's sake, save yourself!" cried they. "If your Majesty were safe, we care not for ourselves."

"Fly!" cried Sir Ambrose, throwing himself upon his knees before her, his white hair streaming almost to the ground; "for God's sake, fly!" It was too late, however, then, had the Queen been disposed to obey him; for, as he spoke, the outer door burst open with tremendous violence; the palace seemed to shake to its foundation with the shock; and in an instant the chamber was filled by the infuriated populace.

"Seize the Queen, but do not injure her!" cried a voice that thrilled through every nerve of Sir Ambrose. "Spare the old man; do not hurt a hair of his head." Sir Ambrose looked up; the voice came from the man in armour; but it was the voice of Edmund. A crowd of overwhelming thoughts rushed through his mind, and, overpowered by their weight, he sank senseless upon the ground. "Take him away!" cried Edmund; (for it was indeed he;) "take him away! but see that ye hurt him not: he dies that injures him."

"Edmund!" cried Elvira, struck also by his voice—

"To prison with her!" exclaimed he.

"To prison, Edmund! do you doom your Queen to prison? Is it thus you treat your Sovereign?"

"I own no Sovereign here but Rosabella."

"But, by what right can she be called your Sovereign?"

"By that which made you Queen. The people's voice. It lies with them to crown or to dethrone!"

"Oh Edmund! mercy!"

"Away with her! I'll hear no more."

The guards seized upon the unfortunate Queen, and, in spite of her entreaties, hurried her away. Edmund did not trust himself to look at her. For a moment he hid his face in his hands; then rousing himself, he exclaimed, "Now to proclaim the Queen!" The people followed him with shouts of applause, and before evening Edmund and Rosabella were unanimously acknowledged as King and Queen of England.

CHAPTER XXX.

Notwithstanding the able manner in which the revolution had been effected, England was still in a state of tumult. Though the army had been seduced by the example of Edmund, and the people had been obliged to submit, they were by no means perfectly satisfied with their new government; and Rosabella found, too late, that though the throne might be compared to a bed of roses, it was not without its thorns. The discontented nobles who had aided her cause were also extremely displeased by what they called the trifling value of the rewards bestowed upon them; though, in fact, they rated their services so high, that Rosabella found her whole kingdom did not possess the power of repaying them to their satisfaction. It was also a considerable grievance of these haughty nobles, to see Prince Ferdinand return to the English Court immediately after the dethronement of Elvira, and be received with open arms by Rosabella, who, with the anxiety to conciliate the friendship of foreign powers, usually displayed by those whose thrones feel far from secure at home, loaded him with favours, and even gave him a post of honour in the command of her own body-guard.

Whilst the unreasonableness of her people thus embittered Rosabella's political life, her domestic happiness seemed to rest upon a yet more unstable foundation. She knew that though she possessed Edmund's hand, his heart was still devoted to Elvira; and jealousy made her view all his actions in a distorted light. If he were sad, she was sure he was thinking of her rival; and if gay, she fancied it a masque put on only to deceive her. She was thus completely miserable, and Edmund was as wretched as herself. He felt that he had sacrificed himself to revenge, and sold his peace for a bauble, which, when obtained, did not seem worth the trouble of possessing. His father too—Sir Ambrose, his doating father, was now entirely estranged from him, as he repeatedly declared he would never forgive a traitor, who could forget his oath of allegiance for his own aggrandizement.

"No!" exclaimed the old man, "I loved, I doted upon Edmund; but the Edmund I loved is vanished. My darling son was brave and noble, not a deceptive scoundrel. No, no, my old heart may break—nay, I hope it will—but never whilst I live shall a deceitful traitor be pressed against this breast."

Edmund was inconsolable; he passionately loved his father, and could not bear his anger; besides, he felt that the reproaches of the old man were seconded by those of his own heart. It is painful at any time to bear the censures of the world, but they fall with double weight when we know that they are deserved. Edmund was dissatisfied with himself, and, consequently, disposed to quarrel with the world. He fancied it looked coldly upon him, and, in return, he affected to despise it. A hundred times a day he repeated that he was perfectly indifferent to every thing that was said of him; whilst his nervous anxiety to peruse the newspapers, and make himself perfectly acquainted with every popular rumour, proved that he was only too sensible to every word that was uttered. Edmund had made the mob his idol, he could not live without its applauses, and wretched indeed are those who thus depend on others for their hopes of happiness.

Edmund's disgust at his new rank and situation was soon still farther increased by a visit from Lord Gustavus, who, with several other lords, was deputed to present to his Majesty the complaints of the Commons. They wanted to be enfranchised, they desired innumerable rights and privileges, and in fact they wanted to be all kings; for if half that they demanded had been granted, Edmund must have made them more powerful than himself. He pointed this out to Lord Gustavus, and condescended to reason with him upon the folly of their desires.

"Impossible!" cried Lord Gustavus. "Your Majesty must excuse me but I cannot listen to such arguments; I came here to defend the liberties of the people. Reform is necessary — without reform, nothing can go on well. Evils must be torn up root and branch."

"Are not my subjects healthy, wealthy, and prosperous?" asked Edmund. "Have they not been successful at home and abroad? Do not the English peasants live as well as most foreign princes, and what more can they require?"

"Liberty, Sire," returned Lord Gustavus. "What are all these pretended advantages without liberty? mere toys; gaudy apples, but rotten at the core. Of what use, indeed, are all the blessings of life, without liberty to give them zest, and radical reform to purge them of all impurities?"

"But listen to reason."

"Reason! Thinking as I think, and as I am sure every rational being must think, your Majesty must forgive me if I assert, that even Reason herself does not deserve to be attended to, when she is basely enlisted upon the side of Tyranny."

"Nay, then," said Edmund, "it is useless to attempt to argue

The Mummy!

with you. I thought you had made Reason your goddess; but if you worship her only as long as it suits your own purposes, I have done. You may retire. I shall take the petition into consideration, and give it an answer when I may think fit."

Edmund, who, from being degraded and debased in his own opinion, no longer possessed that confidence in himself that carried conviction with all he said, had yet sufficient dignity in his manner to awe those to silence who dared to dispute his commands; and Lord Gustavus and his colleagues, not presuming to make farther remonstrance, retired in dudgeon. This incident contributed to sicken Edmund of reigning: he became disgusted with his Queen, his court, his kingdom, and his country, and, secluding himself as much as possible from public life, left the care of managing the affairs of state to Rosabella and Father Morris, who now throwing off the disguise he so long had worn, appeared openly as the dispenser of her favours, and the arbiter of her actions.

The spirit of poor Sir Ambrose was quite broken by these misfortunes. The defection of his son, and the ingratitude of his confessor, stung him to the core. He retired again to the country, where with his friend the duke, Clara, and Father Murphy, he contrived to exist, though but the shadow of his former self. The duke was also grievously changed, and it was melancholy to see these two poor old men wandering about their splendid gardens and magnificent palaces like roaming ghosts, permitted to revisit for a time the scenes of their departed happiness. Clara now became the sole stay that bound these old men to life. Her character had developed itself wonderfully in the midst of the striking events she had witnessed. Firm, courageous, and enterprising, though still gentle—the lively girl seemed changed into the intelligent woman, whose active mind and comprehensive spirit foresaw every thing and provided against every emergency. Clara was still young; but her spirit was mature beyond her years, and her attention to the duke and Sir Ambrose was unremitting.

"Well!" would they often say, "though we have lost much, we ought still to be thankful that Clara is spared to us:" and then with tears trickling down their aged cheeks, they would join in imploring Heaven to shower down blessings upon her head. In the mean time, however, Clara herself was far from happy. She would, it is true, exert herself to appear cheerful, but it was evident it was an exertion; and often, when the duke and Sir Ambrose had seated themselves at a party at chess, she would steal out unobserved and retire to a little pavilion in the garden, near what were formerly the apartments of Father

Morris, as being the most secluded spot she could find; this part of the mansion having been carefully shut up and avoided by every human being, since the departure of the priest, as infectious; the indignation the worthy and attached servants of Sir Ambrose felt towards Father Morris for his desertion of their master, being extended even to the rooms he had occupied.

In this secluded spot Clara often sate for hours, lost in meditation, her head resting upon her hand, and her eyes fixed in vacancy. Winter had now given place to spring, and all nature seemed to revive with that gay and joyous season. The heart of Clara, however, was still lonely; she fancied it could enjoy no second summer; and she felt almost disposed to quarrel with all around her for displaying a gaiety in which she could not participate. Nothing makes a broken heart feel more gloomy than to see all other objects look gay. It turns from them in disgust, and feels its own misery doubled by the sight of their happiness.

One evening as Clara was sitting absorbed in melancholy reflections, she was startled by hearing a deep-drawn sigh heaved heavily behind her. She turned, and fancied she could distinguish a figure in the midst of the twilight but, magnified by the obscurity, the figure seemed of gigantic proportions. Uttering a faint scream, she attempted to fly — when a hand of iron grasped her arm, and arrested her progress. An icy chill shot to her heart, whilst the well-remembered voice of Cheops sounded in her ears.

"Clara," said he, in his deep sepulchral tone, "would you save your Queen?"

"With the sacrifice of my life, if necessary," replied Clara firmly.

"Clara," continued the Mummy, "I have marked you attentively, — and as I do not know any individual possessing more strength of mind and personal courage than yourself, I have fixed upon you to be my assistant in this enterprize. The life of Elvira is in danger; and even my influence cannot much longer save her, if she remain in the power of Father Morris. Besides, the lesson she has already had, has been sufficiently severe. I will aid her to escape, and you must assist me. You shall go to Ireland; and there, if the warlike Roderick be not deaf to the cry of beauty in distress, through his aid Elvira may hope redress, — at least, she must implore his help. — Rosabella is now at a palace near this, and she has brought her rival in her train; for, with the usual jealousy and suspicion of tyrants and usurpers, she scarcely dares to trust her from her sight. Besides this, her diabolical revenge is gratified in making Elvira wait humbly near her throne, and serve in those palaces where she once commanded. Moved by this ungenerous conduct, and the patience with which the unhappy Elvira bears her sufferings, the nobles and people of the realm begin to pity her: and when they are disgusted with the haughtiness and intolerance of Rosabella, they sigh for the return of the gentle Elvira. Father Morris perceives this, and determining to rid Rosabella of her rival, the fair Elvira fades beneath his arts, like a flower withering on its stem."

"She must be saved!" said Clara, with enthusiasm; "she shall be saved! — Point but out the means, and I am devoted to her service."

"You must assume these weeds, and follow me," said Cheops, pointing to a bundle in a corner of the pavilion, which Clara had not before noticed. "In half an hour I will return for you."

"And my sudden disappearance," rejoined Clara, "will it not excite suspicion?"

"The river is deep and rapid," returned Cheops; "some of your clothes left upon its banks — "

"I comprehend," cried Clara eagerly; "but the poor old duke, and Sir Ambrose?"?

"Their anxiety and distress may be great, but cannot be lasting: the feelings of age are blunt, and — "

"Oh, no!" exclaimed Clara, "you are deceived; — nay, I think that age feels grief more acutely than youth. The mind has lost its elasticity — hope is dead within it, and the old brood over their secret sorrow till they destroy their — "

"By Osiris! thou art a most extraordinary girl," said Cheops; "the old do brood over grief, but why say this to me? Do I not know it well — too well?" continued he, looking at her earnestly. Clara turned pale, and trembled — he saw her agitation; and, hastily averting his eyes, continued in a calmer tone, — "Whatever the sufferings of the old men may be for the moment, I suppose even you will allow the life of Elvira more than counterbalances them; — and, by inflicting this temporary pain, you will save them from the more lasting agony they would endure from her death: for Father Morris is so subtle, that it would be dangerous to give them the slightest hint of our intention, lest he should worm it from them. Be ready then, Clara; resign thyself to my instructions, and, above all, fear not."

Clara bent her head in token of assent, and Cheops disappeared. Upon examining the clothes, Clara found them to be the dress of a Greek peasant boy, numbers of whom at this period were rambling over England singing wild romances to their harps or lutes, and telling fortunes in a kind of doggerel rhyme. Exposure to the air tanned most of these wandering minstrels brown, and Clara found a bottle of liquid in the parcel to stain her face and hands. She bound up her flaxen ringlets, and, covering her head with curls of a jetty blackness, she found the metamorphosis so complete that she scarcely knew herself as she saw her figure reflected in a large mirror behind her. It was now nearly dark, but Cheops had left the necessary implements for striking a light, and Clara made her toilette without the least difficulty.

Anxious were the moments, however, that passed after her task was completed, till the arrival of Cheops; and when he did come, she saw he was attired as herself. He grasped her arm, and without speaking led her to the banks of the river. Clara shuddered as she found herself alone in the power of this mysterious being, and saw the river roll deep and dark beneath her feet. Cheops felt her shudder, and cried with one of his horrid laughs, which sounded fearfully amidst the stillness of the night, "What! do even you fear me? Is there no courage in this degenerate race? None? What do you fear? If you dread to trust yourself in my power, or think yourself unequal to the task you have undertaken, retire: there is yet time, and I wish no unwilling agents. Poor child!" continued he, looking at her with feeling; "thou dost not know me, but for worlds I would not harm thee!"

"I will go with you," said Clara resolutely; "I do not shrink. Let what will await me, I will not recede: though unheard-of torments may attend me, I will endure them."

"By the Holy Gods of my forefathers," cried Cheops, "she is a brave girl! Yes, Clara, I will trust thee; and though we should encounter horrors fearful as those which menace the initiati in the dread Isian mysteries, I will not doubt thy courage. A determined spirit, Clara, may subdue even Fate."

As he spoke, he threw the clothes she had brought for the purpose carelessly upon the banks of the river; and then again seizing her arm, he dragged her forward with such rapidity, that in an incredibly short time they approached the palace of Rosabella. The mansion looked the region of enchantment. Brilliantly illuminated, light streamed from every window; and through the colonnade of the great hall, groups of elegantly dressed people were seen gaily moving to and fro, some dancing, and others listening to harmonious music.

Clara, though terrified and exhausted, felt still irresistibly impelled to proceed, and, still guided by her strange companion, entered, unobserved, the outer court of the palace.

"Prince Ferdinand of Germany commands the guard to-night," whispered Cheops, in a low, unnatural voice "it is well, he shall go with us."

"But will he?" asked Clara tremblingly.

"Will he?" returned Cheops, with his peculiar sneer: "dost thou doubt my power, girl?"

Clara and Cheops had now reached a place from whence, unobserved, they could survey the whole of the splendid apartment before them. They had, in fact, entered the hall, and placed themselves in a kind of recess shaded by projecting pillars, from whence they could see every part of the saloon. Clara was astonished to find herself so easily in the presence of the Queen, for she knew not how they had attained their present situation; and she would have spoken to ask Cheops, but he laid his finger upon his lips: and whispering—"Hippocrates was the only son of Isis and Osiris!"—she comprehended he meant that Wisdom and Knowledge produced Silence, and she did not dare to breathe a syllable.

Rosabella sate upon a splendid dais, gorgeously attired; her black eyes flashing with added brilliancy from the deep rouge upon her cheeks; whilst her raven hair was adorned with diamonds, and a splendid tiara of the same precious stones sparkled on her forehead; a robe of crimson velvet, bordered with ermine, fell in graceful folds over her fine figure; whilst her swanlike neck and snowy arms, exposed perhaps more than delicacy might strictly warrant, were also loaded with costly jewels. Around her, stood the ladies of her court, and amongst the rest, Elvira, plainly attired in a robe of dark grey silk. No ornaments shone amongst her golden tresses, and her naturally fair complexion seemed faded to a sickly and unnatural whiteness.

The indignation of Clara could scarcely be restrained at this sight; but Cheops laying his hand upon her arm, they stood suddenly before the Queen.

"Ah! who are these?" cried Rosabella, starting. Cheops took no notice of her surprise; but, tuning his lute, began to sing.

"Loveliest Queen! oh deign to hear

The humblest of thy suppliants' prayer;

Blandly on a stranger smile,

Who has sought thy happy Isle,

To feast his eyes upon that face,

Where majesty combines with grace."

"What means this mummery?" asked Rosabella; "how came these minstrels here?"

"It is doubtless a device of the King," returned some of her ladies, "to amuse your majesty."

Rosabella smiled; attentions were now so rare upon the part of Edmund towards her, that she felt gratified that it should even be supposed he wished to please her, and, addressing the minstrel more graciously, asked what brought him to England. He sung his reply:

"Full often in my native land

I've struck my lute with bolder hand;

But with the liberties of Greece,

Her minstrel's harmony must cease.

Since Iwan with a soldier's frown

Hath seized and worn th' imperial crown,

Those hearts which spurn despotic power

Must wander from their native bower,

And in far distant lands must try

The meaner arts of palmistry.

Give then your hand, fair lady! give,

And let the wandering minstrel live:

The Mummy!

So shall he tell the varied fate

That may that lovely form await.

To other strains his voice is mute;

Broken his heart, unstrung his lute!"

"What say you, ladies," said Rosabella, again smiling, "shall we hear our destiny?"

The ladies, delighted at any thing that promised an interruption to the general gloom which hung over Rosabella's court, gladly assented; and, to Clara's infinite surprise, the Mummy addressed a few doggerel verses to each. When Elvira's turn came, Clara perceived her colour was heightened, and that she trembled excessively, yet the Mummy's verses to her were as unmeaning as to the rest. Whilst this scene was passing, the King and Father Morris approached. The former stood silent and abstracted, apparently quite unconscious of the group before him; whilst Father Morris gazed at them intently, with a satirical sneer upon his countenance, as though in thorough contempt for such folly.

"How can you endure such mummery?" said he to Rosabella, after a short pause.

"Any thing for a change," said she, sighing. The father's dark eye glanced upon the King, and then upon Rosabella, as with a gloomy frown he stalked on. The Queen coloured, and hastily waving her hand to the minstrel, as a sign that he might depart, she turned away, and the disappointed ladies were reluctantly obliged to follow in her train. In a few minutes, however, a page returned with a chain and a purse of gold, which he gave the minstrels, and retired. Clara was upon the point of refusing her share of this bounty, but a look from the Mummy made her sensible of her error, and she took it without uttering a syllable. Her hesitation, however, did not pass unnoticed, and she found, to her infinite horror, when they quitted the palace, that two of the Queen's servants had followed them. Clara trembled excessively, and clung tightly to the Mummy's arm for protection; but that mysterious being still stalked on with the same indifference as before. Clara longed to give him some intimation of the danger that awaited him, but she could not speak; the words seemed to swell in her throat and almost choke her, whilst she found herself dragged along by an irresistible influence, too powerful to admit of her even struggling against it. Inexpressible agony, however, seized her as she found herself hurried on towards the river; and when, as they reached the brink, she beheld Cheops stamp, with almost supernatural force, upon the fragile bridge which stretched across the water, and saw the slender plank sink beneath his weight, she could bear no more, and, screaming with horror, rushed forwards to save him. A strong arm, however, pulled her back; she felt herself whirled round, and for the moment her senses seemed to desert her. The next instant she found she had been dragged under some bushes, and saw their pursuers rush down to the place where the broken bridge had been.

"They are gone, by Jupiter!" said one; "I heard them fall into the water. It was a tremendous crash."

"I heard them," returned the other; "they fell as heavy as lead; and how they screamed!"

"The young one screamed," said the first; "but the old one groaned."

"What does it matter," resumed the second, "whether they screamed or groaned? They are gone to the devil a little before their time, and so we have only to go back as we came. Between ourselves, it was nonsense to take the trouble to watch them. They were evidently only what they seemed to be; and even Father Morris, suspicious as he is, gave us no orders about them."

"Thy dull head cannot see," said the first. "The father's negligence was the very motive of my vigilance. Things are not with him as they have been—he wants to rule the Queen with a rod of iron, and Rosabella will not endure control. Now, it struck me when I saw the youth's hesitation, that all was not right, and, I thought, if I could discover what had escaped him—"

"I see," said the other; "his lifeless trunk might have had the honour of serving as a stepping-stone to enable you to rise."

"It was possible," returned the other, laughing; and they retired, their voices gradually dying away till they became inaudible in the distance. Clara now perceived that the Mummy stood beside her. He did not speak, but pressed his finger upon his lips in token of silence, and for some minutes they stood fixed to the spot:—till, as the last faint echo of the servants' footsteps died away, he again seized the arm of Clara, and hurried her away towards a gloomy cave.

They stopped at the entrance; and though the poor girl was

still too much terrified to speak, yet she felt somewhat relieved by the discovery that the Mummy had evidently saved her from danger, instead of, as she feared, precipitating her into it. She still gazed with awe, however, at his strange unearthly figure, as he stood with his eyes fixed earnestly upon a star, and apparently occupied in muttering prayers addressed to it.

"Clara!" at length said he, his deep, full voice echoing solemnly through the vaulted cave; "Clara!" again he repeated, whilst the blood of his terrified companion seemed to curdle in her veins at the awful sound. She, however, slowly and tremblingly advanced—he grasped her arm—she attempted to shrink back, but seemed fixed as though by magic;—"Hear me," continued the Mummy, in a low, hollow tone, which appeared to rise from the tomb,—"Elvira understood my signal, and she will soon be here; but you must do the rest. Prince Ferdinand keeps guard to-night. Pass through this cave; the outlet will bring you to his station. Throw yourself at his feet, and appeal to his compassion in whatever language the feelings of the moment may inspire. He will readily listen to you, for he has not forgotten your visit to him in prison, and will swear to devote himself to your service. Tell him you accept his offers, and entreat him to convey yourself and the Queen to Ireland—where Roderick will receive and protect you. He will immediately comply; and his being the companion of your flight, will induce the belief that you are gone to Germany, and will consequently prevent the least danger of pursuit."

At this moment a slight figure, wrapped in a large mantle, appeared at the entrance of the cavern. "Elvira!" cried Cheops, and the stranger sprang forward. "Then I am right," exclaimed she, whilst her whole frame trembled with agitation.

"This is your guide," said Cheops, in his deep sepulchral tone; "follow her and you will do well. Farewell! but we shall meet again." Then bending over her, he pressed his lips to her forehead, and to that of Clara.

Both shuddered at the touch of those cold marble lips, and an icy chill ran through their veins, as the fearful conviction that their companion was no earthly being thrilled in their bosoms. Even the strongest minds dread supernatural horrors, and our fair fugitives turned involuntarily away. When they looked again, the Mummy was gone, and the darkness appeared so profound that they were obliged to grope their way cautiously along. Fearing alike to remain or to advance, they proceeded with trembling steps slowly along a narrow passage; their minds filled with that vague sense of danger that generally attends the want of light, when Imagination pictures terrors which do not really exist, and Fancy lends her aid to magnify those which do.

By degrees, however, the Queen and her companion became accustomed to the darkness; and as the pupils of their eyes dilated, they were enabled to discern the objects around them. Innumerable fantastic shapes, however, now appeared to flit before them, and grim giants to frown awfully from every corner of the gloomy vault they were traversing. The dim and indistinct light threw a misty veil round the projecting corners of the rocks that gave them a fearful and unnatural grandeur; whilst the fair friends, overpowered with terror, gazed timidly around, and stood a few moments not daring to advance into the darker abysses of the caverns, and yet dreading alike to remain where they were, or to return.

"We must go on," said Elvira at length, her voice echoing through the cave, till she started at the sound.

"Oh God!" cried Clara; "hark! a thousand mocking demons seem to repeat from every rock—Go on!—"

"Go on!" again rang in a thousand varied tones through the cavern.

"Let us proceed," whispered Elvira, shuddering; "this is a fearful place!"

And they hurried on as fast as their trembling limbs could carry them, along a dark and gloomy passage, leading in the direction pointed out by the Mummy. In a few minutes, however, a bright though glimmering light appeared afar off, like a star, which, gleaming through the darkness, seemed a beacon of hope to guide them on to happiness. A slight current of air, too, now blew freshly in their faces, and their spirits rose, as with quickened steps they hastened onward in the direction from whence it appeared to proceed.

The light now seemed rapidly to enlarge, and the wind blew more freshly, whilst the Queen and her companion distinctly heard the heavy stamping of horses, which vibrated fearfully on the hollow ground, and grew louder and louder every moment as they advanced.

"Ah! what is that?" cried Elvira trembling, clinging closer to her companion.

"It is the bivouack of Prince Ferdinand," replied Clara; "the Mummy told me we should find him here, and that he would aid us."

"Ah, that fearful Mummy," murmured Elvira softly; "if he should deceive us, and this should be only a plan to betray us to our enemies?"

"Fear not," said Clara; "come what may, we must dare the worst."

They had now reached the outlet of the cavern, and found an opening large enough to admit of a single person. Cautiously advancing towards it, they paused for a few moments ere they descended, to gaze upon the scene below. A troop of soldiers were scattered round, in various attitudes of repose, under a small grove of trees, whilst their horses grazed at a little distance. The prince alone seemed awake, and he lay apart from his companions, stretched upon a grassy bank, a thick tree spreading above him, his head resting upon his hand, and his eyes fixed upon the ground. The moon shone brightly, and played upon the prince's polished armour, like summer lightning dancing on a lake. His helmet was thrown aside, and his countenance looked pale and sad, whilst his frequent sighs betrayed the uneasiness of his mind.

"Let us advance," said Clara, "and try to move him to compassion."

Elvira complied; and with light and timid steps, fearing almost to breathe, lest they should break the slumbers of their enemies, they approached the prince. All was still, save the hard breathing of the sleeping soldiers, and the measured champing of the horses; their stately figures strongly relieved by the dark grey sky beyond, and their long manes and tails sweeping the ground. The prince was now listlessly tracing figures in the grass with the scabbard of his sword: he started as they approached, and hastily demanded the cause of their intrusion.

"Mercy!" cried Elvira, sinking upon her knees before him; "mercy!" She could say no more, but gasping for breath, she stretched out her arms imploringly, whilst every thing around seemed to swim before her eyes, and the figures of the prince, the trees, the horses, and the sleeping soldiers, appeared all dilated to gigantic magnitude. She entirely forgot the pathetic appeal she had intended making to the prince's feelings, and every faculty seemed suspended in the intenseness of her anxiety.

"For Heaven's sake, good youth," exclaimed the prince, addressing Clara, "explain the meaning of this scene! Why does this lovely female kneel to me, and why does she implore my mercy?"

"Because she has no other hope, save in that and Heaven," said Clara solemnly; "it is the Queen."

"Elvira!" cried the prince: then raising her eagerly, he continued—"Your Majesty may command my services; only tell me how I can assist you."

A few words from Clara explained the urgency of their situation; and the prince, promising to meet them with horses in an hour, persuaded them to return to the cavern till he should join them. Heavily rolled the minutes of this tedious hour, which seemed destined never to have an end, till the nerves of Elvira and Clara were wrought up to such a pitch of agony, that death would have appeared a blessing. At length, the prince came, bringing with him only his faithful Hans.

The sight of him was sufficient to rouse the almost fainting spirits of the Queen; and, without speaking a single word, she and Clara hurried after their conductors, to the wood where the horses were waiting for them.

They mounted, still in perfect silence, and hurried through the most intricate paths they could find; for, as morning dawned, they feared inevitable destruction. Before it became quite light, however, they had reached a thick wood, near the centre of which, they found a half ruined hut; and here did the ci-devant Queen of England and her suite try to obtain a few hours' repose. But, alas! sleep fled from Elvira's eyes; she could not forget she was a fugitive in her own kingdom, flying with terror from those very people who, but a few months before, had almost worshipped her as a goddess; and not even the exhaustion of her body could overcome the hurry of her spirits, whilst every time she closed her eyes, and felt a soft doze creeping over her troubled senses, she started up again in horror, fancying her pursuers had overtaken her.

Consternation reigned in the palace when the flight of Elvira, and the defection of Prince Ferdinand were made known there. "She is gone to Germany!" was the universal cry, and troops were directly dispatched to all the sea-ports, whilst a whole fleet of balloons were ordered to scour the air in all directions, and arrest every aërial vehicle they should meet with, whose passengers could not give a perfectly satisfactory account of themselves. These commissions were executed to the letter, as the guards now sought by extra diligence to excuse the negligence with which they had suffered the Queen to escape; and numerous were the wandering lovers, absconding clerks, and unfaithful wives, who were brought before the Council instead of Elvira and the German Prince, of whom, however, nothing could be heard, their measures having been taken too well to expose them to detection.

In the mean time, the hat and mantle of Clara having been found upon the banks of the river, the duke and Sir Ambrose were inconsolable; and dispatched emissaries every where in search of her. Amongst the rest, Father Murphy and Abelard were sent to the summer palace of the Queen, to inquire if she had there been heard of. Rosabella and her Court, however, had removed to London immediately upon the flight of Elvira being discovered, and the disconsolate searchers having inquired of every one they met in vain, wandered through the gardens, restless and forlorn, till at last they found the mysterious cavern. The aspect of the place was dreary in the extreme: a few stunted shrubs grew upon the banks of a dark, dull rivulet; and Father Murphy shivered and crossed himself as he looked around.

"Och, murther! and this is an awful place, Mr. Abelard," said he; "and I'm after thinking the sooner we get out of it the better."

"Ah, what is that?" cried the butler, springing forward eagerly, and snatching at something in the bushes that looked white.

"It is Clara's pocket-handkerchief, poor darling!" said the friar; "see, here is her name worked upon it by her own pretty fingers:" and as he turned to examine it, his foot slipped, and he rolled into the water, floundering about like a huge porpoise.

"Oh dear! oh dear!" cried Abelard, "he will certainly be drowned. Submersion in an aqueous fluid is almost always destructive of animal life, and I see little chance that he has of escape."

"Och! and will ye let me drown while ye're talking?" asked the indignant priest. "Before it's the good-natured thing ye'd be doing in pulling me out, will ye let me be suffocated?"

"No, no, certainly not!" returned Abelard; "my agony is unspeakable at your distress. I only doubt how I shall be able to raise you without a lever or pulley. The application of the mechanical powers—"

"May go to the devil," cried Father Murphy, as he crawled out without assistance; "and so you would have let me drown, whilst you were talking of the mechanical powers?"

"Excuse me, father," returned Abelard; "friendship is a powerful affection of the human mind; it invigorates, it warms."

"Does it," said the priest, shaking himself like a water-spaniel; "then I should be very glad to have a little of it at present, for I am shivering with cold; to say nothing of being so hungry that I could eat my fingers."

"I am surprised to hear you talk of being hungry, father," said Abelard; "you are surely too fat to feel any craving for food. Fat, you know, is a kind of intermedium through which the nutritive matter extracted from the food, must pass before it is assimilated to repair the loss of the individual. It thus forms a kind of magazine to supply his wants; and a fat man may abstain from food much longer than another, because, during this abstinence, the collected fat is rapidly re-absorbed."

Father Murphy did not speak, but his look was sufficient, and his teeth clattering in his head afforded an ample commentary upon the text.

"You seem cold also," said the pedantic butler; "but that must be a mistake, for animal oil is universally allowed to be a bad conductor of caloric."

"The devil take your caloric," cried Father Murphy, again forgetting his holy office in his anger; "I suppose you'll want to persuade me that I have no feeling next."

"That is far from impossible," replied Abelard, with the most provoking gravity; "for fat, by surrounding the extremities of the nerves, always obviates inordinate sensibility. At the same time, pray do not let me be misunderstood: — I do not say that fat people can do entirely without eating, for the indivisibility and individuality of the living body can only be maintained by an incessant change of the particles which enter into its composition; though merely part—"

"Hold, hold, for Heaven's sake!" groaned Father Murphy.

"—Part of the animal food is reduced into chyle," resumed Abelard; "and, as you doubtless know, another part becomes bones; in fact, the bones are merely secretory organs encrusted with phosphate of lime. The lymphatic vessels remove this salt—"

"Oh!" groaned Father Murphy, "all this is very fine, but it does not make me one whit less hungry. O that I had a broiled rump-steak at this moment, smoking hot and swimming in gravy, with a lump of fresh butter!"

"Hark!" cried Abelard, "the vibration of the air that strikes upon the tympanum of my ears, gives intimation of the approach of some tangible object."

"Alas! alas!" cried the priest, "it is certainly the spirits returned, that carried away poor Clara. Poor dear girl! that was certainly her pocket-handkerchief."

"I despair of finding her," said the butler.

"Despair is sinful, my son," replied the friar; "misfortunes are sent to try us, and we ought to bear them with resignation, and without uttering a single murmur."

"But I thought you were even now complaining of being hungry, father?" said Abelard with the utmost simplicity.

"True, true!" replied the priest, a little disconcerted by this remark; "but—but—"

"It is one thing to preach, and another to practise," resumed the butler, smiling; "is it not, father? However, I certainly heard a noise; and if any one finds us here, we shall be ruined."

"Och! never mind that," said Father Murphy; "for that we are already, ye know."

"Who have we here?" cried some soldiers, who now descended into the cave; and who as before-mentioned, were particularly alert in performing their duty in examining all strangers.

"And is it me ye are asking that?" demanded Father Murphy—"for if it is, it's of no manner of use; for if I were to set about telling you, it's a hundred to one if ever ye got to the bottom of it."

"Is it possible?" cried one of the soldiers; "surely my ears deceive me, or that is the voice of Father Murphy!"

"Sure and it is!" said the reverend father; "and whose should it be but my own? D'ye think I'd use that of another person?"

"No, no!" returned the soldier, laughing; "but my astonishment was, to find the owner of the voice so near me. Though, now I think of it, it is not at all surprising, as the Duke of Cornwall is at the palace hard by, and you of course are with him."

"And how can I be with him," asked the literal Father Murphy, "when I am here? Now if an Irishman had said such a thing, they'd have called it a bull."

"Well, well, my good friend," said the soldier, "we will not quarrel for words. I suppose you came down with the duke?"

"And if you do, you never were more mistaken in your whole life!"

"I cannot in the least comprehend you."

"I don't know how ye should, for I hav'n't begun to explain myself yet: nor should I finish if I were to work at it all day; and so, as the duke is here, we'll just go to him, if ye plase."

The duke, already miserable at the loss of Clara, had no sooner heard of the escape of his daughter, than he had determined to visit the place where she had been, principally from that restless desire of change which generally haunts the unhappy; and he was now as much surprised as the soldier to see Father Murphy there. He felt grateful, however, to the priest for his assiduous search for Clara; but as the adventure of the handkerchief rested entirely upon the father's conviction of its identity—the handkerchief itself having been lost in the holy father's unfortunate tumble into the water—the duke considered the whole adventure as rather apocryphal. He felt, however, consoled by it, though he scarcely knew why; and returned to his friend Sir Ambrose in much better spirits than he had left him.

In the mean time, the party of Elvira did not dare to leave the hut in which they had remained pent up the whole day; their horses being crowded within its walls, as well as themselves, to prevent the possibility of discovery. At length, the shades of evening began to fall, and they again set forward at a rapid pace. The agony they had suffered all day from fear of detection—the narrow space in which they had been cooped up, together with want of food, had exhausted the Queen so much, that the morning found her unable to proceed without refreshment, and about daybreak they were obliged to approach a cottage to implore assistance.

The cottager and his son were out at work; but the woman of the house agreed to give the fugitives the shelter they requested. The prince, delighted at receiving this permission, flew back to the Queen to lift her from her horse; but, alas! Elvira was not in a state to enjoy even the most welcome tidings. Pale and livid as a corpse, her head hung upon the prince's shoulder as he bore her into the house, and her terrified friends thought she had expired. A little warm milk, however, revived her, and she opened her eyes.

"I am ready—quite ready—to go on," said she, gasping for utterance, and again sinking back in a fainting fit.

"It is impossible she can proceed in this state," said the prince to Clara, in a whisper; "what will become of us?"

"We must remain here quietly, till she is better," said Clara.

"But if we should be pursued and taken?"

"We cannot die better than in such a cause," said the heroic girl.

"It is strange," said the prince, looking at her earnestly, "that the Queen has been able to inspire such enthusiastic devotion in such a mere boy."

Clara blushed, and cast her eyes upon the ground, whilst the prince gazed upon her blushing cheeks still more earnestly, till she turned away from him abashed. He took her hand; "I cannot be mistaken," said he, "it is, it is Miss Montagu!"

Clara's agitation betrayed her. "I must attend the Queen," said she, breaking from him; and the prince, respecting the awkwardness of her situation, forbore to urge her farther: he felt, however, completely happy. Clara was too artless to conceal the interest he had excited in her breast, and it was not in the nature of man to be indifferent to the devotion of so young and lovely a creature. His eyes, however, alone expressed his happiness; and Clara, who felt his delicacy in refraining from making any farther observations on her disguise, found her love for him increased tenfold by his forbearance.

A few hours' repose restored Elvira so much, that she

wished to pursue her journey immediately, and it was with the greatest difficulty that the prince persuaded her to wait till nightfall. "You must recruit your strength," said he, "or you will never be able to plead your cause with Roderick. He is too stern a hero to be won as I was."

"Oh, it is impossible to describe how I dread to meet him," cried Elvira; "I tremble at his name. A being so fierce and stern as he is, will perhaps not even condescend to listen to a woman's prayer, and he will spurn me from him."

"Impossible!" cried the prince; "though, I own, I wish we could do without him."

Whilst the principals were thus employed, the cottager's wife was endeavouring to learn from Hans who and what they were. "That poor lady seemed dreadfully tired," said she. "When she came, she looked just like a drooping daffadowndilly; when the gentleman lifted her from her horse — oh! it was quite moving to see her!"

"Ja!" said Hans.

"However, though her illness should occasion a little delay," continued the cottager; "I opine that you must be unreasonable to grumble, when you consider the delightful occasion it affords you of refreshing your olfactory nerves by partaking of a little of this odoriferous atmosphere."

"My what nerves?" asked Hans.

"Your olfactory nerves," replied the learned cottager, with a look of the greatest possible contempt: "that is, the nerves that line the membrane of the nasal organ. Every child knows that the nasal fossæ are formed to receive sensations, as by their depth and extent a larger surface is given to the pituitary membrane, and these soft sinuses, or cavities, are enabled to retain a greater mass of air loaded with odoriferous matter."

Poor Hans stood aghast at this explanation, which he found something like that said to be given by Dr. Johnson, when he called network a complicated concatenation of rectangular angles; and afraid to speak, lest he should draw upon himself a new volley of words as astounding as the last, he remained silent, staring at his companions with much the same kind of feeling as that with which a wild man of the woods just caught, might be supposed to gaze upon enlightened Europeans.

"Can you give me some more warm milk?" asked Clara, who now descended in search of refreshments for the Queen.

"Do you think so much of the tepid lacteous fluid good for the lady?" asked the cottager, as she put some milk into a saucepan.

"She can take nothing else," returned Clara. "How delightfully that girl sings!" continued she, listening with rapture to a milk-maid, who was chanting an Italian bravura as she was milking her cow.

"Yes," replied the cottager; "Angelica sings well. The parieties of her larynx are in a very tense condition, and her trachea is quite cartilaginous. But here comes my good man," continued she; "he has been hard at work all day in the roads, and I am sure he must want some refreshment."

"I do indeed feel excessive lassitude, missis," said the cottager, as he came in; "and I want something to eat. What have ye got? Do see, will you, for it's dreadful hard work breaking stones; most we had to-day were primitive limestone, but I found a few fine specimens of quartz. The crystals were quite rhomboidal, and I stopped at least half an hour admiring them."

"Rock crystals are often found amongst quartz," said his wife; "so I don't think you had any occasion to lose your time in admiring them, when, you know, you break stones by measure, and your wife and children are starving for want of bread."

"Do not distress yourself upon that head, my good woman," said Clara; "we have money, and our gratitude will not permit you to want any thing that we can give you."

"Thank you, thank you," cried the woman; "it's a pleasure to serve a generous gentleman like your honour."

"What a charming voice you have!" said Clara, turning away to avoid the woman's praises, and addressing herself to the milk-maid; who, having finished her task, now stepped over the stile that divided the field from the garden of the cottage, with a pail of milk upon her head, and advanced gracefully in measured steps towards them.

"I am very happy to have pleased you, Sir," replied the girl, dropping her foot into the fourth position, as she made an elegant curtsy, and then glided gracefully on.

"Stay, stay!" cried Clara; "won't you give us another song before you go?"

"You must excuse me, Sir," said the girl, again gracefully curtsying; "I am exceedingly sorry to be obliged to refuse a gentleman of your appearance; but singing requires an alternate enlargement and contraction of the glottis, an elevation and depression of the larynx, and an elongation and shortening of the neck, very difficult to be performed with a pail of milk upon one's head."

"Set down the pail, then," said Clara.

"Indeed I can't, Sir; for I have not a moment to spare. I just met some gentlemen of my acquaintance on the hill, and as I expect them here every moment, I must snatch an instant or two to arrange my toilette."

"Gentlemen of your acquaintance!" cried the mother; "what gentlemen can you have met with here, child, that know you?"

"My cousin John that went for a soldier some time since, and a party of his companions."

"And what brings them in these parts? No good, I fear; for John was always a wild good-for-nothing lad."

"It is no evil, I assure you, mother," said Angelica pertly; "but you are always fancying the worst. John is become a man of consequence now, and he is at the head of a party of soldiers, searching for some state prisoners. He'll be made a captain if he finds them: and I hope he will, with all my heart."

"Where are they now?" asked the mother.

"In the wood," replied the girl; "and my brother is gone to help them to search, as he'll get a share of the reward if they find the fugitives whilst he is with them."

"And you'd go too, if you'd any wit," said the wife to her husband, who had now seated himself comfortably before the fire, and seemed very unwilling to be disturbed. Inspired, however, by his wife's remonstrances, he roused himself, and, stretching his heavy limbs, rolled rather than walked away. Angelica had also retired, and Clara was left alone with the woman. It has already been mentioned, that presence of mind was one of Clara's distinguishing characteristics; and, perceiving the danger of the Queen, she was aware not a moment was to be lost. The observations of the woman to her husband, and, in fact, her whole manner, showed that avarice was her master passion, and upon this hint Clara spoke. She offered her abundance of gold; she enlarged upon the greediness of the soldiers, who, if she waited for their approach, would perhaps cheat her of her share in the promised reward, or, at least, give her such a trifle as would not to be worth having; and at last drew forth the glittering metal and spread it before her eyes. Gold softens the hardest heart, and the cottager's wife could resist no longer, but promised to connive at their escape.

Clara instantly ordered Hans to prepare the horses; and, informing the prince and Elvira of what had passed, the whole party again set forward on their eventful journey.

CHAPTER XXXI.

In the mean time, Roderick had been completely victorious in Spain. He had reached Madrid and established Don Pedro as King; and was now on his return to Seville, where he had left M. de Mallet and his charming daughter. Edric, of course, accompanied him; but the rest of the army had marched to Cadiz to embark, the Greek page only attending upon his master.

"Well, Edric!" said the King, laughing, as they approached Seville, "does not your heart beat with pleasure at the thought of quitting Spain?"

"How can you torment me so, Roderick?"

"Torment you! why I thought you would be in raptures; though I must own, if you are, they are the most melancholy raptures I ever beheld in my life."

"This raillery is not generous. It is unworthy of you. I own I love Mademoiselle de Mallet—but I despair."

"And why?"

"Alas! how can I ask her to share the fortunes of a banished man?"

"Am not I your friend?"

"I know it; but I cannot brook dependence even upon you."

"I do not wish you to be dependent; but what can I do to serve you? Shall I make war upon this cross old father of yours?"

"Oh, do not speak of him so lightly! Say what you please of me, but spare my father!"

"I respect your feelings; and as I can say no good of him, I will have the discretion to be silent."

Edric felt no inclination to reply to this remark, and they travelled on in perfect silence till they reached Seville. Here they found every thing changed: the town had been partially re-built, and the lovely groves of orange and myrtle trees in the vicinity, glowing with all the rich luxuriance of a southern spring, gave no idea of the scene of ruin and desolation it had before presented. They inquired for the house of M. de Mallet, and upon entering the inner square, or court-yard, they found him seated under the piazza that stretched round it, enjoying the evening breeze, whilst his fair daughter was occupied in reading to him.

A fountain played in the centre of the court, its sparkling spray descending in silvery showers; whilst innumerable orange trees and flowering shrubs, which were placed around, perfumed the air with their delicious fragrance; and a light awning, spread over the roof of the court, mellowed the light to a soft though glowing tinge, which gave an air of voluptuous languor to the whole scene.

The delight felt by M. de Mallet and his daughter at again seeing their deliverers was enthusiastic; and though it was most openly expressed by the father, the burning cheeks and sparkling eyes of Pauline spoke quite as intelligibly her silent transport.

"We have long expected you," said M. de Mallet; "for I cannot describe how anxious we are to leave this country. Pauline has wearied Heaven with prayers for your safety, and as I have felt my strength decay daily, I too have prayed for your return, for I have a secret to confide to you that weighs heavily upon my spirits."

"To confide to us?" cried Edric.

"Yes, to you," said M. de Mallet. "It is true I have not known you long; but some circumstances make men better acquainted in a month than the ordinary routine of life does in years. Thus, the kindness with which you have treated me, and the important events in which I have seen you engaged, have made me consider you as old and tried friends, and have induced me to confide to you a secret which I have hitherto guarded with the utmost scrupulous fidelity."

"What can you mean?" asked Edric in astonishment; whilst Pauline gazed upon her father with a look of the most intense anxiety.

"Pauline is not my child!" said the old man impressively. Pauline uttered a cry of agony that thrilled through the souls of her auditors, and threw herself at his feet, looking up in his face with an expression of the bitterest anguish, as though she implored him not to desert her. M. de Mallet's agitation was equal to her own, and, as he fondly regarded her, he continued:

"Yes, miserable being that I am! I am not her father. Alas! often when I have beheld her enduring hunger and thirst for my sake; when I have seen her delicate frame exhausted with fatigue or shivering with cold, whilst still with angelic sweetness she has seemed to forget her own sufferings, and to think only of alleviating mine—oh, then, how I have burned to tell her that I did not deserve her kindness, and that I was an alien from her blood!"

"Oh father! my dearest father!" cried Pauline, her eyes streaming with tears; "what do you not deserve from me? What is there that I could do, that could half express my love and gratitude? Alas! though I am not your child, the tender care you took of my infancy—your kindness, your affection—" Pauline could not continue, her sobs impeded her utterance.

"My dear child!" said M. de Mallet: and folding her in his arms, he mingled his tears with hers; whilst Roderick and Edric were both too powerfully affected to interrupt their sorrows, and stood gazing upon them in silence, though both ardently desired an explanation of this seeming mastery. After a short pause, M. de Mallet resumed: "I see the astonishment I have caused you, and my heart bleeds for the pain I have been compelled to inflict upon Pauline, but I could not die in peace without disclosing the truth."

"Oh, do not talk of dying!" cried Pauline, still clinging to him with the fondest affection.

"And who are the parents of Mademoiselle de Mallet?" demanded Roderick.

"Alas! I know not," returned the Swiss. "About twenty years ago, I was travelling in England with my wife, who, afflicted with an incurable disease, had been advised to try the skill of English physicians, they being considered the most able in the world. One night, my poor wife being exhausted with fatigue, we stopped at a small inn in a village near the sea coast. The night was tempestuous, and a blazing light in the kitchen tempted us to wait there whilst the parlour was prepared for us. A woman sate near the fire, with a lovely little girl, about two years old, playing at her feet. My poor wife was always passionately fond of children, though Heaven had never blest us with any; and attracted by the exquisite beauty of the little cherub, she took it in her arms and began to caress it.

"'Is your honour fond of children?' asked the woman with an evident affectation of vulgarity.

"'I dote upon them,' replied my wife. 'Oh Louis,' continued she, addressing me in French, 'if I could have such an angel as this to supply my place to you, I think I could be resigned to die.'

"'If your honours like the child, you may have her,' said the woman.

"I started: but recollecting that, from the over education of the lower classes in England, they were all linguists; the circumstance of the woman's understanding what we said, did not appear extraordinary. 'She is my child,' continued the woman; 'I live hard by—and have only taken shelter here from the storm. The landlady knows me very well. My husband has been dead some months; and, as I find it hard work to maintain myself and the child too, I own I shall be glad to place her in hands where she is sure to be taken care of.'

"The woman's tale seemed plausible; and my wife and I were easily induced to conclude the bargain that gave us possession of Pauline! We visited the cottage of this woman the next morning, and found her story true, excepting that she had only lived there a few weeks. This, however, appeared immaterial; as indeed she had not fixed any definite time for the period of her residence, and gave some reason which I have forgotten for having left her former abode when her husband died. Soon after this, we left England, taking Pauline with us: her beauty increased with her years; and when my poor wife died, which she did a few months after our return to Switzerland, Pauline formed the sole consolation of my life. Two or three years afterwards, a friend of mine visiting England called by my desire upon the reputed mother of Pauline. He found the cottage deserted, and the landlady of the inn told him, that the woman had left the place a few hours after we had done so ourselves.

"This circumstance, combined with the evidently affected vulgarity of the woman, and the elegance and delicacy of Pauline, has always induced me to suspect I was the dupe of a deception, and that the child had been stolen from parents in a superior rank of life to that in which I found her. Whether my conjectures are correct, I know not; but when I have surveyed the beauty and graces of my child, my breast has smote me for confining her to my own humble station, and I have determined, whenever circumstances would permit, to take her to England, and endeavour, if possible, to elucidate the mystery that hangs over her destiny."

"Accompany me then to Ireland," said Roderick, "and when you have stayed there till you are tired, if you still wish to prosecute your researches, I will give you letters of introduction to the English Court, and I sincerely hope we may find our fair friend to be a princess of the blood at least."

In the mean time, M. de Mallet's narrative had caused the greatest agitation in the breasts of Edric and Pauline. "Not his daughter!" thought the former; "whose can she be, then?" and his imagination ran wild amongst a variety of dreams and fancies, each more extravagant than the last: for, to suppose the elegant and accomplished Pauline the daughter of a mere peasant was impossible; and the transporting hope that she might yet be his, with the consent of his father and the approbation of all his friends, danced before him; whilst Pauline, uncertain what to think, and unable to analyze her own sensations, felt, even amidst the desolation in which the avowal of M. de Mallet had involved her, a faint emotion of pleasure still throb at her heart, when she reflected that now her country was that of her lover's, and that it was possible — she dared go no farther, for her senses seemed unable to support the intoxicating thoughts of what might follow.

It had been agreed that our friends should remain a few days at Seville, to give the army at Cadiz time to recover from the fatigue of their march previous to their embarkation; but the morning after their arrival, a courier arrived with despatches from England, which made Roderick impatient to leave Spain immediately. He was at breakfast when these letters, which had been forwarded to him from Cadiz, were put into his hands. He changed colour, and, starting from his seat, begged Edric to follow him into the garden.

"Good God, what is the matter?" asked M. de Mallet.

"Nothing, nothing!" replied Roderick; "but that I must return to Ireland immediately."

And waving his hand as though to repel farther inquiry, he left the room; Edric followed in silence. "Edric," said the Irish Monarch, throwing himself into a garden-seat and burying his face in his hands; "Elvira is dethroned, and perhaps murdered, all owing to my cursed folly in remaining so long in Spain."

"Elvira!" exclaimed Edric, looking at his friend in the most profound amazement; for he could not imagine why he took so deep an interest in her fate.

The Mummy!

"I see your astonishment, Edric," resumed the King; "but I have not now time to explain whys and wherefores. Suffice it to say, that I adore Elvira, and if she perish, I will not survive her."

A piercing shriek burst from the thicket as he uttered these words, and both Edric and Roderick sprang involuntarily to the spot—it was vacant; they searched the wood, but no creature was to be seen.

"It was fancy," said Edric.

"It was the Mummy," murmured the King, "come to chide me for doubting his promises for an instant."

"The Mummy!" cried Edric; "good God! what do you mean?" and he gazed with horror upon the wild and haggard countenance of his friend, who he seriously believed had become distracted. His look recalled the fleeting senses of Roderick, and with a ghastly smile he replied, "I am not mad, though I have enough to make me so. We must return to Ireland without a moment's delay, and there reinforce my army. Elvira must be restored immediately, for her life is in danger from every moment's delay."

"I hope not," said Edric; "for, though I detest Rosabella, I do not think her capable of assassination."

"If she be not, Father Morris is," returned Roderick, in a low voice, with a look of intense feeling.

Edric turned pale.—"In the name of God, tell me who and what you are?" said he earnestly; "and how you have obtained this close knowledge of the English Court."

"I am called the Devil's favourite, you know," returned Roderick, smiling, in spite of his distress, at his friend's embarrassment, "and it would be very hard if my patron did not give me a hint now and then upon subjects of importance."

"How can you jest upon such a topic?" asked Edric reproachfully.

"True," returned Roderick; "as you say, the subject is not one to joke upon: for we must quit Seville in a few hours, and leave M. de Mallet and the pretty Pauline to follow us under the escort of my Greek page; or rather, what perhaps you would prefer, you shall stay behind to take care of them, and Alexis and I will proceed alone."

"Oh Roderick!" exclaimed Edric, "how can you imagine I could leave you?"

"Not even for Pauline?" asked the King, smiling.

"Not even for Pauline," repeated Edric firmly; "my love for you surpasses even the devoted love of woman; and whilst I breathe, neither peril nor pleasure shall tear me from your side."

"My dear Edric!" said Roderick; the tears glistening in his eyes: the next instant, however, he dashed them away, and added gaily, "But come, we must go and make our bows, and take our leave like pretty behaved cavaliers; and you may trust my discretion, Edric, that I will not tell Pauline of your want of gallantry."

The Greek page looked the image of despair, when he heard his master's commands that he should remain behind; and passions, dark as the lowering heavens before a storm, hung upon his brow. He offered no opposition, however, to his master's will; and crossing his arms upon his breast, bent his head in token of obedience.

The voyage of Edric and Roderick to Ireland was rapid and favourable in the extreme; and on their arrival, their reception was enthusiastic. The Irish are proverbially warmhearted, and the rapture with which they now greeted their victorious Monarch defies description. Triumphal arches were erected, the walls were hung with tapestry, and the streets strewed with flowers, to greet his entry into his capital. Roderick did not refuse these honours; but it was evident to all who knew him well, that his mind was occupied with other things; and, in fact, he took his measures so promptly and so decidedly, that, by the time his army, with M. de Mallet and his daughter, Dr. Entwerfen, and the Greek page, arrived from Spain, he had assembled a force quite sufficient for the restoration of the Queen.

The very day that Elvira fled in terror from the power of her rival, the combined army of Roderick began its march to hasten to her assistance; and it had nearly advanced through the whole of the tunnel under the sea, which separates the two kingdoms, without opposition. Orders were now given for the soldiers to rest for the night, and tents were rapidly pitched for that purpose. Roderick, however, could not sleep; and he stood with his arms folded, gazing at the singular scene before him, the innumerable torches fixed against the dark sides of the tunnel shedding their lucid light around, and showing distinctly the long line of white tents that stretched as far as the eye could reach; whilst the distant roaring of the sea above their heads, sounded like the hoarse murmur of gathering thunder.

Whilst Roderick was thus engaged, Edric perceived a group of people enter the cavern from the English side, and eagerly inquire for the King. They were brought before him; they were four in number: but one stayed behind, holding their horses, which looked dreadfully jaded and distressed; whilst the other three, a man and two women, approached and threw themselves at Roderick's feet: "Good God! it is Elvira!" exclaimed he.

"Henry Seymour!" screamed the Queen, and fell senseless upon the ground.

In the mean time all was anarchy in England. Disgusted with the world and with himself, the King secluded himself from society, and passed his time entirely upon a small estate adjoining the chateau of his father. Sir Ambrose and he often met; but they never spoke, though their hearts yearned towards each other. With all his good qualities, Sir Ambrose was prejudiced and obstinate; he loved his son passionately, but he could not endure a rebel, and the poor old man was fast sinking into the grave, for want of the very consolation he would not condescend to receive.

Edmund also was wretched: the habits of respect in which he had been always brought up towards his father, prevented his daring to intrude upon him against his will, though he would willingly have relinquished his empty title of King, and have exposed himself to all the miseries of absolute want, to have obtained the privilege of throwing himself upon his father's neck, and receiving his forgiveness. The title of Edmund was, indeed, now only an empty one. Rosabella alone exercised the power of a Sovereign, and her haughty temper and capricious tyranny made her universally detested. Monarchs to be respected must be firm; and whilst they continue to inspire respect, they may sometimes venture to be tyrants. But Rosabella was no longer respected; he was despised; and the Commons finding themselves oppressed, and their complaints completely unattended to, began to regret the gentle sway of Elvira. "She, at least," said they, "treated us with kindness; and if she did refuse our petitions, it was with gentleness. But now we are treated with scorn, and trampled beneath the feet, not only of the Queen, but of her confessor. We will not, we cannot bear it."

Sad and mournful also was the life of the Duke of Cornwall: for days and hours he would wander in the gardens of his chateau with his friend Sir Ambrose, and lament sorrowfully over the complete destruction of his hopes.

In these walks they often saw Edmund, gliding at a distance like a solitary ghost, and plunging amongst the trees when he thought himself observed. "How changed Edmund is become!" said the duke. "Alas! how guilt corrodes the heart! He has destroyed my daughter, and he is now suffering the penalty of his crime."

"Say not so," rejoined Sir Ambrose, who could not bear to hear his son blamed by any one but himself; "if Elvira had not eloped with Prince Ferdinand—"

"Eloped with Prince Ferdinand!" cried the duke,—"I did not expect this. What! can you, Sir Ambrose, join in the general voice? Will you slander poor Elvira? Elvira, whom you have known from her cradle—whom you have loved and fondled as your own child?"

"Patience! patience! my good friend."

"I have no patience, I can have no patience, when I hear my daughter scandalized—my poor motherless girl. Remember, if she should err, she lost her mother in her childhood—she has been always brought up with me, and as she has been the playfellow of your sons, from her earliest infancy, perhaps she may not act according to those rigid restraints imposed upon her sex, by those who have been always secluded from the society of men. But she means well, Sir Ambrose, she means well always, and I'd answer for her virtue with my life. Besides, you know, she has always been used to have an intimate friend of the other sex;—You know Edmund—"

"No one ever blamed her whilst Edmund was her friend."

"And who dares blame her now? No one, I trust, whilst I have an arm and a sword ready to defend her."

"My good friend, you reason like a fond father; who, though he sees, is willing to excuse the faults of his offspring: your judgment condemns Elvira, even more than mine."

"No, no,—if I thought her wrong, I should not blame her as you do. Your partiality to Edmund blinds you, and you fancy my poor child has a thousand faults, because she was not

The Mummy!

sensible to the merit of your son."

"You mistake me quite; my opinion of Elvira would be just the same if Edmund were not in existence: though I acknowledge frankly, that every time I see his fine noble countenance, worn with care—his pale cheeks and sunken eyes—I feel a pang through my inmost soul. It is a strange infatuation that she should repulse my noble boy, and yet elope so readily with a youth she scarcely knew."

"Take care what you say, Sir Ambrose—take care what you say,—I will not have my child insulted."

"I do not wish to insult her—I speak but the truth—I do not even think her guilty, though the whole Court rings with her shame."

"Guilt! shame! And this to me? Oh God! Oh God! I have lived too long! To hear my child thus basely slandered, and be unable to resent it!"

"Base! and is this the conclusion of our long friendship—Base! and have I lived to be called base, for merely blaming a coquettish wanton?"

"Wanton!" cried the duke, and transported by his passion he struck Sir Ambrose violently. The aged baronet could not endure this insult; his sword flew from his scabbard, and in a few seconds these ancient friends were engaged in mortal combat.

It was a shocking thing to see these two old men, their white hair streaming in the wind—their venerable features wrinkled with age, and their feeble frames tottering for support—fighting with all the vindictive fury of youth. How fearful is the storm of passion! How vile the human heart when left to its own workings! Every gentler feeling was extinguished in the breasts of the two veterans, and only brutal rage remained. For some time victory was doubtful; but at last Sir Ambrose fell, and in another moment the sword of his antagonist would have passed through his bosom, had not a powerful arm arrested the stroke. It was Edmund! he had heard the clashing of swords at a distance, and, rushing to the spot, arrived just in time to prevent the fatal blow.

"Oh my father!" cried Edmund with a thrill of horror, "for God's sake, do not die till you have forgiven me! He hears me not!" cried he, wringing his hands in unutterable anguish. "Oh, for mercy's sake, speak! Do not destroy me."

Sir Ambrose feebly opened his languid eyes: "Farewell," said he, faintly: "God bless you!"

"Oh, do you forgive me!" shrieked Edmund, falling upon his knees.

"I do," said Sir Ambrose: "and—the—duke;" the words feebly ebbed from his lips; and, as he spoke, the fearful rattle of death gurgled in his throat, and with a convulsive sob he expired.

Sadly did the duke now gaze upon his fallen foe, but when he found him dead he was distracted. Madly he tore his hair, and threw himself upon the corpse; but his agonies were in vain, the vital spark was extinct. Edmund stood also for some seconds gazing upon the body, without any distinct idea existing in his mind; but when the whole sad reality rushed upon him, he could not endure his own thoughts, and darted away with the velocity of lightning. The duke heeded not his departure; he had thrown himself upon the body of his departed friend, and the whole universe seemed to contain for him only that bloody corpse. "I have killed him! I have killed him!" cried he, "I have killed him!"

His fearful shrieks soon drew many persons to the spot. "I have killed him!" screamed the duke, in answer to all interrogations; "I have killed him!" Abelard was one of the first collected round this mournful spectacle. "What can we do?" said he to Father Murphy,—"the case seems desperate."

"I've killed him!" again screamed the duke in agony.

"He's entirely mad," said Father Murphy, "and there's no doubt of it."

"I've killed him!" repeated the duke, with a still more piercing shriek: "I've killed him!"

"Oh he is mad," cried all the spectators, whilst they attempted to remove him from the spot. With infinite difficulty they succeeded, he still clinging to the corpse, and screaming "I've killed him!" till his voice was lost in the distance.

Whilst these scenes were transacting at the English Court, the army of Roderick marched through the kingdom without opposition, for the people every where, tired of the tyranny of her rival, received Elvira with open arms, and the chief nobility vied with each other in opening their houses to entertain her and her suite as she passed along.

It was a fine evening in March, and the night was clear, though cold, when Elvira, with hurried steps, paced the fine terrace belonging to the castle of one of these noblemen. The Queen was evidently lost in reflection, and as she occasionally stopped, she threw back her long hair and looked up to the sky with an air of intense anxiety. "It is a lovely night!" murmured she: "Heaven grant that peace may still attend us! yet, I fear I know not what of danger. Oh, if the forces of Rosabella should resist—and Roderick should fall—and for me—"

She paused, for the thought seemed too dreadful for endurance. The moon shone brightly in the heavens, and the stars sparkled like diamonds on the clear blue sky; whilst Elvira, raising her eyes to heaven, and clasping her hands together, seemed lost in silent prayer. Her fair face, shaded by her long black veil, looked even more lovely than usual, in the soft light thrown upon it; and, as she stood thus apparently quite absorbed in inward devotion, she seemed almost a celestial being descended for the moment upon earth, and about to remount to her native skies.

A figure, wrapped in a dark long cloak, now appeared at the extremity of the terrace, and advanced slowly towards the Queen. Two other figures also emerged from the shade, and followed, though at a considerable distance. Elvira was not aware of their approach till the first figure stood behind her, and seizing her arms, threw a cloak over her head to stifle her cries; and then, with the help of the others, was hurrying her off. At this moment, Roderick sprang actively upon the terrace, and with one blow from his vigorous arm, felled the first assailant to the ground. Then, drawing his sword, the enraged Monarch would have instantly dispatched him, had not the supposed assassin uttered a piercing scream, and, clinging round his knees, implored mercy. The moon shone full upon the boy's face, and disclosed to Roderick's astonished eyes the features of the dumb page. "Alexis!" cried he.

The boy sprang from the ground.

"Roderick!" screamed he; "then I am ruined!"

"Stay!" returned the King, grasping his arm, and preventing his escape; "who, and what are you? Speak, or dread my vengeance."

The boy's heart beat almost to suffocation; every nerve throbbed with the most violent emotion, and drawing a dagger from his belt, he attempted to plunge it into the heart of Roderick. "Ah!" cried the King, starting aside in time to prevent the blow; whilst ere he could prevent it, the page had buried the weapon in his own bosom.

"Good God!" exclaimed Roderick, "what can this mean?"

The whole of this scene had passed with such rapidity, that Elvira had scarcely time to recover herself, or to be aware of what had happened. The two assistants had fled the moment they perceived the King; and Elvira, with trembling steps and pallid cheeks, approached the spot where Roderick knelt beside the bleeding page.

Kneeling beside him, she attempted to staunch the blood which flowed rapidly from the wound, but in vain; for the boy's life was evidently fast ebbing.

Brian, a servant of the King, who had followed his master to the terrace, aided her endeavours; but Roderick remained fixed and immoveable, his eyes chained as by the power of fascination upon the page, who now slowly unclosed his eyelids, and heaving a deep sigh, fixed his languid eyes upon those of Roderick.

"Zoe!" cried the King.

"Yes," returned the page, gasping for breath, and speaking with difficulty; "Zoe! I am indeed that wretch. I loved you, Roderick; I would have died for you. I do die for you; but—but—Elvira—"

"What meant your outrage upon her?"

"What did it mean?" cried Zoe, her eyes flashing fire, and her whole frame supported by a supernatural energy; "did I not see that you loved her, and could I endure to resign you to another? No," continued she, starting from the ground; "I would have killed her, and, had she perished, I should have died contented."

The violence of the action made the blood gush in torrents from her wound; and, pale and feeble, her failing eyes closed. She staggered a few paces, fell, heaved one convulsive struggle, and Zoe was no more!

Sadly did Roderick gaze upon that form which had so lately

The Mummy!

thrilled with feeling—now cold and inanimate at his feet: the victim of passion lay before him. Her hopes, her fears, her rage, and her love, had passed away, and there her body remained a senseless clod of clay, till it should be resolved into its original elements. By this time, some of the servants of the castle, who had been summoned by Brian, approached; and the old Earl of Warwick, in whose castle the fatal scene had taken place, rushed upon the terrace, calling wildly upon his people to save the Queen.

"Is it the Lady Elvira that ye mane?" asked Brian; "Och an't plase yere honour, and she's safe, every inch of her."

"And what has been the matter?" asked the Earl.

"Och and your lordship may well ask that; but the divil a bit any body can tell you but one, and that's myself. Ye see, my master, his most gracious Majesty, and me were walking in the garden; that is, he was walking and I was watching, for fear any harm should happen to him; for the life of such as he isn't to be trusted to chance in a strange country, and I guess he was thinking of the Queen, though he never said nothing about it. And so when we came near the terrace, it was so dark, ye couldn't see yere hand before you. And then the moon peeped through the clouds, like a pretty face looking through a ground-glass window. And then she came out as bright as a silver mirror; and the Queen looked so pretty as she stood praying, that my master couldn't find it in his heart to interrupt her; and for me, I wasn't the man to be even thinking of such a thing. And then two black-looking spalpeens, bad luck to them! stole out behind her, and there wasn't two, for there were three of them—with never a livin' soul beside, to be seen in respect of being near her: but God never would suffer a rale lady like herself to want a friend to comfort her when she'd be in naad—and my master wouldn't let her be after coming to harm, for he jumped upon the terrace entirely like a hound springing at the deer—and saved her, which nobody but himself could have done like it, for the very life of 'em. And when I came, there was the man lying dead that would have killed the princess, and it turned out he wasn't a man at all, but a woman."

The story of Zoe is soon told. Bred in a warm climate, and naturally enthusiastic in her disposition, she was the child of passion. The misfortunes she had experienced in Greece, by depriving her of all she loved, had thrown her affections back upon her own bosom, and they had preyed upon themselves.

To give vent to the feelings that oppressed her, she created an image of perfection in her own mind, and this she worshipped in secret. When she saw Roderick, however, all was changed; a new world seemed to open upon her. The idol of her fancy, indeed, stood before her; for Roderick realized all her wildest dreams. He became her god. His heroism, his person, his talents, caught her imagination, and the violence of her passions completed the delirium of her soul. Notwithstanding, however, the intensity of her feelings, no thought of grosser texture contaminated her mind. Her love was as that of angels, pure and undefiled:—she regarded Roderick as a thing enshrined, almost too holy for mortal vows to worship; and she would have considered it sacrilege to dare even to think of him as a husband.

With these feelings, she had watched over him, with almost a mother's love; and when she informed him of the conspiracy against him, she resolved, with all the romantic self-devotion of a fond woman, to follow him unknown and in disguise; without any plan, however, but that of being near him, or any hope but that of contributing to his happiness. Money, and the assistance of one or two devoted servants, who contrived to follow in Roderick's train, had enabled her to accomplish this. She had felt a momentary jealousy at his anxiety for Pauline, and she had been half induced to favour the plots of the Spanish general, to take Roderick prisoner; but that feeling had worn away, when she discovered the mutual passion of Edric and the fair Swiss. Now the case was different, and, maddened by the thought of Roderick's devotion to Elvira, she had determined to destroy her. Her trusty Greeks would have assisted her plan, but they fled at her detection.

Inexpressibly shocked at what had taken place, Roderick could scarcely bear again to separate himself, even for an instant, from Elvira. "Do not bid me leave you," said he, looking at her with the fondest affection; "You shall accompany me, even to the field. Oh! would to Heaven you would give me a right to be near you for ever."

"Alas! alas!" replied Elvira; "I tremble for the result of this fatal contest. Oh that I were but a humble peasant!"

"Would to Heaven you were!" cried Roderick, with enthusiasm; "for happy as I always am in your presence, never do I feel so much so, as when we seem, as at present, secluded from the world. Then I could forget your rank, and all the artificial restraints grandeur has thrown around you; and without remembering that I am Roderick, and you Elvira, think only of a pair of simple lovers, whose weightiest care was their attendance upon their flocks, and whose only happiness consisted in loving and being beloved."

"Alas, Roderick!" replied Elvira; "do not speak of love. After the dreadful scene we have just witnessed, I tremble at the passion. No, be my friend, Roderick. Friendship is more sure than love. On that, we may confidently rely; but passion destroys itself with what it feeds upon—intense feelings cannot last."

"Oh Elvira! say not so," cried Roderick, fixing his eyes earnestly upon her blushing countenance—whilst she, trembling and agitated, betrayed by her confusion the passion she would have fain concealed.

How feeble are words to express the transports of such a moment! 'Tis the oasis in the desert of life—the bright gem that casts a radiance even upon the dross with which it is surrounded. Man is born to misery—thick clouds hang over him, and obscure his path—dangers await him at every step. One single ray alone breaks through the gloom—bright as the fairy dreams of childhood; but, alas! equally fleeting. 'Tis love—pure, passionate, unsophisticated love—the only glimpse of heaven vouchsafed on earth to man. And this was what was now felt by Roderick and Elvira, as he, throwing himself at her feet, vowed eternal constancy, and persuaded her to acknowledge that her hopes of earthly happiness centered in him alone.

But why do I profane such a scene, by attempting to describe it? Those who have loved, have only to recollect what they felt upon a similar occasion; and to those who have not,—Heaven help them!—not all the eloquence of Cicero himself could give the least idea of any thing of the kind. Suffice it to say, that before Roderick and Elvira parted, she consented, if success should crown their efforts, to become his bride.

The state of England, at this moment, defies description. The death of Sir Ambrose and the insanity of the Duke of Cornwall were events so shocking in themselves, that it was not surprising they produced a violent effect upon the minds of the people. Edmund had disappeared, and Rosabella, instigated by Father Morris and Marianne, became every day more rapacious and tyrannical; whilst even they quarrelled amongst themselves, and wretchedness prevailed throughout the kingdom.

This was the state of the public mind, when the news of the

invasion of Roderick first reached the ears of Rosabella.

"Marianne!" she exclaimed, "summon Father Morris. We are ruined," continued she, as the reverend father entered—"absolutely ruined. Roderick is invincible, and he supports Elvira! Where is Cheops?"

"Ay!" returned Father Morris, "where is Cheops? It is that accursed fiend that has led us on to destruction! His counsels have destroyed us; for, though plausible in appearance, they have been as deceitful as the oracles of old."

"Yet you trusted him!" said Rosabella. "I hated him from the first; but you trusted him. You thought him all perfection: he flattered your vanity, and you weakly believed every thing that he asserted."

"Weakly!" cried Father Morris, his lips quivering with rage.

"Yes, weakly!" returned Rosabella; "for a child would have seen through his artifices; but you were deceived by them, and have been his dupe, his tool, his plaything."

"This to me!" cried Father Morris, gnashing his teeth together with passion.

"Yes, to you," returned Rosabella coolly; "for why should I longer conceal my sentiments? I will no longer be your slave. You have made me deserted by my husband—hated by my subjects—and detested by myself. I will, therefore, no longer follow your councils; from henceforward I will act for myself. Adieu, we meet no more as friends!"

And as she spoke, she walked out of the room, leaving the priest motionless with astonishment.—"This to me!" cried he to Marianne, as soon as he recovered himself sufficiently to speak—"to me, who have sacrificed every thing for her! Did I not place her on the throne? Have I scrupled even to imbrue my hands in blood for her sake? Have I not committed crimes for her that weigh heavily upon my soul? Did I not poison Claudia? and should I not also have destroyed Elvira, if Cheops had not saved her? Oh, Marianne, am I awake? Is it not a cruel dream? Is it possible it can be Rosabella! Rosabella! my Rosabella! my child! my own Rosabella! that uses me thus?"

"Hush! hush!" cried Marianne; "'tis but the passion of a moment. Be composed. Rosabella still loves you; but, irritated by the desertion of Edmund, and the news she has just heard—"

The Mummy!

"Oh, Marianne!" interrupted the friar in agony, "you may easily reason, for you never had a child; but if Heaven had blessed us with one, you might have felt for my anguish."

"I do feel for you," returned Marianne; "but does she not treat me with equal scorn? Since the absence of Edmund she has become distracted, and I, who know the agonies a woman endures when she finds herself deserted by the man she adores, can feel for her."

"And who first gained her Edmund? Would he ever have become her husband, had not I induced him?"

"I believe not; neither would she have been Queen but for you."

"No—no. Oh! how I have toiled for that ungrateful girl! How I have adored her!"

"You have been a devoted father."

"Have I not, Marianne? I have at least endeavoured to expiate my sin. I have done penance—I have spent nights unnumbered in painful vigils. I have scourged my body, till the feeble flesh has shrunk beneath the torture; yet still my mind remains unappeased. Remorse still gnaws my vitals! Oh, Marianne! how poor is earthly grandeur to a mind diseased!"

In this manner did these companions in iniquity confer; till at length, hating each other and themselves, they gave vent to mutual upbraiding, and parted with undisguised hatred and contempt. Such, indeed, is the disgusting nature of sin, that though a man may shut his eyes to his own defects, or rather, see them through the magic prism of self-love; yet he almost always abhors them when he sees them reflected in another.

Thus it was with Father Morris.—Marianne had been his associate in many scenes of vice; he had, in fact, first led her from the paths of virtue, and, as usual in such cases, he now hated the creature he had made.

Father Morris was indeed that brother of the Duke of Cornwall, whose crimes and punishment have been before slightly hinted at. He had married in early life a beautiful and accomplished woman; but, instigated by the machinations of Marianne, whom he had previously seduced and abandoned, he had become jealous of her, and, in a paroxysm of rage, had deprived her of life. This was the crime he had since endeavoured to expiate by the penance of his whole life. Vain, however, had been his endeavour! The mortification of the body avails little, where the humiliation of the spirit is wanting; and Father Morris, notwithstanding his apparent repentance, was proud, envious, and intolerant.

In a fit of remorse, after the death of his wife, he had embraced a monastic life, and in order to subject himself to a perpetual penance, had placed himself as father confessor to Sir Ambrose. No situation, in fact, could have been more painful to a proud spirit than this; yet this daily misery Father Morris felt a pride in supporting without murmuring.

It is strange, but true, that haughty spirits sometimes feel almost pleasure in trying their powers of endurance to the utmost; for there is a self-satisfaction in thinking we have borne what seems almost too much for mortals, that often consoles a man under the acutest agonies.

This was the case with Father Morris, and the daily tortures which he endured without shrinking, almost reconciled him to himself. Ambition, however, was still his master-passion, and as his monastic vows prevented its indulgence in his own person, he devoted himself to the advancement of his child. How he succeeded, and how he was rewarded, has been already shown.

CHAPTER XXXII.

"Have you heard the news?" asked Lord Maysworth one morning, bustling into the breakfast-room of Lord Gustavus de Montfort.

"What is it?" demanded that noble lord, who was sitting at breakfast with his usual satellites.

"The King of Ireland has arrived at Oxford with an immense army, intending to re-establish Elvira."

"Impossible!" cried Lord Gustavus.

"Impossible!" echoed the satellites.

"Something must be done," said Lord Maysworth.

"Thinking as I think, and as I am confident every one who hears me must think, or at least, ought to think," said Lord Gustavus; "no government can be worse than the one we have at present."

"The Queen has not performed one of her promises," subjoined Dr. Hardman; "and her caprice and cruelty are beyond endurance."

"Her extravagance is unbounded," said Lord Maysworth.

"And her arrogance extreme," rejoined Lord Gustavus.

The satellites shook their heads in chorus.

"In my opinion," said Lord Maysworth, "we had better seek Elvira and try to propitiate her. She was used to be mild and gentle."

"But will she not be too much exasperated with our former desertion, to listen to us?" asked Dr. Hardman.

"I think not," said Lord Gustavus pompously.

The result of this conference may be easily imagined. Rosabella found herself deserted; many who would not have had courage to abandon her cause, had they not found precedents for their conduct, fled in the suite of the rebel lords. Roderick rapidly advanced, and his army was every day augmented by the discontented English.

"I am lost, Marianne!" cried the Queen, when she found the enemy was within a day's march of her capital; "I am ruined past redemption."

"Do not desert yourself," said Marianne, "and you may yet be saved. If you despair, it is a virtual acknowledgment of the weakness of your cause."

"What will become of me?" continued Rosabella, wringing her hands; "no earthly help can save me."

"But courage may," said the deep voice of Cheops, who had entered the room unobserved.

"Ah!" screamed Rosabella; "it is the fiend!"

Cheops laughed, and the unearthly sound rang hoarsely in the ears of his auditors.

"Speak, demon! or whatever thou art," cried Marianne; "shall we perish?"

"You shall meet with your reward!" said the Mummy calmly: "Are you satisfied?"

"Oh, Rosabella!" screamed Father Morris, rushing into the room in an agony of despair; "save her! save my child!"

"Your child?" cried Rosabella; "can it be possible that you are my father?"

"I am — I am; — but fly — fly — and I forgive every thing; only let us fly!"

"Alas!" cried Marianne; "he has but too much reason for his agony. The enemy have entered the city."

"What will become of us?" ejaculated the friar. "Fiend! monster! barbarian!" cried he, addressing Cheops, and seizing him roughly by the arm; "deliver us! It was thy accursed counsels which involved us in ruin. Save us!"

"My counsels that led you to ruin!" returned Cheops, with one of his bitter laughs; "say rather, your own passions. Did I urge you to murder Claudia? Nay, did I not save Elvira? Did I not warn you that the throne and misery were inseparably connected? And have not all my promises been fulfilled to the very letter?"

"Yes, yes; to the letter," returned Father Morris; "but not in spirit."

"By the sacred hawks of Osiris kept at Edfou! I swore Rosabella should be Queen, and you her favourite minister."

"Talk not of what is past," cried the priest impatiently; "tell me how to act. The foe is at the gates of the palace."

"Did you not say there was a secret passage, leading from this chamber?"

"There is! there is!" cried Father Morris, with rapture; "we will there lie concealed, and may surprise them."

Cheops laughed:—"Am I still your foe?" asked he, with his usual bitterness.

"Name it not, name it not!" cried Father Morris; "we have not an instant to lose. Hurry into the subterranean passage. I hear the horses of the enemy in the court of the palace!"

"Thebes was perforated with passages, yet she has fallen," muttered Cheops, as he followed the friar and Rosabella through the opening into the secret chamber; Marianne joined them, and the spring pannel closed.

Nothing could be more flattering than the reception Elvira met with from her people. Roderick had placed her at the head of his army, and the people hailed her appearance with rapture. Not a blow had been struck, for the army of Rosabella had joined her banners; and Elvira advanced to London without opposition. Too mild and forgiving to indulge a single feeling of revenge, she felt rejoiced that her rival had escaped, and wished no pursuit to be instituted.

Edric, however, was not so quiescent. A thousand circumstances flashed upon his mind, to prove that the accession of Rosabella had been long planned by Father Morris, and he felt convinced he had been the dupe of the plans they had laid to induce him to quit the kingdom.

"I will find him," said he, "and expose his infamy. He shall not escape me thus."

Vain, however, was his search, and he returned to the room so lately occupied by Rosabella restless and dispirited. Elvira was now in this splendid chamber, surrounded by her friends;

and, trembling with agitation, was awaiting the expected arrival of her father.

"Oh, Heavens!" exclaimed she, as the poor old man was led in; "Roderick! my beloved Roderick! can we not save him!"

"Alas," returned Roderick, "I fear—but compose yourself, my dearest girl; all may yet go well."

"Where is Elvira? my child, my darling Elvira!" cried the old man: "I did not kill her! No," whispered he, drawing near to Roderick; "I killed him, it is true, but it was for her sake. He slandered my child, and I could not bear that."

"Oh God! oh God!" cried Elvira! "have mercy upon him! It breaks my heart to see him thus. Leave us, I implore you," she continued, addressing her friends; "I cannot bear that even you should see the extent of his malady. Leave him with me, and perhaps my presence may recall his lost recollection."

Finding opposition only increased her anxiety, her friends at length consented; and Elvira was left alone with her father. Kneeling by his side as he lay stretched upon a sofa, the Queen endeavoured to console him; but he knew her not, and wrung her heart by calling vehemently upon Elvira. "If I could see my child," said he, "I should die contented. Call my child! where is Elvira? Yes, yes, I know she is a Queen, and cannot come to me! Yet I think even a Queen might look at her poor old father: I only want her to look at me!"

Whilst this scene was passing, Rosabella and her friends lay concealed in the secret chamber; and, through the moveable pannel, watched every thing that passed.

"Now is the time," cried Father Morris; when he saw that Elvira, exhausted by her grief, had hidden her face in her hands, to indulge her tears unrestrainedly.

"You ensure your own destruction if you kill her!" said Cheops.

"I care not," returned Father Morris; and removing the pannel, he approached. Elvira saw him not: and the shining dagger already was aimed at her breast, when it caught the eye of the maniac; and returning reason flashed through his mind.

"Edgar!" cried he, with a piercing scream, "spare my child!"

The Mummy!

The cry roused the friends of Elvira, who had remained in the antechamber, and they rushed in. In an instant the room was crowded; Father Morris was secured; and his confederates (from his having left the pannel open) discovered.

"Edgar!" cried the duke; "yes, it is Edgar! my brother! my only brother! and this is Elvira. She is not fled; I knew she was not! She is safe!"

"And is it possible," cried Edric, "that you can be Duke Edgar!"

"I am that wretch!" said Father Morris.

"Then Rosabella is—"

"My child! and for her I have become the wretch I am! Yet to her I have done my duty; and if she be spared?"

"Ah!" cried M. de Mallet; "it is, it is—yes, I am not deceived, that is the woman who sold us Pauline."

"Who, which—" exclaimed Edric eagerly.

"There," cried the Swiss, pointing to Marianne.

"Marianne!" exclaimed Edric.

"Yes," said she, "Marianne! He is right; it was I, and now is the moment of my vengeance. Seduced and deserted by this man," pointing to Father Morris, "my passions, always impetuous, panted for revenge. I instigated him to murder the wife for whom he had abandoned me—I stole his child and sold her to a stranger—and I substituted my own wretched offspring, whom I had had by a man he abhorred, in its place."

"What!" cried Father Morris, his livid lips quivering with anguish; "is not Rosabella my child?"

"No," said Marianne; "twenty years ago I sold your child to this gentleman," pointing to M. de Mallet. "He was a foreigner, and I believed, by placing her in his hands, you would never see her more."

"Then who is Rosabella?"

"My child, and by your servant Jacques."

"Curses on thee, woman! What! have I then destroyed myself here and hereafter for the offspring of that wretch? A man I detested, abhorred, despised!"

"Yes," said Marianne, with a fiendish laugh. "You abandoned me, and I swore to be revenged: he heard my oath, and by promising to assist me obtained my consent to be his paramour. By his aid I effected all the rest. He has long been dead, but still I have pursued my plan; and when I saw you risking body and soul for Rosabella, I have gloried, for I was revenged."

"Fiend!" cried the priest; and rushing upon her before any one could prevent him, he stabbed her to the heart, and then instantly withdrawing the dagger buried it in his own bosom. "Still I am revenged!" cried Marianne, as heaving a deep sigh she expired. Father Morris never spoke again.

My tale is nearly closed, for dull must be the mind that cannot picture all the rest. The duke recovered his reason, and enjoyed all the happiness his bosom was yet capable of, in witnessing the union of his daughter and Roderick, whom he had loved as Henry Seymour, and now adored as the hero of Ireland. He gave Pauline a noble fortune, as his niece, and she married Edric; who, in the absence of his brother, took possession of his father's wealth, and fixed his residence in his former dwelling, where, after all his troubles, Dr. Entwerfen found himself comfortably re-established in his ancient chamber; whilst Clara, by becoming the bride of Prince Ferdinand, enchanted her mother, and secured her own happiness.

The coronation of Roderick and Elvira, as King and Queen of the United Kingdoms of Great Britain and Ireland, was superb, and far excelled that in which Elvira had previously been an actress. Taught wisdom by experience, however, she no longer placed implicit reliance upon the shouts of applause that followed her footsteps;—yet, even with the reflection that all the promises she received might be evanescent, she could not resist the emotion of pleasure that swelled her breast, when, after the priest had pronounced the nuptial benediction, she walked with Roderick, the chosen of her heart, through a long line of kneeling subjects, and heard every mouth implore blessings on their heads, and bestow praises on her choice.

Proudly did Elvira look around as she reached the entrance of Westminster Hall; yet, ere she entered it, a rush and bustle in the crowd attracted her attention, and a man, clad like a monk, threw himself before her. Elvira screamed; when the man, throwing back his cowl, fixed his heavy eyes upon her and exclaimed, "Do you not know me, Elvira?" It was Edmund.

"Alas! alas!" cried he, "the demon was right; I trusted in my own strength, and I have fallen, miserably fallen. Though I knew it not, ambition was my god—and every thing else weighed lightly in the scale. Yet, even when my ambition was gratified, I was wretched; for I loved you, Elvira, even whilst I plotted against you;—and as my own heart reproached me, I felt every wrong you suffered far more poignantly than you could yourself. My poor father too!—but all is over now, and I am doomed to bitter expiation of my sins,—bitter indeed, for oh, how far beyond all other sufferings are the never-dying tortures of remorse. One thought alone haunted my mind,—one image alone floated before my senses. I could not die till I had obtained your pardon. Pardon me then, Elvira! See! thus humbly, at thy feet I implore thy forgiveness; crouching in the dust, and bending my neck to be thy footstool!"

"Rise, I entreat you, rise!" said Elvira; "and be assured I forgive you—nay, that I pity you from my inmost soul."

"She pities me!" cried Edmund; "yet I can bear even this: even pity. And am I indeed fallen so low as to be pitied! Yes, yes, I am indeed to be pitied."

"I did not mean to wound your feelings," returned Elvira, "believe me, Edmund. Tell me, what is there I can do for you?"

"Nothing!" cried he wildly; "the world is nothing for me now. Pity that unhappy woman that was my wife; and as for me, forget me!"

"Never!" said Elvira; "for never can I forget your disinterested love and your devoted affection. The heart, however, is capricious; and mine, though sensible to your merits, was destined for another."

"And well does that other deserve your love;—for even jealousy itself must own that Roderick is worthy to be your husband. Yes, to him I can resign you. Farewell, Elvira! you shall never see me more! Let my brother take my inheritance! May you be happy! God bless you! God bless you!"

And starting from his knees, he disappeared, before she could reply.

The spirits of Elvira were agitated by this event, which threw a damp over the remaining festivities of the day; and, trembling and unnerved, she proceeded to the magnificent hall, where a sumptuous banquet was prepared for her reception. For some days after this event, the attention of Roderick and Elvira was occupied in arranging the different affairs of the kingdom; whilst Edric and Pauline, with the old Duke of Cornwall, M. de Mallet, and Father Murphy retired to the house of the former in the country, where Dr. Entwerfen was already comfortably established.

A thousand emotions swelled in the heart of Edric as he approached this venerable mansion, and saw again its well-known turrets peeping through the trees. Strange, indeed, are the feelings that oppress the mind, when the wanderer returns, after a long absence, to the habitation of his forefathers. A mingled crowd of contradictory sensations, of disappointed hopes, of undefined fears, float through his fancy; and, as well-remembered objects recall the visions that formerly delighted him, he starts at the difference the experience of their fallacy has made in himself, and he sighs in vain for a return of the blissful ignorance he formerly despised. All too appears changed! As the human mind judges only by comparison, the eyes become dazzled by distant splendours, and that which to the eyes of youth had appeared superb, seems to the maturer judgment of manhood, tame, vapid, and insipid,—whilst the imagination which had fondly cherished the favourite dreams of childhood, and decked them in all the vivid colours of fancy, feels disappointed and disgusted, though it scarce knows why, to find the reality so different from the image it had pictured to itself.

Such were the feelings of Edric as he entered the grand hall of this residence of his ancestors, and gazed upon the well-remembered faces of the crowd of servants assembled to meet him. At the head of these was Davis; his tall thin figure waving to and fro, and his long thin white hair floating upon his shoulders; and the more spruce and gallant aspects of Abelard and his devoted Eloisa, the late Mrs. Russell, who had blest him with the possession of her fair hand a few days before, and now stood blushing and simpering, with all the affected modesty of a bride of sixty, to receive the congratulations of those around her.

"Welcome! welcome, my dear Edric!" cried Dr. Entwerfen, rushing down-stairs to meet them, his sleeves tucked up, and his wig thrown back, in a very experimental-philosophic manner; "rejoice with me too, for I have recovered my balloon! My darling caoutchouc bottle of inflammability! My immortalizing snuff, and, more than all, my adored galvanic battery! Yes, my compendium of science, my epitome of talent, and my most inestimable treasure, is safe! Not, indeed, that which was employed in galvanizing the Mummy, but its counterpart, its duplicate, its prototype. The Mummy came to England, and the balloon being recognized to be mine, it was placed in my apartment, where it has remained ever since, stowed up in safe but inglorious obscurity, till my return."

"Och! and that's a clear case!" said Father Murphy; "and there's no doubt of it."

Leaving the delighted doctor to show the treasures of his laboratory to M. de Mallet, Edric retired to his chamber, and after surveying again and again the well-known objects it contained, he hurried to his favourite grove.

It is singular how inanimate objects, which have been long unseen, recall the thoughts and train of feelings indulged in when one last beheld them: thus, the house, the groves, the walks, the gardens, and the river, recalled all its former longings to Edric's mind; and he again burnt to converse with a disembodied spirit, as he entered the grove where he had formerly so often ruminated, and indulged dreams wild and improbable as the delusions of delirium. The day was beautiful; it was one of those bright glowing mornings in April, when dew drops hang upon every thorn, when the sun shines brightly through the clear pure air, and all nature seems awaking to new life and vigour from repose.

Edric entered the grove, and threw himself upon that very bank where he had reclined only a few months before, under such different feelings. The river, the grove, the bank, were all the same; he only was changed. "And yet," said he, "is not my mind still as unsettled as before? Am I not still wandering in a labyrinth of doubts? Unknowing where to turn; and yet tormented with a restless desire to discover my way. What can have become of the Mummy, I so strangely resuscitated? It is strange, that since the restoration of Elvira it seems to have vanished, and yet all here speak of it as of a living animated being. Would that I could see it. O Cheops! Cheops—"

Suddenly a strange unearthly voice seemed to murmur harshly in his ear—"Go to the Pyramid! There and there only can thy hopes be gratified." Edric started upon his feet—no one was near him, and not a sound broke the awful stillness that reigned around, save the gentle rippling of the river that flowed at his feet. He gazed wildly on every side, hoping, yet fearing to behold the ghastly being, he fancied his words had conjured up. It was in vain; no dark figure interposed between him and the clear bright sunshine; no gloomy shadow stretched along the plain; all looked gay as youth and happiness; yet still that awful voice rang in his ears, and thrilled through every nerve.

"I will go the Pyramid," cried he energetically; "I will again enter that horrid tomb — but I will go alone."

In pursuance of this sudden, but irresistible desire, Edric hastily prepared to return to Egypt; and feigning that he was called to London by business of importance, to satisfy the anxious curiosity of Pauline, he departed. Indescribable emotions throbbed in his bosom as he took his seat in the stage balloon which was to convey him to Egypt; but when he saw the towers and temples, and, above all, the pyramids of this mysterious country, lying beneath his feet, his agitation increased almost to agony. It was with infinite difficulty that he obtained permission again to visit the objects of his journey; as, since the mysterious disappearance of the Mummy, the tomb of Cheops had been closed from mortal eyes. The interference of the British consul, however, at length obviated all objections, and Edric (whose impatience had become absolute torture from the delay) once more entered that awful receptacle of fallen greatness.

Scarcely a twelvemonth had elapsed since he had last trodden those solemn vaults, yet what a change had taken place in his destiny! When he considered the number and variety of the events that had befallen him, he could scarcely fancy it possible that they had been crowded into so short a space of time; and, instead of a year, centuries seemed to have rolled over his head. His feeling of personal identity seemed confused — his senses became bewildered, and he mechanically followed his conductor almost without knowing whither he was going.

At last the guide stopped — "This is the tomb of Cheops," said he; "I suppose, Sir, you will enter it alone."

Edric started — the words of the guide seemed to ring in his ears as the knell of death, and he shuddered as the thought crossed his mind that some horrid and appalling punishment might even now await him for his presumption. Desperately he snatched the torch from the hands of his guide and advanced alone.

Darkly did those gloomy vaults seem to frown at his

approach, and fearfully did his footsteps resound as he slowly penetrated into their deep recesses. At length, he reached the tomb, but the brazen gates were closed, and he attempted in vain to open them. He placed the torch upon the ground, and again tried to unclose the fatal portal; he exerted his whole strength, but still it resisted his efforts. Rendered desperate, he now threw himself against the gates with almost superhuman force. Suddenly a hollow sound murmured through the cavern, and a current of wind rushed by with mighty and resistless fury. The brazen gates flew open with a fearful clang, and the torch fell and was extinguished. The next moment the sepulchral lamp shot forth a faint gleaming light, which brightened by degrees into a steady flame, whilst heavenly music sounded faintly upon the ear, dying gradually away in murmurs, soft as those of the Æolian harp.

The brilliant light of the lamp now glowed with noon-day radiance, and showed distinctly every corner of the fatal chamber. Edric looked timidly around, and shuddered as each well-remembered object met his eyes; but what was his horror and surprise when, glancing at the marble sarcophagus of Cheops, he beheld the gigantic figure of the Mummy standing erect beside it! It was again simply wrapped in the garments of the tomb, and its glassy eyes, rigid features, and statue-like form, chilled Edric to the heart. He looked at it a few moments in silence, till it raised its arm and seemed about to address him; when, shrinking back with indescribable horror, he uttered a faint shriek, and hid his face in his hands.

"Why dost thou tremble?" asked the Mummy in a deep hollow voice that thrilled through Edric's very soul. "Didst thou not come here to seek me, and dost thou shudder to behold my form? I am now before thee. Ask what thou wilt, I am permitted to reply. Why art thou silent? Why does thy heart seem to wither in my presence? Alas! alas! is no mortal to be found free from the debasing influence of fear? Thou art called bold, courageous, and noble. Thou hast dared to soar above thy fellow-men, and thou hast ardently wished to see me. Behold I am here, and now, weak, fearful, and inconsistent as thou art, thou shunnest my approach."

"I do not shun thee," said Edric, removing his hands, and endeavouring to look calmly on the fearful being before him, though the flesh seemed to quiver on his bones with the effort—"I do not shun thee; but the nerves will shrink though the mind be firm. I did wish to see thee; for ardently do I still desire to know the secrets of the tomb."

Cheops burst into one of his fearful laughs. "Weak, silly worm! are you not satisfied then? How would this knowledge avail you? Has any thing but misery attended your former researches? And can any thing but misery attend the knowledge you now covet? Learn wisdom by experience! Seek not to pry into secrets denied to man! If you wish still, however, to be resolved of your doubts, behold me ready to satisfy them; but, I warn you, wretchedness will wait upon my words."

"Then I no longer seek to hear them; for, even weak as you esteem me, I can learn wisdom from experience. Thus, then, I tear the tormenting doubts, that have so long haunted me, from my mind, and bid them farewell for ever!"

"It is well," said Cheops, his eyes beaming with joy. "Then my task is accomplished. I have at last found a reasonable man. I honour you, for you can command yourself, and now you may command me."

"I wish it not," said Edric.

"Have you no curiosity?" asked the Mummy, with a ghastly smile.

"None," returned Edric; "unless it be that I would fain know your history, and the meaning of the sculptures upon your tomb."

"What are they?" demanded Cheops.

"A youthful warrior is bearing off a beautiful woman in his arms, whilst an old man laments bitterly in the distance."

"I was the warrior," said Cheops; "and the beautiful female was Arsinoë. I loved her, and to gratify my impetuous passion I tore her from the arms of her father by force."

"The warrior is afterwards contending with the old man who falls beneath his blows—"

"He did, he did," cried Cheops; "he died by my hand; and eternal misery haunts me for the deed."

"And this old man was—"

"My father!" cried the Mummy, writhing in agony.

"And Arsinoë—"

The Mummy!

"My sister — my own, my beloved sister!"

A solemn pause followed this speech, for Edric was too much shocked to speak again to the awful being who had avowed such crimes, and upon whose face were traced passions too horrible to be imagined. After a short silence Cheops again exclaimed —

"Yes, yes; I see your horror, and it is just; but think you that I do not suffer? know that a fiend — a wild, never-dying fiend rages here," continued he, pressing his hand upon his breast. "It gnaws my vitals — it burns with unquenchable fire and never ceasing torment. Permitted for a time to revisit earth, I have made use of the powers entrusted to me to assist the good and punish the malevolent. Under pretence of aiding them, I gave them counsels which only plunged them yet deeper in destruction, whilst the evil that my advice appeared to bring upon the good was only like a passing cloud before the sun: it gave lustre to the success that followed. My task is now finished; — be happy, Edric, for happiness is in your power; be wise, for wisdom may be obtained by reflection; and be merciful, for unless we give, how can we expect mercy? Rely not on your own strength — seek not to pry into mysteries designed to be concealed from man; and enjoy the comforts within your reach — for know, that knowledge, above the sphere of man's capacity, produces only wretchedness; and that to be contented with our station, and to make ourselves useful to our fellow-creatures, is the only true path to happiness."

The Mummy ceased to speak, and his features, which had appeared wild and animated during his conversation with Edric, became fixed — the unearthly lustre that had flashed from his eyes, faded away, and gave place to a glassy deadness — his limbs became rigid, and as the light of the lamp gradually sunk to less distinctness, the ghastly form of the Mummy seemed rapidly changing into stone. Edric felt that the moment when it was possible for him to hold communion with this strange being was rapidly passing away, and almost shrieked as he exclaimed, "One question! only one ere it be too late." The Mummy feebly raised his languid eyelids, but Edric felt his blood freeze at the unnatural glare. With a violent effort, however, he roused himself to speak. "Was it a human power that dragged you from the tomb?"

"The power that gave me life could alone restore it," replied the Mummy in slow measured accents, as it sank gradually back into its former tomb. Edric shuddered, and involuntarily rushed forward, but the Mummy no longer lived or breathed.

Cold, pale, and inanimate it lay, as though its sleep of two thousand years had never been broken.

"Oblivion laid him down upon his hearse!"

and no mortal ever more could boast of holding converse with The Mummy.

THE END.

Rappaccini's Daughter

By Nathaniel Hawthorne

A young man, named Giovanni Guasconti, came, very long ago, from the more southern region of Italy, to pursue his studies at the University of Padua. Giovanni, who had but a scanty supply of gold ducats in his pocket, took lodgings in a high and gloomy chamber of an old edifice which looked not unworthy to have been the palace of a Paduan noble, and which, in fact, exhibited over its entrance the armorial bearings of a family long since extinct. The young stranger, who was not unstudied in the great poem of his country, recollected that one of the ancestors of this family, and perhaps an occupant of this very mansion, had been pictured by Dante as a partaker of the immortal agonies of his Inferno. These reminiscences and associations, together with the tendency to heartbreak natural to a young man for the first time out of his native sphere, caused Giovanni to sigh heavily as he looked around the desolate and ill-furnished apartment.

"Holy Virgin, signor!" cried old Dame Lisabetta, who, won by the youth's remarkable beauty of person, was kindly endeavoring to give the chamber a habitable air, "what a sigh was that to come out of a young man's heart! Do you find this old mansion gloomy? For the love of Heaven, then, put your head out of the window, and you will see as bright sunshine as you have left in Naples."

Guasconti mechanically did as the old woman advised, but could not quite agree with her that the Paduan sunshine was as cheerful as that of southern Italy. Such as it was, however, it fell upon a garden beneath the window and expended its fostering influences on a variety of plants, which seemed to have been cultivated with exceeding care.

"Does this garden belong to the house?" asked Giovanni.

"Heaven forbid, signor, unless it were fruitful of better pot herbs than any that grow there now," answered old Lisabetta. "No; that garden is cultivated by the own hands of Signor Giacomo Rappaccini, the famous doctor, who, I warrant him, has been heard of as far as Naples. It is said that he distils these plants into medicines that are as potent as a charm. Oftentimes you may see the signor doctor at work, and perchance the signora, his daughter, too, gathering the strange flowers that grow in the garden."

The old woman had now done what she could for the aspect of the chamber; and, commending the young man to the protection of the saints, took her departure

Giovanni still found no better occupation than to look down into the garden beneath his window. From its appearance, he judged it to be one of those botanic gardens which were of earlier date in Padua than elsewhere in Italy or in the world. Or, not improbably, it might once have been the pleasure-place of an opulent family; for there was the ruin of a marble fountain in the centre, sculptured with rare art, but so wofully shattered that it was impossible to trace the original design from the chaos of remaining fragments. The water, however, continued to gush and sparkle into the sunbeams as cheerfully as ever. A little gurgling sound ascended to the young man's window, and made him feel as if the fountain were an immortal spirit that sung its song unceasingly and without heeding the vicissitudes around it, while one century imbodied it in marble and another scattered the perishable garniture on the soil. All about the pool into which the water subsided grew various plants, that seemed to require a plentiful supply of moisture for the nourishment of gigantic leaves, and in some instances, flowers gorgeously magnificent. There was one shrub in particular, set in a marble vase in the midst of the pool, that bore a profusion of purple blossoms, each of which had the lustre and richness of a gem; and the whole together made a show so resplendent that it seemed enough to illuminate the garden, even had there been no sunshine. Every portion of the soil was peopled with plants and herbs, which, if less beautiful, still bore tokens of assiduous care, as if all had their individual virtues, known to the scientific mind that fostered them. Some were placed in urns, rich with old carving, and others in common garden pots; some crept serpent-like along the ground or climbed on high, using whatever means of ascent was offered them. One plant had wreathed itself round a statue of Vertumnus, which was thus quite veiled and shrouded in a drapery of hanging foliage, so happily arranged that it might have served a sculptor for a study.

While Giovanni stood at the window he heard a rustling behind a screen of leaves, and became aware that a person was at work in the garden. His figure soon emerged into view, and showed itself to be that of no common laborer, but a tall, emaciated, sallow, and sickly-looking man, dressed in a scholar's garb of black. He was beyond the middle term of life, with gray hair, a thin, gray beard, and a face singularly marked with intellect and cultivation, but which could never, even in his more youthful days, have expressed much warmth of heart.

Nothing could exceed the intentness with which this scientific gardener examined every shrub which grew in his path: it seemed as if he was looking into their inmost nature, making observations in regard to their creative essence, and discovering why one leaf grew in this shape and another in that, and wherefore such and such flowers differed among themselves in hue and perfume. Nevertheless, in spite of this deep intelligence on his part, there was no approach to intimacy between himself and these vegetable existences. On the contrary, he avoided their actual touch or the direct inhaling of their odors with a caution that impressed Giovanni most disagreeably; for the man's demeanor was that of one walking among malignant influences, such as savage beasts, or deadly snakes, or evil spirits, which, should he allow them one moment of license, would wreak upon him some terrible fatality. It was strangely frightful to the young man's imagination to see this air of insecurity in a person cultivating a garden, that most simple and innocent of human toils, and which had been alike the joy and labor of the unfallen parents of the race. Was this garden, then, the Eden of the present world? And this man, with such a perception of harm in what his own hands caused to grow,--was he the Adam?

The distrustful gardener, while plucking away the dead leaves or pruning the too luxuriant growth of the shrubs, defended his hands with a pair of thick gloves. Nor were these his only armor. When, in his walk through the garden, he came to the magnificent plant that hung its purple gems beside the marble fountain, he placed a kind of mask over his mouth and nostrils, as if all this beauty did but conceal a deadlier malice; but, finding his task still too dangerous, he drew back, removed the mask, and called loudly, but in the infirm voice of a person affected with inward disease, "Beatrice! Beatrice!"

"Here am I, my father. What would you?" cried a rich and youthful voice from the window of the opposite house--a voice as rich as a tropical sunset, and which made Giovanni, though he knew not why, think of deep hues of purple or crimson and of perfumes heavily delectable. "Are you in the garden?"

"Yes, Beatrice," answered the gardener, "and I need your help."

Soon there emerged from under a sculptured portal the figure of a young girl, arrayed with as much richness of taste as the most splendid of the flowers, beautiful as the day, and with a bloom so deep and vivid that one shade more would have been too much. She looked redundant with life, health, and energy; all of which attributes were bound down and compressed, as it were and girdled tensely, in their luxuriance, by her virgin zone. Yet Giovanni's fancy must have grown morbid while he looked down into the garden; for the impression which the fair stranger made upon him was as if here were another flower, the human sister of those vegetable ones, as beautiful as they, more beautiful than the richest of them, but still to be touched only with a glove, nor to be approached without a mask. As Beatrice came down the garden path, it was observable that she handled and inhaled the odor of several of the plants which her father had most sedulously avoided.

"Here, Beatrice," said the latter, "see how many needful offices require to be done to our chief treasure. Yet, shattered as I am, my life might pay the penalty of approaching it so closely as circumstances demand. Henceforth, I fear, this plant must be consigned to your sole charge."

"And gladly will I undertake it," cried again the rich tones of the young lady, as she bent towards the magnificent plant and opened her arms as if to embrace it. "Yes, my sister, my splendour, it shall be Beatrice's task to nurse and serve thee; and thou shalt reward her with thy kisses and perfumed breath, which to her is as the breath of life."

Then, with all the tenderness in her manner that was so strikingly expressed in her words, she busied herself with such attentions as the plant seemed to require; and Giovanni, at his lofty window, rubbed his eyes and almost doubted whether it were a girl tending her favorite flower, or one sister performing the duties of affection to another. The scene soon terminated. Whether Dr. Rappaccini had finished his labors in the garden, or that his watchful eye had caught the stranger's face, he now took his daughter's arm and retired. Night was already closing in; oppressive exhalations seemed to proceed from the plants and steal upward past the open window; and Giovanni, closing the lattice, went to his couch and dreamed of a rich flower and beautiful girl. Flower and maiden were different, and yet the same, and fraught with some strange peril in either shape.

But there is an influence in the light of morning that tends to rectify whatever errors of fancy, or even of judgment, we may have incurred during the sun's decline, or among the shadows of the night, or in the less wholesome glow of moonshine. Giovanni's first movement, on starting from sleep, was to throw open the window and gaze down into the garden which his dreams had made so fertile of mysteries. He was surprised and a little ashamed to find how real and matter-of-fact an affair it proved to be, in the first rays of the sun which gilded the dew-drops that hung upon leaf and blossom, and, while giving a brighter beauty to each rare flower, brought everything within the limits of ordinary experience. The young man rejoiced that, in the heart of the barren city, he had the privilege of overlooking this spot of lovely and luxuriant vegetation. It would serve, he said to himself, as a symbolic language to keep him in communion with Nature. Neither the sickly and thoughtworn Dr. Giacomo Rappaccini, it is true, nor his brilliant daughter, were now visible; so that Giovanni could not determine how much of the singularity which he attributed to both was due to their own qualities and how much to his wonder-working fancy; but he was inclined to take a most rational view of the whole matter.

In the course of the day he paid his respects to Signor Pietro Baglioni, professor of medicine in the university, a physician of eminent repute to whom Giovanni had brought a letter of introduction. The professor was an elderly personage, apparently of genial nature, and habits that might almost be called jovial. He kept the young man to dinner, and made himself very agreeable by the freedom and liveliness of his conversation, especially when warmed by a flask or two of Tuscan wine. Giovanni, conceiving that men of science, inhabitants of the same city, must needs be on familiar terms with one another, took an opportunity to mention the name of Dr. Rappaccini. But the professor did not respond with so much cordiality as he had anticipated.

"Ill would it become a teacher of the divine art of medicine," said Professor Pietro Baglioni, in answer to a question of Giovanni, "to withhold due and well-considered praise of a physician so eminently skilled as Rappaccini; but, on the other hand, I should answer it but scantily to my conscience were I to permit a worthy youth like yourself, Signor Giovanni, the son of an ancient friend, to imbibe erroneous ideas respecting a man who might hereafter chance to hold your life and death in his hands. The truth is, our worshipful Dr. Rappaccini has as much science as any member of the faculty--with perhaps one single exception--in Padua, or all Italy; but there are certain grave objections to his professional character."

"And what are they?" asked the young man.

"Has my friend Giovanni any disease of body or heart, that he is so inquisitive about physicians?" said the professor, with a smile. "But as for Rappaccini, it is said of him--and I, who know the man well, can answer for its truth--that he cares infinitely more for science than for mankind. His patients are interesting to him only as subjects for some new experiment. He would sacrifice human life, his own among the rest, or whatever else was dearest to him, for the sake of adding so much as a grain of mustard seed to the great heap of his accumulated knowledge."

"Methinks he is an awful man indeed," remarked Guasconti, mentally recalling the cold and purely intellectual aspect of Rappaccini. "And yet, worshipful professor, is it not a noble spirit? Are there many men capable of so spiritual a love of science?"

"God forbid," answered the professor, somewhat testily; "at least, unless they take sounder views of the healing art than those adopted by Rappaccini. It is his theory that all medicinal virtues are comprised within those substances which we term vegetable poisons. These he cultivates with his own hands, and is said even to have produced new varieties of poison, more horribly deleterious than Nature, without the assistance of this learned person, would ever have plagued the world withal. That the signor doctor does less mischief than might be expected with such dangerous substances is undeniable. Now and then, it must be owned, he has effected, or seemed to effect, a marvellous cure; but, to tell you my private mind, Signor Giovanni, he should receive little credit for such instances of success,--they being probably the work of chance, --but should be held strictly accountable for his failures, which may justly be considered his own work."

The youth might have taken Baglioni's opinions with many grains of allowance had he known that there was a professional warfare of long continuance between him and Dr. Rappaccini, in which the latter was generally thought to have gained the advantage. If the reader be inclined to judge for himself, we refer him to certain black-letter tracts on both sides, preserved in the medical department of the University of Padua.

"I know not, most learned professor," returned Giovanni, after musing on what had been said of Rappaccini's exclusive zeal for science,--"I know not how dearly this physician may love his art; but surely there is one object more dear to him. He has a daughter."

Rappaccini's Daughter

"Aha!" cried the professor, with a laugh. "So now our friend Giovanni's secret is out. You have heard of this daughter, whom all the young men in Padua are wild about, though not half a dozen have ever h ad the good hap to see her face. I know little of the Signora Beatrice save that Rappaccini is said to have instructed her deeply in his science, and that, young and beautiful as fame reports her, she is already qualified to fill a professor's chair. Perchance her father destines her for mine! Other absurd rumors there be, not worth talking about or listening to. So now, Signor Giovanni, drink off your glass of lachryma."

Guasconti returned to his lodgings somewhat heated with the wine he had quaffed, and which caused his brain to swim with strange fantasies in reference to Dr. Rappaccini and the beautiful Beatrice. On his way, happening to pass by a florist's, he bought a fresh bouquet of flowers.

Ascending to his chamber, he seated himself near the window, but within the shadow thrown by the depth of the wall, so that he could look down into the garden with little risk of being discovered. All beneath his eye was a solitude. The strange plants were basking in the sunshine, and now and then nodding gently to one another, as if in acknowledgment of sympathy and kindred. In the midst, by the shattered fountain, grew the magnificent shrub, with its purple gems clustering all over it; they glowed in the air, and gleamed back again out of the depths of the pool, which thus seemed to overflow with colored radiance from the rich reflection that was steeped in it. At first, as we have said, the garden was a solitude. Soon, however,--as Giovanni had half hoped, half feared, would be the case,--a figure appeared beneath the antique sculptured portal, and came down between the rows of plants, inhaling their various perfumes as if she were one of those beings of old classic fable that lived upon sweet odors. On again beholding Beatrice, the young man was even startled to perceive how much her beauty exceeded his recollection of it; so brilliant, so vivid, was its character, that she glowed amid the sunlight, and, as Giovanni whispered to himself, positively illuminated the more shadowy intervals of the garden path. Her face being now more revealed than on the former occasion, he was struck by its expression of simplicity and sweetness,--qualities that had not entered into his idea of her character, and which made him ask anew what manner of mortal she might be. Nor did he fail again to observe, or imagine, an analogy between the beautiful girl and the gorgeous shrub that hung its gemlike flowers over the fountain,--a resemblance which Beatrice seemed to have indulged a fantastic humor in heightening, both by the arrangement of her dress and the selection of its hues.

Approaching the shrub, she threw open her arms, as with a passionate ardor, and drew its branches into an intimate embrace--so intimate that her features were hidden in its leafy bosom and her glistening ringlets all intermingled with the flowers

"Give me thy breath, my sister," exclaimed Beatrice; "for I am faint with common air. And give me this flower of thine, which I separate with gentlest fingers from the stem and place it close beside my heart."

With these words the beautiful daughter of Rappaccini plucked one of the richest blossoms of the shrub, and was about to fasten it in her bosom. But now, unless Giovanni's draughts of wine had bewildered his senses, a singular incident occurred. A small orange-colored reptile, of the lizard or chameleon species, chanced to be creeping along the path, just at the feet of Beatrice. It appeared to Giovanni,--but, at the distance from which he gazed, he could scarcely have seen anything so minute,--it appeared to him, however, that a drop or two of moisture from the broken stem of the flower descended upon the lizard's head. For an instant the reptile contorted itself violently, and then lay motionless in the sunshine. Beatrice observed this remarkable phenomenon and crossed herself, sadly, but without surprise; nor did she therefore hesitate to arrange the fatal flower in her bosom. There it blushed, and almost glimmered with the dazzling effect of a precious stone, adding to her dress and aspect the one appropriate charm which nothing else in the world could have supplied. But Giovanni, out of the shadow of his window, bent forward and shrank back, and murmured and trembled.

"Am I awake? Have I my senses?" said he to himself. "What is this being? Beautiful shall I call her, or inexpressibly terrible?"

Beatrice now strayed carelessly through the garden, approaching closer beneath Giovanni's window, so that he was compelled to thrust his head quite out of its concealment in order to gratify the intense and painful curiosity which she excited. At this moment there came a beautiful insect over the garden wall; it had, perhaps, wandered through the city, and found no flowers or verdure among those antique haunts of men until the heavy perfumes of Dr. Rappaccini's shrubs had lured it from afar. Without alighting on the flowers, this winged brightness seemed to be attracted by Beatrice, and lingered in the air and fluttered about her head. Now, here it could not be but that Giovanni Guasconti's eyes deceived him. Be that as it might, he fancied that, while Beatrice was gazing at the insect with childish delight, it grew faint and fell at her feet; its bright wings shivered; it was dead--from no cause that he could discern, unless it were the atmosphere of her breath. Agai n Beatrice crossed herself and sighed heavily as she bent over the dead insect.

An impulsive movement of Giovanni drew her eyes to the window. There she beheld the beautiful head of the young man--rather a Grecian than an Italian head, with fair, regular features, and a glistening of gold among his ringlets--gazing down upon her like a being that hovered in mid air. Scarcely knowing what he did, Giovanni threw down the bouquet which he had hitherto held in his hand.

"Signora," said he, "there are pure and healthful flowers. Wear them for the sake of Giovanni Guasconti."

"Thanks, signor," replied Beatrice, with her rich voice, that came forth as it were like a gush of music, and with a mirthful expression half childish and half woman-like. "I accept your gift, and would fain recompense it with this precious purple flower; but if I toss it into the air it will not reach you. So Signor Guasconti must even content himself with my thanks."

She lifted the bouquet from the ground, and then, as if inwardly ashamed at having stepped aside from her maidenly reserve to respond to a stranger's greeting, passed swiftly homeward through the garden. But few as the moments were, it seemed to Giovanni, when she was on the point of vanishing beneath the sculptured portal, that his beautiful bouquet was already beginning to wither in her grasp. It was an idle thought; there could be no possibility of distinguishing a faded flower from a fresh one at so great a distance.

For many days after this incident the young man avoided the window that looked into Dr. Rappaccini's garden, as if something ugly and monstrous would have blasted his eyesight had he been betrayed into a glance. He felt conscious of having put himself, to a certain e xtent, within the influence of an unintelligible power by the communication which he had opened with Beatrice. The wisest course would have been, if his heart were in any real danger, to quit his lodgings and Padua itself at once; the next wiser, to have accustomed himself, as far as possible, to the familiar and daylight view of Beatrice--thus bringing her rigidly and systematically within the limits of ordinary experience. Least of all, while avoiding her sight, ought Giovanni to have remained so near this extraordinary being that the proximity and possibility even of intercourse should give a kind of substance and reality to the wild vagaries which his imagination ran riot continually in producing. Guasconti had not a deep heart--or, at all events, its depths were not sounded now; but he had a quick fancy, and an ardent southern temperament, which rose every instant to a higher fever pitch. Whether or no Beatrice possessed those terrible attributes, that fatal breath, the affinity with those so beautiful and deadly flowers which were indicated by what Giovanni had witnessed, she had at least instilled a fierce and subtle poison into his system. It was not love, although her rich beauty was a madness to him; nor horror, even while he fancied her spirit to be imbued with the same baneful essence that seemed to pervade her physical frame; but a wild offspring of both love and horror that had each parent in it, and burned like one and shivered like the other. Giovanni knew not what to dread; still less did he know what to hope; yet hope and dread kept a continual warfare in his breast, alternately vanquishing one another and starting up afresh to renew the contest. Blessed are all simple emotions, be they dark or bright! It is the lurid intermixture of the two that produces the illuminating blaze of the infernal regions.

Sometimes he endeavored to assuage the fever of his spirit by a rapid walk through the streets of Padua or beyond its gates: his footsteps kept time with the throbbings of his brain, so that the walk was apt to accelerate itself to a race. One day he found himself arrested; his arm was seized by a portly personage, who had turned back on recognizing the young man and expended much breath in overtaking him.

"Signor Giovanni! Stay, my young friend!" cried he. "Have you forgotten me? That might well be the case if I were as much altered as yourself."

It was Baglioni, whom Giovanni had avoided ever since their first meeting, from a doubt that the professor's sagacity would look too deeply into his secrets. Endeavoring to recover himself, he stared forth wildly from his inner world into the outer one and spoke like a man in a dream.

"Yes; I am Giovanni Guasconti. You are Professor Pietro Baglioni. Now let me pass!"

"Not yet, not yet, Signor Giovanni Guasconti," said the professor, smiling, but at the same time scrutinizing the youth with an earnest glance. "What! did I grow up side by side with your father? and shall his son pass me like a stranger in these old streets of Padua? Stand still, Signor Giovanni; for we must have a word or two before we part."

"Speedily, then, most worshipful professor, speedily," said Giovanni, with feverish impatience. "Does not your worship see that I am in haste?"

Now, while he was speaking there came a man in black along the street, stooping and moving feebly like a person in inferior health. His face was all overspread with a most sickly and sallow hue, but yet so pervaded with an expression of piercing and active intellect that an observer might easily have overlooked the merely physical attributes and have seen only this wonderful energy. As he passed, this person exchanged a cold and distant salutation with Baglioni, but fixed his eyes upon Giovanni with an intentness that seemed to bring out whatever was within him worthy of notice. Nevertheless, there was a peculiar quietness in the look, as if taking merely a speculative, not a human interest, in the young man.

"It is Dr. Rappaccini!" whispered the professor when the stranger had passed. "Has he ever seen your face before?"

"Not that I know," answered Giovanni, starting at the name.

"He HAS seen you! he must have seen you!" said Baglioni, hastily. "For some purpose or other, this man of science is making a study of you. I know that look of his! It is the same that coldly illuminates his face as he bends over a bird, a mouse, or a butterfly, which, in pursuance of some experiment, he has killed by the perfume of a flower; a look as deep as Nature itself, but without Nature's warmth of love. Signor Giovanni, I will stake my life upon it, you are the subject of one of Rappaccini's experiments!"

"Will you make a fool of me?" cried Giovanni, passionately. "THAT, signor professor, were an untoward experiment."

"Patience! patience!" replied the imperturbable professor. "I tell thee, my poor Giovanni, that Rappaccini has a scientific interest in thee. Thou hast fallen into fearful hands! And the Signora Beatrice,--what part does she act in this mystery?"

But Guasconti, finding Baglioni's pertinacity intolerable, here broke away, and was gone before the professor could again seize his arm. He looked after the young man intently and shook his head.

"This must not be," said Baglioni to himself. "The youth is the son of my old friend, and shall not come to any harm from which the arcana of medical science can preserve him. Besides, it is too insufferable an impertinence in Rappaccini, thus to snatch the lad out of my own hands, as I may say, and make use of him for his infernal experiments. This daughter of his! It shall be looked to. Perchance, most learned Rappaccini, I may foil you where you little dream of it!"

Meanwhile Giovanni had pursued a circuitous route, and at length found himself at the door of his lodgings. As he crossed the threshold he was met by old Lisabetta, who smirked and smiled, and was evidently desirous to attract his attention; vainly, however, as the ebullition of his feelings had momentarily subsided into a cold and dull vacuity. He turned his eyes full upon the withered face that was puckering itself into a smile, but seemed to behold it not. The old dame, therefore, laid her grasp upon his cloak.

"Signor! signor!" whispered she, still with a smile over the whole breadth of her visage, so that it looked not unlike a grotesque carving in wood, darkened by centuries. "Listen, signor! There is a private entrance into the garden!"

"What do you say?" exclaimed Giovanni, turning quickly about, as if an inanimate thing should start into feverish life. "A private entrance into Dr. Rappaccini's garden?"

"Hush! hush! not so loud!" whispered Lisabetta, putting her hand over his mouth. "Yes; into the worshipful doctor's garden, where you may see all his fine shrubbery. Many a young man in Padua would give gold to be admitted among those flo wers."

Giovanni put a piece of gold into her hand.

"Show me the way," said he.

A surmise, probably excited by his conversation with Baglioni, crossed his mind, that this interposition of old Lisabetta might perchance be connected with the intrigue, whatever were its nature, in which the professor seemed to suppose that Dr. Rappaccini was involving him. But such a suspicion, though it disturbed Giovanni, was inadequate to restrain him. The instant that he was aware of the possibility of approaching Beatrice, it seemed an absolute necessity of his existence to do so. It mattered not whether she were angel or demon; he was irrevocably within her sphere, and must obey the law that whirled him onward, in ever-lessening circles, towards a result which he did not attempt to foreshadow; and yet, strange to say, there came across him a sudden doubt whether this intense interest on his part were not delusory; whether it were really of so deep and positive a nature as to justify him in now thrusting himself into an incalculable position; whether it were not merely the fantasy of a young man's brain, only slightly or not at all connected with his heart.

He paused, hesitated, turned half about, but again went on. His withered guide led him along several obscure passages, and finally undid a door, through which, as it was opened, there came the sight and sound of rustling leaves, with the broken sunshine glimmering among them. Giovanni stepped forth, and, forcing himself through the entanglement of a shrub that wreathed its tendrils over the hidden entrance, stood beneath his own window in the open area of Dr. Rappaccini's garden.

How often is it the case that, when impossibilities have come to pass and dreams have condensed their misty substance into tangible realities, we find ourselves calm, and even coldly self-possessed, amid circumstances which it would have been a delirium of joy or agony to anticipate! Fate delights to thwart us thus. Passion will choose his own time to rush upon the scene, and lingers sluggishly behind when an appropriate adjustment of events would seem to summon his appearance. So was it now with Giovanni. Day after day his pulses had throbbed with feverish blood at the improbable idea of an interview with Beatrice, and of standing with her, face to face, in this very garden, basking in the Oriental sunshine of her beauty, and snatching from her full gaze the mystery which he deemed the riddle of his own existence. But now there was a singular and untimely equanimity within his breast. He threw a glance around the garden to discover if Beatrice or her father were present, and, perceiving that he was alone, began a critical observation of the plants.

The aspect of one and all of them dissatisfied him; their gorgeousness seemed fierce, passionate, and even unnatural. There was hardly an individual shrub which a wanderer, straying by himself through a forest, would not have been startled to find growing wild, as if an unearthly face had glared at him out of the thicket. Several also would have shocked a delicate instinct by an appearance of artificialness indicating that there had been such commixture, and, as it were, adultery, of various vegetable species, that the production was no longer of God's making, but the monstrous offspring of man's depraved fancy, glowing with only an evil mockery of beauty. They were probably the result of experiment, which in one or two cases had succeeded in mingling plants individually lovely into a compound possessing the questionable and ominous character that distinguished the whole growth of the garden. In fine, Giovanni recognized but two or three plants in the collection, and those of a kind that he well knew to be poisonous. While busy with these contemplations he heard the rustling of a silken garment, and, turning, beheld Beatrice emerging from beneath the sculptured portal.

Giovanni had not considered with himself what should be his deportment; whether he should apologize for his intrusion into the garden, or assume that he was there with the privity at least, if not by the desire, of Dr. Rappaccini or his daughter; but Beatrice's manner placed him at his ease, though leaving him still in doubt by what agency he had gained admittance. She came lightly along the path and met him near the broken fountain. There was surprise in her face, but brightened by a simple and kind expression of pleasure.

"You are a connoisseur in flowers, signor," said Beatrice, with a smile, alluding to the bouquet which he had flung her from the window. "It is no marvel, therefore, if the sight of my father's rare collection has tempted you to take a nearer view. If he were here, he could tell you many strange and interesting facts as to the nature and habits of these shrubs; for he has spent a lifetime in such studies, and this garden is his world."

"And yourself, lady," observed Giovanni, "if fame says true,--you likewise are deeply skilled in the virtues indicated by these rich blossoms and these spicy perfumes. Would you deign to be my instructress, I should prove an apter scholar than if taught by Signor Rappaccini himself."

"Are there such idle rumors?" asked Beatrice, with the music of a pleasant laugh. "Do people say that I am skilled in my father's science of plants? What a jest is there! No; though I have grown up among these flowers, I know no more of them than their hues and perfume; and sometimes methinks I would fain rid myself of even that small knowledge. There are many flowers here, and those not the least brilliant, that shock and offend me when they meet my eye. But pray, signor, do not believe these stories about my science. Believe nothing of me save what you see with your own eyes."

"And must I believe all that I have seen with my own eyes?" asked Giovanni, pointedly, while the recollection of former scenes made him shrink. "No, signora; you demand too little of me. Bid me believe nothing save what comes from your own lips."

It would appear that Beatrice understood him. There came a deep flush to her cheek; but she looked full into Giovanni's eyes, and responded to his gaze of uneasy suspicion with a queenlike haughtiness.

"I do so bid you, signor," she replied. "Forget whatever you may have fancied in regard to me. If true to the outward senses, still it may be false in its essence; but the words of Beatrice Rappaccini's lips are true from the depths of the heart outward. Those you may believe."

A fervor glowed in her whole aspect and beamed upon Giovanni's consciousness like the light of truth itself; but while she spoke there was a fragrance in the atmosphere around her, rich and delightful, though evanescent, yet which the young man, from an indefinable reluctance, scarcely dared to draw into his lungs. It might be the odor of the flowers. Could it be Beatrice's breath which thus embalmed her words with a strange richness, as if by steeping them in her heart? A faintness passed like a shadow over Giovanni and flitted away; he seemed to gaze through the beautiful girl's eyes into her transparent soul, and felt no more doubt or fear.

The tinge of passion that had colored Beat rice's manner vanished; she became gay, and appeared to derive a pure delight from her communion with the youth not unlike what the maiden of a lonely island might have felt conversing with a voyager from the civilized world. Evidently her experience of life had been confined within the limits of that garden. She talked now about matters as simple as the daylight or summer clouds, and now asked questions in reference to the city, or Giovanni's distant home, his friends, his mother, and his sisters--questions indicating such seclusion, and such lack of familiarity with modes and forms, that Giovanni responded as if to an infant. Her spirit gushed out before him like a fresh rill that was just catching its first glimpse of the sunlight and wondering at the reflections of earth and sky which were flung into its bosom. There came thoughts, too, from a deep source, and fantasies of a gemlike brilliancy, as if diamonds and rubies sparkled upward among the bubbles of the fountain. Ever and anon there gleamed across the young man's mind a sense of wonder that he should be walking side by side with the being who had so wrought upon his imagination, whom he had idealized in such hues of terror, in whom he had positively witnessed such manifestations of dreadful attributes,--that he should be conversing with Beatrice like a brother, and should find her so human and so maidenlike. But such reflections were only momentary; the effect of her character was too real not to make itself familiar at once.

In this free intercourse they had strayed through the garden, and now, after many turns among its avenues, were come to the shattered fountain, beside which grew the magnificent shrub, with its treasury of glowing blossoms. A fragrance was diffused from it which Giovanni recognized as identical with that which he had attributed to Beatrice's breath, but incomparably more powerful. As her eyes fell upon it, Giovanni beheld her press her hand to her bosom as if her heart were throbbing suddenly and painfully.

"For the first time in my life," murmured she, addressing the shrub, "I had forgotten thee."

"I remember, signora," said Giovanni, "that you once promised to reward me with one of these living gems for the bouquet which I had the happy boldness to fling to your feet. Permit me now to pluck it as a memorial of this interview."

He made a step towards the shrub with extended hand; but Beatrice darted forward, uttering a shriek that went through his heart like a dagger. She caught his hand and drew it back with the whole force of her slender figure. Giovanni felt her touch thrilling through his fibres.

"Touch it not!" exclaimed she, in a voice of agony. "Not for thy life! It is fatal!"

Then, hiding her face, she fled from him and vanished beneath the sculptured portal. As Giovanni followed her with his eyes, he beheld the emaciated figure and pale intelligence of Dr. Rappaccini, who had been watching the scene, he knew not how long, within the shadow of the entrance.

No sooner was Guasconti alone in his chamber than the image of Beatrice came back to his passionate musings, invested with all the witchery that had been gathering around it ever since his first glimpse of her, and now likewise imbued with a tender warmth of girlish womanhood. She was human; her nature was endowed with all gentle and feminine qualities; she was worthiest to be worshipped; she was capable, surely, on her part, of the height and heroism of love. Those tokens which he had hitherto considered as proofs of a frightful peculiarity in her physical and moral system were now either forgotten, or, by the subtle sophistry of passion transmitted into a golden crown of enchantment, rendering Beatrice the more admirable by so much as she was the more unique. Whatever had looked ugly was now beautiful; or, if incapable of such a change, it stole away and hid itself among those shapeless half ideas which throng the dim region beyond the daylight of our perfect consciousness. Thus did he spend the night, nor fell asleep until the dawn had begun to awake the slumbering flowers in Dr. Rappaccini's garden, whither Giovanni's dreams doubtless led him. Up rose the sun in his due season, and, flinging his beams upon the young man's eyelids, awoke him to a sense of pain. When thoroughly aroused, he became sensible of a burning and tingling agony in his hand--in his right hand--the very hand which Beatrice had grasped in her own when he was on the point of plucking one of the gemlike flowers. On the back of that hand there was now a purple print like that of four small fingers, and the likeness of a slender thumb upon his wrist.

Oh, how stubbornly does love,--or even that cunning semblance of love which flourishes in the imagination, but strikes no depth of root into the heart,--how stubbornly does it hold its faith until the moment comes when it is doomed to vanish into thin mist! Giovanni wrapped a handkerchief about his hand and wondered what evil thing had stung him, and soon forgot his pain in a reverie of Beatrice.

After the first interview, a second was in the inevitable course of what we call fate. A third; a fourth; and a meeting with Beatrice in the garden was no longer an incident in Giovanni's daily life, but the whole space in which he might be said to live; for the anticipation and memory of that ecstatic hour made up the remainder. Nor was it otherwise with the daughter of Rappaccini. She watched for the youth's appearance, and flew to his side with confidence as unreserved as if they had been playmates from early infancy--as if they were such playmates still. If, by any unwonted chance, he failed to come at the appointed moment, she stood beneath the window and sent up the rich sweetness of her tones to float around him in his chamber and echo and reverberate throughout his heart: "Giovanni! Giovanni! Why tarriest thou? Come down!" And down he hastened into that Eden of poisonous flowers.

But, with all this intimate familiarity, there was still a reserve in Beatrice's demeanor, so rigidly and invariably sustained that the idea of infringing it scarcely occurred to his imagination. By all appreciable signs, they loved; they had looked love with eyes that conveyed the holy secret from the depths of one soul into the depths of the other, as if it were too sacred to be whispered by the way; they had even spoken love in those gushes of passion when their spirits darted forth in articulated breath like tongues of long-hidden flame; and yet there had been no seal of lips, no clasp of hands, nor any slightest caress such as love claims and hallows. He had never touched one of the gleaming ringlets of her hair; her garment--so marked was the physical barrier between them--had never been waved against him by a breeze. On the few occasions when Giovanni had seemed tempted to overstep the limit, Beatrice grew so sad, so stern, and withal wore such a look of desolate separation, shuddering at itself, that not a spoken word was requisite to repel him. At such times he was startled at the horrible suspicions that rose, monster-like, out of the caverns of his heart and stared him in the face; his love grew thin and faint as the morning mist, his doubts alone had substance. But, when Beatrice's face brightened again after the momentary shadow, she was transformed at once from the mysterious, questionable being whom he had watched with so much awe and horror; she was now the beautiful and unsophisticated girl whom he felt that his spirit knew with a certainty beyond all other knowledge.

A considerable time had now passed since Giovanni's last meeting with Baglioni. One morning, however, he was disagreeably surprised by a visit from the professor, whom he had scarcely thought of for whole weeks, and would willingly have forgotten still longer. Given up as he had long been to a pervading excitement, he could tolerate no companions except upon condition of their perfect sympathy with his present state of feeling. Such sympathy was not to be expected from Professor Baglioni.

The visitor chatted carelessly for a few moments about the gossip of the city and the university, and then took up another topic.

"I have been reading an old classic author lately," said he, "and met with a story that strangely interested me. Possibly you may remember it. It is of an Indian prince, who sent a beautiful woman as a present to Alexander the Great. She was as lovely as the dawn and gorgeous as the sunset; but what especially distinguished her was a certain rich perfume in her breath--richer than a garden of Persian roses. Alexander, as was natural to a youthful conqueror, fell in love at first sight with this magnificent stranger; but a certain sage physician, happening to be present, discovered a terrible secret in regard to her."

"And what was that?" asked Giovanni, turning his eyes downward to avoid those of the professor

Rappaccini's Daughter

"That this lovely woman," continued Baglioni, with emphasis, "had been nourished with poisons from her birth upward, until her whole nature was so imbued with them that she herself had become the deadliest poison in existence. Poison was her element of life. With that rich perfume of her breath she blasted the very air. Her love would have been poison--her embrace death. Is not this a marvellous tale?"

"A childish fable," answered Giovanni, nervously starting from his chair. "I marvel how your worship finds time to read such nonsense among your graver studies."

"By the by," said the professor, looking uneasily about him, "what singular fragrance is this in your apartment? Is it the perfume of your gloves? It is faint, but delicious; and yet, after all, by no means agreeable. Were I to breathe it long, methinks it would make me ill. It is like the breath of a flower; but I see no flowers in the chamber."

"Nor are there any," replied Giovanni, who had turned pale as the professor spoke; "nor, I think, is there any fragrance except in your worship's imagination. Odors, being a sort of element combined of the sensual and the spiritual, are apt to deceive us in this manner. The recollection of a perfume, the bare idea of it, may easily be mistaken for a present reality."

"Ay; but my sober imagination does not often play such tricks," said Baglioni; "and, were I to fancy any kind of odor, it would be that of some vile apothecary drug, wherewith my fingers are likely enough to be imbued. Our worshipful friend Rappaccini, as I have heard, tinctures his medicaments with odors richer than those of Araby. Doubtless, likewise, the fair and learned Signora Beatrice would minister to her patients with draughts as sweet as a maiden's breath; but woe to him that sips them!"

Giovanni's face evinced many contending emotions. The tone in which the professor alluded to the pure and lovely daughter of Rappaccini was a torture to his soul; and yet the intimation of a view of her character opposite to his own, gave instantaneous distinctness to a thousand dim suspicions, which now grinned at him like so many demons. But he strove hard to quell them and to respond to Baglioni with a true lover's perfect faith.

"Signor professor," said he, "you were my father's friend; perchance, too, it is your purpose to act a friendly part towards his son. I would fain feel nothing towards you save respect and deference; but I pray you to observe, signor, that there is one subject on which we must not speak. You know not the Signora Beatrice. You cannot, therefore, estimate the wrong--the blasphemy, I may even say--that is offered to her character by a light or injurious word."

"Giovanni! my poor Giovanni!" answered the professor, with a calm expression of pity, "I know this wretched girl far better than yourself. You shall hear the truth in respect to the poisoner Rappaccini and his poisonous daughter; yes, poisonous as she is beautiful. Listen; for, even should you do violence to my gray hairs, it shall not silence me. That old fable of the Indian woman has become a truth by the deep and deadly science of Rappaccini and in the person of the lovely Beatrice."

Giovanni groaned and hid his face.

"Her father," continued Baglioni, "was not restrained by natural affection from offering up his child in this horrible manner as the victim of his insane zeal for science; for, let us do him justice, he is as true a man of science as ever distilled his own heart in an alembic. What, then, will be your fate? Beyond a doubt you are selected as the material of some new experiment. Perhaps the result is to be death; perhaps a fate more awful still. Rappaccini, with what he calls the interest of science before his eyes, will hesitate at nothing."

"It is a dream," muttered Giovanni to himself; "surely it is a dream."

"But," resumed the professor, "be of good cheer, son of my friend. It is not yet too late for the rescue. Possibly we may even succeed in bringing back this miserable child within the limits of ordinary nature, from which her father's madness has estranged her. Behold this little silver vase! It was wrought by the hands of the renowned Benvenuto Cellini, and is well worthy to be a love gift to the fairest dame in Italy. But its contents are invaluable. One little sip of this antidote would have rendered the most virulent poisons of the Borgias innocuous. Doubt not that it will be as efficacious against those of Rappaccini. Bestow the vase, and the precious liquid within it, on your Beatrice, and hopefully await the result."

Baglioni laid a small, exquisitely wrought silver vial on the table and withdrew, leaving what he had said to produce its effect upon the young man's mind.

"We will thwart Rappaccini yet," thought he, chuckling to

himself, as he descended the stairs; "but, let us confess the truth of him, he is a wonderful man--a wonderful man indeed; a vile empiric, however, in his practice, and therefore not to be tolerated by those who respect the good old rules of the medical profession."

Throughout Giovanni's whole acquaintance with Beatrice, he had occasionally, as we have said, been haunted by dark surmises as to her character; yet so thoroughly had she made herself felt by him as a simple, natural, most affectionate, and guileless creature, that the image now held up by Professor Baglioni looked as strange and incredible as if it were not in accordance with his own original conception. True, there were ugly recollections connected with his first glimpses of the beautiful girl; he could not quite forget the bouquet that withered in her grasp, and the insect that perished amid the sunny air, by no ostensible agency save the fragrance of her breath. These incidents, however, dissolving in the pure light of her character, had no longer the efficacy of facts, but were acknowledged as mistaken fantasies, by whatever testimony of the senses they might appear to be substantiated. There is something truer and more real than what we can see with the eyes and touch with the finger. On such better evidence had Giovanni founded his confidence in Beatrice, though rather by the necessary force of her high attributes than by any deep and generous faith on his part. But now his spirit was incapable of sustaining itself at the height to which the early enthusiasm of passion had exalted it; he fell down, grovelling among earthly doubts, and defiled therewith the pure whiteness of Beatrice's image. Not that he gave her up; he did but distrust. He resolved to institute some decisive test that should satisfy him, once for all, whether there were those dreadful peculiarities in her physical nature which could not be supposed to exist without some corresponding monstrosity of soul. His eyes, gazing down afar, might have deceived him as to the lizard, the insect, and the flowers; but if he could witness, at the distance of a few paces, the sudden blight of one fresh and healthful flower in Beatrice's hand, there would be room for no further question. With this idea he hastened to the florist's and purchased a bouquet that was still gemmed with the morning dew-drops.

It was now the customary hour of his daily interview with Beatrice. Before descending into the garden, Giovanni failed not to look at his figure in the mirror,--a vanity to be expected in a beautiful young man, yet, as displaying itself at that troubled and feverish moment, the token of a certain shallowness of feeling and insincerity of character. He did gaze, however, and said to himself that his features had never before possessed so rich a grace, nor his eyes such vivacity, nor his cheeks so warm a hue of superabundant life.

"At least," thought he, "her poison has not yet insinuated itself into my system. I am no flower to perish in her grasp."

With that thought he turned his eyes on the bouquet, which he had never once laid aside from his hand. A thrill of indefinable horror shot through his frame on perceiving that those dewy flowers were already beginning to droop; they wore the aspect of things that had been fresh and lovely yesterday. Giovanni grew white as marble, and stood motionless before the mirror, staring at his own reflection there as at the likeness of something frightful. He remembered Baglioni's remark about the fragrance that seemed to pervade the chamber. It must have been the poison in his breath! Then he shuddered--shuddered at himself. Recovering from his stupor, he began to watch with curious eye a spider that was busily at work hanging its web from the antique cornice of the apartment, crossing and recrossing the artful system of interwoven lines--as vigorous and active a spider as ever dangled from an old ceiling. Giovanni bent towards the insect, and emitted a deep, long breath. The spider suddenly ceased its toil; the web vibrated with a tremor originating in the body of the small artisan. Again Giovanni sent forth a breath, deeper, longer, and imbued with a venomous feeling out of his heart: he knew not whether he were wicked, or only desperate. The spider made a convulsive gripe with his limbs and hung dead across the window.

"Accursed! accursed!" muttered Giovanni, addressing himself. "Hast thou grown so poisonous that this deadly insect perishes by thy breath?"

At that moment a rich, sweet voice came floating up from the garden

"Giovanni! Giovanni! It is past the hour! Why tarriest thou? Come down!"

"Yes," muttered Giovanni again. "She is the only being whom my breath may not slay! Would that it might!"

He rushed down, and in an instant was standing before the bright and loving eyes of Beatrice. A moment ago his wrath and despair had been so fierce that he could have desired nothing so much as to wither her by a glance; but with her actual presence there came influences which had too real an existence to be at once shaken off: recollections of the delicate and benign power of her feminine nature, which had so often enveloped him in a religious calm; recollections of many a holy and passionate outgush of her heart, when the pure fountain had been unsealed from its depths and made visible in its transparency to his mental eye; recollections which, had Giovanni known how to estimate them, would have assured him that all th is ugly mystery was but an earthly illusion, and that, whatever mist of evil might seem to have gathered over her, the real Beatrice was a heavenly angel. Incapable as he was of such high faith, still her presence had not utterly lost its magic. Giovanni's rage was quelled into an aspect of sullen insensibility. Beatrice, with a quick spiritual sense, immediately felt that there was a gulf of blackness between them which neither he nor she could pass. They walked on together, sad and silent, and came thus to the marble fountain and to its pool of water on the ground, in the midst of which grew the shrub that bore gem-like blossoms. Giovanni was affrighted at the eager enjoyment--the appetite, as it were--with which he found himself inhaling the fragrance of the flowers.

"Beatrice," asked he, abruptly, "whence came this shrub?"

"My father created it," answered she, with simplicity.

"Created it! created it!" repeated Giovanni. "What mean you, Beatrice?"

"He is a man fearfully acquainted with the secrets of Nature," replied Beatrice; "and, at the hour when I first drew breath, this plant sprang from the soil, the offspring of his science, of his intellect, while I was but his earthly child. Approach it not!" continued she, observing with terror that Giovanni was drawing nearer to the shrub. "It has qualities that you little dream of. But I, dearest Giovanni,--I grew up and blossomed with the plant and was nourished with its breath. It was my sister, and I loved it with a human affection; for, alas!--hast thou not suspected it?--there was an awful doom."

Here Giovanni frowned so darkly upon her th at Beatrice paused and trembled. But her faith in his tenderness reassured her, and made her blush that she had doubted for an instant.

"There was an awful doom," she continued, "the effect of my father's fatal love of science, which estranged me from all society of my kind. Until Heaven sent thee, dearest Giovanni, oh, how lonely was thy poor Beatrice!"

"Was it a hard doom?" asked Giovanni, fixing his eyes upon

her.

"Only of late have I known how hard it was," answered she, tenderly. "Oh, yes; but my heart was torpid, and therefore quiet."

Giovanni's rage broke forth from his sullen gloom like a lightning flash out of a dark cloud.

"Accursed one!" cried he, with venomous scorn and anger. "And, finding thy solitude wearisome, thou hast severed me likewise from all the warmth of life and enticed me into thy region of unspeakable horror!"

"Giovanni!" exclaimed Beatrice, turning her large bright eyes upon his face. The force of his words had not found its way into her mind; she was merely thunderstruck.

"Yes, poisonous thing!" repeated Giovanni, beside himself with passion. "Thou hast done it! Thou hast blasted me! Thou hast filled my veins with poison! Thou hast made me as hateful, as ugly, as loathsome and deadly a creature as thyself--a world's wonder of hideous monstrosity! Now, if our breath be happily as fatal to ourselves as to all others, let us join our lips in one kiss of unutterable hatred, and so die!"

"What has befallen me?" murmured Beatrice, with a low moan out of her heart. "Holy Virgin, pity me, a poor heart-broken child!"

"Thou,--dost thou pray?" cried Giovanni, still with the same fiendish scorn. "Thy very prayers, as they come from thy lips, taint the atmosphere with death. Yes, yes; let us pray! Let us to church and dip our fingers in the holy water at the portal! They that come after us will perish as by a pestilence! Let us sign crosses in the air! It will be scattering curses abroad in the likeness of holy symbols!"

"Giovanni," said Beatrice, calmly, for her grief was beyond passion, "why dost thou join thyself with me thus in those terrible words? I, it is true, am the horrible thing thou namest me. But thou,--what hast thou to do, save with one other shudder at my hideous misery to go forth out of the garden and mingle with thy race, and forget there ever crawled on earth such a monster as poor Beatrice?"

"Dost thou pretend ignorance?" asked Giovanni, scowling upon her. "Behold! this power have I gained from the pure

Rappaccini's Daughter

daughter of Rappaccini.

There was a swarm of summer insects flitting through the air in search of the food promised by the flower odors of the fatal garden. They circled round Giovanni's head, and were evidently attracted towards him by the same influence which had drawn them for an instant within the sphere of several of the shrubs. He sent forth a breath among them, and smiled bitterly at Beatrice as at least a score of the insects fell dead upon the ground.

"I see it! I see it!" shrieked Beatrice. "It is my father's fatal science! No, no, Giovanni; it was not I! Never! never! I dreamed only to love thee and be with thee a little time, and so to let thee pass away, leaving but thine image in mine heart; for, Giovanni, believe it, though my body be nourished with poison, my spirit is God's creature, and craves love as its daily food. But my father,--he has united us in this fearful sympathy. Yes; spurn me, tread upon me, kill me! Oh, what is death after such words as thine? But it was not I. Not for a world of bliss would I have done it."

Giovanni's passion had exhausted itself in its outburst from his lips. There now came across him a sense, mournful, and not without tenderness, of the intimate and peculiar relationship between Beatrice and himself. They stood, as it were, in an utter solitude, which would be made none the less solitary by the densest throng of human life. Ought not, then, the desert of humanity around them to press this insulated pair closer together? If they should be cruel to one another, who was there to be kind to them? Besides, thought Giovanni, might there not still be a hope of his returning within the limits of ordinary nature, and leading Beatrice, the redeemed Beatrice, by the hand? O, weak, and selfish, and unworthy spirit, that could dream of an earthly union and earthly happiness as possible, after such deep love had been so bitterly wronged as was Beatrice's love by Giovanni's blighting words! No, no; there could be no such hope. She must pass heavily, with that broken heart, across the borders of Time--she must bathe her hurts in some fount of paradise, and forget her grief in the light of immortality, and THERE be well.

But Giovanni did not know it.

"Dear Beatrice," said he, approaching her, while she shrank away as always at his approach, but now with a different impulse, "dearest Beatrice, our fate is not yet so desperate. Behold! there is a medicine, potent, as a wise physician has assured me, and almost divine in its efficacy. It is composed of ingredients the most opposite to those by which thy awful father has brought this calamity upon thee and me. It is distilled of blessed herbs. Shall we not quaff it together, and thus be purified from evil?"

"Give it me!" said Beatrice, extending her hand to receive the little silver vial which Giovanni took from his bosom. She added, with a peculiar emphasis, "I will drink; but do thou await the result."

She put Baglioni's antidote to her lips; and, at the same moment, the figure of Rappaccini emerged from the portal and came slowly towards the marble fountain. As he drew near, the pale man of science seemed to gaze with a triumphant expression at the beautiful youth and maiden, as might an artist who should spend his life in achieving a picture or a group of statuary and finally be satisfied with his success. He paused; his bent form grew erect with conscious power; he spread out his hands over them in the attitude of a father imploring a blessing upon his children; but those were the same hands that had thrown poison into the stream of their lives. Giovanni trembled. Beatrice shuddered nervously, and pressed her hand upon her heart.

"My daughter," said Rappaccini, "thou art no longer lonely in the world. Pluck one of those precious gems from thy sister shrub and bid thy bridegroom wear it in his bosom. It will not harm him now. My science and the sympathy between thee and him have so wrought within his system that he now stands apart from common men, as thou dost, daughter of my pride and triumph, from ordinary women. Pass on, then, through the world, most dear to one another and dreadful to all besides!"

"My father," said Beatrice, feebly,--and still as she spoke she kept her hand upon her heart,--"wherefore didst thou inflict this miserable doom upon thy child?"

"Miserable!" exclaimed Rappaccini. "What mean you, foolish girl? Dost thou deem it misery to be endowed with marvellous gifts against which no power nor strength could avail an enemy--misery, to be able to quell the mightiest with a breath--misery, to be as terrible as thou art beautiful? Wouldst thou, then, have preferred the condition of a weak woman, exposed to all evil and capable of none?"

"I would fain have been loved, not feared," murmured Beatrice, sinking down upon the ground. "But now it matters not. I am going, father, where the evil which thou hast striven to mingle with my being will pass away like a dream-like the fragrance of these poisonous flowers, which will no longer taint my breath among the flowers of Eden. Farewell, Giovanni! Thy words of hatred are like lead within my heart; but they, too, will fall away as I ascend. Oh, was there not, from the first, more poison in thy nature than in mine?"

To Beatrice,--so radically had her earthly part been wrought upon by Rappaccini's skill,--as poison had been life, so the powerful antidote was death; and thus the poor victim of man's ingenuity and of thwarted nature, and of the fatality that attends all such efforts of perverted wisdom, perished there, at the feet of her father and Giovanni. Just at that moment Professor Pietro Baglioni looked forth from the window, and called loudly, in a tone of triumph mixed with horror, to the thunderstricken man of science,"Rappaccini! Rappaccini! and is THIS the upshot of your experiment!"

The Scarlet Letter

By Nathaniel Hawthorne

THE CUSTOM-HOUSE

INTRODUCTORY TO "THE SCARLET LETTER"

It is a little remarkable, that—though disinclined to talk overmuch of myself and my affairs at the fireside, and to my personal friends—an autobiographical impulse should twice in my life have taken possession of me, in addressing the public. The first time was three or four years since, when I favoured the reader—inexcusably, and for no earthly reason that either the indulgent reader or the intrusive author could imagine—with a description of my way of life in the deep quietude of an Old Manse. And now—because, beyond my deserts, I was happy enough to find a listener or two on the former occasion—I again seize the public by the button, and talk of my three years' experience in a Custom-House. The example of the famous "P. P., Clerk of this Parish," was never more faithfully followed. The truth seems to be, however, that when he casts his leaves forth upon the wind, the author addresses, not the many who will fling aside his volume, or never take it up, but the few who will understand him better than most of his schoolmates or lifemates. Some authors, indeed, do far more than this, and indulge themselves in such confidential depths of revelation as could fittingly be addressed only and exclusively to the one heart and mind of perfect sympathy; as if the printed book, thrown at large on the wide world, were certain to find out the divided segment of the writer's own nature, and complete his circle of existence by bringing him into communion with it. It is scarcely decorous, however, to speak all, even where we speak impersonally. But, as thoughts are frozen and utterance benumbed, unless the speaker stand in some true relation with his audience, it may be pardonable to imagine that a friend, a kind and apprehensive, though not the closest friend, is listening to our talk; and then, a native reserve being thawed by this genial consciousness, we may prate of the circumstances that lie around us, and even of ourself, but still keep the inmost Me behind its veil. To this extent, and within these limits, an author, methinks, may be autobiographical, without violating either the reader's rights or his own.

It will be seen, likewise, that this Custom-House sketch has a certain propriety, of a kind always recognised in literature, as explaining how a large portion of the following pages came into my possession, and as offering proofs of the authenticity of a narrative therein contained. This, in fact — a desire to put myself in my true position as editor, or very little more, of the most prolix among the tales that make up my volume — this, and no other, is my true reason for assuming a personal relation with the public. In accomplishing the main purpose, it has appeared allowable, by a few extra touches, to give a faint representation of a mode of life not heretofore described, together with some of the characters that move in it, among whom the author happened to make one.

In my native town of Salem, at the head of what, half a century ago, in the days of old King Derby, was a bustling wharf — but which is now burdened with decayed wooden warehouses, and exhibits few or no symptoms of commercial life; except, perhaps, a bark or brig, half-way down its melancholy length, discharging hides; or, nearer at hand, a Nova Scotia schooner, pitching out her cargo of firewood — at the head, I say, of this dilapidated wharf, which the tide often overflows, and along which, at the base and in the rear of the row of buildings, the track of many languid years is seen in a border of unthrifty grass — here, with a view from its front windows adown this not very enlivening prospect, and thence across the harbour, stands a spacious edifice of brick. From the loftiest point of its roof, during precisely three and a half hours of each forenoon, floats or droops, in breeze or calm, the banner of the republic; but with the thirteen stripes turned vertically, instead of horizontally, and thus indicating that a civil, and not a military, post of Uncle Sam's government is here established. Its front is ornamented with a portico of half-a-dozen wooden pillars, supporting a balcony, beneath which a flight of wide granite steps descends towards the street. Over the entrance hovers an enormous specimen of the American eagle, with outspread wings, a shield before her breast, and, if I recollect aright, a bunch of intermingled thunderbolts and barbed arrows in each claw. With the customary infirmity of temper that characterizes this unhappy fowl, she appears by the fierceness of her beak and eye, and the general truculency of her attitude, to threaten mischief to the inoffensive community; and especially to warn all citizens careful of their safety against intruding on the premises which she overshadows with her wings. Nevertheless, vixenly as she looks, many people are seeking at this very moment to shelter themselves under the wing of the federal eagle; imagining, I presume, that her bosom has all the softness and snugness of an eiderdown pillow. But she has no great tenderness even in her best of moods, and, sooner or later—oftener soon than late—is apt to fling off her nestlings with a scratch of her claw, a dab of her beak, or a rankling wound from her barbed arrows.

The pavement round about the above-described edifice—which we may as well name at once as the Custom-House of the port—has grass enough growing in its chinks to show that it has not, of late days, been worn by any multitudinous resort of business. In some months of the year, however, there often chances a forenoon when affairs move onward with a livelier tread. Such occasions might remind the elderly citizen of that period, before the last war with England, when Salem was a port by itself; not scorned, as she is now, by her own merchants and ship-owners, who permit her wharves to crumble to ruin while their ventures go to swell, needlessly and imperceptibly, the mighty flood of commerce at New York or Boston. On some such morning, when three or four vessels happen to have arrived at once usually from Africa or South America—or to be on the verge of their departure thitherward, there is a sound of frequent feet passing briskly up and down the granite steps. Here, before his own wife has greeted him, you may greet the sea-flushed ship-master, just in port, with his vessel's papers under his arm in a tarnished tin box. Here, too, comes his owner, cheerful, sombre, gracious or in the sulks, accordingly as his scheme of the now accomplished voyage has been realized in merchandise that will readily be turned to gold, or has buried him under a bulk of incommodities such as nobody will care to rid him of. Here, likewise—the germ of the wrinkle-browed, grizzly-bearded, careworn merchant—we have the smart young clerk, who gets the taste of traffic as a wolf-cub does of blood, and already sends adventures in his master's ships, when he had better be sailing mimic boats upon a mill-pond. Another figure in the scene is the outward-bound sailor, in quest of a protection; or the recently arrived one, pale and feeble, seeking a passport to the hospital. Nor must we forget the captains of the rusty little schooners that bring firewood from the British provinces; a rough-looking set of tarpaulins, without the alertness of the Yankee aspect, but contributing an item of no slight importance to our decaying trade.

Cluster all these individuals together, as they sometimes were, with other miscellaneous ones to diversify the group, and, for the time being, it made the Custom-House a stirring scene. More frequently, however, on ascending the steps, you would discern— in the entry if it were summer time, or in their appropriate rooms if wintry or inclement weathers—a row of venerable figures, sitting in old-fashioned chairs, which were tipped on their hind legs back against the wall. Oftentimes they were asleep, but occasionally might be heard talking together, in voices between a speech and a snore, and with that lack of energy that distinguishes the occupants of alms-houses, and all other human beings who depend for subsistence on charity, on monopolized labour, or anything else but their own independent exertions. These old gentlemen—seated, like Matthew at the receipt of custom, but not very liable to be summoned thence, like him, for apostolic errands—were Custom-House officers.

Furthermore, on the left hand as you enter the front door, is a certain room or office, about fifteen feet square, and of a lofty height, with two of its arched windows commanding a view of the aforesaid dilapidated wharf, and the third looking across a narrow lane, and along a portion of Derby Street. All three give glimpses of the shops of grocers, block-makers, slop-sellers, and ship-chandlers, around the doors of which are generally to be seen, laughing and gossiping, clusters of old salts, and such other wharf-rats as haunt the Wapping of a seaport. The room itself is cobwebbed, and dingy with old paint; its floor is strewn with grey sand, in a fashion that has elsewhere fallen into long disuse; and it is easy to conclude, from the general slovenliness of the place, that this is a sanctuary into which womankind, with her tools of magic, the broom and mop, has very infrequent access. In the way of furniture, there is a stove with a voluminous funnel; an old pine desk with a three-legged stool beside it; two or three wooden-bottom chairs, exceedingly decrepit and infirm; and—not to forget the library—on some shelves, a score or two of volumes of the Acts of Congress, and a bulky Digest of the Revenue laws. A tin pipe ascends through the ceiling, and forms a medium of vocal communication with other parts of the edifice. And here, some six months ago—pacing from corner to corner, or lounging on the long-legged stool, with his elbow on the desk, and his eyes wandering up and down the columns of the morning newspaper—you might have recognised, honoured reader, the same individual who welcomed you into his cheery little study, where the sunshine glimmered so pleasantly through the willow branches on the western side of the Old Manse. But now, should you go thither to seek him, you would inquire in vain for the Locofoco Surveyor. The besom of reform hath swept him out of office, and a worthier successor wears his dignity and pockets his emoluments.

This old town of Salem—my native place, though I have

dwelt much away from it both in boyhood and maturer years — possesses, or did possess, a hold on my affection, the force of which I have never realized during my seasons of actual residence here. Indeed, so far as its physical aspect is concerned, with its flat, unvaried surface, covered chiefly with wooden houses, few or none of which pretend to architectural beauty — its irregularity, which is neither picturesque nor quaint, but only tame — its long and lazy street, lounging wearisomely through the whole extent of the peninsula, with Gallows Hill and New Guinea at one end, and a view of the alms-house at the other — such being the features of my native town, it would be quite as reasonable to form a sentimental attachment to a disarranged checker-board. And yet, though invariably happiest elsewhere, there is within me a feeling for Old Salem, which, in lack of a better phrase, I must be content to call affection. The sentiment is probably assignable to the deep and aged roots which my family has stuck into the soil. It is now nearly two centuries and a quarter since the original Briton, the earliest emigrant of my name, made his appearance in the wild and forest-bordered settlement which has since become a city. And here his descendants have been born and died, and have mingled their earthly substance with the soil, until no small portion of it must necessarily be akin to the mortal frame wherewith, for a little while, I walk the streets. In part, therefore, the attachment which I speak of is the mere sensuous sympathy of dust for dust. Few of my countrymen can know what it is; nor, as frequent transplantation is perhaps better for the stock, need they consider it desirable to know.

But the sentiment has likewise its moral quality. The figure of that first ancestor, invested by family tradition with a dim and dusky grandeur, was present to my boyish imagination as far back as I can remember. It still haunts me, and induces a sort of home-feeling with the past, which I scarcely claim in reference to the present phase of the town. I seem to have a stronger claim to a residence here on account of this grave, bearded, sable-cloaked, and steeple-crowned progenitor — who came so early, with his Bible and his sword, and trode the unworn street with such a stately port, and made so large a figure, as a man of war and peace — a stronger claim than for myself, whose name is seldom heard and my face hardly known. He was a soldier, legislator, judge; he was a ruler in the Church; he had all the Puritanic traits, both good and evil. He was likewise a bitter persecutor; as witness the Quakers, who have remembered him in their histories, and relate an incident of his hard severity towards a woman of their sect, which will last longer, it is to be feared, than any record of his better deeds, although these were many. His son, too, inherited the persecuting spirit, and made himself so conspicuous in the martyrdom of the witches, that their blood may fairly be said to have left a stain upon him. So deep a stain, indeed, that his dry old bones, in the Charter-street burial-ground, must still retain it, if they have not crumbled utterly to dust! I know not whether these ancestors of mine bethought themselves to repent, and ask pardon of Heaven for their cruelties; or whether they are now groaning under the heavy consequences of them in another state of being. At all events, I, the present writer, as their representative, hereby take shame upon myself for their sakes, and pray that any curse incurred by them—as I have heard, and as the dreary and unprosperous condition of the race, for many a long year back, would argue to exist—may be now and henceforth removed.

Doubtless, however, either of these stern and black-browed Puritans would have thought it quite a sufficient retribution for his sins that, after so long a lapse of years, the old trunk of the family tree, with so much venerable moss upon it, should have borne, as its topmost bough, an idler like myself. No aim that I have ever cherished would they recognise as laudable; no success of mine—if my life, beyond its domestic scope, had ever been brightened by success—would they deem otherwise than worthless, if not positively disgraceful. "What is he?" murmurs one grey shadow of my forefathers to the other. "A writer of story books! What kind of business in life—what mode of glorifying God, or being serviceable to mankind in his day and generation—may that be? Why, the degenerate fellow might as well have been a fiddler!" Such are the compliments bandied between my great grandsires and myself, across the gulf of time! And yet, let them scorn me as they will, strong traits of their nature have intertwined themselves with mine.

Planted deep, in the town's earliest infancy and childhood, by these two earnest and energetic men, the race has ever since subsisted here; always, too, in respectability; never, so far as I have known, disgraced by a single unworthy member; but seldom or never, on the other hand, after the first two generations, performing any memorable deed, or so much as putting forward a claim to public notice. Gradually, they have sunk almost out of sight; as old houses, here and there about the streets, get covered half-way to the eaves by the accumulation of new soil. From father to son, for above a hundred years, they followed the sea; a grey-headed shipmaster, in each generation, retiring from the quarter-deck to the homestead, while a boy of fourteen took the hereditary place before the mast, confronting the salt spray and the gale which had blustered against his sire and grandsire. The boy, also in due time, passed from the forecastle to the cabin, spent a tempestuous manhood, and returned from his world-wanderings, to grow old, and die, and mingle his dust with the natal earth. This long connexion of a family with one spot, as its place of birth and burial, creates a kindred between the human being and the locality, quite independent of any charm in the scenery or moral circumstances that surround him. It is not love but instinct. The new inhabitant—who came himself from a foreign land, or whose father or grandfather came—has little claim to be called a Salemite; he has no conception of the oyster-like tenacity with which an old settler, over whom his third century is creeping, clings to the spot where his successive generations have been embedded. It is no matter that the place is joyless for him; that he is weary of the old wooden houses, the mud and dust, the dead level of site and sentiment, the chill east wind, and the chillest of social atmospheres;—all these, and whatever faults besides he may see or imagine, are nothing to the purpose. The spell survives, and just as powerfully as if the natal spot were an earthly paradise. So has it been in my case. I felt it almost as a destiny to make Salem my home; so that the mould of features and cast of character which had all along been familiar here—ever, as one representative of the race lay down in the grave, another assuming, as it were, his sentry-march along the main street—might still in my little day be seen and recognised in the old town. Nevertheless, this very sentiment is an evidence that the connexion, which has become an unhealthy one, should at last be severed. Human nature will not flourish, any more than a potato, if it be planted and re-planted, for too long a series of generations, in the same worn-out soil. My children have had other birth-places, and, so far as their fortunes may be within my control, shall strike their roots into unaccustomed earth.

On emerging from the Old Manse, it was chiefly this strange, indolent, unjoyous attachment for my native town that brought me to fill a place in Uncle Sam's brick edifice, when I might as well, or better, have gone somewhere else. My doom was on me. It was not the first time, nor the second, that I had gone away—as it seemed, permanently—but yet returned, like the bad halfpenny, or as if Salem were for me the inevitable centre of the universe. So, one fine morning I ascended the flight of granite steps, with the President's commission in my pocket, and was introduced to the corps of gentlemen who were to aid me in my weighty responsibility as chief executive officer of the Custom-House.

I doubt greatly—or, rather, I do not doubt at all—whether any public functionary of the United States, either in the civil or military line, has ever had such a patriarchal body of veterans under his orders as myself. The whereabouts of the Oldest Inhabitant was at once settled when I looked at them. For upwards of twenty years before this epoch, the independent position of the Collector had kept the Salem Custom-House out of the whirlpool of political vicissitude, which makes the tenure of office generally so fragile. A soldier—New England's most distinguished soldier—he stood firmly on the pedestal of his gallant services; and, himself secure in the wise liberality of the successive administrations through which he had held office, he had been the safety of his subordinates in many an hour of danger and heart-quake. General Miller was radically conservative; a man over whose kindly nature habit had no slight influence; attaching himself strongly to familiar faces, and with difficulty moved to change, even when change might have brought unquestionable improvement. Thus, on taking charge of my department, I found few but aged men. They were ancient sea-captains, for the most part, who, after being tossed on every sea, and standing up sturdily against life's tempestuous blast, had finally drifted into this quiet nook, where, with little to disturb them, except the periodical terrors of a Presidential election, they one and all acquired a new lease of existence. Though by no means less liable than their fellow-men to age and infirmity, they had evidently some talisman or other that kept death at bay. Two or three of their number, as I was assured, being gouty and rheumatic, or perhaps bed-ridden, never dreamed of making their appearance at the Custom-House during a large part of the year; but, after a torpid winter, would creep out into the warm sunshine of May or June, go lazily about what they termed duty, and, at their own leisure and convenience, betake themselves to bed again. I must plead guilty to the charge of abbreviating the official breath of more than one of these venerable servants of the republic. They were allowed, on my representation, to rest from their arduous labours, and soon afterwards—as if their sole principle of life had been zeal for their country's service—as I verily believe it was—withdrew to a better world. It is a pious consolation to me that, through my interference, a sufficient space was allowed them for repentance of the evil and corrupt practices into which, as a matter of course, every Custom-House officer must be supposed to fall. Neither the front nor the back entrance of the Custom-House opens on the road to Paradise.

The greater part of my officers were Whigs. It was well for their venerable brotherhood that the new Surveyor was not a politician, and though a faithful Democrat in principle, neither received nor held his office with any reference to political services. Had it been otherwise—had an active politician been put into this influential post, to assume the easy task of making head against a Whig Collector, whose infirmities withheld him from the personal administration of his office—hardly a man of the old corps would have drawn the breath of official life within a month after the exterminating angel had come up the Custom-House steps. According to the received code in such matters, it would have been nothing short of duty, in a politician, to bring every one of those white heads under the axe of the guillotine. It was plain enough to discern that the old fellows dreaded some such discourtesy at my hands. It pained, and at the same time amused me, to behold the terrors that attended my advent, to see a furrowed cheek, weather-beaten by half a century of storm, turn ashy pale at the glance of so harmless an individual as myself; to detect, as one or another addressed me, the tremor of a voice which, in long-past days, had been wont to bellow through a speaking-trumpet, hoarsely enough to frighten Boreas himself to silence. They knew, these excellent old persons, that, by all established rule—and, as regarded some of them, weighed by their own lack of efficiency for business— they ought to have given place to younger men, more orthodox in politics, and altogether fitter than themselves to serve our common Uncle. I knew it, too, but could never quite find in my heart to act upon the knowledge. Much and deservedly to my own discredit, therefore, and considerably to the detriment of my official conscience, they continued, during my incumbency, to creep about the wharves, and loiter up and down the Custom-House steps. They spent a good deal of time, also, asleep in their accustomed corners, with their chairs tilted back against the walls; awaking, however, once or twice in the forenoon, to bore one another with the several thousandth repetition of old sea-stories and mouldy jokes, that had grown to be passwords and countersigns among them.

The discovery was soon made, I imagine, that the new Surveyor had no great harm in him. So, with lightsome hearts and the happy consciousness of being usefully employed—in their own behalf at least, if not for our beloved country—these good old gentlemen went through the various formalities of office. Sagaciously under their spectacles, did they peep into the holds of vessels. Mighty was their fuss about little matters, and marvellous, sometimes, the obtuseness that allowed greater ones to slip between their fingers! Whenever such a mischance occurred—when a waggon-load of valuable merchandise had been smuggled ashore, at noonday, perhaps, and directly beneath their unsuspicious noses—nothing could exceed the vigilance and alacrity with which they proceeded to lock, and double-lock, and secure with tape and sealing-wax, all the avenues of the delinquent vessel. Instead of a reprimand for their previous negligence, the case seemed rather to require an eulogium on their praiseworthy caution after the mischief had happened; a grateful recognition of the promptitude of their zeal the moment that there was no longer any remedy.

Unless people are more than commonly disagreeable, it is my foolish habit to contract a kindness for them. The better part of my companion's character, if it have a better part, is that which usually comes uppermost in my regard, and forms the type whereby I recognise the man. As most of these old Custom-House officers had good traits, and as my position in reference to them, being paternal and protective, was favourable to the growth of friendly sentiments, I soon grew to like them all. It was pleasant in the summer forenoons — when the fervent heat, that almost liquefied the rest of the human family, merely communicated a genial warmth to their half torpid systems — it was pleasant to hear them chatting in the back entry, a row of them all tipped against the wall, as usual; while the frozen witticisms of past generations were thawed out, and came bubbling with laughter from their lips. Externally, the jollity of aged men has much in common with the mirth of children; the intellect, any more than a deep sense of humour, has little to do with the matter; it is, with both, a gleam that plays upon the surface, and imparts a sunny and cheery aspect alike to the green branch and grey, mouldering trunk. In one case, however, it is real sunshine; in the other, it more resembles the phosphorescent glow of decaying wood.

It would be sad injustice, the reader must understand, to represent all my excellent old friends as in their dotage. In the first place, my coadjutors were not invariably old; there were men among them in their strength and prime, of marked ability and energy, and altogether superior to the sluggish and dependent mode of life on which their evil stars had cast them. Then, moreover, the white locks of age were sometimes found to be the thatch of an intellectual tenement in good repair. But, as respects the majority of my corps of veterans, there will be no wrong done if I characterize them generally as a set of wearisome old souls, who had gathered nothing worth preservation from their varied experience of life. They seemed to have flung away all the golden grain of practical wisdom, which they had enjoyed so many opportunities of harvesting, and most carefully to have stored their memory with the husks. They spoke with far more interest and unction of their morning's breakfast, or yesterday's, today's, or tomorrow's dinner, than of the shipwreck of forty or fifty years ago, and all the world's wonders which they had witnessed with their youthful eyes.

Rappaccini's Daughter

The father of the Custom-House—the patriarch, not only of this little squad of officials, but, I am bold to say, of the respectable body of tide-waiters all over the United States—was a certain permanent Inspector. He might truly be termed a legitimate son of the revenue system, dyed in the wool, or rather born in the purple; since his sire, a Revolutionary colonel, and formerly collector of the port, had created an office for him, and appointed him to fill it, at a period of the early ages which few living men can now remember. This Inspector, when I first knew him, was a man of fourscore years, or thereabouts, and certainly one of the most wonderful specimens of winter-green that you would be likely to discover in a lifetime's search. With his florid cheek, his compact figure smartly arrayed in a bright-buttoned blue coat, his brisk and vigorous step, and his hale and hearty aspect, altogether he seemed—not young, indeed—but a kind of new contrivance of Mother Nature in the shape of man, whom age and infirmity had no business to touch. His voice and laugh, which perpetually re-echoed through the Custom-House, had nothing of the tremulous quaver and cackle of an old man's utterance; they came strutting out of his lungs, like the crow of a cock, or the blast of a clarion. Looking at him merely as an animal—and there was very little else to look at—he was a most satisfactory object, from the thorough healthfulness and wholesomeness of his system, and his capacity, at that extreme age, to enjoy all, or nearly all, the delights which he had ever aimed at or conceived of. The careless security of his life in the Custom-House, on a regular income, and with but slight and infrequent apprehensions of removal, had no doubt contributed to make time pass lightly over him. The original and more potent causes, however, lay in the rare perfection of his animal nature, the moderate proportion of intellect, and the very trifling admixture of moral and spiritual ingredients; these latter qualities, indeed, being in barely enough measure to keep the old gentleman from walking on all-fours. He possessed no power of thought, no depth of feeling, no troublesome sensibilities: nothing, in short, but a few commonplace instincts, which, aided by the cheerful temper which grew inevitably out of his physical well-being, did duty very respectably, and to general acceptance, in lieu of a heart. He had been the husband of three wives, all long since dead; the father of twenty children, most of whom, at every age of childhood or maturity, had likewise returned to dust. Here, one would suppose, might have been sorrow enough to imbue the sunniest disposition through and through with a sable tinge. Not so with our old Inspector. One brief sigh sufficed to carry off the entire burden of these dismal reminiscences. The next moment he was as ready for sport as any unbreeched infant: far readier than the Collector's junior clerk, who at nineteen years

Rappaccini's Daughter

was much the elder and graver man of the two.

I used to watch and study this patriarchal personage with, I think, livelier curiosity than any other form of humanity there presented to my notice. He was, in truth, a rare phenomenon; so perfect, in one point of view; so shallow, so delusive, so impalpable such an absolute nonentity, in every other. My conclusion was that he had no soul, no heart, no mind; nothing, as I have already said, but instincts; and yet, withal, so cunningly had the few materials of his character been put together that there was no painful perception of deficiency, but, on my part, an entire contentment with what I found in him. It might be difficult—and it was so—to conceive how he should exist hereafter, so earthly and sensuous did he seem; but surely his existence here, admitting that it was to terminate with his last breath, had been not unkindly given; with no higher moral responsibilities than the beasts of the field, but with a larger scope of enjoyment than theirs, and with all their blessed immunity from the dreariness and duskiness of age.

One point in which he had vastly the advantage over his four-footed brethren was his ability to recollect the good dinners which it had made no small portion of the happiness of his life to eat. His gourmandism was a highly agreeable trait; and to hear him talk of roast meat was as appetizing as a pickle or an oyster. As he possessed no higher attribute, and neither sacrificed nor vitiated any spiritual endowment by devoting all his energies and ingenuities to subserve the delight and profit of his maw, it always pleased and satisfied me to hear him expatiate on fish, poultry, and butcher's meat, and the most eligible methods of preparing them for the table. His reminiscences of good cheer, however ancient the date of the actual banquet, seemed to bring the savour of pig or turkey under one's very nostrils. There were flavours on his palate that had lingered there not less than sixty or seventy years, and were still apparently as fresh as that of the mutton chop which he had just devoured for his breakfast. I have heard him smack his lips over dinners, every guest at which, except himself, had long been food for worms. It was marvellous to observe how the ghosts of bygone meals were continually rising up before him—not in anger or retribution, but as if grateful for his former appreciation, and seeking to reduplicate an endless series of enjoyment, at once shadowy and sensual: a tenderloin of beef, a hind-quarter of veal, a spare-rib of pork, a particular chicken, or a remarkably praiseworthy turkey, which had perhaps adorned his board in the days of the elder Adams, would be remembered; while all the subsequent experience of our race, and all the events that brightened or darkened his individual career, had gone over him with as little permanent effect as the passing breeze. The chief tragic event of the old man's life, so far as I could judge, was his mishap with a certain goose, which lived and died some twenty or forty years ago: a goose of most promising figure, but which, at table, proved so inveterately tough, that the carving-knife would make no impression on its carcase, and it could only be divided with an axe and handsaw.

But it is time to quit this sketch; on which, however, I should be glad to dwell at considerably more length, because of all men whom I have ever known, this individual was fittest to be a Custom-House officer. Most persons, owing to causes which I may not have space to hint at, suffer moral detriment from this peculiar mode of life. The old Inspector was incapable of it; and, were he to continue in office to the end of time, would be just as good as he was then, and sit down to dinner with just as good an appetite.

There is one likeness, without which my gallery of Custom-House portraits would be strangely incomplete, but which my comparatively few opportunities for observation enable me to sketch only in the merest outline. It is that of the Collector, our gallant old General, who, after his brilliant military service, subsequently to which he had ruled over a wild Western territory, had come hither, twenty years before, to spend the decline of his varied and honourable life.

The brave soldier had already numbered, nearly or quite, his three-score years and ten, and was pursuing the remainder of his earthly march, burdened with infirmities which even the martial music of his own spirit-stirring recollections could do little towards lightening. The step was palsied now, that had been foremost in the charge. It was only with the assistance of a servant, and by leaning his hand heavily on the iron balustrade, that he could slowly and painfully ascend the Custom-House steps, and, with a toilsome progress across the floor, attain his customary chair beside the fireplace. There he used to sit, gazing with a somewhat dim serenity of aspect at the figures that came and went, amid the rustle of papers, the administering of oaths, the discussion of business, and the casual talk of the office; all which sounds and circumstances seemed but indistinctly to impress his senses, and hardly to make their way into his inner sphere of contemplation. His countenance, in this repose, was mild and kindly. If his notice was sought, an expression of courtesy and interest gleamed out upon his features, proving that there was light within him, and that it was only the outward medium of the intellectual lamp that obstructed the rays in their passage. The closer you penetrated to the substance of his mind, the sounder it appeared. When no longer called upon to speak or listen — either of which operations cost him an evident effort — his face would briefly subside into its former not uncheerful quietude. It was not painful to behold this look; for, though dim, it had not the imbecility of decaying age. The framework of his nature, originally strong and massive, was not yet crumpled into ruin.

To observe and define his character, however, under such disadvantages, was as difficult a task as to trace out and build up anew, in imagination, an old fortress, like Ticonderoga, from a view of its grey and broken ruins. Here and there, perchance, the walls may remain almost complete; but elsewhere may be only a shapeless mound, cumbrous with its very strength, and overgrown, through long years of peace and neglect, with grass and alien weeds.

Nevertheless, looking at the old warrior with affection — for, slight as was the communication between us, my feeling towards him, like that of all bipeds and quadrupeds who knew him, might not improperly be termed so, — I could discern the main points of his portrait. It was marked with the noble and heroic qualities which showed it to be not a mere accident, but of good right, that he had won a distinguished name. His spirit could never, I conceive, have been characterized by an uneasy activity; it must, at any period of his life, have required an impulse to set him in motion; but once stirred up, with obstacles to overcome, and an adequate object to be attained, it was not in the man to give out or fail. The heat that had formerly pervaded his nature, and which was not yet extinct, was never of the kind that flashes and flickers in a blaze; but rather a deep red glow, as of iron in a furnace. Weight, solidity, firmness — this was the expression of his repose, even in such decay as had crept untimely over him at the period of which I speak. But I could imagine, even then, that, under some excitement which should go deeply into his consciousness — roused by a trumpet's peal, loud enough to awaken all of his energies that were not dead, but only slumbering — he was yet capable of flinging off his infirmities like a sick man's gown, dropping the staff of age to seize a battle-sword, and starting up once more a warrior. And, in so intense a moment his demeanour would have still been calm. Such an exhibition, however, was but to be pictured in fancy; not to be anticipated, nor desired. What I saw in him — as evidently as the indestructible ramparts of Old Ticonderoga, already cited as the most appropriate simile — was the features of stubborn and ponderous endurance, which might well have amounted to obstinacy in his earlier days; of integrity, that, like most of his other endowments, lay in a somewhat heavy mass, and was just as unmalleable or unmanageable as a ton of iron ore; and of benevolence which, fiercely as he led the bayonets on at Chippewa or Fort Erie, I take to be of quite as genuine a stamp as what actuates any or all the polemical philanthropists of the age. He had slain men with his own hand, for aught I know—certainly, they had fallen like blades of grass at the sweep of the scythe before the charge to which his spirit imparted its triumphant energy—but, be that as it might, there was never in his heart so much cruelty as would have brushed the down off a butterfly's wing. I have not known the man to whose innate kindliness I would more confidently make an appeal.

Many characteristics—and those, too, which contribute not the least forcibly to impart resemblance in a sketch—must have vanished, or been obscured, before I met the General. All merely graceful attributes are usually the most evanescent; nor does nature adorn the human ruin with blossoms of new beauty, that have their roots and proper nutriment only in the chinks and crevices of decay, as she sows wall-flowers over the ruined fortress of Ticonderoga. Still, even in respect of grace and beauty, there were points well worth noting. A ray of humour, now and then, would make its way through the veil of dim obstruction, and glimmer pleasantly upon our faces. A trait of native elegance, seldom seen in the masculine character after childhood or early youth, was shown in the General's fondness for the sight and fragrance of flowers. An old soldier might be supposed to prize only the bloody laurel on his brow; but here was one who seemed to have a young girl's appreciation of the floral tribe.

There, beside the fireplace, the brave old General used to sit; while the Surveyor—though seldom, when it could be avoided, taking upon himself the difficult task of engaging him in conversation—was fond of standing at a distance, and watching his quiet and almost slumberous countenance. He seemed away from us, although we saw him but a few yards off; remote, though we passed close beside his chair; unattainable, though we might have stretched forth our hands and touched his own. It might be that he lived a more real life within his thoughts than amid the unappropriate environment of the Collector's office. The evolutions of the parade; the tumult of the battle; the flourish of old heroic music, heard thirty years before—such scenes and sounds, perhaps, were all alive before his intellectual sense. Meanwhile, the merchants and ship-masters, the spruce clerks and uncouth sailors, entered and departed; the bustle of his commercial and Custom-House life kept up its little murmur round about him; and neither with the men nor their affairs did the General appear to sustain the most distant relation. He was as much out of place as an old sword—now rusty, but which had flashed once in the battle's front, and showed still a bright gleam along its blade—would have been among the inkstands, paper-folders, and mahogany rulers on the Deputy Collector's desk.

There was one thing that much aided me in renewing and re-creating the stalwart soldier of the Niagara frontier—the man of true and simple energy. It was the recollection of those memorable words of his—"I'll try, Sir"—spoken on the very verge of a desperate and heroic enterprise, and breathing the soul and spirit of New England hardihood, comprehending all perils, and encountering all. If, in our country, valour were rewarded by heraldic honour, this phrase—which it seems so easy to speak, but which only he, with such a task of danger and glory before him, has ever spoken—would be the best and fittest of all mottoes for the General's shield of arms.

It contributes greatly towards a man's moral and intellectual health to be brought into habits of companionship with individuals unlike himself, who care little for his pursuits, and whose sphere and abilities he must go out of himself to appreciate. The accidents of my life have often afforded me this advantage, but never with more fulness and variety than during my continuance in office. There was one man, especially, the observation of whose character gave me a new idea of talent. His gifts were emphatically those of a man of business; prompt, acute, clear-minded; with an eye that saw through all perplexities, and a faculty of arrangement that made them vanish as by the waving of an enchanter's wand. Bred up from boyhood in the Custom-House, it was his proper field of activity; and the many intricacies of business, so harassing to the interloper, presented themselves before him with the regularity of a perfectly comprehended system. In my contemplation, he stood as the ideal of his class. He was, indeed, the Custom-House in himself; or, at all events, the mainspring that kept its variously revolving wheels in motion; for, in an institution like this, where its officers are appointed to subserve their own profit and convenience, and seldom with a leading reference to their fitness for the duty to be performed, they must perforce seek elsewhere the dexterity which is not in them. Thus, by an inevitable necessity, as a magnet attracts steel-filings, so did our man of business draw to himself the difficulties which everybody met with. With an easy condescension, and kind forbearance towards our stupidity—which, to his order of mind, must have seemed little short of crime—would he forth-with, by the merest touch of his finger, make the incomprehensible as clear as daylight. The merchants valued him not less than we, his esoteric friends. His integrity was perfect; it was a law of nature with him, rather than a choice or a principle; nor can it be otherwise than the main condition of an intellect so remarkably clear and accurate as his to be honest and regular in the administration of affairs. A stain on his conscience, as to anything that came within the range of his vocation, would trouble such a man very much in the same way, though to a far greater degree, than an error in the balance of an account, or an ink-blot on the fair page of a book of record. Here, in a word—and it is a rare instance in my life—I had met with a person thoroughly adapted to the situation which he held.

Such were some of the people with whom I now found myself connected. I took it in good part, at the hands of Providence, that I was thrown into a position so little akin to my past habits; and set myself seriously to gather from it whatever profit was to be had. After my fellowship of toil and impracticable schemes with the dreamy brethren of Brook Farm; after living for three years within the subtle influence of an intellect like Emerson's; after those wild, free days on the Assabeth, indulging fantastic speculations, beside our fire of fallen boughs, with Ellery Channing; after talking with Thoreau about pine-trees and Indian relics in his hermitage at Walden; after growing fastidious by sympathy with the classic refinement of Hillard's culture; after becoming imbued with poetic sentiment at Longfellow's hearthstone—it was time, at length, that I should exercise other faculties of my nature, and nourish myself with food for which I had hitherto had little appetite. Even the old Inspector was desirable, as a change of diet, to a man who had known Alcott. I looked upon it as an evidence, in some measure, of a system naturally well balanced, and lacking no essential part of a thorough organization, that, with such associates to remember, I could mingle at once with men of altogether different qualities, and never murmur at the change.

Literature, its exertions and objects, were now of little moment in my regard. I cared not at this period for books; they were apart from me. Nature—except it were human nature—the nature that is developed in earth and sky, was, in one sense, hidden from me; and all the imaginative delight wherewith it had been spiritualized passed away out of my mind. A gift, a faculty, if it had not been departed, was suspended and inanimate within me. There would have been something sad, unutterably dreary, in all this, had I not been conscious that it lay at my own option to recall whatever was valuable in the past. It might be true, indeed, that this was a life which could not, with impunity, be lived too long; else, it might make me permanently other than I had been, without transforming me into any shape which it would be worth my while to take. But I never considered it as other than a transitory life. There was always a prophetic instinct, a low whisper in my ear, that within no long period, and whenever a new change of custom should be essential to my good, change would come.

Meanwhile, there I was, a Surveyor of the Revenue and, so far as I have been able to understand, as good a Surveyor as need be. A man of thought, fancy, and sensibility (had he ten times the Surveyor's proportion of those qualities), may, at any time, be a man of affairs, if he will only choose to give himself the trouble. My fellow-officers, and the merchants and sea-captains with whom my official duties brought me into any manner of connection, viewed me in no other light, and probably knew me in no other character. None of them, I presume, had ever read a page of my inditing, or would have cared a fig the more for me if they had read them all; nor would it have mended the matter, in the least, had those same unprofitable pages been written with a pen like that of Burns or of Chaucer, each of whom was a Custom-House officer in his day, as well as I. It is a good lesson — though it may often be a hard one — for a man who has dreamed of literary fame, and of making for himself a rank among the world's dignitaries by such means, to step aside out of the narrow circle in which his claims are recognized and to find how utterly devoid of significance, beyond that circle, is all that he achieves, and all he aims at. I know not that I especially needed the lesson, either in the way of warning or rebuke; but at any rate, I learned it thoroughly: nor, it gives me pleasure to reflect, did the truth, as it came home to my perception, ever cost me a pang, or require to be thrown off in a sigh. In the way of literary talk, it is true, the Naval Officer — an excellent fellow, who came into the office with me, and went out only a little later — would often engage me in a discussion about one or the other of his favourite topics, Napoleon or Shakespeare. The Collector's junior clerk, too a young gentleman who, it was whispered occasionally covered a sheet of Uncle Sam's letter paper with what (at the distance of a few yards) looked very much like poetry — used now and then to speak to me of books, as matters with which I might possibly be conversant. This was my all of lettered intercourse; and it was quite sufficient for my necessities.

No longer seeking nor caring that my name should be blasoned abroad on title-pages, I smiled to think that it had now another kind of vogue. The Custom-House marker imprinted it, with a stencil and black paint, on pepper-bags, and baskets of anatto, and cigar-boxes, and bales of all kinds of dutiable merchandise, in testimony that these commodities had paid the impost, and gone regularly through the office. Borne on such queer vehicle of fame, a knowledge of my existence, so far as a name conveys it, was carried where it had never been before, and, I hope, will never go again.

But the past was not dead. Once in a great while, the thoughts that had seemed so vital and so active, yet had been put to rest so quietly, revived again. One of the most remarkable occasions, when the habit of bygone days awoke in me, was that which brings it within the law of literary propriety to offer the public the sketch which I am now writing.

In the second storey of the Custom-House there is a large room, in which the brick-work and naked rafters have never been covered with panelling and plaster. The edifice — originally projected on a scale adapted to the old commercial enterprise of the port, and with an idea of subsequent prosperity destined never to be realized — contains far more space than its occupants know what to do with. This airy hall, therefore, over the Collector's apartments, remains unfinished to this day, and, in spite of the aged cobwebs that festoon its dusky beams, appears still to await the labour of the carpenter and mason. At one end of the room, in a recess, were a number of barrels piled one upon another, containing bundles of official documents. Large quantities of similar rubbish lay lumbering the floor. It was sorrowful to think how many days, and weeks, and months, and years of toil had been wasted on these musty papers, which were now only an encumbrance on earth, and were hidden away in this forgotten corner, never more to be glanced at by human eyes. But then, what reams of other manuscripts — filled, not with the dulness of official formalities, but with the thought of inventive brains and the rich effusion of deep hearts — had gone equally to oblivion; and that, moreover, without serving a purpose in their day, as these heaped-up papers had, and — saddest of all — without purchasing for their writers the comfortable livelihood which the clerks of the Custom-House had gained by these worthless scratchings of the pen. Yet not altogether worthless, perhaps, as materials of local history. Here, no doubt, statistics of the former commerce of Salem might be discovered, and memorials of her princely merchants — old King Derby — old Billy Gray — old Simon Forrester — and many another magnate in his day, whose powdered head, however, was scarcely in the tomb before his mountain pile of wealth began to dwindle. The founders of the greater part of the families which now compose the aristocracy of Salem might here be traced, from the petty and obscure beginnings of their traffic, at periods generally much posterior to the Revolution, upward to what their children look upon as long-established rank.

Prior to the Revolution there is a dearth of records; the earlier documents and archives of the Custom-House having, probably, been carried off to Halifax, when all the king's officials accompanied the British army in its flight from Boston. It has often been a matter of regret with me; for, going back, perhaps, to the days of the Protectorate, those papers must have contained many references to forgotten or remembered men, and to antique customs, which would have affected me with the same pleasure as when I used to pick up Indian arrow-heads in the field near the Old Manse.

But, one idle and rainy day, it was my fortune to make a discovery of some little interest. Poking and burrowing into the heaped-up rubbish in the corner, unfolding one and another document, and reading the names of vessels that had long ago foundered at sea or rotted at the wharves, and those of merchants never heard of now on 'Change, nor very readily decipherable on their mossy tombstones; glancing at such matters with the saddened, weary, half-reluctant interest which we bestow on the corpse of dead activity—and exerting my fancy, sluggish with little use, to raise up from these dry bones an image of the old town's brighter aspect, when India was a new region, and only Salem knew the way thither—I chanced to lay my hand on a small package, carefully done up in a piece of ancient yellow parchment. This envelope had the air of an official record of some period long past, when clerks engrossed their stiff and formal chirography on more substantial materials than at present. There was something about it that quickened an instinctive curiosity, and made me undo the faded red tape that tied up the package, with the sense that a treasure would here be brought to light. Unbending the rigid folds of the parchment cover, I found it to be a commission, under the hand and seal of Governor Shirley, in favour of one Jonathan Pue, as Surveyor of His Majesty's Customs for the Port of Salem, in the Province of Massachusetts Bay. I remembered to have read (probably in Felt's "Annals") a notice of the decease of Mr. Surveyor Pue, about fourscore years ago; and likewise, in a newspaper of recent times, an account of the digging up of his remains in the little graveyard of St. Peter's Church, during the renewal of that edifice. Nothing, if I rightly call to mind, was left of my respected predecessor, save an imperfect skeleton, and some fragments of apparel, and a wig of majestic frizzle, which, unlike the head that it once adorned, was in very satisfactory preservation. But, on examining the papers which the parchment commission served to envelop, I found more traces of Mr. Pue's mental part, and the internal operations of his head, than the frizzled wig had contained of the venerable skull itself.

They were documents, in short, not official, but of a private nature, or, at least, written in his private capacity, and apparently with his own hand. I could account for their being included in the heap of Custom-House lumber only by the fact that Mr. Pue's death had happened suddenly, and that these papers, which he probably kept in his official desk, had never come to the knowledge of his heirs, or were supposed to relate to the business of the revenue. On the transfer of the archives to Halifax, this package, proving to be of no public concern, was left behind, and had remained ever since unopened.

The ancient Surveyor—being little molested, I suppose, at that early day with business pertaining to his office—seems to have devoted some of his many leisure hours to researches as a local antiquarian, and other inquisitions of a similar nature. These supplied material for petty activity to a mind that would otherwise have been eaten up with rust. A portion of his facts, by the by, did me good service in the preparation of the article entitled "MAIN STREET," included in the present volume. The remainder may perhaps be applied to purposes equally valuable hereafter, or not impossibly may be worked up, so far as they go, into a regular history of Salem, should my veneration for the natal soil ever impel me to so pious a task. Meanwhile, they shall be at the command of any gentleman, inclined and competent, to take the unprofitable labour off my hands. As a final disposition I contemplate depositing them with the Essex Historical Society. But the object that most drew my attention to the mysterious package was a certain affair of fine red cloth, much worn and faded, There were traces about it of gold embroidery, which, however, was greatly frayed and defaced, so that none, or very little, of the glitter was left. It had been wrought, as was easy to perceive, with wonderful skill of needlework; and the stitch (as I am assured by ladies conversant with such mysteries) gives evidence of a now forgotten art, not to be discovered even by the process of picking out the threads. This rag of scarlet cloth—for time, and wear, and a sacrilegious moth had reduced it to little other than a rag—on careful examination, assumed the shape of a letter.

It was the capital letter A. By an accurate measurement, each limb proved to be precisely three inches and a quarter in length. It had been intended, there could be no doubt, as an ornamental article of dress; but how it was to be worn, or what rank, honour, and dignity, in by-past times, were signified by it, was a riddle which (so evanescent are the fashions of the world in these particulars) I saw little hope of solving. And yet it strangely interested me. My eyes fastened themselves upon the old scarlet letter, and would not be turned aside. Certainly there was some deep meaning in it most worthy of interpretation, and which, as it were, streamed forth from the mystic symbol, subtly communicating itself to my sensibilities, but evading the analysis of my mind.

When thus perplexed—and cogitating, among other hypotheses, whether the letter might not have been one of those decorations which the white men used to contrive in order to take the eyes of Indians—I happened to place it on my breast. It seemed to me—the reader may smile, but must not doubt my word—it seemed to me, then, that I experienced a sensation not altogether physical, yet almost so, as of burning heat, and as if the letter were not of red cloth, but red-hot iron. I shuddered, and involuntarily let it fall upon the floor.

In the absorbing contemplation of the scarlet letter, I had hitherto neglected to examine a small roll of dingy paper, around which it had been twisted. This I now opened, and had the satisfaction to find recorded by the old Surveyor's pen, a reasonably complete explanation of the whole affair. There were several foolscap sheets, containing many particulars respecting the life and conversation of one Hester Prynne, who appeared to have been rather a noteworthy personage in the view of our ancestors. She had flourished during the period between the early days of Massachusetts and the close of the seventeenth century. Aged persons, alive in the time of Mr. Surveyor Pue, and from whose oral testimony he had made up his narrative, remembered her, in their youth, as a very old, but not decrepit woman, of a stately and solemn aspect. It had been her habit, from an almost immemorial date, to go about the country as a kind of voluntary nurse, and doing whatever miscellaneous good she might; taking upon herself, likewise, to give advice in all matters, especially those of the heart, by which means—as a person of such propensities inevitably must—she gained from many people the reverence due to an angel, but, I should imagine, was looked upon by others as an intruder and a nuisance. Prying further into the manuscript, I found the record of other doings and sufferings of this singular woman, for most of which the reader is referred to the story entitled "THE SCARLET LETTER"; and it should be borne carefully in mind that the main facts of that story are authorized and authenticated by the document of Mr. Surveyor Pue. The original papers, together with the scarlet letter itself — a most curious relic — are still in my possession, and shall be freely exhibited to whomsoever, induced by the great interest of the narrative, may desire a sight of them. I must not be understood affirming that, in the dressing up of the tale, and imagining the motives and modes of passion that influenced the characters who figure in it, I have invariably confined myself within the limits of the old Surveyor's half-a-dozen sheets of foolscap. On the contrary, I have allowed myself, as to such points, nearly, or altogether, as much license as if the facts had been entirely of my own invention. What I contend for is the authenticity of the outline.

This incident recalled my mind, in some degree, to its old track. There seemed to be here the groundwork of a tale. It impressed me as if the ancient Surveyor, in his garb of a hundred years gone by, and wearing his immortal wig — which was buried with him, but did not perish in the grave — had met me in the deserted chamber of the Custom-House. In his port was the dignity of one who had borne His Majesty's commission, and who was therefore illuminated by a ray of the splendour that shone so dazzlingly about the throne. How unlike alas the hangdog look of a republican official, who, as the servant of the people, feels himself less than the least, and below the lowest of his masters. With his own ghostly hand, the obscurely seen, but majestic, figure had imparted to me the scarlet symbol and the little roll of explanatory manuscript. With his own ghostly voice he had exhorted me, on the sacred consideration of my filial duty and reverence towards him — who might reasonably regard himself as my official ancestor — to bring his mouldy and moth-eaten lucubrations before the public. "Do this," said the ghost of Mr. Surveyor Pue, emphatically nodding the head that looked so imposing within its memorable wig; "do this, and the profit shall be all your own. You will shortly need it; for it is not in your days as it was in mine, when a man's office was a life-lease, and oftentimes an heirloom. But I charge you, in this matter of old Mistress Prynne, give to your predecessor's memory the credit which will be rightfully due" And I said to the ghost of Mr. Surveyor Pue — "I will".

On Hester Prynne's story, therefore, I bestowed much thought. It was the subject of my meditations for many an hour, while pacing to and fro across my room, or traversing, with a hundredfold repetition, the long extent from the front door of the Custom-House to the side entrance, and back again. Great were the weariness and annoyance of the old Inspector and the Weighers and Gaugers, whose slumbers were disturbed by the unmercifully lengthened tramp of my passing and returning footsteps. Remembering their own former habits, they used to say that the Surveyor was walking the quarter-deck. They probably fancied that my sole object—and, indeed, the sole object for which a sane man could ever put himself into voluntary motion—was to get an appetite for dinner. And, to say the truth, an appetite, sharpened by the east wind that generally blew along the passage, was the only valuable result of so much indefatigable exercise. So little adapted is the atmosphere of a Custom-house to the delicate harvest of fancy and sensibility, that, had I remained there through ten Presidencies yet to come, I doubt whether the tale of "The Scarlet Letter" would ever have been brought before the public eye. My imagination was a tarnished mirror. It would not reflect, or only with miserable dimness, the figures with which I did my best to people it. The characters of the narrative would not be warmed and rendered malleable by any heat that I could kindle at my intellectual forge. They would take neither the glow of passion nor the tenderness of sentiment, but retained all the rigidity of dead corpses, and stared me in the face with a fixed and ghastly grin of contemptuous defiance. "What have you to do with us?" that expression seemed to say. "The little power you might have once possessed over the tribe of unrealities is gone! You have bartered it for a pittance of the public gold. Go then, and earn your wages!" In short, the almost torpid creatures of my own fancy twitted me with imbecility, and not without fair occasion.

It was not merely during the three hours and a half which Uncle Sam claimed as his share of my daily life that this wretched numbness held possession of me. It went with me on my sea-shore walks and rambles into the country, whenever— which was seldom and reluctantly—I bestirred myself to seek that invigorating charm of Nature which used to give me such freshness and activity of thought, the moment that I stepped across the threshold of the Old Manse. The same torpor, as regarded the capacity for intellectual effort, accompanied me home, and weighed upon me in the chamber which I most absurdly termed my study. Nor did it quit me when, late at night, I sat in the deserted parlour, lighted only by the glimmering coal-fire and the moon, striving to picture forth imaginary scenes, which, the next day, might flow out on the brightening page in many-hued description.

If the imaginative faculty refused to act at such an hour, it might well be deemed a hopeless case. Moonlight, in a familiar room, falling so white upon the carpet, and showing all its figures so distinctly—making every object so minutely visible, yet so unlike a morning or noontide visibility—is a medium the most suitable for a romance-writer to get acquainted with his illusive guests. There is the little domestic scenery of the well-known apartment; the chairs, with each its separate individuality; the centre-table, sustaining a work-basket, a volume or two, and an extinguished lamp; the sofa; the book-case; the picture on the wall—all these details, so completely seen, are so spiritualised by the unusual light, that they seem to lose their actual substance, and become things of intellect. Nothing is too small or too trifling to undergo this change, and acquire dignity thereby. A child's shoe; the doll, seated in her little wicker carriage; the hobby-horse—whatever, in a word, has been used or played with during the day is now invested with a quality of strangeness and remoteness, though still almost as vividly present as by daylight. Thus, therefore, the floor of our familiar room has become a neutral territory, somewhere between the real world and fairy-land, where the Actual and the Imaginary may meet, and each imbue itself with the nature of the other. Ghosts might enter here without affrighting us. It would be too much in keeping with the scene to excite surprise, were we to look about us and discover a form, beloved, but gone hence, now sitting quietly in a streak of this magic moonshine, with an aspect that would make us doubt whether it had returned from afar, or had never once stirred from our fireside.

    The somewhat dim coal fire has an essential Influence in producing the effect which I would describe. It throws its unobtrusive tinge throughout the room, with a faint ruddiness upon the walls and ceiling, and a reflected gleam upon the polish of the furniture. This warmer light mingles itself with the cold spirituality of the moon-beams, and communicates, as it were, a heart and sensibilities of human tenderness to the forms which fancy summons up. It converts them from snow-images into men and women. Glancing at the looking-glass, we behold—deep within its haunted verge—the smouldering glow of the half-extinguished anthracite, the white moon-beams on the floor, and a repetition of all the gleam and shadow of the picture, with one remove further from the actual, and nearer to the imaginative. Then, at such an hour, and with this scene before him, if a man, sitting all alone, cannot dream strange things, and make them look like truth, he need never try to write romances.

    But, for myself, during the whole of my Custom-House experience, moonlight and sunshine, and the glow of firelight, were just alike in my regard; and neither of them was of one whit more avail than the twinkle of a tallow-candle. An entire class of susceptibilities, and a gift connected with them—of no great richness or value, but the best I had—was gone from me.

It is my belief, however, that had I attempted a different order of composition, my faculties would not have been found so pointless and inefficacious. I might, for instance, have contented myself with writing out the narratives of a veteran shipmaster, one of the Inspectors, whom I should be most ungrateful not to mention, since scarcely a day passed that he did not stir me to laughter and admiration by his marvelous gifts as a story-teller. Could I have preserved the picturesque force of his style, and the humourous colouring which nature taught him how to throw over his descriptions, the result, I honestly believe, would have been something new in literature. Or I might readily have found a more serious task. It was a folly, with the materiality of this daily life pressing so intrusively upon me, to attempt to fling myself back into another age, or to insist on creating the semblance of a world out of airy matter, when, at every moment, the impalpable beauty of my soap-bubble was broken by the rude contact of some actual circumstance. The wiser effort would have been to diffuse thought and imagination through the opaque substance of today, and thus to make it a bright transparency; to spiritualise the burden that began to weigh so heavily; to seek, resolutely, the true and indestructible value that lay hidden in the petty and wearisome incidents, and ordinary characters with which I was now conversant. The fault was mine. The page of life that was spread out before me seemed dull and commonplace only because I had not fathomed its deeper import. A better book than I shall ever write was there; leaf after leaf presenting itself to me, just as it was written out by the reality of the flitting hour, and vanishing as fast as written, only because my brain wanted the insight, and my hand the cunning, to transcribe it. At some future day, it may be, I shall remember a few scattered fragments and broken paragraphs, and write them down, and find the letters turn to gold upon the page.

These perceptions had come too late. At the Instant, I was only conscious that what would have been a pleasure once was now a hopeless toil. There was no occasion to make much moan about this state of affairs. I had ceased to be a writer of tolerably poor tales and essays, and had become a tolerably good Surveyor of the Customs. That was all. But, nevertheless, it is anything but agreeable to be haunted by a suspicion that one's intellect is dwindling away, or exhaling, without your consciousness, like ether out of a phial; so that, at every glance, you find a smaller and less volatile residuum. Of the fact there could be no doubt and, examining myself and others, I was led to conclusions, in reference to the effect of public office on the character, not very favourable to the mode of life in question. In some other form, perhaps, I may hereafter develop these effects. Suffice it here to say that a Custom-House officer of long continuance can hardly be a very praiseworthy or respectable personage, for many reasons; one of them, the tenure by which he holds his situation, and another, the very nature of his business, which—though, I trust, an honest one—is of such a sort that he does not share in the united effort of mankind.

An effect—which I believe to be observable, more or less, in every individual who has occupied the position—is, that while he leans on the mighty arm of the Republic, his own proper strength departs from him. He loses, in an extent proportioned to the weakness or force of his original nature, the capability of self-support. If he possesses an unusual share of native energy, or the enervating magic of place do not operate too long upon him, his forfeited powers may be redeemable. The ejected officer—fortunate in the unkindly shove that sends him forth betimes, to struggle amid a struggling world—may return to himself, and become all that he has ever been. But this seldom happens. He usually keeps his ground just long enough for his own ruin, and is then thrust out, with sinews all unstrung, to totter along the difficult footpath of life as he best may. Conscious of his own infirmity—that his tempered steel and elasticity are lost—he for ever afterwards looks wistfully about him in quest of support external to himself. His pervading and continual hope—a hallucination, which, in the face of all discouragement, and making light of impossibilities, haunts him while he lives, and, I fancy, like the convulsive throes of the cholera, torments him for a brief space after death—is, that finally, and in no long time, by some happy coincidence of circumstances, he shall be restored to office. This faith, more than anything else, steals the pith and availability out of whatever enterprise he may dream of undertaking. Why should he toil and moil, and be at so much trouble to pick himself up out of the mud, when, in a little while hence, the strong arm of his Uncle will raise and support him? Why should he work for his living here, or go to dig gold in California, when he is so soon to be made happy, at monthly intervals, with a little pile of glittering coin out of his Uncle's pocket? It is sadly curious to observe how slight a taste of office suffices to infect a poor fellow with this singular disease. Uncle Sam's gold—meaning no disrespect to the worthy old gentleman—has, in this respect, a quality of enchantment like that of the devil's wages. Whoever touches it should look well to himself, or he may find the bargain to go hard against him, involving, if not his soul, yet many of its better attributes; its sturdy force, its courage and constancy, its truth, its self-reliance, and all that gives the emphasis to manly character.

Here was a fine prospect in the distance. Not that the Surveyor brought the lesson home to himself, or admitted that he could be so utterly undone, either by continuance in office or ejectment. Yet my reflections were not the most comfortable. I began to grow melancholy and restless; continually prying into my mind, to discover which of its poor properties were gone, and what degree of detriment had already accrued to the remainder. I endeavoured to calculate how much longer I could stay in the Custom-House, and yet go forth a man. To confess the truth, it was my greatest apprehension—as it would never be a measure of policy to turn out so quiet an individual as myself; and it being hardly in the nature of a public officer to resign—it was my chief trouble, therefore, that I was likely to grow grey and decrepit in the Surveyorship, and become much such another animal as the old Inspector. Might it not, in the tedious lapse of official life that lay before me, finally be with me as it was with this venerable friend—to make the dinner-hour the nucleus of the day, and to spend the rest of it, as an old dog spends it, asleep in the sunshine or in the shade? A dreary look-forward, this, for a man who felt it to be the best definition of happiness to live throughout the whole range of his faculties and sensibilities. But, all this while, I was giving myself very unnecessary alarm. Providence had meditated better things for me than I could possibly imagine for myself.

A remarkable event of the third year of my Surveyorship—to adopt the tone of "P. P."—was the election of General Taylor to the Presidency. It is essential, in order to form a complete estimate of the advantages of official life, to view the incumbent at the incoming of a hostile administration. His position is then one of the most singularly irksome, and, in every contingency, disagreeable, that a wretched mortal can possibly occupy; with seldom an alternative of good on either hand, although what presents itself to him as the worst event may very probably be the best. But it is a strange experience, to a man of pride and sensibility, to know that his interests are within the control of individuals who neither love nor understand him, and by whom, since one or the other must needs happen, he would rather be injured than obliged. Strange, too, for one who has kept his calmness throughout the contest, to observe the bloodthirstiness that is developed in the hour of triumph, and to be conscious that he is himself among its objects! There are few uglier traits of human nature than this tendency—which I now witnessed in men no worse than their neighbours—to grow cruel, merely because they possessed the power of inflicting harm. If the guillotine, as applied to office-holders, were a literal fact, instead of one of the most apt of metaphors, it is my sincere belief that the active members of the victorious party were sufficiently excited to have chopped off all our heads, and have thanked Heaven for the opportunity! It appears to me—who have been a calm and curious observer, as well in victory as defeat—that this fierce and bitter spirit of malice and revenge has never distinguished the many triumphs of my own party as it now did that of the Whigs. The Democrats take the offices, as a general rule, because they need them, and because the practice of many years has made it the law of political warfare, which unless a different system be proclaimed, it was weakness and cowardice to murmur at. But the long habit of victory has made them generous. They know how to spare when they see occasion; and when they strike, the axe may be sharp indeed, but its edge is seldom poisoned with ill-will; nor is it their custom ignominiously to kick the head which they have just struck off.

In short, unpleasant as was my predicament, at best, I saw much reason to congratulate myself that I was on the losing side rather than the triumphant one. If, heretofore, I had been none of the warmest of partisans I began now, at this season of peril and adversity, to be pretty acutely sensible with which party my predilections lay; nor was it without something like regret and shame that, according to a reasonable calculation of chances, I saw my own prospect of retaining office to be better than those of my democratic brethren. But who can see an inch into futurity beyond his nose? My own head was the first that fell.

The moment when a man's head drops off is seldom or never, I am inclined to think, precisely the most agreeable of his life. Nevertheless, like the greater part of our misfortunes, even so serious a contingency brings its remedy and consolation with it, if the sufferer will but make the best rather than the worst, of the accident which has befallen him. In my particular case the consolatory topics were close at hand, and, indeed, had suggested themselves to my meditations a considerable time before it was requisite to use them. In view of my previous weariness of office, and vague thoughts of resignation, my fortune somewhat resembled that of a person who should entertain an idea of committing suicide, and although beyond his hopes, meet with the good hap to be murdered. In the Custom-House, as before in the Old Manse, I had spent three years—a term long enough to rest a weary brain: long enough to break off old intellectual habits, and make room for new ones: long enough, and too long, to have lived in an unnatural state, doing what was really of no advantage nor delight to any human being, and withholding myself from toil that would, at least, have stilled an unquiet impulse in me. Then, moreover, as regarded his unceremonious ejectment, the late Surveyor was not altogether ill-pleased to be recognised by the Whigs as an enemy; since his inactivity in political affairs—his tendency to roam, at will, in that broad and quiet field where all mankind may meet, rather than confine himself to those narrow paths where brethren of the same household must diverge from one another—had sometimes made it questionable with his brother Democrats whether he was a friend. Now, after he had won the crown of martyrdom (though with no longer a head to wear it on), the point might be looked upon as settled. Finally, little heroic as he was, it seemed more decorous to be overthrown in the downfall of the party with which he had been content to stand than to remain a forlorn survivor, when so many worthier men were falling: and at last, after subsisting for four years on the mercy of a hostile administration, to be compelled then to define his position anew, and claim the yet more humiliating mercy of a friendly one.

Meanwhile, the press had taken up my affair, and kept me for a week or two careering through the public prints, in my decapitated state, like Irving's Headless Horseman, ghastly and grim, and longing to be buried, as a political dead man ought. So much for my figurative self. The real human being all this time, with his head safely on his shoulders, had brought himself to the comfortable conclusion that everything was for the best; and making an investment in ink, paper, and steel pens, had opened his long-disused writing desk, and was again a literary man.

Now it was that the lucubrations of my ancient predecessor, Mr. Surveyor Pue, came into play. Rusty through long idleness, some little space was requisite before my intellectual machinery could be brought to work upon the tale with an effect in any degree satisfactory. Even yet, though my thoughts were ultimately much absorbed in the task, it wears, to my eye, a stern and sombre aspect: too much ungladdened by genial sunshine; too little relieved by the tender and familiar influences which soften almost every scene of nature and real life, and undoubtedly should soften every picture of them. This uncaptivating effect is perhaps due to the period of hardly accomplished revolution, and still seething turmoil, in which the story shaped itself. It is no indication, however, of a lack of cheerfulness in the writer's mind: for he was happier while straying through the gloom of these sunless fantasies than at any time since he had quitted the Old Manse. Some of the briefer articles, which contribute to make up the volume, have likewise been written since my involuntary withdrawal from the toils and honours of public life, and the remainder are gleaned from annuals and magazines, of such antique date, that they have gone round the circle, and come back to novelty again. Keeping up the metaphor of the political guillotine, the whole may be considered as the POSTHUMOUS PAPERS OF A DECAPITATED SURVEYOR: and the sketch which I am now bringing to a close, if too autobiographical for a modest person to publish in his lifetime, will readily be excused in a gentleman who writes from beyond the grave. Peace be with all the world! My blessing on my friends! My forgiveness to my enemies! For I am in the realm of quiet!

The life of the Custom-House lies like a dream behind me. The old Inspector—who, by the by, I regret to say, was overthrown and killed by a horse some time ago, else he would certainly have lived for ever—he, and all those other venerable personages who sat with him at the receipt of custom, are but shadows in my view: white-headed and wrinkled images, which my fancy used to sport with, and has now flung aside for ever. The merchants—Pingree, Phillips, Shepard, Upton, Kimball, Bertram, Hunt—these and many other names, which had such classic familiarity for my ear six months ago,—these men of traffic, who seemed to occupy so important a position in the world—how little time has it required to disconnect me from them all, not merely in act, but recollection! It is with an effort that I recall the figures and appellations of these few. Soon, likewise, my old native town will loom upon me through the haze of memory, a mist brooding over and around it; as if it were no portion of the real earth, but an overgrown village in cloud-land, with only imaginary inhabitants to people its wooden houses and walk its homely lanes, and the unpicturesque prolixity of its main street. Henceforth it ceases to be a reality of my life; I am a citizen of somewhere else. My good townspeople will not much regret me, for—though it has been as dear an object as any, in my literary efforts, to be of some importance in their eyes, and to win myself a pleasant memory in this abode and burial-place of so many of my forefathers—there has never been, for me, the genial atmosphere which a literary man requires in order to ripen the best harvest of his mind. I shall do better amongst other faces; and these familiar ones, it need hardly be said, will do just as well without me.

It may be, however—oh, transporting and triumphant thought—that the great-grandchildren of the present race may sometimes think kindly of the scribbler of bygone days, when the antiquary of days to come, among the sites memorable in

Rappaccini's Daughter

the town's history, shall point out the locality of THE TOWN PUMP.

THE SCARLET LETTER

I.

THE PRISON DOOR

A throng of bearded men, in sad-coloured garments and grey steeple-crowned hats, intermixed with women, some wearing hoods, and others bareheaded, was assembled in front of a wooden edifice, the door of which was heavily timbered with oak, and studded with iron spikes.

The founders of a new colony, whatever Utopia of human virtue and happiness they might originally project, have invariably recognised it among their earliest practical necessities to allot a portion of the virgin soil as a cemetery, and another portion as the site of a prison. In accordance with this rule it may safely be assumed that the forefathers of Boston had built the first prison-house somewhere in the vicinity of Cornhill, almost as seasonably as they marked out the first burial-ground, on Isaac Johnson's lot, and round about his grave, which subsequently became the nucleus of all the congregated sepulchres in the old churchyard of King's Chapel. Certain it is that, some fifteen or twenty years after the settlement of the town, the wooden jail was already marked with weather-stains and other indications of age, which gave a yet darker aspect to its beetle-browed and gloomy front. The rust on the ponderous iron-work of its oaken door looked more antique than anything else in the New World. Like all that pertains to crime, it seemed never to have known a youthful era. Before this ugly edifice, and between it and the wheel-track of the street, was a grass-plot, much overgrown with burdock, pig-weed, apple-pern, and such unsightly vegetation, which evidently found something congenial in the soil that had so early borne the black flower of civilised society, a prison. But on one side of the portal, and rooted almost at the threshold, was a wild rose-bush, covered, in this month of June, with its delicate gems, which might be imagined to offer their fragrance and fragile beauty to the prisoner as he went in, and to the condemned criminal as he came forth to his doom, in token that the deep heart of Nature could pity and be kind to him.

This rose-bush, by a strange chance, has been kept alive in history; but whether it had merely survived out of the stern old wilderness, so long after the fall of the gigantic pines and oaks that originally overshadowed it, or whether, as there is fair authority for believing, it had sprung up under the footsteps of

Rappaccini's Daughter

the sainted Ann Hutchinson as she entered the prison-door, we shall not take upon us to determine. Finding it so directly on the threshold of our narrative, which is now about to issue from that inauspicious portal, we could hardly do otherwise than pluck one of its flowers, and present it to the reader. It may serve, let us hope, to symbolise some sweet moral blossom that may be found along the track, or relieve the darkening close of a tale of human frailty and sorrow.

II.

THE MARKET-PLACE

The grass-plot before the jail, in Prison Lane, on a certain summer morning, not less than two centuries ago, was occupied by a pretty large number of the inhabitants of Boston, all with their eyes intently fastened on the iron-clamped oaken door. Amongst any other population, or at a later period in the history of New England, the grim rigidity that petrified the bearded physiognomies of these good people would have augured some awful business in hand. It could have betokened nothing short of the anticipated execution of some noted culprit, on whom the sentence of a legal tribunal had but confirmed the verdict of public sentiment. But, in that early severity of the Puritan character, an inference of this kind could not so indubitably be drawn. It might be that a sluggish bond-servant, or an undutiful child, whom his parents had given over to the civil authority, was to be corrected at the whipping-post. It might be that an Antinomian, a Quaker, or other heterodox religionist, was to be scourged out of the town, or an idle or vagrant Indian, whom the white man's firewater had made riotous about the streets, was to be driven with stripes into the shadow of the forest. It might be, too, that a witch, like old Mistress Hibbins, the bitter-tempered widow of the magistrate, was to die upon the gallows. In either case, there was very much the same solemnity of demeanour on the part of the spectators, as befitted a people among whom religion and law were almost identical, and in whose character both were so thoroughly interfused, that the mildest and severest acts of public discipline were alike made venerable and awful. Meagre, indeed, and cold, was the sympathy that a transgressor might look for, from such bystanders, at the scaffold. On the other hand, a penalty which, in our days, would infer a degree of mocking infamy and ridicule, might then be invested with almost as stern a dignity as the punishment of death itself.

It was a circumstance to be noted on the summer morning when our story begins its course, that the women, of whom there were several in the crowd, appeared to take a peculiar interest in whatever penal infliction might be expected to ensue. The age had not so much refinement, that any sense of impropriety restrained the wearers of petticoat and farthingale from stepping forth into the public ways, and wedging their not unsubstantial persons, if occasion were, into the throng nearest to the scaffold at an execution. Morally, as well as materially, there was a coarser fibre in those wives and maidens of old

English birth and breeding than in their fair descendants, separated from them by a series of six or seven generations; for, throughout that chain of ancestry, every successive mother had transmitted to her child a fainter bloom, a more delicate and briefer beauty, and a slighter physical frame, if not character of less force and solidity than her own. The women who were now standing about the prison-door stood within less than half a century of the period when the man-like Elizabeth had been the not altogether unsuitable representative of the sex. They were her countrywomen: and the beef and ale of their native land, with a moral diet not a whit more refined, entered largely into their composition. The bright morning sun, therefore, shone on broad shoulders and well-developed busts, and on round and ruddy cheeks, that had ripened in the far-off island, and had hardly yet grown paler or thinner in the atmosphere of New England. There was, moreover, a boldness and rotundity of speech among these matrons, as most of them seemed to be, that would startle us at the present day, whether in respect to its purport or its volume of tone.

"Goodwives," said a hard-featured dame of fifty, "I'll tell ye a piece of my mind. It would be greatly for the public behoof if we women, being of mature age and church-members in good repute, should have the handling of such malefactresses as this Hester Prynne. What think ye, gossips? If the hussy stood up for judgment before us five, that are now here in a knot together, would she come off with such a sentence as the worshipful magistrates have awarded? Marry, I trow not."

"People say," said another, "that the Reverend Master Dimmesdale, her godly pastor, takes it very grievously to heart that such a scandal should have come upon his congregation."

"The magistrates are God-fearing gentlemen, but merciful overmuch—that is a truth," added a third autumnal matron. "At the very least, they should have put the brand of a hot iron on Hester Prynne's forehead. Madame Hester would have winced at that, I warrant me. But she—the naughty baggage—little will she care what they put upon the bodice of her gown! Why, look you, she may cover it with a brooch, or such like heathenish adornment, and so walk the streets as brave as ever!"

"Ah, but," interposed, more softly, a young wife, holding a child by the hand, "let her cover the mark as she will, the pang of it will be always in her heart."

"What do we talk of marks and brands, whether on the

bodice of her gown or the flesh of her forehead?" cried another female, the ugliest as well as the most pitiless of these self-constituted judges. "This woman has brought shame upon us all, and ought to die; is there not law for it? Truly there is, both in the Scripture and the statute-book. Then let the magistrates, who have made it of no effect, thank themselves if their own wives and daughters go astray."

"Mercy on us, goodwife!" exclaimed a man in the crowd, "is there no virtue in woman, save what springs from a wholesome fear of the gallows? That is the hardest word yet! Hush now, gossips for the lock is turning in the prison-door, and here comes Mistress Prynne herself."

The door of the jail being flung open from within there appeared, in the first place, like a black shadow emerging into sunshine, the grim and grisly presence of the town-beadle, with a sword by his side, and his staff of office in his hand. This personage prefigured and represented in his aspect the whole dismal severity of the Puritanic code of law, which it was his business to administer in its final and closest application to the offender. Stretching forth the official staff in his left hand, he laid his right upon the shoulder of a young woman, whom he thus drew forward, until, on the threshold of the prison-door, she repelled him, by an action marked with natural dignity and force of character, and stepped into the open air as if by her own free will. She bore in her arms a child, a baby of some three months old, who winked and turned aside its little face from the too vivid light of day; because its existence, heretofore, had brought it acquaintance only with the grey twilight of a dungeon, or other darksome apartment of the prison.

When the young woman—the mother of this child—stood fully revealed before the crowd, it seemed to be her first impulse to clasp the infant closely to her bosom; not so much by an impulse of motherly affection, as that she might thereby conceal a certain token, which was wrought or fastened into her dress. In a moment, however, wisely judging that one token of her shame would but poorly serve to hide another, she took the baby on her arm, and with a burning blush, and yet a haughty smile, and a glance that would not be abashed, looked around at her townspeople and neighbours. On the breast of her gown, in fine red cloth, surrounded with an elaborate embroidery and fantastic flourishes of gold thread, appeared the letter A. It was so artistically done, and with so much fertility and gorgeous luxuriance of fancy, that it had all the effect of a last and fitting decoration to the apparel which she wore, and which was of a splendour in accordance with the taste of the age, but greatly beyond what was allowed by the sumptuary regulations of the colony.

The young woman was tall, with a figure of perfect elegance on a large scale. She had dark and abundant hair, so glossy that it threw off the sunshine with a gleam; and a face which, besides being beautiful from regularity of feature and richness of complexion, had the impressiveness belonging to a marked brow and deep black eyes. She was ladylike, too, after the manner of the feminine gentility of those days; characterised by a certain state and dignity, rather than by the delicate, evanescent, and indescribable grace which is now recognised as its indication. And never had Hester Prynne appeared more ladylike, in the antique interpretation of the term, than as she issued from the prison. Those who had before known her, and had expected to behold her dimmed and obscured by a disastrous cloud, were astonished, and even startled, to perceive how her beauty shone out, and made a halo of the misfortune and ignominy in which she was enveloped. It may be true that, to a sensitive observer, there was some thing exquisitely painful in it. Her attire, which indeed, she had wrought for the occasion in prison, and had modelled much after her own fancy, seemed to express the attitude of her spirit, the desperate recklessness of her mood, by its wild and picturesque peculiarity. But the point which drew all eyes, and, as it were, transfigured the wearer—so that both men and women who had been familiarly acquainted with Hester Prynne were now impressed as if they beheld her for the first time—was that SCARLET LETTER, so fantastically embroidered and illuminated upon her bosom. It had the effect of a spell, taking her out of the ordinary relations with humanity, and enclosing her in a sphere by herself.

"She hath good skill at her needle, that's certain," remarked one of her female spectators; "but did ever a woman, before this brazen hussy, contrive such a way of showing it? Why, gossips, what is it but to laugh in the faces of our godly magistrates, and make a pride out of what they, worthy gentlemen, meant for a punishment?"

"It were well," muttered the most iron-visaged of the old dames, "if we stripped Madame Hester's rich gown off her dainty shoulders; and as for the red letter which she hath stitched so curiously, I'll bestow a rag of mine own rheumatic flannel to make a fitter one!"

"Oh, peace, neighbours—peace!" whispered their youngest companion; "do not let her hear you! Not a stitch in that embroidered letter but she has felt it in her heart."

The grim beadle now made a gesture with his staff. "Make way, good people—make way, in the King's name!" cried he. "Open a passage; and I promise ye, Mistress Prynne shall be set where man, woman, and child may have a fair sight of her brave apparel from this time till an hour past meridian. A blessing on the righteous colony of the Massachusetts, where iniquity is dragged out into the sunshine! Come along, Madame Hester, and show your scarlet letter in the market-place!"

A lane was forthwith opened through the crowd of spectators. Preceded by the beadle, and attended by an irregular procession of stern-browed men and unkindly visaged women, Hester Prynne set forth towards the place appointed for her punishment. A crowd of eager and curious schoolboys, understanding little of the matter in hand, except that it gave them a half-holiday, ran before her progress, turning their heads continually to stare into her face and at the winking baby in her arms, and at the ignominious letter on her breast. It was no great distance, in those days, from the prison door to the market-place. Measured by the prisoner's experience, however, it might be reckoned a journey of some length; for haughty as her demeanour was, she perchance underwent an agony from every footstep of those that thronged to see her, as if her heart had been flung into the street for them all to spurn and trample upon. In our nature, however, there is a provision, alike marvellous and merciful, that the sufferer should never know the intensity of what he endures by its present torture, but chiefly by the pang that rankles after it. With almost a serene deportment, therefore, Hester Prynne passed through this portion of her ordeal, and came to a sort of scaffold, at the western extremity of the market-place. It stood nearly beneath the eaves of Boston's earliest church, and appeared to be a fixture there.

In fact, this scaffold constituted a portion of a penal machine, which now, for two or three generations past, has been merely historical and traditionary among us, but was held, in the old time, to be as effectual an agent, in the promotion of good citizenship, as ever was the guillotine among the terrorists of France. It was, in short, the platform of the pillory; and above it rose the framework of that instrument of discipline, so fashioned as to confine the human head in its tight grasp, and thus hold it up to the public gaze. The very ideal of ignominy was embodied and made manifest in this contrivance of wood and iron. There can be no outrage, methinks, against our common nature—whatever be the delinquencies of the individual—no outrage more flagrant than to forbid the culprit to hide his face for shame; as it was the essence of this punishment to do. In Hester Prynne's instance, however, as not unfrequently in other cases, her sentence bore that she should stand a certain time upon the platform, but without undergoing that gripe about the neck and confinement of the head, the proneness to which was the most devilish characteristic of this ugly engine. Knowing well her part, she ascended a flight of wooden steps, and was thus displayed to the surrounding multitude, at about the height of a man's shoulders above the street.

Had there been a Papist among the crowd of Puritans, he might have seen in this beautiful woman, so picturesque in her attire and mien, and with the infant at her bosom, an object to remind him of the image of Divine Maternity, which so many illustrious painters have vied with one another to represent; something which should remind him, indeed, but only by contrast, of that sacred image of sinless motherhood, whose infant was to redeem the world. Here, there was the taint of deepest sin in the most sacred quality of human life, working such effect, that the world was only the darker for this woman's beauty, and the more lost for the infant that she had borne.

The scene was not without a mixture of awe, such as must always invest the spectacle of guilt and shame in a fellow-creature, before society shall have grown corrupt enough to smile, instead of shuddering at it. The witnesses of Hester Prynne's disgrace had not yet passed beyond their simplicity. They were stern enough to look upon her death, had that been the sentence, without a murmur at its severity, but had none of the heartlessness of another social state, which would find only a theme for jest in an exhibition like the present. Even had there been a disposition to turn the matter into ridicule, it must have been repressed and overpowered by the solemn presence of men no less dignified than the governor, and several of his counsellors, a judge, a general, and the ministers of the town, all of whom sat or stood in a balcony of the meeting-house, looking down upon the platform. When such personages could constitute a part of the spectacle, without risking the majesty, or reverence of rank and office, it was safely to be inferred that the infliction of a legal sentence would have an earnest and effectual meaning. Accordingly, the crowd was sombre and grave. The unhappy culprit sustained herself as best a woman might, under the heavy weight of a thousand unrelenting eyes, all fastened upon her, and concentrated at her bosom. It was almost intolerable to be borne. Of an impulsive and passionate nature, she had fortified herself to encounter the stings and venomous stabs of public contumely, wreaking itself in every variety of insult; but there was a quality so much more terrible in the solemn mood of the popular mind, that she longed rather to behold all those rigid countenances contorted with scornful merriment, and herself the object. Had a roar of laughter burst from the multitude—each man, each woman, each little shrill-voiced child, contributing their individual parts—Hester Prynne might have repaid them all with a bitter and disdainful smile. But, under the leaden infliction which it was her doom to endure, she felt, at moments, as if she must needs shriek out with the full power of her lungs, and cast herself from the scaffold down upon the ground, or else go mad at once.

Yet there were intervals when the whole scene, in which she was the most conspicuous object, seemed to vanish from her eyes, or, at least, glimmered indistinctly before them, like a mass of imperfectly shaped and spectral images. Her mind, and especially her memory, was preternaturally active, and kept bringing up other scenes than this roughly hewn street of a little town, on the edge of the western wilderness: other faces than were lowering upon her from beneath the brims of those steeple-crowned hats. Reminiscences, the most trifling and immaterial, passages of infancy and school-days, sports, childish quarrels, and the little domestic traits of her maiden years, came swarming back upon her, intermingled with recollections of whatever was gravest in her subsequent life; one picture precisely as vivid as another; as if all were of similar importance, or all alike a play. Possibly, it was an instinctive device of her spirit to relieve itself by the exhibition of these phantasmagoric forms, from the cruel weight and hardness of the reality.

Be that as it might, the scaffold of the pillory was a point of view that revealed to Hester Prynne the entire track along which she had been treading, since her happy infancy. Standing on that miserable eminence, she saw again her native village, in Old England, and her paternal home: a decayed house of grey stone, with a poverty-stricken aspect, but retaining a half obliterated shield of arms over the portal, in token of antique gentility. She saw her father's face, with its bold brow, and reverend white beard that flowed over the old-fashioned Elizabethan ruff; her mother's, too, with the look of heedful and anxious love which it always wore in her remembrance, and which, even since her death, had so often laid the impediment of a gentle remonstrance in her daughter's pathway. She saw her own face, glowing with girlish beauty, and illuminating all the interior of the dusky mirror in which she had been wont to gaze at it. There she beheld another countenance, of a man well stricken in years, a pale, thin, scholar-like visage, with eyes dim and bleared by the lamp-light that had served them to pore over many ponderous books. Yet those same bleared optics had a strange, penetrating power, when it was their owner's purpose to read the human soul. This figure of the study and the cloister, as Hester Prynne's womanly fancy failed not to recall, was slightly deformed, with the left shoulder a trifle higher than the right. Next rose before her in memory's picture-gallery, the intricate and narrow thoroughfares, the tall, grey houses, the huge cathedrals, and the public edifices, ancient in date and quaint in architecture, of a continental city; where new life had awaited her, still in connexion with the misshapen scholar: a new life, but feeding itself on time-worn materials, like a tuft of green moss on a crumbling wall. Lastly, in lieu of these shifting scenes, came back the rude market-place of the Puritan settlement, with all the townspeople assembled, and levelling their stern regards at Hester Prynne — yes, at herself — who stood on the scaffold of the pillory, an infant on her arm, and the letter A, in scarlet, fantastically embroidered with gold thread, upon her bosom.

Could it be true? She clutched the child so fiercely to her breast that it sent forth a cry; she turned her eyes downward at the scarlet letter, and even touched it with her finger, to assure herself that the infant and the shame were real. Yes these were her realities — all else had vanished!

III.

THE RECOGNITION

From this intense consciousness of being the object of severe and universal observation, the wearer of the scarlet letter was at length relieved, by discerning, on the outskirts of the crowd, a figure which irresistibly took possession of her thoughts. An Indian in his native garb was standing there; but the red men were not so infrequent visitors of the English settlements that one of them would have attracted any notice from Hester Prynne at such a time; much less would he have excluded all other objects and ideas from her mind. By the Indian's side, and evidently sustaining a companionship with him, stood a white man, clad in a strange disarray of civilized and savage costume.

He was small in stature, with a furrowed visage, which as yet could hardly be termed aged. There was a remarkable intelligence in his features, as of a person who had so cultivated his mental part that it could not fail to mould the physical to itself and become manifest by unmistakable tokens. Although, by a seemingly careless arrangement of his heterogeneous garb, he had endeavoured to conceal or abate the peculiarity, it was sufficiently evident to Hester Prynne that one of this man's shoulders rose higher than the other. Again, at the first instant of perceiving that thin visage, and the slight deformity of the figure, she pressed her infant to her bosom with so convulsive a force that the poor babe uttered another cry of pain. But the mother did not seem to hear it.

At his arrival in the market-place, and some time before she saw him, the stranger had bent his eyes on Hester Prynne. It was carelessly at first, like a man chiefly accustomed to look inward, and to whom external matters are of little value and import, unless they bear relation to something within his mind. Very soon, however, his look became keen and penetrative. A writhing horror twisted itself across his features, like a snake gliding swiftly over them, and making one little pause, with all its wreathed intervolutions in open sight. His face darkened with some powerful emotion, which, nevertheless, he so instantaneously controlled by an effort of his will, that, save at a single moment, its expression might have passed for calmness. After a brief space, the convulsion grew almost imperceptible, and finally subsided into the depths of his nature. When he found the eyes of Hester Prynne fastened on his own, and saw that she appeared to recognize him, he slowly and calmly raised his finger, made a gesture with it in the air, and laid it on his lips.

Then touching the shoulder of a townsman who stood near to him, he addressed him in a formal and courteous manner:

"I pray you, good Sir," said he, "who is this woman? — and wherefore is she here set up to public shame?"

"You must needs be a stranger in this region, friend," answered the townsman, looking curiously at the questioner and his savage companion, "else you would surely have heard of Mistress Hester Prynne and her evil doings. She hath raised a great scandal, I promise you, in godly Master Dimmesdale's church."

"You say truly," replied the other; "I am a stranger, and have been a wanderer, sorely against my will. I have met with grievous mishaps by sea and land, and have been long held in bonds among the heathen-folk to the southward; and am now brought hither by this Indian to be redeemed out of my captivity. Will it please you, therefore, to tell me of Hester Prynne's — have I her name rightly? — of this woman's offences, and what has brought her to yonder scaffold?"

"Truly, friend; and methinks it must gladden your heart, after your troubles and sojourn in the wilderness," said the townsman, "to find yourself at length in a land where iniquity is searched out and punished in the sight of rulers and people, as here in our godly New England. Yonder woman, Sir, you must know, was the wife of a certain learned man, English by birth, but who had long ago dwelt in Amsterdam, whence some good time agone he was minded to cross over and cast in his lot with us of the Massachusetts. To this purpose he sent his wife before him, remaining himself to look after some necessary affairs. Marry, good Sir, in some two years, or less, that the woman has been a dweller here in Boston, no tidings have come of this learned gentleman, Master Prynne; and his young wife, look you, being left to her own misguidance—"

"Ah! — aha! — I conceive you," said the stranger with a bitter smile. "So learned a man as you speak of should have learned this too in his books. And who, by your favour, Sir, may be the father of yonder babe — it is some three or four months old, I should judge — which Mistress Prynne is holding in her arms?"

"Of a truth, friend, that matter remaineth a riddle; and the Daniel who shall expound it is yet a-wanting," answered the townsman. "Madame Hester absolutely refuseth to speak, and the magistrates have laid their heads together in vain. Peradventure the guilty one stands looking on at this sad spectacle, unknown of man, and forgetting that God sees him."

"The learned man," observed the stranger with another smile, "should come himself to look into the mystery."

"It behoves him well if he be still in life," responded the townsman. "Now, good Sir, our Massachusetts magistracy, bethinking themselves that this woman is youthful and fair, and doubtless was strongly tempted to her fall, and that, moreover, as is most likely, her husband may be at the bottom of the sea, they have not been bold to put in force the extremity of our righteous law against her. The penalty thereof is death. But in their great mercy and tenderness of heart they have doomed Mistress Prynne to stand only a space of three hours on the platform of the pillory, and then and thereafter, for the remainder of her natural life to wear a mark of shame upon her bosom."

"A wise sentence," remarked the stranger, gravely, bowing his head. "Thus she will be a living sermon against sin, until the ignominious letter be engraved upon her tombstone. It irks me, nevertheless, that the partner of her iniquity should not at least, stand on the scaffold by her side. But he will be known—he will be known!—he will be known!"

He bowed courteously to the communicative townsman, and whispering a few words to his Indian attendant, they both made their way through the crowd.

While this passed, Hester Prynne had been standing on her pedestal, still with a fixed gaze towards the stranger—so fixed a gaze that, at moments of intense absorption, all other objects in the visible world seemed to vanish, leaving only him and her. Such an interview, perhaps, would have been more terrible than even to meet him as she now did, with the hot mid-day sun burning down upon her face, and lighting up its shame; with the scarlet token of infamy on her breast; with the sin-born infant in her arms; with a whole people, drawn forth as to a festival, staring at the features that should have been seen only in the quiet gleam of the fireside, in the happy shadow of a home, or beneath a matronly veil at church. Dreadful as it was, she was conscious of a shelter in the presence of these thousand witnesses. It was better to stand thus, with so many betwixt him and her, than to greet him face to face—they two alone. She fled for refuge, as it were, to the public exposure, and dreaded the moment when its protection should be withdrawn from her.

Involved in these thoughts, she scarcely heard a voice behind her until it had repeated her name more than once, in a loud and solemn tone, audible to the whole multitude.

"Hearken unto me, Hester Prynne!" said the voice.

It has already been noticed that directly over the platform on which Hester Prynne stood was a kind of balcony, or open gallery, appended to the meeting-house. It was the place whence proclamations were wont to be made, amidst an assemblage of the magistracy, with all the ceremonial that attended such public observances in those days. Here, to witness the scene which we are describing, sat Governor Bellingham himself with four sergeants about his chair, bearing halberds, as a guard of honour. He wore a dark feather in his hat, a border of embroidery on his cloak, and a black velvet tunic beneath—a gentleman advanced in years, with a hard experience written in his wrinkles. He was not ill-fitted to be the head and representative of a community which owed its origin and progress, and its present state of development, not to the impulses of youth, but to the stern and tempered energies of manhood and the sombre sagacity of age; accomplishing so much, precisely because it imagined and hoped so little. The other eminent characters by whom the chief ruler was surrounded were distinguished by a dignity of mien, belonging to a period when the forms of authority were felt to possess the sacredness of Divine institutions. They were, doubtless, good men, just and sage. But, out of the whole human family, it would not have been easy to select the same number of wise and virtuous persons, who should be less capable of sitting in judgment on an erring woman's heart, and disentangling its mesh of good and evil, than the sages of rigid aspect towards whom Hester Prynne now turned her face. She seemed conscious, indeed, that whatever sympathy she might expect lay in the larger and warmer heart of the multitude; for, as she lifted her eyes towards the balcony, the unhappy woman grew pale, and trembled.

The voice which had called her attention was that of the reverend and famous John Wilson, the eldest clergyman of Boston, a great scholar, like most of his contemporaries in the profession, and withal a man of kind and genial spirit. This last attribute, however, had been less carefully developed than his intellectual gifts, and was, in truth, rather a matter of shame than self-congratulation with him. There he stood, with a border of grizzled locks beneath his skull-cap, while his grey eyes, accustomed to the shaded light of his study, were winking, like those of Hester's infant, in the unadulterated sunshine. He looked like the darkly engraved portraits which we see prefixed to old volumes of sermons, and had no more right than one of those portraits would have to step forth, as he now did, and meddle with a question of human guilt, passion, and anguish.

"Hester Prynne," said the clergyman, "I have striven with my young brother here, under whose preaching of the Word you have been privileged to sit"—here Mr. Wilson laid his hand on the shoulder of a pale young man beside him—"I have sought, I say, to persuade this godly youth, that he should deal with you, here in the face of Heaven, and before these wise and upright rulers, and in hearing of all the people, as touching the vileness and blackness of your sin. Knowing your natural temper better than I, he could the better judge what arguments to use, whether of tenderness or terror, such as might prevail over your hardness and obstinacy, insomuch that you should no longer hide the name of him who tempted you to this grievous fall. But he opposes to me—with a young man's over-softness, albeit wise beyond his years—that it were wronging the very nature of woman to force her to lay open her heart's secrets in such broad daylight, and in presence of so great a multitude. Truly, as I sought to convince him, the shame lay in the commission of the sin, and not in the showing of it forth. What say you to it, once again, brother Dimmesdale? Must it be thou, or I, that shall deal with this poor sinner's soul?"

There was a murmur among the dignified and reverend occupants of the balcony; and Governor Bellingham gave expression to its purport, speaking in an authoritative voice, although tempered with respect towards the youthful clergyman whom he addressed:

"Good Master Dimmesdale," said he, "the responsibility of this woman's soul lies greatly with you. It behoves you, therefore, to exhort her to repentance and to confession, as a proof and consequence thereof."

The directness of this appeal drew the eyes of the whole crowd upon the Reverend Mr. Dimmesdale—young clergyman, who had come from one of the great English universities, bringing all the learning of the age into our wild forest land. His eloquence and religious fervour had already given the earnest of high eminence in his profession. He was a person of very striking aspect, with a white, lofty, and impending brow; large, brown, melancholy eyes, and a mouth which, unless when he forcibly compressed it, was apt to be tremulous, expressing both nervous sensibility and a vast power of self restraint. Notwithstanding his high native gifts and scholar-like attainments, there was an air about this young minister—an apprehensive, a startled, a half-frightened look—as of a being who felt himself quite astray, and at a loss in the pathway of human existence, and could only be at ease in some seclusion of his own. Therefore, so far as his duties would permit, he trod in the shadowy by-paths, and thus kept himself simple and childlike, coming forth, when occasion was, with a freshness, and fragrance, and dewy purity of thought, which, as many people said, affected them like the speech of an angel.

Such was the young man whom the Reverend Mr. Wilson and the Governor had introduced so openly to the public notice, bidding him speak, in the hearing of all men, to that mystery of a woman's soul, so sacred even in its pollution. The trying nature of his position drove the blood from his cheek, and made his lips tremulous.

"Speak to the woman, my brother," said Mr. Wilson. "It is of moment to her soul, and, therefore, as the worshipful Governor says, momentous to thine own, in whose charge hers is. Exhort her to confess the truth!"

The Reverend Mr. Dimmesdale bent his head, in silent prayer, as it seemed, and then came forward.

"Hester Prynne," said he, leaning over the balcony and looking down steadfastly into her eyes, "thou hearest what this good man says, and seest the accountability under which I labour. If thou feelest it to be for thy soul's peace, and that thy earthly punishment will thereby be made more effectual to salvation, I charge thee to speak out the name of thy fellow-sinner and fellow-sufferer! Be not silent from any mistaken pity and tenderness for him; for, believe me, Hester, though he were to step down from a high place, and stand there beside thee, on thy pedestal of shame, yet better were it so than to hide a guilty heart through life. What can thy silence do for him, except it tempt him—yea, compel him, as it were—to add hypocrisy to sin? Heaven hath granted thee an open ignominy, that thereby thou mayest work out an open triumph over the evil within thee and the sorrow without. Take heed how thou deniest to him—who, perchance, hath not the courage to grasp it for himself—the bitter, but wholesome, cup that is now presented to thy lips!"

The young pastor's voice was tremulously sweet, rich, deep, and broken. The feeling that it so evidently manifested, rather than the direct purport of the words, caused it to vibrate within all hearts, and brought the listeners into one accord of sympathy. Even the poor baby at Hester's bosom was affected by the same influence, for it directed its hitherto vacant gaze towards Mr. Dimmesdale, and held up its little arms with a half-pleased, half-plaintive murmur. So powerful seemed the minister's appeal that the people could not believe but that Hester Prynne would speak out the guilty name, or else that the guilty one himself in whatever high or lowly place he stood, would be drawn forth by an inward and inevitable necessity, and compelled to ascend the scaffold.

Hester shook her head.

"Woman, transgress not beyond the limits of Heaven's mercy!" cried the Reverend Mr. Wilson, more harshly than before. "That little babe hath been gifted with a voice, to second and confirm the counsel which thou hast heard. Speak out the name! That, and thy repentance, may avail to take the scarlet letter off thy breast."

"Never," replied Hester Prynne, looking, not at Mr. Wilson, but into the deep and troubled eyes of the younger clergyman. "It is too deeply branded. Ye cannot take it off. And would that I might endure his agony as well as mine!"

"Speak, woman!" said another voice, coldly and sternly, proceeding from the crowd about the scaffold, "Speak; and give your child a father!"

"I will not speak!" answered Hester, turning pale as death, but responding to this voice, which she too surely recognised. "And my child must seek a heavenly father; she shall never know an earthly one!"

"She will not speak!" murmured Mr. Dimmesdale, who, leaning over the balcony, with his hand upon his heart, had awaited the result of his appeal. He now drew back with a long respiration. "Wondrous strength and generosity of a woman's heart! She will not speak!"

Discerning the impracticable state of the poor culprit's mind, the elder clergyman, who had carefully prepared himself for the occasion, addressed to the multitude a discourse on sin, in all its branches, but with continual reference to the ignominious letter. So forcibly did he dwell upon this symbol, for the hour or more during which his periods were rolling over the people's heads, that it assumed new terrors in their imagination, and seemed to derive its scarlet hue from the flames of the infernal pit. Hester Prynne, meanwhile, kept her place upon the pedestal of shame, with glazed eyes, and an air of weary indifference. She had borne that morning all that nature could endure; and as her temperament was not of the order that escapes from too intense suffering by a swoon, her spirit could only shelter itself beneath a stony crust of insensibility, while the faculties of animal life remained entire. In this state, the voice of the preacher thundered remorselessly, but unavailingly, upon her ears. The infant, during the latter portion of her ordeal, pierced the air with its wailings and screams; she strove to hush it mechanically, but seemed scarcely to sympathise with its trouble. With the same hard demeanour, she was led back to prison, and vanished from the public gaze within its iron-clamped portal. It was whispered by those who peered after her that the scarlet letter threw a lurid gleam along the dark passage-way of the interior.

IV.

THE INTERVIEW

After her return to the prison, Hester Prynne was found to be in a state of nervous excitement, that demanded constant watchfulness, lest she should perpetrate violence on herself, or do some half-frenzied mischief to the poor babe. As night approached, it proving impossible to quell her insubordination by rebuke or threats of punishment, Master Brackett, the jailer, thought fit to introduce a physician. He described him as a man of skill in all Christian modes of physical science, and likewise familiar with whatever the savage people could teach in respect to medicinal herbs and roots that grew in the forest. To say the truth, there was much need of professional assistance, not merely for Hester herself, but still more urgently for the child — who, drawing its sustenance from the maternal bosom, seemed to have drank in with it all the turmoil, the anguish and despair, which pervaded the mother's system. It now writhed in convulsions of pain, and was a forcible type, in its little frame, of the moral agony which Hester Prynne had borne throughout the day.

Closely following the jailer into the dismal apartment, appeared that individual, of singular aspect whose presence in the crowd had been of such deep interest to the wearer of the scarlet letter. He was lodged in the prison, not as suspected of any offence, but as the most convenient and suitable mode of disposing of him, until the magistrates should have conferred with the Indian sagamores respecting his ransom. His name was announced as Roger Chillingworth. The jailer, after ushering him into the room, remained a moment, marvelling at the comparative quiet that followed his entrance; for Hester Prynne had immediately become as still as death, although the child continued to moan.

"Prithee, friend, leave me alone with my patient," said the practitioner. "Trust me, good jailer, you shall briefly have peace in your house; and, I promise you, Mistress Prynne shall hereafter be more amenable to just authority than you may have found her heretofore."

"Nay, if your worship can accomplish that," answered Master Brackett, "I shall own you for a man of skill, indeed! Verily, the woman hath been like a possessed one; and there lacks little that I should take in hand, to drive Satan out of her with stripes."

The stranger had entered the room with the characteristic quietude of the profession to which he announced himself as belonging. Nor did his demeanour change when the withdrawal of the prison keeper left him face to face with the woman, whose absorbed notice of him, in the crowd, had intimated so close a relation between himself and her. His first care was given to the child, whose cries, indeed, as she lay writhing on the trundle-bed, made it of peremptory necessity to postpone all other business to the task of soothing her. He examined the infant carefully, and then proceeded to unclasp a leathern case, which he took from beneath his dress. It appeared to contain medical preparations, one of which he mingled with a cup of water.

"My old studies in alchemy," observed he, "and my sojourn, for above a year past, among a people well versed in the kindly properties of simples, have made a better physician of me than many that claim the medical degree. Here, woman! The child is yours — she is none of mine — neither will she recognise my voice or aspect as a father's. Administer this draught, therefore, with thine own hand."

Hester repelled the offered medicine, at the same time gazing with strongly marked apprehension into his face. "Wouldst thou avenge thyself on the innocent babe?" whispered she.

"Foolish woman!" responded the physician, half coldly, half soothingly. "What should ail me to harm this misbegotten and miserable babe? The medicine is potent for good, and were it my child — yea, mine own, as well as thine! I could do no better for it."

As she still hesitated, being, in fact, in no reasonable state of mind, he took the infant in his arms, and himself administered the draught. It soon proved its efficacy, and redeemed the leech's pledge. The moans of the little patient subsided; its convulsive tossings gradually ceased; and in a few moments, as is the custom of young children after relief from pain, it sank into a profound and dewy slumber. The physician, as he had a fair right to be termed, next bestowed his attention on the mother. With calm and intent scrutiny, he felt her pulse, looked into her eyes — a gaze that made her heart shrink and shudder, because so familiar, and yet so strange and cold — and, finally, satisfied with his investigation, proceeded to mingle another draught.

"I know not Lethe nor Nepenthe," remarked he; "but I have

learned many new secrets in the wilderness, and here is one of them—a recipe that an Indian taught me, in requital of some lessons of my own, that were as old as Paracelsus. Drink it! It may be less soothing than a sinless conscience. That I cannot give thee. But it will calm the swell and heaving of thy passion, like oil thrown on the waves of a tempestuous sea."

He presented the cup to Hester, who received it with a slow, earnest look into his face; not precisely a look of fear, yet full of doubt and questioning as to what his purposes might be. She looked also at her slumbering child.

"I have thought of death," said she—"have wished for it—would even have prayed for it, were it fit that such as I should pray for anything. Yet, if death be in this cup, I bid thee think again, ere thou beholdest me quaff it. See! it is even now at my lips."

"Drink, then," replied he, still with the same cold composure. "Dost thou know me so little, Hester Prynne? Are my purposes wont to be so shallow? Even if I imagine a scheme of vengeance, what could I do better for my object than to let thee live—than to give thee medicines against all harm and peril of life—so that this burning shame may still blaze upon thy bosom?" As he spoke, he laid his long forefinger on the scarlet letter, which forthwith seemed to scorch into Hester's breast, as if it had been red hot. He noticed her involuntary gesture, and smiled. "Live, therefore, and bear about thy doom with thee, in the eyes of men and women—in the eyes of him whom thou didst call thy husband—in the eyes of yonder child! And, that thou mayest live, take off this draught."

Without further expostulation or delay, Hester Prynne drained the cup, and, at the motion of the man of skill, seated herself on the bed, where the child was sleeping; while he drew the only chair which the room afforded, and took his own seat beside her. She could not but tremble at these preparations; for she felt that—having now done all that humanity, or principle, or, if so it were, a refined cruelty, impelled him to do for the relief of physical suffering—he was next to treat with her as the man whom she had most deeply and irreparably injured.

"Hester," said he, "I ask not wherefore, nor how thou hast fallen into the pit, or say, rather, thou hast ascended to the pedestal of infamy on which I found thee. The reason is not far to seek. It was my folly, and thy weakness. I—a man of thought—the book-worm of great libraries—a man already in decay, having given my best years to feed the hungry dream of knowledge—what had I to do with youth and beauty like thine own? Misshapen from my birth-hour, how could I delude myself with the idea that intellectual gifts might veil physical deformity in a young girl's fantasy? Men call me wise. If sages were ever wise in their own behoof, I might have foreseen all this. I might have known that, as I came out of the vast and dismal forest, and entered this settlement of Christian men, the very first object to meet my eyes would be thyself, Hester Prynne, standing up, a statue of ignominy, before the people. Nay, from the moment when we came down the old church-steps together, a married pair, I might have beheld the bale-fire of that scarlet letter blazing at the end of our path!"

"Thou knowest," said Hester—for, depressed as she was, she could not endure this last quiet stab at the token of her shame—"thou knowest that I was frank with thee. I felt no love, nor feigned any."

"True," replied he. "It was my folly! I have said it. But, up to that epoch of my life, I had lived in vain. The world had been so cheerless! My heart was a habitation large enough for many guests, but lonely and chill, and without a household fire. I longed to kindle one! It seemed not so wild a dream—old as I was, and sombre as I was, and misshapen as I was—that the simple bliss, which is scattered far and wide, for all mankind to gather up, might yet be mine. And so, Hester, I drew thee into my heart, into its innermost chamber, and sought to warm thee by the warmth which thy presence made there!"

"I have greatly wronged thee," murmured Hester.

"We have wronged each other," answered he. "Mine was the first wrong, when I betrayed thy budding youth into a false and unnatural relation with my decay. Therefore, as a man who has not thought and philosophised in vain, I seek no vengeance, plot no evil against thee. Between thee and me, the scale hangs fairly balanced. But, Hester, the man lives who has wronged us both! Who is he?"

"Ask me not!" replied Hester Prynne, looking firmly into his face. "That thou shalt never know!"

"Never, sayest thou?" rejoined he, with a smile of dark and self-relying intelligence. "Never know him! Believe me, Hester, there are few things whether in the outward world, or, to a certain depth, in the invisible sphere of thought—few things hidden from the man who devotes himself earnestly and unreservedly to the solution of a mystery. Thou mayest cover up thy secret from the prying multitude. Thou mayest conceal it, too, from the ministers and magistrates, even as thou didst this day, when they sought to wrench the name out of thy heart, and give thee a partner on thy pedestal. But, as for me, I come to the inquest with other senses than they possess. I shall seek this man, as I have sought truth in books: as I have sought gold in alchemy. There is a sympathy that will make me conscious of him. I shall see him tremble. I shall feel myself shudder, suddenly and unawares. Sooner or later, he must needs be mine."

The eyes of the wrinkled scholar glowed so intensely upon her, that Hester Prynne clasped her hand over her heart, dreading lest he should read the secret there at once.

"Thou wilt not reveal his name? Not the less he is mine," resumed he, with a look of confidence, as if destiny were at one with him. "He bears no letter of infamy wrought into his garment, as thou dost, but I shall read it on his heart. Yet fear not for him! Think not that I shall interfere with Heaven's own method of retribution, or, to my own loss, betray him to the gripe of human law. Neither do thou imagine that I shall contrive aught against his life; no, nor against his fame, if as I judge, he be a man of fair repute. Let him live! Let him hide himself in outward honour, if he may! Not the less he shall be mine!"

"Thy acts are like mercy," said Hester, bewildered and appalled; "but thy words interpret thee as a terror!"

"One thing, thou that wast my wife, I would enjoin upon thee," continued the scholar. "Thou hast kept the secret of thy paramour. Keep, likewise, mine! There are none in this land that know me. Breathe not to any human soul that thou didst ever call me husband! Here, on this wild outskirt of the earth, I shall pitch my tent; for, elsewhere a wanderer, and isolated from human interests, I find here a woman, a man, a child, amongst whom and myself there exist the closest ligaments. No matter whether of love or hate: no matter whether of right or wrong! Thou and thine, Hester Prynne, belong to me. My home is where thou art and where he is. But betray me not!"

"Wherefore dost thou desire it?" inquired Hester, shrinking, she hardly knew why, from this secret bond. "Why not announce thyself openly, and cast me off at once?"

"It may be," he replied, "because I will not encounter the dishonour that besmirches the husband of a faithless woman. It may be for other reasons. Enough, it is my purpose to live and die unknown. Let, therefore, thy husband be to the world as one already dead, and of whom no tidings shall ever come. Recognise me not, by word, by sign, by look! Breathe not the secret, above all, to the man thou wottest of. Shouldst thou fail me in this, beware! His fame, his position, his life will be in my hands. Beware!"

"I will keep thy secret, as I have his," said Hester.

"Swear it!" rejoined he.

And she took the oath.

"And now, Mistress Prynne," said old Roger Chillingworth, as he was hereafter to be named, "I leave thee alone: alone with thy infant and the scarlet letter! How is it, Hester? Doth thy sentence bind thee to wear the token in thy sleep? Art thou not afraid of nightmares and hideous dreams?"

"Why dost thou smile so at me?" inquired Hester, troubled at the expression of his eyes. "Art thou like the Black Man that haunts the forest round about us? Hast thou enticed me into a bond that will prove the ruin of my soul?"

"Not thy soul," he answered, with another smile. "No, not thine!"

V.

HESTER AT HER NEEDLE

Hester Prynne's term of confinement was now at an end. Her prison-door was thrown open, and she came forth into the sunshine, which, falling on all alike, seemed, to her sick and morbid heart, as if meant for no other purpose than to reveal the scarlet letter on her breast. Perhaps there was a more real torture in her first unattended footsteps from the threshold of the prison than even in the procession and spectacle that have been described, where she was made the common infamy, at which all mankind was summoned to point its finger. Then, she was supported by an unnatural tension of the nerves, and by all the combative energy of her character, which enabled her to convert the scene into a kind of lurid triumph. It was, moreover, a separate and insulated event, to occur but once in her lifetime, and to meet which, therefore, reckless of economy, she might call up the vital strength that would have sufficed for many quiet years. The very law that condemned her — a giant of stern features but with vigour to support, as well as to annihilate, in his iron arm — had held her up through the terrible ordeal of her ignominy. But now, with this unattended walk from her prison door, began the daily custom; and she must either sustain and carry it forward by the ordinary resources of her nature, or sink beneath it. She could no longer borrow from the future to help her through the present grief. Tomorrow would bring its own trial with it; so would the next day, and so would the next: each its own trial, and yet the very same that was now so unutterably grievous to be borne. The days of the far-off future would toil onward, still with the same burden for her to take up, and bear along with her, but never to fling down; for the accumulating days and added years would pile up their misery upon the heap of shame. Throughout them all, giving up her individuality, she would become the general symbol at which the preacher and moralist might point, and in which they might vivify and embody their images of woman's frailty and sinful passion. Thus the young and pure would be taught to look at her, with the scarlet letter flaming on her breast — at her, the child of honourable parents — at her, the mother of a babe that would hereafter be a woman — at her, who had once been innocent — as the figure, the body, the reality of sin. And over her grave, the infamy that she must carry thither would be her only monument.

It may seem marvellous that, with the world before her — kept by no restrictive clause of her condemnation within the limits of the Puritan settlement, so remote and so obscure—free to return to her birth-place, or to any other European land, and there hide her character and identity under a new exterior, as completely as if emerging into another state of being—and having also the passes of the dark, inscrutable forest open to her, where the wildness of her nature might assimilate itself with a people whose customs and life were alien from the law that had condemned her—it may seem marvellous that this woman should still call that place her home, where, and where only, she must needs be the type of shame. But there is a fatality, a feeling so irresistible and inevitable that it has the force of doom, which almost invariably compels human beings to linger around and haunt, ghost-like, the spot where some great and marked event has given the colour to their lifetime; and, still the more irresistibly, the darker the tinge that saddens it. Her sin, her ignominy, were the roots which she had struck into the soil. It was as if a new birth, with stronger assimilations than the first, had converted the forest-land, still so uncongenial to every other pilgrim and wanderer, into Hester Prynne's wild and dreary, but life-long home. All other scenes of earth—even that village of rural England, where happy infancy and stainless maidenhood seemed yet to be in her mother's keeping, like garments put off long ago—were foreign to her, in comparison. The chain that bound her here was of iron links, and galling to her inmost soul, but could never be broken.

It might be, too—doubtless it was so, although she hid the secret from herself, and grew pale whenever it struggled out of her heart, like a serpent from its hole—it might be that another feeling kept her within the scene and pathway that had been so fatal. There dwelt, there trode, the feet of one with whom she deemed herself connected in a union that, unrecognised on earth, would bring them together before the bar of final judgment, and make that their marriage-altar, for a joint futurity of endless retribution. Over and over again, the tempter of souls had thrust this idea upon Hester's contemplation, and laughed at the passionate and desperate joy with which she seized, and then strove to cast it from her. She barely looked the idea in the face, and hastened to bar it in its dungeon. What she compelled herself to believe—what, finally, she reasoned upon as her motive for continuing a resident of New England—was half a truth, and half a self-delusion. Here, she said to herself had been the scene of her guilt, and here should be the scene of her earthly punishment; and so, perchance, the torture of her daily shame would at length purge her soul, and work out another purity than that which she had lost: more saint-like, because the result of martyrdom.

Hester Prynne, therefore, did not flee. On the outskirts of the town, within the verge of the peninsula, but not in close vicinity to any other habitation, there was a small thatched cottage. It had been built by an earlier settler, and abandoned, because the soil about it was too sterile for cultivation, while its comparative remoteness put it out of the sphere of that social activity which already marked the habits of the emigrants. It stood on the shore, looking across a basin of the sea at the forest-covered hills, towards the west. A clump of scrubby trees, such as alone grew on the peninsula, did not so much conceal the cottage from view, as seem to denote that here was some object which would fain have been, or at least ought to be, concealed. In this little lonesome dwelling, with some slender means that she possessed, and by the licence of the magistrates, who still kept an inquisitorial watch over her, Hester established herself, with her infant child. A mystic shadow of suspicion immediately attached itself to the spot. Children, too young to comprehend wherefore this woman should be shut out from the sphere of human charities, would creep nigh enough to behold her plying her needle at the cottage-window, or standing in the doorway, or labouring in her little garden, or coming forth along the pathway that led townward, and, discerning the scarlet letter on her breast, would scamper off with a strange contagious fear.

Lonely as was Hester's situation, and without a friend on earth who dared to show himself, she, however, incurred no risk of want. She possessed an art that sufficed, even in a land that afforded comparatively little scope for its exercise, to supply food for her thriving infant and herself. It was the art, then, as now, almost the only one within a woman's grasp—of needle-work. She bore on her breast, in the curiously embroidered letter, a specimen of her delicate and imaginative skill, of which the dames of a court might gladly have availed themselves, to add the richer and more spiritual adornment of human ingenuity to their fabrics of silk and gold. Here, indeed, in the sable simplicity that generally characterised the Puritanic modes of dress, there might be an infrequent call for the finer productions of her handiwork. Yet the taste of the age, demanding whatever was elaborate in compositions of this kind, did not fail to extend its influence over our stern progenitors, who had cast behind them so many fashions which it might seem harder to dispense with.

Public ceremonies, such as ordinations, the installation of magistrates, and all that could give majesty to the forms in which a new government manifested itself to the people, were, as a matter of policy, marked by a stately and well-conducted ceremonial, and a sombre, but yet a studied magnificence. Deep ruffs, painfully wrought bands, and gorgeously embroidered gloves, were all deemed necessary to the official state of men assuming the reins of power, and were readily allowed to individuals dignified by rank or wealth, even while sumptuary laws forbade these and similar extravagances to the plebeian order. In the array of funerals, too—whether for the apparel of the dead body, or to typify, by manifold emblematic devices of sable cloth and snowy lawn, the sorrow of the survivors—there was a frequent and characteristic demand for such labour as Hester Prynne could supply. Baby-linen—for babies then wore robes of state—afforded still another possibility of toil and emolument.

By degrees, not very slowly, her handiwork became what would now be termed the fashion. Whether from commiseration for a woman of so miserable a destiny; or from the morbid curiosity that gives a fictitious value even to common or worthless things; or by whatever other intangible circumstance was then, as now, sufficient to bestow, on some persons, what others might seek in vain; or because Hester really filled a gap which must otherwise have remained vacant; it is certain that she had ready and fairly requited employment for as many hours as she saw fit to occupy with her needle. Vanity, it may be, chose to mortify itself, by putting on, for ceremonials of pomp and state, the garments that had been wrought by her sinful hands. Her needle-work was seen on the ruff of the Governor; military men wore it on their scarfs, and the minister on his band; it decked the baby's little cap; it was shut up, to be mildewed and moulder away, in the coffins of the dead. But it is not recorded that, in a single instance, her skill was called in to embroider the white veil which was to cover the pure blushes of a bride. The exception indicated the ever relentless vigour with which society frowned upon her sin.

Hester sought not to acquire anything beyond a subsistence, of the plainest and most ascetic description, for herself, and a simple abundance for her child. Her own dress was of the coarsest materials and the most sombre hue, with only that one ornament—the scarlet letter—which it was her doom to wear. The child's attire, on the other hand, was distinguished by a fanciful, or, we may rather say, a fantastic ingenuity, which served, indeed, to heighten the airy charm that early began to develop itself in the little girl, but which appeared to have also a deeper meaning. We may speak further of it hereafter. Except for that small expenditure in the decoration of her infant, Hester bestowed all her superfluous means in charity, on wretches less miserable than herself, and who not unfrequently insulted the hand that fed them. Much of the time, which she might readily have applied to the better efforts of her art, she employed in making coarse garments for the poor. It is probable that there was an idea of penance in this mode of occupation, and that she offered up a real sacrifice of enjoyment in devoting so many hours to such rude handiwork. She had in her nature a rich, voluptuous, Oriental characteristic—a taste for the gorgeously beautiful, which, save in the exquisite productions of her needle, found nothing else, in all the possibilities of her life, to exercise itself upon. Women derive a pleasure, incomprehensible to the other sex, from the delicate toil of the needle. To Hester Prynne it might have been a mode of expressing, and therefore soothing, the passion of her life. Like all other joys, she rejected it as sin. This morbid meddling of conscience with an immaterial matter betokened, it is to be feared, no genuine and steadfast penitence, but something doubtful, something that might be deeply wrong beneath.

In this manner, Hester Prynne came to have a part to perform in the world. With her native energy of character and rare capacity, it could not entirely cast her off, although it had set a mark upon her, more intolerable to a woman's heart than that which branded the brow of Cain. In all her intercourse with society, however, there was nothing that made her feel as if she belonged to it. Every gesture, every word, and even the silence of those with whom she came in contact, implied, and often expressed, that she was banished, and as much alone as if she inhabited another sphere, or communicated with the common nature by other organs and senses than the rest of human kind. She stood apart from mortal interests, yet close beside them, like a ghost that revisits the familiar fireside, and can no longer make itself seen or felt; no more smile with the household joy, nor mourn with the kindred sorrow; or, should it succeed in manifesting its forbidden sympathy, awakening only terror and horrible repugnance. These emotions, in fact, and its bitterest scorn besides, seemed to be the sole portion that she retained in the universal heart. It was not an age of delicacy; and her position, although she understood it well, and was in little danger of forgetting it, was often brought before her vivid self-perception, like a new anguish, by the rudest touch upon the tenderest spot. The poor, as we have already said, whom she sought out to be the objects of her bounty, often reviled the hand that was stretched forth to succour them. Dames of elevated rank, likewise, whose doors she entered in the way of her occupation, were accustomed to distil drops of bitterness into her heart; sometimes through that alchemy of quiet malice, by which women can concoct a subtle poison from ordinary trifles; and sometimes, also, by a coarser expression, that fell upon the sufferer's defenceless breast like a rough blow upon an ulcerated wound. Hester had schooled herself long and well; and she never responded to these attacks, save by a flush of crimson that rose irrepressibly over her pale cheek, and again subsided into the depths of her bosom. She was patient—a martyr, indeed—but she forebore to pray for enemies, lest, in spite of her forgiving aspirations, the words of the blessing should stubbornly twist themselves into a curse.

Continually, and in a thousand other ways, did she feel the innumerable throbs of anguish that had been so cunningly contrived for her by the undying, the ever-active sentence of the Puritan tribunal. Clergymen paused in the streets, to address words of exhortation, that brought a crowd, with its mingled grin and frown, around the poor, sinful woman. If she entered a church, trusting to share the Sabbath smile of the Universal Father, it was often her mishap to find herself the text of the discourse. She grew to have a dread of children; for they had imbibed from their parents a vague idea of something horrible in this dreary woman gliding silently through the town, with never any companion but one only child. Therefore, first allowing her to pass, they pursued her at a distance with shrill cries, and the utterances of a word that had no distinct purport to their own minds, but was none the less terrible to her, as proceeding from lips that babbled it unconsciously. It seemed to argue so wide a diffusion of her shame, that all nature knew of it; it could have caused her no deeper pang had the leaves of the trees whispered the dark story among themselves—had the summer breeze murmured about it—had the wintry blast shrieked it aloud! Another peculiar torture was felt in the gaze of a new eye. When strangers looked curiously at the scarlet letter—and none ever failed to do so—they branded it afresh in Hester's soul; so that, oftentimes, she could scarcely refrain, yet always did refrain, from covering the symbol with her hand. But then, again, an accustomed eye had likewise its own anguish to inflict. Its cool stare of familiarity was intolerable. From first to last, in short, Hester Prynne had always this dreadful agony in feeling a human eye upon the token; the spot never grew callous; it seemed, on the contrary, to grow more sensitive with daily torture.

But sometimes, once in many days, or perchance in many months, she felt an eye—a human eye—upon the ignominious brand, that seemed to give a momentary relief, as if half of her agony were shared. The next instant, back it all rushed again, with still a deeper throb of pain; for, in that brief interval, she had sinned anew. (Had Hester sinned alone?)

Her imagination was somewhat affected, and, had she been

of a softer moral and intellectual fibre would have been still more so, by the strange and solitary anguish of her life. Walking to and fro, with those lonely footsteps, in the little world with which she was outwardly connected, it now and then appeared to Hester — if altogether fancy, it was nevertheless too potent to be resisted — she felt or fancied, then, that the scarlet letter had endowed her with a new sense. She shuddered to believe, yet could not help believing, that it gave her a sympathetic knowledge of the hidden sin in other hearts. She was terror-stricken by the revelations that were thus made. What were they? Could they be other than the insidious whispers of the bad angel, who would fain have persuaded the struggling woman, as yet only half his victim, that the outward guise of purity was but a lie, and that, if truth were everywhere to be shown, a scarlet letter would blaze forth on many a bosom besides Hester Prynne's? Or, must she receive those intimations — so obscure, yet so distinct — as truth? In all her miserable experience, there was nothing else so awful and so loathsome as this sense. It perplexed, as well as shocked her, by the irreverent inopportuneness of the occasions that brought it into vivid action. Sometimes the red infamy upon her breast would give a sympathetic throb, as she passed near a venerable minister or magistrate, the model of piety and justice, to whom that age of antique reverence looked up, as to a mortal man in fellowship with angels. "What evil thing is at hand?" would Hester say to herself. Lifting her reluctant eyes, there would be nothing human within the scope of view, save the form of this earthly saint! Again a mystic sisterhood would contumaciously assert itself, as she met the sanctified frown of some matron, who, according to the rumour of all tongues, had kept cold snow within her bosom throughout life. That unsunned snow in the matron's bosom, and the burning shame on Hester Prynne's — what had the two in common? Or, once more, the electric thrill would give her warning — "Behold Hester, here is a companion!" and, looking up, she would detect the eyes of a young maiden glancing at the scarlet letter, shyly and aside, and quickly averted, with a faint, chill crimson in her cheeks as if her purity were somewhat sullied by that momentary glance. O Fiend, whose talisman was that fatal symbol, wouldst thou leave nothing, whether in youth or age, for this poor sinner to revere? — such loss of faith is ever one of the saddest results of sin. Be it accepted as a proof that all was not corrupt in this poor victim of her own frailty, and man's hard law, that Hester Prynne yet struggled to believe that no fellow-mortal was guilty like herself.

The vulgar, who, in those dreary old times, were always contributing a grotesque horror to what interested their imaginations, had a story about the scarlet letter which we might readily work up into a terrific legend. They averred that the symbol was not mere scarlet cloth, tinged in an earthly dye-pot, but was red-hot with infernal fire, and could be seen glowing all alight whenever Hester Prynne walked abroad in the night-time. And we must needs say it seared Hester's bosom so deeply, that perhaps there was more truth in the rumour than our modern incredulity may be inclined to admit.

VI.

PEARL

We have as yet hardly spoken of the infant; that little creature, whose innocent life had sprung, by the inscrutable decree of Providence, a lovely and immortal flower, out of the rank luxuriance of a guilty passion. How strange it seemed to the sad woman, as she watched the growth, and the beauty that became every day more brilliant, and the intelligence that threw its quivering sunshine over the tiny features of this child! Her Pearl—for so had Hester called her; not as a name expressive of her aspect, which had nothing of the calm, white, unimpassioned lustre that would be indicated by the comparison. But she named the infant "Pearl," as being of great price—purchased with all she had—her mother's only treasure! How strange, indeed! Man had marked this woman's sin by a scarlet letter, which had such potent and disastrous efficacy that no human sympathy could reach her, save it were sinful like herself. God, as a direct consequence of the sin which man thus punished, had given her a lovely child, whose place was on that same dishonoured bosom, to connect her parent for ever with the race and descent of mortals, and to be finally a blessed soul in heaven! Yet these thoughts affected Hester Prynne less with hope than apprehension. She knew that her deed had been evil; she could have no faith, therefore, that its result would be good. Day after day she looked fearfully into the child's expanding nature, ever dreading to detect some dark and wild peculiarity that should correspond with the guiltiness to which she owed her being.

Certainly there was no physical defect. By its perfect shape, its vigour, and its natural dexterity in the use of all its untried limbs, the infant was worthy to have been brought forth in Eden: worthy to have been left there to be the plaything of the angels after the world's first parents were driven out. The child had a native grace which does not invariably co-exist with faultless beauty; its attire, however simple, always impressed the beholder as if it were the very garb that precisely became it best. But little Pearl was not clad in rustic weeds. Her mother, with a morbid purpose that may be better understood hereafter, had bought the richest tissues that could be procured, and allowed her imaginative faculty its full play in the arrangement and decoration of the dresses which the child wore before the public eye. So magnificent was the small figure when thus arrayed, and such was the splendour of Pearl's own proper beauty, shining through the gorgeous robes which might have extinguished a paler loveliness, that there was an absolute circle of radiance around her on the darksome cottage floor. And yet a russet gown, torn and soiled with the child's rude play, made a picture of her just as perfect. Pearl's aspect was imbued with a spell of infinite variety; in this one child there were many children, comprehending the full scope between the wild-flower prettiness of a peasant-baby, and the pomp, in little, of an infant princess. Throughout all, however, there was a trait of passion, a certain depth of hue, which she never lost; and if in any of her changes, she had grown fainter or paler, she would have ceased to be herself — it would have been no longer Pearl!

This outward mutability indicated, and did not more than fairly express, the various properties of her inner life. Her nature appeared to possess depth, too, as well as variety; but — or else Hester's fears deceived her — it lacked reference and adaptation to the world into which she was born. The child could not be made amenable to rules. In giving her existence a great law had been broken; and the result was a being whose elements were perhaps beautiful and brilliant, but all in disorder, or with an order peculiar to themselves, amidst which the point of variety and arrangement was difficult or impossible to be discovered. Hester could only account for the child's character — and even then most vaguely and imperfectly — by recalling what she herself had been during that momentous period while Pearl was imbibing her soul from the spiritual world, and her bodily frame from its material of earth. The mother's impassioned state had been the medium through which were transmitted to the unborn infant the rays of its moral life; and, however white and clear originally, they had taken the deep stains of crimson and gold, the fiery lustre, the black shadow, and the untempered light of the intervening substance. Above all, the warfare of Hester's spirit at that epoch was perpetuated in Pearl. She could recognize her wild, desperate, defiant mood, the flightiness of her temper, and even some of the very cloud-shapes of gloom and despondency that had brooded in her heart. They were now illuminated by the morning radiance of a young child's disposition, but, later in the day of earthly existence, might be prolific of the storm and whirlwind.

The discipline of the family in those days was of a far more rigid kind than now. The frown, the harsh rebuke, the frequent application of the rod, enjoined by Scriptural authority, were used, not merely in the way of punishment for actual offences, but as a wholesome regimen for the growth and promotion of all childish virtues. Hester Prynne, nevertheless, the loving mother of this one child, ran little risk of erring on the side of undue severity. Mindful, however, of her own errors and misfortunes, she early sought to impose a tender but strict control over the infant immortality that was committed to her charge. But the task was beyond her skill. After testing both smiles and frowns, and proving that neither mode of treatment possessed any calculable influence, Hester was ultimately compelled to stand aside and permit the child to be swayed by her own impulses. Physical compulsion or restraint was effectual, of course, while it lasted. As to any other kind of discipline, whether addressed to her mind or heart, little Pearl might or might not be within its reach, in accordance with the caprice that ruled the moment. Her mother, while Pearl was yet an infant, grew acquainted with a certain peculiar look, that warned her when it would be labour thrown away to insist, persuade or plead.

It was a look so intelligent, yet inexplicable, perverse, sometimes so malicious, but generally accompanied by a wild flow of spirits, that Hester could not help questioning at such moments whether Pearl was a human child. She seemed rather an airy sprite, which, after playing its fantastic sports for a little while upon the cottage floor, would flit away with a mocking smile. Whenever that look appeared in her wild, bright, deeply black eyes, it invested her with a strange remoteness and intangibility: it was as if she were hovering in the air, and might vanish, like a glimmering light that comes we know not whence and goes we know not whither. Beholding it, Hester was constrained to rush towards the child — to pursue the little elf in the flight which she invariably began — to snatch her to her bosom with a close pressure and earnest kisses — not so much from overflowing love as to assure herself that Pearl was flesh and blood, and not utterly delusive. But Pearl's laugh, when she was caught, though full of merriment and music, made her mother more doubtful than before.

Heart-smitten at this bewildering and baffling spell, that so often came between herself and her sole treasure, whom she had bought so dear, and who was all her world, Hester sometimes burst into passionate tears. Then, perhaps — for there was no foreseeing how it might affect her — Pearl would frown, and clench her little fist, and harden her small features into a stern, unsympathising look of discontent. Not seldom she would laugh anew, and louder than before, like a thing incapable and unintelligent of human sorrow. Or — but this more rarely happened — she would be convulsed with rage of grief and sob out her love for her mother in broken words, and seem intent on proving that she had a heart by breaking it. Yet Hester was hardly safe in confiding herself to that gusty tenderness: it passed as suddenly as it came. Brooding over all these matters, the mother felt like one who has evoked a spirit, but, by some irregularity in the process of conjuration, has failed to win the master-word that should control this new and incomprehensible intelligence. Her only real comfort was when the child lay in the placidity of sleep. Then she was sure of her, and tasted hours of quiet, sad, delicious happiness; until — perhaps with that perverse expression glimmering from beneath her opening lids — little Pearl awoke!

How soon — with what strange rapidity, indeed — did Pearl arrive at an age that was capable of social intercourse beyond the mother's ever-ready smile and nonsense-words! And then what a happiness would it have been could Hester Prynne have heard her clear, bird-like voice mingling with the uproar of other childish voices, and have distinguished and unravelled her own darling's tones, amid all the entangled outcry of a group of sportive children. But this could never be. Pearl was a born outcast of the infantile world. An imp of evil, emblem and product of sin, she had no right among christened infants. Nothing was more remarkable than the instinct, as it seemed, with which the child comprehended her loneliness: the destiny that had drawn an inviolable circle round about her: the whole peculiarity, in short, of her position in respect to other children. Never since her release from prison had Hester met the public gaze without her. In all her walks about the town, Pearl, too, was there: first as the babe in arms, and afterwards as the little girl, small companion of her mother, holding a forefinger with her whole grasp, and tripping along at the rate of three or four footsteps to one of Hester's. She saw the children of the settlement on the grassy margin of the street, or at the domestic thresholds, disporting themselves in such grim fashions as the Puritanic nurture would permit; playing at going to church, perchance, or at scourging Quakers; or taking scalps in a sham fight with the Indians, or scaring one another with freaks of imitative witchcraft. Pearl saw, and gazed intently, but never sought to make acquaintance. If spoken to, she would not speak again. If the children gathered about her, as they sometimes did, Pearl would grow positively terrible in her puny wrath, snatching up stones to fling at them, with shrill, incoherent exclamations, that made her mother tremble, because they had so much the sound of a witch's anathemas in some unknown tongue.

The truth was, that the little Puritans, being of the most intolerant brood that ever lived, had got a vague idea of something outlandish, unearthly, or at variance with ordinary fashions, in the mother and child, and therefore scorned them in their hearts, and not unfrequently reviled them with their tongues. Pearl felt the sentiment, and requited it with the bitterest hatred that can be supposed to rankle in a childish bosom. These outbreaks of a fierce temper had a kind of value, and even comfort for the mother; because there was at least an intelligible earnestness in the mood, instead of the fitful caprice that so often thwarted her in the child's manifestations. It appalled her, nevertheless, to discern here, again, a shadowy reflection of the evil that had existed in herself. All this enmity and passion had Pearl inherited, by inalienable right, out of Hester's heart. Mother and daughter stood together in the same circle of seclusion from human society; and in the nature of the child seemed to be perpetuated those unquiet elements that had distracted Hester Prynne before Pearl's birth, but had since begun to be soothed away by the softening influences of maternity.

At home, within and around her mother's cottage, Pearl wanted not a wide and various circle of acquaintance. The spell of life went forth from her ever-creative spirit, and communicated itself to a thousand objects, as a torch kindles a flame wherever it may be applied. The unlikeliest materials—a stick, a bunch of rags, a flower—were the puppets of Pearl's witchcraft, and, without undergoing any outward change, became spiritually adapted to whatever drama occupied the stage of her inner world. Her one baby-voice served a multitude of imaginary personages, old and young, to talk withal. The pine-trees, aged, black, and solemn, and flinging groans and other melancholy utterances on the breeze, needed little transformation to figure as Puritan elders; the ugliest weeds of the garden were their children, whom Pearl smote down and uprooted most unmercifully. It was wonderful, the vast variety of forms into which she threw her intellect, with no continuity, indeed, but darting up and dancing, always in a state of preternatural activity—soon sinking down, as if exhausted by so rapid and feverish a tide of life—and succeeded by other shapes of a similar wild energy. It was like nothing so much as the phantasmagoric play of the northern lights. In the mere exercise of the fancy, however, and the sportiveness of a growing mind, there might be a little more than was observable in other children of bright faculties; except as Pearl, in the dearth of human playmates, was thrown more upon the visionary throng which she created. The singularity lay in the hostile feelings with which the child regarded all these offsprings of her own heart and mind. She never created a friend, but seemed always to be sowing broadcast the dragon's teeth, whence sprung a harvest of armed enemies, against whom she rushed to battle. It was inexpressibly sad—then what depth of sorrow to a mother, who felt in her own heart the cause—to observe, in one so young, this constant recognition of an adverse world, and so fierce a training of the energies that were to make good her cause in the contest that must ensue.

Gazing at Pearl, Hester Prynne often dropped her work upon her knees, and cried out with an agony which she would fain have hidden, but which made utterance for itself betwixt speech and a groan—"O Father in Heaven—if Thou art still my Father—what is this being which I have brought into the world?" And Pearl, overhearing the ejaculation, or aware through some more subtle channel, of those throbs of anguish, would turn her vivid and beautiful little face upon her mother, smile with sprite-like intelligence, and resume her play.

One peculiarity of the child's deportment remains yet to be told. The very first thing which she had noticed in her life, was—what?—not the mother's smile, responding to it, as other babies do, by that faint, embryo smile of the little mouth, remembered so doubtfully afterwards, and with such fond discussion whether it were indeed a smile. By no means! But that first object of which Pearl seemed to become aware was— shall we say it?—the scarlet letter on Hester's bosom! One day, as her mother stooped over the cradle, the infant's eyes had been caught by the glimmering of the gold embroidery about the letter; and putting up her little hand she grasped at it, smiling, not doubtfully, but with a decided gleam, that gave her face the look of a much older child. Then, gasping for breath, did Hester Prynne clutch the fatal token, instinctively endeavouring to tear it away, so infinite was the torture inflicted by the intelligent touch of Pearl's baby-hand. Again, as if her mother's agonised gesture were meant only to make sport for her, did little Pearl look into her eyes, and smile. From that epoch, except when the child was asleep, Hester had never felt a moment's safety: not a moment's calm enjoyment of her. Weeks, it is true, would sometimes elapse, during which Pearl's gaze might never once be fixed upon the scarlet letter; but then, again, it would come at unawares, like the stroke of sudden death, and always with that peculiar smile and odd expression of the eyes.

Once this freakish, elvish cast came into the child's eyes while Hester was looking at her own image in them, as mothers are fond of doing; and suddenly—for women in solitude, and with troubled hearts, are pestered with unaccountable delusions—she fancied that she beheld, not her own miniature portrait, but another face in the small black mirror of Pearl's eye. It was a face, fiend-like, full of smiling malice, yet bearing the semblance of features that she had known full well, though seldom with a smile, and never with malice in them. It was as if an evil spirit possessed the child, and had just then peeped forth in mockery. Many a time afterwards had Hester been tortured, though less vividly, by the same illusion.

In the afternoon of a certain summer's day, after Pearl grew big enough to run about, she amused herself with gathering handfuls of wild flowers, and flinging them, one by one, at her mother's bosom; dancing up and down like a little elf whenever she hit the scarlet letter. Hester's first motion had been to cover her bosom with her clasped hands. But whether from pride or resignation, or a feeling that her penance might best be wrought out by this unutterable pain, she resisted the impulse, and sat erect, pale as death, looking sadly into little Pearl's wild eyes. Still came the battery of flowers, almost invariably hitting the mark, and covering the mother's breast with hurts for which she could find no balm in this world, nor knew how to seek it in another. At last, her shot being all expended, the child stood still and gazed at Hester, with that little laughing image of a fiend peeping out — or, whether it peeped or no, her mother so imagined it — from the unsearchable abyss of her black eyes.

"Child, what art thou?" cried the mother.

"Oh, I am your little Pearl!" answered the child.

But while she said it, Pearl laughed, and began to dance up and down with the humoursome gesticulation of a little imp, whose next freak might be to fly up the chimney.

"Art thou my child, in very truth?" asked Hester.

Nor did she put the question altogether idly, but, for the moment, with a portion of genuine earnestness; for, such was Pearl's wonderful intelligence, that her mother half doubted whether she were not acquainted with the secret spell of her existence, and might not now reveal herself.

"Yes; I am little Pearl!" repeated the child, continuing her antics.

"Thou art not my child! Thou art no Pearl of mine!" said the mother half playfully; for it was often the case that a sportive impulse came over her in the midst of her deepest suffering. "Tell me, then, what thou art, and who sent thee hither?"

"Tell me, mother!" said the child, seriously, coming up to

Hester, and pressing herself close to her knees. "Do thou tell me!"

"Thy Heavenly Father sent thee!" answered Hester Prynne.

But she said it with a hesitation that did not escape the acuteness of the child. Whether moved only by her ordinary freakishness, or because an evil spirit prompted her, she put up her small forefinger and touched the scarlet letter.

"He did not send me!" cried she, positively. "I have no Heavenly Father!"

"Hush, Pearl, hush! Thou must not talk so!" answered the mother, suppressing a groan. "He sent us all into the world. He sent even me, thy mother. Then, much more thee! Or, if not, thou strange and elfish child, whence didst thou come?"

"Tell me! Tell me!" repeated Pearl, no longer seriously, but laughing and capering about the floor. "It is thou that must tell me!"

But Hester could not resolve the query, being herself in a dismal labyrinth of doubt. She remembered—betwixt a smile and a shudder—the talk of the neighbouring townspeople, who, seeking vainly elsewhere for the child's paternity, and observing some of her odd attributes, had given out that poor little Pearl was a demon offspring: such as, ever since old Catholic times, had occasionally been seen on earth, through the agency of their mother's sin, and to promote some foul and wicked purpose. Luther, according to the scandal of his monkish enemies, was a brat of that hellish breed; nor was Pearl the only child to whom this inauspicious origin was assigned among the New England Puritans.

VII.

THE GOVERNOR'S HALL

Hester Prynne went one day to the mansion of Governor Bellingham, with a pair of gloves which she had fringed and embroidered to his order, and which were to be worn on some great occasion of state; for, though the chances of a popular election had caused this former ruler to descend a step or two from the highest rank, he still held an honourable and influential place among the colonial magistracy.

Another and far more important reason than the delivery of a pair of embroidered gloves, impelled Hester, at this time, to seek an interview with a personage of so much power and activity in the affairs of the settlement. It had reached her ears that there was a design on the part of some of the leading inhabitants, cherishing the more rigid order of principles in religion and government, to deprive her of her child. On the supposition that Pearl, as already hinted, was of demon origin, these good people not unreasonably argued that a Christian interest in the mother's soul required them to remove such a stumbling-block from her path. If the child, on the other hand, were really capable of moral and religious growth, and possessed the elements of ultimate salvation, then, surely, it would enjoy all the fairer prospect of these advantages by being transferred to wiser and better guardianship than Hester Prynne's. Among those who promoted the design, Governor Bellingham was said to be one of the most busy. It may appear singular, and, indeed, not a little ludicrous, that an affair of this kind, which in later days would have been referred to no higher jurisdiction than that of the select men of the town, should then have been a question publicly discussed, and on which statesmen of eminence took sides. At that epoch of pristine simplicity, however, matters of even slighter public interest, and of far less intrinsic weight than the welfare of Hester and her child, were strangely mixed up with the deliberations of legislators and acts of state. The period was hardly, if at all, earlier than that of our story, when a dispute concerning the right of property in a pig not only caused a fierce and bitter contest in the legislative body of the colony, but resulted in an important modification of the framework itself of the legislature.

Full of concern, therefore—but so conscious of her own right that it seemed scarcely an unequal match between the public on the one side, and a lonely woman, backed by the sympathies of nature, on the other—Hester Prynne set forth from her solitary cottage. Little Pearl, of course, was her companion. She was now of an age to run lightly along by her mother's side, and, constantly in motion from morn till sunset, could have accomplished a much longer journey than that before her. Often, nevertheless, more from caprice than necessity, she demanded to be taken up in arms; but was soon as imperious to be let down again, and frisked onward before Hester on the grassy pathway, with many a harmless trip and tumble. We have spoken of Pearl's rich and luxuriant beauty—a beauty that shone with deep and vivid tints, a bright complexion, eyes possessing intensity both of depth and glow, and hair already of a deep, glossy brown, and which, in after years, would be nearly akin to black. There was fire in her and throughout her: she seemed the unpremeditated offshoot of a passionate moment. Her mother, in contriving the child's garb, had allowed the gorgeous tendencies of her imagination their full play, arraying her in a crimson velvet tunic of a peculiar cut, abundantly embroidered in fantasies and flourishes of gold thread. So much strength of colouring, which must have given a wan and pallid aspect to cheeks of a fainter bloom, was admirably adapted to Pearl's beauty, and made her the very brightest little jet of flame that ever danced upon the earth.

But it was a remarkable attribute of this garb, and indeed, of the child's whole appearance, that it irresistibly and inevitably reminded the beholder of the token which Hester Prynne was doomed to wear upon her bosom. It was the scarlet letter in another form: the scarlet letter endowed with life! The mother herself—as if the red ignominy were so deeply scorched into her brain that all her conceptions assumed its form—had carefully wrought out the similitude, lavishing many hours of morbid ingenuity to create an analogy between the object of her affection and the emblem of her guilt and torture. But, in truth, Pearl was the one as well as the other; and only in consequence of that identity had Hester contrived so perfectly to represent the scarlet letter in her appearance.

As the two wayfarers came within the precincts of the town, the children of the Puritans looked up from their play,—or what passed for play with those sombre little urchins—and spoke gravely one to another.

"Behold, verily, there is the woman of the scarlet letter: and of a truth, moreover, there is the likeness of the scarlet letter running along by her side! Come, therefore, and let us fling mud at them!"

But Pearl, who was a dauntless child, after frowning, stamping her foot, and shaking her little hand with a variety of threatening gestures, suddenly made a rush at the knot of her enemies, and put them all to flight. She resembled, in her fierce pursuit of them, an infant pestilence—the scarlet fever, or some such half-fledged angel of judgment—whose mission was to punish the sins of the rising generation. She screamed and shouted, too, with a terrific volume of sound, which, doubtless, caused the hearts of the fugitives to quake within them. The victory accomplished, Pearl returned quietly to her mother, and looked up, smiling, into her face.

Without further adventure, they reached the dwelling of Governor Bellingham. This was a large wooden house, built in a fashion of which there are specimens still extant in the streets of our older towns now moss-grown, crumbling to decay, and melancholy at heart with the many sorrowful or joyful occurrences, remembered or forgotten, that have happened and passed away within their dusky chambers. Then, however, there was the freshness of the passing year on its exterior, and the cheerfulness, gleaming forth from the sunny windows, of a human habitation, into which death had never entered. It had, indeed, a very cheery aspect, the walls being overspread with a kind of stucco, in which fragments of broken glass were plentifully intermixed; so that, when the sunshine fell aslant-wise over the front of the edifice, it glittered and sparkled as if diamonds had been flung against it by the double handful. The brilliancy might have befitted Aladdin's palace rather than the mansion of a grave old Puritan ruler. It was further decorated with strange and seemingly cabalistic figures and diagrams, suitable to the quaint taste of the age which had been drawn in the stucco, when newly laid on, and had now grown hard and durable, for the admiration of after times.

Pearl, looking at this bright wonder of a house began to caper and dance, and imperatively required that the whole breadth of sunshine should be stripped off its front, and given her to play with.

"No, my little Pearl!" said her mother; "thou must gather thine own sunshine. I have none to give thee!"

They approached the door, which was of an arched form, and flanked on each side by a narrow tower or projection of the edifice, in both of which were lattice-windows, the wooden shutters to close over them at need. Lifting the iron hammer that hung at the portal, Hester Prynne gave a summons, which was answered by one of the Governor's bond-servants—a free-born

Englishman, but now a seven years' slave. During that term he was to be the property of his master, and as much a commodity of bargain and sale as an ox, or a joint-stool. The serf wore the customary garb of serving-men at that period, and long before, in the old hereditary halls of England.

"Is the worshipful Governor Bellingham within?" inquired Hester.

"Yea, forsooth," replied the bond-servant, staring with wide-open eyes at the scarlet letter, which, being a new-comer in the country, he had never before seen. "Yea, his honourable worship is within. But he hath a godly minister or two with him, and likewise a leech. Ye may not see his worship now."

"Nevertheless, I will enter," answered Hester Prynne; and the bond-servant, perhaps judging from the decision of her air, and the glittering symbol in her bosom, that she was a great lady in the land, offered no opposition.

So the mother and little Pearl were admitted into the hall of entrance. With many variations, suggested by the nature of his building materials, diversity of climate, and a different mode of social life, Governor Bellingham had planned his new habitation after the residences of gentlemen of fair estate in his native land. Here, then, was a wide and reasonably lofty hall, extending through the whole depth of the house, and forming a medium of general communication, more or less directly, with all the other apartments. At one extremity, this spacious room was lighted by the windows of the two towers, which formed a small recess on either side of the portal. At the other end, though partly muffled by a curtain, it was more powerfully illuminated by one of those embowed hall windows which we read of in old books, and which was provided with a deep and cushioned seat. Here, on the cushion, lay a folio tome, probably of the Chronicles of England, or other such substantial literature; even as, in our own days, we scatter gilded volumes on the centre table, to be turned over by the casual guest. The furniture of the hall consisted of some ponderous chairs, the backs of which were elaborately carved with wreaths of oaken flowers; and likewise a table in the same taste, the whole being of the Elizabethan age, or perhaps earlier, and heirlooms, transferred hither from the Governor's paternal home. On the table — in token that the sentiment of old English hospitality had not been left behind — stood a large pewter tankard, at the bottom of which, had Hester or Pearl peeped into it, they might have seen the frothy remnant of a recent draught of ale.

On the wall hung a row of portraits, representing the forefathers of the Bellingham lineage, some with armour on their breasts, and others with stately ruffs and robes of peace. All were characterised by the sternness and severity which old portraits so invariably put on, as if they were the ghosts, rather than the pictures, of departed worthies, and were gazing with harsh and intolerant criticism at the pursuits and enjoyments of living men.

At about the centre of the oaken panels that lined the hall was suspended a suit of mail, not, like the pictures, an ancestral relic, but of the most modern date; for it had been manufactured by a skilful armourer in London, the same year in which Governor Bellingham came over to New England. There was a steel head-piece, a cuirass, a gorget and greaves, with a pair of gauntlets and a sword hanging beneath; all, and especially the helmet and breastplate, so highly burnished as to glow with white radiance, and scatter an illumination everywhere about upon the floor. This bright panoply was not meant for mere idle show, but had been worn by the Governor on many a solemn muster and training field, and had glittered, moreover, at the head of a regiment in the Pequod war. For, though bred a lawyer, and accustomed to speak of Bacon, Coke, Noye, and Finch, as his professional associates, the exigencies of this new country had transformed Governor Bellingham into a soldier, as well as a statesman and ruler.

Little Pearl, who was as greatly pleased with the gleaming armour as she had been with the glittering frontispiece of the house, spent some time looking into the polished mirror of the breastplate.

"Mother," cried she, "I see you here. Look! Look!"

Hester looked by way of humouring the child; and she saw that, owing to the peculiar effect of this convex mirror, the scarlet letter was represented in exaggerated and gigantic proportions, so as to be greatly the most prominent feature of her appearance. In truth, she seemed absolutely hidden behind it. Pearl pointed upwards also, at a similar picture in the head-piece; smiling at her mother, with the elfish intelligence that was so familiar an expression on her small physiognomy. That look of naughty merriment was likewise reflected in the mirror, with so much breadth and intensity of effect, that it made Hester Prynne feel as if it could not be the image of her own child, but of an imp who was seeking to mould itself into Pearl's shape.

"Come along, Pearl," said she, drawing her away, "Come

and look into this fair garden. It may be we shall see flowers there; more beautiful ones than we find in the woods."

Pearl accordingly ran to the bow-window, at the further end of the hall, and looked along the vista of a garden walk, carpeted with closely-shaven grass, and bordered with some rude and immature attempt at shrubbery. But the proprietor appeared already to have relinquished as hopeless, the effort to perpetuate on this side of the Atlantic, in a hard soil, and amid the close struggle for subsistence, the native English taste for ornamental gardening. Cabbages grew in plain sight; and a pumpkin-vine, rooted at some distance, had run across the intervening space, and deposited one of its gigantic products directly beneath the hall window, as if to warn the Governor that this great lump of vegetable gold was as rich an ornament as New England earth would offer him. There were a few rose-bushes, however, and a number of apple-trees, probably the descendants of those planted by the Reverend Mr. Blackstone, the first settler of the peninsula; that half mythological personage who rides through our early annals, seated on the back of a bull.

Pearl, seeing the rose-bushes, began to cry for a red rose, and would not be pacified.

"Hush, child—hush!" said her mother, earnestly. "Do not cry, dear little Pearl! I hear voices in the garden. The Governor is coming, and gentlemen along with him."

In fact, adown the vista of the garden avenue, a number of persons were seen approaching towards the house. Pearl, in utter scorn of her mother's attempt to quiet her, gave an eldritch scream, and then became silent, not from any notion of obedience, but because the quick and mobile curiosity of her disposition was excited by the appearance of those new personages.

VIII.

THE ELF-CHILD AND THE MINISTER

Governor Bellingham, in a loose gown and easy cap—such as elderly gentlemen loved to endue themselves with, in their domestic privacy—walked foremost, and appeared to be showing off his estate, and expatiating on his projected improvements. The wide circumference of an elaborate ruff, beneath his grey beard, in the antiquated fashion of King James's reign, caused his head to look not a little like that of John the Baptist in a charger. The impression made by his aspect, so rigid and severe, and frost-bitten with more than autumnal age, was hardly in keeping with the appliances of worldly enjoyment wherewith he had evidently done his utmost to surround himself. But it is an error to suppose that our great forefathers—though accustomed to speak and think of human existence as a state merely of trial and warfare, and though unfeignedly prepared to sacrifice goods and life at the behest of duty—made it a matter of conscience to reject such means of comfort, or even luxury, as lay fairly within their grasp. This creed was never taught, for instance, by the venerable pastor, John Wilson, whose beard, white as a snow-drift, was seen over Governor Bellingham's shoulders, while its wearer suggested that pears and peaches might yet be naturalised in the New England climate, and that purple grapes might possibly be compelled to flourish against the sunny garden-wall. The old clergyman, nurtured at the rich bosom of the English Church, had a long established and legitimate taste for all good and comfortable things, and however stern he might show himself in the pulpit, or in his public reproof of such transgressions as that of Hester Prynne, still, the genial benevolence of his private life had won him warmer affection than was accorded to any of his professional contemporaries.

Behind the Governor and Mr. Wilson came two other guests—one, the Reverend Arthur Dimmesdale, whom the reader may remember as having taken a brief and reluctant part in the scene of Hester Prynne's disgrace; and, in close companionship with him, old Roger Chillingworth, a person of great skill in physic, who for two or three years past had been settled in the town. It was understood that this learned man was the physician as well as friend of the young minister, whose health had severely suffered of late by his too unreserved self-sacrifice to the labours and duties of the pastoral relation.

The Governor, in advance of his visitors, ascended one or

two steps, and, throwing open the leaves of the great hall window, found himself close to little Pearl. The shadow of the curtain fell on Hester Prynne, and partially concealed her.

"What have we here?" said Governor Bellingham, looking with surprise at the scarlet little figure before him. "I profess, I have never seen the like since my days of vanity, in old King James's time, when I was wont to esteem it a high favour to be admitted to a court mask! There used to be a swarm of these small apparitions in holiday time, and we called them children of the Lord of Misrule. But how gat such a guest into my hall?"

"Ay, indeed!" cried good old Mr. Wilson. "What little bird of scarlet plumage may this be? Methinks I have seen just such figures when the sun has been shining through a richly painted window, and tracing out the golden and crimson images across the floor. But that was in the old land. Prithee, young one, who art thou, and what has ailed thy mother to bedizen thee in this strange fashion? Art thou a Christian child—ha? Dost know thy catechism? Or art thou one of those naughty elfs or fairies whom we thought to have left behind us, with other relics of Papistry, in merry old England?"

"I am mother's child," answered the scarlet vision, "and my name is Pearl!"

"Pearl?—Ruby, rather—or Coral!—or Red Rose, at the very least, judging from thy hue!" responded the old minister, putting forth his hand in a vain attempt to pat little Pearl on the cheek. "But where is this mother of thine? Ah! I see," he added; and, turning to Governor Bellingham, whispered, "This is the selfsame child of whom we have held speech together; and behold here the unhappy woman, Hester Prynne, her mother!"

"Sayest thou so?" cried the Governor. "Nay, we might have judged that such a child's mother must needs be a scarlet woman, and a worthy type of her of Babylon! But she comes at a good time, and we will look into this matter forthwith."

Governor Bellingham stepped through the window into the hall, followed by his three guests.

"Hester Prynne," said he, fixing his naturally stern regard on the wearer of the scarlet letter, "there hath been much question concerning thee of late. The point hath been weightily discussed, whether we, that are of authority and influence, do well discharge our consciences by trusting an immortal soul, such as there is in yonder child, to the guidance of one who hath stumbled and fallen amid the pitfalls of this world. Speak thou, the child's own mother! Were it not, thinkest thou, for thy little one's temporal and eternal welfare that she be taken out of thy charge, and clad soberly, and disciplined strictly, and instructed in the truths of heaven and earth? What canst thou do for the child in this kind?"

"I can teach my little Pearl what I have learned from this!" answered Hester Prynne, laying her finger on the red token.

"Woman, it is thy badge of shame!" replied the stern magistrate. "It is because of the stain which that letter indicates that we would transfer thy child to other hands."

"Nevertheless," said the mother, calmly, though growing more pale, "this badge hath taught me—it daily teaches me—it is teaching me at this moment—lessons whereof my child may be the wiser and better, albeit they can profit nothing to myself."

"We will judge warily," said Bellingham, "and look well what we are about to do. Good Master Wilson, I pray you, examine this Pearl—since that is her name—and see whether she hath had such Christian nurture as befits a child of her age."

The old minister seated himself in an arm-chair and made an effort to draw Pearl betwixt his knees. But the child, unaccustomed to the touch or familiarity of any but her mother, escaped through the open window, and stood on the upper step, looking like a wild tropical bird of rich plumage, ready to take flight into the upper air. Mr. Wilson, not a little astonished at this outbreak—for he was a grandfatherly sort of personage, and usually a vast favourite with children—essayed, however, to proceed with the examination.

"Pearl," said he, with great solemnity, "thou must take heed to instruction, that so, in due season, thou mayest wear in thy bosom the pearl of great price. Canst thou tell me, my child, who made thee?"

Now Pearl knew well enough who made her, for Hester Prynne, the daughter of a pious home, very soon after her talk with the child about her Heavenly Father, had begun to inform her of those truths which the human spirit, at whatever stage of immaturity, imbibes with such eager interest. Pearl, therefore—so large were the attainments of her three years' lifetime—could have borne a fair examination in the New England Primer, or the first column of the Westminster Catechisms, although unacquainted with the outward form of either of those celebrated works. But that perversity, which all children have more or less of, and of which little Pearl had a tenfold portion, now, at the most inopportune moment, took thorough possession of her, and closed her lips, or impelled her to speak words amiss. After putting her finger in her mouth, with many ungracious refusals to answer good Mr. Wilson's question, the child finally announced that she had not been made at all, but had been plucked by her mother off the bush of wild roses that grew by the prison-door.

This phantasy was probably suggested by the near proximity of the Governor's red roses, as Pearl stood outside of the window, together with her recollection of the prison rose-bush, which she had passed in coming hither.

Old Roger Chillingworth, with a smile on his face, whispered something in the young clergyman's ear. Hester Prynne looked at the man of skill, and even then, with her fate hanging in the balance, was startled to perceive what a change had come over his features — how much uglier they were, how his dark complexion seemed to have grown duskier, and his figure more misshapen — since the days when she had familiarly known him. She met his eyes for an instant, but was immediately constrained to give all her attention to the scene now going forward.

"This is awful!" cried the Governor, slowly recovering from the astonishment into which Pearl's response had thrown him. "Here is a child of three years old, and she cannot tell who made her! Without question, she is equally in the dark as to her soul, its present depravity, and future destiny! Methinks, gentlemen, we need inquire no further."

Hester caught hold of Pearl, and drew her forcibly into her arms, confronting the old Puritan magistrate with almost a fierce expression. Alone in the world, cast off by it, and with this sole treasure to keep her heart alive, she felt that she possessed indefeasible rights against the world, and was ready to defend them to the death.

"God gave me the child!" cried she. "He gave her in requital of all things else which ye had taken from me. She is my happiness — she is my torture, none the less! Pearl keeps me here in life! Pearl punishes me, too! See ye not, she is the scarlet letter, only capable of being loved, and so endowed with a millionfold the power of retribution for my sin? Ye shall not take her! I will die first!"

"My poor woman," said the not unkind old minister, "the child shall be well cared for—far better than thou canst do for it."

"God gave her into my keeping!" repeated Hester Prynne, raising her voice almost to a shriek. "I will not give her up!" And here by a sudden impulse, she turned to the young clergyman, Mr. Dimmesdale, at whom, up to this moment, she had seemed hardly so much as once to direct her eyes. "Speak thou for me!" cried she. "Thou wast my pastor, and hadst charge of my soul, and knowest me better than these men can. I will not lose the child! Speak for me! Thou knowest—for thou hast sympathies which these men lack—thou knowest what is in my heart, and what are a mother's rights, and how much the stronger they are when that mother has but her child and the scarlet letter! Look thou to it! I will not lose the child! Look to it!"

At this wild and singular appeal, which indicated that Hester Prynne's situation had provoked her to little less than madness, the young minister at once came forward, pale, and holding his hand over his heart, as was his custom whenever his peculiarly nervous temperament was thrown into agitation. He looked now more careworn and emaciated than as we described him at the scene of Hester's public ignominy; and whether it were his failing health, or whatever the cause might be, his large dark eyes had a world of pain in their troubled and melancholy depth.

"There is truth in what she says," began the minister, with a voice sweet, tremulous, but powerful, insomuch that the hall re-echoed and the hollow armour rang with it—"truth in what Hester says, and in the feeling which inspires her! God gave her the child, and gave her, too, an instinctive knowledge of its nature and requirements—both seemingly so peculiar—which no other mortal being can possess. And, moreover, is there not a quality of awful sacredness in the relation between this mother and this child?"

"Ay—how is that, good Master Dimmesdale?" interrupted the Governor. "Make that plain, I pray you!"

"It must be even so," resumed the minister. "For, if we deem it otherwise, do we not thereby say that the Heavenly Father, the creator of all flesh, hath lightly recognised a deed of sin, and made of no account the distinction between unhallowed lust and holy love? This child of its father's guilt and its mother's shame has come from the hand of God, to work in many ways upon her heart, who pleads so earnestly and with such bitterness of spirit the right to keep her. It was meant for a blessing—for the one blessing of her life! It was meant, doubtless, the mother herself hath told us, for a retribution, too; a torture to be felt at many an unthought-of moment; a pang, a sting, an ever-recurring agony, in the midst of a troubled joy! Hath she not expressed this thought in the garb of the poor child, so forcibly reminding us of that red symbol which sears her bosom?"

"Well said again!" cried good Mr. Wilson. "I feared the woman had no better thought than to make a mountebank of her child!"

"Oh, not so!—not so!" continued Mr. Dimmesdale. "She recognises, believe me, the solemn miracle which God hath wrought in the existence of that child. And may she feel, too—what, methinks, is the very truth—that this boon was meant, above all things else, to keep the mother's soul alive, and to preserve her from blacker depths of sin into which Satan might else have sought to plunge her! Therefore it is good for this poor, sinful woman, that she hath an infant immortality, a being capable of eternal joy or sorrow, confided to her care—to be trained up by her to righteousness, to remind her, at every moment, of her fall, but yet to teach her, as if it were by the Creator's sacred pledge, that, if she bring the child to heaven, the child also will bring its parents thither! Herein is the sinful mother happier than the sinful father. For Hester Prynne's sake, then, and no less for the poor child's sake, let us leave them as Providence hath seen fit to place them!"

"You speak, my friend, with a strange earnestness," said old Roger Chillingworth, smiling at him.

"And there is a weighty import in what my young brother hath spoken," added the Rev. Mr. Wilson.

"What say you, worshipful Master Bellingham? Hath he not pleaded well for the poor woman?"

"Indeed hath he," answered the magistrate; "and hath adduced such arguments, that we will even leave the matter as it now stands; so long, at least, as there shall be no further scandal in the woman. Care must be had nevertheless, to put the child to due and stated examination in the catechism, at thy hands or Master Dimmesdale's. Moreover, at a proper season, the tithing-men must take heed that she go both to school and to meeting."

The young minister, on ceasing to speak had withdrawn a few steps from the group, and stood with his face partially concealed in the heavy folds of the window-curtain; while the shadow of his figure, which the sunlight cast upon the floor, was tremulous with the vehemence of his appeal. Pearl, that wild and flighty little elf stole softly towards him, and taking his hand in the grasp of both her own, laid her cheek against it; a caress so tender, and withal so unobtrusive, that her mother, who was looking on, asked herself—"Is that my Pearl?" Yet she knew that there was love in the child's heart, although it mostly revealed itself in passion, and hardly twice in her lifetime had been softened by such gentleness as now. The minister—for, save the long-sought regards of woman, nothing is sweeter than these marks of childish preference, accorded spontaneously by a spiritual instinct, and therefore seeming to imply in us something truly worthy to be loved—the minister looked round, laid his hand on the child's head, hesitated an instant, and then kissed her brow. Little Pearl's unwonted mood of sentiment lasted no longer; she laughed, and went capering down the hall so airily, that old Mr. Wilson raised a question whether even her tiptoes touched the floor.

"The little baggage hath witchcraft in her, I profess," said he to Mr. Dimmesdale. "She needs no old woman's broomstick to fly withal!"

"A strange child!" remarked old Roger Chillingworth. "It is easy to see the mother's part in her. Would it be beyond a philosopher's research, think ye, gentlemen, to analyse that child's nature, and, from it make a mould, to give a shrewd guess at the father?"

"Nay; it would be sinful, in such a question, to follow the clue of profane philosophy," said Mr. Wilson. "Better to fast and pray upon it; and still better, it may be, to leave the mystery as we find it, unless Providence reveal it of its own accord. Thereby, every good Christian man hath a title to show a father's kindness towards the poor, deserted babe."

The affair being so satisfactorily concluded, Hester Prynne, with Pearl, departed from the house. As they descended the steps, it is averred that the lattice of a chamber-window was thrown open, and forth into the sunny day was thrust the face of Mistress Hibbins, Governor Bellingham's bitter-tempered sister, and the same who, a few years later, was executed as a witch.

"Hist, hist!" said she, while her ill-omened physiognomy

seemed to cast a shadow over the cheerful newness of the house. "Wilt thou go with us tonight? There will be a merry company in the forest; and I well-nigh promised the Black Man that comely Hester Prynne should make one."

"Make my excuse to him, so please you!" answered Hester, with a triumphant smile. "I must tarry at home, and keep watch over my little Pearl. Had they taken her from me, I would willingly have gone with thee into the forest, and signed my name in the Black Man's book too, and that with mine own blood!"

"We shall have thee there anon!" said the witch-lady, frowning, as she drew back her head.

But here—if we suppose this interview betwixt Mistress Hibbins and Hester Prynne to be authentic, and not a parable—was already an illustration of the young minister's argument against sundering the relation of a fallen mother to the offspring of her frailty. Even thus early had the child saved her from Satan's snare.

IX.

THE LEECH

Under the appellation of Roger Chillingworth, the reader will remember, was hidden another name, which its former wearer had resolved should never more be spoken. It has been related, how, in the crowd that witnessed Hester Prynne's ignominious exposure, stood a man, elderly, travel-worn, who, just emerging from the perilous wilderness, beheld the woman, in whom he hoped to find embodied the warmth and cheerfulness of home, set up as a type of sin before the people. Her matronly fame was trodden under all men's feet. Infamy was babbling around her in the public market-place. For her kindred, should the tidings ever reach them, and for the companions of her unspotted life, there remained nothing but the contagion of her dishonour; which would not fail to be distributed in strict accordance and proportion with the intimacy and sacredness of their previous relationship. Then why — since the choice was with himself — should the individual, whose connexion with the fallen woman had been the most intimate and sacred of them all, come forward to vindicate his claim to an inheritance so little desirable? He resolved not to be pilloried beside her on her pedestal of shame. Unknown to all but Hester Prynne, and possessing the lock and key of her silence, he chose to withdraw his name from the roll of mankind, and, as regarded his former ties and interest, to vanish out of life as completely as if he indeed lay at the bottom of the ocean, whither rumour had long ago consigned him. This purpose once effected, new interests would immediately spring up, and likewise a new purpose; dark, it is true, if not guilty, but of force enough to engage the full strength of his faculties.

In pursuance of this resolve, he took up his residence in the Puritan town as Roger Chillingworth, without other introduction than the learning and intelligence of which he possessed more than a common measure. As his studies, at a previous period of his life, had made him extensively acquainted with the medical science of the day, it was as a physician that he presented himself and as such was cordially received. Skilful men, of the medical and chirurgical profession, were of rare occurrence in the colony. They seldom, it would appear, partook of the religious zeal that brought other emigrants across the Atlantic. In their researches into the human frame, it may be that the higher and more subtle faculties of such men were materialised, and that they lost the spiritual view of existence amid the intricacies of that wondrous mechanism, which seemed to involve art enough to comprise all of life within itself. At all events, the health of the good town of Boston, so far as medicine had aught to do with it, had hitherto lain in the guardianship of an aged deacon and apothecary, whose piety and godly deportment were stronger testimonials in his favour than any that he could have produced in the shape of a diploma. The only surgeon was one who combined the occasional exercise of that noble art with the daily and habitual flourish of a razor. To such a professional body Roger Chillingworth was a brilliant acquisition. He soon manifested his familiarity with the ponderous and imposing machinery of antique physic; in which every remedy contained a multitude of far-fetched and heterogeneous ingredients, as elaborately compounded as if the proposed result had been the Elixir of Life. In his Indian captivity, moreover, he had gained much knowledge of the properties of native herbs and roots; nor did he conceal from his patients that these simple medicines, Nature's boon to the untutored savage, had quite as large a share of his own confidence as the European Pharmacopœia, which so many learned doctors had spent centuries in elaborating.

This learned stranger was exemplary as regarded at least the outward forms of a religious life; and early after his arrival, had chosen for his spiritual guide the Reverend Mr. Dimmesdale. The young divine, whose scholar-like renown still lived in Oxford, was considered by his more fervent admirers as little less than a heavenly ordained apostle, destined, should he live and labour for the ordinary term of life, to do as great deeds, for the now feeble New England Church, as the early Fathers had achieved for the infancy of the Christian faith. About this period, however, the health of Mr. Dimmesdale had evidently begun to fail. By those best acquainted with his habits, the paleness of the young minister's cheek was accounted for by his too earnest devotion to study, his scrupulous fulfilment of parochial duty, and more than all, to the fasts and vigils of which he made a frequent practice, in order to keep the grossness of this earthly state from clogging and obscuring his spiritual lamp. Some declared, that if Mr. Dimmesdale were really going to die, it was cause enough that the world was not worthy to be any longer trodden by his feet. He himself, on the other hand, with characteristic humility, avowed his belief that if Providence should see fit to remove him, it would be because of his own unworthiness to perform its humblest mission here on earth. With all this difference of opinion as to the cause of his decline, there could be no question of the fact. His form grew emaciated; his voice, though still rich and sweet, had a certain melancholy prophecy of decay in it; he was often observed, on any slight alarm or other sudden accident, to put his hand over his heart with first a flush and then a paleness, indicative of pain.

Such was the young clergyman's condition, and so imminent the prospect that his dawning light would be extinguished, all untimely, when Roger Chillingworth made his advent to the town. His first entry on the scene, few people could tell whence, dropping down as it were out of the sky or starting from the nether earth, had an aspect of mystery, which was easily heightened to the miraculous. He was now known to be a man of skill; it was observed that he gathered herbs and the blossoms of wild-flowers, and dug up roots and plucked off twigs from the forest-trees like one acquainted with hidden virtues in what was valueless to common eyes. He was heard to speak of Sir Kenelm Digby and other famous men — whose scientific attainments were esteemed hardly less than supernatural — as having been his correspondents or associates. Why, with such rank in the learned world, had he come hither? What, could he, whose sphere was in great cities, be seeking in the wilderness? In answer to this query, a rumour gained ground — and however absurd, was entertained by some very sensible people — that Heaven had wrought an absolute miracle, by transporting an eminent Doctor of Physic from a German university bodily through the air and setting him down at the door of Mr. Dimmesdale's study! Individuals of wiser faith, indeed, who knew that Heaven promotes its purposes without aiming at the stage-effect of what is called miraculous interposition, were inclined to see a providential hand in Roger Chillingworth's so opportune arrival.

This idea was countenanced by the strong interest which the physician ever manifested in the young clergyman; he attached himself to him as a parishioner, and sought to win a friendly regard and confidence from his naturally reserved sensibility. He expressed great alarm at his pastor's state of health, but was anxious to attempt the cure, and, if early undertaken, seemed not despondent of a favourable result. The elders, the deacons, the motherly dames, and the young and fair maidens of Mr. Dimmesdale's flock, were alike importunate that he should make trial of the physician's frankly offered skill. Mr. Dimmesdale gently repelled their entreaties.

"I need no medicine," said he.

But how could the young minister say so, when, with every successive Sabbath, his cheek was paler and thinner, and his voice more tremulous than before — when it had now become a constant habit, rather than a casual gesture, to press his hand over his heart? Was he weary of his labours? Did he wish to die? These questions were solemnly propounded to Mr. Dimmesdale by the elder ministers of Boston, and the deacons of his church, who, to use their own phrase, "dealt with him," on the sin of rejecting the aid which Providence so manifestly held out. He listened in silence, and finally promised to confer with the physician.

"Were it God's will," said the Reverend Mr. Dimmesdale, when, in fulfilment of this pledge, he requested old Roger Chillingworth's professional advice, "I could be well content that my labours, and my sorrows, and my sins, and my pains, should shortly end with me, and what is earthly of them be buried in my grave, and the spiritual go with me to my eternal state, rather than that you should put your skill to the proof in my behalf."

"Ah," replied Roger Chillingworth, with that quietness, which, whether imposed or natural, marked all his deportment, "it is thus that a young clergyman is apt to speak. Youthful men, not having taken a deep root, give up their hold of life so easily! And saintly men, who walk with God on earth, would fain be away, to walk with him on the golden pavements of the New Jerusalem."

"Nay," rejoined the young minister, putting his hand to his heart, with a flush of pain flitting over his brow, "were I worthier to walk there, I could be better content to toil here."

"Good men ever interpret themselves too meanly," said the physician.

In this manner, the mysterious old Roger Chillingworth became the medical adviser of the Reverend Mr. Dimmesdale. As not only the disease interested the physician, but he was strongly moved to look into the character and qualities of the patient, these two men, so different in age, came gradually to spend much time together. For the sake of the minister's health, and to enable the leech to gather plants with healing balm in them, they took long walks on the sea-shore, or in the forest; mingling various walks with the splash and murmur of the waves, and the solemn wind-anthem among the tree-tops. Often, likewise, one was the guest of the other in his place of study and retirement. There was a fascination for the minister in the company of the man of science, in whom he recognised an intellectual cultivation of no moderate depth or scope; together with a range and freedom of ideas, that he would have vainly looked for among the members of his own profession. In truth, he was startled, if not shocked, to find this attribute in the physician. Mr. Dimmesdale was a true priest, a true religionist, with the reverential sentiment largely developed, and an order of mind that impelled itself powerfully along the track of a creed, and wore its passage continually deeper with the lapse of time. In no state of society would he have been what is called a man of liberal views; it would always be essential to his peace to feel the pressure of a faith about him, supporting, while it confined him within its iron framework. Not the less, however, though with a tremulous enjoyment, did he feel the occasional relief of looking at the universe through the medium of another kind of intellect than those with which he habitually held converse. It was as if a window were thrown open, admitting a freer atmosphere into the close and stifled study, where his life was wasting itself away, amid lamp-light, or obstructed day-beams, and the musty fragrance, be it sensual or moral, that exhales from books. But the air was too fresh and chill to be long breathed with comfort. So the minister, and the physician with him, withdrew again within the limits of what their Church defined as orthodox.

Thus Roger Chillingworth scrutinised his patient carefully, both as he saw him in his ordinary life, keeping an accustomed pathway in the range of thoughts familiar to him, and as he appeared when thrown amidst other moral scenery, the novelty of which might call out something new to the surface of his character. He deemed it essential, it would seem, to know the man, before attempting to do him good. Wherever there is a heart and an intellect, the diseases of the physical frame are tinged with the peculiarities of these. In Arthur Dimmesdale, thought and imagination were so active, and sensibility so intense, that the bodily infirmity would be likely to have its groundwork there. So Roger Chillingworth—the man of skill, the kind and friendly physician—strove to go deep into his patient's bosom, delving among his principles, prying into his recollections, and probing everything with a cautious touch, like a treasure-seeker in a dark cavern. Few secrets can escape an investigator, who has opportunity and licence to undertake such a quest, and skill to follow it up. A man burdened with a secret should especially avoid the intimacy of his physician. If the latter possess native sagacity, and a nameless something more,—let us call it intuition; if he show no intrusive egotism, nor disagreeable prominent characteristics of his own; if he have the power, which must be born with him, to bring his mind into such affinity with his patient's, that this last shall unawares have spoken what he imagines himself only to have thought; if such revelations be received without tumult, and acknowledged not so often by an uttered sympathy as by silence, an inarticulate breath, and here and there a word to indicate that all is understood; if to these qualifications of a confidant be joined the advantages afforded by his recognised character as a physician;—then, at some inevitable moment, will the soul of the sufferer be dissolved, and flow forth in a dark but transparent stream, bringing all its mysteries into the daylight.

Roger Chillingworth possessed all, or most, of the attributes above enumerated. Nevertheless, time went on; a kind of intimacy, as we have said, grew up between these two cultivated minds, which had as wide a field as the whole sphere of human thought and study to meet upon; they discussed every topic of ethics and religion, of public affairs, and private character; they talked much, on both sides, of matters that seemed personal to themselves; and yet no secret, such as the physician fancied must exist there, ever stole out of the minister's consciousness into his companion's ear. The latter had his suspicions, indeed, that even the nature of Mr. Dimmesdale's bodily disease had never fairly been revealed to him. It was a strange reserve!

After a time, at a hint from Roger Chillingworth, the friends of Mr. Dimmesdale effected an arrangement by which the two were lodged in the same house; so that every ebb and flow of the minister's life-tide might pass under the eye of his anxious and attached physician. There was much joy throughout the town when this greatly desirable object was attained. It was held to be the best possible measure for the young clergyman's welfare; unless, indeed, as often urged by such as felt authorised to do so, he had selected some one of the many blooming damsels, spiritually devoted to him, to become his devoted wife. This latter step, however, there was no present prospect that Arthur Dimmesdale would be prevailed upon to take; he rejected all suggestions of the kind, as if priestly celibacy were one of his articles of Church discipline. Doomed by his own choice, therefore, as Mr. Dimmesdale so evidently was, to eat his unsavoury morsel always at another's board, and endure the life-long chill which must be his lot who seeks to warm himself only at another's fireside, it truly seemed that this sagacious, experienced, benevolent old physician, with his concord of paternal and reverential love for the young pastor, was the very man, of all mankind, to be constantly within reach of his voice.

The new abode of the two friends was with a pious widow, of good social rank, who dwelt in a house covering pretty nearly the site on which the venerable structure of King's

Chapel has since been built. It had the graveyard, originally Isaac Johnson's home-field, on one side, and so was well adapted to call up serious reflections, suited to their respective employments, in both minister and man of physic. The motherly care of the good widow assigned to Mr. Dimmesdale a front apartment, with a sunny exposure, and heavy window-curtains, to create a noontide shadow when desirable. The walls were hung round with tapestry, said to be from the Gobelin looms, and, at all events, representing the Scriptural story of David and Bathsheba, and Nathan the Prophet, in colours still unfaded, but which made the fair woman of the scene almost as grimly picturesque as the woe-denouncing seer. Here the pale clergyman piled up his library, rich with parchment-bound folios of the Fathers, and the lore of Rabbis, and monkish erudition, of which the Protestant divines, even while they vilified and decried that class of writers, were yet constrained often to avail themselves. On the other side of the house, old Roger Chillingworth arranged his study and laboratory: not such as a modern man of science would reckon even tolerably complete, but provided with a distilling apparatus and the means of compounding drugs and chemicals, which the practised alchemist knew well how to turn to purpose. With such commodiousness of situation, these two learned persons sat themselves down, each in his own domain, yet familiarly passing from one apartment to the other, and bestowing a mutual and not incurious inspection into one another's business.

And the Reverend Arthur Dimmesdale's best discerning friends, as we have intimated, very reasonably imagined that the hand of Providence had done all this for the purpose—besought in so many public and domestic and secret prayers—of restoring the young minister to health. But, it must now be said, another portion of the community had latterly begun to take its own view of the relation betwixt Mr. Dimmesdale and the mysterious old physician. When an uninstructed multitude attempts to see with its eyes, it is exceedingly apt to be deceived. When, however, it forms its judgment, as it usually does, on the intuitions of its great and warm heart, the conclusions thus attained are often so profound and so unerring as to possess the character of truth supernaturally revealed. The people, in the case of which we speak, could justify its prejudice against Roger Chillingworth by no fact or argument worthy of serious refutation. There was an aged handicraftsman, it is true, who had been a citizen of London at the period of Sir Thomas Overbury's murder, now some thirty years agone; he testified to having seen the physician, under some other name, which the narrator of the story had now forgotten, in company with Dr.

Forman, the famous old conjurer, who was implicated in the affair of Overbury. Two or three individuals hinted that the man of skill, during his Indian captivity, had enlarged his medical attainments by joining in the incantations of the savage priests, who were universally acknowledged to be powerful enchanters, often performing seemingly miraculous cures by their skill in the black art. A large number—and many of these were persons of such sober sense and practical observation that their opinions would have been valuable in other matters—affirmed that Roger Chillingworth's aspect had undergone a remarkable change while he had dwelt in town, and especially since his abode with Mr. Dimmesdale. At first, his expression had been calm, meditative, scholar-like. Now there was something ugly and evil in his face, which they had not previously noticed, and which grew still the more obvious to sight the oftener they looked upon him. According to the vulgar idea, the fire in his laboratory had been brought from the lower regions, and was fed with infernal fuel; and so, as might be expected, his visage was getting sooty with the smoke.

To sum up the matter, it grew to be a widely diffused opinion that the Rev. Arthur Dimmesdale, like many other personages of special sanctity, in all ages of the Christian world, was haunted either by Satan himself or Satan's emissary, in the guise of old Roger Chillingworth. This diabolical agent had the Divine permission, for a season, to burrow into the clergyman's intimacy, and plot against his soul. No sensible man, it was confessed, could doubt on which side the victory would turn. The people looked, with an unshaken hope, to see the minister come forth out of the conflict transfigured with the glory which he would unquestionably win. Meanwhile, nevertheless, it was sad to think of the perchance mortal agony through which he must struggle towards his triumph.

Alas! to judge from the gloom and terror in the depth of the poor minister's eyes, the battle was a sore one, and the victory anything but secure.

X.

THE LEECH AND HIS PATIENT

Old Roger Chillingworth, throughout life, had been calm in temperament, kindly, though not of warm affections, but ever, and in all his relations with the world, a pure and upright man. He had begun an investigation, as he imagined, with the severe and equal integrity of a judge, desirous only of truth, even as if the question involved no more than the air-drawn lines and figures of a geometrical problem, instead of human passions, and wrongs inflicted on himself. But, as he proceeded, a terrible fascination, a kind of fierce, though still calm, necessity, seized the old man within its gripe, and never set him free again until he had done all its bidding. He now dug into the poor clergyman's heart, like a miner searching for gold; or, rather, like a sexton delving into a grave, possibly in quest of a jewel that had been buried on the dead man's bosom, but likely to find nothing save mortality and corruption. Alas, for his own soul, if these were what he sought!

Sometimes a light glimmered out of the physician's eyes, burning blue and ominous, like the reflection of a furnace, or, let us say, like one of those gleams of ghastly fire that darted from Bunyan's awful doorway in the hillside, and quivered on the pilgrim's face. The soil where this dark miner was working had perchance shown indications that encouraged him.

"This man," said he, at one such moment, to himself, "pure as they deem him—all spiritual as he seems—hath inherited a strong animal nature from his father or his mother. Let us dig a little further in the direction of this vein!"

Then after long search into the minister's dim interior, and turning over many precious materials, in the shape of high aspirations for the welfare of his race, warm love of souls, pure sentiments, natural piety, strengthened by thought and study, and illuminated by revelation—all of which invaluable gold was perhaps no better than rubbish to the seeker—he would turn back, discouraged, and begin his quest towards another point. He groped along as stealthily, with as cautious a tread, and as wary an outlook, as a thief entering a chamber where a man lies only half asleep—or, it may be, broad awake—with purpose to steal the very treasure which this man guards as the apple of his eye. In spite of his premeditated carefulness, the floor would now and then creak; his garments would rustle; the shadow of his presence, in a forbidden proximity, would be thrown across his victim. In other words, Mr. Dimmesdale, whose sensibility of nerve often produced the effect of spiritual intuition, would become vaguely aware that something inimical to his peace had thrust itself into relation with him. But Old Roger Chillingworth, too, had perceptions that were almost intuitive; and when the minister threw his startled eyes towards him, there the physician sat; his kind, watchful, sympathising, but never intrusive friend.

Yet Mr. Dimmesdale would perhaps have seen this individual's character more perfectly, if a certain morbidness, to which sick hearts are liable, had not rendered him suspicious of all mankind. Trusting no man as his friend, he could not recognize his enemy when the latter actually appeared. He therefore still kept up a familiar intercourse with him, daily receiving the old physician in his study, or visiting the laboratory, and, for recreation's sake, watching the processes by which weeds were converted into drugs of potency.

One day, leaning his forehead on his hand, and his elbow on the sill of the open window, that looked towards the graveyard, he talked with Roger Chillingworth, while the old man was examining a bundle of unsightly plants.

"Where," asked he, with a look askance at them—for it was the clergyman's peculiarity that he seldom, now-a-days, looked straight forth at any object, whether human or inanimate, "where, my kind doctor, did you gather those herbs, with such a dark, flabby leaf?"

"Even in the graveyard here at hand," answered the physician, continuing his employment. "They are new to me. I found them growing on a grave, which bore no tombstone, no other memorial of the dead man, save these ugly weeds, that have taken upon themselves to keep him in remembrance. They grew out of his heart, and typify, it may be, some hideous secret that was buried with him, and which he had done better to confess during his lifetime."

"Perchance," said Mr. Dimmesdale, "he earnestly desired it, but could not."

"And wherefore?" rejoined the physician.

"Wherefore not; since all the powers of nature call so earnestly for the confession of sin, that these black weeds have sprung up out of a buried heart, to make manifest, an outspoken crime?"

"That, good sir, is but a phantasy of yours," replied the minister. "There can be, if I forbode aright, no power, short of the Divine mercy, to disclose, whether by uttered words, or by type or emblem, the secrets that may be buried in the human heart. The heart, making itself guilty of such secrets, must perforce hold them, until the day when all hidden things shall be revealed. Nor have I so read or interpreted Holy Writ, as to understand that the disclosure of human thoughts and deeds, then to be made, is intended as a part of the retribution. That, surely, were a shallow view of it. No; these revelations, unless I greatly err, are meant merely to promote the intellectual satisfaction of all intelligent beings, who will stand waiting, on that day, to see the dark problem of this life made plain. A knowledge of men's hearts will be needful to the completest solution of that problem. And, I conceive moreover, that the hearts holding such miserable secrets as you speak of, will yield them up, at that last day, not with reluctance, but with a joy unutterable."

"Then why not reveal it here?" asked Roger Chillingworth, glancing quietly aside at the minister. "Why should not the guilty ones sooner avail themselves of this unutterable solace?"

"They mostly do," said the clergyman, griping hard at his breast, as if afflicted with an importunate throb of pain. "Many, many a poor soul hath given its confidence to me, not only on the death-bed, but while strong in life, and fair in reputation. And ever, after such an outpouring, oh, what a relief have I witnessed in those sinful brethren! even as in one who at last draws free air, after a long stifling with his own polluted breath. How can it be otherwise? Why should a wretched man—guilty, we will say, of murder—prefer to keep the dead corpse buried in his own heart, rather than fling it forth at once, and let the universe take care of it!"

"Yet some men bury their secrets thus," observed the calm physician.

"True; there are such men," answered Mr. Dimmesdale. "But not to suggest more obvious reasons, it may be that they are kept silent by the very constitution of their nature. Or—can we not suppose it?—guilty as they may be, retaining, nevertheless, a zeal for God's glory and man's welfare, they shrink from displaying themselves black and filthy in the view of men; because, thenceforward, no good can be achieved by them; no evil of the past be redeemed by better service. So, to their own unutterable torment, they go about among their fellow-creatures, looking pure as new-fallen snow, while their hearts are all speckled and spotted with iniquity of which they cannot rid themselves."

"These men deceive themselves," said Roger Chillingworth, with somewhat more emphasis than usual, and making a slight gesture with his forefinger. "They fear to take up the shame that rightfully belongs to them. Their love for man, their zeal for God's service—these holy impulses may or may not coexist in their hearts with the evil inmates to which their guilt has unbarred the door, and which must needs propagate a hellish breed within them. But, if they seek to glorify God, let them not lift heavenward their unclean hands! If they would serve their fellowmen, let them do it by making manifest the power and reality of conscience, in constraining them to penitential self-abasement! Would thou have me to believe, O wise and pious friend, that a false show can be better—can be more for God's glory, or man's welfare—than God's own truth? Trust me, such men deceive themselves!"

"It may be so," said the young clergyman, indifferently, as waiving a discussion that he considered irrelevant or unseasonable. He had a ready faculty, indeed, of escaping from any topic that agitated his too sensitive and nervous temperament.—"But, now, I would ask of my well-skilled physician, whether, in good sooth, he deems me to have profited by his kindly care of this weak frame of mine?"

Before Roger Chillingworth could answer, they heard the clear, wild laughter of a young child's voice, proceeding from the adjacent burial-ground. Looking instinctively from the open window—for it was summer-time—the minister beheld Hester Prynne and little Pearl passing along the footpath that traversed the enclosure. Pearl looked as beautiful as the day, but was in one of those moods of perverse merriment which, whenever they occurred, seemed to remove her entirely out of the sphere of sympathy or human contact. She now skipped irreverently from one grave to another; until coming to the broad, flat, armorial tombstone of a departed worthy—perhaps of Isaac Johnson himself—she began to dance upon it. In reply to her mother's command and entreaty that she would behave more decorously, little Pearl paused to gather the prickly burrs from a tall burdock which grew beside the tomb. Taking a handful of these, she arranged them along the lines of the scarlet letter that decorated the maternal bosom, to which the burrs, as their nature was, tenaciously adhered. Hester did not pluck them off.

Roger Chillingworth had by this time approached the window and smiled grimly down.

"There is no law, nor reverence for authority, no regard for human ordinances or opinions, right or wrong, mixed up with that child's composition," remarked he, as much to himself as to his companion. "I saw her, the other day, bespatter the Governor himself with water at the cattle-trough in Spring Lane. What, in heaven's name, is she? Is the imp altogether evil? Hath she affections? Hath she any discoverable principle of being?"

"None, save the freedom of a broken law," answered Mr. Dimmesdale, in a quiet way, as if he had been discussing the point within himself, "Whether capable of good, I know not."

The child probably overheard their voices, for, looking up to the window with a bright, but naughty smile of mirth and intelligence, she threw one of the prickly burrs at the Rev. Mr. Dimmesdale. The sensitive clergyman shrank, with nervous dread, from the light missile. Detecting his emotion, Pearl clapped her little hands in the most extravagant ecstacy. Hester Prynne, likewise, had involuntarily looked up, and all these four persons, old and young, regarded one another in silence, till the child laughed aloud, and shouted—"Come away, mother! Come away, or yonder old black man will catch you! He hath got hold of the minister already. Come away, mother or he will catch you! But he cannot catch little Pearl!"

So she drew her mother away, skipping, dancing, and frisking fantastically among the hillocks of the dead people, like a creature that had nothing in common with a bygone and buried generation, nor owned herself akin to it. It was as if she had been made afresh out of new elements, and must perforce be permitted to live her own life, and be a law unto herself without her eccentricities being reckoned to her for a crime.

"There goes a woman," resumed Roger Chillingworth, after a pause, "who, be her demerits what they may, hath none of that mystery of hidden sinfulness which you deem so grievous to be borne. Is Hester Prynne the less miserable, think you, for that scarlet letter on her breast?"

"I do verily believe it," answered the clergyman. "Nevertheless, I cannot answer for her. There was a look of pain in her face which I would gladly have been spared the sight of. But still, methinks, it must needs be better for the sufferer to be free to show his pain, as this poor woman Hester is, than to cover it up in his heart."

There was another pause, and the physician began anew to

examine and arrange the plants which he had gathered.

"You inquired of me, a little time agone," said he, at length, "my judgment as touching your health."

"I did," answered the clergyman, "and would gladly learn it. Speak frankly, I pray you, be it for life or death."

"Freely then, and plainly," said the physician, still busy with his plants, but keeping a wary eye on Mr. Dimmesdale, "the disorder is a strange one; not so much in itself nor as outwardly manifested,—in so far, at least as the symptoms have been laid open to my observation. Looking daily at you, my good sir, and watching the tokens of your aspect now for months gone by, I should deem you a man sore sick, it may be, yet not so sick but that an instructed and watchful physician might well hope to cure you. But I know not what to say, the disease is what I seem to know, yet know it not."

"You speak in riddles, learned sir," said the pale minister, glancing aside out of the window.

"Then, to speak more plainly," continued the physician, "and I crave pardon, sir, should it seem to require pardon, for this needful plainness of my speech. Let me ask as your friend, as one having charge, under Providence, of your life and physical well being, hath all the operation of this disorder been fairly laid open and recounted to me?"

"How can you question it?" asked the minister. "Surely it were child's play to call in a physician and then hide the sore!"

"You would tell me, then, that I know all?" said Roger Chillingworth, deliberately, and fixing an eye, bright with intense and concentrated intelligence, on the minister's face. "Be it so! But again! He to whom only the outward and physical evil is laid open, knoweth, oftentimes, but half the evil which he is called upon to cure. A bodily disease, which we look upon as whole and entire within itself, may, after all, be but a symptom of some ailment in the spiritual part. Your pardon once again, good sir, if my speech give the shadow of offence. You, sir, of all men whom I have known, are he whose body is the closest conjoined, and imbued, and identified, so to speak, with the spirit whereof it is the instrument."

"Then I need ask no further," said the clergyman, somewhat hastily rising from his chair. "You deal not, I take it, in medicine for the soul!"

"Thus, a sickness," continued Roger Chillingworth, going on, in an unaltered tone, without heeding the interruption, but standing up and confronting the emaciated and white-cheeked minister, with his low, dark, and misshapen figure,—"a sickness, a sore place, if we may so call it, in your spirit hath immediately its appropriate manifestation in your bodily frame. Would you, therefore, that your physician heal the bodily evil? How may this be unless you first lay open to him the wound or trouble in your soul?"

"No, not to thee! not to an earthly physician!" cried Mr. Dimmesdale, passionately, and turning his eyes, full and bright, and with a kind of fierceness, on old Roger Chillingworth. "Not to thee! But, if it be the soul's disease, then do I commit myself to the one Physician of the soul! He, if it stand with His good pleasure, can cure, or he can kill. Let Him do with me as, in His justice and wisdom, He shall see good. But who art thou, that meddlest in this matter? that dares thrust himself between the sufferer and his God?"

With a frantic gesture he rushed out of the room.

"It is as well to have made this step," said Roger Chillingworth to himself, looking after the minister, with a grave smile. "There is nothing lost. We shall be friends again anon. But see, now, how passion takes hold upon this man, and hurrieth him out of himself! As with one passion so with another. He hath done a wild thing ere now, this pious Master Dimmesdale, in the hot passion of his heart."

It proved not difficult to re-establish the intimacy of the two companions, on the same footing and in the same degree as heretofore. The young clergyman, after a few hours of privacy, was sensible that the disorder of his nerves had hurried him into an unseemly outbreak of temper, which there had been nothing in the physician's words to excuse or palliate. He marvelled, indeed, at the violence with which he had thrust back the kind old man, when merely proffering the advice which it was his duty to bestow, and which the minister himself had expressly sought. With these remorseful feelings, he lost no time in making the amplest apologies, and besought his friend still to continue the care which, if not successful in restoring him to health, had, in all probability, been the means of prolonging his feeble existence to that hour. Roger Chillingworth readily assented, and went on with his medical supervision of the minister; doing his best for him, in all good faith, but always quitting the patient's apartment, at the close of the professional interview, with a mysterious and puzzled smile upon his lips.

This expression was invisible in Mr. Dimmesdale's presence, but grew strongly evident as the physician crossed the threshold.

"A rare case," he muttered. "I must needs look deeper into it. A strange sympathy betwixt soul and body! Were it only for the art's sake, I must search this matter to the bottom."

It came to pass, not long after the scene above recorded, that the Reverend Mr. Dimmesdale, at noonday, and entirely unawares, fell into a deep, deep slumber, sitting in his chair, with a large black-letter volume open before him on the table. It must have been a work of vast ability in the somniferous school of literature. The profound depth of the minister's repose was the more remarkable, inasmuch as he was one of those persons whose sleep ordinarily is as light as fitful, and as easily scared away, as a small bird hopping on a twig. To such an unwonted remoteness, however, had his spirit now withdrawn into itself that he stirred not in his chair when old Roger Chillingworth, without any extraordinary precaution, came into the room. The physician advanced directly in front of his patient, laid his hand upon his bosom, and thrust aside the vestment, that hitherto had always covered it even from the professional eye.

Then, indeed, Mr. Dimmesdale shuddered, and slightly stirred.

After a brief pause, the physician turned away.

But with what a wild look of wonder, joy, and horror! With what a ghastly rapture, as it were, too mighty to be expressed only by the eye and features, and therefore bursting forth through the whole ugliness of his figure, and making itself even riotously manifest by the extravagant gestures with which he threw up his arms towards the ceiling, and stamped his foot upon the floor! Had a man seen old Roger Chillingworth, at that moment of his ecstasy, he would have had no need to ask how Satan comports himself when a precious human soul is lost to heaven, and won into his kingdom.

But what distinguished the physician's ecstasy from Satan's was the trait of wonder in it!

XI.

THE INTERIOR OF A HEART

After the incident last described, the intercourse between the clergyman and the physician, though externally the same, was really of another character than it had previously been. The intellect of Roger Chillingworth had now a sufficiently plain path before it. It was not, indeed, precisely that which he had laid out for himself to tread. Calm, gentle, passionless, as he appeared, there was yet, we fear, a quiet depth of malice, hitherto latent, but active now, in this unfortunate old man, which led him to imagine a more intimate revenge than any mortal had ever wreaked upon an enemy. To make himself the one trusted friend, to whom should be confided all the fear, the remorse, the agony, the ineffectual repentance, the backward rush of sinful thoughts, expelled in vain! All that guilty sorrow, hidden from the world, whose great heart would have pitied and forgiven, to be revealed to him, the Pitiless—to him, the Unforgiving! All that dark treasure to be lavished on the very man, to whom nothing else could so adequately pay the debt of vengeance!

The clergyman's shy and sensitive reserve had balked this scheme. Roger Chillingworth, however, was inclined to be hardly, if at all, less satisfied with the aspect of affairs, which Providence—using the avenger and his victim for its own purposes, and, perchance, pardoning, where it seemed most to punish—had substituted for his black devices. A revelation, he could almost say, had been granted to him. It mattered little for his object, whether celestial or from what other region. By its aid, in all the subsequent relations betwixt him and Mr. Dimmesdale, not merely the external presence, but the very inmost soul of the latter, seemed to be brought out before his eyes, so that he could see and comprehend its every movement. He became, thenceforth, not a spectator only, but a chief actor in the poor minister's interior world. He could play upon him as he chose. Would he arouse him with a throb of agony? The victim was for ever on the rack; it needed only to know the spring that controlled the engine: and the physician knew it well. Would he startle him with sudden fear? As at the waving of a magician's wand, up rose a grisly phantom—up rose a thousand phantoms—in many shapes, of death, or more awful shame, all flocking round about the clergyman, and pointing with their fingers at his breast!

All this was accomplished with a subtlety so perfect, that the minister, though he had constantly a dim perception of some evil influence watching over him, could never gain a knowledge of its actual nature. True, he looked doubtfully, fearfully—even, at times, with horror and the bitterness of hatred—at the deformed figure of the old physician. His gestures, his gait, his grizzled beard, his slightest and most indifferent acts, the very fashion of his garments, were odious in the clergyman's sight; a token implicitly to be relied on of a deeper antipathy in the breast of the latter than he was willing to acknowledge to himself. For, as it was impossible to assign a reason for such distrust and abhorrence, so Mr. Dimmesdale, conscious that the poison of one morbid spot was infecting his heart's entire substance, attributed all his presentiments to no other cause. He took himself to task for his bad sympathies in reference to Roger Chillingworth, disregarded the lesson that he should have drawn from them, and did his best to root them out. Unable to accomplish this, he nevertheless, as a matter of principle, continued his habits of social familiarity with the old man, and thus gave him constant opportunities for perfecting the purpose to which—poor forlorn creature that he was, and more wretched than his victim—the avenger had devoted himself.

While thus suffering under bodily disease, and gnawed and tortured by some black trouble of the soul, and given over to the machinations of his deadliest enemy, the Reverend Mr. Dimmesdale had achieved a brilliant popularity in his sacred office. He won it indeed, in great part, by his sorrows. His intellectual gifts, his moral perceptions, his power of experiencing and communicating emotion, were kept in a state of preternatural activity by the prick and anguish of his daily life. His fame, though still on its upward slope, already overshadowed the soberer reputations of his fellow-clergymen, eminent as several of them were. There are scholars among them, who had spent more years in acquiring abstruse lore, connected with the divine profession, than Mr. Dimmesdale had lived; and who might well, therefore, be more profoundly versed in such solid and valuable attainments than their youthful brother. There were men, too, of a sturdier texture of mind than his, and endowed with a far greater share of shrewd, hard iron, or granite understanding; which, duly mingled with a fair proportion of doctrinal ingredient, constitutes a highly respectable, efficacious, and unamiable variety of the clerical species. There were others again, true saintly fathers, whose faculties had been elaborated by weary toil among their books, and by patient thought, and etherealised, moreover, by spiritual communications with the better world, into which their purity of life had almost introduced these holy personages, with their garments of mortality still clinging to them. All that they lacked was, the gift that descended upon the chosen disciples at Pentecost, in tongues of flame; symbolising, it would seem, not the power of speech in foreign and unknown languages, but that of addressing the whole human brotherhood in the heart's native language. These fathers, otherwise so apostolic, lacked Heaven's last and rarest attestation of their office, the Tongue of Flame. They would have vainly sought—had they ever dreamed of seeking—to express the highest truths through the humblest medium of familiar words and images. Their voices came down, afar and indistinctly, from the upper heights where they habitually dwelt.

Not improbably, it was to this latter class of men that Mr. Dimmesdale, by many of his traits of character, naturally belonged. To the high mountain peaks of faith and sanctity he would have climbed, had not the tendency been thwarted by the burden, whatever it might be, of crime or anguish, beneath which it was his doom to totter. It kept him down on a level with the lowest; him, the man of ethereal attributes, whose voice the angels might else have listened to and answered! But this very burden it was that gave him sympathies so intimate with the sinful brotherhood of mankind; so that his heart vibrated in unison with theirs, and received their pain into itself and sent its own throb of pain through a thousand other hearts, in gushes of sad, persuasive eloquence. Oftenest persuasive, but sometimes terrible! The people knew not the power that moved them thus. They deemed the young clergyman a miracle of holiness. They fancied him the mouth-piece of Heaven's messages of wisdom, and rebuke, and love. In their eyes, the very ground on which he trod was sanctified. The virgins of his church grew pale around him, victims of a passion so imbued with religious sentiment, that they imagined it to be all religion, and brought it openly, in their white bosoms, as their most acceptable sacrifice before the altar. The aged members of his flock, beholding Mr. Dimmesdale's frame so feeble, while they were themselves so rugged in their infirmity, believed that he would go heavenward before them, and enjoined it upon their children that their old bones should be buried close to their young pastor's holy grave. And all this time, perchance, when poor Mr. Dimmesdale was thinking of his grave, he questioned with himself whether the grass would ever grow on it, because an accursed thing must there be buried!

It is inconceivable, the agony with which this public veneration tortured him. It was his genuine impulse to adore the truth, and to reckon all things shadow-like, and utterly devoid of weight or value, that had not its divine essence as the life within their life. Then what was he?—a substance?—or the dimmest of all shadows? He longed to speak out from his own pulpit at the full height of his voice, and tell the people what he was. "I, whom you behold in these black garments of the priesthood—I, who ascend the sacred desk, and turn my pale face heavenward, taking upon myself to hold communion in your behalf with the Most High Omniscience—I, in whose daily life you discern the sanctity of Enoch—I, whose footsteps, as you suppose, leave a gleam along my earthly track, whereby the Pilgrims that shall come after me may be guided to the regions of the blest—I, who have laid the hand of baptism upon your children—I, who have breathed the parting prayer over your dying friends, to whom the Amen sounded faintly from a world which they had quitted—I, your pastor, whom you so reverence and trust, am utterly a pollution and a lie!"

More than once, Mr. Dimmesdale had gone into the pulpit, with a purpose never to come down its steps until he should have spoken words like the above. More than once he had cleared his throat, and drawn in the long, deep, and tremulous breath, which, when sent forth again, would come burdened with the black secret of his soul. More than once—nay, more than a hundred times—he had actually spoken! Spoken! But how? He had told his hearers that he was altogether vile, a viler companion of the vilest, the worst of sinners, an abomination, a thing of unimaginable iniquity, and that the only wonder was that they did not see his wretched body shrivelled up before their eyes by the burning wrath of the Almighty! Could there be plainer speech than this? Would not the people start up in their seats, by a simultaneous impulse, and tear him down out of the pulpit which he defiled? Not so, indeed! They heard it all, and did but reverence him the more. They little guessed what deadly purport lurked in those self-condemning words. "The godly youth!" said they among themselves. "The saint on earth! Alas! if he discern such sinfulness in his own white soul, what horrid spectacle would he behold in thine or mine!" The minister well knew—subtle, but remorseful hypocrite that he was!—the light in which his vague confession would be viewed. He had striven to put a cheat upon himself by making the avowal of a guilty conscience, but had gained only one other sin, and a self-acknowledged shame, without the momentary relief of being self-deceived. He had spoken the very truth, and transformed it into the veriest falsehood. And yet, by the constitution of his nature, he loved the truth, and loathed the lie, as few men ever did. Therefore, above all things else, he loathed his miserable self!

His inward trouble drove him to practices more in accordance with the old, corrupted faith of Rome than with the better light of the church in which he had been born and bred. In Mr. Dimmesdale's secret closet, under lock and key, there was a bloody scourge. Oftentimes, this Protestant and Puritan divine had plied it on his own shoulders, laughing bitterly at himself the while, and smiting so much the more pitilessly because of that bitter laugh. It was his custom, too, as it has been that of many other pious Puritans, to fast—not however, like them, in order to purify the body, and render it the fitter medium of celestial illumination—but rigorously, and until his knees trembled beneath him, as an act of penance. He kept vigils, likewise, night after night, sometimes in utter darkness, sometimes with a glimmering lamp, and sometimes, viewing his own face in a looking-glass, by the most powerful light which he could throw upon it. He thus typified the constant introspection wherewith he tortured, but could not purify himself. In these lengthened vigils, his brain often reeled, and visions seemed to flit before him; perhaps seen doubtfully, and by a faint light of their own, in the remote dimness of the chamber, or more vividly and close beside him, within the looking-glass. Now it was a herd of diabolic shapes, that grinned and mocked at the pale minister, and beckoned him away with them; now a group of shining angels, who flew upward heavily, as sorrow-laden, but grew more ethereal as they rose. Now came the dead friends of his youth, and his white-bearded father, with a saint-like frown, and his mother turning her face away as she passed by. Ghost of a mother—thinnest fantasy of a mother—methinks she might yet have thrown a pitying glance towards her son! And now, through the chamber which these spectral thoughts had made so ghastly, glided Hester Prynne leading along little Pearl, in her scarlet garb, and pointing her forefinger, first at the scarlet letter on her bosom, and then at the clergyman's own breast.

   None of these visions ever quite deluded him. At any moment, by an effort of his will, he could discern substances through their misty lack of substance, and convince himself that they were not solid in their nature, like yonder table of carved oak, or that big, square, leather-bound and brazen-clasped volume of divinity. But, for all that, they were, in one sense, the truest and most substantial things which the poor minister now dealt with. It is the unspeakable misery of a life so false as his, that it steals the pith and substance out of whatever realities there are around us, and which were meant by Heaven to be the spirit's joy and nutriment. To the untrue man, the whole universe is false—it is impalpable—it shrinks to nothing within his grasp. And he himself in so far as he shows himself in a false light, becomes a shadow, or, indeed, ceases to exist. The only truth that continued to give Mr. Dimmesdale a real existence on this earth was the anguish in his inmost soul, and the undissembled expression of it in his aspect. Had he once found power to smile, and wear a face of gaiety, there would have been no such man!

On one of those ugly nights, which we have faintly hinted at, but forborne to picture forth, the minister started from his chair. A new thought had struck him. There might be a moment's peace in it. Attiring himself with as much care as if it had been for public worship, and precisely in the same manner, he stole softly down the staircase, undid the door, and issued forth.

XII.

THE MINISTER'S VIGIL

Walking in the shadow of a dream, as it were, and perhaps actually under the influence of a species of somnambulism, Mr. Dimmesdale reached the spot where, now so long since, Hester Prynne had lived through her first hours of public ignominy. The same platform or scaffold, black and weather-stained with the storm or sunshine of seven long years, and foot-worn, too, with the tread of many culprits who had since ascended it, remained standing beneath the balcony of the meeting-house. The minister went up the steps.

It was an obscure night in early May. An unvaried pall of cloud muffled the whole expanse of sky from zenith to horizon. If the same multitude which had stood as eye-witnesses while Hester Prynne sustained her punishment could now have been summoned forth, they would have discerned no face above the platform nor hardly the outline of a human shape, in the dark grey of the midnight. But the town was all asleep. There was no peril of discovery. The minister might stand there, if it so pleased him, until morning should redden in the east, without other risk than that the dank and chill night air would creep into his frame, and stiffen his joints with rheumatism, and clog his throat with catarrh and cough; thereby defrauding the expectant audience of tomorrow's prayer and sermon. No eye could see him, save that ever-wakeful one which had seen him in his closet, wielding the bloody scourge. Why, then, had he come hither? Was it but the mockery of penitence? A mockery, indeed, but in which his soul trifled with itself! A mockery at which angels blushed and wept, while fiends rejoiced with jeering laughter! He had been driven hither by the impulse of that Remorse which dogged him everywhere, and whose own sister and closely linked companion was that Cowardice which invariably drew him back, with her tremulous gripe, just when the other impulse had hurried him to the verge of a disclosure. Poor, miserable man! what right had infirmity like his to burden itself with crime? Crime is for the iron-nerved, who have their choice either to endure it, or, if it press too hard, to exert their fierce and savage strength for a good purpose, and fling it off at once! This feeble and most sensitive of spirits could do neither, yet continually did one thing or another, which intertwined, in the same inextricable knot, the agony of heaven-defying guilt and vain repentance.

And thus, while standing on the scaffold, in this vain show

of expiation, Mr. Dimmesdale was overcome with a great horror of mind, as if the universe were gazing at a scarlet token on his naked breast, right over his heart. On that spot, in very truth, there was, and there had long been, the gnawing and poisonous tooth of bodily pain. Without any effort of his will, or power to restrain himself, he shrieked aloud: an outcry that went pealing through the night, and was beaten back from one house to another, and reverberated from the hills in the background; as if a company of devils, detecting so much misery and terror in it, had made a plaything of the sound, and were bandying it to and fro.

"It is done!" muttered the minister, covering his face with his hands. "The whole town will awake and hurry forth, and find me here!"

But it was not so. The shriek had perhaps sounded with a far greater power, to his own startled ears, than it actually possessed. The town did not awake; or, if it did, the drowsy slumberers mistook the cry either for something frightful in a dream, or for the noise of witches, whose voices, at that period, were often heard to pass over the settlements or lonely cottages, as they rode with Satan through the air. The clergyman, therefore, hearing no symptoms of disturbance, uncovered his eyes and looked about him. At one of the chamber-windows of Governor Bellingham's mansion, which stood at some distance, on the line of another street, he beheld the appearance of the old magistrate himself with a lamp in his hand a white night-cap on his head, and a long white gown enveloping his figure. He looked like a ghost evoked unseasonably from the grave. The cry had evidently startled him. At another window of the same house, moreover appeared old Mistress Hibbins, the Governor's sister, also with a lamp, which even thus far off revealed the expression of her sour and discontented face. She thrust forth her head from the lattice, and looked anxiously upward. Beyond the shadow of a doubt, this venerable witch-lady had heard Mr. Dimmesdale's outcry, and interpreted it, with its multitudinous echoes and reverberations, as the clamour of the fiends and night-hags, with whom she was well known to make excursions in the forest.

Detecting the gleam of Governor Bellingham's lamp, the old lady quickly extinguished her own, and vanished. Possibly, she went up among the clouds. The minister saw nothing further of her motions. The magistrate, after a wary observation of the darkness—into which, nevertheless, he could see but little further than he might into a mill-stone—retired from the window.

The minister grew comparatively calm. His eyes, however, were soon greeted by a little glimmering light, which, at first a long way off was approaching up the street. It threw a gleam of recognition, on here a post, and there a garden fence, and here a latticed window-pane, and there a pump, with its full trough of water, and here again an arched door of oak, with an iron knocker, and a rough log for the door-step. The Reverend Mr. Dimmesdale noted all these minute particulars, even while firmly convinced that the doom of his existence was stealing onward, in the footsteps which he now heard; and that the gleam of the lantern would fall upon him in a few moments more, and reveal his long-hidden secret. As the light drew nearer, he beheld, within its illuminated circle, his brother clergyman — or, to speak more accurately, his professional father, as well as highly valued friend — the Reverend Mr. Wilson, who, as Mr. Dimmesdale now conjectured, had been praying at the bedside of some dying man. And so he had. The good old minister came freshly from the death-chamber of Governor Winthrop, who had passed from earth to heaven within that very hour. And now surrounded, like the saint-like personage of olden times, with a radiant halo, that glorified him amid this gloomy night of sin — as if the departed Governor had left him an inheritance of his glory, or as if he had caught upon himself the distant shine of the celestial city, while looking thitherward to see the triumphant pilgrim pass within its gates — now, in short, good Father Wilson was moving homeward, aiding his footsteps with a lighted lantern! The glimmer of this luminary suggested the above conceits to Mr. Dimmesdale, who smiled — nay, almost laughed at them — and then wondered if he was going mad.

As the Reverend Mr. Wilson passed beside the scaffold, closely muffling his Geneva cloak about him with one arm, and holding the lantern before his breast with the other, the minister could hardly restrain himself from speaking —

"A good evening to you, venerable Father Wilson. Come up hither, I pray you, and pass a pleasant hour with me!"

Good Heavens! Had Mr. Dimmesdale actually spoken? For one instant he believed that these words had passed his lips. But they were uttered only within his imagination. The venerable Father Wilson continued to step slowly onward, looking carefully at the muddy pathway before his feet, and never once turning his head towards the guilty platform. When the light of the glimmering lantern had faded quite away, the minister discovered, by the faintness which came over him, that the last few moments had been a crisis of terrible anxiety, although his mind had made an involuntary effort to relieve itself by a kind of lurid playfulness.

Shortly afterwards, the like grisly sense of the humorous again stole in among the solemn phantoms of his thought. He felt his limbs growing stiff with the unaccustomed chilliness of the night, and doubted whether he should be able to descend the steps of the scaffold. Morning would break and find him there. The neighbourhood would begin to rouse itself. The earliest riser, coming forth in the dim twilight, would perceive a vaguely-defined figure aloft on the place of shame; and half-crazed betwixt alarm and curiosity, would go knocking from door to door, summoning all the people to behold the ghost—as he needs must think it—of some defunct transgressor. A dusky tumult would flap its wings from one house to another. Then—the morning light still waxing stronger—old patriarchs would rise up in great haste, each in his flannel gown, and matronly dames, without pausing to put off their night-gear. The whole tribe of decorous personages, who had never heretofore been seen with a single hair of their heads awry, would start into public view with the disorder of a nightmare in their aspects. Old Governor Bellingham would come grimly forth, with his King James' ruff fastened askew, and Mistress Hibbins, with some twigs of the forest clinging to her skirts, and looking sourer than ever, as having hardly got a wink of sleep after her night ride; and good Father Wilson too, after spending half the night at a death-bed, and liking ill to be disturbed, thus early, out of his dreams about the glorified saints. Hither, likewise, would come the elders and deacons of Mr. Dimmesdale's church, and the young virgins who so idolized their minister, and had made a shrine for him in their white bosoms, which now, by the by, in their hurry and confusion, they would scantly have given themselves time to cover with their kerchiefs. All people, in a word, would come stumbling over their thresholds, and turning up their amazed and horror-stricken visages around the scaffold. Whom would they discern there, with the red eastern light upon his brow? Whom, but the Reverend Arthur Dimmesdale, half-frozen to death, overwhelmed with shame, and standing where Hester Prynne had stood!

Carried away by the grotesque horror of this picture, the minister, unawares, and to his own infinite alarm, burst into a great peal of laughter. It was immediately responded to by a light, airy, childish laugh, in which, with a thrill of the heart—but he knew not whether of exquisite pain, or pleasure as acute—he recognised the tones of little Pearl.

"Pearl! Little Pearl!" cried he, after a moment's pause; then, suppressing his voice—"Hester! Hester Prynne! Are you there?"

"Yes; it is Hester Prynne!" she replied, in a tone of surprise; and the minister heard her footsteps approaching from the sidewalk, along which she had been passing. "It is I, and my little Pearl."

"Whence come you, Hester?" asked the minister. "What sent you hither?"

"I have been watching at a death-bed," answered Hester Prynne "at Governor Winthrop's death-bed, and have taken his measure for a robe, and am now going homeward to my dwelling."

"Come up hither, Hester, thou and little Pearl," said the Reverend Mr. Dimmesdale. "Ye have both been here before, but I was not with you. Come up hither once again, and we will stand all three together."

She silently ascended the steps, and stood on the platform, holding little Pearl by the hand. The minister felt for the child's other hand, and took it. The moment that he did so, there came what seemed a tumultuous rush of new life, other life than his own pouring like a torrent into his heart, and hurrying through all his veins, as if the mother and the child were communicating their vital warmth to his half-torpid system. The three formed an electric chain.

"Minister!" whispered little Pearl.

"What wouldst thou say, child?" asked Mr. Dimmesdale.

"Wilt thou stand here with mother and me, tomorrow noontide?" inquired Pearl.

"Nay; not so, my little Pearl," answered the minister; for, with the new energy of the moment, all the dread of public exposure, that had so long been the anguish of his life, had returned upon him; and he was already trembling at the conjunction in which—with a strange joy, nevertheless—he now found himself—"not so, my child. I shall, indeed, stand with thy mother and thee one other day, but not tomorrow."

Pearl laughed, and attempted to pull away her hand. But the minister held it fast.

"A moment longer, my child!" said he.

"But wilt thou promise," asked Pearl, "to take my hand, and mother's hand, tomorrow noontide?"

"Not then, Pearl," said the minister; "but another time."

"And what other time?" persisted the child.

"At the great judgment day," whispered the minister; and, strangely enough, the sense that he was a professional teacher of the truth impelled him to answer the child so. "Then, and there, before the judgment-seat, thy mother, and thou, and I must stand together. But the daylight of this world shall not see our meeting!"

Pearl laughed again.

But before Mr. Dimmesdale had done speaking, a light gleamed far and wide over all the muffled sky. It was doubtless caused by one of those meteors, which the night-watcher may so often observe burning out to waste, in the vacant regions of the atmosphere. So powerful was its radiance, that it thoroughly illuminated the dense medium of cloud betwixt the sky and earth. The great vault brightened, like the dome of an immense lamp. It showed the familiar scene of the street with the distinctness of mid-day, but also with the awfulness that is always imparted to familiar objects by an unaccustomed light. The wooden houses, with their jutting storeys and quaint gable-peaks; the doorsteps and thresholds with the early grass springing up about them; the garden-plots, black with freshly-turned earth; the wheel-track, little worn, and even in the market-place margined with green on either side—all were visible, but with a singularity of aspect that seemed to give another moral interpretation to the things of this world than they had ever borne before. And there stood the minister, with his hand over his heart; and Hester Prynne, with the embroidered letter glimmering on her bosom; and little Pearl, herself a symbol, and the connecting link between those two. They stood in the noon of that strange and solemn splendour, as if it were the light that is to reveal all secrets, and the daybreak that shall unite all who belong to one another.

There was witchcraft in little Pearl's eyes; and her face, as she glanced upward at the minister, wore that naughty smile which made its expression frequently so elvish. She withdrew her hand from Mr. Dimmesdale's, and pointed across the street. But he clasped both his hands over his breast, and cast his eyes towards the zenith.

Nothing was more common, in those days, than to interpret all meteoric appearances, and other natural phenomena that occurred with less regularity than the rise and set of sun and moon, as so many revelations from a supernatural source. Thus, a blazing spear, a sword of flame, a bow, or a sheaf of arrows seen in the midnight sky, prefigured Indian warfare. Pestilence was known to have been foreboded by a shower of crimson light. We doubt whether any marked event, for good or evil, ever befell New England, from its settlement down to revolutionary times, of which the inhabitants had not been previously warned by some spectacle of its nature. Not seldom, it had been seen by multitudes. Oftener, however, its credibility rested on the faith of some lonely eye-witness, who beheld the wonder through the coloured, magnifying, and distorted medium of his imagination, and shaped it more distinctly in his after-thought. It was, indeed, a majestic idea that the destiny of nations should be revealed, in these awful hieroglyphics, on the cope of heaven. A scroll so wide might not be deemed too expensive for Providence to write a people's doom upon. The belief was a favourite one with our forefathers, as betokening that their infant commonwealth was under a celestial guardianship of peculiar intimacy and strictness. But what shall we say, when an individual discovers a revelation addressed to himself alone, on the same vast sheet of record. In such a case, it could only be the symptom of a highly disordered mental state, when a man, rendered morbidly self-contemplative by long, intense, and secret pain, had extended his egotism over the whole expanse of nature, until the firmament itself should appear no more than a fitting page for his soul's history and fate.

We impute it, therefore, solely to the disease in his own eye and heart that the minister, looking upward to the zenith, beheld there the appearance of an immense letter—the letter A—marked out in lines of dull red light. Not but the meteor may have shown itself at that point, burning duskily through a veil of cloud, but with no such shape as his guilty imagination gave it, or, at least, with so little definiteness, that another's guilt might have seen another symbol in it.

There was a singular circumstance that characterised Mr. Dimmesdale's psychological state at this moment. All the time that he gazed upward to the zenith, he was, nevertheless, perfectly aware that little Pearl was pointing her finger towards old Roger Chillingworth, who stood at no great distance from the scaffold. The minister appeared to see him, with the same glance that discerned the miraculous letter. To his feature as to all other objects, the meteoric light imparted a new expression; or it might well be that the physician was not careful then, as at all other times, to hide the malevolence with which he looked upon his victim. Certainly, if the meteor kindled up the sky, and disclosed the earth, with an awfulness that admonished Hester Prynne and the clergyman of the day of judgment, then might Roger Chillingworth have passed with them for the arch-fiend, standing there with a smile and scowl, to claim his own. So vivid was the expression, or so intense the minister's perception of it, that it seemed still to remain painted on the darkness after the meteor had vanished, with an effect as if the street and all things else were at once annihilated.

"Who is that man, Hester?" gasped Mr. Dimmesdale, overcome with terror. "I shiver at him! Dost thou know the man? I hate him, Hester!"

She remembered her oath, and was silent.

"I tell thee, my soul shivers at him!" muttered the minister again. "Who is he? Who is he? Canst thou do nothing for me? I have a nameless horror of the man!"

"Minister," said little Pearl, "I can tell thee who he is!"

"Quickly, then, child!" said the minister, bending his ear close to her lips. "Quickly, and as low as thou canst whisper."

Pearl mumbled something into his ear that sounded, indeed, like human language, but was only such gibberish as children may be heard amusing themselves with by the hour together. At all events, if it involved any secret information in regard to old Roger Chillingworth, it was in a tongue unknown to the erudite clergyman, and did but increase the bewilderment of his mind. The elvish child then laughed aloud.

"Dost thou mock me now?" said the minister.

"Thou wast not bold! — thou wast not true!" answered the child. "Thou wouldst not promise to take my hand, and mother's hand, tomorrow noontide!"

"Worthy sir," answered the physician, who had now advanced to the foot of the platform — "pious Master Dimmesdale! can this be you? Well, well, indeed! We men of study, whose heads are in our books, have need to be straitly looked after! We dream in our waking moments, and walk in our sleep. Come, good sir, and my dear friend, I pray you let me lead you home!"

"How knewest thou that I was here?" asked the minister, fearfully.

"Verily, and in good faith," answered Roger Chillingworth, "I knew nothing of the matter. I had spent the better part of the night at the bedside of the worshipful Governor Winthrop, doing what my poor skill might to give him ease. He, going home to a better world, I, likewise, was on my way homeward, when this light shone out. Come with me, I beseech you, Reverend sir, else you will be poorly able to do Sabbath duty tomorrow. Aha! see now how they trouble the brain — these books! — these books! You should study less, good sir, and take a little pastime, or these night whimsies will grow upon you."

"I will go home with you," said Mr. Dimmesdale.

With a chill despondency, like one awakening, all nerveless, from an ugly dream, he yielded himself to the physician, and was led away.

The next day, however, being the Sabbath, he preached a discourse which was held to be the richest and most powerful, and the most replete with heavenly influences, that had ever proceeded from his lips. Souls, it is said, more souls than one, were brought to the truth by the efficacy of that sermon, and vowed within themselves to cherish a holy gratitude towards Mr. Dimmesdale throughout the long hereafter. But as he came down the pulpit steps, the grey-bearded sexton met him, holding up a black glove, which the minister recognised as his own.

"It was found," said the Sexton, "this morning on the scaffold where evil-doers are set up to public shame. Satan dropped it there, I take it, intending a scurrilous jest against your reverence. But, indeed, he was blind and foolish, as he ever and always is. A pure hand needs no glove to cover it!"

"Thank you, my good friend," said the minister, gravely, but startled at heart; for so confused was his remembrance, that he had almost brought himself to look at the events of the past night as visionary.

"Yes, it seems to be my glove, indeed!"

"And, since Satan saw fit to steal it, your reverence must

needs handle him without gloves henceforward," remarked the old sexton, grimly smiling. "But did your reverence hear of the portent that was seen last night? a great red letter in the sky—the letter A, which we interpret to stand for Angel. For, as our good Governor Winthrop was made an angel this past night, it was doubtless held fit that there should be some notice thereof!"

"No," answered the minister; "I had not heard of it."

XIII.

ANOTHER VIEW OF HESTER

In her late singular interview with Mr. Dimmesdale, Hester Prynne was shocked at the condition to which she found the clergyman reduced. His nerve seemed absolutely destroyed. His moral force was abased into more than childish weakness. It grovelled helpless on the ground, even while his intellectual faculties retained their pristine strength, or had perhaps acquired a morbid energy, which disease only could have given them. With her knowledge of a train of circumstances hidden from all others, she could readily infer that, besides the legitimate action of his own conscience, a terrible machinery had been brought to bear, and was still operating, on Mr. Dimmesdale's well-being and repose. Knowing what this poor fallen man had once been, her whole soul was moved by the shuddering terror with which he had appealed to her—the outcast woman—for support against his instinctively discovered enemy. She decided, moreover, that he had a right to her utmost aid. Little accustomed, in her long seclusion from society, to measure her ideas of right and wrong by any standard external to herself, Hester saw—or seemed to see—that there lay a responsibility upon her in reference to the clergyman, which she owned to no other, nor to the whole world besides. The links that united her to the rest of humankind—links of flowers, or silk, or gold, or whatever the material—had all been broken. Here was the iron link of mutual crime, which neither he nor she could break. Like all other ties, it brought along with it its obligations.

Hester Prynne did not now occupy precisely the same position in which we beheld her during the earlier periods of her ignominy. Years had come and gone. Pearl was now seven years old. Her mother, with the scarlet letter on her breast, glittering in its fantastic embroidery, had long been a familiar object to the townspeople. As is apt to be the case when a person stands out in any prominence before the community, and, at the same time, interferes neither with public nor individual interests and convenience, a species of general regard had ultimately grown up in reference to Hester Prynne. It is to the credit of human nature that, except where its selfishness is brought into play, it loves more readily than it hates. Hatred, by a gradual and quiet process, will even be transformed to love, unless the change be impeded by a continually new irritation of the original feeling of hostility. In this matter of Hester Prynne there was neither irritation nor irksomeness. She never battled with the public, but submitted uncomplainingly to its worst usage; she made no claim upon it in requital for what she suffered; she did not weigh upon its sympathies. Then, also, the blameless purity of her life during all these years in which she had been set apart to infamy was reckoned largely in her favour. With nothing now to lose, in the sight of mankind, and with no hope, and seemingly no wish, of gaining anything, it could only be a genuine regard for virtue that had brought back the poor wanderer to its paths.

It was perceived, too, that while Hester never put forward even the humblest title to share in the world's privileges — further than to breathe the common air and earn daily bread for little Pearl and herself by the faithful labour of her hands — she was quick to acknowledge her sisterhood with the race of man whenever benefits were to be conferred. None so ready as she to give of her little substance to every demand of poverty, even though the bitter-hearted pauper threw back a gibe in requital of the food brought regularly to his door, or the garments wrought for him by the fingers that could have embroidered a monarch's robe. None so self-devoted as Hester when pestilence stalked through the town. In all seasons of calamity, indeed, whether general or of individuals, the outcast of society at once found her place. She came, not as a guest, but as a rightful inmate, into the household that was darkened by trouble, as if its gloomy twilight were a medium in which she was entitled to hold intercourse with her fellow-creature. There glimmered the embroidered letter, with comfort in its unearthly ray. Elsewhere the token of sin, it was the taper of the sick chamber. It had even thrown its gleam, in the sufferer's hard extremity, across the verge of time. It had shown him where to set his foot, while the light of earth was fast becoming dim, and ere the light of futurity could reach him. In such emergencies Hester's nature showed itself warm and rich — a well-spring of human tenderness, unfailing to every real demand, and inexhaustible by the largest. Her breast, with its badge of shame, was but the softer pillow for the head that needed one. She was self-ordained a Sister of Mercy, or, we may rather say, the world's heavy hand had so ordained her, when neither the world nor she looked forward to this result. The letter was the symbol of her calling. Such helpfulness was found in her — so much power to do, and power to sympathise — that many people refused to interpret the scarlet A by its original signification. They said that it meant Able, so strong was Hester Prynne, with a woman's strength.

It was only the darkened house that could contain her. When sunshine came again, she was not there. Her shadow had faded across the threshold. The helpful inmate had departed, without one backward glance to gather up the meed of gratitude, if any were in the hearts of those whom she had served so zealously. Meeting them in the street, she never raised her head to receive their greeting. If they were resolute to accost her, she laid her finger on the scarlet letter, and passed on. This might be pride, but was so like humility, that it produced all the softening influence of the latter quality on the public mind. The public is despotic in its temper; it is capable of denying common justice when too strenuously demanded as a right; but quite as frequently it awards more than justice, when the appeal is made, as despots love to have it made, entirely to its generosity. Interpreting Hester Prynne's deportment as an appeal of this nature, society was inclined to show its former victim a more benign countenance than she cared to be favoured with, or, perchance, than she deserved.

The rulers, and the wise and learned men of the community, were longer in acknowledging the influence of Hester's good qualities than the people. The prejudices which they shared in common with the latter were fortified in themselves by an iron frame-work of reasoning, that made it a far tougher labour to expel them. Day by day, nevertheless, their sour and rigid wrinkles were relaxing into something which, in the due course of years, might grow to be an expression of almost benevolence. Thus it was with the men of rank, on whom their eminent position imposed the guardianship of the public morals. Individuals in private life, meanwhile, had quite forgiven Hester Prynne for her frailty; nay, more, they had begun to look upon the scarlet letter as the token, not of that one sin for which she had borne so long and dreary a penance, but of her many good deeds since. "Do you see that woman with the embroidered badge?" they would say to strangers. "It is our Hester—the town's own Hester—who is so kind to the poor, so helpful to the sick, so comfortable to the afflicted!" Then, it is true, the propensity of human nature to tell the very worst of itself, when embodied in the person of another, would constrain them to whisper the black scandal of bygone years. It was none the less a fact, however, that in the eyes of the very men who spoke thus, the scarlet letter had the effect of the cross on a nun's bosom. It imparted to the wearer a kind of sacredness, which enabled her to walk securely amid all peril. Had she fallen among thieves, it would have kept her safe. It was reported, and believed by many, that an Indian had drawn his arrow against the badge, and that the missile struck it, and fell harmless to the ground.

The effect of the symbol—or rather, of the position in respect to society that was indicated by it—on the mind of Hester Prynne herself was powerful and peculiar. All the light and graceful foliage of her character had been withered up by this red-hot brand, and had long ago fallen away, leaving a bare and harsh outline, which might have been repulsive had she possessed friends or companions to be repelled by it. Even the attractiveness of her person had undergone a similar change. It might be partly owing to the studied austerity of her dress, and partly to the lack of demonstration in her manners. It was a sad transformation, too, that her rich and luxuriant hair had either been cut off, or was so completely hidden by a cap, that not a shining lock of it ever once gushed into the sunshine. It was due in part to all these causes, but still more to something else, that there seemed to be no longer anything in Hester's face for Love to dwell upon; nothing in Hester's form, though majestic and statue-like, that Passion would ever dream of clasping in its embrace; nothing in Hester's bosom to make it ever again the pillow of Affection. Some attribute had departed from her, the permanence of which had been essential to keep her a woman. Such is frequently the fate, and such the stern development, of the feminine character and person, when the woman has encountered, and lived through, an experience of peculiar severity. If she be all tenderness, she will die. If she survive, the tenderness will either be crushed out of her, or—and the outward semblance is the same—crushed so deeply into her heart that it can never show itself more. The latter is perhaps the truest theory. She who has once been a woman, and ceased to be so, might at any moment become a woman again, if there were only the magic touch to effect the transformation. We shall see whether Hester Prynne were ever afterwards so touched and so transfigured.

Much of the marble coldness of Hester's impression was to be attributed to the circumstance that her life had turned, in a great measure, from passion and feeling to thought. Standing alone in the world—alone, as to any dependence on society, and with little Pearl to be guided and protected—alone, and hopeless of retrieving her position, even had she not scorned to consider it desirable—she cast away the fragment of a broken chain. The world's law was no law for her mind. It was an age in which the human intellect, newly emancipated, had taken a more active and a wider range than for many centuries before. Men of the sword had overthrown nobles and kings. Men bolder than these had overthrown and rearranged—not actually, but within the sphere of theory, which was their most real abode—the whole system of ancient prejudice, wherewith was linked much of ancient principle. Hester Prynne imbibed this spirit. She assumed a freedom of speculation, then common enough on the other side of the Atlantic, but which our forefathers, had they known it, would have held to be a deadlier crime than that stigmatised by the scarlet letter. In her lonesome cottage, by the sea-shore, thoughts visited her such as dared to enter no other dwelling in New England; shadowy guests, that would have been as perilous as demons to their entertainer, could they have been seen so much as knocking at her door.

It is remarkable that persons who speculate the most boldly often conform with the most perfect quietude to the external regulations of society. The thought suffices them, without investing itself in the flesh and blood of action. So it seemed to be with Hester. Yet, had little Pearl never come to her from the spiritual world, it might have been far otherwise. Then she might have come down to us in history, hand in hand with Ann Hutchinson, as the foundress of a religious sect. She might, in one of her phases, have been a prophetess. She might, and not improbably would, have suffered death from the stern tribunals of the period, for attempting to undermine the foundations of the Puritan establishment. But, in the education of her child, the mother's enthusiasm of thought had something to wreak itself upon. Providence, in the person of this little girl, had assigned to Hester's charge, the germ and blossom of womanhood, to be cherished and developed amid a host of difficulties. Everything was against her. The world was hostile. The child's own nature had something wrong in it which continually betokened that she had been born amiss—the effluence of her mother's lawless passion—and often impelled Hester to ask, in bitterness of heart, whether it were for ill or good that the poor little creature had been born at all.

Indeed, the same dark question often rose into her mind with reference to the whole race of womanhood. Was existence worth accepting even to the happiest among them? As concerned her own individual existence, she had long ago decided in the negative, and dismissed the point as settled. A tendency to speculation, though it may keep women quiet, as it does man, yet makes her sad. She discerns, it may be, such a hopeless task before her. As a first step, the whole system of society is to be torn down and built up anew. Then the very nature of the opposite sex, or its long hereditary habit, which has become like nature, is to be essentially modified before woman can be allowed to assume what seems a fair and suitable position. Finally, all other difficulties being obviated, woman cannot take advantage of these preliminary reforms until she herself shall have undergone a still mightier change, in which, perhaps, the ethereal essence, wherein she has her truest life, will be found to have evaporated. A woman never overcomes these problems by any exercise of thought. They are not to be solved, or only in one way. If her heart chance to come uppermost, they vanish. Thus Hester Prynne, whose heart had lost its regular and healthy throb, wandered without a clue in the dark labyrinth of mind; now turned aside by an insurmountable precipice; now starting back from a deep chasm. There was wild and ghastly scenery all around her, and a home and comfort nowhere. At times a fearful doubt strove to possess her soul, whether it were not better to send Pearl at once to Heaven, and go herself to such futurity as Eternal Justice should provide.

The scarlet letter had not done its office. Now, however, her interview with the Reverend Mr. Dimmesdale, on the night of his vigil, had given her a new theme of reflection, and held up to her an object that appeared worthy of any exertion and sacrifice for its attainment. She had witnessed the intense misery beneath which the minister struggled, or, to speak more accurately, had ceased to struggle. She saw that he stood on the verge of lunacy, if he had not already stepped across it. It was impossible to doubt that, whatever painful efficacy there might be in the secret sting of remorse, a deadlier venom had been infused into it by the hand that proffered relief. A secret enemy had been continually by his side, under the semblance of a friend and helper, and had availed himself of the opportunities thus afforded for tampering with the delicate springs of Mr. Dimmesdale's nature. Hester could not but ask herself whether there had not originally been a defect of truth, courage, and loyalty on her own part, in allowing the minister to be thrown into a position where so much evil was to be foreboded and nothing auspicious to be hoped. Her only justification lay in the fact that she had been able to discern no method of rescuing him from a blacker ruin than had overwhelmed herself except by acquiescing in Roger Chillingworth's scheme of disguise. Under that impulse she had made her choice, and had chosen, as it now appeared, the more wretched alternative of the two. She determined to redeem her error so far as it might yet be possible. Strengthened by years of hard and solemn trial, she felt herself no longer so inadequate to cope with Roger Chillingworth as on that night, abased by sin and half-maddened by the ignominy that was still new, when they had talked together in the prison-chamber. She had climbed her way since then to a higher point. The old man, on the other hand, had brought himself nearer to her level, or, perhaps, below it, by the revenge which he had stooped for.

In fine, Hester Prynne resolved to meet her former husband, and do what might be in her power for the rescue of the victim on whom he had so evidently set his gripe. The occasion was not long to seek. One afternoon, walking with Pearl in a retired part of the peninsula, she beheld the old physician with a basket on one arm and a staff in the other hand, stooping along the ground in quest of roots and herbs to concoct his medicine withal.

XIV.

HESTER AND THE PHYSICIAN

Hester bade little Pearl run down to the margin of the water, and play with the shells and tangled sea-weed, until she should have talked awhile with yonder gatherer of herbs. So the child flew away like a bird, and, making bare her small white feet went pattering along the moist margin of the sea. Here and there she came to a full stop, and peeped curiously into a pool, left by the retiring tide as a mirror for Pearl to see her face in. Forth peeped at her, out of the pool, with dark, glistening curls around her head, and an elf-smile in her eyes, the image of a little maid whom Pearl, having no other playmate, invited to take her hand and run a race with her. But the visionary little maid on her part, beckoned likewise, as if to say—"This is a better place; come thou into the pool." And Pearl, stepping in mid-leg deep, beheld her own white feet at the bottom; while, out of a still lower depth, came the gleam of a kind of fragmentary smile, floating to and fro in the agitated water.

Meanwhile her mother had accosted the physician. "I would speak a word with you," said she—"a word that concerns us much."

"Aha! and is it Mistress Hester that has a word for old Roger Chillingworth?" answered he, raising himself from his stooping posture. "With all my heart! Why, mistress, I hear good tidings of you on all hands! No longer ago than yester-eve, a magistrate, a wise and godly man, was discoursing of your affairs, Mistress Hester, and whispered me that there had been question concerning you in the council. It was debated whether or no, with safety to the commonweal, yonder scarlet letter might be taken off your bosom. On my life, Hester, I made my intreaty to the worshipful magistrate that it might be done forthwith."

"It lies not in the pleasure of the magistrates to take off the badge," calmly replied Hester. "Were I worthy to be quit of it, it would fall away of its own nature, or be transformed into something that should speak a different purport."

"Nay, then, wear it, if it suit you better," rejoined he, "A woman must needs follow her own fancy touching the adornment of her person. The letter is gaily embroidered, and shows right bravely on your bosom!"

All this while Hester had been looking steadily at the old man, and was shocked, as well as wonder-smitten, to discern what a change had been wrought upon him within the past seven years. It was not so much that he had grown older; for though the traces of advancing life were visible, he bore his age well, and seemed to retain a wiry vigour and alertness. But the former aspect of an intellectual and studious man, calm and quiet, which was what she best remembered in him, had altogether vanished, and been succeeded by an eager, searching, almost fierce, yet carefully guarded look. It seemed to be his wish and purpose to mask this expression with a smile, but the latter played him false, and flickered over his visage so derisively that the spectator could see his blackness all the better for it. Ever and anon, too, there came a glare of red light out of his eyes, as if the old man's soul were on fire and kept on smouldering duskily within his breast, until by some casual puff of passion it was blown into a momentary flame. This he repressed as speedily as possible, and strove to look as if nothing of the kind had happened.

In a word, old Roger Chillingworth was a striking evidence of man's faculty of transforming himself into a devil, if he will only, for a reasonable space of time, undertake a devil's office. This unhappy person had effected such a transformation by devoting himself for seven years to the constant analysis of a heart full of torture, and deriving his enjoyment thence, and adding fuel to those fiery tortures which he analysed and gloated over.

The scarlet letter burned on Hester Prynne's bosom. Here was another ruin, the responsibility of which came partly home to her.

"What see you in my face," asked the physician, "that you look at it so earnestly?"

"Something that would make me weep, if there were any tears bitter enough for it," answered she. "But let it pass! It is of yonder miserable man that I would speak."

"And what of him?" cried Roger Chillingworth, eagerly, as if he loved the topic, and were glad of an opportunity to discuss it with the only person of whom he could make a confidant. "Not to hide the truth, Mistress Hester, my thoughts happen just now to be busy with the gentleman. So speak freely and I will make answer."

"When we last spake together," said Hester, "now seven

years ago, it was your pleasure to extort a promise of secrecy as touching the former relation betwixt yourself and me. As the life and good fame of yonder man were in your hands there seemed no choice to me, save to be silent in accordance with your behest. Yet it was not without heavy misgivings that I thus bound myself, for, having cast off all duty towards other human beings, there remained a duty towards him, and something whispered me that I was betraying it in pledging myself to keep your counsel. Since that day no man is so near to him as you. You tread behind his every footstep. You are beside him, sleeping and waking. You search his thoughts. You burrow and rankle in his heart! Your clutch is on his life, and you cause him to die daily a living death, and still he knows you not. In permitting this I have surely acted a false part by the only man to whom the power was left me to be true!"

"What choice had you?" asked Roger Chillingworth. "My finger, pointed at this man, would have hurled him from his pulpit into a dungeon, thence, peradventure, to the gallows!"

"It had been better so!" said Hester Prynne.

"What evil have I done the man?" asked Roger Chillingworth again. "I tell thee, Hester Prynne, the richest fee that ever physician earned from monarch could not have bought such care as I have wasted on this miserable priest! But for my aid his life would have burned away in torments within the first two years after the perpetration of his crime and thine. For, Hester, his spirit lacked the strength that could have borne up, as thine has, beneath a burden like thy scarlet letter. Oh, I could reveal a goodly secret! But enough. What art can do, I have exhausted on him. That he now breathes and creeps about on earth is owing all to me!"

"Better he had died at once!" said Hester Prynne.

"Yea, woman, thou sayest truly!" cried old Roger Chillingworth, letting the lurid fire of his heart blaze out before her eyes. "Better had he died at once! Never did mortal suffer what this man has suffered. And all, all, in the sight of his worst enemy! He has been conscious of me. He has felt an influence dwelling always upon him like a curse. He knew, by some spiritual sense—for the Creator never made another being so sensitive as this—he knew that no friendly hand was pulling at his heartstrings, and that an eye was looking curiously into him, which sought only evil, and found it. But he knew not that the eye and hand were mine! With the superstition common to his brotherhood, he fancied himself given over to a fiend, to be tortured with frightful dreams and desperate thoughts, the sting of remorse and despair of pardon, as a foretaste of what awaits him beyond the grave. But it was the constant shadow of my presence, the closest propinquity of the man whom he had most vilely wronged, and who had grown to exist only by this perpetual poison of the direst revenge! Yea, indeed, he did not err, there was a fiend at his elbow! A mortal man, with once a human heart, has become a fiend for his especial torment."

The unfortunate physician, while uttering these words, lifted his hands with a look of horror, as if he had beheld some frightful shape, which he could not recognise, usurping the place of his own image in a glass. It was one of those moments — which sometimes occur only at the interval of years — when a man's moral aspect is faithfully revealed to his mind's eye. Not improbably he had never before viewed himself as he did now.

"Hast thou not tortured him enough?" said Hester, noticing the old man's look. "Has he not paid thee all?"

"No, no! He has but increased the debt!" answered the physician, and as he proceeded, his manner lost its fiercer characteristics, and subsided into gloom. "Dost thou remember me, Hester, as I was nine years agone? Even then I was in the autumn of my days, nor was it the early autumn. But all my life had been made up of earnest, studious, thoughtful, quiet years, bestowed faithfully for the increase of mine own knowledge, and faithfully, too, though this latter object was but casual to the other — faithfully for the advancement of human welfare. No life had been more peaceful and innocent than mine; few lives so rich with benefits conferred. Dost thou remember me? Was I not, though you might deem me cold, nevertheless a man thoughtful for others, craving little for himself — kind, true, just and of constant, if not warm affections? Was I not all this?"

"All this, and more," said Hester.

"And what am I now?" demanded he, looking into her face, and permitting the whole evil within him to be written on his features. "I have already told thee what I am — a fiend! Who made me so?"

"It was myself," cried Hester, shuddering. "It was I, not less than he. Why hast thou not avenged thyself on me?"

"I have left thee to the scarlet letter," replied Roger Chillingworth. "If that has not avenged me, I can do no more!"

He laid his finger on it with a smile.

"It has avenged thee," answered Hester Prynne.

"I judged no less," said the physician. "And now what wouldst thou with me touching this man?"

"I must reveal the secret," answered Hester, firmly. "He must discern thee in thy true character. What may be the result I know not. But this long debt of confidence, due from me to him, whose bane and ruin I have been, shall at length be paid. So far as concerns the overthrow or preservation of his fair fame and his earthly state, and perchance his life, he is in my hands. Nor do I—whom the scarlet letter has disciplined to truth, though it be the truth of red-hot iron entering into the soul—nor do I perceive such advantage in his living any longer a life of ghastly emptiness, that I shall stoop to implore thy mercy. Do with him as thou wilt! There is no good for him, no good for me, no good for thee. There is no good for little Pearl. There is no path to guide us out of this dismal maze."

"Woman, I could well-nigh pity thee," said Roger Chillingworth, unable to restrain a thrill of admiration too, for there was a quality almost majestic in the despair which she expressed. "Thou hadst great elements. Peradventure, hadst thou met earlier with a better love than mine, this evil had not been. I pity thee, for the good that has been wasted in thy nature."

"And I thee," answered Hester Prynne, "for the hatred that has transformed a wise and just man to a fiend! Wilt thou yet purge it out of thee, and be once more human? If not for his sake, then doubly for thine own! Forgive, and leave his further retribution to the Power that claims it! I said, but now, that there could be no good event for him, or thee, or me, who are here wandering together in this gloomy maze of evil, and stumbling at every step over the guilt wherewith we have strewn our path. It is not so! There might be good for thee, and thee alone, since thou hast been deeply wronged and hast it at thy will to pardon. Wilt thou give up that only privilege? Wilt thou reject that priceless benefit?"

"Peace, Hester—peace!" replied the old man, with gloomy sternness—"it is not granted me to pardon. I have no such power as thou tellest me of. My old faith, long forgotten, comes back to me, and explains all that we do, and all we suffer. By thy first step awry, thou didst plant the germ of evil; but since that moment it has all been a dark necessity. Ye that have wronged me are not sinful, save in a kind of typical illusion; neither am I fiend-like, who have snatched a fiend's office from his hands. It is our fate. Let the black flower blossom as it may! Now, go thy ways, and deal as thou wilt with yonder man."

He waved his hand, and betook himself again to his employment of gathering herbs.

XV.

HESTER AND PEARL

So Roger Chillingworth—a deformed old figure with a face that haunted men's memories longer than they liked—took leave of Hester Prynne, and went stooping away along the earth. He gathered here and there a herb, or grubbed up a root and put it into the basket on his arm. His gray beard almost touched the ground as he crept onward. Hester gazed after him a little while, looking with a half fantastic curiosity to see whether the tender grass of early spring would not be blighted beneath him and show the wavering track of his footsteps, sere and brown, across its cheerful verdure. She wondered what sort of herbs they were which the old man was so sedulous to gather. Would not the earth, quickened to an evil purpose by the sympathy of his eye, greet him with poisonous shrubs of species hitherto unknown, that would start up under his fingers? Or might it suffice him that every wholesome growth should be converted into something deleterious and malignant at his touch? Did the sun, which shone so brightly everywhere else, really fall upon him? Or was there, as it rather seemed, a circle of ominous shadow moving along with his deformity whichever way he turned himself? And whither was he now going? Would he not suddenly sink into the earth, leaving a barren and blasted spot, where, in due course of time, would be seen deadly nightshade, dogwood, henbane, and whatever else of vegetable wickedness the climate could produce, all flourishing with hideous luxuriance? Or would he spread bat's wings and flee away, looking so much the uglier the higher he rose towards heaven?

"Be it sin or no," said Hester Prynne, bitterly, as still she gazed after him, "I hate the man!"

She upbraided herself for the sentiment, but could not overcome or lessen it. Attempting to do so, she thought of those long-past days in a distant land, when he used to emerge at eventide from the seclusion of his study and sit down in the firelight of their home, and in the light of her nuptial smile. He needed to bask himself in that smile, he said, in order that the chill of so many lonely hours among his books might be taken off the scholar's heart. Such scenes had once appeared not otherwise than happy, but now, as viewed through the dismal medium of her subsequent life, they classed themselves among her ugliest remembrances. She marvelled how such scenes could have been! She marvelled how she could ever have been wrought upon to marry him! She deemed it her crime most to be repented of, that she had ever endured and reciprocated the lukewarm grasp of his hand, and had suffered the smile of her lips and eyes to mingle and melt into his own. And it seemed a fouler offence committed by Roger Chillingworth than any which had since been done him, that, in the time when her heart knew no better, he had persuaded her to fancy herself happy by his side.

"Yes, I hate him!" repeated Hester more bitterly than before. "He betrayed me! He has done me worse wrong than I did him!"

Let men tremble to win the hand of woman, unless they win along with it the utmost passion of her heart! Else it may be their miserable fortune, as it was Roger Chillingworth's, when some mightier touch than their own may have awakened all her sensibilities, to be reproached even for the calm content, the marble image of happiness, which they will have imposed upon her as the warm reality. But Hester ought long ago to have done with this injustice. What did it betoken? Had seven long years, under the torture of the scarlet letter, inflicted so much of misery and wrought out no repentance?

The emotion of that brief space, while she stood gazing after the crooked figure of old Roger Chillingworth, threw a dark light on Hester's state of mind, revealing much that she might not otherwise have acknowledged to herself.

He being gone, she summoned back her child.

"Pearl! Little Pearl! Where are you?"

Pearl, whose activity of spirit never flagged, had been at no loss for amusement while her mother talked with the old gatherer of herbs. At first, as already told, she had flirted fancifully with her own image in a pool of water, beckoning the phantom forth, and—as it declined to venture—seeking a passage for herself into its sphere of impalpable earth and unattainable sky. Soon finding, however, that either she or the image was unreal, she turned elsewhere for better pastime. She made little boats out of birch-bark, and freighted them with snailshells, and sent out more ventures on the mighty deep than any merchant in New England; but the larger part of them foundered near the shore. She seized a live horse-shoe by the tail, and made prize of several five-fingers, and laid out a jelly-fish to melt in the warm sun. Then she took up the white foam that streaked the line of the advancing tide, and threw it upon the breeze, scampering after it with winged footsteps to catch the great snowflakes ere they fell. Perceiving a flock of beach-birds that fed and fluttered along the shore, the naughty child picked up her apron full of pebbles, and, creeping from rock to rock after these small sea-fowl, displayed remarkable dexterity in pelting them. One little gray bird, with a white breast, Pearl was almost sure had been hit by a pebble, and fluttered away with a broken wing. But then the elf-child sighed, and gave up her sport, because it grieved her to have done harm to a little being that was as wild as the sea-breeze, or as wild as Pearl herself.

Her final employment was to gather seaweed of various kinds, and make herself a scarf or mantle, and a head-dress, and thus assume the aspect of a little mermaid. She inherited her mother's gift for devising drapery and costume. As the last touch to her mermaid's garb, Pearl took some eel-grass and imitated, as best she could, on her own bosom the decoration with which she was so familiar on her mother's. A letter — the letter A — but freshly green instead of scarlet. The child bent her chin upon her breast, and contemplated this device with strange interest, even as if the one only thing for which she had been sent into the world was to make out its hidden import.

"I wonder if mother will ask me what it means?" thought Pearl.

Just then she heard her mother's voice, and, flitting along as lightly as one of the little sea-birds, appeared before Hester Prynne dancing, laughing, and pointing her finger to the ornament upon her bosom.

"My little Pearl," said Hester, after a moment's silence, "the green letter, and on thy childish bosom, has no purport. But dost thou know, my child, what this letter means which thy mother is doomed to wear?"

"Yes, mother," said the child. "It is the great letter A. Thou hast taught me in the horn-book."

Hester looked steadily into her little face; but though there was that singular expression which she had so often remarked in her black eyes, she could not satisfy herself whether Pearl really attached any meaning to the symbol. She felt a morbid desire to ascertain the point.

"Dost thou know, child, wherefore thy mother wears this letter?"

"Truly do I!" answered Pearl, looking brightly into her mother's face. "It is for the same reason that the minister keeps his hand over his heart!"

"And what reason is that?" asked Hester, half smiling at the absurd incongruity of the child's observation; but on second thoughts turning pale.

"What has the letter to do with any heart save mine?"

"Nay, mother, I have told all I know," said Pearl, more seriously than she was wont to speak. "Ask yonder old man whom thou hast been talking with, — it may be he can tell. But in good earnest now, mother dear, what does this scarlet letter mean? — and why dost thou wear it on thy bosom? — and why does the minister keep his hand over his heart?"

She took her mother's hand in both her own, and gazed into her eyes with an earnestness that was seldom seen in her wild and capricious character. The thought occurred to Hester, that the child might really be seeking to approach her with childlike confidence, and doing what she could, and as intelligently as she knew how, to establish a meeting-point of sympathy. It showed Pearl in an unwonted aspect. Heretofore, the mother, while loving her child with the intensity of a sole affection, had schooled herself to hope for little other return than the waywardness of an April breeze, which spends its time in airy sport, and has its gusts of inexplicable passion, and is petulant in its best of moods, and chills oftener than caresses you, when you take it to your bosom; in requital of which misdemeanours it will sometimes, of its own vague purpose, kiss your cheek with a kind of doubtful tenderness, and play gently with your hair, and then be gone about its other idle business, leaving a dreamy pleasure at your heart. And this, moreover, was a mother's estimate of the child's disposition. Any other observer might have seen few but unamiable traits, and have given them a far darker colouring. But now the idea came strongly into Hester's mind, that Pearl, with her remarkable precocity and acuteness, might already have approached the age when she could have been made a friend, and intrusted with as much of her mother's sorrows as could be imparted, without irreverence either to the parent or the child. In the little chaos of Pearl's character there might be seen emerging and could have been from the very first — the steadfast principles of an unflinching courage — an uncontrollable will — sturdy pride, which might be disciplined into self-respect — and a bitter scorn of many things which, when examined, might be found to have the taint of falsehood in them. She possessed affections, too, though hitherto acrid and disagreeable, as are the richest flavours of unripe fruit. With all these sterling attributes, thought Hester, the evil which she inherited from her mother must be great indeed, if a noble woman do not grow out of this elfish child.

Pearl's inevitable tendency to hover about the enigma of the scarlet letter seemed an innate quality of her being. From the earliest epoch of her conscious life, she had entered upon this as her appointed mission. Hester had often fancied that Providence had a design of justice and retribution, in endowing the child with this marked propensity; but never, until now, had she bethought herself to ask, whether, linked with that design, there might not likewise be a purpose of mercy and beneficence. If little Pearl were entertained with faith and trust, as a spirit messenger no less than an earthly child, might it not be her errand to soothe away the sorrow that lay cold in her mother's heart, and converted it into a tomb? — and to help her to overcome the passion, once so wild, and even yet neither dead nor asleep, but only imprisoned within the same tomb-like heart?

Such were some of the thoughts that now stirred in Hester's mind, with as much vivacity of impression as if they had actually been whispered into her ear. And there was little Pearl, all this while, holding her mother's hand in both her own, and turning her face upward, while she put these searching questions, once and again, and still a third time.

"What does the letter mean, mother? and why dost thou wear it? and why does the minister keep his hand over his heart?"

"What shall I say?" thought Hester to herself. "No! if this be the price of the child's sympathy, I cannot pay it."

Then she spoke aloud—

"Silly Pearl," said she, "what questions are these? There are many things in this world that a child must not ask about. What know I of the minister's heart? And as for the scarlet letter, I wear it for the sake of its gold thread."

In all the seven bygone years, Hester Prynne had never before been false to the symbol on her bosom. It may be that it was the talisman of a stern and severe, but yet a guardian spirit, who now forsook her; as recognising that, in spite of his strict watch over her heart, some new evil had crept into it, or some old one had never been expelled. As for little Pearl, the earnestness soon passed out of her face.

But the child did not see fit to let the matter drop. Two or three times, as her mother and she went homeward, and as often at supper-time, and while Hester was putting her to bed, and once after she seemed to be fairly asleep, Pearl looked up, with mischief gleaming in her black eyes.

"Mother," said she, "what does the scarlet letter mean?"

And the next morning, the first indication the child gave of being awake was by popping up her head from the pillow, and making that other enquiry, which she had so unaccountably connected with her investigations about the scarlet letter—

"Mother!—Mother!—Why does the minister keep his hand over his heart?"

"Hold thy tongue, naughty child!" answered her mother, with an asperity that she had never permitted to herself before. "Do not tease me; else I shall put thee into the dark closet!"

XVI.

A FOREST WALK

Hester Prynne remained constant in her resolve to make known to Mr. Dimmesdale, at whatever risk of present pain or ulterior consequences, the true character of the man who had crept into his intimacy. For several days, however, she vainly sought an opportunity of addressing him in some of the meditative walks which she knew him to be in the habit of taking along the shores of the Peninsula, or on the wooded hills of the neighbouring country. There would have been no scandal, indeed, nor peril to the holy whiteness of the clergyman's good fame, had she visited him in his own study, where many a penitent, ere now, had confessed sins of perhaps as deep a dye as the one betokened by the scarlet letter. But, partly that she dreaded the secret or undisguised interference of old Roger Chillingworth, and partly that her conscious heart imparted suspicion where none could have been felt, and partly that both the minister and she would need the whole wide world to breathe in, while they talked together—for all these reasons Hester never thought of meeting him in any narrower privacy than beneath the open sky.

At last, while attending a sick chamber, whither the Rev. Mr. Dimmesdale had been summoned to make a prayer, she learnt that he had gone, the day before, to visit the Apostle Eliot, among his Indian converts. He would probably return by a certain hour in the afternoon of the morrow. Betimes, therefore, the next day, Hester took little Pearl—who was necessarily the companion of all her mother's expeditions, however inconvenient her presence—and set forth.

The road, after the two wayfarers had crossed from the Peninsula to the mainland, was no other than a footpath. It straggled onward into the mystery of the primeval forest. This hemmed it in so narrowly, and stood so black and dense on either side, and disclosed such imperfect glimpses of the sky above, that, to Hester's mind, it imaged not amiss the moral wilderness in which she had so long been wandering. The day was chill and sombre. Overhead was a gray expanse of cloud, slightly stirred, however, by a breeze; so that a gleam of flickering sunshine might now and then be seen at its solitary play along the path. This flitting cheerfulness was always at the further extremity of some long vista through the forest. The sportive sunlight—feebly sportive, at best, in the predominant pensiveness of the day and scene—withdrew itself as they came nigh, and left the spots where it had danced the drearier, because they had hoped to find them bright.

"Mother," said little Pearl, "the sunshine does not love you. It runs away and hides itself, because it is afraid of something on your bosom. Now, see! There it is, playing a good way off. Stand you here, and let me run and catch it. I am but a child. It will not flee from me—for I wear nothing on my bosom yet!"

"Nor ever will, my child, I hope," said Hester.

"And why not, mother?" asked Pearl, stopping short, just at the beginning of her race. "Will not it come of its own accord when I am a woman grown?"

"Run away, child," answered her mother, "and catch the sunshine. It will soon be gone."

Pearl set forth at a great pace, and as Hester smiled to perceive, did actually catch the sunshine, and stood laughing in the midst of it, all brightened by its splendour, and scintillating with the vivacity excited by rapid motion. The light lingered about the lonely child, as if glad of such a playmate, until her mother had drawn almost nigh enough to step into the magic circle too.

"It will go now," said Pearl, shaking her head.

"See!" answered Hester, smiling; "now I can stretch out my hand and grasp some of it."

As she attempted to do so, the sunshine vanished; or, to judge from the bright expression that was dancing on Pearl's features, her mother could have fancied that the child had absorbed it into herself, and would give it forth again, with a gleam about her path, as they should plunge into some gloomier shade. There was no other attribute that so much impressed her with a sense of new and untransmitted vigour in Pearl's nature, as this never failing vivacity of spirits: she had not the disease of sadness, which almost all children, in these latter days, inherit, with the scrofula, from the troubles of their ancestors. Perhaps this, too, was a disease, and but the reflex of the wild energy with which Hester had fought against her sorrows before Pearl's birth. It was certainly a doubtful charm, imparting a hard, metallic lustre to the child's character. She wanted—what some people want throughout life—a grief that should deeply touch her, and thus humanise and make her capable of sympathy. But there was time enough yet for little Pearl.

"Come, my child!" said Hester, looking about her from the

spot where Pearl had stood still in the sunshine—"we will sit down a little way within the wood, and rest ourselves."

"I am not aweary, mother," replied the little girl. "But you may sit down, if you will tell me a story meanwhile."

"A story, child!" said Hester. "And about what?"

"Oh, a story about the Black Man," answered Pearl, taking hold of her mother's gown, and looking up, half earnestly, half mischievously, into her face.

"How he haunts this forest, and carries a book with him a big, heavy book, with iron clasps; and how this ugly Black Man offers his book and an iron pen to everybody that meets him here among the trees; and they are to write their names with their own blood; and then he sets his mark on their bosoms. Didst thou ever meet the Black Man, mother?"

"And who told you this story, Pearl," asked her mother, recognising a common superstition of the period.

"It was the old dame in the chimney corner, at the house where you watched last night," said the child. "But she fancied me asleep while she was talking of it. She said that a thousand and a thousand people had met him here, and had written in his book, and have his mark on them. And that ugly tempered lady, old Mistress Hibbins, was one. And, mother, the old dame said that this scarlet letter was the Black Man's mark on thee, and that it glows like a red flame when thou meetest him at midnight, here in the dark wood. Is it true, mother? And dost thou go to meet him in the nighttime?"

"Didst thou ever awake and find thy mother gone?" asked Hester.

"Not that I remember," said the child. "If thou fearest to leave me in our cottage, thou mightest take me along with thee. I would very gladly go! But, mother, tell me now! Is there such a Black Man? And didst thou ever meet him? And is this his mark?"

"Wilt thou let me be at peace, if I once tell thee?" asked her mother.

"Yes, if thou tellest me all," answered Pearl.

"Once in my life I met the Black Man!" said her mother.

"This scarlet letter is his mark!"

Thus conversing, they entered sufficiently deep into the wood to secure themselves from the observation of any casual passenger along the forest track. Here they sat down on a luxuriant heap of moss; which at some epoch of the preceding century, had been a gigantic pine, with its roots and trunk in the darksome shade, and its head aloft in the upper atmosphere. It was a little dell where they had seated themselves, with a leaf-strewn bank rising gently on either side, and a brook flowing through the midst, over a bed of fallen and drowned leaves. The trees impending over it had flung down great branches from time to time, which choked up the current, and compelled it to form eddies and black depths at some points; while, in its swifter and livelier passages there appeared a channel-way of pebbles, and brown, sparkling sand. Letting the eyes follow along the course of the stream, they could catch the reflected light from its water, at some short distance within the forest, but soon lost all traces of it amid the bewilderment of tree-trunks and underbrush, and here and there a huge rock covered over with gray lichens. All these giant trees and boulders of granite seemed intent on making a mystery of the course of this small brook; fearing, perhaps, that, with its never-ceasing loquacity, it should whisper tales out of the heart of the old forest whence it flowed, or mirror its revelations on the smooth surface of a pool. Continually, indeed, as it stole onward, the streamlet kept up a babble, kind, quiet, soothing, but melancholy, like the voice of a young child that was spending its infancy without playfulness, and knew not how to be merry among sad acquaintance and events of sombre hue.

"Oh, brook! Oh, foolish and tiresome little brook!" cried Pearl, after listening awhile to its talk, "Why art thou so sad? Pluck up a spirit, and do not be all the time sighing and murmuring!"

But the brook, in the course of its little lifetime among the forest trees, had gone through so solemn an experience that it could not help talking about it, and seemed to have nothing else to say. Pearl resembled the brook, inasmuch as the current of her life gushed from a well-spring as mysterious, and had flowed through scenes shadowed as heavily with gloom. But, unlike the little stream, she danced and sparkled, and prattled airily along her course.

"What does this sad little brook say, mother?" inquired she.

"If thou hadst a sorrow of thine own, the brook might tell

thee of it," answered her mother, "even as it is telling me of mine. But now, Pearl, I hear a footstep along the path, and the noise of one putting aside the branches. I would have thee betake thyself to play, and leave me to speak with him that comes yonder."

"Is it the Black Man?" asked Pearl.

"Wilt thou go and play, child?" repeated her mother, "But do not stray far into the wood. And take heed that thou come at my first call."

"Yes, mother," answered Pearl, "But if it be the Black Man, wilt thou not let me stay a moment, and look at him, with his big book under his arm?"

"Go, silly child!" said her mother impatiently. "It is no Black Man! Thou canst see him now, through the trees. It is the minister!"

"And so it is!" said the child. "And, mother, he has his hand over his heart! Is it because, when the minister wrote his name in the book, the Black Man set his mark in that place? But why does he not wear it outside his bosom, as thou dost, mother?"

"Go now, child, and thou shalt tease me as thou wilt another time," cried Hester Prynne. "But do not stray far. Keep where thou canst hear the babble of the brook."

The child went singing away, following up the current of the brook, and striving to mingle a more lightsome cadence with its melancholy voice. But the little stream would not be comforted, and still kept telling its unintelligible secret of some very mournful mystery that had happened—or making a prophetic lamentation about something that was yet to happen—within the verge of the dismal forest. So Pearl, who had enough of shadow in her own little life, chose to break off all acquaintance with this repining brook. She set herself, therefore, to gathering violets and wood-anemones, and some scarlet columbines that she found growing in the crevice of a high rock.

When her elf-child had departed, Hester Prynne made a step or two towards the track that led through the forest, but still remained under the deep shadow of the trees. She beheld the minister advancing along the path entirely alone, and leaning on a staff which he had cut by the wayside. He looked haggard and feeble, and betrayed a nerveless despondency in his air, which had never so remarkably characterised him in his walks about the settlement, nor in any other situation where he deemed himself liable to notice. Here it was wofully visible, in this intense seclusion of the forest, which of itself would have been a heavy trial to the spirits. There was a listlessness in his gait, as if he saw no reason for taking one step further, nor felt any desire to do so, but would have been glad, could he be glad of anything, to fling himself down at the root of the nearest tree, and lie there passive for evermore. The leaves might bestrew him, and the soil gradually accumulate and form a little hillock over his frame, no matter whether there were life in it or no. Death was too definite an object to be wished for or avoided.

To Hester's eye, the Reverend Mr. Dimmesdale exhibited no symptom of positive and vivacious suffering, except that, as little Pearl had remarked, he kept his hand over his heart.

XVII.

THE PASTOR AND HIS PARISHIONER

Slowly as the minister walked, he had almost gone by before Hester Prynne could gather voice enough to attract his observation. At length she succeeded.

"Arthur Dimmesdale!" she said, faintly at first, then louder, but hoarsely — "Arthur Dimmesdale!"

"Who speaks?" answered the minister. Gathering himself quickly up, he stood more erect, like a man taken by surprise in a mood to which he was reluctant to have witnesses. Throwing his eyes anxiously in the direction of the voice, he indistinctly beheld a form under the trees, clad in garments so sombre, and so little relieved from the gray twilight into which the clouded sky and the heavy foliage had darkened the noontide, that he knew not whether it were a woman or a shadow. It may be that his pathway through life was haunted thus by a spectre that had stolen out from among his thoughts.

He made a step nigher, and discovered the scarlet letter.

"Hester! Hester Prynne!", said he; "is it thou? Art thou in life?"

"Even so." she answered. "In such life as has been mine these seven years past! And thou, Arthur Dimmesdale, dost thou yet live?"

It was no wonder that they thus questioned one another's actual and bodily existence, and even doubted of their own. So strangely did they meet in the dim wood that it was like the first encounter in the world beyond the grave of two spirits who had been intimately connected in their former life, but now stood coldly shuddering in mutual dread, as not yet familiar with their state, nor wonted to the companionship of disembodied beings. Each a ghost, and awe-stricken at the other ghost. They were awe-stricken likewise at themselves, because the crisis flung back to them their consciousness, and revealed to each heart its history and experience, as life never does, except at such breathless epochs. The soul beheld its features in the mirror of the passing moment. It was with fear, and tremulously, and, as it were, by a slow, reluctant necessity, that Arthur Dimmesdale put forth his hand, chill as death, and touched the chill hand of Hester Prynne. The grasp, cold as it was, took away what was dreariest in the interview. They now felt themselves, at least, inhabitants of the same sphere.

Without a word more spoken—neither he nor she assuming the guidance, but with an unexpressed consent—they glided back into the shadow of the woods whence Hester had emerged, and sat down on the heap of moss where she and Pearl had before been sitting. When they found voice to speak, it was at first only to utter remarks and inquiries such as any two acquaintances might have made, about the gloomy sky, the threatening storm, and, next, the health of each. Thus they went onward, not boldly, but step by step, into the themes that were brooding deepest in their hearts. So long estranged by fate and circumstances, they needed something slight and casual to run before and throw open the doors of intercourse, so that their real thoughts might be led across the threshold.

After awhile, the minister fixed his eyes on Hester Prynne's.

"Hester," said he, "hast thou found peace?"

She smiled drearily, looking down upon her bosom.

"Hast thou?" she asked.

"None—nothing but despair!" he answered. "What else could I look for, being what I am, and leading such a life as mine? Were I an atheist—a man devoid of conscience—a wretch with coarse and brutal instincts—I might have found peace long ere now. Nay, I never should have lost it. But, as matters stand with my soul, whatever of good capacity there originally was in me, all of God's gifts that were the choicest have become the ministers of spiritual torment. Hester, I am most miserable!"

"The people reverence thee," said Hester. "And surely thou workest good among them! Doth this bring thee no comfort?"

"More misery, Hester!—Only the more misery!" answered the clergyman with a bitter smile. "As concerns the good which I may appear to do, I have no faith in it. It must needs be a delusion. What can a ruined soul like mine effect towards the redemption of other souls?—or a polluted soul towards their purification? And as for the people's reverence, would that it were turned to scorn and hatred! Canst thou deem it, Hester, a consolation that I must stand up in my pulpit, and meet so many eyes turned upward to my face, as if the light of heaven were beaming from it!—must see my flock hungry for the truth, and listening to my words as if a tongue of Pentecost were speaking! — and then look inward, and discern the black reality of what they idolise? I have laughed, in bitterness and agony of heart, at the contrast between what I seem and what I am! And Satan laughs at it!"

"You wrong yourself in this," said Hester gently. "You have deeply and sorely repented. Your sin is left behind you in the days long past. Your present life is not less holy, in very truth, than it seems in people's eyes. Is there no reality in the penitence thus sealed and witnessed by good works? And wherefore should it not bring you peace?"

"No, Hester — no!" replied the clergyman. "There is no substance in it! It is cold and dead, and can do nothing for me! Of penance, I have had enough! Of penitence, there has been none! Else, I should long ago have thrown off these garments of mock holiness, and have shown myself to mankind as they will see me at the judgment-seat. Happy are you, Hester, that wear the scarlet letter openly upon your bosom! Mine burns in secret! Thou little knowest what a relief it is, after the torment of a seven years' cheat, to look into an eye that recognises me for what I am! Had I one friend — or were it my worst enemy! — to whom, when sickened with the praises of all other men, I could daily betake myself, and be known as the vilest of all sinners, methinks my soul might keep itself alive thereby. Even thus much of truth would save me! But now, it is all falsehood! — all emptiness! — all death!"

Hester Prynne looked into his face, but hesitated to speak. Yet, uttering his long-restrained emotions so vehemently as he did, his words here offered her the very point of circumstances in which to interpose what she came to say. She conquered her fears, and spoke:

"Such a friend as thou hast even now wished for," said she, "with whom to weep over thy sin, thou hast in me, the partner of it!" Again she hesitated, but brought out the words with an effort. — "Thou hast long had such an enemy, and dwellest with him, under the same roof!"

The minister started to his feet, gasping for breath, and clutching at his heart, as if he would have torn it out of his bosom.

"Ha! What sayest thou?" cried he. "An enemy! And under mine own roof! What mean you?"

Hester Prynne was now fully sensible of the deep injury for

which she was responsible to this unhappy man, in permitting him to lie for so many years, or, indeed, for a single moment, at the mercy of one whose purposes could not be other than malevolent. The very contiguity of his enemy, beneath whatever mask the latter might conceal himself, was enough to disturb the magnetic sphere of a being so sensitive as Arthur Dimmesdale. There had been a period when Hester was less alive to this consideration; or, perhaps, in the misanthropy of her own trouble, she left the minister to bear what she might picture to herself as a more tolerable doom. But of late, since the night of his vigil, all her sympathies towards him had been both softened and invigorated. She now read his heart more accurately. She doubted not that the continual presence of Roger Chillingworth—the secret poison of his malignity, infecting all the air about him—and his authorised interference, as a physician, with the minister's physical and spiritual infirmities—that these bad opportunities had been turned to a cruel purpose. By means of them, the sufferer's conscience had been kept in an irritated state, the tendency of which was, not to cure by wholesome pain, but to disorganize and corrupt his spiritual being. Its result, on earth, could hardly fail to be insanity, and hereafter, that eternal alienation from the Good and True, of which madness is perhaps the earthly type.

Such was the ruin to which she had brought the man, once—nay, why should we not speak it?—still so passionately loved! Hester felt that the sacrifice of the clergyman's good name, and death itself, as she had already told Roger Chillingworth, would have been infinitely preferable to the alternative which she had taken upon herself to choose. And now, rather than have had this grievous wrong to confess, she would gladly have laid down on the forest leaves, and died there, at Arthur Dimmesdale's feet.

"Oh, Arthur!" cried she, "forgive me! In all things else, I have striven to be true! Truth was the one virtue which I might have held fast, and did hold fast, through all extremity; save when thy good—thy life—thy fame—were put in question! Then I consented to a deception. But a lie is never good, even though death threaten on the other side! Dost thou not see what I would say? That old man!—the physician!—he whom they call Roger Chillingworth!—he was my husband!"

The minister looked at her for an instant, with all that violence of passion, which—intermixed in more shapes than one with his higher, purer, softer qualities—was, in fact, the portion of him which the devil claimed, and through which he sought to win the rest. Never was there a blacker or a fiercer frown than Hester now encountered. For the brief space that it lasted, it was a dark transfiguration. But his character had been so much enfeebled by suffering, that even its lower energies were incapable of more than a temporary struggle. He sank down on the ground, and buried his face in his hands.

"I might have known it," murmured he—"I did know it! Was not the secret told me, in the natural recoil of my heart at the first sight of him, and as often as I have seen him since? Why did I not understand? Oh, Hester Prynne, thou little, little knowest all the horror of this thing! And the shame!—the indelicacy!—the horrible ugliness of this exposure of a sick and guilty heart to the very eye that would gloat over it! Woman, woman, thou art accountable for this!—I cannot forgive thee!"

"Thou shalt forgive me!" cried Hester, flinging herself on the fallen leaves beside him. "Let God punish! Thou shalt forgive!"

With sudden and desperate tenderness she threw her arms around him, and pressed his head against her bosom, little caring though his cheek rested on the scarlet letter. He would have released himself, but strove in vain to do so. Hester would not set him free, lest he should look her sternly in the face. All the world had frowned on her—for seven long years had it frowned upon this lonely woman—and still she bore it all, nor ever once turned away her firm, sad eyes. Heaven, likewise, had frowned upon her, and she had not died. But the frown of this pale, weak, sinful, and sorrow-stricken man was what Hester could not bear, and live!

"Wilt thou yet forgive me?" she repeated, over and over again. "Wilt thou not frown? Wilt thou forgive?"

"I do forgive you, Hester," replied the minister at length, with a deep utterance, out of an abyss of sadness, but no anger. "I freely forgive you now. May God forgive us both. We are not, Hester, the worst sinners in the world. There is one worse than even the polluted priest! That old man's revenge has been blacker than my sin. He has violated, in cold blood, the sanctity of a human heart. Thou and I, Hester, never did so!"

"Never, never!" whispered she. "What we did had a consecration of its own. We felt it so! We said so to each other. Hast thou forgotten it?"

"Hush, Hester!" said Arthur Dimmesdale, rising from the ground. "No; I have not forgotten!"

They sat down again, side by side, and hand clasped in hand, on the mossy trunk of the fallen tree. Life had never brought them a gloomier hour; it was the point whither their pathway had so long been tending, and darkening ever, as it stole along—and yet it unclosed a charm that made them linger upon it, and claim another, and another, and, after all, another moment. The forest was obscure around them, and creaked with a blast that was passing through it. The boughs were tossing heavily above their heads; while one solemn old tree groaned dolefully to another, as if telling the sad story of the pair that sat beneath, or constrained to forbode evil to come.

And yet they lingered. How dreary looked the forest-track that led backward to the settlement, where Hester Prynne must take up again the burden of her ignominy and the minister the hollow mockery of his good name! So they lingered an instant longer. No golden light had ever been so precious as the gloom of this dark forest. Here seen only by his eyes, the scarlet letter need not burn into the bosom of the fallen woman! Here seen only by her eyes, Arthur Dimmesdale, false to God and man, might be, for one moment true!

He started at a thought that suddenly occurred to him.

"Hester!" cried he, "here is a new horror! Roger Chillingworth knows your purpose to reveal his true character. Will he continue, then, to keep our secret? What will now be the course of his revenge?"

"There is a strange secrecy in his nature," replied Hester, thoughtfully; "and it has grown upon him by the hidden practices of his revenge. I deem it not likely that he will betray the secret. He will doubtless seek other means of satiating his dark passion."

"And I!—how am I to live longer, breathing the same air with this deadly enemy?" exclaimed Arthur Dimmesdale, shrinking within himself, and pressing his hand nervously against his heart—a gesture that had grown involuntary with him. "Think for me, Hester! Thou art strong. Resolve for me!"

"Thou must dwell no longer with this man," said Hester, slowly and firmly. "Thy heart must be no longer under his evil eye!"

"It were far worse than death!" replied the minister. "But how to avoid it? What choice remains to me? Shall I lie down again on these withered leaves, where I cast myself when thou didst tell me what he was? Must I sink down there, and die at once?"

"Alas! what a ruin has befallen thee!" said Hester, with the tears gushing into her eyes. "Wilt thou die for very weakness? There is no other cause!"

"The judgment of God is on me," answered the conscience-stricken priest. "It is too mighty for me to struggle with!"

"Heaven would show mercy," rejoined Hester, "hadst thou but the strength to take advantage of it."

"Be thou strong for me!" answered he. "Advise me what to do."

"Is the world, then, so narrow?" exclaimed Hester Prynne, fixing her deep eyes on the minister's, and instinctively exercising a magnetic power over a spirit so shattered and subdued that it could hardly hold itself erect. "Doth the universe lie within the compass of yonder town, which only a little time ago was but a leaf-strewn desert, as lonely as this around us? Whither leads yonder forest-track? Backward to the settlement, thou sayest! Yes; but, onward, too! Deeper it goes, and deeper into the wilderness, less plainly to be seen at every step; until some few miles hence the yellow leaves will show no vestige of the white man's tread. There thou art free! So brief a journey would bring thee from a world where thou hast been most wretched, to one where thou mayest still be happy! Is there not shade enough in all this boundless forest to hide thy heart from the gaze of Roger Chillingworth?"

"Yes, Hester; but only under the fallen leaves!" replied the minister, with a sad smile.

"Then there is the broad pathway of the sea!" continued Hester. "It brought thee hither. If thou so choose, it will bear thee back again. In our native land, whether in some remote rural village, or in vast London—or, surely, in Germany, in France, in pleasant Italy—thou wouldst be beyond his power and knowledge! And what hast thou to do with all these iron men, and their opinions? They have kept thy better part in bondage too long already!"

"It cannot be!" answered the minister, listening as if he were called upon to realise a dream. "I am powerless to go. Wretched and sinful as I am, I have had no other thought than to drag on my earthly existence in the sphere where Providence hath placed me. Lost as my own soul is, I would still do what I may for other human souls! I dare not quit my post, though an unfaithful sentinel, whose sure reward is death and dishonour, when his dreary watch shall come to an end!"

"Thou art crushed under this seven years' weight of misery," replied Hester, fervently resolved to buoy him up with her own energy. "But thou shalt leave it all behind thee! It shall not cumber thy steps, as thou treadest along the forest-path: neither shalt thou freight the ship with it, if thou prefer to cross the sea. Leave this wreck and ruin here where it hath happened. Meddle no more with it! Begin all anew! Hast thou exhausted possibility in the failure of this one trial? Not so! The future is yet full of trial and success. There is happiness to be enjoyed! There is good to be done! Exchange this false life of thine for a true one. Be, if thy spirit summon thee to such a mission, the teacher and apostle of the red men. Or, as is more thy nature, be a scholar and a sage among the wisest and the most renowned of the cultivated world. Preach! Write! Act! Do anything, save to lie down and die! Give up this name of Arthur Dimmesdale, and make thyself another, and a high one, such as thou canst wear without fear or shame. Why shouldst thou tarry so much as one other day in the torments that have so gnawed into thy life? that have made thee feeble to will and to do? that will leave thee powerless even to repent? Up, and away!"

"Oh, Hester!" cried Arthur Dimmesdale, in whose eyes a fitful light, kindled by her enthusiasm, flashed up and died away, "thou tellest of running a race to a man whose knees are tottering beneath him! I must die here! There is not the strength or courage left me to venture into the wide, strange, difficult world alone!"

It was the last expression of the despondency of a broken spirit. He lacked energy to grasp the better fortune that seemed within his reach.

He repeated the word — "Alone, Hester!"

"Thou shall not go alone!" answered she, in a deep whisper. Then, all was spoken!

XVIII.

A FLOOD OF SUNSHINE

Arthur Dimmesdale gazed into Hester's face with a look in which hope and joy shone out, indeed, but with fear betwixt them, and a kind of horror at her boldness, who had spoken what he vaguely hinted at, but dared not speak.

But Hester Prynne, with a mind of native courage and activity, and for so long a period not merely estranged, but outlawed from society, had habituated herself to such latitude of speculation as was altogether foreign to the clergyman. She had wandered, without rule or guidance, in a moral wilderness, as vast, as intricate, and shadowy as the untamed forest, amid the gloom of which they were now holding a colloquy that was to decide their fate. Her intellect and heart had their home, as it were, in desert places, where she roamed as freely as the wild Indian in his woods. For years past she had looked from this estranged point of view at human institutions, and whatever priests or legislators had established; criticising all with hardly more reverence than the Indian would feel for the clerical band, the judicial robe, the pillory, the gallows, the fireside, or the church. The tendency of her fate and fortunes had been to set her free. The scarlet letter was her passport into regions where other women dared not tread. Shame, Despair, Solitude! These had been her teachers—stern and wild ones—and they had made her strong, but taught her much amiss.

The minister, on the other hand, had never gone through an experience calculated to lead him beyond the scope of generally received laws; although, in a single instance, he had so fearfully transgressed one of the most sacred of them. But this had been a sin of passion, not of principle, nor even purpose. Since that wretched epoch, he had watched with morbid zeal and minuteness, not his acts—for those it was easy to arrange—but each breath of emotion, and his every thought. At the head of the social system, as the clergymen of that day stood, he was only the more trammelled by its regulations, its principles, and even its prejudices. As a priest, the framework of his order inevitably hemmed him in. As a man who had once sinned, but who kept his conscience all alive and painfully sensitive by the fretting of an unhealed wound, he might have been supposed safer within the line of virtue than if he had never sinned at all.

Thus we seem to see that, as regarded Hester Prynne, the whole seven years of outlaw and ignominy had been little other than a preparation for this very hour. But Arthur Dimmesdale! Were such a man once more to fall, what plea could be urged in extenuation of his crime? None; unless it avail him somewhat that he was broken down by long and exquisite suffering; that his mind was darkened and confused by the very remorse which harrowed it; that, between fleeing as an avowed criminal, and remaining as a hypocrite, conscience might find it hard to strike the balance; that it was human to avoid the peril of death and infamy, and the inscrutable machinations of an enemy; that, finally, to this poor pilgrim, on his dreary and desert path, faint, sick, miserable, there appeared a glimpse of human affection and sympathy, a new life, and a true one, in exchange for the heavy doom which he was now expiating. And be the stern and sad truth spoken, that the breach which guilt has once made into the human soul is never, in this mortal state, repaired. It may be watched and guarded, so that the enemy shall not force his way again into the citadel, and might even in his subsequent assaults, select some other avenue, in preference to that where he had formerly succeeded. But there is still the ruined wall, and near it the stealthy tread of the foe that would win over again his unforgotten triumph.

The struggle, if there were one, need not be described. Let it suffice that the clergyman resolved to flee, and not alone.

"If in all these past seven years," thought he, "I could recall one instant of peace or hope, I would yet endure, for the sake of that earnest of Heaven's mercy. But now—since I am irrevocably doomed—wherefore should I not snatch the solace allowed to the condemned culprit before his execution? Or, if this be the path to a better life, as Hester would persuade me, I surely give up no fairer prospect by pursuing it! Neither can I any longer live without her companionship; so powerful is she to sustain—so tender to soothe! O Thou to whom I dare not lift mine eyes, wilt Thou yet pardon me?"

"Thou wilt go!" said Hester calmly, as he met her glance.

The decision once made, a glow of strange enjoyment threw its flickering brightness over the trouble of his breast. It was the exhilarating effect—upon a prisoner just escaped from the dungeon of his own heart—of breathing the wild, free atmosphere of an unredeemed, unchristianised, lawless region. His spirit rose, as it were, with a bound, and attained a nearer prospect of the sky, than throughout all the misery which had kept him grovelling on the earth. Of a deeply religious temperament, there was inevitably a tinge of the devotional in his mood.

"Do I feel joy again?" cried he, wondering at himself. "Methought the germ of it was dead in me! Oh, Hester, thou art my better angel! I seem to have flung myself—sick, sin-stained, and sorrow-blackened—down upon these forest leaves, and to have risen up all made anew, and with new powers to glorify Him that hath been merciful! This is already the better life! Why did we not find it sooner?"

"Let us not look back," answered Hester Prynne. "The past is gone! Wherefore should we linger upon it now? See! With this symbol I undo it all, and make it as if it had never been!"

So speaking, she undid the clasp that fastened the scarlet letter, and, taking it from her bosom, threw it to a distance among the withered leaves. The mystic token alighted on the hither verge of the stream. With a hand's-breadth further flight, it would have fallen into the water, and have given the little brook another woe to carry onward, besides the unintelligible tale which it still kept murmuring about. But there lay the embroidered letter, glittering like a lost jewel, which some ill-fated wanderer might pick up, and thenceforth be haunted by strange phantoms of guilt, sinkings of the heart, and unaccountable misfortune.

The stigma gone, Hester heaved a long, deep sigh, in which the burden of shame and anguish departed from her spirit. O exquisite relief! She had not known the weight until she felt the freedom! By another impulse, she took off the formal cap that confined her hair, and down it fell upon her shoulders, dark and rich, with at once a shadow and a light in its abundance, and imparting the charm of softness to her features. There played around her mouth, and beamed out of her eyes, a radiant and tender smile, that seemed gushing from the very heart of womanhood. A crimson flush was glowing on her cheek, that had been long so pale. Her sex, her youth, and the whole richness of her beauty, came back from what men call the irrevocable past, and clustered themselves with her maiden hope, and a happiness before unknown, within the magic circle of this hour. And, as if the gloom of the earth and sky had been but the effluence of these two mortal hearts, it vanished with their sorrow. All at once, as with a sudden smile of heaven, forth burst the sunshine, pouring a very flood into the obscure forest, gladdening each green leaf, transmuting the yellow fallen ones to gold, and gleaming adown the gray trunks of the solemn trees. The objects that had made a shadow hitherto, embodied the brightness now. The course of the little brook might be traced by its merry gleam afar into the wood's heart of mystery, which had become a mystery of joy.

Such was the sympathy of Nature—that wild, heathen Nature of the forest, never subjugated by human law, nor illumined by higher truth—with the bliss of these two spirits! Love, whether newly-born, or aroused from a death-like slumber, must always create a sunshine, filling the heart so full of radiance, that it overflows upon the outward world. Had the forest still kept its gloom, it would have been bright in Hester's eyes, and bright in Arthur Dimmesdale's!

Hester looked at him with a thrill of another joy.

"Thou must know Pearl!" said she. "Our little Pearl! Thou hast seen her—yes, I know it!—but thou wilt see her now with other eyes. She is a strange child! I hardly comprehend her! But thou wilt love her dearly, as I do, and wilt advise me how to deal with her!"

"Dost thou think the child will be glad to know me?" asked the minister, somewhat uneasily. "I have long shrunk from children, because they often show a distrust—a backwardness to be familiar with me. I have even been afraid of little Pearl!"

"Ah, that was sad!" answered the mother. "But she will love thee dearly, and thou her. She is not far off. I will call her. Pearl! Pearl!"

"I see the child," observed the minister. "Yonder she is, standing in a streak of sunshine, a good way off, on the other side of the brook. So thou thinkest the child will love me?"

Hester smiled, and again called to Pearl, who was visible at some distance, as the minister had described her, like a bright-apparelled vision in a sunbeam, which fell down upon her through an arch of boughs. The ray quivered to and fro, making her figure dim or distinct—now like a real child, now like a child's spirit—as the splendour went and came again. She heard her mother's voice, and approached slowly through the forest.

Pearl had not found the hour pass wearisomely while her mother sat talking with the clergyman. The great black forest—stern as it showed itself to those who brought the guilt and troubles of the world into its bosom—became the playmate of the lonely infant, as well as it knew how. Sombre as it was, it put on the kindest of its moods to welcome her. It offered her the partridge-berries, the growth of the preceding autumn, but ripening only in the spring, and now red as drops of blood upon the withered leaves. These Pearl gathered, and was pleased with their wild flavour. The small denizens of the wilderness hardly took pains to move out of her path. A partridge, indeed, with a brood of ten behind her, ran forward threateningly, but soon repented of her fierceness, and clucked to her young ones not to be afraid. A pigeon, alone on a low branch, allowed Pearl to come beneath, and uttered a sound as much of greeting as alarm. A squirrel, from the lofty depths of his domestic tree, chattered either in anger or merriment—for the squirrel is such a choleric and humorous little personage, that it is hard to distinguish between his moods—so he chattered at the child, and flung down a nut upon her head. It was a last year's nut, and already gnawed by his sharp tooth. A fox, startled from his sleep by her light footstep on the leaves, looked inquisitively at Pearl, as doubting whether it were better to steal off, or renew his nap on the same spot. A wolf, it is said—but here the tale has surely lapsed into the improbable—came up and smelt of Pearl's robe, and offered his savage head to be patted by her hand. The truth seems to be, however, that the mother-forest, and these wild things which it nourished, all recognised a kindred wilderness in the human child.

And she was gentler here than in the grassy-margined streets of the settlement, or in her mother's cottage. The flowers appeared to know it, and one and another whispered as she passed, "Adorn thyself with me, thou beautiful child, adorn thyself with me!"—and, to please them, Pearl gathered the violets, and anemones, and columbines, and some twigs of the freshest green, which the old trees held down before her eyes. With these she decorated her hair and her young waist, and became a nymph child, or an infant dryad, or whatever else was in closest sympathy with the antique wood. In such guise had Pearl adorned herself, when she heard her mother's voice, and came slowly back.

Slowly—for she saw the clergyman!

XIX.

THE CHILD AT THE BROOKSIDE

"Thou wilt love her dearly," repeated Hester Prynne, as she and the minister sat watching little Pearl. "Dost thou not think her beautiful? And see with what natural skill she has made those simple flowers adorn her! Had she gathered pearls, and diamonds, and rubies in the wood, they could not have become her better! She is a splendid child! But I know whose brow she has!"

"Dost thou know, Hester," said Arthur Dimmesdale, with an unquiet smile, "that this dear child, tripping about always at thy side, hath caused me many an alarm? Methought—oh, Hester, what a thought is that, and how terrible to dread it!—that my own features were partly repeated in her face, and so strikingly that the world might see them! But she is mostly thine!"

"No, no! Not mostly!" answered the mother, with a tender smile. "A little longer, and thou needest not to be afraid to trace whose child she is. But how strangely beautiful she looks with those wild flowers in her hair! It is as if one of the fairies, whom we left in dear old England, had decked her out to meet us."

It was with a feeling which neither of them had ever before experienced, that they sat and watched Pearl's slow advance. In her was visible the tie that united them. She had been offered to the world, these seven past years, as the living hieroglyphic, in which was revealed the secret they so darkly sought to hide—all written in this symbol—all plainly manifest—had there been a prophet or magician skilled to read the character of flame! And Pearl was the oneness of their being. Be the foregone evil what it might, how could they doubt that their earthly lives and future destinies were conjoined when they beheld at once the material union, and the spiritual idea, in whom they met, and were to dwell immortally together; thoughts like these—and perhaps other thoughts, which they did not acknowledge or define— threw an awe about the child as she came onward.

"Let her see nothing strange—no passion or eagerness—in thy way of accosting her," whispered Hester. "Our Pearl is a fitful and fantastic little elf sometimes. Especially she is generally intolerant of emotion, when she does not fully comprehend the why and wherefore. But the child hath strong affections! She loves me, and will love thee!"

"Thou canst not think," said the minister, glancing aside at Hester Prynne, "how my heart dreads this interview, and yearns for it! But, in truth, as I already told thee, children are not readily won to be familiar with me. They will not climb my knee, nor prattle in my ear, nor answer to my smile, but stand apart, and eye me strangely. Even little babes, when I take them in my arms, weep bitterly. Yet Pearl, twice in her little lifetime, hath been kind to me! The first time — thou knowest it well! The last was when thou ledst her with thee to the house of yonder stern old Governor."

"And thou didst plead so bravely in her behalf and mine!" answered the mother. "I remember it; and so shall little Pearl. Fear nothing. She may be strange and shy at first, but will soon learn to love thee!"

By this time Pearl had reached the margin of the brook, and stood on the further side, gazing silently at Hester and the clergyman, who still sat together on the mossy tree-trunk waiting to receive her. Just where she had paused, the brook chanced to form a pool so smooth and quiet that it reflected a perfect image of her little figure, with all the brilliant picturesqueness of her beauty, in its adornment of flowers and wreathed foliage, but more refined and spiritualized than the reality. This image, so nearly identical with the living Pearl, seemed to communicate somewhat of its own shadowy and intangible quality to the child herself. It was strange, the way in which Pearl stood, looking so steadfastly at them through the dim medium of the forest gloom, herself, meanwhile, all glorified with a ray of sunshine, that was attracted thitherward as by a certain sympathy. In the brook beneath stood another child — another and the same — with likewise its ray of golden light. Hester felt herself, in some indistinct and tantalizing manner, estranged from Pearl, as if the child, in her lonely ramble through the forest, had strayed out of the sphere in which she and her mother dwelt together, and was now vainly seeking to return to it.

There were both truth and error in the impression; the child and mother were estranged, but through Hester's fault, not Pearl's. Since the latter rambled from her side, another inmate had been admitted within the circle of the mother's feelings, and so modified the aspect of them all, that Pearl, the returning wanderer, could not find her wonted place, and hardly knew where she was.

"I have a strange fancy," observed the sensitive minister, "that this brook is the boundary between two worlds, and that thou canst never meet thy Pearl again. Or is she an elfish spirit, who, as the legends of our childhood taught us, is forbidden to cross a running stream? Pray hasten her, for this delay has already imparted a tremor to my nerves."

"Come, dearest child!" said Hester encouragingly, and stretching out both her arms. "How slow thou art! When hast thou been so sluggish before now? Here is a friend of mine, who must be thy friend also. Thou wilt have twice as much love henceforward as thy mother alone could give thee! Leap across the brook and come to us. Thou canst leap like a young deer!"

Pearl, without responding in any manner to these honey-sweet expressions, remained on the other side of the brook. Now she fixed her bright wild eyes on her mother, now on the minister, and now included them both in the same glance, as if to detect and explain to herself the relation which they bore to one another. For some unaccountable reason, as Arthur Dimmesdale felt the child's eyes upon himself, his hand—with that gesture so habitual as to have become involuntary—stole over his heart. At length, assuming a singular air of authority, Pearl stretched out her hand, with the small forefinger extended, and pointing evidently towards her mother's breast. And beneath, in the mirror of the brook, there was the flower-girdled and sunny image of little Pearl, pointing her small forefinger too.

"Thou strange child! why dost thou not come to me?" exclaimed Hester.

Pearl still pointed with her forefinger, and a frown gathered on her brow—the more impressive from the childish, the almost baby-like aspect of the features that conveyed it. As her mother still kept beckoning to her, and arraying her face in a holiday suit of unaccustomed smiles, the child stamped her foot with a yet more imperious look and gesture. In the brook, again, was the fantastic beauty of the image, with its reflected frown, its pointed finger, and imperious gesture, giving emphasis to the aspect of little Pearl.

"Hasten, Pearl, or I shall be angry with thee!" cried Hester Prynne, who, however, inured to such behaviour on the elf-child's part at other seasons, was naturally anxious for a more seemly deportment now. "Leap across the brook, naughty child, and run hither! Else I must come to thee!"

But Pearl, not a whit startled at her mother's threats any more than mollified by her entreaties, now suddenly burst into a fit of passion, gesticulating violently, and throwing her small figure into the most extravagant contortions. She accompanied this wild outbreak with piercing shrieks, which the woods reverberated on all sides, so that, alone as she was in her childish and unreasonable wrath, it seemed as if a hidden multitude were lending her their sympathy and encouragement. Seen in the brook once more was the shadowy wrath of Pearl's image, crowned and girdled with flowers, but stamping its foot, wildly gesticulating, and, in the midst of all, still pointing its small forefinger at Hester's bosom.

"I see what ails the child," whispered Hester to the clergyman, and turning pale in spite of a strong effort to conceal her trouble and annoyance, "Children will not abide any, the slightest, change in the accustomed aspect of things that are daily before their eyes. Pearl misses something that she has always seen me wear!"

"I pray you," answered the minister, "if thou hast any means of pacifying the child, do it forthwith! Save it were the cankered wrath of an old witch like Mistress Hibbins," added he, attempting to smile, "I know nothing that I would not sooner encounter than this passion in a child. In Pearl's young beauty, as in the wrinkled witch, it has a preternatural effect. Pacify her if thou lovest me!"

Hester turned again towards Pearl with a crimson blush upon her cheek, a conscious glance aside at the clergyman, and then a heavy sigh, while, even before she had time to speak, the blush yielded to a deadly pallor.

"Pearl," said she sadly, "look down at thy feet! There! — before thee! — on the hither side of the brook!"

The child turned her eyes to the point indicated, and there lay the scarlet letter so close upon the margin of the stream that the gold embroidery was reflected in it.

"Bring it hither!" said Hester.

"Come thou and take it up!" answered Pearl.

"Was ever such a child!" observed Hester aside to the minister. "Oh, I have much to tell thee about her! But, in very truth, she is right as regards this hateful token. I must bear its torture yet a little longer — only a few days longer — until we shall have left this region, and look back hither as to a land which we have dreamed of. The forest cannot hide it! The mid-ocean shall take it from my hand, and swallow it up for ever!"

With these words she advanced to the margin of the brook, took up the scarlet letter, and fastened it again into her bosom. Hopefully, but a moment ago, as Hester had spoken of drowning it in the deep sea, there was a sense of inevitable doom upon her as she thus received back this deadly symbol from the hand of fate. She had flung it into infinite space! she had drawn an hour's free breath! and here again was the scarlet misery glittering on the old spot! So it ever is, whether thus typified or no, that an evil deed invests itself with the character of doom. Hester next gathered up the heavy tresses of her hair and confined them beneath her cap. As if there were a withering spell in the sad letter, her beauty, the warmth and richness of her womanhood, departed like fading sunshine, and a gray shadow seemed to fall across her.

When the dreary change was wrought, she extended her hand to Pearl.

"Dost thou know thy mother now, child?", asked she, reproachfully, but with a subdued tone. "Wilt thou come across the brook, and own thy mother, now that she has her shame upon her—now that she is sad?"

"Yes; now I will!" answered the child, bounding across the brook, and clasping Hester in her arms "Now thou art my mother indeed! and I am thy little Pearl!"

In a mood of tenderness that was not usual with her, she drew down her mother's head, and kissed her brow and both her cheeks. But then—by a kind of necessity that always impelled this child to alloy whatever comfort she might chance to give with a throb of anguish—Pearl put up her mouth and kissed the scarlet letter, too.

"That was not kind!" said Hester. "When thou hast shown me a little love, thou mockest me!"

"Why doth the minister sit yonder?" asked Pearl.

"He waits to welcome thee," replied her mother. "Come thou, and entreat his blessing! He loves thee, my little Pearl, and loves thy mother, too. Wilt thou not love him? Come he longs to greet thee!"

"Doth he love us?" said Pearl, looking up with acute intelligence into her mother's face. "Will he go back with us, hand in hand, we three together, into the town?"

"Not now, my child," answered Hester. "But in days to come he will walk hand in hand with us. We will have a home and fireside of our own; and thou shalt sit upon his knee; and he will teach thee many things, and love thee dearly. Thou wilt love him — wilt thou not?"

"And will he always keep his hand over his heart?" inquired Pearl.

"Foolish child, what a question is that!" exclaimed her mother. "Come, and ask his blessing!"

But, whether influenced by the jealousy that seems instinctive with every petted child towards a dangerous rival, or from whatever caprice of her freakish nature, Pearl would show no favour to the clergyman. It was only by an exertion of force that her mother brought her up to him, hanging back, and manifesting her reluctance by odd grimaces; of which, ever since her babyhood, she had possessed a singular variety, and could transform her mobile physiognomy into a series of different aspects, with a new mischief in them, each and all. The minister — painfully embarrassed, but hoping that a kiss might prove a talisman to admit him into the child's kindlier regards — bent forward, and impressed one on her brow. Hereupon, Pearl broke away from her mother, and, running to the brook, stooped over it, and bathed her forehead, until the unwelcome kiss was quite washed off and diffused through a long lapse of the gliding water. She then remained apart, silently watching Hester and the clergyman; while they talked together and made such arrangements as were suggested by their new position and the purposes soon to be fulfilled.

And now this fateful interview had come to a close. The dell was to be left in solitude among its dark, old trees, which, with their multitudinous tongues, would whisper long of what had passed there, and no mortal be the wiser. And the melancholy brook would add this other tale to the mystery with which its little heart was already overburdened, and whereof it still kept up a murmuring babble, with not a whit more cheerfulness of tone than for ages heretofore.

XX.

THE MINISTER IN A MAZE

As the minister departed, in advance of Hester Prynne and little Pearl, he threw a backward glance, half expecting that he should discover only some faintly traced features or outline of the mother and the child, slowly fading into the twilight of the woods. So great a vicissitude in his life could not at once be received as real. But there was Hester, clad in her gray robe, still standing beside the tree-trunk, which some blast had overthrown a long antiquity ago, and which time had ever since been covering with moss, so that these two fated ones, with earth's heaviest burden on them, might there sit down together, and find a single hour's rest and solace. And there was Pearl, too, lightly dancing from the margin of the brook—now that the intrusive third person was gone—and taking her old place by her mother's side. So the minister had not fallen asleep and dreamed!

In order to free his mind from this indistinctness and duplicity of impression, which vexed it with a strange disquietude, he recalled and more thoroughly defined the plans which Hester and himself had sketched for their departure. It had been determined between them that the Old World, with its crowds and cities, offered them a more eligible shelter and concealment than the wilds of New England or all America, with its alternatives of an Indian wigwam, or the few settlements of Europeans scattered thinly along the sea-board. Not to speak of the clergyman's health, so inadequate to sustain the hardships of a forest life, his native gifts, his culture, and his entire development would secure him a home only in the midst of civilization and refinement; the higher the state the more delicately adapted to it the man. In furtherance of this choice, it so happened that a ship lay in the harbour; one of those unquestionable cruisers, frequent at that day, which, without being absolutely outlaws of the deep, yet roamed over its surface with a remarkable irresponsibility of character. This vessel had recently arrived from the Spanish Main, and within three days' time would sail for Bristol. Hester Prynne—whose vocation, as a self-enlisted Sister of Charity, had brought her acquainted with the captain and crew—could take upon herself to secure the passage of two individuals and a child with all the secrecy which circumstances rendered more than desirable.

The minister had inquired of Hester, with no little interest, the precise time at which the vessel might be expected to depart.

It would probably be on the fourth day from the present. "This is most fortunate!" he had then said to himself. Now, why the Reverend Mr. Dimmesdale considered it so very fortunate we hesitate to reveal. Nevertheless—to hold nothing back from the reader—it was because, on the third day from the present, he was to preach the Election Sermon; and, as such an occasion formed an honourable epoch in the life of a New England Clergyman, he could not have chanced upon a more suitable mode and time of terminating his professional career. "At least, they shall say of me," thought this exemplary man, "that I leave no public duty unperformed or ill-performed!" Sad, indeed, that an introspection so profound and acute as this poor minister's should be so miserably deceived! We have had, and may still have, worse things to tell of him; but none, we apprehend, so pitiably weak; no evidence, at once so slight and irrefragable, of a subtle disease that had long since begun to eat into the real substance of his character. No man, for any considerable period, can wear one face to himself and another to the multitude, without finally getting bewildered as to which may be the true.

    The excitement of Mr. Dimmesdale's feelings as he returned from his interview with Hester, lent him unaccustomed physical energy, and hurried him townward at a rapid pace. The pathway among the woods seemed wilder, more uncouth with its rude natural obstacles, and less trodden by the foot of man, than he remembered it on his outward journey. But he leaped across the plashy places, thrust himself through the clinging underbrush, climbed the ascent, plunged into the hollow, and overcame, in short, all the difficulties of the track, with an unweariable activity that astonished him. He could not but recall how feebly, and with what frequent pauses for breath he had toiled over the same ground, only two days before. As he drew near the town, he took an impression of change from the series of familiar objects that presented themselves. It seemed not yesterday, not one, not two, but many days, or even years ago, since he had quitted them. There, indeed, was each former trace of the street, as he remembered it, and all the peculiarities of the houses, with the due multitude of gable-peaks, and a weather-cock at every point where his memory suggested one. Not the less, however, came this importunately obtrusive sense of change. The same was true as regarded the acquaintances whom he met, and all the well-known shapes of human life, about the little town. They looked neither older nor younger now; the beards of the aged were no whiter, nor could the creeping babe of yesterday walk on his feet today; it was impossible to describe in what respect they differed from the individuals on whom he had so recently bestowed a parting glance; and yet the minister's deepest sense seemed to inform him of their mutability. A similar impression struck him most remarkably as he passed under the walls of his own church. The edifice had so very strange, and yet so familiar an aspect, that Mr. Dimmesdale's mind vibrated between two ideas; either that he had seen it only in a dream hitherto, or that he was merely dreaming about it now.

This phenomenon, in the various shapes which it assumed, indicated no external change, but so sudden and important a change in the spectator of the familiar scene, that the intervening space of a single day had operated on his consciousness like the lapse of years. The minister's own will, and Hester's will, and the fate that grew between them, had wrought this transformation. It was the same town as heretofore, but the same minister returned not from the forest. He might have said to the friends who greeted him—"I am not the man for whom you take me! I left him yonder in the forest, withdrawn into a secret dell, by a mossy tree trunk, and near a melancholy brook! Go, seek your minister, and see if his emaciated figure, his thin cheek, his white, heavy, pain-wrinkled brow, be not flung down there, like a cast-off garment!" His friends, no doubt, would still have insisted with him—"Thou art thyself the man!" but the error would have been their own, not his.

Before Mr. Dimmesdale reached home, his inner man gave him other evidences of a revolution in the sphere of thought and feeling. In truth, nothing short of a total change of dynasty and moral code, in that interior kingdom, was adequate to account for the impulses now communicated to the unfortunate and startled minister. At every step he was incited to do some strange, wild, wicked thing or other, with a sense that it would be at once involuntary and intentional, in spite of himself, yet growing out of a profounder self than that which opposed the impulse. For instance, he met one of his own deacons. The good old man addressed him with the paternal affection and patriarchal privilege which his venerable age, his upright and holy character, and his station in the church, entitled him to use and, conjoined with this, the deep, almost worshipping respect, which the minister's professional and private claims alike demanded. Never was there a more beautiful example of how the majesty of age and wisdom may comport with the obeisance and respect enjoined upon it, as from a lower social rank, and inferior order of endowment, towards a higher. Now, during a conversation of some two or three moments between the Reverend Mr. Dimmesdale and this excellent and hoary-bearded deacon, it was only by the most careful self-control that the former could refrain from uttering certain blasphemous suggestions that rose into his mind, respecting the communion-supper. He absolutely trembled and turned pale as ashes, lest his tongue should wag itself in utterance of these horrible matters, and plead his own consent for so doing, without his having fairly given it. And, even with this terror in his heart, he could hardly avoid laughing, to imagine how the sanctified old patriarchal deacon would have been petrified by his minister's impiety.

Again, another incident of the same nature. Hurrying along the street, the Reverend Mr. Dimmesdale encountered the eldest female member of his church, a most pious and exemplary old dame, poor, widowed, lonely, and with a heart as full of reminiscences about her dead husband and children, and her dead friends of long ago, as a burial-ground is full of storied gravestones. Yet all this, which would else have been such heavy sorrow, was made almost a solemn joy to her devout old soul, by religious consolations and the truths of Scripture, wherewith she had fed herself continually for more than thirty years. And since Mr. Dimmesdale had taken her in charge, the good grandam's chief earthly comfort—which, unless it had been likewise a heavenly comfort, could have been none at all—was to meet her pastor, whether casually, or of set purpose, and be refreshed with a word of warm, fragrant, heaven-breathing Gospel truth, from his beloved lips, into her dulled, but rapturously attentive ear. But, on this occasion, up to the moment of putting his lips to the old woman's ear, Mr. Dimmesdale, as the great enemy of souls would have it, could recall no text of Scripture, nor aught else, except a brief, pithy, and, as it then appeared to him, unanswerable argument against the immortality of the human soul. The instilment thereof into her mind would probably have caused this aged sister to drop down dead, at once, as by the effect of an intensely poisonous infusion. What he really did whisper, the minister could never afterwards recollect. There was, perhaps, a fortunate disorder in his utterance, which failed to impart any distinct idea to the good widow's comprehension, or which Providence interpreted after a method of its own. Assuredly, as the minister looked back, he beheld an expression of divine gratitude and ecstasy that seemed like the shine of the celestial city on her face, so wrinkled and ashy pale.

Again, a third instance. After parting from the old church member, he met the youngest sister of them all. It was a maiden newly-won—and won by the Reverend Mr. Dimmesdale's own sermon, on the Sabbath after his vigil—to barter the transitory pleasures of the world for the heavenly hope that was to assume brighter substance as life grew dark around her, and which would gild the utter gloom with final glory. She was fair and pure as a lily that had bloomed in Paradise. The minister knew well that he was himself enshrined within the stainless sanctity of her heart, which hung its snowy curtains about his image, imparting to religion the warmth of love, and to love a religious purity. Satan, that afternoon, had surely led the poor young girl away from her mother's side, and thrown her into the pathway of this sorely tempted, or—shall we not rather say?—this lost and desperate man. As she drew nigh, the arch-fiend whispered him to condense into small compass, and drop into her tender bosom a germ of evil that would be sure to blossom darkly soon, and bear black fruit betimes. Such was his sense of power over this virgin soul, trusting him as she did, that the minister felt potent to blight all the field of innocence with but one wicked look, and develop all its opposite with but a word. So—with a mightier struggle than he had yet sustained—he held his Geneva cloak before his face, and hurried onward, making no sign of recognition, and leaving the young sister to digest his rudeness as she might. She ransacked her conscience—which was full of harmless little matters, like her pocket or her work-bag—and took herself to task, poor thing! for a thousand imaginary faults, and went about her household duties with swollen eyelids the next morning.

Before the minister had time to celebrate his victory over this last temptation, he was conscious of another impulse, more ludicrous, and almost as horrible. It was—we blush to tell it—it was to stop short in the road, and teach some very wicked words to a knot of little Puritan children who were playing there, and had but just begun to talk. Denying himself this freak, as unworthy of his cloth, he met a drunken seaman, one of the ship's crew from the Spanish Main. And here, since he had so valiantly forborne all other wickedness, poor Mr. Dimmesdale longed at least to shake hands with the tarry blackguard, and recreate himself with a few improper jests, such as dissolute sailors so abound with, and a volley of good, round, solid, satisfactory, and heaven-defying oaths! It was not so much a better principle, as partly his natural good taste, and still more his buckramed habit of clerical decorum, that carried him safely through the latter crisis.

"What is it that haunts and tempts me thus?" cried the minister to himself, at length, pausing in the street, and striking his hand against his forehead.

"Am I mad? or am I given over utterly to the fiend? Did I make a contract with him in the forest, and sign it with my blood? And does he now summon me to its fulfilment, by suggesting the performance of every wickedness which his most foul imagination can conceive?"

At the moment when the Reverend Mr. Dimmesdale thus communed with himself, and struck his forehead with his hand, old Mistress Hibbins, the reputed witch-lady, is said to have been passing by. She made a very grand appearance, having on a high head-dress, a rich gown of velvet, and a ruff done up with the famous yellow starch, of which Anne Turner, her especial friend, had taught her the secret, before this last good lady had been hanged for Sir Thomas Overbury's murder. Whether the witch had read the minister's thoughts or no, she came to a full stop, looked shrewdly into his face, smiled craftily, and—though little given to converse with clergymen—began a conversation.

"So, reverend sir, you have made a visit into the forest," observed the witch-lady, nodding her high head-dress at him. "The next time I pray you to allow me only a fair warning, and I shall be proud to bear you company. Without taking overmuch upon myself my good word will go far towards gaining any strange gentleman a fair reception from yonder potentate you wot of."

"I profess, madam," answered the clergyman, with a grave obeisance, such as the lady's rank demanded, and his own good breeding made imperative—"I profess, on my conscience and character, that I am utterly bewildered as touching the purport of your words! I went not into the forest to seek a potentate, neither do I, at any future time, design a visit thither, with a view to gaining the favour of such personage. My one sufficient object was to greet that pious friend of mine, the Apostle Eliot, and rejoice with him over the many precious souls he hath won from heathendom!"

"Ha, ha, ha!" cackled the old witch-lady, still nodding her high head-dress at the minister. "Well, well! we must needs talk thus in the daytime! You carry it off like an old hand! But at midnight, and in the forest, we shall have other talk together!"

She passed on with her aged stateliness, but often turning back her head and smiling at him, like one willing to recognise a secret intimacy of connexion.

"Have I then sold myself," thought the minister, "to the fiend whom, if men say true, this yellow-starched and velveted old hag has chosen for her prince and master?"

The wretched minister! He had made a bargain very like it! Tempted by a dream of happiness, he had yielded himself with deliberate choice, as he had never done before, to what he knew was deadly sin. And the infectious poison of that sin had been thus rapidly diffused throughout his moral system. It had stupefied all blessed impulses, and awakened into vivid life the whole brotherhood of bad ones. Scorn, bitterness, unprovoked malignity, gratuitous desire of ill, ridicule of whatever was good and holy, all awoke to tempt, even while they frightened him. And his encounter with old Mistress Hibbins, if it were a real incident, did but show its sympathy and fellowship with wicked mortals, and the world of perverted spirits.

He had by this time reached his dwelling on the edge of the burial-ground, and, hastening up the stairs, took refuge in his study. The minister was glad to have reached this shelter, without first betraying himself to the world by any of those strange and wicked eccentricities to which he had been continually impelled while passing through the streets. He entered the accustomed room, and looked around him on its books, its windows, its fireplace, and the tapestried comfort of the walls, with the same perception of strangeness that had haunted him throughout his walk from the forest dell into the town and thitherward. Here he had studied and written; here gone through fast and vigil, and come forth half alive; here striven to pray; here borne a hundred thousand agonies! There was the Bible, in its rich old Hebrew, with Moses and the Prophets speaking to him, and God's voice through all.

There on the table, with the inky pen beside it, was an unfinished sermon, with a sentence broken in the midst, where his thoughts had ceased to gush out upon the page two days before. He knew that it was himself, the thin and white-cheeked minister, who had done and suffered these things, and written thus far into the Election Sermon! But he seemed to stand apart, and eye this former self with scornful pitying, but half-envious curiosity. That self was gone. Another man had returned out of the forest—a wiser one—with a knowledge of hidden mysteries which the simplicity of the former never could have reached. A bitter kind of knowledge that!

While occupied with these reflections, a knock came at the door of the study, and the minister said, "Come in!"—not wholly devoid of an idea that he might behold an evil spirit. And so he did! It was old Roger Chillingworth that entered. The minister stood white and speechless, with one hand on the Hebrew Scriptures, and the other spread upon his breast.

"Welcome home, reverend sir," said the physician. "And how found you that godly man, the Apostle Eliot? But methinks, dear sir, you look pale, as if the travel through the wilderness had been too sore for you. Will not my aid be requisite to put you in heart and strength to preach your Election Sermon?"

"Nay, I think not so," rejoined the Reverend Mr. Dimmesdale. "My journey, and the sight of the holy Apostle yonder, and the free air which I have breathed have done me good, after so long confinement in my study. I think to need no more of your drugs, my kind physician, good though they be, and administered by a friendly hand."

All this time Roger Chillingworth was looking at the minister with the grave and intent regard of a physician towards his patient. But, in spite of this outward show, the latter was almost convinced of the old man's knowledge, or, at least, his confident suspicion, with respect to his own interview with Hester Prynne. The physician knew then that in the minister's regard he was no longer a trusted friend, but his bitterest enemy. So much being known, it would appear natural that a part of it should be expressed. It is singular, however, how long a time often passes before words embody things; and with what security two persons, who choose to avoid a certain subject, may approach its very verge, and retire without disturbing it. Thus the minister felt no apprehension that Roger Chillingworth would touch, in express words, upon the real position which they sustained towards one another. Yet did the physician, in his dark way, creep frightfully near the secret.

"Were it not better," said he, "that you use my poor skill tonight? Verily, dear sir, we must take pains to make you strong and vigorous for this occasion of the Election discourse. The people look for great things from you, apprehending that another year may come about and find their pastor gone."

"Yes, to another world," replied the minister with pious resignation. "Heaven grant it be a better one; for, in good sooth, I hardly think to tarry with my flock through the flitting seasons of another year! But touching your medicine, kind sir, in my present frame of body I need it not."

"I joy to hear it," answered the physician. "It may be that my remedies, so long administered in vain, begin now to take due effect. Happy man were I, and well deserving of New England's gratitude, could I achieve this cure!"

"I thank you from my heart, most watchful friend," said the Reverend Mr. Dimmesdale with a solemn smile. "I thank you, and can but requite your good deeds with my prayers."

"A good man's prayers are golden recompense!" rejoined old Roger Chillingworth, as he took his leave. "Yea, they are the current gold coin of the New Jerusalem, with the King's own mint mark on them!"

Left alone, the minister summoned a servant of the house, and requested food, which, being set before him, he ate with ravenous appetite. Then flinging the already written pages of the Election Sermon into the fire, he forthwith began another, which he wrote with such an impulsive flow of thought and emotion, that he fancied himself inspired; and only wondered that Heaven should see fit to transmit the grand and solemn music of its oracles through so foul an organ pipe as he. However, leaving that mystery to solve itself, or go unsolved for ever, he drove his task onward with earnest haste and ecstasy.

Thus the night fled away, as if it were a winged steed, and he careering on it; morning came, and peeped, blushing, through the curtains; and at last sunrise threw a golden beam into the study, and laid it right across the minister's bedazzled eyes. There he was, with the pen still between his fingers, and a vast, immeasurable tract of written space behind him!

XXI.

THE NEW ENGLAND HOLIDAY

Betimes in the morning of the day on which the new Governor was to receive his office at the hands of the people, Hester Prynne and little Pearl came into the market-place. It was already thronged with the craftsmen and other plebeian inhabitants of the town, in considerable numbers, among whom, likewise, were many rough figures, whose attire of deer-skins marked them as belonging to some of the forest settlements, which surrounded the little metropolis of the colony.

On this public holiday, as on all other occasions for seven years past, Hester was clad in a garment of coarse gray cloth. Not more by its hue than by some indescribable peculiarity in its fashion, it had the effect of making her fade personally out of sight and outline; while again the scarlet letter brought her back from this twilight indistinctness, and revealed her under the moral aspect of its own illumination. Her face, so long familiar to the townspeople, showed the marble quietude which they were accustomed to behold there. It was like a mask; or, rather like the frozen calmness of a dead woman's features; owing this dreary resemblance to the fact that Hester was actually dead, in respect to any claim of sympathy, and had departed out of the world with which she still seemed to mingle.

It might be, on this one day, that there was an expression unseen before, nor, indeed, vivid enough to be detected now; unless some preternaturally gifted observer should have first read the heart, and have afterwards sought a corresponding development in the countenance and mien. Such a spiritual seer might have conceived, that, after sustaining the gaze of the multitude through several miserable years as a necessity, a penance, and something which it was a stern religion to endure, she now, for one last time more, encountered it freely and voluntarily, in order to convert what had so long been agony into a kind of triumph. "Look your last on the scarlet letter and its wearer!" — the people's victim and lifelong bond-slave, as they fancied her, might say to them. "Yet a little while, and she will be beyond your reach! A few hours longer and the deep, mysterious ocean will quench and hide for ever the symbol which ye have caused to burn on her bosom!" Nor were it an inconsistency too improbable to be assigned to human nature, should we suppose a feeling of regret in Hester's mind, at the moment when she was about to win her freedom from the pain which had been thus deeply incorporated with her being. Might there not be an irresistible desire to quaff a last, long, breathless draught of the cup of wormwood and aloes, with which nearly all her years of womanhood had been perpetually flavoured. The wine of life, henceforth to be presented to her lips, must be indeed rich, delicious, and exhilarating, in its chased and golden beaker, or else leave an inevitable and weary languor, after the lees of bitterness wherewith she had been drugged, as with a cordial of intensest potency.

Pearl was decked out with airy gaiety. It would have been impossible to guess that this bright and sunny apparition owed its existence to the shape of gloomy gray; or that a fancy, at once so gorgeous and so delicate as must have been requisite to contrive the child's apparel, was the same that had achieved a task perhaps more difficult, in imparting so distinct a peculiarity to Hester's simple robe. The dress, so proper was it to little Pearl, seemed an effluence, or inevitable development and outward manifestation of her character, no more to be separated from her than the many-hued brilliancy from a butterfly's wing, or the painted glory from the leaf of a bright flower. As with these, so with the child; her garb was all of one idea with her nature. On this eventful day, moreover, there was a certain singular inquietude and excitement in her mood, resembling nothing so much as the shimmer of a diamond, that sparkles and flashes with the varied throbbings of the breast on which it is displayed. Children have always a sympathy in the agitations of those connected with them: always, especially, a sense of any trouble or impending revolution, of whatever kind, in domestic circumstances; and therefore Pearl, who was the gem on her mother's unquiet bosom, betrayed, by the very dance of her spirits, the emotions which none could detect in the marble passiveness of Hester's brow.

This effervescence made her flit with a bird-like movement, rather than walk by her mother's side.

She broke continually into shouts of a wild, inarticulate, and sometimes piercing music. When they reached the market-place, she became still more restless, on perceiving the stir and bustle that enlivened the spot; for it was usually more like the broad and lonesome green before a village meeting-house, than the centre of a town's business.

"Why, what is this, mother?" cried she. "Wherefore have all the people left their work today? Is it a play-day for the whole world? See, there is the blacksmith! He has washed his sooty face, and put on his Sabbath-day clothes, and looks as if he would gladly be merry, if any kind body would only teach him how! And there is Master Brackett, the old jailer, nodding and smiling at me. Why does he do so, mother?"

"He remembers thee a little babe, my child," answered Hester.

"He should not nod and smile at me, for all that—the black, grim, ugly-eyed old man!" said Pearl. "He may nod at thee, if he will; for thou art clad in gray, and wearest the scarlet letter. But see, mother, how many faces of strange people, and Indians among them, and sailors! What have they all come to do, here in the market-place?"

"They wait to see the procession pass," said Hester. "For the Governor and the magistrates are to go by, and the ministers, and all the great people and good people, with the music and the soldiers marching before them."

"And will the minister be there?" asked Pearl. "And will he hold out both his hands to me, as when thou ledst me to him from the brook-side?"

"He will be there, child," answered her mother, "but he will not greet thee today, nor must thou greet him."

"What a strange, sad man is he!" said the child, as if speaking partly to herself. "In the dark nighttime he calls us to him, and holds thy hand and mine, as when we stood with him on the scaffold yonder! And in the deep forest, where only the old trees can hear, and the strip of sky see it, he talks with thee, sitting on a heap of moss! And he kisses my forehead, too, so that the little brook would hardly wash it off! But, here, in the sunny day, and among all the people, he knows us not; nor must we know him! A strange, sad man is he, with his hand always over his heart!"

"Be quiet, Pearl—thou understandest not these things," said her mother. "Think not now of the minister, but look about thee, and see how cheery is everybody's face today. The children have come from their schools, and the grown people from their workshops and their fields, on purpose to be happy, for, today, a new man is beginning to rule over them; and so—as has been the custom of mankind ever since a nation was first gathered— they make merry and rejoice: as if a good and golden year were at length to pass over the poor old world!"

It was as Hester said, in regard to the unwonted jollity that brightened the faces of the people. Into this festal season of the year—as it already was, and continued to be during the greater part of two centuries—the Puritans compressed whatever mirth and public joy they deemed allowable to human infirmity; thereby so far dispelling the customary cloud, that, for the space of a single holiday, they appeared scarcely more grave than most other communities at a period of general affliction.

But we perhaps exaggerate the gray or sable tinge, which undoubtedly characterized the mood and manners of the age. The persons now in the market-place of Boston had not been born to an inheritance of Puritanic gloom. They were native Englishmen, whose fathers had lived in the sunny richness of the Elizabethan epoch; a time when the life of England, viewed as one great mass, would appear to have been as stately, magnificent, and joyous, as the world has ever witnessed. Had they followed their hereditary taste, the New England settlers would have illustrated all events of public importance by bonfires, banquets, pageantries, and processions. Nor would it have been impracticable, in the observance of majestic ceremonies, to combine mirthful recreation with solemnity, and give, as it were, a grotesque and brilliant embroidery to the great robe of state, which a nation, at such festivals, puts on. There was some shadow of an attempt of this kind in the mode of celebrating the day on which the political year of the colony commenced. The dim reflection of a remembered splendour, a colourless and manifold diluted repetition of what they had beheld in proud old London—we will not say at a royal coronation, but at a Lord Mayor's show—might be traced in the customs which our forefathers instituted, with reference to the annual installation of magistrates. The fathers and founders of the commonwealth—the statesman, the priest, and the soldier—seemed it a duty then to assume the outward state and majesty, which, in accordance with antique style, was looked upon as the proper garb of public and social eminence. All came forth to move in procession before the people's eye, and thus impart a needed dignity to the simple framework of a government so newly constructed.

Then, too, the people were countenanced, if not encouraged, in relaxing the severe and close application to their various modes of rugged industry, which at all other times, seemed of the same piece and material with their religion. Here, it is true, were none of the appliances which popular merriment would so readily have found in the England of Elizabeth's time, or that of James—no rude shows of a theatrical kind; no minstrel, with his harp and legendary ballad, nor gleeman with an ape dancing to his music; no juggler, with his tricks of mimic witchcraft; no

Rappaccini's Daughter

Merry Andrew, to stir up the multitude with jests, perhaps a hundred years old, but still effective, by their appeals to the very broadest sources of mirthful sympathy. All such professors of the several branches of jocularity would have been sternly repressed, not only by the rigid discipline of law, but by the general sentiment which give law its vitality. Not the less, however, the great, honest face of the people smiled—grimly, perhaps, but widely too. Nor were sports wanting, such as the colonists had witnessed, and shared in, long ago, at the country fairs and on the village-greens of England; and which it was thought well to keep alive on this new soil, for the sake of the courage and manliness that were essential in them. Wrestling matches, in the different fashions of Cornwall and Devonshire, were seen here and there about the market-place; in one corner, there was a friendly bout at quarterstaff; and—what attracted most interest of all—on the platform of the pillory, already so noted in our pages, two masters of defence were commencing an exhibition with the buckler and broadsword. But, much to the disappointment of the crowd, this latter business was broken off by the interposition of the town beadle, who had no idea of permitting the majesty of the law to be violated by such an abuse of one of its consecrated places.

It may not be too much to affirm, on the whole, (the people being then in the first stages of joyless deportment, and the offspring of sires who had known how to be merry, in their day), that they would compare favourably, in point of holiday keeping, with their descendants, even at so long an interval as ourselves. Their immediate posterity, the generation next to the early emigrants, wore the blackest shade of Puritanism, and so darkened the national visage with it, that all the subsequent years have not sufficed to clear it up. We have yet to learn again the forgotten art of gaiety.

The picture of human life in the market-place, though its general tint was the sad gray, brown, or black of the English emigrants, was yet enlivened by some diversity of hue. A party of Indians—in their savage finery of curiously embroidered deerskin robes, wampum-belts, red and yellow ochre, and feathers, and armed with the bow and arrow and stone-headed spear—stood apart with countenances of inflexible gravity, beyond what even the Puritan aspect could attain. Nor, wild as were these painted barbarians, were they the wildest feature of the scene. This distinction could more justly be claimed by some mariners—a part of the crew of the vessel from the Spanish Main—who had come ashore to see the humours of Election Day. They were rough-looking desperadoes, with sun-blackened faces, and an immensity of beard; their wide short trousers were confined about the waist by belts, often clasped with a rough plate of gold, and sustaining always a long knife, and in some instances, a sword. From beneath their broad-brimmed hats of palm-leaf, gleamed eyes which, even in good-nature and merriment, had a kind of animal ferocity. They transgressed without fear or scruple, the rules of behaviour that were binding on all others: smoking tobacco under the beadle's very nose, although each whiff would have cost a townsman a shilling; and quaffing at their pleasure, draughts of wine or aqua-vitæ from pocket flasks, which they freely tendered to the gaping crowd around them. It remarkably characterised the incomplete morality of the age, rigid as we call it, that a licence was allowed the seafaring class, not merely for their freaks on shore, but for far more desperate deeds on their proper element. The sailor of that day would go near to be arraigned as a pirate in our own. There could be little doubt, for instance, that this very ship's crew, though no unfavourable specimens of the nautical brotherhood, had been guilty, as we should phrase it, of depredations on the Spanish commerce, such as would have perilled all their necks in a modern court of justice.

But the sea in those old times heaved, swelled, and foamed very much at its own will, or subject only to the tempestuous wind, with hardly any attempts at regulation by human law. The buccaneer on the wave might relinquish his calling and become at once if he chose, a man of probity and piety on land; nor, even in the full career of his reckless life, was he regarded as a personage with whom it was disreputable to traffic or casually associate. Thus the Puritan elders in their black cloaks, starched bands, and steeple-crowned hats, smiled not unbenignantly at the clamour and rude deportment of these jolly seafaring men; and it excited neither surprise nor animadversion when so reputable a citizen as old Roger Chillingworth, the physician, was seen to enter the market-place in close and familiar talk with the commander of the questionable vessel.

The latter was by far the most showy and gallant figure, so far as apparel went, anywhere to be seen among the multitude. He wore a profusion of ribbons on his garment, and gold lace on his hat, which was also encircled by a gold chain, and surmounted with a feather. There was a sword at his side and a sword-cut on his forehead, which, by the arrangement of his hair, he seemed anxious rather to display than hide. A landsman could hardly have worn this garb and shown this face, and worn and shown them both with such a galliard air, without undergoing stern question before a magistrate, and probably incurring a fine or imprisonment, or perhaps an exhibition in the stocks. As regarded the shipmaster, however, all was looked upon as pertaining to the character, as to a fish his glistening scales.

After parting from the physician, the commander of the Bristol ship strolled idly through the market-place; until happening to approach the spot where Hester Prynne was standing, he appeared to recognise, and did not hesitate to address her. As was usually the case wherever Hester stood, a small vacant area — a sort of magic circle — had formed itself about her, into which, though the people were elbowing one another at a little distance, none ventured or felt disposed to intrude. It was a forcible type of the moral solitude in which the scarlet letter enveloped its fated wearer; partly by her own reserve, and partly by the instinctive, though no longer so unkindly, withdrawal of her fellow-creatures. Now, if never before, it answered a good purpose by enabling Hester and the seaman to speak together without risk of being overheard; and so changed was Hester Prynne's repute before the public, that the matron in town, most eminent for rigid morality, could not have held such intercourse with less result of scandal than herself.

"So, mistress," said the mariner, "I must bid the steward make ready one more berth than you bargained for! No fear of scurvy or ship fever this voyage. What with the ship's surgeon and this other doctor, our only danger will be from drug or pill; more by token, as there is a lot of apothecary's stuff aboard, which I traded for with a Spanish vessel."

"What mean you?" inquired Hester, startled more than she permitted to appear. "Have you another passenger?"

"Why, know you not," cried the shipmaster, "that this physician here — Chillingworth he calls himself — is minded to try my cabin-fare with you? Ay, ay, you must have known it; for he tells me he is of your party, and a close friend to the gentleman you spoke of — he that is in peril from these sour old Puritan rulers."

"They know each other well, indeed," replied Hester, with a mien of calmness, though in the utmost consternation. "They have long dwelt together."

Nothing further passed between the mariner and Hester Prynne. But at that instant she beheld old Roger Chillingworth himself, standing in the remotest corner of the market-place and smiling on her; a smile which — across the wide and bustling square, and through all the talk and laughter, and various thoughts, moods, and interests of the crowd—conveyed secret and fearful meaning.

XXII.

THE PROCESSION

Before Hester Prynne could call together her thoughts, and consider what was practicable to be done in this new and startling aspect of affairs, the sound of military music was heard approaching along a contiguous street. It denoted the advance of the procession of magistrates and citizens on its way towards the meeting-house: where, in compliance with a custom thus early established, and ever since observed, the Reverend Mr. Dimmesdale was to deliver an Election Sermon.

Soon the head of the procession showed itself, with a slow and stately march, turning a corner, and making its way across the market-place. First came the music. It comprised a variety of instruments, perhaps imperfectly adapted to one another, and played with no great skill; but yet attaining the great object for which the harmony of drum and clarion addresses itself to the multitude—that of imparting a higher and more heroic air to the scene of life that passes before the eye. Little Pearl at first clapped her hands, but then lost for an instant the restless agitation that had kept her in a continual effervescence throughout the morning; she gazed silently, and seemed to be borne upward like a floating sea-bird on the long heaves and swells of sound. But she was brought back to her former mood by the shimmer of the sunshine on the weapons and bright armour of the military company, which followed after the music, and formed the honorary escort of the procession. This body of soldiery—which still sustains a corporate existence, and marches down from past ages with an ancient and honourable fame—was composed of no mercenary materials. Its ranks were filled with gentlemen who felt the stirrings of martial impulse, and sought to establish a kind of College of Arms, where, as in an association of Knights Templars, they might learn the science, and, so far as peaceful exercise would teach them, the practices of war. The high estimation then placed upon the military character might be seen in the lofty port of each individual member of the company. Some of them, indeed, by their services in the Low Countries and on other fields of European warfare, had fairly won their title to assume the name and pomp of soldiership. The entire array, moreover, clad in burnished steel, and with plumage nodding over their bright morions, had a brilliancy of effect which no modern display can aspire to equal.

And yet the men of civil eminence, who came immediately

behind the military escort, were better worth a thoughtful observer's eye. Even in outward demeanour they showed a stamp of majesty that made the warrior's haughty stride look vulgar, if not absurd. It was an age when what we call talent had far less consideration than now, but the massive materials which produce stability and dignity of character a great deal more. The people possessed by hereditary right the quality of reverence, which, in their descendants, if it survive at all, exists in smaller proportion, and with a vastly diminished force in the selection and estimate of public men. The change may be for good or ill, and is partly, perhaps, for both. In that old day the English settler on these rude shores — having left king, nobles, and all degrees of awful rank behind, while still the faculty and necessity of reverence was strong in him — bestowed it on the white hair and venerable brow of age — on long-tried integrity — on solid wisdom and sad-coloured experience — on endowments of that grave and weighty order which gave the idea of permanence, and comes under the general definition of respectability. These primitive statesmen, therefore — Bradstreet, Endicott, Dudley, Bellingham, and their compeers — who were elevated to power by the early choice of the people, seem to have been not often brilliant, but distinguished by a ponderous sobriety, rather than activity of intellect. They had fortitude and self-reliance, and in time of difficulty or peril stood up for the welfare of the state like a line of cliffs against a tempestuous tide. The traits of character here indicated were well represented in the square cast of countenance and large physical development of the new colonial magistrates. So far as a demeanour of natural authority was concerned, the mother country need not have been ashamed to see these foremost men of an actual democracy adopted into the House of Peers, or make the Privy Council of the Sovereign.

Next in order to the magistrates came the young and eminently distinguished divine, from whose lips the religious discourse of the anniversary was expected. His was the profession at that era in which intellectual ability displayed itself far more than in political life; for — leaving a higher motive out of the question — it offered inducements powerful enough in the almost worshipping respect of the community, to win the most aspiring ambition into its service. Even political power — as in the case of Increase Mather — was within the grasp of a successful priest.

It was the observation of those who beheld him now, that never, since Mr. Dimmesdale first set his foot on the New England shore, had he exhibited such energy as was seen in the gait and air with which he kept his pace in the procession. There was no feebleness of step as at other times; his frame was not bent, nor did his hand rest ominously upon his heart. Yet, if the clergyman were rightly viewed, his strength seemed not of the body. It might be spiritual and imparted to him by angelical ministrations. It might be the exhilaration of that potent cordial which is distilled only in the furnace-glow of earnest and long-continued thought. Or perchance his sensitive temperament was invigorated by the loud and piercing music that swelled heavenward, and uplifted him on its ascending wave. Nevertheless, so abstracted was his look, it might be questioned whether Mr. Dimmesdale even heard the music. There was his body, moving onward, and with an unaccustomed force. But where was his mind? Far and deep in its own region, busying itself, with preternatural activity, to marshal a procession of stately thoughts that were soon to issue thence; and so he saw nothing, heard nothing, knew nothing of what was around him; but the spiritual element took up the feeble frame and carried it along, unconscious of the burden, and converting it to spirit like itself. Men of uncommon intellect, who have grown morbid, possess this occasional power of mighty effort, into which they throw the life of many days and then are lifeless for as many more.

Hester Prynne, gazing steadfastly at the clergyman, felt a dreary influence come over her, but wherefore or whence she knew not, unless that he seemed so remote from her own sphere, and utterly beyond her reach. One glance of recognition she had imagined must needs pass between them. She thought of the dim forest, with its little dell of solitude, and love, and anguish, and the mossy tree-trunk, where, sitting hand-in-hand, they had mingled their sad and passionate talk with the melancholy murmur of the brook. How deeply had they known each other then! And was this the man? She hardly knew him now! He, moving proudly past, enveloped as it were, in the rich music, with the procession of majestic and venerable fathers; he, so unattainable in his worldly position, and still more so in that far vista of his unsympathizing thoughts, through which she now beheld him! Her spirit sank with the idea that all must have been a delusion, and that, vividly as she had dreamed it, there could be no real bond betwixt the clergyman and herself. And thus much of woman was there in Hester, that she could scarcely forgive him—least of all now, when the heavy footstep of their approaching Fate might be heard, nearer, nearer, nearer! —for being able so completely to withdraw himself from their mutual world—while she groped darkly, and stretched forth her cold hands, and found him not.

Pearl either saw and responded to her mother's feelings, or

herself felt the remoteness and intangibility that had fallen around the minister. While the procession passed, the child was uneasy, fluttering up and down, like a bird on the point of taking flight. When the whole had gone by, she looked up into Hester's face —

"Mother," said she, "was that the same minister that kissed me by the brook?"

"Hold thy peace, dear little Pearl!" whispered her mother. "We must not always talk in the market-place of what happens to us in the forest."

"I could not be sure that it was he — so strange he looked," continued the child. "Else I would have run to him, and bid him kiss me now, before all the people, even as he did yonder among the dark old trees. What would the minister have said, mother? Would he have clapped his hand over his heart, and scowled on me, and bid me begone?"

"What should he say, Pearl," answered Hester, "save that it was no time to kiss, and that kisses are not to be given in the market-place? Well for thee, foolish child, that thou didst not speak to him!"

Another shade of the same sentiment, in reference to Mr. Dimmesdale, was expressed by a person whose eccentricities — insanity, as we should term it — led her to do what few of the townspeople would have ventured on — to begin a conversation with the wearer of the scarlet letter in public. It was Mistress Hibbins, who, arrayed in great magnificence, with a triple ruff, a broidered stomacher, a gown of rich velvet, and a gold-headed cane, had come forth to see the procession. As this ancient lady had the renown (which subsequently cost her no less a price than her life) of being a principal actor in all the works of necromancy that were continually going forward, the crowd gave way before her, and seemed to fear the touch of her garment, as if it carried the plague among its gorgeous folds. Seen in conjunction with Hester Prynne — kindly as so many now felt towards the latter — the dread inspired by Mistress Hibbins had doubled, and caused a general movement from that part of the market-place in which the two women stood.

"Now, what mortal imagination could conceive it?" whispered the old lady confidentially to Hester. "Yonder divine man! That saint on earth, as the people uphold him to be, and as — I must needs say — he really looks! Who, now, that saw him pass in the procession, would think how little while it is since he went forth out of his study—chewing a Hebrew text of Scripture in his mouth, I warrant—to take an airing in the forest! Aha! we know what that means, Hester Prynne! But truly, forsooth, I find it hard to believe him the same man. Many a church member saw I, walking behind the music, that has danced in the same measure with me, when Somebody was fiddler, and, it might be, an Indian powwow or a Lapland wizard changing hands with us! That is but a trifle, when a woman knows the world. But this minister. Couldst thou surely tell, Hester, whether he was the same man that encountered thee on the forest path?"

"Madam, I know not of what you speak," answered Hester Prynne, feeling Mistress Hibbins to be of infirm mind; yet strangely startled and awe-stricken by the confidence with which she affirmed a personal connexion between so many persons (herself among them) and the Evil One. "It is not for me to talk lightly of a learned and pious minister of the Word, like the Reverend Mr. Dimmesdale."

"Fie, woman—fie!" cried the old lady, shaking her finger at Hester. "Dost thou think I have been to the forest so many times, and have yet no skill to judge who else has been there? Yea, though no leaf of the wild garlands which they wore while they danced be left in their hair! I know thee, Hester, for I behold the token. We may all see it in the sunshine! and it glows like a red flame in the dark. Thou wearest it openly, so there need be no question about that. But this minister! Let me tell thee in thine ear! When the Black Man sees one of his own servants, signed and sealed, so shy of owning to the bond as is the Reverend Mr. Dimmesdale, he hath a way of ordering matters so that the mark shall be disclosed, in open daylight, to the eyes of all the world! What is that the minister seeks to hide, with his hand always over his heart? Ha, Hester Prynne?"

"What is it, good Mistress Hibbins?" eagerly asked little Pearl. "Hast thou seen it?"

"No matter, darling!" responded Mistress Hibbins, making Pearl a profound reverence. "Thou thyself wilt see it, one time or another. They say, child, thou art of the lineage of the Prince of Air! Wilt thou ride with me some fine night to see thy father? Then thou shalt know wherefore the minister keeps his hand over his heart!"

Laughing so shrilly that all the market-place could hear her, the weird old gentlewoman took her departure.

By this time the preliminary prayer had been offered in the meeting-house, and the accents of the Reverend Mr. Dimmesdale were heard commencing his discourse. An irresistible feeling kept Hester near the spot. As the sacred edifice was too much thronged to admit another auditor, she took up her position close beside the scaffold of the pillory. It was in sufficient proximity to bring the whole sermon to her ears, in the shape of an indistinct but varied murmur and flow of the minister's very peculiar voice.

This vocal organ was in itself a rich endowment, insomuch that a listener, comprehending nothing of the language in which the preacher spoke, might still have been swayed to and fro by the mere tone and cadence. Like all other music, it breathed passion and pathos, and emotions high or tender, in a tongue native to the human heart, wherever educated. Muffled as the sound was by its passage through the church walls, Hester Prynne listened with such intenseness, and sympathized so intimately, that the sermon had throughout a meaning for her, entirely apart from its indistinguishable words. These, perhaps, if more distinctly heard, might have been only a grosser medium, and have clogged the spiritual sense. Now she caught the low undertone, as of the wind sinking down to repose itself; then ascended with it, as it rose through progressive gradations of sweetness and power, until its volume seemed to envelop her with an atmosphere of awe and solemn grandeur. And yet, majestic as the voice sometimes became, there was for ever in it an essential character of plaintiveness. A loud or low expression of anguish—the whisper, or the shriek, as it might be conceived, of suffering humanity, that touched a sensibility in every bosom! At times this deep strain of pathos was all that could be heard, and scarcely heard sighing amid a desolate silence. But even when the minister's voice grew high and commanding—when it gushed irrepressibly upward—when it assumed its utmost breadth and power, so overfilling the church as to burst its way through the solid walls, and diffuse itself in the open air—still, if the auditor listened intently, and for the purpose, he could detect the same cry of pain. What was it? The complaint of a human heart, sorrow-laden, perchance guilty, telling its secret, whether of guilt or sorrow, to the great heart of mankind; beseeching its sympathy or forgiveness,—at every moment,—in each accent,—and never in vain! It was this profound and continual undertone that gave the clergyman his most appropriate power.

During all this time, Hester stood, statue-like, at the foot of the scaffold. If the minister's voice had not kept her there, there would, nevertheless, have been an inevitable magnetism in that spot, whence she dated the first hour of her life of ignominy. There was a sense within her—too ill-defined to be made a thought, but weighing heavily on her mind—that her whole orb of life, both before and after, was connected with this spot, as with the one point that gave it unity.

Little Pearl, meanwhile, had quitted her mother's side, and was playing at her own will about the market-place. She made the sombre crowd cheerful by her erratic and glistening ray, even as a bird of bright plumage illuminates a whole tree of dusky foliage by darting to and fro, half seen and half concealed amid the twilight of the clustering leaves. She had an undulating, but oftentimes a sharp and irregular movement. It indicated the restless vivacity of her spirit, which today was doubly indefatigable in its tip-toe dance, because it was played upon and vibrated with her mother's disquietude. Whenever Pearl saw anything to excite her ever active and wandering curiosity, she flew thitherward, and, as we might say, seized upon that man or thing as her own property, so far as she desired it, but without yielding the minutest degree of control over her motions in requital. The Puritans looked on, and, if they smiled, were none the less inclined to pronounce the child a demon offspring, from the indescribable charm of beauty and eccentricity that shone through her little figure, and sparkled with its activity. She ran and looked the wild Indian in the face, and he grew conscious of a nature wilder than his own. Thence, with native audacity, but still with a reserve as characteristic, she flew into the midst of a group of mariners, the swarthy-cheeked wild men of the ocean, as the Indians were of the land; and they gazed wonderingly and admiringly at Pearl, as if a flake of the sea-foam had taken the shape of a little maid, and were gifted with a soul of the sea-fire, that flashes beneath the prow in the night-time.

One of these seafaring men the shipmaster, indeed, who had spoken to Hester Prynne was so smitten with Pearl's aspect, that he attempted to lay hands upon her, with purpose to snatch a kiss. Finding it as impossible to touch her as to catch a humming-bird in the air, he took from his hat the gold chain that was twisted about it, and threw it to the child. Pearl immediately twined it around her neck and waist with such happy skill, that, once seen there, it became a part of her, and it was difficult to imagine her without it.

"Thy mother is yonder woman with the scarlet letter," said the seaman, "Wilt thou carry her a message from me?"

"If the message pleases me, I will," answered Pearl.

"Then tell her," rejoined he, "that I spake again with the black-a-visaged, hump shouldered old doctor, and he engages to bring his friend, the gentleman she wots of, aboard with him. So let thy mother take no thought, save for herself and thee. Wilt thou tell her this, thou witch-baby?"

"Mistress Hibbins says my father is the Prince of the Air!" cried Pearl, with a naughty smile. "If thou callest me that ill-name, I shall tell him of thee, and he will chase thy ship with a tempest!"

Pursuing a zigzag course across the market-place, the child returned to her mother, and communicated what the mariner had said. Hester's strong, calm steadfastly-enduring spirit almost sank, at last, on beholding this dark and grim countenance of an inevitable doom, which at the moment when a passage seemed to open for the minister and herself out of their labyrinth of misery — showed itself with an unrelenting smile, right in the midst of their path.

With her mind harassed by the terrible perplexity in which the shipmaster's intelligence involved her, she was also subjected to another trial. There were many people present from the country round about, who had often heard of the scarlet letter, and to whom it had been made terrific by a hundred false or exaggerated rumours, but who had never beheld it with their own bodily eyes. These, after exhausting other modes of amusement, now thronged about Hester Prynne with rude and boorish intrusiveness. Unscrupulous as it was, however, it could not bring them nearer than a circuit of several yards. At that distance they accordingly stood, fixed there by the centrifugal force of the repugnance which the mystic symbol inspired. The whole gang of sailors, likewise, observing the press of spectators, and learning the purport of the scarlet letter, came and thrust their sunburnt and desperado-looking faces into the ring. Even the Indians were affected by a sort of cold shadow of the white man's curiosity and, gliding through the crowd, fastened their snake-like black eyes on Hester's bosom, conceiving, perhaps, that the wearer of this brilliantly embroidered badge must needs be a personage of high dignity among her people. Lastly, the inhabitants of the town (their own interest in this worn-out subject languidly reviving itself, by sympathy with what they saw others feel) lounged idly to the same quarter, and tormented Hester Prynne, perhaps more than all the rest, with their cool, well-acquainted gaze at her familiar shame. Hester saw and recognized the selfsame faces of that group of matrons, who had awaited her forthcoming from the prison-door seven years ago; all save one, the youngest and only compassionate among them, whose burial-robe she had since made. At the final hour, when she was so soon to fling aside the burning letter, it had strangely become the centre of more remark and excitement, and was thus made to sear her breast more painfully, than at any time since the first day she put it on.

While Hester stood in that magic circle of ignominy, where the cunning cruelty of her sentence seemed to have fixed her for ever, the admirable preacher was looking down from the sacred pulpit upon an audience whose very inmost spirits had yielded to his control. The sainted minister in the church! The woman of the scarlet letter in the market-place! What imagination would have been irreverent enough to surmise that the same scorching stigma was on them both!

XXIII.

THE REVELATION OF THE SCARLET LETTER

The eloquent voice, on which the souls of the listening audience had been borne aloft as on the swelling waves of the sea, at length came to a pause. There was a momentary silence, profound as what should follow the utterance of oracles. Then ensued a murmur and half-hushed tumult, as if the auditors, released from the high spell that had transported them into the region of another's mind, were returning into themselves, with all their awe and wonder still heavy on them. In a moment more the crowd began to gush forth from the doors of the church. Now that there was an end, they needed more breath, more fit to support the gross and earthly life into which they relapsed, than that atmosphere which the preacher had converted into words of flame, and had burdened with the rich fragrance of his thought.

In the open air their rapture broke into speech. The street and the market-place absolutely babbled, from side to side, with applauses of the minister. His hearers could not rest until they had told one another of what each knew better than he could tell or hear.

According to their united testimony, never had man spoken in so wise, so high, and so holy a spirit, as he that spake this day; nor had inspiration ever breathed through mortal lips more evidently than it did through his. Its influence could be seen, as it were, descending upon him, and possessing him, and continually lifting him out of the written discourse that lay before him, and filling him with ideas that must have been as marvellous to himself as to his audience. His subject, it appeared, had been the relation between the Deity and the communities of mankind, with a special reference to the New England which they were here planting in the wilderness. And, as he drew towards the close, a spirit as of prophecy had come upon him, constraining him to its purpose as mightily as the old prophets of Israel were constrained, only with this difference, that, whereas the Jewish seers had denounced judgments and ruin on their country, it was his mission to foretell a high and glorious destiny for the newly gathered people of the Lord. But, throughout it all, and through the whole discourse, there had been a certain deep, sad undertone of pathos, which could not be interpreted otherwise than as the natural regret of one soon to pass away. Yes; their minister whom they so loved—and who so loved them all, that he could not depart heavenward without a sigh — had the foreboding of untimely death upon him, and would soon leave them in their tears. This idea of his transitory stay on earth gave the last emphasis to the effect which the preacher had produced; it was as if an angel, in his passage to the skies, had shaken his bright wings over the people for an instant — at once a shadow and a splendour — and had shed down a shower of golden truths upon them.

Thus, there had come to the Reverend Mr. Dimmesdale — as to most men, in their various spheres, though seldom recognised until they see it far behind them — an epoch of life more brilliant and full of triumph than any previous one, or than any which could hereafter be. He stood, at this moment, on the very proudest eminence of superiority, to which the gifts or intellect, rich lore, prevailing eloquence, and a reputation of whitest sanctity, could exalt a clergyman in New England's earliest days, when the professional character was of itself a lofty pedestal. Such was the position which the minister occupied, as he bowed his head forward on the cushions of the pulpit at the close of his Election Sermon. Meanwhile Hester Prynne was standing beside the scaffold of the pillory, with the scarlet letter still burning on her breast!

Now was heard again the clamour of the music, and the measured tramp of the military escort issuing from the church door. The procession was to be marshalled thence to the town hall, where a solemn banquet would complete the ceremonies of the day.

Once more, therefore, the train of venerable and majestic fathers were seen moving through a broad pathway of the people, who drew back reverently, on either side, as the Governor and magistrates, the old and wise men, the holy ministers, and all that were eminent and renowned, advanced into the midst of them. When they were fairly in the market-place, their presence was greeted by a shout. This — though doubtless it might acquire additional force and volume from the child-like loyalty which the age awarded to its rulers — was felt to be an irrepressible outburst of enthusiasm kindled in the auditors by that high strain of eloquence which was yet reverberating in their ears. Each felt the impulse in himself, and in the same breath, caught it from his neighbour. Within the church, it had hardly been kept down; beneath the sky it pealed upward to the zenith. There were human beings enough, and enough of highly wrought and symphonious feeling to produce that more impressive sound than the organ tones of the blast, or the thunder, or the roar of the sea; even that mighty swell of many voices, blended into one great voice by the universal impulse which makes likewise one vast heart out of the many. Never, from the soil of New England had gone up such a shout! Never, on New England soil had stood the man so honoured by his mortal brethren as the preacher!

How fared it with him, then? Were there not the brilliant particles of a halo in the air about his head? So etherealised by spirit as he was, and so apotheosised by worshipping admirers, did his footsteps, in the procession, really tread upon the dust of earth?

As the ranks of military men and civil fathers moved onward, all eyes were turned towards the point where the minister was seen to approach among them. The shout died into a murmur, as one portion of the crowd after another obtained a glimpse of him. How feeble and pale he looked, amid all his triumph! The energy — or say, rather, the inspiration which had held him up, until he should have delivered the sacred message that had brought its own strength along with it from heaven — was withdrawn, now that it had so faithfully performed its office. The glow, which they had just before beheld burning on his cheek, was extinguished, like a flame that sinks down hopelessly among the late decaying embers. It seemed hardly the face of a man alive, with such a death-like hue: it was hardly a man with life in him, that tottered on his path so nervously, yet tottered, and did not fall!

One of his clerical brethren — it was the venerable John Wilson — observing the state in which Mr. Dimmesdale was left by the retiring wave of intellect and sensibility, stepped forward hastily to offer his support. The minister tremulously, but decidedly, repelled the old man's arm. He still walked onward, if that movement could be so described, which rather resembled the wavering effort of an infant, with its mother's arms in view, outstretched to tempt him forward. And now, almost imperceptible as were the latter steps of his progress, he had come opposite the well-remembered and weather-darkened scaffold, where, long since, with all that dreary lapse of time between, Hester Prynne had encountered the world's ignominious stare. There stood Hester, holding little Pearl by the hand! And there was the scarlet letter on her breast! The minister here made a pause; although the music still played the stately and rejoicing march to which the procession moved. It summoned him onward — inward to the festival! — but here he made a pause.

Bellingham, for the last few moments, had kept an anxious

eye upon him. He now left his own place in the procession, and advanced to give assistance judging, from Mr. Dimmesdale's aspect that he must otherwise inevitably fall. But there was something in the latter's expression that warned back the magistrate, although a man not readily obeying the vague intimations that pass from one spirit to another. The crowd, meanwhile, looked on with awe and wonder. This earthly faintness, was, in their view, only another phase of the minister's celestial strength; nor would it have seemed a miracle too high to be wrought for one so holy, had he ascended before their eyes, waxing dimmer and brighter, and fading at last into the light of heaven!

He turned towards the scaffold, and stretched forth his arms.

"Hester," said he, "come hither! Come, my little Pearl!"

It was a ghastly look with which he regarded them; but there was something at once tender and strangely triumphant in it. The child, with the bird-like motion, which was one of her characteristics, flew to him, and clasped her arms about his knees. Hester Prynne — slowly, as if impelled by inevitable fate, and against her strongest will — likewise drew near, but paused before she reached him. At this instant old Roger Chillingworth thrust himself through the crowd — or, perhaps, so dark, disturbed, and evil was his look, he rose up out of some nether region — to snatch back his victim from what he sought to do! Be that as it might, the old man rushed forward, and caught the minister by the arm.

"Madman, hold! what is your purpose?" whispered he. "Wave back that woman! Cast off this child! All shall be well! Do not blacken your fame, and perish in dishonour! I can yet save you! Would you bring infamy on your sacred profession?"

"Ha, tempter! Methinks thou art too late!" answered the minister, encountering his eye, fearfully, but firmly. "Thy power is not what it was! With God's help, I shall escape thee now!"

He again extended his hand to the woman of the scarlet letter.

"Hester Prynne," cried he, with a piercing earnestness, "in the name of Him, so terrible and so merciful, who gives me grace, at this last moment, to do what — for my own heavy sin and miserable agony — I withheld myself from doing seven years ago, come hither now, and twine thy strength about me!

Thy strength, Hester; but let it be guided by the will which God hath granted me! This wretched and wronged old man is opposing it with all his might!—with all his own might, and the fiend's! Come, Hester—come! Support me up yonder scaffold."

The crowd was in a tumult. The men of rank and dignity, who stood more immediately around the clergyman, were so taken by surprise, and so perplexed as to the purport of what they saw—unable to receive the explanation which most readily presented itself, or to imagine any other—that they remained silent and inactive spectators of the judgement which Providence seemed about to work. They beheld the minister, leaning on Hester's shoulder, and supported by her arm around him, approach the scaffold, and ascend its steps; while still the little hand of the sin-born child was clasped in his. Old Roger Chillingworth followed, as one intimately connected with the drama of guilt and sorrow in which they had all been actors, and well entitled, therefore to be present at its closing scene.

"Hadst thou sought the whole earth over," said he looking darkly at the clergyman, "there was no one place so secret—no high place nor lowly place, where thou couldst have escaped me—save on this very scaffold!"

"Thanks be to Him who hath led me hither!" answered the minister.

Yet he trembled, and turned to Hester, with an expression of doubt and anxiety in his eyes, not the less evidently betrayed, that there was a feeble smile upon his lips.

"Is not this better," murmured he, "than what we dreamed of in the forest?"

"I know not! I know not!" she hurriedly replied. "Better? Yea; so we may both die, and little Pearl die with us!"

"For thee and Pearl, be it as God shall order," said the minister; "and God is merciful! Let me now do the will which He hath made plain before my sight. For, Hester, I am a dying man. So let me make haste to take my shame upon me!"

Partly supported by Hester Prynne, and holding one hand of little Pearl's, the Reverend Mr. Dimmesdale turned to the dignified and venerable rulers; to the holy ministers, who were his brethren; to the people, whose great heart was thoroughly appalled yet overflowing with tearful sympathy, as knowing that some deep life-matter—which, if full of sin, was full of anguish and repentance likewise—was now to be laid open to them. The sun, but little past its meridian, shone down upon the clergyman, and gave a distinctness to his figure, as he stood out from all the earth, to put in his plea of guilty at the bar of Eternal Justice.

"People of New England!" cried he, with a voice that rose over them, high, solemn, and majestic—yet had always a tremor through it, and sometimes a shriek, struggling up out of a fathomless depth of remorse and woe—"ye, that have loved me! —ye, that have deemed me holy!—behold me here, the one sinner of the world! At last—at last!—I stand upon the spot where, seven years since, I should have stood, here, with this woman, whose arm, more than the little strength wherewith I have crept hitherward, sustains me at this dreadful moment, from grovelling down upon my face! Lo, the scarlet letter which Hester wears! Ye have all shuddered at it! Wherever her walk hath been—wherever, so miserably burdened, she may have hoped to find repose—it hath cast a lurid gleam of awe and horrible repugnance round about her. But there stood one in the midst of you, at whose brand of sin and infamy ye have not shuddered!"

It seemed, at this point, as if the minister must leave the remainder of his secret undisclosed. But he fought back the bodily weakness—and, still more, the faintness of heart—that was striving for the mastery with him. He threw off all assistance, and stepped passionately forward a pace before the woman and the children.

"It was on him!" he continued, with a kind of fierceness; so determined was he to speak out the whole. "God's eye beheld it! The angels were for ever pointing at it! (The Devil knew it well, and fretted it continually with the touch of his burning finger!) But he hid it cunningly from men, and walked among you with the mien of a spirit, mournful, because so pure in a sinful world!—and sad, because he missed his heavenly kindred! Now, at the death-hour, he stands up before you! He bids you look again at Hester's scarlet letter! He tells you, that, with all its mysterious horror, it is but the shadow of what he bears on his own breast, and that even this, his own red stigma, is no more than the type of what has seared his inmost heart! Stand any here that question God's judgment on a sinner! Behold! Behold, a dreadful witness of it!"

With a convulsive motion, he tore away the ministerial band from before his breast. It was revealed! But it were irreverent to describe that revelation. For an instant, the gaze of the horror-stricken multitude was concentrated on the ghastly miracle; while the minister stood, with a flush of triumph in his face, as one who, in the crisis of acutest pain, had won a victory. Then, down he sank upon the scaffold! Hester partly raised him, and supported his head against her bosom. Old Roger Chillingworth knelt down beside him, with a blank, dull countenance, out of which the life seemed to have departed.

"Thou hast escaped me!" he repeated more than once. "Thou hast escaped me!"

"May God forgive thee!" said the minister. "Thou, too, hast deeply sinned!"

He withdrew his dying eyes from the old man, and fixed them on the woman and the child.

"My little Pearl," said he, feebly and there was a sweet and gentle smile over his face, as of a spirit sinking into deep repose; nay, now that the burden was removed, it seemed almost as if he would be sportive with the child — "dear little Pearl, wilt thou kiss me now? Thou wouldst not, yonder, in the forest! But now thou wilt?"

Pearl kissed his lips. A spell was broken. The great scene of grief, in which the wild infant bore a part had developed all her sympathies; and as her tears fell upon her father's cheek, they were the pledge that she would grow up amid human joy and sorrow, nor forever do battle with the world, but be a woman in it. Towards her mother, too, Pearl's errand as a messenger of anguish was fulfilled.

"Hester," said the clergyman, "farewell!"

"Shall we not meet again?" whispered she, bending her face down close to his. "Shall we not spend our immortal life together? Surely, surely, we have ransomed one another, with all this woe! Thou lookest far into eternity, with those bright dying eyes! Then tell me what thou seest!"

"Hush, Hester — hush!" said he, with tremulous solemnity. "The law we broke! — the sin here awfully revealed! — let these alone be in thy thoughts! I fear! I fear! It may be, that, when we forgot our God — when we violated our reverence each for the other's soul — it was thenceforth vain to hope that we could meet hereafter, in an everlasting and pure reunion. God knows; and He is merciful! He hath proved his mercy, most of all, in my afflictions. By giving me this burning torture to bear upon my breast! By sending yonder dark and terrible old man, to keep the torture always at red-heat! By bringing me hither, to die this death of triumphant ignominy before the people! Had either of these agonies been wanting, I had been lost for ever! Praised be His name! His will be done! Farewell!"

That final word came forth with the minister's expiring breath. The multitude, silent till then, broke out in a strange, deep voice of awe and wonder, which could not as yet find utterance, save in this murmur that rolled so heavily after the departed spirit.

XXIV.

CONCLUSION

After many days, when time sufficed for the people to arrange their thoughts in reference to the foregoing scene, there was more than one account of what had been witnessed on the scaffold.

Most of the spectators testified to having seen, on the breast of the unhappy minister, a SCARLET LETTER—the very semblance of that worn by Hester Prynne—imprinted in the flesh. As regarded its origin there were various explanations, all of which must necessarily have been conjectural. Some affirmed that the Reverend Mr. Dimmesdale, on the very day when Hester Prynne first wore her ignominious badge, had begun a course of penance—which he afterwards, in so many futile methods, followed out—by inflicting a hideous torture on himself. Others contended that the stigma had not been produced until a long time subsequent, when old Roger Chillingworth, being a potent necromancer, had caused it to appear, through the agency of magic and poisonous drugs. Others, again and those best able to appreciate the minister's peculiar sensibility, and the wonderful operation of his spirit upon the body—whispered their belief, that the awful symbol was the effect of the ever-active tooth of remorse, gnawing from the inmost heart outwardly, and at last manifesting Heaven's dreadful judgment by the visible presence of the letter. The reader may choose among these theories. We have thrown all the light we could acquire upon the portent, and would gladly, now that it has done its office, erase its deep print out of our own brain, where long meditation has fixed it in very undesirable distinctness.

It is singular, nevertheless, that certain persons, who were spectators of the whole scene, and professed never once to have removed their eyes from the Reverend Mr. Dimmesdale, denied that there was any mark whatever on his breast, more than on a new-born infant's. Neither, by their report, had his dying words acknowledged, nor even remotely implied, any—the slightest—connexion on his part, with the guilt for which Hester Prynne had so long worn the scarlet letter. According to these highly-respectable witnesses, the minister, conscious that he was dying—conscious, also, that the reverence of the multitude placed him already among saints and angels—had desired, by yielding up his breath in the arms of that fallen woman, to express to the world how utterly nugatory is the choicest of man's own righteousness. After exhausting life in his efforts for mankind's spiritual good, he had made the manner of his death a parable, in order to impress on his admirers the mighty and mournful lesson, that, in the view of Infinite Purity, we are sinners all alike. It was to teach them, that the holiest amongst us has but attained so far above his fellows as to discern more clearly the Mercy which looks down, and repudiate more utterly the phantom of human merit, which would look aspiringly upward. Without disputing a truth so momentous, we must be allowed to consider this version of Mr. Dimmesdale's story as only an instance of that stubborn fidelity with which a man's friends—and especially a clergyman's—will sometimes uphold his character, when proofs, clear as the midday sunshine on the scarlet letter, establish him a false and sin-stained creature of the dust.

The authority which we have chiefly followed—a manuscript of old date, drawn up from the verbal testimony of individuals, some of whom had known Hester Prynne, while others had heard the tale from contemporary witnesses fully confirms the view taken in the foregoing pages. Among many morals which press upon us from the poor minister's miserable experience, we put only this into a sentence:—"Be true! Be true! Be true! Show freely to the world, if not your worst, yet some trait whereby the worst may be inferred!"

Nothing was more remarkable than the change which took place, almost immediately after Mr. Dimmesdale's death, in the appearance and demeanour of the old man known as Roger Chillingworth. All his strength and energy—all his vital and intellectual force—seemed at once to desert him, insomuch that he positively withered up, shrivelled away and almost vanished from mortal sight, like an uprooted weed that lies wilting in the sun. This unhappy man had made the very principle of his life to consist in the pursuit and systematic exercise of revenge; and when, by its completest triumph consummation that evil principle was left with no further material to support it—when, in short, there was no more Devil's work on earth for him to do, it only remained for the unhumanised mortal to betake himself whither his master would find him tasks enough, and pay him his wages duly. But, to all these shadowy beings, so long our near acquaintances—as well Roger Chillingworth as his companions we would fain be merciful. It is a curious subject of observation and inquiry, whether hatred and love be not the same thing at bottom. Each, in its utmost development, supposes a high degree of intimacy and heart-knowledge; each renders one individual dependent for the food of his affections and spiritual fife upon another: each leaves the passionate lover, or the no less passionate hater, forlorn and desolate by the withdrawal of his subject. Philosophically considered, therefore, the two passions seem essentially the same, except that one happens to be seen in a celestial radiance, and the other in a dusky and lurid glow. In the spiritual world, the old physician and the minister—mutual victims as they have been—may, unawares, have found their earthly stock of hatred and antipathy transmuted into golden love.

Leaving this discussion apart, we have a matter of business to communicate to the reader. At old Roger Chillingworth's decease, (which took place within the year), and by his last will and testament, of which Governor Bellingham and the Reverend Mr. Wilson were executors, he bequeathed a very considerable amount of property, both here and in England to little Pearl, the daughter of Hester Prynne.

So Pearl—the elf child—the demon offspring, as some people up to that epoch persisted in considering her—became the richest heiress of her day in the New World. Not improbably this circumstance wrought a very material change in the public estimation; and had the mother and child remained here, little Pearl at a marriageable period of life might have mingled her wild blood with the lineage of the devoutest Puritan among them all. But, in no long time after the physician's death, the wearer of the scarlet letter disappeared, and Pearl along with her. For many years, though a vague report would now and then find its way across the sea—like a shapeless piece of driftwood tossed ashore with the initials of a name upon it—yet no tidings of them unquestionably authentic were received. The story of the scarlet letter grew into a legend. Its spell, however, was still potent, and kept the scaffold awful where the poor minister had died, and likewise the cottage by the sea-shore where Hester Prynne had dwelt. Near this latter spot, one afternoon some children were at play, when they beheld a tall woman in a gray robe approach the cottage-door. In all those years it had never once been opened; but either she unlocked it or the decaying wood and iron yielded to her hand, or she glided shadow-like through these impediments—and, at all events, went in.

On the threshold she paused—turned partly round—for perchance the idea of entering alone and all so changed, the home of so intense a former life, was more dreary and desolate than even she could bear. But her hesitation was only for an instant, though long enough to display a scarlet letter on her breast.

And Hester Prynne had returned, and taken up her long-forsaken shame! But where was little Pearl? If still alive she must now have been in the flush and bloom of early womanhood. None knew—nor ever learned with the fulness of perfect certainty—whether the elf-child had gone thus untimely to a maiden grave; or whether her wild, rich nature had been softened and subdued and made capable of a woman's gentle happiness. But through the remainder of Hester's life there were indications that the recluse of the scarlet letter was the object of love and interest with some inhabitant of another land. Letters came, with armorial seals upon them, though of bearings unknown to English heraldry. In the cottage there were articles of comfort and luxury such as Hester never cared to use, but which only wealth could have purchased and affection have imagined for her. There were trifles too, little ornaments, beautiful tokens of a continual remembrance, that must have been wrought by delicate fingers at the impulse of a fond heart. And once Hester was seen embroidering a baby-garment with such a lavish richness of golden fancy as would have raised a public tumult had any infant thus apparelled, been shown to our sober-hued community.

In fine, the gossips of that day believed—and Mr. Surveyor Pue, who made investigations a century later, believed—and one of his recent successors in office, moreover, faithfully believes—that Pearl was not only alive, but married, and happy, and mindful of her mother; and that she would most joyfully have entertained that sad and lonely mother at her fireside.

But there was a more real life for Hester Prynne, here, in New England, than in that unknown region where Pearl had found a home. Here had been her sin; here, her sorrow; and here was yet to be her penitence. She had returned, therefore, and resumed—of her own free will, for not the sternest magistrate of that iron period would have imposed it—resumed the symbol of which we have related so dark a tale. Never afterwards did it quit her bosom. But, in the lapse of the toilsome, thoughtful, and self-devoted years that made up Hester's life, the scarlet letter ceased to be a stigma which attracted the world's scorn and bitterness, and became a type of something to be sorrowed over, and looked upon with awe, yet with reverence too. And, as Hester Prynne had no selfish ends, nor lived in any measure for her own profit and enjoyment, people brought all their sorrows and perplexities, and besought her counsel, as one who had herself gone through a mighty trouble. Women, more especially—in the continually recurring trials of wounded, wasted, wronged, misplaced, or erring and sinful passion—or with the dreary burden of a heart unyielded, because unvalued and unsought came to Hester's cottage, demanding why they were so wretched, and what the remedy! Hester comforted and counselled them, as best she might. She assured them, too, of her firm belief that, at some brighter period, when the world should have grown ripe for it, in Heaven's own time, a new truth would be revealed, in order to establish the whole relation between man and woman on a surer ground of mutual happiness. Earlier in life, Hester had vainly imagined that she herself might be the destined prophetess, but had long since recognised the impossibility that any mission of divine and mysterious truth should be confided to a woman stained with sin, bowed down with shame, or even burdened with a life-long sorrow. The angel and apostle of the coming revelation must be a woman, indeed, but lofty, pure, and beautiful, and wise; moreover, not through dusky grief, but the ethereal medium of joy; and showing how sacred love should make us happy, by the truest test of a life successful to such an end.

So said Hester Prynne, and glanced her sad eyes downward at the scarlet letter. And, after many, many years, a new grave was delved, near an old and sunken one, in that burial-ground beside which King's Chapel has since been built. It was near that old and sunken grave, yet with a space between, as if the dust of the two sleepers had no right to mingle. Yet one tombstone served for both. All around, there were monuments carved with armorial bearings; and on this simple slab of slate — as the curious investigator may still discern, and perplex himself with the purport — there appeared the semblance of an engraved escutcheon. It bore a device, a herald's wording of which may serve for a motto and brief description of our now concluded legend; so sombre is it, and relieved only by one ever-glowing point of light gloomier than the shadow:—

"ON A FIELD, SABLE, THE LETTER A, GULES."

Milton Keynes UK
Ingram Content Group UK Ltd.
UKHW021938081024
449407UK00008B/154